OLD MONEY

WORLDS APART

By the same author

THE GIRLS
IN LOVE
BRIDIE CLIMBING
A WOMAN LIKE US
THE PERFECT WIFE AND MOTHER
THE DAUGHTERS OF THE HOUSE
WHERE THE RIVERS MEET
AFFAIRS OF LOVE
THE ENCHANTRESS SAGA
CHAMPAGNE
PRIDE OF PLACE
SWIFT FLOWS THE RIVER
BIRD OF PASSAGE
THE RECTOR'S DAUGHTER
CHAMPAGNE GOLD
A WIND IN SUMMER
SILK
PROFIT AND LOSS
TROPHY WIFE
REPOSSESSION
WORLDS APART

The Askham Chronicles

NEVER SUCH INNOCENCE
YESTERDAY'S PROMISES
BRIGHT MORNING
A PLACE IN THE SUN

NICOLA THORNE

OLD MONEY

WORLDS APART

HarperCollins*Publishers*

This omnibus edition published in 1999 by HarperCollins*Publishers*

HarperCollins*Publishers*
77-85 Fulham Palace Road,
Hammersmith, London W6 8JB

This novel is entirely a work of fiction.
The names, characters and incidents portrayed in it are
the work of the author's imagination. Any resemblance to
actual persons, living or dead, events of localities is
entirely coincidental.

ISBN 0 261 67228 2

Set in Bembo

Printed and bound in Great Britain by
Caledonian International Book Manufacturing Ltd, Glasgow

This book is dedicated
to the memory of
Dr Enid Legrange,
a much loved, admired
and most courageous woman

CONTENTS

PART I

Man of the Match: Nick

CHAPTER 1

There was always something superior about the Harveys; a feeling of class, old money.

However much Lydia Constantine tried to feel on equal terms with them, she couldn't. And, God knows, she'd tried. Tried for years.

It wasn't that the Harveys were visually smart or ostentatious. Valerie Harvey was downright shabby, seemed to delight in wearing old clothes. Old but good; the sort of thing you bought at Harrods or Harvey Nicks, or sometimes second-hand at the Oxfam shop.

Lydia shopped in little boutiques in Knightsbridge, Bond Street or Hampstead, sometimes in St John's Wood. Places where you didn't ask the price, and, my, how you would be looked down upon if you did. Lydia was sure Valerie would ask the price of everything, but this wouldn't diminish the fact that she had class; generations, maybe centuries, of breeding which enabled people to do that sort of thing, and get away with it. Lydia and her friends assumed that, if you had to ask the price of something, you couldn't afford it.

The Harveys and the Constantines sat next to one another in comfortable deck chairs on the edge of the field, their eyes on the main characters, Giles and Nick, who were fielding with the rest of the school team. It was the annual match between the school and the old boys, and Edmund Harvey was wearing whites because he might be called upon to bat. He hoped not, because he was going in at number eight and didn't want to make a fool of himself and disgrace his son, because if he was called upon as late as that it would be with the object of saving the side, and he didn't think he had much of a chance.

The old boys had just come in to bat after lunch, a good lunch, during which the wine flowed, thus making the chances of beating the school, who had scored two hundred and fifty off fifty overs, practically zero. Giles had got fifty, Nick had been out for a duck. The Constantines had wriggled uncomfortably, the Harveys had been profuse in their sympathies during the lunch break.

'Bad luck, old boy.' A firm handclasp on the shoulder, a rueful shake of the head from Edmund. 'Jolly bad luck.'

Nick had smiled deprecatingly, glancing at his feet. Inwardly Lydia had seethed. Always that feeling of being patronised by the Harveys; Giles just that little bit one up on Nick.

Wasn't it always the way, especially when there was an audience, that the Constantines came off worse than the Harveys?

Bad luck every time.

Andreas Constantine was not an old boy of the school. He wore flannels, a white shirt and a blazer, a tie adorned with the crest of some club or other. Certainly it wasn't an old school tie. The sparse education he'd received in the local elementary school in Camden Town, where he'd been born the year the war ended, 1945, had been frequently interrupted by periods of truancy, indiscipline and downright rebellion, until his father hauled him into his little business at the age of fourteen, whereupon Andreas saw the light and buckled down to work.

As if to make up for his batting failure, Nick not only fielded well but got two of the old boys out for a duck. Nick seemed to shine on the field whereas Giles remained near the boundary, arms folded, with the air of a man enjoying the sun, content, perhaps deliberately, to let his friend take the glory that his batting prowess had eluded.

The contrast in their styles of play was reflected in their appearances. Although close friends, they were completely unalike physically. Nick was shorter than Giles, slim, elegantly built, intense, olive skin, warm brown eyes and tightly-curled black hair.

Giles seemed the archetypal, laconic Englishman; extremely tall, straight fair hair, pale skin, deep-blue eyes, and the air of one at ease with himself, sure of himself, as if continually amused and entertained by the follies of the world.

Whatever chemistry had brought Giles and Nick together emphasised their contrasting looks as well as personalities. It was an attraction of opposites, yet they were deeply compatible. Perhaps it was their intelligence, their swiftness of mind and shared sense of humour that had not only attracted them to each other in the first place, but had maintained and strengthened their friendship through boyhood and adolescence. Each was sure that, as it had been, so it would continue for the rest of their lives.

By tea-time it looked as though Edmund would indeed be called upon to bat, and he fortified himself with a stiff gin and tonic in the refreshment tent while Valerie looked on with disapproval, nudging him in the ribs and hissing: 'You'll fall flat on your face if you're not careful!'

'Nonsense!' Edmund hissed back and, leaning over the bar, asked for a refill.

Edmund, however, acquitted himself well, scoring fifteen not out before the last batsman was despatched by Nick, who had got three wickets for forty-five runs, two catches in the field, and was declared man of the match despite his poor performance as a batsman.

Giles, as captain of the school team, received the cup from the chairman of governors, made a graceful speech of thanks, congratulated the old boys on a splendid effort, particularly his father (broad smiles and claps), and then paid tribute to his best friend Nick Constantine, deservedly man of the match.

There was applause, shuffling of feet, and as people began to move towards the bar, Giles held up his hands calling for order.

'Just one more thing, ladies and gentlemen,' he said as soon as he had their attention. 'This is the last time I shall have an opportunity to address an audience at this school, because in two weeks' time I'll be leaving it.' He paused and looked about him. 'It is a very sad occasion for me and for those like me to whom the school has come to mean such a lot, to whom it has given opportunities not only academically but in the field of sports and social activities in general. This school has a fine name, as so many of you old boys can testify.' He paused, face flustered, and looked around: 'Schools like this exist not, as some people say, as bastions of privilege but to turn out well-rounded citizens of a largely classless society, a society based on sexual and racial equality, and I shall be proud to be one of its distinguished corps of old boys.'

Giles appeared momentarily overcome by emotion, and then the Head came over to him and vigorously shook his hand. Then he held up an arm gesturing for silence.

'Ladies and gentlemen,' he began, 'this very unexpected, and gratifying, speech of Giles Harvey has left me, for once, very nearly speechless myself. As I know many of you – particularly the players – are anxious to slake your thirst, I will not detain you any longer except to thank Giles for his kind words, sentiments I strongly echo, and may I say that here,' he paused and looked at Giles, 'we have one of the finest representatives this school can produce to take its work and philosophy out into the world at large. Giles has a distinguished academic career, he has a conditional place at

Oxford, he has been captain of rugger and cricket. He has enjoyed enormous popularity with both staff and his fellow students and I wish him and all the sixth formers who are leaving us this term the best of success and happiness in the future.'

There was further applause, stamping of feet, followed by a rush to the bar. There Edmund Harvey was the first to procure a bottle of champagne which he opened with a flourish before proceeding to pour the contents into glasses, holding out the first two to Nick and Giles.

'Splendid speech,' he turned proudly towards his son. 'I didn't know you had it in you.'

'Well done, darling,' Giles's mother Valerie said, her clipped upper-class vowels imperceptibly raising her voice above the crowd. '*I* knew you had it in you.' She reached up to peck his cheek and Giles gave her his glass of champagne, then turned to his father for another. At that moment Andreas Constantine emerged from the crush round the bar clutching a bottle of champagne in each hand.

'I thought I'd add to the celebration,' he said, handing a bottle to Nick to uncork. 'I think we can be proud of our two boys today, Edmund. They have done us, and the school, proud. I agree that was a very good speech, Giles. I'm sure you've both got a lot to offer the world, and look,' he paused to take the other open bottle from Nick and refilled Edmund's already half-empty glass, 'can't we persuade you to spend part of the vacation on our boat? We've asked you before . . .'

Edmund pulled a wry face.

'Valerie's not a very good sailor.'

'It's *you* who doesn't want to go on the boat,' Valerie retorted indignantly. 'I think you're the one who's afraid of being seasick.'

'I am *not* afraid of being seasick,' Edmund hissed. 'I simply don't like boats.'

Emma Constantine, Nick's sister, slipped quietly in beside her mother.

'Sorry I'm late,' she gulped. 'Sorry I missed the match. Did we win?'

'It depends who you mean by "we",' Giles laughed.

'Well "we". You and Nick.'

'We won.' Nick turned to offer her a glass of champagne.

Little Alice Harvey, who was standing shyly beside her father, her hand tightly clenched in his, piped up.

'Daddy was *fifteen* not out.'

'Is that good?' Emma, tall and languid, dark and good looking like Nick, her twin, pretended to affect ignorance of all sport.

'It means he retired with honour.' Giles smiled at Emma and then looked across the room to where his younger brother, Paul, was tentatively edging his way towards them.

'Sorry I'm late,' he said. 'Sorry I missed the match. But I managed to hear the speeches. Did you bat, Dad?' Paul accepted a glass from Nick. 'I see we're celebrating.'

'You missed a very good match.' Edmund looked disapprovingly at his younger son. 'I suppose you'd consider it impertinent of me to ask where you've been.'

'Like me, Paul can't stand cricket.' Emma gave him a conspiratorial smile. 'Why pretend?'

'Why pretend indeed?' Nick was anxious to lower the temperature which, in this over-heated, over-crowded room, was rapidly rising. He felt nervous, strangely depressed, and he had a headache. He felt uneasy, as he always did, when his family and the Harveys were together. Dad was anxious to show off – trust him to buy two bottles of champagne – and his mother usually talked too much. Although today she'd hardly said a word. He smiled at her fondly. She looked terrific, impeccably groomed as always, beautifully dressed, elegant, her fine features just a trifle set. He knew how she felt about the Harveys.

'We're trying to persuade your family to join our boat in Monte Carlo for a few days in the summer.' Andreas turned to Paul. 'I'm sure you like the sea.'

'*I'd* love to come,' Paul, usually the most laid-back member of the family, replied eagerly.

'We've asked you before . . .'

'Oh, Andreas,' Lydia burst out impatiently, 'if they don't want to come, they don't want to come.'

'It isn't that we don't *want* to come,' Valerie said carefully, passing her glass to Nick for a refill. 'It's . . . well, we usually do other things in the summer.'

'I'd *love* to go,' Alice said. '*Please*, Daddy?'

'We'll have to think about it.' Edmund looked down at his youngest, then across to Andreas. 'It's very kind of you to ask.'

It was always very kind of them to ask, and they asked often. They asked them to dinner, to parties and, of course, to go on this goddamned boat. As they left the gathering the Harveys said that, of course it was *very* kind of the Constantines to ask, could they let them know later as they had so many other things to consider.

'Of course. There's no hurry. Give us a ring,' Andreas said. 'And no doubt we'll see you again before the end of term.'

The Constantines' long, sleek Rolls was parked at the end of the row in the car park. Even from a distance, it looked ostentatious. The Harveys' Volvo, a good, sensible family car, a few years old, looked indistinguishable from the rest, but there was no mistaking the pale-blue Rolls with the yellow numberplate, AND CON 1.

The two families waved goodbye, and the Constantines strolled towards the Rolls while the Harveys made their way to their car, their progress frequently interrupted as they stopped to greet numerous friends or acquaintances.

On occasions like these, Nick was assailed by a feeling of

isolation as though, when his family visited the school, they were outcasts, people who stood apart. Of course the Harveys had been associated with the school for years. Not only was Edmund Harvey an old boy, but his father had been one too. A Harvey had attended the school when it was founded in the mid-nineteenth century, well over a hundred years before.

Andreas was usually too busy to attend school functions, but Lydia was assiduous. Yet when she was in a crowd, like today, she sometimes retreated into a shell, dwarfed, as usual, by the Harveys who knew everyone. And everyone seemed to know them.

In a way, Nick knew he would be glad to leave the school.

'Thank God there will be no more "dos" like this,' he said, throwing his bags into the boot which he shut firmly.

Lydia looked sharply at him as she stood waiting for Andreas to open the door. 'I thought you enjoyed it. You seemed to.'

'And why do you always have to bring the Rolls?' he went on. 'I feel such an ass.'

Andreas had arrived late, having dropped his wife off earlier en route to a business meeting. Nick and Emma had made their way separately to the school.

'I'll drive what car I like,' Andreas said huffily, 'without advice from you, my lad. I am not ashamed to be able to afford to drive a Rolls, or own a yacht based in Monte for that matter.'

'And to buy *two* bottles of champagne,' Nick was undeterred. 'I thought you overdid it. It's so over the top.'

Lydia glanced nervously at her husband. 'Oh don't start rowing you two.' She got wearily into the car and settled in to her seat while Andreas got in beside her. Emma and Nick sat at the back.

Lydia placed a hand gingerly against her brow. 'I think I have one of my heads coming on.'

'What Nick *means,*' Emma said, 'is that there is something so patronising about the Harveys.'

'No, I don't know what he means.' Andreas adjusted the driving mirror, then started the engine.

'You *do* know what we mean, Dad.' Emma glanced at her father who was looking at her in the mirror. 'We never feel comfortable when we are all together, especially in the school. That's what Nick means by saying he is glad there will be no more "dos". Isn't it, Nick?'

'I don't know why you always have to invite them on the boat.' Nick gazed moodily out of the window. 'It's obvious they don't want to come.'

'Well, I shan't ask them again,' Andreas said, his pride wounded, as he slowly manoeuvred the large car out of the school car park. 'If that's how you feel.'

'Frankly,' Lydia sighed, settling back into her seat, 'I shouldn't be sorry if I never saw the Harveys again. And now that Nick is leaving, let's hope we don't have to. Except Giles,' she glanced quickly at Nick slumped in the back seat. 'I've always liked Giles. If only the rest of the family were like Giles.'

It was early evening when the Harveys arrived home. As usual, they met so many people they hadn't seen for ages, and now that Giles was about to leave it might be a long time before they met again. Paul had failed the Common Entrance exam and had been unable to follow his brother to the school which was a blow to the family pride, as well as its finances, because an expensive boarding school had to be found for him in the Home Counties.

There was an air of anticlimax after the excitement of the day. Giles went up to his room to change out of his whites while his father kept his on and went into the drawing room. After helping himself to a drink, he wandered onto the patio and sank into a lounger, watching Alice at play in the garden.

Valerie went immediately into the kitchen to prepare supper, much of which had been left ready in the fridge: cold meats and a selection of salads. She, too, helped herself to a glass of wine from an open bottle on the kitchen table.

'Shall we eat outside?' she called from the window and, receiving no answer, put her head out to discover Edmund fast asleep in the lounger, his empty glass by his side. Alice was sitting in her swing gazing thoughtfully at her father.

'Darling, come and help,' Valerie called, whereupon Alice obediently got down from her swing just as Giles appeared in the kitchen now dressed in jeans and a T-shirt.

'Where's Paul?' his mother asked, as she carefully laid slices of beef and ham on the serving plate.

'Upstairs,' Giles replied, 'in his room.'

'I do wish Paul would try and be more pleasant when he's at home. After all, he got special weekend leave for the match and then missed it.'

Giles shrugged. 'I guess it was just an excuse to get away from school. We know he doesn't like cricket.'

'But your *last* match for the school. I do think . . .'

'Mum, what is the use of thinking?' Giles began to slice bread and arrange them in a bread basket. Giles, in every way the antithesis of Paul, was helpful in the house. 'You know what Paul's like. You're always expecting him to be something he's not.'

True. Paul was the weak link in the family chain. Ten-year-old Alice was the perfect daughter: pretty, compliant, obedient yet spirited too, and Giles was almost the perfect son. Almost. Because he and his father did not entirely hit it off. Edmund, a bastion of the Tory party, didn't approve of Giles's Leftish leanings, voiced too frequently for his liking. Valerie so wished Giles would respect Edmund's views more, and keep his own opinions to himself. It made Edmund so choleric, and also contributed to his consumption of alcohol, already high enough.

'Giles, would you go and wake Daddy and tell him we're having supper on the patio? And call Paul? Alice is outside in the garden. Oh, and just take these things out for me,' and she thrust a tray into Giles's hands.

The Harvey residence was a substantial thirties building in a good part of Hampstead. It had been a gift to the young Harveys on their marriage from Valerie's parents, and was in a leafy road off Frognal. It had a small garden at the front, and a substantial one to the rear, part of which was paved to patio and the rest remained lawn. They did not number gardening among their many interests.

There was also a house in Somerset which had been in Edmund Harvey's family for several generations. It was rather dilapidated and not much visited, though they kept horses there which were looked after by a resident groomsman whose wife acted as housekeeper. They always spent Christmas and part of the summer holidays in Somerset, and it was the excuse they always gave for not joining the Constantines on their boat.

That night as they sat eating supper on the patio, the day's events were very much in their thoughts. They kept on returning to the match, the sadness of the last days at school and, inevitably, the boat.

'I think that just once we should accept.' Valerie flung her napkin on the table and sat back. 'It's been on my mind.'

'But why?' Edmund began.

'It seems so rude to keep on saying "no". After all, it's not as though we'll be seeing all that much of them in future, as the boys will no longer be at school together. Oxford will be different.'

'*If* we get into Oxford,' Giles said.

'Oh, you'll get into Oxford, no question.' His mother seemed astonished by his remark. 'Your interview went well, didn't it? But still it's not the same. I mean there won't be all those "dos" that parents have to go to.'

'You didn't *have* to go.' Giles sounded peeved.

'No, darling, we wanted to. I mean it's part of one's duty to take part in school events, fund raising activities, that sort of thing. I must have seen Lydia Constantine a couple of times a month at least. Really, I *like* her. I do. She's very generous, hardworking . . .'

'Don't sound so patronising, Mum,' Paul said, pushing his chair back.

'I am *not* patronising,' Valerie said indignantly.

'You are. You know you don't really like them. You patronise them and it shows. Just because Andreas Constantine is the son of a Greek import merchant . . .'

'There is nothing wrong with being an import merchant,' Edmund said indignantly. 'Anyway, that man's a millionaire several times over. He could probably buy and sell us.'

'His father was a barrow boy or something, wasn't he?' Valerie, looking vague, fluttered her hands in the air.

'His grandfather,' Giles corrected her. 'His grandfather came from Greece and had a market stall, I think in Leather Lane in those days. It was his father who started to import wine and olives and that sort of thing. It's a multimillion pound business now. And yes I guess they *can* buy and sell us.'

'But it's breeding that counts.' Paul slyly eyed his father. 'Isn't it, Dad? The old school tie? By the way, Giles, while we're on the subject, I thought your speech was soppy and sentimental.'

'Thank *you*!' The colour slowly suffused Giles's cheeks.

'Not at all; but it's what I have against the public schools. Play up, play up and play the game. No questions asked. It's what made so many young men glad, nay eager, to lay down their lives for King and Empire. I guess the same thing would happen again if there were a war, and Giles would be the first to volunteer . . .'

'I don't see why I should have to put up with your cheek,' Giles retorted angrily.

'I think you should apologise to your brother.' Edmund stared sternly at Paul. 'That, or go to your room.'

'I thought *that* heavy parental attitude went out years ago.'

'Not in this house.' Edmund thumped the table with his fist. 'I'm just about sick of your lip, Paul, your iconoclasm. You're going to one of the most expensive private schools in the country, draining me in the process incidentally, just because you haven't the intelligence to get into the same school as your brother, yet you have the nerve to insult him . . .'

'Really, Dad, I don't mind.' Giles agitatedly rubbed a hand over his face. 'Let's forget it. This is getting right out of hand.'

'I apologise,' Paul said with a charming smile.

'I accept,' Giles smiled back. 'What were we talking about?'

'I was hoping to get off the subject . . .' Valerie began.

'The old school tie.' Paul seemed intent on driving his point home. 'Breeding and the Constantines, or rather the lack of it.'

'Now that sort of thing *did* go out ages ago.' Edmund speared a piece of cheese with his knife and conveyed it to his mouth. 'I've absolutely nothing against Andreas Constantine, but then I've nothing in common with him either. Nick is another matter. Nick is educated. Nick is the fortunate generation benefiting from the sacrifice of his forebears. I don't have to like Andreas Constantine to respect him, and I do. If you were to ask him, he would probably say the same thing about me.'

'I still think it would be nice to go on the yacht.' Paul got up and threw himself onto the lounger previously occupied by his father. 'I'd like it, and Giles would like it, and Alice would love it . . .'

'Oh, yes!' Alice cried, squeezing her eyes shut with rapture and clasping her hands.

'I think it would be a nice gesture,' Giles said, tight-lipped.

'Well . . .' Valerie paused and looked across at her husband. 'What do you say, Ed?'

'It appears I'm outvoted.' Edmund gave a deep sigh. 'For the sake of family harmony it seems I have to say "yes".'

CHAPTER 2

A welcoming hand reached out to help Edmund up the gangplank.

'Welcome aboard.'

'Nice to see you, Andreas.' With surprising agility Edmund Harvey jumped onto the deck.

'Call me Andy.' The hand moved to his shoulder and gave it a chummy squeeze. 'Everyone calls me Andy.'

'Nice to see you, Andy.' Valerie now seized the proffered hand and was hauled aboard. Behind her was Alice, then Paul and finally Giles who stood at the bottom of the gangplank on the quayside talking to Nick.

Behind Andreas, also wearing nautical attire, was Lydia, and behind her was an assortment of people, one or two who were obviously crew, and another couple who were quite clearly guests. The yacht anchored in the harbour at Monte Carlo seemed huge, a seventy-two footer with lights blazing, while the sun simultaneously set across the bay, illuminating the famous castle of the Grimaldis, high on the hill.

Nick had gone to the airport in Nice to meet them in a large Range Rover which he had driven overland. At first, the idea had been that Giles should accompany him and Emma, but Edmund had insisted that the first part of the holiday should follow the hallowed family tradition of the ritual visit to Somerset where the family foregathered: various aunts, uncles, cousins and Valerie's mother and father who were still alive.

Edmund's mother had died soon after he was born, and he had been brought up in the country, largely by his grandfather and grandmother.

From the quay, Nick and Giles watched the Harvey family clamber aboard and listened to the chatter as they were introduced to the other guests who had preceded them. 'How many people have you got altogether?' Giles asked his friend.

'Just another couple, the Thompsons, plus you. We're picking up others along the way as we cruise to Majorca.'

'It's *huge,*' Giles gazed admiringly at the boat. 'I'd no idea it would be as large as this. It must be as big as Onassis's?'

Nick grinned.

'I think Dad rather hoped it would be bigger.'

'Did he know him?'

Nick shook his head. 'I don't think so. Maybe my grandfather did. Onassis was a generation older than Dad.'

'Of course.'

The conversation seemed stilted, awkward. Giles, who had been looking forward to the trip, now began slightly to regret that he'd come. Nick and he were never easy in the company of their parents, and now that they would be together for five days, close together in the restricted confines of a ship, even a vessel as large as this one. And on the last day of the holiday, the A level results were due.

'Shall we go aboard?' Nick pointed towards the gangplank and, taking his holdall, Giles sprinted along towards the hand held out to him.

'Welcome aboard, Giles. Nice to see you.'

'Thanks, Andreas.' Giles gripped the hand of his host.

'Call me Andy. Everyone calls me Andy.'

'Nice to see you, Andy.'

'And very nice to see you, Giles. Emma and my chief steward have taken your parents, and Paul and Alice to their cabins. You're sharing with Nick. Is that alright?'

'That's fine.' Giles smiled. 'As long as it's OK with Nick.'

'Promise not to snore?'

'Welcome aboard, Giles.' Lydia took his hand and then, drawing him towards her self-consciously, kissed his cheek. She wore a white trouser suit over a red top with a rounded neck and, with her dark hair and tanned skin, looked quite stunning. Of course they had already been here for five weeks: Giles thought that, if it were him, he'd soon get very bored entertaining various guests and spending five weeks at sea. 'Let me introduce you to your fellow guests.' Lydia indicated a couple who stood awkwardly by the gangplank. 'Frank and Sally Thompson. Frank is in the same business as Andy. Giles is Nick's best friend,' she explained. 'They're hoping to go to Oxford together.'

'How exciting.' Sally Thompson was about forty, her husband maybe five years older. She too was tanned, dressed in shorts and a sun top, and looked as though she spent a lot of time in beauty salons.

Once she had completed the introductions, Lydia studied her watch. 'We'll meet in about half an hour for drinks on deck. Did you bring a dinner jacket, Giles?'

'Oh!' Giles clapped a hand to his mouth.

Lydia looked reproachfully at her son. 'Nick should have reminded you. We always like to dress for dinner.'

'I, well . . .' Giles looked around. 'I didn't realise it would be quite as posh as this. I don't think Dad has brought a dinner jacket either.'

A shadow flitted across Lydia's face.

'Never mind,' she said. 'Tonight at least we'll dress informally.'

'Well,' Giles shuffled his feet, 'maybe tomorrow we can slip into Monte and hire something.'

Andreas looked vaguely embarrassed, while Lydia, eyebrows raised, gazed despairingly across at her guests. How like the Harveys, she seemed to be saying, to attempt to belittle their hosts even so far from home, and in their own environment.

The gentle motion of the boat on the water momentarily disoriented Giles as he woke from sleep, making him wonder where he was. The light of the water was reflected on the ceiling of the cabin and danced about as the boat swayed with the tide. The cabin was fairly large and contained not bunks, as Giles had expected, but ordinary beds bolted to the floor. There was a dressing table, a chest of drawers, two chairs and *en suite* loo and shower. His parents' room was even grander with a full size double bed and mahogany, possibly antique, furniture. It was more like a hotel than a yacht, incredibly luxurious, and must have cost a fortune.

Giles glanced over towards Nick's bed and saw that he was still fast asleep. His watch told him it was just after six, and he wished they were anchored in some remote cove where he could jump out of bed and dive into the sea for a long refreshing dip.

He felt he couldn't wait now for them to go to sea, to put some distance between the yacht and the rather oppressive atmosphere of Monte. Or was it not rather the close confines of the yacht and the oddly assorted mixture of people that were oppressive?

He thought back to the dinner party the night before: the stilted conversation, the over-indulgence of his father in drink, and his mother's disapproving looks. The fact that the women wore their finery while the men wore either blazers and flannels, or lounge suits. He didn't think his father, as ill-prepared as the rest of the family for formality, had even brought a tie, and he wore a cricket club cravat tucked into the neck of his open white shirt.

As for his mother, she had worn a shirt-waisted cotton dress that had seen better summers, inevitably a purchase from her favourite Oxfam nearly-new store. She'd thrown it in at the last minute. Was it arrogance or stupidity that had made none of his family, including himself, realise that sailing was a dressy affair, and that people like the Constantines would enjoy showing off, not only their own finery, but that of their guests?

People 'like' the Constantines. What did he mean by that? People not like us, not like the Harveys who put very little store by what people thought about them, cocooned as they were in their own innate sense of superiority?

Suddenly he hated himself and his family, and everything to do with the idea of class, epitomised so aptly by what Paul had said when he criticised his brother's speech the day of the old boys versus the school cricket match.

Giles got out of bed, and his action woke Nick who raised his head and, blinking, looked over at him.

'What's the time?'

'Six.'

'Six! Golly!' Nick turned over and thumped his pillow. 'Couldn't you sleep?'

'I thought it would be nice to go for a swim.'

'The bay is probably polluted.'

'Tomorrow, maybe. We are sailing today, aren't we?'

'About noon, Dad said.'

'It's all very exciting.' Giles perched on the side of the bed and rubbed his hands together. 'I'm looking forward to it. Do you know I've never been on a boat like this before?' As Nick remained silent he said: 'I expect it shows.'

'How do you mean?' Nick, instantly awake, looked across at him.

'Well our behaviour is rather naive.'

'*Your* behaviour naive?' Nick sat upright on the bed, leaning on his elbows. 'I thought we were the ones who were naive.'

Giles gazed at the floor. 'I don't know what you mean.'

'You know what I mean. I really don't know why you came. Your father said he didn't like boats.'

Giles said nothing, dismayed by the bitterness in Nick's voice.

'I suppose you felt you should,' Nick went on. 'After all, we invited you every year, and this was our last at the school. Perhaps your father, or maybe your mother, said: "Really, we better. They ask us every year and . . ."' Nick made a feeble attempt to mimic Valerie's rather high-pitched voice.

'Oh, do shut up, Nick,' Giles burst out suddenly. 'Why do you bring all this up now?'

'Because last night was so awful. Everyone was on their best behaviour.'

'My father drank too much. I thought he made a fool of himself.'

'And my mother talked too much, as if she was afraid of an awkward silence.'

It was true Lydia had gone on and on, and Giles had begun to wonder if she'd had too much to drink too. The Thompsons had remained largely silent and it was, surprisingly, Paul who kept up a spirited and intelligent conversation with Emma on his right, who also seemed absolutely oblivious to the tensions surrounding her.

In fact, Paul and Emma had been the most relaxed and normal people present.

'Look,' Giles went over to Nick's bed and sat on the side, 'let's make the best of this. We're here for almost a week. We can't go back. It would look awful. Besides, we don't want to. I think Dad and Mum genuinely wanted to come out here, but it's not the sort of thing they're used to and they don't know how to behave, or to dress. I apologise on their behalf.'

'They're more used to horsey gatherings in the country.'

'Yes, if you like, and Mum has never been much of a dresser. She has no fashion sense at all, and no interest in clothes. It's nothing to do with class. It's the way she is.'

There it was, out at last, that word 'class'. They stared at each other, as if they'd committed blasphemy or a social solecism. 'That's what we're talking about, isn't it, Nick?' Giles said softly.

'I suppose it is.' Nick nodded. 'I always feel awkward when your parents are about. Always have. At one point I thought it would destroy our friendship. But somehow we always managed to steer clear of it and, besides, you were always so normal. I don't believe you're affected by class at all.'

'Except for that idiotic speech I made at the last cricket match, all about love of school and country.'

Nick grinned. 'Oh, so you did think it was idiotic?'

'Well, not at the time. Paul drew my attention to the fact that it was sentimental gush, and then I did feel ashamed. I think I must have had a rush of blood to the brain. I think that was Dad speaking, not me. Look, I honestly don't believe in class distinction, and if it does exist, I think our generation should do all it can to get rid of it.'

'My parents have got too much money,' Nick said. 'They are really the first generation to have so much, and they think it can buy them anything. Yet it can't buy them education, and it can't buy them confidence. People like your mother and father make them feel ill at ease. They want to show them that they are every bit as good as them.'

'Well, they are . . .'

'Yes, but you know the way I mean. Dad might not be admitted to the Pavilion at Lords, or Whites. He thinks to rub noses with the Harveys is a social cachet. He knows, on the other hand, that we've probably got more money than you have, and he wants to show you his Rolls and his yacht . . .' Nick put a hand over his face. 'Frankly, the whole thing makes me sick – and ashamed – because I know that in my way I'm looking down on a family who have given me everything in life, and without whom I would not be where I am today. And I love them. I love them and I'm ashamed of them. There, doesn't that make me an unworthy son?'

Giles simply didn't know what to say and, rising, went and peered out of the porthole.

'It's a lovely day,' he said. 'Let's try and make this week a good one.' And turning round he managed a smile, but Nick remained lying on his back staring at the ceiling.

'Come in,' Edmund called, and paused in the act of putting on his loafers. He looked up as the door opened, and Giles put his head round.

'Hi! Sleep well?'

'Very well, considering.'

'Considering what?'

'Considering that we are not on dry land.'

'Where's Mum?'

Edmund pointed to the shower, and that moment, a towel draped round her from her bosom to her knees, Valerie emerged, shaking her wet hair.

'Hello, darling. Did you sleep well?'

'Fine. Did you, Mum?'

'Better than I expected.'

'Because of the sea?'

'Something like that.'

'Well, we sail at noon, Nick says.'

'Good. I'm looking forward to it.' His shoes on, Edmund stood up and, going over to the dressing table, carefully examined his appearance in the mirror. Seeming pleased, he turned to his son: 'Do I look nautical enough?'

'Every inch the sailor, Dad; but I have bad news.'

'Oh!' Valerie looked up from towelling her hair, concern showing on her face.

'We have to go into town before we sail and hire monkey suits.'

'Are we going to a ball?'

'No, but they expect it.'

'But that's absurd.' Edmund's expression of self-satisfaction vanished immediately.

'Why is it absurd, Dad?' Giles perched on the bed and looked at his father.

'Because this is an informal boating holiday, at least that was what I thought.'

'Yes, but they like to dress for dinner. It's part of the form at sea. Like dressing up for a cricket match. We should have realised it. You know all those films you see about people who own large yachts. They're always in dinner jackets, swanning about.'

'But I've nothing to wear either,' Valerie wailed.

'Maybe you could buy a dress, Mum.'

'I don't see why I should. It will cost the earth.'

'I think you should out of politeness.'

'Well, if we'd been told in advance, I could have brought something.'

'I think we should have been warned,' Edmund agreed. 'Colossal expense, just for a few days.'

'Well, what do you want to do?' Giles stood up.

'I think we should have a word with, what's his name, Andy, and tell him. We were perfectly well attired last night.'

'I thought the women were overdressed.' Valerie flopped on the bed with a sigh. 'Now I know why.'

'I'm quite willing to have a word with Andy.'

'What will you say?'

'I shall apologise and point out that we know nothing about yachting. Put it down to ignorance and all that.'

'That still needn't stop us getting dinner jackets, Dad. Personally I'd like to. They've put themselves out, and I think we should show appreciation by fitting in with their customs.'

'You'd think we were talking about savages, some rare species,' Edmund grumbled.

'You mentioned a ball, Dad. Well, if people came to stay with us and there was a hunt ball . . .'

'Yes, but we'd tell them there was a ball, not expect them to know instinctively.'

'I feel now, with hindsight, that we should have realised they would dress for dinner on a smart yacht, and I think it would be polite and good mannered to slink off into town after breakfast and hire dinner jackets for us, and for Mum to buy a rather smarter frock.'

When the three members of the Harvey family got to the stern of the boat where a table, hovered over by an attentive, white-coated steward, was laid for breakfast, only Sally Thompson was there. Valerie looked round apologetically. 'Are we terribly late?'

'Not at all.' Sally Thompson looked up from the *Daily Mail* with a smile. 'Frank has gone with Andy to find a doctor.'

'Oh, dear!' Valerie exclaimed with concern as she sat down in the chair held out for her by the steward. 'Is someone ill?'

'Lydia has come down with some sort of bug. Apparently she was ill all night.'

'Oh, I *am* sorry.' Valerie, startled, looked at Edmund who also registered his concern.

'Andy insists we are not to let it spoil our day. His plan is still to leave by noon, if possible.'

'But only if Lydia is well enough?'

'That goes without saying.'

'Well.' Edmund, tucking his napkin into the top of his shirt, looked from one to the other as the steward handed round menus. 'We were going into Monte to hire dinner suits. Apparently dressing up for dinner is *de rigueur*.'

'I think they think it adds a holiday flavour,' Sally Thompson said diplomatically. 'I mean, it's nice to splash out occasionally.'

'Well, if we may not be sailing . . .' Edmund ignored her remark.

'Oh, I don't think it's as bad as that. Just a tummy upset. But maybe you should wait to see what the doctor says.'

There was an air of unease around the breakfast table, and conversation was desultory. Every now and then they glanced at the quay to see if there was any sign of Andreas and the doctor.

They were soon joined by Paul, Emma and Alice, who apologised for sleeping late. Emma didn't know her mother was ill and, on hearing the news and that her brother hadn't yet joined the group at the table, excused herself and disappeared below. Edmund and the younger people present ordered full English breakfasts. Valerie settled for her usual tea and toast.

'No,' she said firmly, in answer to the steward's polite enquiry, 'toast, not croissant. I'm sure you have the facility for serving toast in the English way.'

'Of course, madam.'

As Emma and Nick failed to appear, the atmosphere grew more tense. There was also no sign of Andreas and Frank.

'I say, it will be a hoot if the holiday ends before it began.' Paul poured himself orange juice from the jug in front of him.

'I don't think it will be a hoot at all.' Alice sounded distressed. 'I was *so* looking forward . . .'

'Now, no point in anticipation.' Edmund looked up in pleasure as the steward appeared bearing aloft a large tray. 'No one said anything about the holiday ending.'

'I'm sure, even if we don't sail, we'll be able to stay on board.' Sally peered out again from the pages of the *Daily Mail* which appeared engrossing. 'Andreas is *so* hospitable. We shan't be thrown out.'

At that moment there was a movement on the quay. A car drew up beside the boat and Andreas emerged, followed by Frank Thompson and a stranger who, presumably, was the doctor. Without looking at the group assembled in the stern of the boat, they hurried aboard.

The atmosphere of tension increased. Although it didn't prevent any of them from enjoying a hearty breakfast, it seemed to put a dampener on the conversation, which was sparse.

Finally, after what seemed a long time, the doctor was seen running down the gangplank, accompanied by Andreas, who paused by the side of the doctor's car for some sort of conference. He then shook the man's hand, waved him off and slowly ascended the gangplank, coming round the side of the yacht to his guests.

'I'm terribly sorry about all this,' he said before anyone could say a word. 'Lydia had a very nasty attack of sickness during the night and is not at all well. However, the doctor thinks it is nothing serious and has given her medication. There's nothing to prevent us sailing as planned.'

'Oh, but surely it's wiser to wait until Lydia has recovered?' Valerie looked at him with concern.

'No, this stuff will settle her tummy. He thinks she'll be as right as rain by tomorrow. Anyway, we won't go too far away, just in case. I'd thought of popping over to Sardinia, but maybe we'll hug the coast for a day or two. I don't intend for a moment to let this spoil your holiday. It's the last thing that Lydia wants too; but she will stay in her cabin for the time being.'

'Does Lydia get this sort of thing often?' Valerie enquired.

'Well.' Andreas scratched his head. 'Occasionally. It depends on the circumstances. She's very nervous, you know.'

Edmund looked at Valerie and then at his host.

'Andreas, before we sail we thought we should go into Monte and hire dinner jackets. Valerie would also like to buy some sort of more formal dress for evening.'

'Oh, but it's not necessary,' Andreas exclaimed. 'I *assume* you are quite happy to dress informally for the duration of the cruise?'

'No, we'd *like* to conform,' Edmund insisted. 'We had no idea you dressed for dinner. It was silly of us not to ask. You must blame our ignorance of the high life.'

Even this remark sounded patronising, Nick thought. With his sister he had appeared on deck and had stood silently listening to the conversation. Now he came forward to take his place at the table, while Emma slid into a seat next to Paul.

'We're really quite simple people,' Valerie continued, taking her cue from her husband, clearly unaware that she was making an awkward situation worse. 'Used to country life and messing around in wellies, you know the sort of thing.'

Andreas appeared abashed.

'Well, this isn't exactly the high life. We like sailing, and it's nice to have a boat and be able to keep it in a place like Monte. We like to entertain our friends and give them a good time, but that certainly doesn't mean that if they come without dinner suits or evening dresses that they have to go out and hire them. Anyway, as long as Lydia isn't well, it will be nice to remain as informal as we can.'

'Well, if you insist.' Edmund drew a cigar from the case he carried in his breast pocket.

'I do,' Andreas nodded. 'And now I'll go and give orders for the crew to get ready to sail.' He rose with the air of a weary man, pale and tired looking, obviously from the effects of a sleepless night. Beckoning the steward he said: 'Charles, I want you to look after our guests and give them a good time. See that they have everything they want.'

'Yes, sir.' The steward bowed smartly.

'Coffee, champagne, whatever they want. Lunch as usual at one. Alright?'

'Yes, sir.' The steward bowed again.

'I'll see you on deck.' He addressed the assembled company. 'By mid-afternoon we should be well out to sea, but tonight we'll anchor in some pretty little cove, maybe Antibes or Agay.'

'The bay at Agay is lovely for swimming.' Nick looked at Giles and then at his father. 'Giles said this morning that he wished he could swim.'

'Well, tomorrow you can swim all you like.' Andreas pressed Giles's shoulder. 'Be sure you enjoy yourself now.'

As she felt the engines of the yacht judder into life, aware that it was slowly leaving the safety of the quay, Lydia's insides once more started to heave and, leaning over the side of the bed, she retched into the bowl strategically placed on a table. But there was really nothing there except a thin stream of bile. For a moment she lay with her head hanging over the side, and then she righted herself, flopped back exhausted on the bed and, taking a damp cloth from the bedside table, ran it over her face, brushing back her hair.

She really wished she were dead.

The humiliation of collapsing like this just when the Harveys – the *Harveys* of all people – were aboard, was really too much, too humiliating, and Andy was furious. He had begged her to make an effort, pull herself together, even tried to tug her out of bed, but no. It had been useless. As hard as she tried, whenever she attempted to stand on her two feet she felt an overwhelming sensation of nausea, a knowledge that unless she lay down again she would fall flat on her face.

She closed her eyes and, with the gentle motion of the boat as it pulled out to sea, felt herself drifting off to sleep. Blessed sleep. If only she could never wake up again. But wake she did, and when she opened her eyes Nick was gazing down at her, eyes clouded with concern.

'How are you, Mum?'

'I . . .' Lydia put a hand on her head, looked at the clock by the bed. 'I really don't know,' she said bravely, attempting a weak smile. 'I feel pretty washed out. I'm *terribly* sorry.'

'That's absolutely alright. There's nothing to worry about . . .'

'But the *Harveys* . . . '

'The Harveys are perfectly OK, Mum. They're getting along like a house on fire with the Thompsons.'

'Oh, good.' Lydia's hand fluttered in front of her face. 'Thank God for that. I worried so much whether they'd get on. You know how difficult the Harveys are, and . . .' She paused, and looked anxiously at her son.

'And what, Mum?'

'Well, I thought the Harveys might consider the Thompsons, you know, a bit common. Well, let's face it, that's how they consider us. Jumped up working class, nouveau riche.'

'That's a horrible way to talk.' Nick nervously bit his lip, thinking how much his mother's words echoed his own thoughts.

'But you know it's true, dear. Frank and Sally Thompson are people like us, self-made, not much education. I don't think we should have asked them on the yacht with the Harveys, but frankly,' her tone of voice grew heated, 'I felt I needed some support. Another couple to take some of the load. Besides, I much *prefer* them to the Harveys. You know where you are with Frank and Sally. I shall never know where I am with Edmund and Valerie. The truth is we should never have asked them. It was just your father's desire to show off. As a matter of fact . . .' Lydia, her voice calmer now, groped under her pillow for her handkerchief and blew her nose. 'I think all this has been brought on by worry about the Harveys. I mean, we all ate the same thing last night. It's not food poisoning. Can't be.'

'You mean you think it's all due to nerves?' Nick sat on

the side of her bunk and tenderly stroked her hair back from her damp brow.

'Yes, I do. And so does your father. Well *he* was the one who wanted to ask them. Why, I can't think. They have always snubbed us, humiliated us and now . . .'

'Valerie is very concerned about you. Wants to come and see you.'

'Oh my God! No!' Lydia pulled her sheet up to her chin and gazed white-faced at her son. 'Please, please don't let her in here.'

'Of course I won't if you don't want me to. But she's very nice. She really is. I think you're mistaken about them. You're far too sensitive about this stupid class business. It's all in the past, Mum, and people are equal now.' As Lydia gave a derisive snort, Nick continued: 'Valerie is doing all she can to make everyone feel at ease. If she came for a friendly little chat, it might help. Maybe if you got to know her better . . .'

'My dear boy.' Lydia vigorously blew her nose again. 'I have known Mrs Harvey well, if not intimately, for at least five years, and I don't think I will ever know her better if I live until I'm ninety, seeing her every day . . .'

'Most unlikely.' Nick gave a weak laugh and, removing his hand, left his mother and stood gazing reflectively out of the porthole towards the receding shoreline.

'Quite. That woman just does something to me. I don't know what it is, or why. She's nothing to look at – in fact, she's rather plain – she has no dress sense whatsoever; but there it is.' Lydia spread her outstretched palm by the side of the bed about a foot from the level of the floor. 'She makes me feel about this high. I tell you, Nick, I don't think my tummy will ever feel right until we have seen the back of the Harveys. I just can't wait for this cruise to be over.'

CHAPTER 3

The yacht rode at anchor in the calm still waters of the bay at Agay, dominated by the tall white tower of its lighthouse. Below them in the water the children splashed about, diving from a dinghy in which the 'grown up' men of the party had been rowed ashore. Nick and Giles were making serious attempts to snorkle, but their efforts were playfully interrupted by the antics of the younger siblings abetted by Emma who had been persuaded to abandon her predilection for lying on deck, scantily clad, soaking up the sun.

Watching the proceedings from the deck were Valerie and Lydia, the latter, despite the heat, well wrapped up as though she was afraid of catching cold. In fact she seemed to be shivering all the time, but it was indiscernible from the outside and she felt it came from some primitive source, deep inside her. She had made such an effort for everything to be right for the Harveys and it was deeply humiliating for her to have spent almost the entire trip with them shut up in her cabin. The outfits and dresses she'd bought for the occasion hung unworn in her wardrobe, and fine meals she'd discussed with the chef remained uneaten, at least by her.

It was even further humiliating to realise that, despite her absence, they all in fact seem to have had a very good time, revelling in the informality, not dressing for dinner, even to the extent of remaining in the shorts or sports attire worn during the day. She'd heard sounds of revelry coming from the afterdeck and continuing until well into the night. The three men walking on the shore also seemed to be having a very good time, gusts of laughter reached her across the water. Spirals of smoke rose in the air from long, expensive cigars.

Andreas walked in the middle. He wore white shorts, a white top not tucked into the pants and espadrilles on bare feet. He was the shortest of the three, with thinning hair, not a beauty, but it was generally acknowledged that he made up for his looks by his dynamism and charm.

Andreas was a great life enhancer. People enjoyed his company. He liked parties and was a good dancer. He was considered a ruthless businessman, but what successful man in these hard days could be otherwise? He drove a tough bargain. His widowed father, Theo, had semi retired to a large house in the leafy countryside of Oxfordshire. But he kept an eye on the business which was run by his three sons, Andreas and his brothers, Tony and George, both of whom were younger than he was, so that Andreas was chairman of the company.

Both Tony and George were married with children but, except for weddings, christenings and funerals, Easter and Christmas, the family saw little of one another socially. On these occasions, after church, they all foregathered at Andreas's house and, although they'd all been born in England, except Theo, it seemed to a stranger, and at these times Lydia felt like a stranger, that they were all back in Greece again.

Since leaving school without qualifications, Andreas had educated himself. He read, he enjoyed music and opera, he kept abreast of events. His company contributed substantially to the funds of the Conservative Party because it equated conservatism with prosperity and stability.

He was extraordinarily proud of his children, particularly Nick, because Nick had got brains and used them. He was determined that Nick would go a long way. He didn't mind that Emma, although she too had brains, kept them idling at the back of her head. Both children had got their good looks from their mother, and Emma's beauty combined with her father's money, meant that she would never have to work or be financially restricted, and she could take her time about finding a suitable husband. Of the three men walking on the shore, none was handsome in the strict sense of the word, but the best looking was Edmund. He was tall and had the sort of lean, spare frame sometimes associated with members of his profession. He stooped a little, maybe because of his height, and his hairline too was receding though not to the same extent as Andreas's. He had the fine, lined features of a thoroughbred; the sort of face that, over the centuries, had looked imperiously down from family portraits lining the walls of country houses. He wore blue jeans, a blue check shirt, and an old pair of trainers on bare feet.

On the other side, Frank Thompson was of medium height, vastly overweight, blue jowled, unremarkable in every way except that he had a keen, penetrating business brain of which those who worked with him were all too aware. He supplied produce from Middle Eastern countries, including Greece, Turkey and Israel to supermarkets, and was probably nearly as wealthy as Andreas and his brothers collectively.

The one missing member of the party, his wife Sally, was sunbathing in a secluded part of the foredeck, having taken advantage of the absence of the men to remove her bikini top which allowed her taut full breasts to be exposed to the sun.

The crew were below stairs, preparing lunch.

Valerie and Lydia sipped their coffee, saying little, their attention taken either by the men walking on the shore or the younger members of the party frolicking about in the water. To her reflections Lydia added the strange fact that neither the Thompsons nor the Harveys were what you might call great friends. They knew the Thompsons from business, and the Harveys from school. Andreas always considered the yacht a valuable asset for cementing useful relationships, rather than giving close friends or family a good time. It was strange, but it was a fact. Maybe he considered it a waste of money to have his yacht, with its costly upkeep, plying the Mediterranean with people he couldn't impress.

Lydia glanced guiltily across at Valerie as if wondering if she could read her thoughts, but Valerie's eyes were fixed either on the shore or on the young people having such a good time in the sea.

Surreptitiously, Lydia studied her.

Her guest had on a cotton skirt and sun top, her waist exposed, feet bare. She had the fine features of a rather faded English rose. Her hair, once blonde, was now a pepper and salt mixture that would probably remain so for many years. She had intensely blue eyes, but her face was lined and this made her seem older than her forty-two years. She had never paid much attention to her appearance and all the make-up and skincare products she used was a moisturiser at night and a trace of lipstick first thing in the morning. This had to last all day. Valerie exuded an air of self-satisfaction which many people, including Lydia Constantine, interpreted with some justification as the kind of arrogance peculiar to the upper classes.

When she had finished her coffee she put her cup and saucer down and lay full length, eyes closed, hands folded across her stomach.

'This is bliss,' she said. 'I don't feel I ever want to go home.'

Lydia started guiltily. She had just been thinking what bliss it would be, what perfect bliss, when the Harveys and the Thompsons had gone and she and her family had the boat to themselves.

'You must come again,' she said. 'Only I hope next time I shan't be such a poor hostess.'

'Oh, but we've had a *marvellous* time!' Valerie raised her head and, shielding her eyes from the sun, stared at her companion. 'Don't think you've spoiled it. I just feel sorry for poor old you.' She peered at her more closely. 'I must say you still look a bit peaky.'

And this was despite loads of make-up! Lydia felt rather affronted. It was true she had had little or nothing to eat for the past three days. Yesterday she'd started to drink tea, and this morning she had toast for breakfast.

'And your husband is a wonderful bridge player,' Valerie enthused. 'We beat the Thompsons hollow.'

'So I heard. Unfortunately I don't play, so poor Andy doesn't often get a game.'

Valerie was about to say that they must do something about that when they were all in London again but stopped herself just in time. After all, did she *really* want to keep up the acquaintanceship when they got back?

'Does your husband play?' Lydia enquired.

'He's not very good. He does when he has to, when we can't find a four.'

In fact the bridge and the sun and the food had made the holiday much more fun than Valerie had expected, and she realised that, in a way, the absence of Lydia had contributed to that. She guessed, if the first night had been anything to go by, that on board the yacht, her own territory, and probably in her own home as well, Lydia would be a bit of a martinet, a stickler for convention. For doing what she perceived to be the right thing, like dressing for dinner, when everyone else would much rather lounge around in their day clothes as, indeed, they were doing. There had been a general lack of organisation and an emphasis on doing one's own thing. Valerie also suspected that, without Lydia to keep an eye on him, Andy was much more fun.

'The children have got on so well,' Lydia murmured. 'Nick and Emma will miss them.'

'Oh, they'll hate going back. It's been wonderful for them.'

'Then couldn't you leave them here?'

Valerie stared at Lydia.

'I mean, just for a few days more, if they've nothing else to do?'

'I couldn't leave Alice,' Valerie said doubtfully.

'But why not?'

'Well, she doesn't really fit in, does she? The others are terribly good with her. Besides, Edmund would worry about her too much. He adores her. The baby you know.'

Yes, it was quite obvious how much Edmund doted on his youngest.

'Well, it's up to you. Of course they might not want to stay.'

'But are you sure?'

'Perfectly sure. I mean, if we can fix up about the flight and so on.'

'Oh, yes, there's that.'

'I'm sure Andy will be able to fix it when we get to Marseilles. Andy can fix anything.'

It had been planned that the guests would disembark at Marseilles and take the train back to Nice, where they would get their plane, while the yacht carried on round the coast and then cross to the Balearics before taking on more guests in Majorca.

'Of course we'll have to ask the children. I'm sure they'll want to stay, Giles and Paul will at least. Alice is a bit clingy. Of course Giles and Nick have loads of time before they go up to Oxford. It will be exciting for them to be together.'

'Don't the results come out soon?' Shielding her eyes, Lydia looked towards the shore where the men seemed to be signalling for the dinghy to come over and collect them. They had by now all taken off their shoes, those wearing trousers had them rolled up and were paddling in the water.

'Very soon.' Valerie, oblivious to what was happening on the shore, put her hands behind her head. 'I don't think we've got anything to worry about.'

'Oh, I don't think Nick's all that confident.' Lydia looked doubtful. If only she could have the certainty Valerie had.

'But Giles says he's sure to do well.'

'Well, if hard work merits doing well, then he should.'

'Giles spent a lot of time on the cricket field as usual.' Valerie sighed deeply. 'But everything comes so easily to him. Always has. Sometimes I think it's a bit of a disadvantage in life being an all-rounder. I mean, he doesn't know anything about struggling. Do you know what I mean?'

'I certainly do.' Lydia gave a rueful smile, then she looked intently at the woman next to her. 'Do *you* know a lot about struggling?'

'Do *I*?' Valerie appeared taken aback by the question. 'Why, I never thought about it. No I don't suppose I've had much of a struggle in life; but then it's different for a man. Don't you think? I mean, I know it sounds rather old-fashioned to say that, and Giles would have a fit if he heard me, but they still have to make their way in life much more than a woman. Oh, I know that these days women have careers and all that sort of thing, much more so even than when we were young, but it's so important for a man to make something of his life even if he has money behind him. I mean we'd hate them to be idlers, wouldn't we?'

Lydia, thinking of her daughter, nodded. There was no question of Emma struggling to pursue a career. All she wanted to do was have a good time and, her mother supposed, hang around and wait for a suitable partner to turn up.

'In many ways it makes them more of a worry,' she said slowly. 'I mean, I worry about Emma much more than Nick. Emma is so directionless.'

Valerie laughed.

'She's so pretty. She doesn't have to have a direction!'

'I still wish she were motivated to do *something*. When I was her age I learned shorthand and typing and became a secretary when I was seventeen. That's how I met Andy.'

'Oh? I wondered . . .' Valerie paused, as if she didn't like being thought nosey.

'Yes, I worked in the import department of the family firm. How did you meet Edmund?'

'Well.' Valerie cracked her knuckles one by one above her head. 'I knew him of course. The families were neighbours in Somerset. Our fathers belonged to the same hunt. You know . . .' She looked sideways at Lydia. 'It was that sort of world.'

'Privileged?' Lydia suggested.

'Yes, I suppose you could call it privileged in a way. But we had our ups and downs. Most people do.'

Old money, Lydia thought, smiling to herself. It cushioned you. You could always tell. You could even smell it. It made you so confident, so sure that things would turn out as you expected them to. Whereas she was racked by anxiety, always fearing the worst: that the business would go bust and they would be flung out of their lovely home, that Andy would die young of a heart attack, that Nick would fail his exams and Emma end up going to the bad. That was why she tried so hard always to look her best, to keep up appearances, to dress for dinner on the yacht, to show people that standards mattered. And it was this desire for perfection that always let her down, that caused the headaches, the sickness in the stomach that prevented her from fulfilling the role that she yearned for. So that on this occasion (as on others in the past) she had had to take to her bed just when she wanted to shine, to demonstrate to the Harveys, for so long a source of real pain and jealousy, that she was their equal.

In a way, Lydia Constantine was a lonely woman, lacking

close friends, people with whom she had a bond, in whom she could confide. Sometimes she felt that she and her friends, such as they were, were playing at charades, unable really to communicate to one another their true feelings, pretending that life was very different from what it actually was. Sometimes she felt that if she worried enough about something, it wouldn't happen, it was a way of prevention, a kind of charm against the unexpected. Whereas she could never imagine Valerie being beset by the doubts and anxieties, the morbidity that sometimes seemed almost to ruin her life. Valerie, with her firm base in the upper-middle classes, the county set, years, generations of privilege and tradition, seemed to have no fears at all, to be certain of her place in the world and assured that nothing would happen to disturb it.

Dripping wet, the children clambered aboard in the wake of the male party from the shore, who had been rowed back to the yacht by Giles. As the last of them, Nick, came on deck Sally Thompson appeared from the stern of the boat discreetly doing up the back of her bikini top. Suddenly the deck seemed very crowded, everyone in high good humour, especially the younger ones who had been frolicking in the water. Charles, the steward, hurried out with more deckchairs and Andy, who seemed in a particularly good mood, asked for drinks to be served. Lydia got to her feet and said she thought she'd had enough fresh air and should get back to her cabin.

'How are you feeling, my dear?' Andy asked, the expression on his face one of tender concern, although indeed he too had been beset by anxiety about the success of the holiday.

'I think I'm a little better,' Lydia said without much conviction. 'Oh, by the way, Andy, I thought it would be nice if the Harvey children – I suppose I mustn't call them children – stayed on for a few days to keep ours company.'

'What a good idea!' Andy exclaimed looking round, while Alice beamed.

'Oh, do you mean it? Oh, *may* we, Daddy?'

Lydia thought it significant that she sought her father's permission rather than that of her mother.

'Well!' Edmund had sat down and, removing his shoes, was examining the sole of one of his feet.

'Anything wrong, Ed?' Valerie enquired, looking down.

'I think I trod on something in the water,' Edmund said.

'Maybe a jellyfish,' Giles said with relish. 'I believe they're poisonous out here, Dad.'

'Thank you.' Edmund rubbed his foot and examined it again.

'Nonsense,' Andy said robustly. 'No poisonous jellyfish out here, I assure you.'

'Well . . .' Edmund went on rubbing his foot and Lydia realised that, as the announcement had taken him by surprise, he had been playing for time. 'I don't really think we should presume on the hospitality of the Constantines for much longer. No, I think we'd all better go back to London as planned the day after tomorrow.'

'Oh, *Dad*!'

There was an instant chorus of dismay during which Andreas, also looking rather perplexed, held up his hand.

'We'd *love* to have them. It's no trouble I assure you. In fact we'd love to have you all stay on. It's been such fun . . .'

'Out of the question I'm afraid.' Edmund shook his head vigorously. 'I have to be back at work on Monday.'

'We'd really *like* to stay, Dad.' Paul's tone was wheedling. 'Please.'

'Giles?' His father looked at him.

'Well, of course I'd like to stay, Dad.'

'And they've got Oxford to discuss,' Lydia added. 'It's all quite exciting.'

'He's got Oxford to prepare for.' Edmund looked dubiously at Valerie.

'Dad, I don't go up for over a month. There is absolutely nothing to do.'

'Well . . .' Edmund slowly began putting his shoes back on. 'I really don't know what to say. It seems an imposition and,' he glanced at his daughter, 'I am not happy about Alice staying on.'

'That's what I thought you'd say,' Valerie nodded.

'Oh, Daddy . . . Mummy . . . please!' Alice looked as though she was about to burst into tears.

'We will take very good care of her,' Sally Thompson intervened. 'I'll be sure that Alice is accompanied by someone wherever she goes.'

The Thompsons were staying on until Majorca where they were meeting their son for a villa holiday.

'Perhaps we ought to talk about it?' Valerie looked meaningfully at Edmund and indicated that they might go below deck.

'There is really nothing to talk about,' Andreas said. 'The children want to stay. We want them to stay. It's all settled.'

'But the tickets . . .'

'I'll see to all that,' Andreas said, looking at his watch. 'I'll get on to them this very moment.' And, as he abruptly left the deck Valerie shrugged and looked apologetically at Edmund as though there was really nothing left to say.

The rest of the day, as the yacht sailed towards the port of Marseilles, was spent in various activities. After lunch the children devised games on deck, and Sally resumed her sunbathing, only this time with her top on. Frank stayed in his cabin sleeping and reading. Lydia stayed in hers doing the same thing, although to this she added fretting, while Andreas went to his office, occupying himself with various business affairs including the exchange of tickets which proved to be more complicated than he anticipated because, unlike the Constantines, the Harveys had come out on a special package deal. In the end, although he didn't tell them, because he didn't want to lose face, Andreas had to pay the difference himself which amounted to several hundred pounds.

Valerie and Edmund retired to their cabin after lunch where he immediately slumped on his bed, removed his shoe and examined the sole of his foot again.

'It hurts like blazes,' he said. 'I really think I trod on something. Maybe it was a poisonous jellyfish.'

'Don't be silly.' Valerie sat down beside him and looked at the foot. It was true, it was very red and did look sore. 'We'd better ask them for something to put on it,' she said. 'They're sure to have a very extensive medical cabinet.'

'Oh, wait until we get home.' Edmund gave the foot a final rub and lay full out on the bed. 'I'm really not at all happy about the children staying here.'

'Why not?'

'Well, it's like we owe the Constantines, and I'm not sure that I want that.'

'What do you mean "owe"?'

'Well, we don't want to spend the rest of our lives being grateful.'

'Grateful for what? I think we're doing *them* a favour. If you ask me, they want company for Nick and Emma.'

'Then that doesn't mean that Alice should stay. I am very unhappy about Alice.'

'I'm not too happy about her either.'

'Then why didn't you put your foot down?'

'How could I? It was so difficult. Anyway, Sally says she'll look after her and we can telephone every day. We can't do anything about it, Edmund. Andreas has rearranged the tickets.'

'I can't understand how he did it without having to pay

extra. You can't change those bookings. It says so in the rules.'

'Well, don't let's worry about it.' Valerie stretched out beside him, fanning her face. 'My, it's hot today. I rather wish we were staying on.'

'Well, why don't you? You could look after Alice.'

'Too late now.'

'I don't know why we didn't think of that before.'

'You mean you go back on your own?'

'Why not?'

Valerie wriggled on the bed. 'Well it *is* too late now. No question. Anyway, Giles will make perfectly sure that Alice is looked after. He's very responsible.'

Valerie turned on her side and prepared to go to sleep. But Edmund lay with his hands beneath his head staring at the reflection of the water on the ceiling, thoughtful.

It seemed to him that they were getting a whole lot closer to the Constantines than he wanted to. Instead of saying 'Goodbye' it seemed as though, after all these years, they were saying, 'Hello and welcome'.

On the other hand, he had enjoyed himself, no question. It had been relaxed, informal and even if Frank Thompson was a bit of a bore, he realised that Andy was an intelligent and clever man. He found his views interesting if not always compatible with his own. Added to which, they were both staunch supporters of the Tory Party. Andreas was very much in favour of Europe whereas Edmund was less optimistic about the advantages of too close an association with our European allies.

Andy was a little boastful, over-anxious to please and impress, but he was also unstuffy, informative about his family's origins and not ashamed of them. Perfectly reasonable. Why should he be?

However, when all was said and done, the Constantines were rather brash, rather ostentatious. They oozed new money, and their values were not quite those of the Harveys. Difficult to put into words without sounding snobbish. They were not one of us and, moreover, they never could be. Maybe their son would, eventually. With his public school and Oxford education, his accent, his polished manners in addition to the fortune he would undoubtedly inherit, he might qualify for admission to that stratum of society in which the Harveys believed themselves to inhabit: upper-middle, the criteria of which were good breeding; years of education and public service; old money.

But Nick's mother and father? Never.

That night, an air of festivity prevailed, beginning with drinks before dinner on deck. For once they all dressed, not in the clothes they'd worn during the day, but something different. The children wore jeans and clean T-shirts, the grown-up men blazers and flannels, white shirts and ties – rather similar to what they'd worn on the first night. Valerie trotted out her Oxfam dress, Sally's was an expensive black number sparkling with sequins and Lydia, making her first appearance for four days, outshone them all in a backless creation in pink and cream tulle with a low, scalloped front, by one of London's top couturiers. Lydia had spent a considerable amount of time on her appearance, although she still didn't feel completely well, in order to make up for the lost days, the dreadful days, lying in bed feeling ill, resentful and sorry for herself – a heady mixture which had done little to aid her recovery.

After dinner there was dancing on deck to music from a stereo. Lydia sat out most of the time, but Valerie and Sally both danced energetically, swapping partners with enthusiasm, and Andreas, who loved dancing, never sat out once. The evening ended with Greek dances performed by everyone with hands flung high above heads and plates sent crashing onto the decks or into the sea.

'What a lovely way to end a holiday,' Valerie said, flinging herself into a chair and gasping for breath. She felt slightly tipsy too. 'We really have had the most super time.'

'We must make this something we do every year.' Andreas flopped down beside her. 'Definitely an annual event. What do you say, Edmund?'

Andreas looked at Edmund who was leaning against the rail, glass in hand.

'Cheers!' Edmund raised his glass.

'I mean, to it happening every year?'

'A lot can happen in a year,' Edmund replied enigmatically and then, shooting his cuff back, he looked at his watch. 'We're all going to be dead tired tomorrow. Time for bed.'

Despite the lateness of the hour at which they finally turned off the light Valerie was awake early and, by the time Edmund woke up, she had finished packing. 'Wasser time?' he asked, blinking in the light.

'It's past eight. We're due in Marseilles at noon.'

'What's the hurry?'

'Well, we have to have our breakfast, say our goodbyes. Make sure the children keep in touch. Incidentally, do we know exactly when they're coming home? Don't forget Alice starts school in a couple of weeks.'

'I think he's putting them off at Barcelona. They've got some new guests coming on then.'

'But how can they fly back from Barcelona if they've tickets from Nice?'

'Oh, Andreas has arranged it all.' Edmund threw back the sheet and, drawing his foot up towards his face, began intently to examine it.

'How's your foot?'

'It's still pretty painful.' Edmund looked at it carefully. 'I'm rather glad we're going back and I can get it seen to. Look how swollen it is.' Valerie glanced at it without much concern. Her husband always took such an exaggerated interest in his health. She perched on the side of the bed.

'Do you mean to tell me Andreas has achieved all this without paying extra?'

'He told me he'd fixed it.'

'That means, don't you see, he's paid a fortune!'

'Look,' Edmund said impatiently, 'he has his pride. If he wants to pay, let him. He can afford it. I don't want to start cross-examining him. It's too infra dig. Besides, I'm damned if I want to pay extra. We've enough on our plates.'

'What do you mean?'

'We've enough expense. None of the kids is independent. I have school fees for Paul and Alice, and we've got to keep Giles through three years at least at Oxford. I haven't got a bottomless purse you know.'

'Time for breakfast!' Giles put his head round the door. 'You two arguing?'

'Just having a discussion,' Valerie replied haughtily. 'Look, how long are you staying on for?'

'I think a week. Until we get to Barcelona.'

'Well, be careful.' Valerie held up her cheek for a kiss. 'And don't dare take your eyes off Alice.'

'Mum, you worry,' Giles said fondly, and then to his father, 'Dad, how's your foot?'

'Painful,' Edmund replied. 'Glad I'm going home.'

'Well,' Giles looked at his watch, 'you've got about five minutes to get up, shower and appear in time for breakfast.'

Giles was in ebullient mood as he propelled his mother along the deck to the stern where the table was laid as usual. As usual, too, it was a lovely morning, the surface of the sea calm as the yacht ploughed towards the coast at a steady rate of knots.

Frank and Sally were already at the table, studying the menu that had been handed to them by Charles.

'Sleep well?'

'Fine. And you?'

'Fine.'

'We shall miss you,' Frank said, handing the menu to the steward and murmuring that he would have the usual, which was a full English breakfast complete with sausages and fried bread. 'You've been great sports.'

'Maybe we'll see you next year?' Valerie smiled sweetly.

'Better still, why don't we get together in London?' Sally suggested.

'That's a great idea.' Frank sounded enthusiastic. 'We could have a night out. Do a show.'

'I'm sure we'd love that.' Valerie's tone was lukewarm. Then she looked anxiously over at Sally. 'You will keep an eye on Alice, won't you? She's so young.'

'My dear,' Sally put a reassuring hand on Valerie's arm, 'you need have no fear about your little one. We shall all make sure she comes to no harm.'

'Mum, I'm going to be here you know.' Giles sounded aggrieved. 'I'm perfectly capable . . .' He stopped as Andreas appeared, walking slowly along the deck studying a paper in his hand. Behind him was Nick whose expression was solemn.

'Bad news? Something wrong?' Frank enquired as Andreas stopped by his chair. 'The stock market taken a dive?'

'We got the results of the A levels,' Andreas mumbled, handing the paper to Giles. 'I phoned the school.'

Giles took the paper from his hand and studied it. Then he looked up at Nick.

'Congratulations.'

Nick nodded, but said nothing. An unaccustomed stab of fear, of doubt, clutched at Valerie's heart. 'Well?' she enquired, looking at Giles.

'Not as good as expected, Mum. Nick got four straight As.' Heads turned towards Nick, yet the smiles of pleasure only seemed to hide an underlying feeling of tension that had suddenly permeated the atmosphere. Giles's eyes remained fixedly on the paper. 'I got three Bs and a C, and I think that means I can't take up the conditional offer from Oxford.'

'Conditional?' Frank looked puzzled. 'You must forgive me. Not being a university man . . .'

'Conditional on A level results,' Giles explained. 'Nick and I decided not to take the Oxbridge entrance exam, but to concentrate on A levels. A lot of people do this, but you then have to rely on your success at the interview plus the A level results. I think I did well at my interview, and I was given an offer of a place providing I got a minimum of two grades at Standard A and one at B.'

'Surely three Bs . . .' Sally's expression tried vainly to be encouraging, but Giles shook his head.

'Ain't good enough, I'm afraid.' He continued to shake his head, obviously utterly bewildered by the results. 'I can't understand it. I never thought they'd be as bad as this.'

'But, darling . . .' Valerie reached over and took the paper from him. 'Why, something must be wrong. Are you *sure*, Andreas?'

'I made them repeat it. I talked to the Head. They're as incredulous as I know Giles must be. The Head said he was one of the stars of the sixth form.'

'He can retake,' Valerie said firmly. 'Or maybe Oxford will still admit him?'

'Because he's a Harvey,' Nick intoned, and then his hand flew to his mouth. 'Sorry. Stupid attempt at humour.'

Giles appeared unoffended by the remark, a slight smile of disparagement flickering across his face. 'I'm sure even being a Harvey isn't enough to get them to admit me. But I'll telephone them. If not, it will have to be another university, if it's not too late.'

'But did you apply to any others?' His mother still looked in a state of shock as Giles shook his head.

By this time Edmund had hobbled up, followed by Paul, and they both stood behind Giles gaping over Valerie's shoulder at the paper.

'It's not the end of the world,' Edmund said finally.

'It means I may not be able to go up to Oxford with Nick. In fact, I'm sure of it. Too many good students competing for places.'

'There must be something we can do,' Andreas slumped at the table next to Valerie.

'I don't think even you can fix this, Dad.'

'No need to be rude, Nick.'

'I didn't mean to be. I just feel a bit shocked. I'm sorry. I'm saying all the wrong things this morning.'

Giles put a hand on his shoulder and gave him a sympathetic smile.

'I think I'm more shocked than you,' Nick said to him. 'I always thought we'd go to Oxford together. I don't know if I can face it without you.'

'Don't be silly. Of course you can.'

'But what will you do?'

'He'll retake,' Valerie said firmly.

'Mother, I could still not go to Oxford this year whatever I did. Also, I don't want to retake or stay on at school. I'll have to go through the clearing.'

'Whatever's that?'

'It's the system that finds places for those who failed to get into the university of their choice.'

'You'll easily get in somewhere with those grades.'

'But we don't want you to go to *any* university. We want you to go to Oxford.' Valerie sounded near to tears. 'Like Daddy and Grandpa.'

'We'll certainly have to discuss all this.' Edmund sat down heavily.

'In the meantime I'll have to come back with you, Dad. I can't stay on here on holiday.'

'Oh!' Alice, who too had silently joined the company assembled on deck with Emma, began to wail. 'Oh, *no*!'

'Well, you can stay on . . .'

'Oh, no, she can't,' Valerie said firmly. 'That is for sure. In fact, the whole family will have to go home.'

'It's a pity you rang the damn school, Andy.' Edmund cast him a reproachful glance. 'What, with this and my painful foot, it's ruined the whole damn holiday.'

Lydia, who had been listening to the drama unfold while standing unnoticed behind a pillar, quietly turned and disappeared along the deck in the direction of her cabin. She had made a special effort to pull herself together and attend breakfast in honour of the departing guests. Had put on a glamorous tracksuit and lots of make-up to conceal her pallor. She began to retch as she got to the door of her cabin, and just made it in time to the lavatory before emptying the contents of her stomach down the pan.

This was really the last straw in their Herculean effort to ingratiate themselves with the wretched Harveys, that their son should get into Oxford while Giles, to whom everything came so easily, had failed.

Then she rose from her supine position, threw water on her face and patted it dry. She felt, to her surprise, not only a whole lot better, she felt something else too: a sense of triumph which seemed to surge through her veins.

CHAPTER 4

The room was full of flowers, and among them was a particularly large arrangement of choice blooms that must have cost the earth. Edmund had wanted to throw them out or send them to a public ward, but Valerie had said how dreadful it would be if the Constantines paid a visit and there was no sign of their flowers. After all, she reasoned, it wasn't as though what had happened to him was their fault. He had stood on a poisonous jellyfish that were particularly prominent in the south of France that summer, and it had happened on the shore, and not on the yacht. No one could possibly blame the Constantines.

But Edmund did blame the Constantines. He had gone through a lot of pain and not a little fear, and he wanted to blame someone. His foot had swelled up to the size of a football, his leg came to resemble the trunk of a tree and before he was carted off to hospital with a high temperature as an emergency, he had indeed been very very afraid.

Now he was better, definitely out of danger but feeling cantankerous. His leg was still swollen, he was still in pain; but he was in no danger.

Never one at coping with illness, something of a hypochondriac, Edmund was a bad patient. Valerie had been rather glad that he was a hospital case, though of course worried and anxious at the same time, and she made up for her feelings of relief by bringing him lots of little gifts and home-made dishes of his favourite food.

Edmund was dozing in the late-afternoon sunlight that crept into his hospital room over the roofs of the adjacent complex in north London. He was of course a private patient, and had the privilege of his own comfortable room in a separate wing of the hospital. Valerie had made her visit for the day, had brought him home-made custard tarts, a great favourite, to have with his tea, and a good claret to have with his supper. Paul might or might not visit him in the evening, Giles was away, and endless hours of boredom stretched in front of him. There was a tap on the door. Edmund started from a state that was part snooze, part reverie.

'Come in,' he called and sat up expecting to see one of the nurses or doctors.

'Hello, Edmund.' The tone of voice was timid, uncertain in its welcome, and Edmund said sharply: 'Come in and close the door.' Then, when the woman had done his bidding, 'Did anyone see you coming?'

The woman didn't reply, but approached his bed as tentatively as she had entered the room, and laid a large bunch of flowers on the table next to it. She stooped and planted a kiss on his forehead, to which he gracefully submitted. Then she stepped back and gazed at him.

'You don't look too bad, Edmund. I was terribly worried.'

Edmund pointed to his leg which hung in a crane suspended from pulleys.

'And all that caused by a little jellyfish?'

Edmund extended his hands to embrace an imaginary sea creature. 'They're whoppers.'

'It's a wonder you didn't see it.'

'I was in the water wading out to the dinghy that had been sent to fetch us from the shore.'

'Didn't you *feel* it, Edmund?' Nervously the woman perched on the side of the bed.

'I felt something, but it wasn't until later that I realised my foot had swollen. Oh, really, Mary,' he reached out and put his hand over hers, 'it was a dreadful holiday . . .'

'I thought you were having a good time. You said you were on your card.'

'Well,' he shook his head ruefully, 'all the bad things happened at the end. I got this sting on my foot and we had the A level results and Giles has failed to get into Oxford.'

'Oh; but that's *terrible.*' Mary clutched his hand. 'How did that happen?'

'His grades weren't good enough. I think he took too much for granted,' Edmund said sternly. 'Didn't work hard enough, that's obvious. The worst thing was that the Constantines' son Nick got *four* As.'

'Oh, well done him!' Mary exclaimed and then stopped, faltered when she saw the expression on Edmund's face. 'But you always *liked* him, Ed, didn't you? He was Giles's best friend.'

'We liked him, of course we did and still do; but we would like our son to have got into Oxford as well.'

'Naturally.'

'Secretly the Constantines crowed. You could see it, though they tried to hide it. They made a point of announcing the results on deck so that everyone on board heard it. I'm sure it was done deliberately to humiliate Giles.'

'But why should they do that, Ed?' Mary tucked his hand firmly in hers.

'Oh, Mary, don't be so *irritating,*' Edmund said, wrenching his hand away. 'Because that's the sort of people they are. Nouveau riche. No manners and no tact.'

'I see,' Mary nodded, 'is that the definition of nouveau riche?'

Edmund looked at her suspiciously. 'You're trying to wind me up, Mary. Please don't. I haven't been well, you know. I've been very ill. I could have died.'

Mary leaned forward impulsively. 'Oh, Ed, don't you think

I've been worried sick? Not knowing anything? Not being able to find out.'

'Sorry, Mary. I couldn't let you know.'

'It made me realise the precariousness of my situation.'

'Well, Mary, you knew that some time ago,' Edmund said with the gravity of a judge delivering a verdict. 'No one tried to force you. You can't say you didn't know what you were doing. No one forced you into a relationship with me.'

Mary Rogers gazed searchingly at her long-time lover. No one forces anyone to fall in love. It was one of those inexplicable things which defied any amount of psychological or physical analysis.

Certainly, in hindsight, it seemed foolish to have fallen in love with a married man, especially one as entrenched in his marriage as Edmund, who never had the slightest intention of leaving his wife on whom he was not only dependent, but of whom he was also a little afraid.

'It never quite hit me like this, Ed. You've never been ill before. You might have died . . .' and she began to weep, as though all her pent-up worry could no longer be contained, her face buried in the bedclothes. Edmund, embarrassed and confused, put one arm round her shoulder and with his other free hand gently stroked her hair.

His relationship with Mary Rogers was more than a decade old. She had been his secretary, a highly qualified, intelligent and attractive woman. Many in the firm, in which he then worked, had thought her too intelligent and attractive to become involved with a man who clearly was only looking for something on the side.

A complicating factor, which happened two years into the affair, was that Mary became pregnant and, despite the entreaties of Edmund to abort, gave birth to a son, Adam, now eight years old.

Edmund had been too much of a gentleman to desert Mary, and after some initial resentment, he not only came to accept Adam but to love him. He was an appealing little chap, with a loveable, trusting, rather vulnerable nature.

However, Edmund felt and continued to feel, guilty about Mary, guiltier still about Adam who did not enjoy the advantages, educational and otherwise, of his legitimate sons. Adam went to the local state junior school. He was bright, but he struggled against asthma. He was also myopic. He was a dear, brave little boy whose timidity contrasted strongly with the extroversion and glamour, the good looks of the other Harvey boys.

Mary wept and Edmund patted her shoulder. But he was anxious, and kept casting furtive glances at the door. What if Paul should arrive? Well, they all knew Mary had once been his secretary. Would it seem strange that she should visit him now? There were all these questions one had to anticipate, subterfuges one had to consider, when the discovery of an illicit relationship could spell possible disaster.

Mary really was an embarrassment. He dearly wished she wasn't there, that he had never given in to the momentary temptation to slip his hand up her skirt one day when she was leaning over his desk. That had started the whole thing off. Moments of frank eroticism begun in the office culminated in a bedroom in Maida Vale where Mary still lived, supported to some extent by Edmund. She eked out his meagre allowance by working as a freelance legal typist.

'There, there,' he said, 'there, there.'

But 'there, there' wasn't enough. Edmund had never been ill before and Mary, alone in her ugly little flat in the desert that was Maida Vale, had felt lonely and cut off in a way she never had before. She'd only found out what had happened by telephoning his office from which she occasionally got legal work. It wasn't enough when you had a long term lover and a child by him.

She threw back her tear-stained face and thumped the bed with clenched fist.

'It isn't *enough*, Edmund . . .'

'What isn't enough?' He looked confused.

'All this,' she gestured wildly. 'Being out on a limb, left in ignorance of the most mundane things, having no *rights* . . . the other woman.'

'Oh, Mary,' he petulantly drew his arm away. 'This is no time to throw a tantrum. It's selfish of you. I've been very ill, *dangerously* ill . . .'

'I know that, Edmund, and don't you think I was worried sick? Hard on me. Hard on Adam.'

Yes it was hard, especially on Adam. He had a deep affection for this youngest child, flawed, illegitimate but with such a loving, trusting nature. He knew that Adam and Alice would get on well; but he also knew that it could never be. He was too established, too settled, too married, also too timid if the truth be known, to upset the applecart.

'We'll have to talk about all this when you get well, Ed.' She vigorously pushed back her hair from her face.

'Talk about what?'

'The situation. It can't go on.'

'Oh, Mary, be reasonable.'

'I *am* being reasonable.' Her lower lip started to tremble, and he thought she was going to burst into tears again. 'I've just been reasonable for too damn long. What is my life, Ed? Did you ever think of that?'

'You should have thought about it before we began, Mary,' he said, eyeing her. 'It took two of us to fall into bed, you know. You can't talk about seducers and seduced. Not in this day and age, not in a time of equality like now. You wanted an affair and you wanted Adam. You said if you didn't have him it would be too late.'

It was true. Adam's conception might have been accidental but maybe because, instinctively or not, she wasn't sure, she had wished it. But had she wished it for herself, or in the hope that it would bind Edmund more strongly to her? Did she even remotely imagine, even then, that he would abandon home, wife, family just for her?

'It's not only all this secrecy, Ed.' Mary tossed back her head, looked him boldly in the eyes. 'I don't think Adam is getting the opportunities he ought to have.'

'What opportunities?' Edmund looked alarmed and, as the pain made his foot begin to throb again, sank back on his pillows.

'*You* know what opportunities, Ed. Adam is bright but he is being held back by being at a state school.'

'It's a very good school.'

'It is not a very good school. It's an adequate school, but from there he goes on to the comp and that has not got a good reputation. I want Adam to have the same opportunities that your other children have. I want him to go to a private school too. I want the best for our son, Ed.'

'Why bring it all up now?'

'Because things have come to a head. I've had enough, enough of being cast to one side, treated like a pariah, my son a second-class citizen . . .'

'You're being over-dramatic, Mary.' Edmund began to sweat and pointed to his foot. 'Look I'm going to have to take some medication. My foot is throbbing dreadfully. I shall have to call the nurse.' His hand reached towards the bell and then halted in mid-air.

'I'm afraid you're going to have to go, Mary.'

'Why?'

'You know why . . .'

'Because I'm the mistress and you don't want people to know about me . . .'

'Don't be silly. Be sensible, please. I beg you. Look, I'm in pain. I've been very ill. I promise you that when I'm better we'll talk again, go into the whole thing . . .'

'We'd better, Ed,' Mary said, getting up. The look of desperation on her face had now been replaced by a curious amalgam of determination and spite. 'I don't want to go back to where we were. I want it all out in the open, otherwise I'm afraid I shall have to tell Valerie . . .'

'You wouldn't.'

'I would. Believe me, Ed, I would and, frankly, I think I'd enjoy seeing the supercilious, know-it-all look on her face replaced by what? Would she be surprised, Ed? Horrified?'

Helplessly, Edmund shook his head.

'I think I know Valerie, Ed. She'd divorce you. She wouldn't put up with it, to know she'd been cuckolded all these years by you, that you had a son she knew nothing about. I tell you I'm absolutely serious. This is crunch time, Ed.' She gathered up her things and made for the door, pausing just before she opened it and looking back at him. 'Think about it.'

'Manchester!' Edmund bellowed. 'What do you want to go to Manchester for?'

'Because it's a good university and they offered me a place. Also, incidentally, it's considered a trendy place to be.'

'But Manchester itself is a terrible town.'

'When were you last there, Dad?'

'Everyone knows Manchester's a terrible town.'

'Terrible in what way?'

Giles knew there would be a fuss so had determined in advance to try and keep his patience.

Edmund didn't reply. His sojourn in hospital was behind him, but his foot and leg were still swollen and he was in a fair amount of pain. The doctors had assured him the infection was cured, and now all that remained was to keep taking the tablets to complete the healing process.

Edmund fretted at the enforced inactivity. He was not a good patient. His legal practice was a one-man band, and although his clerk and secretary faxed him important material and information, he nevertheless worried.

Valerie sat by Edmund's side, her eyes cast downwards, studying her rings, her expression thoughtful. Finally she looked up at Giles.

'Manchester is very disappointing. You must see our point of view, Giles.'

'Frankly, I don't. I think you're being snobbish, just as you were with the Constantines.'

'Oh, for God's sake don't bring that up again,' Edmund roared, his nerves clearly on edge. 'I've heard enough of the bloody Constantines. Just now they seem to me responsible for all our woes.'

Giles perched on the arm of the chair opposite his parents. They were in the family living room, the scene of many such dramas in the past and, no doubt, many more to come. Although a loving and cohesive family, they were also one riven by differences largely owing to the temperament and personalities of its members. Most of the dramas in recent years had been about Paul being a disappointment; about his general attitude, his lack of ambition.

'That's a very unjust remark, Dad.'

'If we hadn't gone on that yacht, none of this would have happened.' Edmund gazed soulfully at his bandaged foot.

'You might not have stood on a jellyfish, Dad, but I would still not have got into Oxford. Nothing can help that.'

'It was the way it was announced, before *everyone* on deck. Even the steward heard.'

'Oh, *that's* what this is about?' Giles stood up and nodded his head several times. 'Wounded pride. Now I understand.'

'It certainly *wasn't* very nice,' Valerie inclined towards her husband. 'Had you both done well it would have been a different matter. It seemed to me that the Constantines were crowing.'

'I didn't think that at all. I don't think Andy really understood the implications. He didn't realise I wouldn't get into Oxford with Nick.'

'He understood the implications alright. Or if he didn't, Nick had explained them to him. They both looked extremely solemn. Remember?'

Giles remembered. It was hard not to agree that Andy must have known the effect of his announcement; but he still found it hard to think it had been made with any malice.

Not even the teeniest, weeniest desire to humiliate people who, according to Nick, always made his family feel inferior?

After the unsatisfactory conversation with his parents, Giles went up to his room, changed into a tracksuit and trainers and, putting his squash racquet and towel into his sports bag, ran back down the stairs and out of the house to the car that had been a seventeenth birthday present from his parents. It was a vintage MG and he was very proud of it. What a dash, he had thought, he would cut in Oxford roaring down the High. But it was not to be.

Instead he would be roaring up the M1 to a far less salubrious town in the north.

It was true that a great deal had been done to improve the image of northern towns since the days of L S Lowry, and his depiction of the dark Satanic mills of Salford. Manchester was a fine city with a great tradition. It was the home of a famous orchestra, the Hallé, had a magnificent library, and was a centre for the arts. Most of the important plays in London discovered the prospect of failure or success during trial runs in front of the critical audiences Manchester had to offer. But Manchester, although prestigious, with a good university, had not quite the cachet of Oxford, that city of dreaming spires, of poets, writers and many Nobel laureates.

Giles had sustained a shock which, in the circumstances, he had been at pains to conceal from his parents. It was true, the latter days of the holiday had been a disaster. The cruise, although enjoyable, had been rather too full of tension thanks also to Lydia's illness, and the feeling that somehow one ought not to be having such a good time when one's hostess was languishing on her sick bed.

Then there was the fact that, although barriers to some extent did break down, the atmosphere between his parents and Andreas was cordial rather than overtly friendly. Everyone seemed to be making too much of an effort, and then when the chance had come to relax a bit on the holiday after his parents had gone home came double disaster: his father's mishap and the results, the consequent abandonment of plans for the Harvey children to continue with their holiday. The terrible fuss and mix-up about plane tickets which Andreas somehow managed to settle.

Fortunately it wasn't until his father had got home that the extent of the damage to his foot became apparent, although it was still not too late for him to blame the Constantines.

When he got to the school Nick was waiting for him at the gates, swinging his squash racquet as though hitting the ball. As old boys they were entitled to the use of the school sports facilities and, as school had finished for the day and everyone had gone home, they almost had the place to themselves. They greeted each other, exchanging only platitudes, and after changing played a vigorous game of squash which, as usual, was won by Giles. They then took a dip in the school pool where they found a few old boys and members of staff, stopped and chatted to them before going to the dressing room to change. After that they set off as usual to the local for a beer before going, as planned, back to the Constantines for a meal. They were silent as they walked through the school grounds and out of the gates, as if self-consciously aware of their new-found status in the world. Only Giles paused for a moment and looked back.

'Very odd to think this is no longer the place where we go every day.'

'We can still come back in the hols.'

It was only a week to the beginning of the academic term.

'They were good days.' Nick put an arm loosely round Giles's shoulder. 'I shall miss you.'

'Ditto, like hell,' Giles grunted.

'Term's only eight weeks.'

'Long enough to grow apart.'

'I was thinking . . .' Nick paused again halfway up the hill to the pub and gazed at his friend. 'I wouldn't mind going to Manchester myself.'

Giles's mouth fell open.

'I'm not kidding. I'm serious. Oxford *is* very elitist. We always said it. Well now is the time to put my principles to the test.'

'But you wouldn't do this if I'd got in.'

'Maybe not. But I can't think Oxford without you will be much fun.'

'And I can't think Manchester without you will be much fun either.'

There was an air of mounting excitement between the two young men as they reached the doors of the pub.

'Let's go tell my parents,' Nick said.

'You're assuming you'll get into Manchester at this late stage?'

'I'll get in for *something*.'

'It could ruin your career.'

'Not a chance. Worth a try?'

'I dread to think what your parents will say. Look maybe I should not come back to dinner?'

'They're expecting you. Besides I need the support.'

'I think we need a half a pint to steady our nerves.' With a grin Giles pushed open the door of the pub and Nick followed him.

The Constantine house stood back from the leafy road in one of the best parts of St John's Wood. It was a low, gabled two-storey house built, maybe, towards the end of the nineteenth century and to which an extension had been added some time in the thirties. Like all the houses in the road, it had a small front garden and a path leading up to a porch and a double front door which was manned by a complex system of security devices including a camera. To one side was a garage big enough for three cars and, behind, a large garden backed onto the high wall of an embassy of an important Middle Eastern state. Unlike the Harvey house, which was casually shabby – the furniture good but old and worn by the passage of time, animals and children; the carpets best-quality Wilton or Axminster but largely threadbare, the inevitable stains that had appeared over the years covered by equally threadbare Persian rugs – the Constantine house was sumptuous in its restrained elegance. Lydia Constantine had extremely good taste, and an abundant purse had enabled her to exercise to the full her gift for interior decoration which, every five to seven years was completely renewed: the colour schemes in the various rooms changed, the walls relined, new curtains hung and sometimes new carpets laid. Good pictures, evidence of a discriminating taste, hung on the walls; there were a few books, not many, but plenty of large coffee table tomes and glossy magazines scattered about and the impression was of a comfortable, affluent rather than an intellectual or cultured home.

Lydia was extremely fastidious and nothing escaped her. Besides, as well as the means, she had the advantage of plenty of time to indulge her passions for personal shopping, interior redecoration and the acquisition of works of art.

Recently returned from the Mediterranean, Andreas, Lydia and Emma were already in the drawing room having drinks when Nick and Giles arrived. They had not 'dressed' for dinner but they looked smart, the women in pretty dresses with jewellery, and Andreas in a business suit. Remembering the episode on the boat, Giles apologised for being in a tracksuit and offered to go home and change. Andreas replied that of course they wouldn't hear of it and told Nick, who looked uncomfortable, not to change either. Giles realised that once again an awkward situation had been set up on account of a member of his family, this time himself. In the years he and Nick had known each other, he had seldom been invited for an evening meal.

'Silly of me, I should have thought,' he said, accepting a drink from Andreas who gestured towards a chair.

'Not at all, not at all. We realised you were coming from the squash court. Who won?' He raised his glass to his lips.

'Giles won, of course.' Nick poured himself a beer. 'Always does.'

'How's your father, Giles?' Andreas spoke in a reverential tone. 'I can't tell you how bad I felt about all that.'

'It wasn't *your* fault. It was his.' Giles smiled encouragingly. 'He trod on the jellyfish.'

'Yes, but I felt in a way responsible. You can understand that, can't you? I mean the holiday hadn't exactly gone with a swing, and we so wanted you to have a good time.'

'We did have a good time. We had a marvellous time.' Giles looked apologetically at Lydia. 'I mean we were all sorry Lydia was unwell, and it took the gilt off the gingerbread, but apart from that we had a wonderful time. I assure you.'

'Oh, good!' A look of relief spread across Andreas's face. 'And he got the flowers?'

'They were magnificent. He'll be writing to you once he gets back to work.'

'No need.'

'In fact, he should have scribbled a note.'

'I expect he got so many.'

'A good few.'

Giles felt embarrassed, but wasn't that always the case? Wasn't there always that slight, almost intangible, feeling of guilt, of awkwardness when it came to relations between the families?

As if to prevent further conversation on the subject, Nick turned excitedly to his father. 'Dad, we've had a brainwave . . .'

He looked so happy that Andreas's worried expression vanished, and he perched on the arm of one of the chairs as Lydia and Emma looked on expectantly.

'Sounds interesting,' he smiled encouragingly, looking from one young man to the other.

'I decided I'm going to give up the place at Oxford and apply to Manchester . . .'

Giles knew immediately that the timing was wrong and lowered his eyes to avoid seeing the reaction of the family. In the event, he didn't need to look. He could feel it. Now that the words were out, the idea immediately seemed ridiculous. He looked up at Nick and shook his head as Andreas, desperately trying to recover his composure, said: 'I don't think I'm hearing you right.'

'It was just a notion,' Giles mumbled. 'It seems rather foolish now.'

'I should think it *is* foolish,' Andreas said. 'Unless you have some very good reason, Nick, for saying what you just said.'

'We'd like to go on being together. We'd miss each other too much. We've been mates for such a long time . . .'

'And of course,' Lydia's tone was icy, 'as Giles failed to get a place at Oxford *you* would be the one to make the sacrifice.'

'It wouldn't be a sacrifice. Oxford is elitist anyway.'

'Then why did you apply to go there?'

Silence as the two younger men studied the floor.

Andreas rose, went over to the bar and shakily helped himself to another whisky.

'I'm quite unable to understand what's going on,' he said in a strangulated voice. 'What are you two telling me? You're a couple of gays or what?'

'*Daddy*!' Emma exclaimed. 'What a horrible thing to say.'

'Well, it's all the acceptable thing now, isn't it?' Andreas shrugged. 'You've got to face facts.'

'We didn't say anything about being gay, Dad.' Nick spoke very quietly. 'You can have a friendship without being homosexual.'

'Well, I think it's a very *odd* friendship, if you don't mind me saying, when two men can't bear to be separated to such an extent that one has to give up a much desired place at Oxford in order to be with the other.' He turned and looked steadily at Giles. 'Would you, Giles, for instance be prepared to make a similar sacrifice, and what do your parents make of this suggestion?'

'They don't know about it. Nick brought it up literally about an hour ago. It never occurred to me, but I guess neither of us thought it through. At the time it seemed a good idea.'

'I imagine it did. Then you wouldn't feel so bad about failing to get into Oxford. Make you feel better would it?'

Giles felt the colour rush to his face.

'That wasn't the case at all, Andreas.' He put down his glass and stood up. 'I'm sorry Nick suggested it, and I'm sorry he brought it up when he did. I didn't know he was going to so soon. It was a silly idea and I'm sorry. Look, maybe I better not stay for dinner.'

'No, stay!' Emma jumped up, a look of outrage on her face as she turned to her father. 'Dad, I don't know how you could say the things you said.'

'And I don't know how Nick could say what *he* said. He would be the first member of our family to go to any university, never mind Oxford. It's all I ever dreamed of. I feel a personal sense of outrage that after all we've done, all our sacrifices and encouragement, Nick should even entertain such an idea. Naturally I want to know what is behind it.'

'I can understand that two friends would want to be together,' Emma went on. 'I'd feel the same.'

'Well, I can't, and that's it.' Andreas turned to his son. 'I apologise, Nick, if what I said offended you.'

'I'm not offended because it's not true.'

'I've nothing against gays.'

'Except that you don't want one as your son.'

'Obviously. I think any parent would say that if they were honest. The trouble is so many of them aren't.'

'You're not discussing the issue.' Emma angrily stamped her foot. 'It's about Nick going to Manchester.'

'I can see that he won't be,' Giles said. 'And I think you're right. It was a crazy idea. Manchester may not be Oxford but it's a good university and I think all the places available will be taken up. I don't think there would be the slightest chance that he'd get a place so late now anyway. We didn't think it through. We didn't think about it at all. We simply got carried away.' He looked straight at Andreas. 'We're not gay, but we like each other. We'll miss each other. That's all.'

As Giles turned to go Lydia rose abruptly and, crossing the room, barred his way to the door.

'Giles, please stay.' She held out her hands towards him as if in a kind of supplication, but he shook his head.

'Really, I think it's better . . .'

'But we'd *like* you to stay, Giles, truly.'

'Besides, I'm not properly dressed.' He looked down at his tracksuit top.

'It really doesn't matter.'

'All the same . . .' He gave an embarrassed, deprecating smile.

Sensing defeat, and possible humiliation again, Lydia deftly stepped aside. 'I hope you'll come again soon,' she said. 'Nick will see you out.'

Silently Nick and Giles walked along the hall and out of the front door, pausing beside Giles's car which was parked by the pavement. Nick ruefully scratched his head.

'I really don't know what to say . . .'

'No need to say anything.' Briefly, Giles placed a hand on Nick's shoulder. 'We both know it doesn't matter. But I really couldn't stay for dinner after that.'

'I know. I think you were right. I don't know what got into Dad.'

'If I'd thought you were going to bring it up immediately I'd have cautioned you to wait until everyone had eaten.'

'You're right. I just blurted it out. I simply didn't think.'

'*We* didn't think. Anyway the whole idea was crazy.' Giles turned towards his car, a hand upraised. 'See you.'

'See you soon.'

Watching him sadly as he drove away, Nick knew that more than a friendship had changed that night, and he wandered for some time around the garden until the chill evening air drove him inside to rejoin his family.

PART II

The Girl in the Quad: Laura

CHAPTER 5

Nick stood at the window of his room looking down into the quad. He'd seen the girl before, watched her as she emerged from the door leading to staircase F, wondering who the lucky sod was whose room she was coming from.

She walked across the quad to the gate, well wrapped up against the chill blast of the keen January wind.

He'd seen her in other places as well, caught glimpses of her through a crowd: in a pub, a coffee bar, once walking along the High with another female, deep in conversation.

It was difficult to know what attracted him to her in a city, a university, where there were so many girls to choose from. Maybe there was something about her that suggested an answer to his loneliness?

She had bronze curly hair cut slightly above shoulder length. It was an amazing colour, like molten gold. She was about five feet nine or ten, of athletic build, and she walked gracefully as though she might once have trained for the ballet before her height outstripped her. Very tall women sometimes had rather a clumsy gait, but hers was unusually graceful.

He had never been really close enough to discern her features with any certainty, but the general impression was of a rather pale face, arresting bone structure and deep-set eyes that could have been green or kingfisher blue.

She reminded him of a quattrocento painting, and he very much wanted to get to know her.

Then she disappeared off the horizon and he began to panic. He had somehow assumed that, one day, inevitably, they would meet, that theirs was a linked destiny. He spent a lot of time at his window; looking for her in the street; in various meeting places; but the girl with the green or kingfisher blue eyes failed to materialise.

He had begun to wonder whether she'd left the university, or even if she'd ever belonged to it.

Would he spend the rest of his life chasing a dream? Maybe he would be one of those people who never married because of the memory of some fruitless, unconsummated love.

Nick wondered if he was obsessed with the girl he had never met because he was so unhappy at Oxford? The row with his parents over Giles, so soon before he joined the university, had distressed him. That combined with natural nerves at the prospect of such an important change, seemed to set the tone for the first term. He had felt uneasy and unhappy. He found it difficult to form new friendships, and he spent a lot of time in his room gazing out of the window, like today, watching the girl stop by the gate for a word with the porter.

Then, suddenly, he acted. He felt exhilarated at seeing her again, and if he allowed her to disappear this time, it might be for good.

He slipped out of his room, ran down the steep winding staircase and walked swiftly across the quad, just as she had done, keeping her in sight. As he approached the gate he saw her wave to the porter and then she turned right. Nick sped after her, but as he drew abreast of the porter's lodge he heard his name.

'Mr Constantine . . .'

'I'll be back in a moment,' he said waving an arm, and as he turned the corner she was still there, about a hundred yards ahead. He felt rather like a stalker as he followed her, slowing down when she slowed down, quickening his pace when she quickened hers. It was nearly four in the afternoon and he saw her pause, consult her watch and then turn abruptly into a coffee bar.

He waited a few seconds and then followed her inside.

As she made her way to the self-service counter, he caught a glimpse of her close-up, and she was even more beautiful than he had imagined, with the most amazing grey-green eyes. He watched her as she gazed into the display cabinet as if deciding whether to have a cake and, if so, which one. Finally she selected a piece of cheesecake, put it with her coffee on a tray and sat at the only available table by the window at the far side of the shop.

Nick also had a coffee, paid for it and made as though he was looking round for somewhere to sit. Finally he approached the table by the window: 'Do you mind?'

'Not at all,' she replied, looked at him for a second, smiled and, lowering her head, went on eating her cheesecake. Nick's mouth dried up. He swallowed some coffee.

'Haven't I seen you somewhere before?' he said at last, and again she looked up with the most fleeting of smiles.

'Sounds familiar.'

'OK. It's a pick-up,' Nick grinned.

'I think we have met before,' she said. 'Laura Chase.'

'Nick Constantine.'

They shook hands across the table. Nick felt easier, more relaxed, crossed his legs and bent his head to drink his coffee. Laura finished eating and, groping in her pockets, produced a packet of cigarettes and a lighter. She held out the packet to Nick. 'Do you?'

'No, I don't.'

'I don't suppose I should either.' She clicked open the lighter and inhaled. Then exhaling she looked at him through smoke.

'I saw you at Michael Marsden's party. Are you at his college?'

'Yes, I am.'

'I know who you are. They say you're very clever.'

He felt a childish pleasure in the fact that she knew something about him.

'I don't think I'm cleverer than anyone else.'

'They say you're brilliant.'

It was thrilling to think that, somehow, she knew so much about him, maybe more than he knew about her.

'Can I get you another coffee?' he said, looking at her cup.

'Thanks.' She smiled again and held out her cup and saucer.

She had a pleasantly deep voice with a distinct northern accent. She wore no make-up except orange lipstick, and her skin glowed. As he came back with the coffees balanced on a tray he saw that she was watching him.

'Is Mike Marsden a particular friend of yours?' he asked.

'We're both doing English Lit,' she said. 'We share a tutor.'

'Is that why you go to his rooms?'

'Ah, ah!' She smiled, spooning sugar into her coffee and stirring it.

'My window faces F block. Sometimes I see you come out.'

She lit another cigarette. 'I assure you it's for the purposes of academic research. What's your subject?'

'PPE. Philosophy, politics and economics.'

'First or second year?'

'First.'

'Me, too. Are you from London?'

'Does it show?'

'No, but most people seem to come from London. I'm from Salford. That's part of Greater Manchester.'

'Oh!' Nick looked interested. 'My best friend went up to Manchester University. I'd like to have gone there too.'

'Why didn't you?'

'My parents wanted me to come to Oxford.'

'Mine, too. I was the first member of our family to go to

university so they were extremely chuffed when I got into Oxford.'

'Me, too.'

'I guess our families must be kind of similar.' She smiled. 'My father is an ex-mill worker. He was made redundant when the cotton mills started to close and he hasn't worked since. My mother's one of those downtrodden characters people make fun of.'

'I'm sure you don't make fun of her.'

'I certainly don't. In fact, I hate leaving her. Sometimes I wish I'd gone to Manchester too. Then I could have stayed at home and helped her.'

'Haven't you brothers and sisters?'

'I've got two brothers. Gordon, is fifteen and still at school. Gary is twenty-one and is a car mechanic, and my sister Sharon is twenty-three, married with two children. So I'm an auntie.'

Nick was very glad she was called Laura and not Sharon.

'Laura's a pretty name,' he mused.

'Tell me about your family.'

'Well, my father's family were Greek – hence the name Nicolas spelled without an "h". My father's grandfather, that is *my* great-grandfather, came from the Peloponnese and had a stall at a market in London.'

'Oh, so you're working class too.' Laura looked relieved. 'That's good. Somehow I thought you weren't.'

'They don't have the market stall any more,' Nick said hurriedly. 'My grandfather started to import stuff from Greece: olives, oil, wine. The business took off after the war when delicatessens began to flourish, and did well.'

'I suppose you've got a shop or something?' Laura looked up, interested.

'No, it's an import/export business with headquarters in the City, near Smithfield as a matter of fact. You know, the meat market.'

'Are you going into the business?'

Nick shook his head. 'Oh, no. I don't think so.'

'What are you going to do?'

'I'd quite like to be an academic if I do well enough.'

'Won't your Dad mind?'

'I don't think so.'

'Have you brothers and sisters?'

'One sister, Emma. She's a twin.'

'Oh, a twin.' Laura seemed to think that interesting. 'Are you alike?'

'To look at?' he smiled. 'Not very. She's much better looking than I am.'

Privately Laura thought that unlikely. To her, he seemed very dishy indeed.

'Are you close then? They always say twins are close.'

'I think we're close, but we're also very different. Emma likes a good time.' He paused nervously, not wishing to put her off. 'People *say* that I'm much more serious.'

This seemed to amuse Laura, and Nick felt a surge of relief. For a first encounter surely it was all going extremely well.

'So what does she do?'

Nick smiled. 'Nothing very much. Look, she's coming down next week. Maybe you'd like to meet her?'

Suddenly it seemed a very good way to develop the acquaintanceship.

'That would be really nice,' Laura said with her enticing, enchanting smile, and Nick thought that she was pleased at this idea of developing the relationship too.

Emma stood with her hands in the pockets of her jeans taking careful stock of Nick's room. His was one of the most ancient of Oxford colleges and, although some new buildings had been added since its foundation in the sixteenth century, Nick's room was in one of the original structures of the college. It was timbered, panelled and cosy.

It was the first time Emma had been to visit. She had recently joined up with friends to cross to North Africa and had then travelled through Africa by jeep. She'd returned feeling restless, and rather envied Nick his dedication to study. She knew that she had the capability of being almost as clever academically as Nick, but lacked the staying power.

Emma had always been very conscious of women's role in the Greek community.

It was a long time ago since her great grandfather had sailed from Corinth with a wife and a baby to seek his fortune in a strange land. There was now no longer a traditional community as such to which the Constantines belonged. They had severed their ties from the strong bonds that bound expatriates. Neither Andreas nor his children could speak any Greek. They were British, born in Britain.

Yet there were certain habits, deeply ingrained, that remained. Greek women from good families were not expected to work. They were expected to marry well, to reflect the industry and wealth of their fathers, to be a credit to the family and pass on the genes of thrift, industry and hard work.

Of course there were exceptions, but Emma was not one of them. She had grown up, assured of her place in the sun; cocooned, loved and protected. It had been a happy close-knit home; her parents were a devoted couple and it is doubtful if, despite the legendary sexual voracity of Greek males, her father had ever eyed up another woman.

Although she knew there was wealth, she and her brother were also taught the value of money. Extravagance was not encouraged; there was no showing off to school friends, being dropped at the gates in chauffeur-driven cars. They travelled like most other children, either by bus or tube.

That said, it was accepted that her father and mother liked the best of everything. They could send their children to the best schools; they could afford fine pictures, costly and elaborate furnishings, good seats at the opera, and first class restaurants. Because he thought it was the supreme example of the manufacturer's craft, Andreas could not resist adding a Rolls to his stable of cars and, eventually, acquire the yacht moored in the bay at Monte Carlo.

Although Emma was slightly bored with her life, she was not envious of Nick. She knew that she herself craved endless excitement and she would not find it in the close confines of academia. She felt flat after the African trip, felt restless and was constantly in search of a good time. Nick's room was neat, compact, with everything that he needed near at hand. It had a bed, a desk, chest of drawers, bookshelf, and a hi-fi with speakers, a stack of classical tapes by its side. It was a scholarly room, a thinker's room, one pleasant and restful to be in.

Nick was serious, purposeful. Emma was not. Yet they had so much in common. Although not identical twins, they had shared that close, confined space in their mother's womb for nine months before they were born.

Emma flopped down on Nick's neatly made bed and picked up the most recent issue of *The Economist* that lay by the side. Underneath that was a weighty tome on the politics of oppression and also, for lighter reading, a well-thumbed copy of Dostoevsky's *The Idiot*.

Nick was at a seminar. Emma had arrived in Oxford the previous evening, was staying at the Randolph and they'd dined there together. It was a happy evening, in the course of which Nick told her about Laura.

She had seldom seen the cautious, sensible Nick so excited; so transformed. Nick, as far as she knew, had never had a serious girlfriend. Over the past few months she had begun to wonder whether her father's intemperate suggestion that Nick might be gay had some foundation. What if he were? Would she have minded? As an emancipated, enlightened woman of the nineties, she liked to think she wouldn't. But, in her heart of hearts, she knew she would. And loving Nick like she did, she knew she would support him anyway. Nothing would change that.

Emma flicked through *The Economist*, found little in it to rivet her attention and, casting it aside, was about to doze off when there was a tap on the door. Thinking it was the scout or someone with a message she rose hastily, sat on the edge of the bed and called out 'come in'.

The door slowly opened and a strange face cautiously peered round it.

'Oh, sorry,' a voice said, and the person was about to withdraw when Emma hurried over and opened the door wide.

'Can I help you?'

'Well, I was wondering if Nick . . .'

'He's at a seminar.' Emma held out a hand at the same time drawing the woman into the room. 'I'm his sister, Emma.'

'I'm Laura,' the girl said.

'Come in, Laura.' Emma stood back to let her pass and then shut the door behind her. 'Do sit down,' she pointed to a chair and then once again sprawled on the bed. 'I'm awfully pleased to meet you.'

'Oh!' Laura looked relieved. 'Nick did mention me? I wasn't sure.'

Emma regarded the young woman with interest. So this was Laura. Not quite what she had expected. Not quite as beautiful as Nick's euphoric description but certainly, with an interesting, intelligent face, and she was so tall! Together they would make an arresting couple; heads would turn wherever they went.

'Nick hardly stopped talking about you,' Emma said. 'You made quite an impression.'

Laura gave a shy smile. 'He's awfully nice. It was so odd the way we met, by chance in a coffee bar.'

So he hadn't told her about his pursuit of her along

the High, of the hours he'd spent gazing out of his window waiting for her to appear. Just as well not to wear your heart on your sleeve, at least at the beginning of a relationship.

Laura, sitting comfortably back in the chair, her arms folded round her knees, was also looking at Emma with curiosity. This was the twin sister about whom Nick talked constantly: the bold adventurous, outward going Emma beside whom he seemed to consider himself rather dull. Opposites in everything, he told her. It would have been impossible, unless one knew it, to believe that they were twins.

'I hear you've been to Africa,' she said.

'Just come back.'

'It sounds very exciting.' Laura now hugged her knees. 'Do you know, I've never been abroad?'

'Really?' Emma looked interested. 'We must soon remedy that. Nick must invite you to come on our yacht. I think we're going to Greece and Turkey this year.'

'On a yacht?'

'Yes.'

'Did you say it was yours?'

'Well ours, that is the family's. It's moored at Monte Carlo. Nick didn't tell you about the yacht?' Nor the Rolls, Emma imagined.

'Nick told me very little about his family. He talked a lot about you. He told me what his father did. I told him what my father did. The usual thing.' Laura paused and looked at her solemnly. 'He didn't tell me about the yacht.'

'No particular reason why he should.' Emma was determined to sound offhand. 'Except that we haven't had it very long and it's a bit like an exciting new toy. I only mentioned it because of going abroad.'

'Of course.'

'I mean, you don't need a yacht to go abroad. I went through Africa in a jeep.'

'It must have been very exciting.' Laura sounded envious.

'It was.'

'And dangerous?'

'Not these days. Providing you've got all your jabs, all you need is your American Express card.'

Once again Laura appeared not to understand, and Emma decided that, for all her apparent sophistication, her height and good looks, she was really rather a naive young woman when it came to experience of the ways of the world. She didn't want to get on the wrong side of someone who might have an important place in Nick's life, and was just wishing he would return when the door slowly began to open and she sprang up and, rushing over to it, flung it open.

'Hi, there . . .' she began. 'Giles!' she exclaimed, and, flinging her arms round his neck, pulled him into the room. 'Giles! Nick didn't say you were coming.'

'Nick didn't know.' Giles, his arms loosely round Emma's waist, looked down at her eager face. 'I thought I'd surprise him but I didn't think I'd find you . . . and' he looked enquiringly round at Laura who had remained where she was.

'This is Laura, a friend of Nick's.'

'How do you do, Laura?' Giles reached down and shook her hand.

'Giles is Nick's best friend,' Emma began to explain but Laura nodded.

'I know. Nick told me about him. Aren't you at Manchester University?'

'Yes,' Giles said eagerly. 'Are you?'

'No, but I come from Salford. You can tell, I expect, from my accent.'

Giles smiled. 'I can't exactly distinguish a Salford accent from a Mancunian one yet, but I guessed you came from the north.'

'So Nick doesn't know you're here?' Emma looked at Giles who shook his head and then smiled apologetically in Laura's direction. 'I'm afraid I got so sick of Manchester.'

'But term's just begun . . .'

'Besides, it never stops raining.'

'It rains here too,' Laura said and stood up. 'I shall have to go. I have a tutorial. Tell Nick that, well . . . I was here.'

'I'm sure we'll meet up with you later,' Emma began to walk her to the door.

'Where are you staying?'

'The Randolph.'

'Oh!'

'I'll tell Nick to give you a ring.'

'See you.' Giles smiled as he watched her proceed to the door and, after Emma had shut it: 'Interesting girl.'

'Oh, you think so too? Nick's had a *coup de foudre*.'

'He didn't tell me.'

'It only happened in the last few days.'

'Really?'

'He followed her along the High and finally accosted her in a coffee bar. He's terribly smitten.'

'Well, I don't know.' Giles's expression was reflective. It was true that, although he himself was a bit of a flirt, Nick had never shown a serious interest in girls.

'I think he's been terribly lonely in Oxford.'

'And I've been terribly lonely in Manchester.'

'Missed each other, I guess?' Emma sounded sympathetic.

'It's ridiculous but true I suppose.' Giles sat on the edge of the bed and stared at the floor. 'I thought I could easily make friends, but I've found it hard.'

'Any particular reason?' Emma looked curiously at him.

'I think I've just known so many people well for so long, chums at school, Nick, that sort of thing. I haven't the ease with strangers I thought I would have had or, to be frank, that people seemed to expect of me. Also, I'm in digs a long way from the campus. They're mostly older students. All the freshers like me are in residential halls and I think that helps to get to know people, make friends. Because I applied so late I couldn't get a place. Digs can be very lonely. I miss the camaraderie of the school days, of London and being surrounded by people I'd known most of my life. Part of the pack.

'I shouldn't really be here now, but I thought I'd surprise Nick. Never guessed you would be here too. That's a bonus.' He looked at her fondly. She was, after all, a great mate. Perhaps more. But somehow it had always been difficult to make a pass at your best friend's sister. Difficult and, unwise too.

'How was Africa?'

'Africa was great.'

Emma sat on the floor cross-legged and began to tell him about it while they waited for Nick's return.

Later they foregathered at an Italian restaurant in the centre of the town. Laura watched the three who had known one another for so long, from whom she was excluded, inevitably, as a stranger, excitedly exchanging news in which, of course, she had no part.

Emma was the most vivacious, the most talkative, delighting in male attention. Laura was interested in her because she was closest to Nick. Yes, they were alike to look at, but it was impossible to tell that they were twins. Both were dark, handsome, but Emma's appearance was less Mediterranean than Nick's. Her skin was quite fair and with her thick, quite long, wavy black hair, dark brown eyes and full red lips, her clever but subtle use of make-up, she looked exotic, exciting; surely extremely attractive to men? She was certainly more lively than Nick who could be given to long, seemingly introspective but not unfriendly periods of silence while Emma and Giles animatedly chatted to each other. However it was easy to tell the twins were close. They had an obvious rapport. They kept on glancing at each other, exchanging looks and smiles and then they would try and draw Laura into the conversation. But it was difficult. In their company she felt shy. Besides, she had nothing to say. She had not travelled by jeep the length of Africa or shared a yachting holiday the previous summer in the Mediterranean.

But, most of all, she had not grown up with these attractive, gifted, exciting young people who not only seemed to share a common bond but, as she now knew, also had a background of wealth and privilege that most certainly excluded her.

And Giles fitted in so well. It was easy to see that he and Nick were intimates, friends, apparently, from the age of thirteen when they went to the London public day school. How many shared memories were there here? Hundreds, thousands; moments of intimacy from which she would be forever excluded.

She saw them as waves coming together, separating for a moment and then joining up again.

They deferred to her; they were nice to her but she felt strangely depressed and apart from the vast expanse of Nick's life before they had met.

Throughout the meal Laura was largely silent, watching.

It was after midnight when they saw Emma and Giles, who was also staying there, back to the Randolph. They lingered for some time in the lobby saying their goodbyes and making plans for the following day. Nick kissed Emma goodnight, Giles and Laura politely shook hands and then Giles and Emma saw them to the door waving as they descended the steps and began to walk towards Carfax.

It was very cold. Nick put his arms around her shoulders and she huddled against him.

'Enjoy the evening?' he asked, bending to look closely at her face.

'Very much.'

'I wondered . . .' he paused.

'Yes?' She looked up at him. 'What did you wonder?'

'I wondered if you felt a bit out of it?'

'Yes, I did, but don't worry. It was nice of you to ask me.'

'I'm just sorry I wasn't there when you, Emma and Giles met up.'

'It didn't matter. Seriously. I liked Emma.'

'And she liked you,' he paused. 'And Giles?'

'Oh, I liked Giles. He's *very* nice. So easy to get on with.'

'Then I'm glad.' Nick squeezed her shoulder hard. 'Those are the two people who mean most in the world to me.'

'Not your mum and dad?' She looked up at him. In the murky light from the street lamps his face looked very solemn.

'Yes, more than my mum and dad. Oh, I love them of course.'

'Is there anything between Giles and Emma?' Laura asked, as they recommenced their stroll, Nick's arm tightly round her waist.

'You mean anything romantic?'

She nodded.

'No.'

'They seem very close.'

'No, they're just good friends,' Nick laughed, 'I know it sounds trite, but in this case it's true.'

Laura appeared to ponder. She halted, detached herself from his arm and gazed at him. 'Nick?'

'Yes?'

'You didn't tell me you were rich.'

'Well!' Nick scratched his head, looked up at the night sky. 'It's not the sort of thing one talks about. It's not important anyway.'

'I mean seriously rich, with a yacht.'

'It's not my yacht. It's my dad's.'

'The jet-set life and all that,' she went on as though she hadn't heard him.

'Does it matter very much to you?'

'It doesn't matter to *me*, but it matters, doesn't it?'

'Why does it matter?'

'In general it matters. Class matters. My parents are working class and we live on a council estate in Salford. My father hasn't worked for over ten years. He's a bitter, frustrated man on the dole.'

'But that doesn't matter to *us*, Laura,' Nick pleaded. 'Keep it in proportion.'

'I just feel rather shocked that I am mixing with people whose father owns a yacht and who stay at the Randolph when they come to Oxford. I hadn't even been in the Randolph until tonight.'

'I don't think I have either.'

'You know what I mean, Nick.'

'No, I don't.' He began to feel rather angry. 'I don't know why you're bringing all this up, letting it interfere with our relationship which I thought was going well. I don't believe in class, don't believe it matters at all. I'm sorry you know about the yacht, but you would have found out about it sooner or later, and then you'd have said I was concealing it from you. As a matter of fact it might amuse you to know that Giles's family are very class conscious. Giles isn't, but his mother and father are. They regard my family as nouveau riche and we didn't have a particularly good time on the yacht.'

'You sounded as though you had a *very* good time.'

'Parts of it were very good. But there was a lot of tension, the end was awful and that clouded the rest. Giles's father trod on a jellyfish and got blood poisoning and Giles learned he hadn't got good enough grades to get into Oxford. We were to be separated and it made us very unhappy. It coloured the whole holiday. But the main thing is that my mother has always felt patronised by the Harveys, Giles's family, and the fact that they were on board made her ill.'

'Then why did you ask them?'

'My father wants to try and impress them, show them that he is as good as they are.'

'Are they very rich too?'

'I don't think they're badly off, but perhaps not quite as well off as my dad. And I stress it *is* my dad. The money is his. It's not mine.'

'I can't tell with you, but I can tell with Emma. The way she behaves, her self-confidence. She's the same age as me, yet she seems much older. Money has given her that particular poise.'

'No, I just think Emma's like that. Actually she's not terribly happy and I think she probably rather envies you.'

'Envies *me*?' Laura looked amazed.

'That you've got into Oxford, that you're clever enough, have a goal. Emma doesn't really know where she's going. She's restless. That's why she seems so sophisticated because she's always on the move, doing things, seeing new places, meeting new people. You see, Emma is really very insecure, and you're the lucky one.'

As if to emphasise this, Nick's arm tightened round her shoulder again, and Laura found herself slipping easily into the comfort of his embrace, feeling reassured by his words, and that already, in a way, she belonged, if not to his family, then to Nick.

CHAPTER 6

Valerie had never liked sex, although before she and Edmund were married she had seemed very keen on it indeed. When Edmund proposed, he felt that he was marrying not only a wealthy woman but a sexy one too. She was neither pretty nor plain, but had the sort of well-bred looks of women of his class, women he was used to and with whom he felt comfortable. She was uninterested in her appearance and always had been. In fact, in the years they'd been married, nothing about Valerie had changed very much except that she had gone off sex after Giles was born, and ever after that was doing him a favour.

It was no wonder he'd strayed, Edmund thought, as he eased himself off his lover and looked down at her face: eyes closed, cheeks suffused, every indication of rapture. There was even the trace of tears. Tears, after all these years. He didn't know whether it was a tribute to his prowess as a lover, or Mary's skills as a mistress.

But whether she pretended or not, Mary managed to invest their love life with something he had never had with his wife: a continual sense of excitement.

Edmund was forty-six and Mary was two years younger. When he had first known her, she was already divorced from her husband, Sam Rogers, an officer in the Merchant Navy who had abused her every time he came home on leave. He led her a wretched life, and finally she left him.

Mary had been petite, blonde, wore a lot of make-up

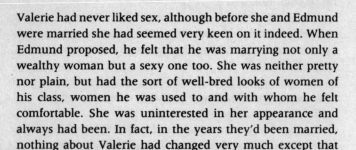

skilfully applied, dressed smartly and was in every way the antithesis of Valerie. And she was wonderfully sexy.

Very shortly after their affair began, Edmund decided to set up a legal practice on his own, having fallen out with his partners. Mary stayed on with his old firm until she became pregnant with Adam.

Edmund had never dreamt Mary would have the child, or that she wanted one. He had tried to persuade her with every inducement, except marriage, to have an abortion, but she refused. Edmund was too much of a gentleman to abandon her, but for a time their relationship had cooled, and he only visited out of a sense of guilt. The child was not only premature but sickly, and Mary was struggling away on her own, determined to be cheerful, keeping up appearances. It was difficult for her, but she coped.

Mary was the sort who coped, and in this she partly resembled Valerie who possessed similar traits. It seemed to go with the characteristics of a certain type of British woman. Edmund didn't love Mary now, and didn't think he ever had. He had found her very attractive, and still did. In a way, he was too calculating a man to fall in love with anyone. He could never quite abandon himself to the loss of emotional control that falling in love seemed to bring. Could never understand it in other chaps.

Parental love he did understand, and he thought that when his daughter Alice was born he had fallen in love for the first time. He simply adored her. There was nothing unpleasant or incestuous about this love, nothing unnatural. It was pure, unadulterated and he would have given his life for her. He was not certain he would have given it either for Valerie or Mary.

Mary stirred and Edmund, who had been lying on his stomach, head in his hands, turned and gazed at her.

It was a Saturday afternoon, about the only free time in the week that Edmund got. It was a toss between playing with Adam, or doing something educational with him like taking him to a film or a museum, or making love. Love won about one Saturday in three. Occasionally there was a late evening when Adam was safely in bed and asleep.

It wasn't much of a life for Mary, but she rarely complained. It was very difficult in fact to know what went on in her mind, and the outburst at the hospital had not been typical. She seldom showed her feelings, but he imagined that they were well bottled up and that sex was for her, as it was for him, a much needed release.

'Heard from Giles?' Mary said, turning over on her stomach too.

'Not for ages.'

'How's he settling down in Manchester?'

'I don't think he's very happy. He has only himself to blame.'

Edmund turned over and patted his stomach, looked at the clock by the side of the bed.

'Why is that?' Mary turned round too, aware that any moment he would say he must be off. Mary thought she would eventually get used to that kind of thing, but somehow she never did and went on wishing that he would stay because he wanted to and not because she nagged.

It wasn't much of a life and she'd often thought in the past ten years that she would have been better off on her own, but then she wouldn't have had Adam and she did adore him. It never occurred to her that she might have met someone else and had a different sort of life altogether. One that would not necessarily have excluded children. On the other hand, when she'd met Edmund she had been alone for six years and celibate for most of that time. That wasn't much of a life either.

Edmund turned his eyes from the clock to the ceiling; his fingers continued drumming on his stomach. Mary wondered if he'd heard her.

'I said, Ed . . .'

'Yes, I heard you, Mary. I was just thinking.'

'You said he only had himself to blame. Is that because he failed to get in to Oxford . . .'

'Well, we warned him Manchester wasn't much of a place.'

'I believe it's come along an awful lot since . . .'

'Yes, but it's not Oxford, or London. It's the provinces. Valerie suggested to Giles that he should retake, but he wouldn't. He was too impatient.'

'Does he still see Nick?'

'I don't really know as he hardly communicates. I know he didn't much at Christmas, if at all, because we were in Somerset and the Constantines, naturally, were in Gstaad.'

'Why do you say "naturally", Ed?'

'Because that's the sort of place people like them go to for Christmas.'

'Whereas people like you go to the country?'

He looked at her suspiciously, uncertain as to whether or not he could detect a note of sarcasm.

'And people like me stay in town,' she went on bitterly, 'because we've nowhere else to go.'

It was difficult, Edmund thought, to believe that a few moments before she'd been in tears from the emotion of their lovemaking. Women were strange creatures.

To add to the guilt Edmund felt, Mary had no close relations. She was an only child and an orphan. Well, he was an only child too, and his mother and father were also dead; but he had an extended family from Valerie's huge brood of relations, not only both parents alive but brothers and sisters, nieces and nephews, aunts, uncles and cousins galore. In Somerset the place heaved with Valerie's kith and kin, in all shapes and sizes, all invariably dressed in Barbours and green wellies, and all devoted to sport and country pursuits.

Edmund heaved himself out of bed and sat on the side,

scratching his head. He was very lean and going thin on top, and strands of hair protruded from his scalp. Mary suddenly thought he looked at the same time both lovable and oddly pathetic.

'Must go,' he said, then turning to her, 'pointless having this sort of conversation, Mary. We seem to have had it so often before. I mean, look, if you feel so discontented, break it off by all means.'

'You mean you wouldn't care?'

'Of *course* I'd care, dammit! But I don't want this continual complaining when there's nothing I can do.'

'I do not "continually" complain,' Mary said indignantly, also sitting up. 'I merely asked how Giles was.'

'And then you brought up the business of having nowhere to go for Christmas. I had the feeling you were on the verge of complaining, let's put it like that.'

Edmund began to put on his underpants and socks.

'About Adam's schooling,' Mary began.

'Oh, that's it.'

'You said you would think about it.'

No reply. Edmund went on dressing.

'I have found a school that will take him after Easter, Ed. No need to wait until September. They gave him a test and they think he's bright. The longer he stays on at a state school the more difficult it will be to get into the private system. They say it will be impossible for him to take Common Entrance if he tries from the comprehensive system. The teaching is quite different.' Mary paused. 'Ed . . .'

'Yes, I'm listening.' Edmund buttoned up his shirt. As it was the weekend he wasn't wearing a tie.

'I know you don't want to discuss it, Ed, but my mind is made up. I *told* them I was a single parent and they will accept a reduced fee. They were very nice. They know about his asthma . . .'

Edmund sat down on the edge of the bed and gazed at

Mary whose hands were hugging her knees, making a tent in the duvet. Her hair was scraped back, her face shiny and flushed, but this time through passion of another kind. Passion for her son, her first and last born, her only child. It was a very strong and determined passion, and Edmund knew already that he had lost.

'How much?' he asked.

'Oh, Ed, you mean you'd consider it?'

'I shall have to.'

'Fifteen hundred a term.'

Edmund whistled. 'Plus uniform, books, music lessons, games kits and extra classes for this and that.' He held up a hand. 'Oh, don't tell me, Mary. I know all about the "hidden extras". We're looking at five or six thousand a year at least. Oh, and then there are excursions; overseas holidays, cub and scout camp . . .'

'You're being pessimistic.'

'I'm being *realistic*, Mary. Believe me, I can't afford it.'

'But with Giles . . .'

'Giles only gets his fees paid. I have to pay for maintenance. I have to pay full fees for Paul and Alice. This could break me, Mary.' He tried to make his voice sound gentle, wheedling, but inside he was boiling.

Mary's voice was steely-edged.

'But Adam is your son too, Ed.'

'Yes, but I didn't ask for him to be born. It was your decision.'

'You accepted the responsibility. You always said you would, and that you loved him.'

'Which I do.' He reached over and took her hand. 'Believe me, Mary, I do.'

'Then you will have to fork out the fees, Ed,' she said. 'I am not messing about. I've accepted a place. I have never claimed maintenance from you, Ed, never dreamt of taking you to court, you know that. I thought if a thing wasn't voluntary it wasn't worthwhile. I wanted our relationship to be based on mutual trust and affection; but now I've had enough. I really have. My mind is made up. I want Adam to be properly educated. He has not much going for him. He's illegitimate and he's not good looking. He's short-sighted and asthmatic. He's not wealthy. He's going to have to fight his way in life and I want him in there with a chance. That chance is education.'

'I'll see what I can do.' Edmund glanced at his watch and rose from the bed.

'If you haven't got the money, Ed, and I find that hard to believe, better ask Valerie. We know she's got plenty.'

When he looked at her Edmund saw a tight, mean smile on Mary's face that made it difficult for him to recall the rapture, the tears. What a fleeting thing sex was, Edmund thought, as he vowed to himself to try, oh to try so hard, never to make love to her again.

Mary stood by the window watching Edmund get into his car. She noticed his humped shoulders, the frown on his forehead, the air of weariness. She recalled how sad he'd looked, perched on the edge of her bed. He did not look a happy man, whereas she always felt exhilarated after sex and the effect took some time to wear off. But then the phrase *post coitus tristus est* was always, she believed, inferred to refer to men and not to women. Maybe it was coined in the days before women were supposed to enjoy sex at all.

After he got into the car Edmund sat there for some time as though thinking, undecided what to do or, maybe, where to go. Yet he always maintained this fiction of being a very busy man, always in a hurry. A hurry to get away after his fill of sex, because she knew he didn't get any from Valerie. A hurry maybe now to get away from her endless nagging about Adam, about the unsatisfactory nature of their relationship, away from the threats that were a recent intrusion into their life together. Yes, Mary felt exhilarated after sex, lifted onto another plane but, after a while there was a process of winding down, a sense of disillusion. She felt let down too because of the lack of follow up: the post-coital embraces, the endearments, the frolicking in and out of the bath; maybe dinner later followed by the theatre, or vice-versa. She and Edmund seldom went anywhere because he was so afraid of being seen or maybe they'd scuttle round to a local bistro and even then he spent most of his time furtively watching the door. It would have been nice, for example, to have gone to collect Adam from the friends he was with, given him the joy of seeing his mother and father arrive together. But it was never to be, maybe because Edmund was afraid even there of meeting someone he knew, someone who would see him exposed as an adulterer.

Their affair was certainly not satisfactory; it was second or even third best, but Mary was helped by the fact that she couldn't stand Valerie: her air of swank, her patronising manner, the sheer effrontery of a rather plain, drab woman having the nerve to lord it over her.

In the days when Mary worked for Edmund, Valerie used to bray on the phone: 'May I speak to my husband, please?' without taking the trouble to announce who she was or say 'Good morning' or 'Good afternoon'. She was the sort of woman Mary instinctively disliked so she didn't mind carrying on with her husband. In fact she rather enjoyed it.

Maybe it was because Valerie had sensed her as a rival all those years ago that she was so rude to her? She was perfectly civil and polite to everyone else. The upper classes usually were, their hypocrisy concealed behind a display of good manners.

Mary knew she wouldn't betray Edmund to the authorities, to his wife or to anyone else. That was just bluff; but she also enjoyed making him anxious getting, maybe, an understandable satisfaction out of seeing him suffer.

Finally Edmund leaned over the wheel, put the car into gear and shot off round the corner never once looking up to the window, from which a rather sad woman watched him. Mary turned back into the sitting room which seemed a lonely and deserted place now that he was no longer there.

Adam was spending the weekend with his friends, so Mary had lots of time to herself in which to do nothing but think. Still in her gown, she wandered aimlessly about the room, plumping up cushions, blowing imaginary specks of dust off the furniture, wondering precisely how to fill the time. In the corner by her word processor were a couple of legal documents from Edmund's old office that needed typing.

She could call a girlfriend, of whom she had a good few in similar situations; that is they were not necessarily having affairs with married men but they were either divorced or without partners.

Maida Vale was a cheerless part of London; long tree-lined streets comprising huge dreary blocks of flats or tall, once graceful Victorian family houses. Some of these bore an air of decrepitude, and were converted into bed-sitting rooms or apartments. One resembled the other, and the area seemed to attract the flotsam and jetsam of the population, those not rich enough to live in Hampstead or St John's Wood and not poor enough for the less salubrious parts of Paddington or the areas off the Edgware or Finchley roads.

There were a lot of foreigners: waiters, waitresses, students either with work permits or without, some resident, some itinerant, an awful lot of retired elderly people who had lived there all their lives and passed through various stages of fortune and misfortune. And then there were people like her, middle-aged, middle class, who had somehow become stuck in a rut without any chance of escape.

She had lived in the flat since her marriage to Sam. They'd rented it, and then, after the divorce, she had bought it with some money her mother had left her. She hadn't bought it outright of course, but there was enough for a mortgage.

It was a dreary flat then and it was a dreary flat now. It was dark because the front faced north and a line of tall trees prevented the sun ever penetrating the kitchen, the bathroom or Adam's bedroom which faced south at the back.

The mansion block, which comprised over a hundred identical flats, lined the whole side of the street, each entrance alike. Built of red brick in the thirties, and fitted out with cheap materials, it boasted a complete lack of artistic or architectural inspiration.

The entrance to Mary's flat was from a long corridor, the walls of which were painted a sickly mixture of cream and brown, the floor covered with a dull orange carpet, discoloured with age. The front door led into a small, very dark internal hall where the light was permanently switched on. From this were doors to the sitting room, the two bedrooms, one much smaller than the other, kitchen and bathroom.

It had now been Mary's home for nearly twenty years and she didn't suppose she would ever leave it. Like her elderly neighbours, she would sink quietly into genteel poverty and live there trying bravely to keep up appearances, to maintain standards either until she died or was carted off to a home for old people, or something worse.

Mary looked round at her sitting room, aware that depression was setting in. One must fight it, could fight it. She would take a bath and ring up one of her girlfriends who were always available on a Saturday night for a meal or a film in the Edgware Road or at the Odeon Swiss Cottage.

She would do that soon, but not just yet.

Laura walked along the High, happily swinging her bag stuffed with the books and papers she needed for her tutorial. She was going to be a bit late. She often was these days and, as usual, her tutor would be annoyed with her.

Laura didn't care, borne aloft as she was on the wings of

love. A romance that started in a coffee bar had become an all-consuming passion. Her first love affair, Nick's too. They were both nineteen, yet they were old enough and wise enough to know that such things were not supposed to last. It was impossible now to say that it could last forever, though they both knew it would. Nick was kind and gentle, he was also powerful and passionate, deeply satisfying as a lover.

In this profound and intimate knowledge of each other they felt completely wrapped up in themselves and lost to the world. Laura knew it showed in her work, in her attitude to her studies, to her friends. She had once enthusiastically embraced Oxford and all it had to offer. Already in her first term she had shown the promise of a future high-flyer.

And now people were saying she was throwing it all away. She had dropped out from many of the activities in which she was formerly so active, turned down a small part in her college drama production. Her friends said she was missing out, mistaking the rapture of first love for the real thing. Laura didn't care.

Laura stopped in front of the coffee bar where she and Nick had first met. She could recall with the utmost clarity every second of that first encounter. She saw him after ordering coffee from the counter, look around, come up to her table.

'Do you mind?' he'd said looking down.

'Not at all,' she'd replied, and had gone on munching her cheesecake.

'Haven't I seen you somewhere before?'

All so corny, all so enjoyable.

They'd discussed since, many times, whether there was such a thing as predestination, if people were meant for each other. They were both logical, rational people, and they still couldn't decide the answer. Since then they'd lived only to be together. It was such a short time, barely two months and yet it seemed like years.

Platitudes, all platitudes.

The woman who was sitting at the same table as Laura had been when she met Nick, looked at her rather curiously. Laura smiled at her and waved, making the expression on the face of the young woman watching her even more comical. Laura wanted to transfer her joy through the huge plate glass windows, but doubtless her youthful contemporary thought she was crazy.

Laura skipped off down the street and continued her way towards her tutor's lodgings which were in an old house tucked between Christ Church and Merton.

It was still cold, but not as bitter as it had been in January when she and Nick had met. Now it was blustery, with the promise of spring in the air. In two weeks' time, term would end and she would be back in Salford. Nick wanted her to come to London and meet his parents but she didn't think the time was right. Well, she'd see. First she felt she should see her own, convince them that an Oxford education didn't mean she was severing her roots. Soon enough to tell them that her new boyfriend was the son of a millionaire, if she bothered to tell them that at all. She couldn't yet decide.

Laura clattered up the stairs of her tutor's lodgings, paused breathlessly outside the door for a second or two and then knocked. On being told to enter she did. Her tutor was sitting by the window apparently engrossed in some document on her lap – maybe Laura's last essay – and removing her tortoiseshell glasses looked up as Laura gently closed the door behind her.

'Sorry I'm late, Maggie.'

'Late *again*, Laura.' Margaret James, lecturer in English Literature at Laura's college, emphasised the word 'again'.

'Sorry.'

Laura took off her coat, unwound her scarf and, still rather breathless, sat down in the chair opposite her tutor. Yes, the essay on her lap, heavily scored, Laura could now see, was hers. Margaret was a clever young don not much more than thirty. Everyone called her Maggie. She smoked and liked a drink and was considered a good sort. Laura had felt privileged to have her as a tutor. She was an expert in nineteenth-century English Literature which was Laura's speciality. They both adored Hardy.

Margaret watched Laura while she sat down and composed herself and, as she did, it was easy to see she was annoyed.

'Sorry,' Laura said again, producing a copy of the essay from her bag. 'Wasn't it any good?' She looked anxiously at the paper on Margaret's lap. She knew they disagreed about Hardy and women, but she didn't think that was the topic pre-eminently on Maggie's mind.

'I know I'm easy-going, Laura, but that doesn't mean you should take advantage of me.' Maggie resumed her spectacles and gazed severely at Laura over the rim.

'Oh, I don't, Maggie,' Laura assured her, grateful that she didn't have a tutor like Doctor Stokes who was rigid and set in her ways, not to say her views. She was also vindictive. Those who failed to find favour with her invariably failed their exams whereas Maggie was known to be exceptionally fair-minded, and just as good a scholar as Winifred Stokes. She was also quite pretty, not tall but with an open, good-natured freckled face and fair curly hair. She invariably wore jeans and didn't seem much interested in her appearance.

'I set great store on punctuality, Laura. Time is precious. I mean, I'm prepared to forgive the odd lapse but,' she consulted the watch on her wrist, 'you're a quarter of an hour late and I have two more tutorials after you and a lecture to deliver at two.'

'Sorry.' Laura knew she was sounding repetitive. 'I will make an effort. I really will.' She threw back her head and smiled, wishing Maggie would now get on with the purpose of the tutorial. But Maggie hadn't finished. She held up Laura's essay and brandished it at her.

'This is indicative of what I mean by your attitude, Laura. It isn't good enough. It is slapdash, slipshod. You haven't followed any of your themes through. I doubt if you even read *A Pair of Blue Eyes* critically.'

'I did.'

'Well, it doesn't show. It seems to me that you leafed through it and scribbled the first ideas that came into your head. This is worth about minus C, if that, and frankly, Laura, it is not the work of an Oxford scholar who sailed through her Oxbridge entrance.'

This time Laura stayed silent, rather staggered by Maggie's words. Maggie cleared her throat and went on.

'If I were saying this in your first term, Laura, I might have wondered about the wisdom of giving you a place. But in your first term your work was so exceptionally good that what staggers me now is how much it has deteriorated. I think we know why, don't we, Laura?'

As Maggie looked at her, Laura lowered her head. Of course, Maggie had been told all about Nick.

'It is since your affair with Nick began.'

'You can't blame *him*!'

'On the contrary, I blame you. It is perfectly possible to be in love and deliver good work. The two are not incompatible. I thought during the first few weeks it was understandable, but now it is nearly two months. Time to settle down, Laura, or I'm afraid that if you fail your exams you might find yourself being sent down.'

Laura looked at Maggie aghast.

'As bad as that?'

'As bad as that.' She handed her back her essay. 'Badly thought out, badly written. It could have been the work of a fifth-form schoolgirl.' Maggie's features softened. 'Laura, I know Doug Gentle, Nick's tutor, and Nick is not having similar difficulties. He still produces excellent work, well above average . . .'

Laura turned scarlet. 'I really don't think you've any business discussing me with Nick's tutor.'

'I did not discuss you with Doug. Doug brought it up. He said what a fine young man Nick was and that you were a nice couple. I agreed. I didn't mention the deterioration in your work at all, but Doug went on to enthuse about Nick saying what an excellent scholar he was and his hopes of a First and so on. I kept quiet about you, Laura.'

'Thanks.' Laura's brows knitted together.

'I can see you don't believe me. It's true.' Maggie sat back and lit a cigarette. All pretences at a tutorial had now gone. 'Frankly, I'd be ashamed to admit to anyone that your work had deteriorated. I'd think that it would reflect too much on us as females. It is true that in a love affair we tend to let it take over. "Man's love is of man's life . . ." and so on. It doesn't seem to have changed since Byron's day. Look, I've had my moments, Laura. I'm not immune to matters of the heart. I guess I've been able to call a halt if it affected my work.' She leaned forward and gazed earnestly at the by now troubled young woman sitting opposite her, the earlier euphoria having well and truly departed. 'You know I like you, Laura. I'm speaking to you as a friend, which a good tutor is meant to be: part instructor, part guide. You are supposed to come to us with any problems and I'm telling you that you have a problem, even if you don't know it, or didn't until now. Now you do and believe me, my dear, it is time to take stock before you ruin your career.'

'Does she have a man?' Nick asked.

'I don't know.' Laura snuggled up closer to him. 'She said something about Doug Gentle.'

'Doug's married.'

'Well, I don't know. I think she's quite attractive, don't you?' She looked at him, and he appeared to consider the question.

'Well, she's not my type, but she's not bad. Anyway let's not be sexist.'

'Why is it sexist?'

'It is rather, don't you think? Talking about types and all that? Whether or not a woman "has" a man?'

'Well, you brought it up.'

'I know, and I shouldn't have.'

'You're simply thinking she might be jealous? I mean, we're allowed to think that, aren't we?'

Nick grunted, as if he didn't want to commit himself.

It was three in the afternoon and they were in bed in Nick's room, whither Laura had gone after her aborted tutorial. Fled would have been a better word. Maggie's lecture had upset her, and the thought of being sent down after the first year was too awful to contemplate.

Nick took her to the pub for bread and cheese and a glass of wine and they went back to his room and made love.

It helped, but not much. It was Nick's love and support that mattered more than the physical side, at least this afternoon. Usually the physical side mattered a great deal, but today she had felt too tense to enjoy it and she let Nick come without coming herself, which upset him.

They talked again about Maggie and what she'd said, and it was then that Nick had asked if she had a man.

Laura thought that in a way Maggie was right, and the relationship between the sexes hadn't changed all that much over the centuries, long before Lord Byron and his ideas about love being a woman's whole existence. The newness and excitement about their affair had destroyed her ability to concentrate or produce good work, while Nick's work was apparently, if anything, even better.

Nick tenderly kissed her cheek and stroked her back, his fingers gently massaging her spine, his touch featherlight.

'I'm sorry about asking if Maggie had a man. By implication it *was* sexist.'

'I know what you meant. You wondered if she understood about being in love. I'm sure she does. I mean, if she hasn't got a lover at present, she did have one at some time. She told me she wasn't immune to matters of the heart. She was simply telling me she didn't let it affect her work. I can see that. She's strong. I'm weak.'

Nick kissed her back. His lips moved up to her neck. His arms closing around her, his hands cupping her breasts. She began to relax, feel desire, tremble with the need for him.

'Shall I make you come now?' he whispered, and gently lowered her onto her back.

CHAPTER 7

The dining table was beautifully laid: silver on mahogany, candles in their sconces gleaming on its highly-polished surface.

Andreas sat at one end of the long table, Lydia at the other. In the middle on one side Nick and Laura sat next to each other, their knees occasionally touching. Emma sat facing them, knowing quite well that they were playing footsie under the table.

In the end Laura, hating to be parted so soon from Nick, and for such a long time, had agreed to go with him to meet his parents. They had arrived earlier in the day, been given a warm greeting. Laura had been shown to her room which overlooked the garden at the back and which was down the hall from Nick's. Neither had said anything about the separation, but had exchanged looks while Lydia twittered, slightly uncomfortable at meeting Nick's only acknowledged girlfriend for the first time. By 'acknowledged' they meant that this was the first time Nick had openly said he had a girlfriend, who she was, what she did and all about her. Information which had been supplemented by Emma when she returned home after meeting Laura at Oxford.

Andreas was absolutely delighted to hear that his son was romantically linked with a woman. Ever since the business of Giles wanting Nick to give up Oxford for Manchester (he was quite sure that Giles was behind that idea and not vice versa, as Nick had insisted), ever since then he had nursed, however reluctantly, the idea that his son might indeed be homosexual, an idea that was abhorrent to a macho father. Thus he had welcomed Laura with open arms even if she was not quite what he expected, or would have liked.

Andreas preferred women who were openly feminine, who wore pretty dresses, lots of make-up and made themselves look attractive, and thus available to men, at all times. Andreas thought that in exchange for this you looked after women; you cocooned them, protected them and loved them. He thought it was a fair exchange which benefited both parties because marriage was essentially a partnership. In most partnerships there was a junior partner and a senior one and in marriage it was the man who predominated. Andreas didn't object to intelligent women so much as women who were overtly intellectual and Laura, as he might have feared, came into this category. Of course, being at Oxford, it was perhaps inevitable.

Lydia was the perfect stereotype of Andreas's favourite kind of woman and it was because of this, he was sure, that his marriage was so successful. Outwardly they were partners, but essentially he led and Lydia followed.

He had been greatly relieved that his individualistic and strong-minded daughter had not shone academically and had shown no inclination to follow her brother to university. Despite her stubbornness and strength of character, Emma's father was convinced that she would follow the example set by her mother: make a suitable marriage, bear children, possess a fine home, be a good hostess and lead a happy and exemplary life. It was true that Lydia worried, was over-anxious to impress, but not everyone was perfect and these deficiencies might be ironed out by her daughter with her advantages of a better education, and cushioned by wealth.

Laura had changed into a skirt and chunky sweater. It was the best she could do to look smart as she invariably wore trousers or jeans. Her only make-up was a dash of lipstick. Lydia and Emma were, as usual, impeccably turned out; Lydia in a couture dress of soft mohair, jewellery at ears, throat and wrist; Emma in a trendy purple two-piece, made of incredibly soft suede. She wore earrings and a large gold bangle, and looked as though she was dressed to go out after dinner.

Andreas wore a business suit, white shirt and silk tie. Nick was in flannels, a blue shirt, blazer and tie.

Laura had never really experienced anything like the formality of the proceedings, and for most of the meal remained tongue-tied. There was a live-in Filipino domestic called Maria, who served the dinner which had been prepared by the chef. He commuted daily from the outskirts of London. Maria's husband, Marco, did the gardening, odd jobs around the house and acted as waiter when there were large parties. Laura was completely overawed by the luxury, the style of the whole thing and wished Nick had prepared her better, though he had advised her to bring a skirt which, luckily, she possessed, having bought it as a concession for her Oxford interview the previous year.

'Nick tells me this is your first visit to London,' Andreas said, in an attempt to draw Laura into the conversation which, until then, had been largely about family matters. He had soon discovered that Laura was not much of a one for small talk.

'Yes.'

'And how do you like it?'

'Well . . .'

'We only just arrived, Dad.' Nick came to the rescue. 'I intend to show her round tomorrow.'

'Well, we hope you'll stay a few days, Laura,' Lydia said brightly. 'There's a fashion show tomorrow at Harrods. Emma and I thought of going. I wonder if you . . .'

'I don't think that's quite up Laura's street, Mum.'

'Why not?' Emma looked challengingly at her brother. 'Anything wrong with fashion shows?'

'Nothing at all.' Nick scratched his head and, turning sideways, looked at Laura. 'Interested?'

Laura shook her head. 'Though it's kind of you to ask me, I'm a traditional working-class girl,' she said with a wry smile, as though gaining confidence. 'Nick will have told you that I come from a very ordinary family, and my father's unemployed.' She looked defiantly round the table and then at Nick.

Andreas came to his rescue.

'Nick didn't tell us anything about you, Laura, except that you were a very nice girl he'd met and he'd like to bring you to meet us.' He leaned towards her. 'I'm glad he did, and believe me, we have no "side" here. My grandfather was a penniless immigrant from Greece, and we've made our money by hard work and the sweat of our brows. I don't want you to think we have any airs and graces just because we live in a nice house and can afford the best. My children have been brought up democratically, and to realise that there are many others not as fortunate as ourselves.' Andreas paused. 'All of which I may have put very awkwardly, I am not an educated man like my son. What I mean is I don't want you to feel in any way uncomfortable . . .' His flow was interrupted by the opening of the door and Maria sidled in.

'Mr Harvey is in the hall, sir.'

'Mr Harvey?' Andreas jumped up. '*Edmund* Harvey?'

'It's the young man, sir.' The girl looked over at Nick. 'Mr Nick's friend.'

'Giles!' Nick rose and, going over to the door, flung it open. 'Giles, we're in here having dinner.'

'Oh, ask him to join us!' Lydia called, and gestured to Maria to lay another place.

Giles appeared in the doorway with Nick, the customary rueful expression on his face. As usual he was clad in tracksuit and trainers and he threw his arms helplessly in the air. 'Yet again you find me in a compromising position, Lydia. I didn't expect you to be eating. I just called round to see Nick.' Then suddenly he noticed Laura and his eyes immediately lit up.

'Oh, hi, Laura! I didn't know you were here.' He crossed the room and warmly shook her hand. Then he turned to Andreas and shook his more formally, finally stooping to kiss Lydia on the cheek and give a cheery wave to Emma. 'Hi!'

'Hi!' Emma said with a smile and a similar gesture. 'Have something to eat.'

'I've eaten,' Giles said and then, in reply to Lydia's look of disbelief, 'no really. I wondered if there was any chance of you coming out afterwards Nick, but I didn't know that Laura was with you.'

'Well, we're just getting to know Laura,' Andreas said firmly. 'I think they'll be staying in this evening, but why don't you stay too and have a drink with us?'

'No, really . . .'

'Look, we've almost finished,' Andreas indicated the pudding on his plate and then the empty chair next to him. 'Why don't you take a pew? Relax, Giles. We don't mind the tracksuit.' He smiled broadly. 'Really. You seem to have got this fixation that we always dress for dinner.'

Giles slid self-consciously into his chair. 'Well, you always look very smart to me and it makes me feel a bit of a bum . . .'

'Ever since the yacht . . .'

'No, it's nothing to do with the yacht. Honestly.'

'Well, to change the subject,' Andreas leaned back magisterially in his chair. 'How's Manchester? You didn't get the chance to tell us at Christmas as we were abroad.'

'Manchester is fine.' Giles glanced at Laura.

'Like the course?'

'Yes.' His tone seemed to indicate that he wasn't too sure.

'Psychology is it you're doing?'

'Yes.'

'Laura was telling us she is from Manchester. You've met Laura already, I gather?'

'I told you, Daddy,' Emma looked sharply at her father, 'when I went to see Nick at the beginning of term. I met Laura, and Giles turned up too. We had rather a good weekend, didn't we, Giles?'

'We did.' Giles smiled.

'Tell you what,' Nick said, glancing at his watch, 'would you mind very much, Mum and Dad, if we did just pop round to the pub after dinner – Emma, Giles, Laura and I? Promise not to be late.'

After coffee, when the young people had made their exit, Lydia and Andreas sat looking at each other. For a few moments they said nothing. Andreas had a large cigar between his fingers and he frequently and absent-mindedly kept tapping the ash into a cut-glass ashtray. He gave a deep sigh and crossed one leg over the other.

'What do you think of the girl?'

Lydia pursed her lips as though she were anxious not to say the wrong thing. 'Ordinary,' she said after a while. 'Very ordinary.'

'Oh, I wouldn't have said that.'

'Not the sort of person I'd expect Nick to have chosen.'

'She's very pretty.'

'Oh, do you think so?'

'Striking.'

'Yes, but that *accent*!'

'You mustn't be so prejudiced, darling.'

'I'm not in the least prejudiced.'

'Well, I think you are.'

'Well, I'm not, Andy, I assure you. She sounds like someone in Coronation Street.'

Andreas shrugged.

'She has a regional accent, so what?'

'I just hoped that Nick would choose someone with more class. Of all the young women in Oxford, why does it have to be her?'

'I think that's a very unfortunate remark, dear, if I may say so.' Andreas had let his cigar go out and attempted to relight it. 'She's intelligent, she's most attractive. I can see why she did appeal to him. Just because she doesn't appeal to you . . .'

'I don't think I have the slightest thing in common with her. As for that speech about being working class . . . frankly, I think it was untimely and in bad taste. You can be an inverted snob you know, Andy.'

'You mean she's actually proud of being working class?'

'Exactly! And wants to ram it down our throats.'

Andreas rose, walked over to the television set and switched it on.

'I think you're taking the whole thing too seriously, Lydia. It's not as though they're going to get married. Time for the news.'

Laura snuggled up to Nick in bed. She felt cold despite the heat of his body, the warmth of the house.

'I don't think your parents like me very much,' she said.

'Nonsense.'

'I think I was silly to talk about my father being unemployed.'

'Maybe you came on a bit strong.' He kissed her cheek.

'I just wasn't prepared for all this, Nick.'

'All what?'

'The house, the style, the maid. I mean your folks are posh. This is a posh place. I felt very uneasy in my chunky sweater and my only skirt.'

'You looked very nice.'

'Your mother's dress was so gorgeous. I bet it cost a

bomb, and that suit of Emma's . . .' Laura emitted a low whistle.

Nick sat up in bed and switched on the light. They were in Laura's bed in the guest room. He had come to her because his was a single bed while Laura's was for two. It was wonderful to have the luxury of a double bed. He'd slunk along the corridor when he'd guessed his parents had turned out the light. Emma was still out, having decided to go clubbing in Soho with Giles. Nick hadn't wanted to upset his parents by being late in on Laura's first night, as the situation was fraught enough already. He had found the atmosphere at dinner almost unbearably tense, the reason why he'd wanted to go out for a breather.

Maybe bringing one's girlfriend home for the first time would be tense anyway, daunting for anyone. Everyone wanted to impress, except perhaps Laura who was determined to be herself. Nick had been a little annoyed by the vigour of her working-class speech, almost as though she relished it. In his view that had been absolutely unnecessary.

Nick put his arms round his legs and looked at Laura, so tousled and adorable beside him.

'Laura, these are the nineteen nineties. We're not living in the age of Queen Victoria.'

'So?' She looked up at him.

'I find all this talk of class and so on obnoxious.'

'I didn't mention class.'

'You said my parents were "posh". It's the same thing.'

'It isn't.'

'Well, you introduced class by talking about your home being very ordinary.'

'Well . . .' her gaze became defiant. 'It is. I am.'

'Then you're the one to introduce class. We don't. I never have.'

'For God's sake,' she exploded, 'your dad has a Rolls Royce *and* a yacht.'

'Then you wish you'd never met me?' His voice had gone very quiet.

'I never said that.'

'You're creating a barrier. I am what I am. My parents are what they are. You're class-conscious, not me, not us.'

'I still don't think your parents like me, especially your mum.'

'I think that's unfair. You've only known them a few hours.'

'You can tell. I can.'

Laura also sat up, raised her knees and, leaning her head on them looked sideways at Nick.

'Maybe it was too soon to visit your house?'

'Don't be silly,' Nick said roughly, putting his arm round her, desiring her intensely, drawing her close. But inside, he wondered if perhaps she was right.

Laura lay listening to the distant rumble of traffic as it trundled up the arterial road to and from the great conurbation that was Manchester and its environs. There was always that steady swish of traffic, day and night, and she supposed that when she was young, sharing this bedroom with her sister, she had got used to it. Certainly it had never disturbed her as it did now.

In Oxford in the spring, she awoke to the sound of birdsong coming from the college park. In winter and at other times of the year there was a profound silence, broken occasionally by the sound of a car or lorry on the Woodstock Road. But never that heavy, continuous sound of the industrial north. Although Salford no longer had the same density of huge smoking chimneys depicted by Lowry, a pall seemed to hang over it, generated by mechanisation and the industrial ghosts of the past. In those days, workers tramped in the pre-dawn along cobbled pavements to the cotton mills to begin the early morning shift.

Salford no longer possessed that historical image. But it was still, to Laura, grim despite the fact that now it had its own university, its streets were cleaner than they ever had been, and it had high-rise apartment blocks of doubtful socio-economic benefit and little or no architectural merit. Salford belonged to childhood and adolescence, and both were full of bad memories.

Maybe it was because the Chase family still lived in one of those narrow passages depicted by Lowry, where kids still played, and loose dogs roamed and housewives hung their washing out on a Monday. 'Housewife' of course was a euphemism for the women who lived on the street; hard-working wives and mothers who ran the family home and held down a job as well. People like her mother who would soon be getting up to get the boys their breakfast before she left for her own job as a tea lady in a large office block where, three nights a week, she also cleaned.

Laura turned restlessly in bed and looked at the clock. Five-thirty. She had no idea what had woken her because her mother didn't get up until six, and usually she slept well. Five-thirty, and in the tree-lined road in St John's Wood Nick would be asleep in his bed, and when he woke it would be to silence or to the sound of birds on nearby Primrose Hill.

There was something working class and industrial about being so close to a main arterial road with lorries thundering past. Something calming and civilised about Oxford or St John's Wood. Here there were no birds except a few scrawny pigeons or dusty sparrows who scavenged hopefully among the bins and black refuse sacks left out in the back passages for scraps that might have escaped the attention of the dustmen.

Maybe she'd woken because she missed Nick, missed his morning embrace, the coming together of their bodies. The exultation of making love, of loving and being loved, of living all day in its memory and being transformed by this unique experience that two people shared.

Laura had never been in love before; never messed about with the fellows or hung around in clubs or on street corners as her sister and brothers had. That was how Sharon, at the age of seventeen, had managed to get herself pregnant and already, at the age of twenty-three, and with two children, had the world-wearied air of an old married woman.

Laura had been different, never fitted in, a cuckoo in the nest. She was bookish and was always to be found in a corner reading, despite the fact that there was not a single volume in the family home.

Laura's mother had been a local beauty who had also fallen for a baby when she was in her teens, the father being the man she married, the then dashing and eminently presentable, indeed handsome, Albert Chase. Their children had inherited their looks. It was very odd to think that a quarter of a century ago, her now sickly and bad tempered father and overworked, dispirited mother, had known the rapture of the flesh that she had shared with Nick.

Or had they? It was almost impossible to know and, certainly, to ask.

Laura was different, always had been. Yet she was not awkward or difficult, but rather shy and sweet tempered, easily put upon. The family was amazed when she got a place at Oxford, yet they were terribly proud of her but, at the same time, resentful that she had left them behind.

'Our' Laura was no longer one of us.

Laura heard the sounds of gentle tapping on the door of the room next to hers, and the quiet voice of her mother urging her brothers to get up. They were temporarily sharing the same bedroom, as she and Sharon had. Now this was Gary's room which he gave up to her when she was at home.

The familiar tapping on the door: 'Get up boys, you'll be late for work.'

Sharon had always been the last one down. She, Laura, was the first, eager in a way to be off, preferring the environment of school to home, though she would never have admitted it. Now Oxford represented freedom, and every time she came home she realised how trapped she felt and had from very early days, as though she didn't belong.

With a feeling of guilt Laura leapt out of bed, dressed quickly – she would wash later when the bathroom was free – and went downstairs where her mother was making sandwiches for the boys, and probably herself. 'Hi, Mum!' she said, but without a kiss. They were not a demonstrative family, and her mother would have thought it odd if any of her children kissed her, either good morning or good night. Kissing, Laura thought, recalling all the kissing and touching and calling of endearments that had gone on in the Constantine home, was for the middle classes.

'Did you sleep well, love?' her mother asked without looking up.

'Very well. And you?'

Laura took the slices her mother was buttering and put on the cheese spread. In the Chase household, when there were women about the men were not expected to help with any of the domestic chores, including getting their own food. Hilda Chase did everything, unless either of the girls were around, when they helped out.

Her mother nodded but said nothing. Laura thought she looked tired and gazed at her with concern.

'Mum, you are looking peaky, you know. You sure you're sleeping well?'

'Take your dad up a cup of tea, would you, Laura,' her mother glanced at the clock on the wall, 'and give the boys another knock? Oh, by the way, someone called you last night.'

'Nick?' Laura, in the act of putting on the kettle, spun round.

'No, someone called Giles. Said he'd ring again.'

'Giles!' Laura murmured, mystified.

'Don't you know him?'

'He's a friend of Nick's. Why should he call me?' Her mother, uncurious, shrugged her shoulders, finished her task and began to put the sandwiches in plastic boxes. In each she also placed an apple. Then she put on the lids, secured them with elastic bands and laid them on the table.

'Do you want a cup of tea, Mum?'

Hilda nodded.

'Best get that up to your father first or he'll be angry.'

Angry! Laura felt indignation mount as she climbed the stairs and knocked on the door of her parents' room. Her mother was only forty-two yet she was going grey. She looked like a woman well into her fifties.

Her father didn't reply to her knock so she opened the door and went in. The large bed practically filled the room. There was very little space for any other furniture. Her father lay with his back to the door, seemingly asleep. She shook him roughly by the shoulder.

'Here's your tea, Dad.'

He shook himself as though to say he didn't want any, pulled the eiderdown more firmly round his shoulders.

One of Dad's off days.

Laura felt the anger surge up in her, as well as a kind of despair that she should consider this behaviour in any way unusual. After all, her father had been unemployed since she was a child and she had never really known anything else. Most days he wouldn't come downstairs until about noon, and anyone who was in the house had to get him something to eat. If there was no one around he would go to the pub, have bread and cheese and a pint with his mates. He would then come home and watch television all afternoon, usually sport if there was any on, before going to the

British Legion or the working man's club where he would spend the evening playing darts.

Her father was not a great drinker. Laura had seldom seen him drunk. His normal state was one of melancholy. He was a very silent man and yet apparently he enjoyed the company of his men friends. As far as she could see, her mother and father led pretty separate lives. Hilda was close to Sharon and enjoyed her grandchildren. She had two sisters who lived nearby, and she would often visit them after work, or go round to the pub with them for a natter over a port and lemon.

Laura wondered what the Constantines would make of all this as she banged on the door of her brothers' room shouting to them to get up. It was school holidays but Gordon Chase had a job in the local supermarket. Downstairs there was breakfast on the table – bread which the boys toasted if they wanted – and cereal. Hilda was putting on her coat saying she would be late for work.

'I'll see you tonight, love,' she said, pausing at the door. 'This Giles sounded ever so posh. You must have a whole new set of friends now, Laura, love. You'll soon not be wanting to come home at all.'

'Don't be silly, Mum, I do,' Laura said, conveying her mother to the front door and wishing that they were more tactile, that she could embrace her. But she couldn't. She couldn't embrace her and she couldn't really talk to her.

Too late to break the habit of a lifetime.

'Did Giles leave a telephone number?' Laura asked as her mother prepared to leave.

'He said he'd ring again.'

'Or what he wanted?'

'Haven't a clue. Tra'aa,' her mother said, closing the door.

After the boys had gone, Laura tidied up. She wasn't going to hang around and get her father lunch. She had plenty of work to do and intended to spend the remainder of the day in the library. The rest of the vac seemed to stretch interminably in front of her, and yet she knew it was a valuable opportunity to make up for time lost because of her involvement with Nick. Maggie had given her another grim warning just before the end of term.

'Time to get a hold on yourself, Laura, or it'll be too late.'

Most of her former schoolfriends worked; one had married, one had a baby without being married and another had gone to one of the new universities, formerly a polytechnic. They were the only two in the whole school who had shone academically. The pass rate at A level had been abysmally poor.

Laura had almost been ashamed of her success. Yet she was still close enough to one or two of them, but socialising would have to wait until evening. A night out with the girls would be the order of the day on Saturday just so that she could prove going to Oxford hadn't turned her into a snob.

Laura was about to leave the house when the telephone rang. She was going to let it ring and then she thought it was a funny time for anyone to telephone, unless it was for her. Nick maybe! She rushed to pick up the phone and a voice said, rather hesitantly: 'Is that you, Laura?'

'Giles! My mother said you'd rung. Where are you?'

'I'm here. In Manchester.'

'Whatever are you doing in Manchester?'

'I'm working.'

'What, you've got a job?' Laura sounded incredulous.

'No, I'm working for my exams.'

'Me, too.'

'I say, Laura, I wondered if we could meet up.'

'That would be nice. When?'

'Today?'

'*Today*?' The question was quite unexpected. 'You mean like now?'

'Why not?'

'I thought you said you were working?'

'Well, today's a nice day. Maybe it will rain tomorrow.'

Maybe it would.

'Laura?'

'Alright. I was actually going to work, but I'll meet you if you like. Where?'

'Well, I'll pick you up. We'll go somewhere.'

'No. I'll come into Manchester to meet you.'

'OK. If you prefer. Where?'

'Outside the library.'

'Right.' Giles sounded pleased. 'When?'

'Give me an hour.'

'Fine, Laura. I'll see you then outside the Central library at about eleven.'

Laura put the telephone down and remained where she was for a few moments, head hung in thought.

It wasn't that she was ashamed of her home or of where she lived. She just didn't want Giles to meet her father.

As if able to read her mind, at that moment her father appeared, putting his head round the door of the kitchen.

'Any chance of anything to eat, love?'

'I'm just going out, Dad,' Laura said.

Her father came slowly into the kitchen and sat down heavily in a chair at the table.

'I don't feel very well today, Laura. I think it's my heart you know.'

'I thought you had your heart tested, Dad. They said there was nothing wrong with it.'

Her father shook his head. 'You can't really trust the doctors, Laura. They don't know what they're talking about.'

This was an old, familiar refrain of her father's. He had on his dressing gown and a pair of very old, scuffed slippers. A few grey hairs stuck out from the top of his open pyjama jacket, his chin was unshaven and his eyes rheumy as though from lack of sleep, or maybe too much of it. The effect produced was often the same.

He looked like a tired old man and yet he was only forty-five, about the same age as Nick's father who didn't look his age either, only much younger. Andreas Constantine looked about ten years younger than Bert Chase, almost his exact contemporary.

You would have to be hard not to be moved by the plight of a man who hadn't worked for years and who had little, if any, self-esteem except in his home where he was undisputed boss. Even if he wheedled and whined to ask favours it was because he expected them to be carried out. If they weren't, he turned nasty.

Even as she was thinking about him, resenting him, Laura was hastily buttering bread, getting cheese out of the fridge and putting on the kettle.

'Where are you going, Laura?' her father asked, noting approvingly that she was doing what he wanted without argument.

'I'm meeting a friend.'

'I thought you were working, Laura?' Her father drew the chair up to the table and tackled the bread and cheese she'd laid before him.

'I was. I mean I am . . .'

'Was that who the phone call was from?'

'Yes.'

'Someone from university, I expect.'

'Yes.'

'You don't have much time these days for your old friends, do you, Laura?'

'I do have time, Dad. But they work during the day.' She put a teacup and saucer next to her father's plate and poured his tea.

'Of course,' he nodded. 'Is it a man or a woman, Laura?'

'Oh, *Dad*!'

'Just wondered. Your life's your own, you know that, and we are very proud of you. But it's bound to be that one of these days you'll draw further and further away from your family until you forget us altogether.'

Now he was getting maudlin. It was only an attempt to keep her there. He was a lonely man who, she knew, felt neglected by his family. Maybe he was frightened too. His only solace seemed to be with his male friends. But she felt now that he had gone too far along the line to be helped. He was sad, but he was despicable too, and as she tore out of the house to keep her date, the old familiar feeling of guilt raged in her heart.

She seemed to have so much and he so little.

They sat on the dry-stone wall by the side of the road looking down into the valley. It was interspersed here and there with copses, a farm and farm buildings and bisected by a stream, a tributary of the River Dove. Nearby, to the right, in a corner of the field was a gypsy caravan which someone had converted, probably, as a weekend retreat. It was surrounded by a wooden fence with a gate, and there were colourful red check curtains at the windows. Laura sighed a little enviously. The Manifold Valley was a beautiful part of Derbyshire which she knew well from camping here when she was at school, coming first with the Brownies and then the Guides.

'I'm surprised to hear you were a Guide.' Giles turned to her with amusement, surreptitiously studying her face.

'Why?' She looked curiously at him.

'Because you seem so non-conformist.'

'Oh, no. I'm very conformist. I was always very good at school. I am not a rebel.'

'You wanted to succeed?'

'Yes. I wanted to get away from my working-class environment, and I knew that education was the only way to do it.'

Giles, surprised by her candour, didn't quite know how to

reply. He expected that if he waited more information would be forthcoming, but her next remark was unexpected.

'Tell me about Nick's yacht.'

'Nick's yacht?' he asked.

'You know what I mean. His father's yacht. Where you spent the summer holidays.'

Giles was nonplussed.

'About what exactly? The size?'

'No!' Laura sounded cross. 'What it's like. He wants me to go in the summer. Is it very posh?'

'Well,' Giles paused, 'you know his mother.'

'How do you mean?'

'Well, she likes everything to be just so.'

'Was it the first time you'd visited?'

'Yes. My parents weren't keen.'

'But they enjoyed it?'

Giles remained silent, looking across the valley.

'*Did* they enjoy it, Giles?' Laura persisted.

'Oh, yeah, we had a great time. I don't know that Lydia enjoyed it much. She had a tummy bug and remained in her cabin . . . Oh, and at the end, my dad trod on a jellyfish . . .'

Laura burst out laughing. He thought how attractive the laughter lines made her face. He longed to put his arm around her, but he knew he mustn't. This was Nick's girl and Nick was his friend. In all his life he had never encountered a situation like it.

But was it strange after all that two friends, who had so much in common, should fall in love with the same girl?

'No, seriously,' he said, lightly putting a hand on her arm, 'he was very ill. He had to go to hospital.'

Laura clapped a hand to her mouth. 'Oh, I'm sorry.'

'Then I got the news I wouldn't be going to Oxford. All in all, the memories left by the holiday aren't good. So you see, you can't really judge it by what happened to us. I'm sure you'll have a good time.'

'Well, nothing's decided . . .' Laura ran a finger thoughtfully along the wall. 'I don't really know what his parents thought about me.'

'I'm sure they liked you.'

'I'm not so sure.' She glanced up at him. 'I think they would have liked something better for Nick.'

'Oh, come . . .'

'Seriously. His mum especially. I quite liked his dad, but you see I had no idea Nick's family had all that money. It gave me quite a shock. My family is very ordinary, working class. I'm not ashamed of it but I'm aware of it, especially since I went to Oxford. Somehow Nick doesn't strike you like that . . .'

'Like what?'

'Rich.'

'No, he doesn't. And it doesn't matter to him. It's not important. It mustn't matter to you, Laura. These days accents and all that kind of thing don't matter. In fact, it's quite fashionable to have one.'

'I know that. I'm aware of it. If it wasn't Nick's family I wouldn't care. But I care what they think about me. And how I behave with them, on a yacht and all that kind of thing, is another matter.'

Giles lowered his head. 'It really is very serious then?'

'Oh, you think it's calf love too, do you?'

'No, I don't, not at all. But it's early days. Things change. I mean you could say you scarcely know each other. I'm not saying it's not important, believe me. Anyway I wouldn't let his parents upset you.'

'Have you been in love ever, Giles?'

He paused. Then: 'I've known a few girls, but I don't think I have. Not really.'

'I hadn't either. But I do love Nick so much.'

'I know you do. Hey!' he said as if wishing to change the subject. 'Why don't we walk a bit? Explore the valley? They say Dovedale is very beautiful.'

'I'll show it to you.' Laura jumped off the wall and dusted her bottom. Giles jumped off too, and as he landed on the soft earth he missed his footing and leaned heavily on Laura for support. As she helped him regain his balance he put an arm round her waist and left it there. She looked at him, thought his expression strange, very direct and quizzical as he looked unfalteringly into her eyes. 'Nick's such a lucky guy,' he murmured. Then abruptly he removed his arm, leaving Laura feeling confused, suddenly anxious.

'Maybe we best be getting back?' she said.

'But it's still early,' he pleaded, looking at the sky.

'I have to see my sister tonight.' Her tone grew stubborn.

'OK.'

He knew that he'd overstepped the mark, and that Laura knew it. He felt foolish and stupid, disloyal. They went back to the car park behind the pub where they'd left the car, and Giles didn't attempt to get her to change her mind, but drove swiftly away from the valley, through Buxton and on towards Manchester saying little.

Laura guided him through the streets of Salford to her house and, as they stopped outside, he pulled on the hand-brake, switched off the ignition and looked at her.

'Sorry,' he said.

'Nothing to be sorry about.'

'It's just that I wish I'd got there first.'

Laura shrugged and gazed at the house, almost as if she hadn't heard him, seeming preoccupied. 'Look,' she said, 'do you mind if I don't ask you in? I know it's rude but . . .' she smiled at him, 'I'll explain some day.'

'It's perfectly OK. Say, maybe we can go out again? It's just that I am quite lonely up here. Nothing will happen I promise you. You're Nick's girl and Nick is my friend.'

Laura got out of the car as Giles remained where he was.

'I don't think so,' she said, peering through the window. The stubborn tone had returned again. 'But thanks, I enjoyed it. I like you too, you know, but . . .' Then, as if embarrassed by her candour, she stepped back and gave him a little wave.

'See you,' she said.

'See you,' he said, waving back, suddenly, despite her refusal to see him again, aware of a feeling of hope.

CHAPTER 8

Laura folded the letter and tucked it hurriedly between the pages of her book as the door opened and Nick put his head round.

'Hi!'

'Hi!' she said, turning to him with a smile.

'Busy?' He bent his head to kiss her and, after their kiss, she let her hand linger on his cheek drawing him down beside her.

'Pretty busy.'

'No time for . . .' he looked suggestively at her crotch and his hand wandered to the fastener of her jeans.

'You're a sexy beast,' she said playfully, smacking his hand.

'Would Hardy have approved?' Nick looked at the title of her book which had fallen to the floor. *The Life and Work of Thomas Hardy* by Michael Millgate. By now her jeans were almost off and, fully aroused, Laura lifted her T-shirt over her head.

'Hardy was quite sexy.' Laura stretched full length on the bed, jeans, T-shirt and knickers in a heap on the floor by the side. 'He liked pretty ladies, but we don't quite know whether he had affairs. Probably not.'

Nick was staring at Millgate's celebrated biography and at the letter which had fallen out of it and which now lay beside it on the floor. Laura saw his expression and, with a sudden guilty start, sat up. Too late.

'Uh, uh,' she muttered and fell back on the bed, covering her face with her hands.

'A letter from Giles?' Nick didn't seem to understand and looked at her. 'Is it for you?'

She nodded. 'I wouldn't be reading a letter meant for you.'

'No, of course not.' Still bemused, he picked it up and shook it open.

'May I read it?' His voice had gone very polite and formal, and he still had all his clothes on. Laura felt rather idiotic and she drew over herself the Indian throw she draped on the bed during the day to turn it into a sofa. Desire had swiftly ebbed at the possibility of a dramatic and damaging revelation.

She reached out and snatched the letter from him.

'I'd rather you didn't, Nick.'

'Why?' His face had a chalky whiteness, and he clenched his fists, as if digging his nails into the palms of his hands.

'It's a personal letter. I don't think you'd understand.'

She hauled herself off the bed and began to dress hurriedly. 'God, what a *stupid thing to happen,*' she added, stamping a foot on the floor in anger.

Nick stood up and, going over to the window, stood with his hands in his pockets looking out across the quad of the girls' college, a much more modern affair than his, yet built in the nineteenth century on architectural principles which emulated an earlier age and style.

'I simply don't understand what's going on, Laura.' He turned and looked at her, his face drawn with pain. 'Are you having an affair with Giles?'

'Of course I'm not!'

'Then why the letter? I mean, I think I'm entitled to an answer. He is my friend and you've only met him with me, as far as I know. Or isn't that so?'

'He looked me up in Manchester during the break.'

'I see.' Nick's tone was very quiet.

'It was completely innocent.'

'Then why didn't you tell me?'

'I should have.'

'If it was completely innocent I can't think why you didn't.' He slumped down on the bed, head between his hands.

'Neither can I.' She sat down beside him and attempted to take his hand. He remained cold and unresponsive to her pressure.

'If he writes you a letter you don't want me to see, something is going on. Must be.'

Laura handed him the letter. 'Read it out,' she said. Nick took it from her – it was a single page – shook it open and with a deep frown of concentration on his face studied it.

'Go on. Aloud,' Laura urged.

Nick cleared his throat.

'Dear Laura,' he read.

'A word of apology for what happened that day in Longnor. I know it upset you, and in retrospect, it upset me. I wouldn't like you to think the worse of me, or for it to affect my relationship with Nick whom I love like a brother.

'The fact is that I have been very lonely and unhappy all the time I've been in Manchester. I'm usually a pretty sociable guy, yet I've been unable to make friends or to establish a relationship with someone of the opposite sex.

'I like you very much, and I guess that day I was drawn to you and went further than I should.

'I am sorry, and please don't let it affect our friendship. I know it won't affect your love for Nick.

'Incidentally, I've decided to leave the university and probably travel abroad. I'm trying to get up the courage to go and tell my parents. After that, maybe

I'll come to Oxford to see Nick, so please don't tell him yet.

'I think you're a great girl,'

Here Nick paused, swallowed and glanced at Laura who was staring at the bed, listening.

'and that Nick's a lucky lucky guy.

'Yours ever . . .'

Nick stopped without saying Giles's name. Then he folded the letter and handed it back to Laura. 'I guess he's in love with you,' he said in an unemotional tone.

'Don't be stupid.'

'Seriously, that's what it looks like to me.'

'Nick, don't be so dramatic.'

'As a matter of fact I guessed that he fancied you. I could tell when he looked at you, especially when he arrived that night we were having dinner in London with Emma and my parents. His eyes lit up when he saw you.'

It was true. Laura had noticed it too.

'I think it was rather despicable of him to try and chat you up in Manchester.' He paused again, as if debating whether or not to say what was on his mind. 'What happened then, Laura?'

'Nothing happened.' Her tone was emphatic. 'He called me and asked if we could go out for the day. I was bored, fed up at home, so I agreed. I suggested that we go to a place called Longnor which is a pretty village in Derbyshire where I used to go to Brownie and Guide camp, so it had a nostalgic association for me. It's about an hour's run from Manchester. There's a nice pub there where we had a ploughman's and a pint. Then we sat on a wall looking at the valley and talked.'

'What about?'

'Just this and that. Then Giles suggested we take a walk and as we got down from the wall he stumbled and put an arm round my waist and told me he thought you were lucky. I realised there was some tension there and suggested we should go back. I had to see my sister anyway, and it was getting late as we'd taken our time over lunch. He drove me home. I didn't ask him in. He didn't touch me again. He didn't try to kiss me. We said goodbye and that was that. I forgot about it and spent the next ten days in the local library. I didn't see Giles again and thought nothing more until this' – she held out the letter – 'arrived this morning. I promise. Now, it's no big deal, is it?'

'I would never have known anything about this if I hadn't come in at this moment and found this letter.'

'Probably not, and just as well too. It would be dreadful if it upset your relationship with Giles. I honestly think he's lonely and unhappy and he just wanted a friend, someone who was close to his best friend.'

'How did he get your telephone number?'

'I have no idea. Maybe in the telephone book. We're listed, Nick.' She held out a hand. 'Let's go back to when you came in.'

'You feel like it?'

'I do, and forgetting all about this.'

She tore the letter into tiny pieces and threw them into the bin.

It was not easy for Nick to forget the letter, or the fact that his best friend was attracted to his girl, because that is what it amounted to. He felt in a sense rather betrayed by Giles, and yet he knew that their friendship was too important to be broken in this manner. A certain amount of magnanimity was called for. He knew that Giles had been hurt by his failure to get into Oxford, yet he didn't think he'd retaliate by trying to take his girl away from him.

Nick believed Laura when she said that nothing had happened from her point of view. But he didn't find it hard to believe that Giles, with whom he had so much in common, was attracted to the same sort of girl as he was.

Later in the day Nick left Laura working, but he felt restless and unable to work himself. He went for a walk in the Meadows and stood for a while watching the college crews practise on the Cherwell for the Head of the River races. He had never been attracted to rowing but he knew that if Giles had gone to Oxford he may well have been selected to row for his college. He'd rowed for the school in the same way that he'd played cricket and rugby for it.

Giles, the complete all-rounder, would have revelled in life at Oxford as Nick never had. Laura, too, had enjoyed Oxford life to the full until she met him. Now she'd dropped out of everything and even her work was suffering. Her tutor kept on lecturing her about it. In many ways Laura and Giles were alike; they enjoyed the same things. They were slightly larger than life, flamboyant characters. And he, Nick, seemed to be the catalyst for change. Only he had not changed Giles and prevented him from getting into Oxford. It was Giles, the all-rounder, who had seen to that, who in his A level years had fitted in too many other activities. Meanwhile Nick had applied himself relentlessly to his work, ambitious to succeed but in a different way from Giles: to prove himself to his family, whereas Giles had no need of that, and thought he had no need until he failed to follow the distinguished line of Harvey forebears to Oxbridge.

Nick watched the sleek boats propelled by the earnest oarsmen glide swiftly through the water. He felt curiously depressed as though he had under-achieved himself. Yet why? His work he knew was good. A first in PPE would provide him with any number of promising careers: the Civil Service, the Diplomatic, maybe a Fellowship at All Souls and the chance to shine in academia. He had Laura, a wonderful girl, who loved him. He'd never had money worries, like so many fellow students, didn't know what they were. He had a close, loving family, understanding parents. What, then, made him depressed?

He went back to his room and, sitting down, wrote a letter to Giles. It took him about an hour, after which he read it through carefully several times and then tore it up, fragmenting the pieces very carefully so that they could never be reassembled, and threw them into the wastepaper basket.

He then left his room and, ignoring the telephones in the downstairs lobby in case anyone overheard him, went into the town and, slipping into a public call box, punched in Giles's telephone number.

Giles answered the phone.

'Hi!' Nick said. 'I wasn't sure you'd be in.' Giles shared a house in Didsbury, near Manchester, with some fellow students.

'Nick!' Giles's tone was equivocal, as though he wasn't sure whether or not to be glad to hear Nick's voice.

'Thought I'd call you.'

'That's great. Anything up?'

'Well,' Nick paused, 'there's a big inter-collegiate cricket match next Saturday and I wondered if you'd like to come. It would be great to see you.'

There was silence at the other end of the line. Then: 'Are you playing?'

'Yes. I think my parents and Emma will be here too. I thought we could have a kind of reunion.'

'That sounds great. Nick . . .'

'Yes?'

'I'm going to leave the university.'

Taken unawares, Nick didn't know how to respond.

'Did you hear what I said, Nick?'

'Yes, I heard you. It's a bit of a shock, isn't it?'

'Well, I don't think so. I never settled here and I think I

chose the wrong subject. I'm really not a psychologist.'

Giles had chosen psychology, because when he had applied, the law faculty was full.

'What are you going to do?'

'I think I'll go abroad for a year. Travel. I don't know what I want out of life. It all seems to have gone wrong. I never seemed able to settle, make friends or take an interest in my work.'

'I'm sorry. Did you tell your parents?'

'Not yet. I don't think they'll mind. I may actually decide to do law at a school and go in with my dad. I think he'd like that. You know they were never very keen on Manchester.'

Nick managed a laugh. 'Well, if you can come next week we'll talk about it.'

'Good idea. I really will try and come.' Pause. 'How's Laura?'

'Laura's fine.'

'Working hard?'

'I think so.'

'Give her my . . .' Giles seemed about to say 'love' and then changed it to 'regards.'

'I will.'

Nick thought that it was the only false note in the conversation. When he got back to his room he still felt depressed, and began to wonder why he did what he'd just done.

Was he tempting fate?

It was the kind of classic English occasion, enjoyed in perfect weather, that is the stuff of legend, of story books and nostalgia. A patch of beautifully kept sward, emerald green, elegant young men in traditional whites going about their tasks in that leisurely, unhurried way that seems to be the hallmark of cricket. The fielders lolled about, arms folded, while they waited for the batsmen to inspect the crease, consult each other with mysterious signals and then position themselves before the wicket ready to receive the ball from the bowler who, bent on intimidation, endeavoured to mould his features into the resemblance of a ferocious panther preparing for the kill as he began to make his run.

For Laura, seated between Nick's parents, it was a strange ritual, one that had never attracted either of her brothers. Gary played football, even in the summer, and Gordon was bookish, myopic and not keen on sport. Laura hoped that he would be the second member of the family to follow her to university. What happened in the Test Matches was a matter of supreme indifference to the entire Chase household, none of whom could have named a single English player.

And there was Nick standing in the field, not far away from her, looking splendid in his whites, arms folded, chatting to a fellow fielder as they waited for the batsman who was just coming in to try and improve the score for his side.

Next to Lydia Constantine sat Giles, who had arrived the night before and was staying in the room of a neighbour on Nick's corridor who was away for the weekend. The Constantines, with Emma, had also arrived the night before and were staying at the Randolph. There had been a family dinner party which Laura had declined to attend, using the pretext that she was working, and also she said she felt Nick should be with his family. There would be another one tonight which she would attend.

Giles had greeted her, at first politely rather than with warmth. He paid a lot of attention to Emma whom he kissed on the cheek. He didn't attempt to kiss Laura, who hadn't replied to his letter. She hadn't been looking forward to the weekend and she wondered why Nick had invited Giles. It seemed perverse.

However, just before they wandered onto the field Giles had caught her by the arm and, unseen by the others, drew her to one side. His manner was completely different from the almost casual way he'd first greeted her. He seemed excited, conspiratorial.

'Hey,' he said, 'how are you?'

'I'm fine.' She looked at him without smiling.

'Did you get my letter?'

'Yes, thanks.'

'I thought you might have answered it.'

'I didn't know what to say. By the way, Nick saw it.'

'You showed it to *Nick*?' Giles looked aghast.

'No, he found it. I'd put it in a book and it dropped out.'

'Oh, Christ!' Giles put his hand to his mouth. 'Couldn't you have been more careful?'

'Look!' Laura felt a sense of indignation. '*I* didn't do anything.'

'Nobody did anything wrong. Two friends had a day out, that's all.'

But they both knew that it wasn't quite like that.

'Nick didn't say anything to me on the phone. I wonder why?'

'Nick doesn't like confrontation. Besides he's very fond of you.'

'Maybe he wants to talk about it this weekend?'

'I don't think so. Anyway there's nothing to talk about, is there? I explained to him that there was nothing between us. Nothing happened, but I think it's naughty of you, Giles, to complicate the situation in this way.'

'In what way?'

'You should never have telephoned me.'

'And you should never have accepted.'

He smiled at her as if to say 'touché'. Then he relented.

'OK, Laura. I'm awfully sorry. I rang you on impulse, I tried to explain about being lonely and it was true. But I am attracted to you and what I did was wrong. Nick is the best friend in the world. I never meant to hurt either of you. I tried to explain in the letter which I never knew he'd see. Somehow I thought you'd take more care of it, hide it.'

'I'd only just received it!' she said indignantly. 'Nick came in and I shoved it inside the book I was studying. Look, Giles, our relationship is difficult enough. Nick is a lovely person, couldn't be lovelier. He's also kind and good, but I've got this thing about money, about his family being so *rich*. It's a barrier. I know that.'

'You shouldn't have.'

'I know, but I have. I find his parents terribly false and I know they don't like me. I'm dreading the weekend.'

'Bear up,' Giles said, noticing Andreas and Lydia coming towards them. 'Look, if I don't have the chance to talk to you this weekend I'll call when I get back.'

'I wish you wouldn't,' Laura had replied, but she didn't think he'd heard her.

She also didn't know if she really meant it. Suddenly, Giles with his warmth, friendliness and understanding seemed a bulwark against the Constantine family.

And now here they were all together on this perfect summer's day with the sound of leather on willow, a satisfying 'plop' that seemed to happen every few seconds, punctuated or accompanied by calls of 'Well done' in gently modulated tones or a sprinkling of polite hand-clapping that echoed faintly round the ground.

Lydia Constantine smiled at Laura.

'Do you enjoy cricket?'

'I know very little about it.'

'Oh! Your father and brothers don't play?'

Laura shook her head.

'Neither does my husband, but Nick's very keen. Giles is *very good*. It's such a pity Giles didn't get to Oxford.' She shook her head sadly. 'You can't help feeling it would have done more for him than Manchester.' She glanced at Laura, murmuring sotto voce, 'You've heard he's leaving?'

Laura nodded.

'I can't think what his parents will say.' Lydia sighed and, as if disappointed at the lack of gossipy response on the part of her son's girlfriend, laid her head against the back of the chair and closed her eyes.

Lydia did not like cricket. She thought it the most boring game imaginable, but she liked the ceremony surrounding it: the whites worn by the players, the ritual of going in to bat, the breaks for lunch and tea, the possible excitement at the end if a match was close. She especially liked Lords, its aura of upper-class decadence, the distinguished elderly members with bald heads and moustaches, the elegance of the ladies who came to support the players, but who, of course, were not allowed in the Long Room, the pink and yellow ties of the members, some of whom had been on the waiting list for over half their lives, many since birth. Lydia liked the snobbery of cricket while reluctantly acknowledging the fact that it was a universal game, and that some of the best players were working-class men from disadvantaged backgrounds.

Cricket meant to Lydia what sending Nick to public school meant, what Oxford, having money and a house in St John's Wood, a Rolls in the garage and a yacht in Monte, meant: status, privilege, the chance to be above some and equal with others. Just as good as the Harveys, if not better.

And now Nick had got himself tied up with a working-class girl from a northern industrial town with an accent you could cut with a knife and whose family didn't play cricket.

The day was a success. Although Nick's college lost the match, he acquitted himself without disgrace. Lunch in the marquee for players and their families and friends was excellent: asparagus, cold beef and ham, a variety of exciting salads, excellent strawberries and cream and plenty of sparkling wines but no champagne. Andreas offered to get some but Nick, in a whisper in his ear, begged his father not to show off and was obeyed.

Tea, too, was good: more strawberries, a variety of delicious cakes, and the chance to talk with some of the parents of Nick's fellow students; most of the fathers had attended Oxford too. Lydia found it all highly satisfying, not unlike similar occasions at Nick's school, an added bonus on this occasion being that Giles's parents weren't there, even if Giles was.

More food followed later at dinner in an expensive French restaurant where, the social niceties with well-bred strangers out of the way, the talk was mainly about Giles and his decision to leave university. Lydia felt strangely excited about it, almost pleased, as if this could set Giles on the slippery slope to failure and disgrace. She realised then that she didn't really like Giles any more than she liked his family. The habit he had of always arriving half-dressed, as though appearances didn't matter, almost as if deliberately to annoy her, and the sort of casual, well-bred arrogance of his manner. There was always that air about him of 'them' and 'us', imperceptible maybe, but inevitably reminding her of his mother.

All her niceness to him over the years had really been pretence for Nick's sake. With any luck, once he went abroad, they would never see him or his family again, or at least not for a very long time.

And then to her horror she heard the word 'yacht' mentioned and there was Andy inviting Giles to join them once again *with* his family and, he hoped, looking in her direction, Laura.

'I hope your father has forgiven me for last year, Giles,' Andreas was saying when Lydia tuned in.

'Of course he has,' Giles exclaimed. 'Nothing to forgive. We had a wonderful time.'

'Giles's father trod on a jellyfish and his foot became infected,' Andreas explained to Laura.

'Yes, I heard.'

'Oh, you heard. I expect Nick told you.'

'I expect he did.'

Nick looked hard at Giles, but Giles merely smiled.

'We do hope you'll be able to come, Laura,' Lydia said graciously, 'and, of *course*, your parents are very welcome if they care to join in.'

The idea of her father on board a luxury yacht in Monte Carlo was a notion so bizarre to Laura that she burst out laughing.

'Oh, do forgive me,' she exclaimed apologetically to Lydia, seeing her expression, 'but my father has never been further south than Manchester.'

'Well, now is the time to start,' Andreas said. 'I'll write to him myself if you like.'

'What about your mother?' Emma chipped in. 'Maybe she'd enjoy it?'

'Oh, I think my mother would, but she's terribly shy.'

'*Do* try and persuade your parents,' Lydia murmured, signalling to the waiter to serve coffee. 'We'd *love* to have them.'

'I do find your parents rather insincere,' Laura said. 'They can't *possibly* want my mother and father on the boat.'

Nick stood by the college gate looking at Laura in the dim light from the lamp over the porch. He felt that the day had been farcical, full of tension, and bitterly regretted his impulse to make it a kind of family reunion, a means of reconciliation with Giles and a way for his mother, father and sister to get to know Laura better.

In fact, they knew Laura no better, or maybe they did. Maybe they now saw her in a light not as favourable as the one he would have wished. He felt she hadn't acquitted herself well. She was not the Laura he knew; clearly ill at ease, silent for the most part, yet almost aggressively defensive. But then there was also at the same time a faintly mocking air about her, as though she was observing the *dramatis personae* and finding them wanting, didn't care if they knew it. At times Laura made him angry that she made so little effort to endear herself to the people he loved.

'Say something,' Laura said, worried by his silence, aware that she'd offended him.

'I really don't know what to say. I'm quite confused. You keep on saying they don't like you, now you say because they make an effort to be nice and friendly not only to you but to your parents you find them insincere. *I* find that hurtful.'

Yes it was very hurtful, but she hadn't meant it like that. She tried to explain.

'I'm sorry. It sounded rude and I didn't mean it like that.' She stretched out a hand and touched his chest. 'I suppose I found *myself* terribly false. I mean, I feel I'm acting a part with them, was in London, too. Look, your folks are rather grand and terribly rich. I'm not used to that scene at all.'

'You're being snobbish in your own way,' Nick replied. 'My parents are being nice and you're unpleasant.' As she withdrew her hand sharply he clutched it and said, 'Sorry, I didn't mean that. I guess it was a mistake to arrange this weekend. I wanted it to be successful and it's been a disaster. We all tried too hard. I think they genuinely do want your parents on the boat. They were very keen to invite Giles's. They don't just want to show off. My father in particular likes people to be happy. He wants to give them a good time, and then he's unhappy if they don't have one. My mother is a bit of a social climber I'll admit. But basically she is a good woman full of doubts and insecurities and I love her.'

'I'm sorry.' Laura bowed her head and planted a kiss on the back of the hand which still held hers. 'We've got all mixed up this evening. Tomorrow will be better.'

Tomorrow after all, the parents were leaving in the afternoon. And so was Giles.

When Nick got back to college he found Giles lying on his bed reading. Giles put his book, page down, on his chest and looked at him.

'Nice day,' he said.

'I'm glad you think so.' Nick slumped dejectedly into a chair.

'Something wrong?'

'I think I'm trying too hard.'

'Come again?' Giles sat up, put the book on the table next to the bed and lit a cigarette.

'I want everyone to get on, love one another.'

'Don't we all?' Giles lay back again, and exhaled smoke. It rose in a cloud above his head and he tried to blow holes in it but it drifted away towards the half-open window. 'I gather you know about the letter?'

'Letter?'

'My letter to Laura.'

'Oh, that letter. Do you really think now is the time to talk about it?'

'I wondered why you asked me this weekend? In the circumstances I find it rather strange.' Giles idly examined the tip of his cigarette. He seemed perfectly relaxed and at ease with himself, whereas Nick felt in the grip of inner turmoil.

'I mean,' Giles went on, 'I found it particularly strange when Laura told me you had seen the letter.'

'I wasn't meant to.'

'So she told me. But you did.'

It seemed to Nick that somehow Giles had seized the initiative, was on top and it was all wrong. He was the guilty one and here he was acting like prosecuting counsel.

'I guess you're in love with Laura yourself,' Nick said. 'If you weren't you wouldn't have come. You wanted to see her and I know how you felt because that's what I feel. I want to see her all the time. I wanted to see you because we are such old mates. We have to work it out.'

'Nothing to work out,' Giles said offhandedly. 'I'd never pinch your girl.' He looked over at Nick. 'You've got it wrong. I like and admire her but I don't think I'm in love with her. I find her very attractive, very sexy – why deny it? – but that's not love, is it? I'd be a very cynical chap if I made a play for Laura knowing how much it would hurt you.'

'I think she likes you too.'

'But that's not "love" is it? I mean one can on an impulse want to touch a girl or kiss her, and I'll admit that's what happened, which is why I wrote the letter to apologise. I didn't want her to misunderstand.'

'It certainly changed Laura.'

'In what way?'

'She's different. Our relationship is different. Something's not the same since you saw her in Manchester. I feel I'm trying to cling onto something that simply isn't there any more. It's like staring into an empty space.'

Giles was silent. The revelation that Laura apparently felt something for him was not a surprise; but he was sure it wasn't recent or connected with the episode in Derbyshire. It had been there from the time they first met. A *coup de foudre*, an attraction, and what was an attraction if it wasn't sexual? That's why he'd gone back to Manchester early in the holiday, why he'd called her and why she'd agreed to come.

More importantly, it was why he'd come down this weekend, just to be sure.

Giles sighed. There seemed little more to say on the subject that wasn't insincere.

He was conscious of violent and warring emotions, feelings he was sure he had never in his life experienced before. He had always believed himself to be a nice bloke who played by the rules, a loyal, good friend who would never do anything mean or underhand: a man like his father, straightforward and honest.

Was he being honest now with his best friend, Nick? And how much did Nick believe his denials and, for that matter, how much did he?

For his sense of elation, the smell of victory overcame his scruples, and after some more casual conversation in which Laura was not referred to again, the two young men retired to their respective beds.

PART III

The Old School Tie: Giles

CHAPTER 9

Giles stood looking round the large room he had inhabited for just over eight months, the span of his short university career. It was at the back of the house overlooking the large garden of what had at one time been a prosperous Victorian mansion occupied, doubtless, by the large family of a woollen or cotton merchant, or one of the barons of the emerging industrial enterprises, which helped in that age of expansion to make Manchester great. Now it belonged to the university and had been converted into bedsits for the use of its students. In addition to the individual study bedrooms there was a common room and a large kitchen. In the summer it would be possible to sit out and work in the garden, away from the noise and bustle surrounding the university in its central location.

It was a nice room and Giles had found his fellow inmates pleasant. But he had not been happy here, because he had not been happy at the university. The reason for this was not the fault of the institution, or the course of study he was pursuing, or the city of Manchester, or the people he met, or the comfortable digs in suburban Didsbury.

Giles Harvey had simply failed to find his niche.

Until the A level results, life had been kind to Giles. He had been a good all-rounder: clever, popular, good at games, reasonably ambitious. He had a solid base in his home, and although he knew they were not wealthy in the way that the Constantines were – 'filthy rich' as his father contemptuously called them – he knew they were alright. He came from a line of solid, achieving, public-service minded, successful, landowning members of the upper-middle class. The Harvey family, past and present, had its place in the sun. No question about it. It had been presumed that Giles would ultimately follow his father into the legal profession, perhaps as a barrister rather than a solicitor. But with his late application he had found all the law faculties full, and opted instead for psychology, a subject he had never studied, knew little about and, he decided, did not really interest him.

Giles's interest in Laura had coincided with his disenchantment with university life, with the company of his fellow students and his general lack of an objective. Like his best friend, Nick, he had found her immediately attractive, compelling, interesting, different from any girl he had met before. Not to beat about the bush too much, she was certainly sexy too.

He had tried to analyse why Laura affected him like she did; to rationalise whether it was jealousy of his friend or plain concupiscence on his part, whether it was love or lust, but so far he had been unable to come up with any solution to the numerous questions he posed himself. However, on his way north from the weekend in Oxford he had realised that the situation was impossible. He would have to distance himself from Laura and Nick for some time. He would have to go abroad. Sort himself out.

Thus his dilemma made him decide to do what he had wanted to do anyway: give up psychology, say farewell to Manchester and its university, the pleasant house in Didsbury and the people he had met there.

Giles picked up his suitcase and a holdall and stole downstairs, feeling rather like a thief in the night, though it was broad daylight. Most, if not all, of the inhabitants of the house were attending lectures or classes and the place was deserted. He had not said goodbye to them, but he knew he would not be returning. He felt his parents had to be told first, and then letters would follow: to the university, to his tutor and to a guy called Henry who was on his course and lived in the same house. He knew Henry Harris better than most. He was a bit of a fish out of water too, which was maybe why they got on.

He would send Henry Harris his room and house keys, and that would be that.

No regrets? None at all. Giles closed the front door, went down the path to where his car was parked and drove off.

Edmund felt trapped by this room. It seemed in a way to typify his relationship with Mary. He felt trapped by her too, bowed down by an overwhelming sense of obligation, of guilt. What really would have suited him would have been a pretty, undemanding, not too well educated, sexy little number of about twenty-five. But he didn't think they existed nowadays. They were too conscious of their rights, about equality between the sexes, about their careers, mobile phones and getting ahead.

He was sure that when the affair had begun, Mary had marriage in mind. They had been very sexually attracted, they got on well, laughed a lot (that seemed hard to believe now), had a good time when they were together, most of it spent in bed. He thought Mary had Adam deliberately to hurry this process along, but after that she gradually changed into the rather sad, dejected, constantly whining person she was now.

Understandable really. She didn't have much fun, and he felt guilty about her.

Edmund shifted in the bed, glanced at the woman at his side and saw that she was still asleep. They had both fallen asleep after lovemaking which, for once, had occurred during the day while Adam was at school. Edmund had business in the area, and after lunch with his client had dropped in to see Mary who was working from home.

Edmund lay on his back, head propped in his hands, and looked around. Mary had taken an awful lot of trouble to try and make the bedroom into a pretty little feminine boudoir with white furniture, Laura Ashley wallpaper and matching curtains. It didn't come off. It was completely out of character with the overall gloom of the building: the dark corridors, the hideous cream and brown walls and orange carpet.

Edmund felt depressed whenever he entered it, and didn't know how Mary could continue to live there. Sometimes she talked about moving out of London and he wished she would, but they both knew she wouldn't.

'Ed,' Mary said, suddenly wide awake, as though she could read his thoughts, 'Adam's Head says he needs a lot of extra coaching.'

Edmund groaned audibly.

'I was wondering when that would come. I knew it.'

'Well, you can understand it,' she said peevishly. 'They don't get much of an education from the State. It's quite different. He's behind in Maths, English and he doesn't know any French. The Maths they do in the State schools is quite different.'

'I thought Maths was Maths anywhere,' Edmund grumbled.

'They have a different system. The Head said the State teachers made it up themselves. The system, that is. The Head has offered to coach Adam himself. He says he has a lot of innate intelligence.'

'I suppose *he* doesn't come cheap.' Edmund looked once more at the clock and swung his legs over the bed. 'How much?'

'He says he'll do it for ten pounds a lesson. Very reasonable really.'

'And how many lessons does he have to have?'

'Oh, Ed, don't be so petty.' Mary turned on her stomach and thumped the pillows. 'I find you *very* petty these days. I don't know what has got into you.'

'Worry is what has got into me, Mary. I have a lot of worries. Especially financial worries. Business is not good. People are taking to the cheap conveyancing and we're losing a lot of work. More than half my business was conveyancing and now people can do it themselves, on the cheap.'

'You should never have left Burrows,' Mary said sniffily. Burrows, Walters and Carter was the firm they had worked for when they both met.

'I have never regretted leaving Burrows.'

'That's because you're stubborn and won't admit you're wrong.'

Edmund began to dress, looking angrily at himself in the mirror while he knotted his tie. His hair was getting thinner and his wrinkles seemed to be multiplying. This was what stress did to a person. Made them old before their time. He turned to the bed and looked down at her.

'I have to go now, Mary. I've got an appointment.'

'What about the money, Ed, for the coaching? What shall I say?'

'To whom?'

'To the Head.'

Edmund flopped on the bed beside her, stretched out his hand to touch her, but she moved away.

'Can it wait a bit, Mary, until I've got some things sorted out?'

'What things?' She looked at him suspiciously.

'Some business matters. I can't be specific.'

'I would have thought your son's schooling was a matter of prime importance. Or is it because he's not like the other sons . . .'

'Don't be silly.' Edmund got up and went to the door

where he stopped, turning to look at her again.

'I do wish you'd try and understand,' he said.

'Ed, you make me sick, you really do.' Mary thumped the pillows hard, and when she heard the front door close she thumped them even harder, as if she was beating the life out of Ed.

Outside, Edmund stood looking up and down the road, just in case he saw anyone he knew. It was kind of instinctive and also, he realised, rather pathetic and unnecessary. After all, he could have been seeing a client. Edmund was a man whose worry and nervousness seemed to increase with the years.

Sometimes he wished he had someone to whom he could turn, but he hadn't. Neither his wife nor his mistress understood him, and his children were too young, too inexperienced, to confide in.

He got into his car, adjusted his driving mirror, scanning the tree-lined road again, and drove away. As he did, his feeling of oppression seemed to lighten, and he realised that a lot of it was due to Mary. The further he got away from her the better he felt, such was the burden of guilt he carried about her and Adam.

He wished they could cease their lovemaking and become platonic friends, but Mary would feel rejected, and he felt that some sex was, after all, better than none. It was better than doing without, looking round for another woman with more complications in an already complex life, or going to prostitutes, even decorous houses which he knew existed. The curious thing was that he and Mary still satisfied each other sexually, which gave a base to an otherwise stultifying and unsatisfactory relationship.

But what to do about increasing school fees he didn't know. And as for all his other problems . . . He started to sweat. God only knew how he was going to resolve those.

Edmund didn't have another appointment. It was now five

and he thought he'd go home early and maybe take Alice to the Heath for a walk. His daughter was the one person he truly cherished and whose company he craved. She was his consolation for an altogether unhappy and troublesome life.

With Alice skipping along by his side it was possible to believe that life was simple, uncomplicated and peaceful, like her.

In a better frame of mind Edmund cast aside thoughts of his troublesome mistress, his disadvantaged natural son and his money worries, and turned off the Finchley Road and drove up the hill that wound towards his home.

Outside the house was Valerie's car and in front of it was Giles's familiar MG. It took him a second or two to wonder what Giles's car was doing there and he also felt a momentary annoyance because it occupied the place where he usually parked his car, the neighbours tacitly agreeing to leave it free out of deference to him. In expensive, high density Hampstead, few houses had garages and most of its residents had to park in the street.

Edmund parked his car further up the road, removed his briefcase and walked towards the house. If Giles had come home it would be very difficult to suggest a walk to Alice; but why should the three of them not go while Valerie got the dinner? A family outing, a rare event. He was not a very imaginative man, and he couldn't think of any reason why Giles should come home in the middle of term, but it didn't worry him.

Edmund ran up the steps of the house, put his key in the door and let himself in. It all seemed very silent. He put his briefcase down in the hall and went into the living room which was also empty. The living room led into a conservatory, and Edmund noticed that the conservatory doors were open and beyond them he could see Valerie and Giles standing under one of the poplar trees in the garden. They had their backs to the house, heads bent, deep in conversation. Of Alice there was no sign.

He stood for a while watching them, and then they turned and, seeing him, waved.

'Hi!' he said, going towards them and stretching out a hand to Giles. 'To what do we owe the unexpected pleasure?'

'Hi, Dad!' Giles awkwardly grasped his father's hand and Valerie murmured, 'I'll leave you two to talk.'

'Something wrong?' Edmund, sensing tension, was now all concern. 'Where's Alice?'

'It's nothing to do with Alice, dear,' Valerie said soothingly. 'She's having tea with her little friend, Philippa.' As Valerie prepared to cross the lawn to the house Giles held her back.

'I'd rather you stayed, Mum, really.'

'Something *is* wrong,' Edmund said with a resigned sigh. 'Let's go into the house. I could actually do with a drink.'

Now that it came to confrontation with his father, Giles felt less sure of himself. His mother seemed instinctively to understand, as he knew she would. She was not the most demonstrative of women, but she had no need to show what he knew and had always known, that she loved him.

Giles led the way into the house, back into the living room and studied the array of bottles on the drinks table.

'Usual for you, Dad? Whisky?'

'Yes, please.' Edmund slumped into a chair and ran his hands over his face.

'And for me too, please,' Valerie said, sitting next to her husband.

Giles gave his parents their drinks, said he'd have a beer and then went into the kitchen to find one. He returned to the living room and as he opened the bottle and poured the beer into a glass he realised that his hand was shaking. He hadn't for a moment thought it would be so difficult.

'Dad,' he said, still standing by the drinks table. 'Not to beat around the bush too much . . .'

'Please don't,' his father said.

'It's nothing dreadful . . .'

'Get on with it, Giles.'

'I've decided to leave university.'

Edmund took a sip from his glass and balanced it on the arm of his chair. Then he folded his hands on his lap.

'To do what?' he asked.

'I'm not quite sure.' Giles's brow puckered. 'I thought I might travel for a while.'

'Oh, I see.' Edmund's tone was sarcastic. 'A gentleman of leisure?'

'Not quite, Dad.' Giles took a chair opposite his father. 'I don't really enjoy psychology.'

'Then why did you do it?'

'Oh, *Edmund*!' Valerie exclaimed impatiently, leaning forward, hands round her knees. 'Don't make things difficult for Giles. He's finding it hard enough telling you as it is.'

'But why did he do it?' Edmund turned to her with an air of surprise. 'I mean, it's cost me a small fortune to keep him at university, and now he's telling me that he's throwing it all away to "travel". No plans, apparently, for a job or a career. Do I get my money back I ask myself? Or am I supposed to go on forking out while he bums round the world.'

'I find you very unreasonable, Ed,' Valerie said. 'Giles simply made a mistake. He didn't like Manchester much either. We said he wouldn't.'

'He should have done what you suggested and tried for higher grades. Then he could have been going to Oxford in a few months from now instead of wasting all this time.'

'I might not have got in, Dad.'

'Of course you'd have got in!' Edmund exclaimed wrathfully. 'You wouldn't have been wasting all your time on the rugger pitch and the cricket ground. You would have applied yourself to your studies and you would have got straight As. I simply can't understand you.'

Edmund drained his glass and, with another exclamation, rose and refilled it. Then he stood by the drinks table and glared at his son.

'And who is paying for this trip round the world? Me, I suppose?'

'I thought he could use the money your father left, Ed.' Valerie spoke placatingly. Edmund's father, who had died years before, had left the bulk of his estate to Edmund, but a small sum of money to each of his grandchildren.

'That money is invested.'

'Yes, but only shares. He can sell them.'

'Then he'll have nothing for a rainy day.'

'This is a rainy day, Dad.' Giles felt discouragement seep through him.

'It is indeed. It's a *very* rainy day. There we have Nick Constantine of whom, frankly, I never expected anything very much, covering himself with glory at Oxford, all set on a good career, whereas you who I always considered had far more ability and considerably more personality, flounder around.'

'Please don't bring Nick into this, Ed.' Valerie unfastened her hands and leaned back in her chair. 'Nick is a *very* nice boy. He worked hard and he did well but I don't think he is covering himself with glory as you suggest, and Giles is certainly not "floundering around". He has made a mistake. I think we half expected this. I'm not surprised. The only thing that does surprise me is that you are. Travel broadens the mind. I think selling the shares and using the money to travel a very good idea. Your father would have approved. If he gets short I think maybe I can help out a little. Then he can come back and go to law school. He wants to do that. Don't you, Giles?' As Giles nodded, she continued. 'He can live at home. That will save a lot of money and when he's finished he can do his articles with you and join you, which is what you've always wanted. All in all,' Valerie stood up and looked at her watch, 'I think it's a very good idea. Things may have turned out for the best.' Before she left the room she turned and gave her menfolk a bright, encouraging smile. 'You know they often do. Dinner in an hour.'

Dinner was a rather strained, silent affair, brightened by the patter of Alice who was delighted to see her elder brother at home. She was such an uncomplicated child that her presence was always a tonic. Edmund visibly relaxed and afterwards went off with her to help her with her homework.

Giles stayed in the kitchen helping his mother to fill the dishwasher and clear away.

'Thanks for your support, Mum,' he said, stooping to kiss her.

Momentarily she leaned against him and put an arm round his waist. She often wondered if Giles realised how much she depended on him. She had missed him living at home already, and knew how much worse it would be if he did go abroad.

'I do think Daddy *was* a bit unreasonable. After all, we all make mistakes and change our minds.' Valerie straightened up from the dishwasher and frowned.

'Daddy is terribly out of sorts lately. Sometimes I worry about him.'

Giles was immediately concerned.

'Is he ill?'

'Oh, no, I don't think it's anything like that. At least I don't *think* it's anything physical. It's more mental or emotional.' She paused and flopped down at the kitchen table. 'Somehow I think it's to do with money. I think he's worried about money, which is why he flew off the handle with you.'

'*Money*!' Giles also sat down and stared across the table at his mother. 'But I thought we were OK? I mean private schools, a good lifestyle. Not a yacht maybe but . . .' he laughed, 'we can't all be the Constantines.'

'No, we can't.' His mother smiled too. Then she frowned. 'I would have said we were OK. I mean he's never mentioned any difficulties to me. It's something we never talk about. Of course I have a small income of my own, you know that. I am not totally dependent on your father and never have been. Daddy has never given me an allowance or paid my dress bills, not that I have many!' She laughed self-consciously, acknowledging the fact that her family regarded her total lack of interest in clothes as an amusing and endearing eccentricity. 'I help with the housekeeping. In fact, I pay a lot of the bills, but Daddy takes care of school fees and so on, household repairs, car maintenance, holidays, Whiteboys (Whiteboys was the Somerset house), and so on. All in all, I should think our annual expenditure is quite considerable, but I would have thought we were able to meet it without much difficulty.'

'But shouldn't you talk about it, Mum?' Giles's expression was one of bewilderment.

'Yes, I suppose we should.' She nervously clasped and unclasped her hands. 'But somehow we never do. I mean, I've asked him if things are alright and he said of course they are and brushed my question aside. You know how brusque, how stiff-upper-lip and all that Dad can be. However I think I'll ask him again after the outburst tonight. I mean, I can help quite a bit if necessary. I just wanted my money to go to you children. After I've gone there will be quite a lot, especially if my parents go before me which I suppose they will.'

Giles rose to get a beer out of the fridge and, breaking open the can, put it to his lips, his expression thoughtful.

'Maybe I should have a chat with Dad?'

'Oh, no, please don't! He wouldn't like that at all. He'll get over this and we'll work something out. He just doesn't like surprises. But he would be very upset if he thought I'd brought up the subject of money.'

'But,' Giles insisted, 'he brought up the subject of money. He made quite a meal of it, asking if I expected him to pay.'

'I know he did; but still he would be very upset if you asked him if things were OK financially. I know he would. Now, darling,' she looked at the clock on the kitchen wall and began to remove her apron, 'it's nearly time for the nine o'clock news. I hope Daddy has made sure that Alice is in bed.'

Edmund sat by the bedside of his daughter for a long time after she'd gone to sleep listening to the gentle sound of her breathing. He recalled the time he used to read to her every night when she was small, the rapt expression on her face as he turned the pages, sometimes the tears when a well-loved story reached the end. Those intimate moments between father and daughter had been very precious to him, still were, though now he had to drag her away from the television set or fetch her from some school friend with whom she had been having tea. Alice was now eleven and Edmund reflected, rather sadly, on how quickly children grew up and matured, how swiftly the years of childhood seemed to vanish behind them.

He leaned forward and, putting out the light by the side of her bed, tiptoed away. As soon as he closed the door his sense of peace and euphoria vanished and the worry, the feeling of dread, returned. He crept along the hall to his study and shut the door, leaning against it for a moment, trying to subdue the mounting panic that sometimes threatened to overwhelm him. At these dark moments he would see the collapse of his life; his work, his home; everything in ruins.

Edmund took a few deep breaths and then, hurrying to his desk, unlocked a drawer and drew from it a notebook which he considered for several seconds, flicking over the pages.

Finally he scribbled a number on his blotter, drew the

telephone towards him and tapped the keys, keeping the handset close to his ear as he heard the ringing tone at the other end.

No one there. He let it ring for several seconds and was about to replace the handset when a voice at the other end said: 'Hello?'

Edmund cleared his throat. 'Hello! Mr Davies?'

'Jeremy Davies speaking.'

'Mr Davies, my name is Edmund Harvey. You don't know me, but your name has been given to me by a mutual acquaintance.'

'May I ask who?'

'Philip Petersen.'

'Oh, yes.' The tone of voice, which had been cautious, even suspicious, relaxed. 'How is Philip?'

'Very well when I saw him which was at lunch today. I understand,' Edmund cleared his throat again, 'that is, he *gave* me to understand you might be looking for some capital to expand your business, a high risk investment which I understand the banks are reluctant to accommodate.'

'May I ask the nature of your interest, Mr Harvey?' The tone was brusque and unfriendly again.

'Certainly. I have funds at my disposal which I invest on behalf of clients who are prepared to take a risk in exchange for high profits. Naturally I would much prefer to discuss this in person rather than over the telephone.'

'There's nothing funny about it, is there?' Mr Davies demanded suspiciously.

'On the contrary,' Edmund replied haughtily. 'I am a lawyer with an international reputation and with over twenty years' experience, largely in commercial affairs. I can call on considerable sums of money available, surprisingly, at substantially lower rates than you might expect in today's climate. The service is also completely confidential, and if we do not come to an arrangement all documentation is destroyed and the matter forgotten. It is absolutely bona fide. I only deal through personal recommendation, and between my clients and myself there is an atmosphere of complete trust.'

'Do you mind if I check you out with Petersen?'

'Not at all.' The receiver was beginning to slip from Edmund's clammy hand, and he transferred it to the other side, wiping his hand on his knee. 'Check it out and call me back. Not tonight as it's getting late. I'll give you my office number.'

'Good of you to get in touch with me, Mr Harvey. I appreciate it.' The tone of voice had now mollified.

'Not at all. I hope we can do business.'

'I hope so.'

Edmund gave Davies his office number, there were more expressions of cordiality and then he replaced the receiver and sat where he was for several minutes, his head bent, his hands shaking.

Valerie finished clearing up in the kitchen, to which she had returned after watching the news with Giles and having a chat. He then decided to go to the pub to see if any of his friends were about, and Valerie went back to the kitchen to remove the dishes from the dishwasher, put them away and lay the table for breakfast which the family usually had together. After doing her chores Valerie sat for a few minutes at the kitchen table reading the *Evening Standard*. After glancing at the clock and seeing it was after ten, she decided to go to bed. Edmund often worked in his study at night, sometimes until quite late. Valerie put out all the downstairs lights and slowly climbed the stairs. She was in a thoughtful and not altogether happy mood. She had tried to make light of Giles's news, but it was really a matter of putting on a brave front. She was no less unhappy about it than her husband, but she was more expert at concealing her feelings.

Valerie was a conventional woman, with conventional ideas, and thought it was the role of the woman to mend relationships in families, and where possible, keep things on an even keel. She reached the first-floor landing and paused at the door of Alice's room. She gently turned the handle and peeped inside. Alice always slept with the window open and the curtains drawn back, and it was possible to see her still form in the bed.

Hopefully, with life ahead of her, her dreams were the happy, untroubled ones of youth.

Valerie closed the door as gently as she had opened it and continued walking along the corridor. Then, seeing a light under the door, she paused outside Edmund's study. She was about to turn the handle when she heard his voice, a low murmur, then silence, then he started to speak in hushed tones again. She turned the handle gently so as not to disturb him, but the door was locked. This rather shocked her and she stood back looking fixedly at the door. She wondered why he was talking so quietly, as though he didn't want to be heard but, above all, why the door was locked in a house where there were few secrets, or had been until now. Valerie climbed the stairs to the second floor where there were the boys' bedrooms, hers and Edmund's and the guest room.

Still thoughtful, she got undressed, washed and did her teeth, cleansed her face, ran a comb through her hair – Valerie's routine at night, like the morning, was brief and basic.

She climbed into her bed, took her book from the bedside table and donned her reading glasses. But she was still preoccupied and the words seemed to blur on the page. Suddenly the house seemed a house of secrets, of discord, possible disaster. The comfortable certainty of years past seemed no longer there. The order and routine she was used to had gone. It was not the first time she'd paused outside Ed's study and heard him speaking quietly on the phone as if he had a hand over his mouth to prevent himself being heard. But it was the first time she'd tried the door – because she had wanted to talk to him about Giles – and found it locked. Maybe he always locked it? That was a thought.

After several attempts to restart her book, Valerie gave up and turned to put out the light. She and Edmund had slept in twin beds for years, so when he came to bed he wouldn't disturb her. She lay for a few moments but realised that she was still too wide awake, too nervous, to contemplate sleep. She put on the light again and was about to pick up the book when Edmund came in and seemed surprised to see her still awake. He turned and closed the door and was about to go into the bathroom when she called out to him: 'Ed, come over here for a minute.' She patted the bed and Edmund, looking very weary and beginning to unfasten his tie, came over to her.

'Yes, dear?' he said, looking down at her.

'Ed, is there anything the matter?'

'The matter?' Edmund appeared nonplussed by her question and shook his head.

'I mean,' Valerie went on, 'is there anything wrong? Be honest, Ed.'

'How do you mean, Valerie?' He perched on the side of her bed, his tie in his hand.

'What do you do in your office, murmuring away on the phone so late at night?'

'My dear, you know I have a lot of business to do at home.'

'Why lock the door?'

'So that I'm not disturbed.'

'Why?'

'Because,' he made as if to get up, clearly irritated, but she put out a hand and held on to his arm.

'Are you worried about anything, Ed?'

'No.' He was clearly getting annoyed and tried to get up again.

'You can tell me you know, confide in me. I'm your wife

and if there is anything wrong I want to know. Maybe I can help?'

'There is nothing wrong,' he insisted, this time succeeding in dragging himself away, and got to his feet. Then he appeared to relent. 'Well, alright, if you like I *am* worried about Giles.'

'But you've only just heard about Giles, and you have been like this for weeks, maybe months. Preoccupied, as if you're worried or unhappy. Also, I know you don't sleep. You're very restless. Is everything alright at the office, Ed? Is it money? If it is I have a bit put by, you know, and perhaps I can help.'

'Look, Valerie,' Edmund said wearily, 'I do appreciate your concern, but there is *nothing* wrong, *nothing* you can do. And if it was money, which it isn't, you know I would never touch your money. I've told you that before. Look, it's very late. I'm tired and you look tired. So let's talk about Giles tomorrow, eh?'

He smiled at her and, suddenly, as if on impulse, bent down and kissed her on the brow.

As an expression of husbandly tenderness, that was as far as he had gone for quite some time.

CHAPTER 10

Laura, white-faced, sat with bowed head trying to hide the tears, the bitter tears of chagrin and failure.

'I'm terribly sorry, Laura,' Maggie said, finding it hard to hide her own feeling of disappointment at the failure of a promising student, but angry at the same time that Laura was responsible for her own predicament, 'but I feel you have only yourself to blame. You admit that you did very little work, and that showed in the exam results. However,' she leaned back in her chair and lit a cigarette, 'the College Head has agreed to take you back if, after a year away, you can satisfy us that you have recovered your ability to work by passing next year's exams. Maybe a year away from Nick will be a good thing to bring you to your senses.'

'Nick had absolutely nothing to do with it,' Laura retorted, eyes smarting.

'Well, Nick's results were alright, I hear,' she said, adding sarcastically, 'obviously he was able to put passion on one side and concentrate on work.'

'That's a horrible thing to say!' Laura leapt from her chair.

'Nevertheless it's true, isn't it, Laura?' Maggie's tone became gentle, more understanding. 'We talked about this before, if you remember. "Man's love is of man's life a thing apart . . ." It's awful to have to quote it in the nineteen-nineties, when it was written over a hundred and fifty years ago, but in many ways it still remains true, at least among some of my students. Not all of them, thank heaven.' She looked up with a smile. 'Some of them are sensible enough to balance their work with their love life. I hope that when you return to us, Laura, and I'm sure you will, that this is a valuable lesson you've learned, and one that will stand you in good stead for the rest of your life.'

Maggie rose and put a hand on her student's shoulder. 'I'm sure this year off will be of inestimable benefit to you, Laura. I know that you won't like me saying this, but in many ways you are immature. I think that's why your first love affair knocked you sideways. Some of my more experienced students were able to cope . . .'

'I suppose because they came from better families,' Laura burst out. 'Most people from Oxford do.'

Maggie paused by the door.

'I think that's rather a silly thing to say. Wherever they came from – and not all were by any means well off – they had a sense of priority which you unfortunately lacked. It has nothing to do with money or class. Just plain common sense.' She gave Laura a final tap on the shoulder and opened the door. 'Come and see me before you go. You've a first-class brain and I want you to use it in the year ahead.'

Nick stood at the room window looking out into the quad, waiting for that girl to appear again, swinging across in easy strides just as he used to observe her before he fell in love with her. Maybe he was in love with her then: love at first sight? It had been a tremendous experience, their love affair. Mind blowing, staggering, all the usual adjectives, yet none of them sufficiently adequate to express what he and Laura meant to each other.

But now he was rather frightened. Laura had been summoned by Maggie and she had been away a long time. Laura had been anxious about her results and so had he about his; but he got through, no sweat. There had been a mild ticking off from his tutor because, though good, the results were not of a sufficiently high standard for a first. No chance of an All Souls Fellowship unless he improved on these.

Nick thought if she'd done well she'd have charged back. But it was impossible to think that she'd failed.

He paced restlessly round the room, tried to read, and he was about to set off and look for her, starting with the tutor's lodgings when, glancing out of the window, he saw that familiar, beloved figure hurrying across the quad. He bounded to the door and, racing down the stairs, greeted her at the entrance. She looked up at him and her stark expression told him the worst. He folded her in his arms and helped her up the stairs.

Laura threw herself onto the bed and stared at the ceiling. She still hadn't said a word, catatonic shock. Nick began to worry about her.

'I'll make tea,' he said, finally getting up from the side of the bed where he'd been sitting holding her hand.

Laura spoke at last. 'A drink would be nice. I failed, Nick. I'm to be sent down.' Nick stood in front of the kettle, not quite taking it in. He plugged it in, then went to a cupboard where there was a bottle of brandy and poured her a good measure. She sat up as he approached and took the proffered glass with the ghost of a smile.

'Sorry. I'm being an ass.'

Nick sat down again and took her free hand.

'They can't send you down.'

'They can, and I am. They need the place for someone else, someone who is prepared to work and benefit from being at this great university.' Laura rolled her eyes to the ceiling and finished the brandy in her glass in a gulp.

'It's my fault,' Nick said.

'No, it isn't. It's mine. You managed to be in love and work. I didn't.'

'I thought you knew your Hardy and your Eliot inside out?'

'I thought I did too, but not with sufficient "maturity" to satisfy the examiners, that is Maggie. She said my scholarship, such as it was, was too shallow, no depth. I suppose I could say she is a frustrated old bitch, but I shan't. I think she's right.' Laura sat up on the bed, put down her glass and linked her hands round her knees.

'You know what the worst part is? Having to tell my family that I failed. Got into Oxford and got chucked out.'

'Can't you say you're having a year off?' Even as he said it, Nick knew the excuse sounded rather lame.

Laura went on as though she hadn't heard him. 'We're a family of failures, low achievers, and I thought I was different.'

'You're not a low achiever, you're not a failure.'

Laura continued regardless. 'Maggie said some of her students managed to combine love with success in exams. I cheapened the whole thing by dragging in class, rather as I did that night we had dinner with your folks. I guess I have a lot to learn, Nick. Stop blaming others, for a start.'

Nick poured hot water onto his tea bag, stirred it in his mug and then added milk.

It would mean Oxford without her, not seeing her every day, not making love to her at every opportunity. And that he supposed was the truth of the matter: what had inspired and fired him had drained her. That was the only explanation he could think of. It was a disaster.

'You could stay on in Oxford,' he said. 'I mean in town. Living in Oxford. We could share a house. I don't mind leaving college. It is a bit like being in a boarding school. We . . .' He began to get excited.

'And what would I use for money? The dole would hardly pay the rent.'

'Laura,' Nick paused, then went on diffidently. 'You know money is no problem. I could keep you. You can get all the benefits you're entitled to and I'll take care of the rest.'

'What *would* your mum and dad say?' Laura's tone was heavy with sarcasm.

Nick shrugged.

'Given that they don't like me very much,' Laura continued.

'That's your idea.'

'It's true. Then if at the end you don't get your fellowship they'll blame me.'

'They won't. Look, if you like, we needn't even tell them. I mean that you've been sent down. We can just say we're sharing a house. No need for them to know.'

'They'll find out. Emma will tell them. Giles will tell them. Hey!' Laura paused and looked thoughtfully at Nick. 'Now Giles and I are in the same situation. Isn't that a coincidence?'

By the look on Nick's face she realised she'd made a mistake even mentioning it.

In the age of corporate identity: large multiple stores and chains dominating the high streets, Boothroyds the Chemists was, if not unique, an increasingly rare sight to behold. Round the corner from the Chase household, it occupied a central position in a modest road, which also had a greengrocer, a butcher, a paper shop and a small supermarket where Gordon worked during the holidays.

Laura had worked for Boothroyds since the age of thirteen or so, on Saturdays and during the school holidays. Mr and Mrs Boothroyd, who lived in a flat over the shop, had become almost as close as her own family. Even so, she couldn't tell them that she had been rusticated from Oxford because they had shared the pride of the family and school when she had got a place. 'Our' Laura had been the toast of everyone. Mr Boothroyd was pleased, if a little surprised, to see Laura asking for her old job during the long vacation. Mrs Boothroyd was a lady who literally enjoyed bad health, made the most of her many complaints, and was in and out of the doctor's surgery and hospital out-patients clinics as fast as they could accommodate her. Maybe it was marriage to a pharmacist that had made her so concerned about her health, and she was forever trying out the free samples of this medicine and that with which her husband was deluged from the drug companies.

Mr Boothroyd was a gentle, patient man, tolerant of his wife's hypochondria, and Laura was devoted to him, more devoted, if the truth be told, than she was to her own father. She enjoyed being back in the shop, behind the counter in her white coat while Mr Boothroyd remained in the dispensary and Mrs Boothroyd, relieved of her duties in the shop, found more time for her trips to the many clinics she could persuade to take an interest in her health problems.

Laura had left Oxford early and had been working at the shop for about a month during which time Mr Boothroyd had gradually come to the conclusion that all was not well with his favourite. Laura had always been a bright, effervescent girl and now she was strangely silent and withdrawn; she had always been of a confiding nature and now she was secretive, buttoned up. Mr Boothroyd tried to get her to talk, but it was useless. He decided that when she had something to say she would tell him, in her own good time.

Laura finished serving the last customer, advising her on the best colour of lipstick from the variety on offer, saw her to the door, changed the 'Open' sign to 'Closed', locked the door and took the keys to Mr Boothroyd who was busy cashing up.

'Quite a good day, Laura,' he said with a smile, and she agreed, smiling back. It was so nice to see her joyful expression that he ventured to comment further. 'Laura, I haven't seen you smile very much these days. Is there anything the matter?' Laura shook her head and he could sense her clamming up. 'Maybe the work at Oxford is harder than you realised, Laura?' Mr Boothroyd suggested, following

Laura to the back of the shop where she removed her white coat and collected her cardigan from a hook and her shopping bag from a chair. Laura turned to him and shook her head.

'Nothing's wrong at all, Mr Boothroyd, thanks. I'll see you tomorrow.'

'Right, Laura.' Mr Boothroyd smiled philosophically and saw her to the door, which he unlocked to allow her out and then relocked again.

Laura thought that if Mr Boothroyd continued to be so nosey she would leave and get a job elsewhere. Somewhere no one knew her, where they were not so curious. She knew he only meant it kindly, but she resented this intrusion in her private life. Laura was grieving and she wanted to keep herself to herself. She was grieving for her ruined career at Oxford and the shame she would have brought on her family if they'd known. She was grieving for her relationship with Nick and for the hurt she'd caused him by leaving Oxford without telling him. She was grieving for all the missed chances, for being nearly twenty and, in a short time, having lost so much.

Laura got home and, to her surprise, found her mother already in the kitchen preparing the tea. Thursday was usually the day Hilda stayed at the office to clean, and Laura took over the maternal role and prepared tea for her father and brothers. Today she'd bought mince at the butcher's and was going to make hamburgers and chips, a favourite of the boys, naturally.

'Hello, Mum,' Laura said, closing the door and putting her shopping on the table. 'Didn't expect to see you. I bought some mince to make hamburgers for tea.' Laura began to get her parcels from her bag and looked up to see her mother staring at her. 'Is there anything wrong, Mum?'

'Well,' Hilda put down the bread knife with which she'd been slicing bread and sat down heavily on a nearby chair. 'I arranged to work tomorrow because I wanted to talk to you, Laura. I want to tell you before I tell the boys, and they'll both be late in this evening. Sharon knows already.'

'Mum, are you ill?' Laura said with concern, aware that suddenly the misery she'd felt about herself had been transferred to something else. She sat down opposite her mother, scrutinising every nuance of expression on her face.

'I'm not ill, Laura.' Hilda flicked away a lock of hair that had fallen over her eye. Laura noticed that her eyes were very bright. Her face was also flushed and there was an air of agitation about her which was unusual. Usually her mother was the embodiment of stoicism and calm.

'Laura, I'm going to leave your father!' Hilda raised her head and looked her daughter boldly in the eyes. 'It hasn't been an easy decision, but I've been thinking about it for a long time. I've told your dad, of course, discussed it with him. He won't take me seriously, but I am serious.'

'Mum! Is there someone else?'

Hilda laughed, raised her eyes to the ceiling. 'How nice it would be if there was, love. No there's no one else. I just can't stomach your father any more, his loutishness, his selfish ways. There's absolutely nothing *wrong* with him, you know.'

'Like Mrs Boothroyd,' Laura murmured and, in reply to her mother's unspoken question, 'there's nothing wrong with her either.'

'Your father's a lazy useless old bugger and I am just sick to death of slaving away all day and having to look after him.'

'But, Mum, where will you go?' As the implication of her mother's words began to sink in, Laura felt aghast.

'Well, I shall go to our Sharon's to start off with, or to my sister Marjorie. Then I'm applying for a council flat, to be rehoused. I know my rights. I've been planning this for a long time. I wanted to see you settled and on the way to a career. The boys can stay with their father. They'll be alright.

They'll cope. I'm so proud that you got into Oxford, Laura.'

Laura sat studying her clenched hands on her lap.

'This is a terrible shock, Mum. You can't think how much.'

Hilda looked surprised.

'But had you no idea, love, how I felt about your father?'

'Well, I knew you weren't very happy, but I never thought you'd leave him.' Laura looked round. 'Where is he tonight, by the way?'

'He's gone to his sister's to have a moan, no doubt. I told him I was going to tell you of my decision and he could stop away as long as he liked. I'm going to Sharon's tonight. I'm not sleeping in this house again. I know it's a shock, but my mind is made up. It's best to make the break, and make it quick, and while you're here you can help your father and brothers get accustomed to the situation. By the time you go back to Oxford they'll be used to it.'

As soon as Laura came into the shop the following morning, Mr Boothroyd knew that something had happened. She was always in good time, but this morning she was particularly early. He had hardly started work himself, Mrs Boothroyd having already left to keep an appointment at the hospital.

Mr Boothroyd, shrugging on his white coat as he let Laura in, said: 'You're early, Laura. Couldn't sleep?' It was meant as a joke, but Laura nodded as she took off her cardigan and hung it on its hook.

'I've had some terrible news, Mr Boothroyd.' As she turned to him tears sprang to her eyes. 'My mum is leaving my dad.'

'Oh, dear, Laura, I'm *very* sorry to hear that.' Mr Boothroyd's expression was immediately one of sympathy, and he put an avuncular hand on her arm. 'Whatever made her decide to do that?'

'They never got on, Mr Boothroyd.' Laura sank into the

chair under the clothes peg. 'My father, as you know, hasn't worked for years, is not in the best of health, though my mum thinks he puts a lot of it on.' She glanced fleetingly at Mr Boothroyd, but his expression didn't change.

'It's a very big step to take, Laura.' Mr Boothroyd sighed. 'Though perhaps, in this day and age, sadly, not all that uncommon. One must expect it. There isn't another . . .' he paused delicately. Laura shook her head.

'Oh, no, no one else. My mum's not like that. She just wants her independence. She's going to stop with my sister or my Auntie Marjorie until the council get her a flat. She's got it all worked out. She's been planning it for months, maybe years. In fact, last night she didn't sleep at home.'

'She's gone just like that?' Mr Boothroyd looked surprised.

'Just like that. Thought it was best. She'd already taken most of her things to Sharon's. It was a very strange feeling when my father and brothers came home. For a while no one mentioned it. My father can't believe it. My brother Gary is probably going to move in with his girlfriend anyway. They've been thinking of it for some time.'

'Good thing they've got you, Laura,' Mr Boothroyd said and then gazed at her. 'Is that what you've had on your mind recently?'

Laura shook her head but remained silent.

'There has been something, hasn't there?'

'It's not that Mr Boothroyd . . .' Laura had entwined the fingers of both hands and sat there twisting them. 'It came as a complete surprise to me. I could never see my Mum leaving the family. No, what . . . what has been the matter,' her voice faltered then went on with a rush, 'I've been sent down from Oxford. I failed my exams and I've had to leave the university.'

'Oh, Laura!' Mr Boothroyd grasped her shoulder so hard that she almost winced, jumped in pain. 'Oh, Laura, I am so sorry . . .'

'I can go back,' she hurried on, 'if I pass next year. But I haven't been able to tell the family. I couldn't tell anyone. I felt so ashamed after all they, and people like you, expected of me.'

'But, Laura, how did it happen? You were so bright. Didn't you work?'

'Not hard enough . . . I fell in love, Mr Boothroyd. There was, is, a man, Nick.'

'Ah!' Mr Boothroyd assumed the tactful, sagacious expression he kept for customers who sought his advice on the intricacies of various methods of contraception. 'Is he still about?'

'Oh, yes! And it wasn't his fault. It was mine. He didn't fail his exams. I think it was all just too much for me. I was very silly. Very weak. My tutor had warned me my work wasn't good enough, but I thought I had it in me to make up.' She shook her head. 'Oxford is very hard, very tough. It's not like school, and the tutors aren't like our teachers who have known us for years. I lived in a cocoon and now I know what the real world is like. You understand that I couldn't tell Mum and Dad, don't you?'

'Poor Laura,' Mr Boothroyd said, still stroking her arm. 'And now you have your home breaking up too. Nowhere to turn. It doesn't seem fair, does it?'

The summer for Laura was one long purgatory from which, unlike the souls who, so legend says, ultimately ascend to heaven, she could see no escape. It was also the summer she turned twenty and became at the same time the mother of the family, fitting into her mother's role, taking her place almost instinctively. She rose early in the morning, took her father his tea, prepared her brothers' breakfasts, washed up, made the beds and left the house just before nine to go to the chemist, returning at five-thirty when she began the cooking and cleaning routine all over again.

It never occurred to the men to offer to help her and it never occurred to her to ask, which was strange for a seemingly liberated university-educated woman. But what applied to other people did not apply to her.

Her father, as if to prove that he really was ill, had what seemed to be a minor heart attack. He developed chest pains in the middle of the night and was taken to hospital, but released after a few days. The doctor seemed to think it was brought on by anxiety about the possibility that Laura might leave him. He was put on medication and Laura felt more imprisoned than ever.

Maybe she would never return to Oxford and would spend the rest of her days looking after her family, all of whom she now realised suffered from various degrees of selfishness, including her mother, whom she only saw when she visited her sister, and who had no regrets about what she had done.

Someone at least had achieved freedom.

She and Nick spoke on the phone regularly until he went to the family yacht in Monte after failing to get her to agree to join him. He tried to come up for her birthday, but she didn't want him to see where she lived, or how she lived. Above all, she didn't want him to meet her father. It was dreadful to be ashamed of her family, but she was. Her sense of low self-esteem was further enhanced by a feeling of disgust at her attitude; but then she thought of the house in St John's Wood, the Rolls in the garage, the yacht in Monte and the splendid youthful-looking parents, and she knew she couldn't help herself.

Laura remembered what Maggie had said about a year away from Nick doing her good, and she wondered if Maggie was right. It was, of course, not Nick's fault that she had fallen in love or failed her exams, but if he hadn't been there it wouldn't have happened. She would be going back to Oxford, some compensation for the wretched life she was leading.

Maybe, deep down, there was a core of resentment against him there.

Sometimes Nick would phone from the boat and he wrote regularly, but his letters were curiously passionless, as if he'd had second thoughts too, as if their love was finally dying.

Towards the end of August of that dreadful, endless summer, Laura was at the back of the shop checking in new stock that had been delivered earlier in the day when the bell that hung over the door jangled to announce the arrival of a customer. Mr Boothroyd called: 'Shop, Laura,' from the dispensary.

Laura, notepad and pencil in hand, went through the curtain into the shop and looked straight into the face smiling at her across the counter – that familiar, laid-back countenance. A great surge of unexpected joy rose up like a fountain inside her.

'Giles!' she cried, and she felt like rushing round and giving him a huge hug.

'Hey, Laura!' He seemed glad that she was so obviously pleased to see him, and held out his hand across the counter. 'How are you?'

She wanted to say something silly like, 'All the better for seeing you', but didn't, because at that moment Mr Boothroyd's face appeared round the dispensary door, his eyebrows raised in enquiry.

'It's alright, Mr Boothroyd. Just a friend.'

'Someone from the university?' Mr Boothroyd looked curiously at Giles.

'A friend of Nick's.'

'Ah!' Mr Boothroyd held out a hand across the counter. 'How do you do . . .'

'Giles Harvey,' Giles said jovially, clasping Mr Boothroyd's proffered hand. 'How do you do, sir?'

'I'm very well thank you, young man.' Laura could tell that Mr Boothroyd approved of Giles with his wide, friendly smile, superior accent and nice manners. 'Have you come from London just to see Laura?'

'Well, no. I had business in the area,' Giles explained, 'and I thought I'd look her up. Say,' he glanced at his watch, 'can we have lunch?'

Laura looked at Mr Boothroyd who nodded. 'It's not quite lunch time, Laura, but by all means go now.' And while Laura ran into the back to put a comb through her hair and get her cardigan she could hear Giles and Mr Boothroyd chatting amiably away in the shop.

'I'll be back in an hour,' she promised, and Giles, opening the door, stood back politely to let her pass.

'Now,' he said, following her, hands in his pockets, looking around, 'anywhere near here you can recommend?'

'I think it will have to be the pub,' she said. 'Unless we go into town, there's nothing much here.'

'Let it be the pub.' Giles fell in beside her with his easy stride.

The pub was on the other side of the street and, as usual, it was full of lunch-time drinkers.

They ordered a bar meal, cottage pie and chips, and Giles had a beer while Laura drank tonic water. The woman behind the bar said she would bring their food to them, and after Giles had paid they took their drinks to the far side of the dark saloon, as far away as possible from the jarring sound of the jukebox and the flashing lights of the garish slot machine. For a moment they sat staring at each other.

'Sure you didn't want anything stronger?' Giles asked, indicating her glass.

Laura shook her head and laughed. 'I have to work. Oh, Giles, it is *so* good to see you. You don't know how good.' She paused. 'How did you know where to find me?'

'I called at your home. Your father was there and he told me where you worked. I hope you don't mind?'

'No, I don't mind.' Laura shook her head but as she put her glass to her lips she knew she was blushing. 'I should actually go back and get my father some lunch.'

'I told him I'd be asking you out to lunch. He didn't seem to mind.'

'Seriously, Giles, what are you doing up here?'

'I came to see you,' he said, staring at her. 'Honestly.'

'Didn't you have business at the university?'

'No.'

'Oh!' She did not know what to say and felt hot again.

'I'm terribly sorry about your exams, Laura. Do you know that I haven't seen you since you left Oxford?'

'Yes, I know.'

'And you haven't seen Nick either?'

'No.' She bowed her head. 'I've hurt Nick. I'm aware of it and I'm sorry. He wanted to come up here but I told him not to. He wanted me to go on the yacht but I couldn't consider it. I find it hard to communicate and I don't think he understands, but it's been a very difficult time for me and it was hard for me to explain. I told you before that I think Nick's wealth comes between us. The wealth and the environment in which he lives. Nick is such a nice fellow and he would be horrified to know how I feel, so I can't tell him. I feel our lifestyles, our backgrounds, are so different. Honestly, I didn't even want you to see where I live. Now you have and I don't really care; but I've never seen your home or met your folks, so it doesn't bother me except that I don't feel the same differences with you that separate me from Nick. I can't explain that either.

'My mother left home recently, and I've had to look after the family, take her place. I didn't want to and I didn't mean to, but it was somehow forced on me. They were all so desolate without her, so lost. Then my father had a mild heart attack, and he needs extra special care.'

'Poor Laura.' Giles's hand closed tightly over hers. She

didn't say anything or try to remove her hand. 'Nick feels very cut up about all this.'

She nodded.

'How do you feel?'

'Cut up, too.' She raised her head and looked at him. 'How was the yacht?'

'We didn't go. My father's in a funny sort of mood and said he couldn't leave his work. I don't think things are too good, but I don't know why. Maybe it's money. My younger brother was going to Venice with the school, and my mother wanted to spend the summer at our house in Somerset. My parents are thinking of selling it.'

'Oh! Will you mind?'

Giles shrugged. 'I shan't mind at all. We hardly ever go there and it's falling to pieces. Look, Laura,' his hand tightened on hers, 'I've got a proposition to make to you. Oh . . .' seeing her expression, 'not *that* sort, well not yet, anyway. But I'm going to go abroad. I thought of going to Australia for six months, maybe a year, backpacking you know. I don't terribly want to go on my own and I wondered if you'd like to join me?'

'To Australia?' she gasped.

'Why not?'

'I couldn't possibly afford it. I haven't any money.'

'I've enough for the fare and a bit more, and then we can live cheaply. I've got some money left to me by my grandfather.'

'I couldn't. Nick wants me to live with him in Oxford. I couldn't even accept that. I'm not a concubine.'

Giles smiled at the old-fashioned word.

'I know you're not, and I don't regard you as one. But I guess you're depressed and I would like a companion for the journey. You can, if you like, regard the money as a loan and pay it back in future years as and when you like.'

'I want to go back to Oxford next year.'

'I know you do. No reason why you can't.'

'Did you talk to Nick?'

'Oh, no.' Giles gave a wry smile. 'Not yet. Not until I hear what you say.'

'But my father, my family . . .'

'Look, Laura, this is your life. You don't want to throw it away on them. They can look after themselves. If you went back to Oxford they'd have to.'

'They don't know that I'm not going back to Oxford. I could never pluck up the courage to tell them.'

'Well, then. This sounds just the thing to do. It's an opportunity you may never get again, Laura. Take a chance.'

Laura thought of the grim little terraced house, her father's insistent demands, the selfishness of her brothers. Who really cared anything about her? And the thought of going on like this, keeping house, working at the chemist for the next year, possibly longer, was unendurable. She would have a nervous breakdown, and who would look after *her*?

And if she regarded the money from Giles as a loan, why, it made her so much more independent. It altered the complexion of the whole thing.

She looked at Giles and her heart lifted.

'Seize the hour!' she said.

CHAPTER 11

Valerie opened the door of Edmund's study and stood looking in. He was sitting at his desk, working on some papers.

'Darling,' Valerie said, 'there's an odd bod waiting to see you.'

Edmund turned and looked questioningly at her.

'What sort of "odd bod", dear?'

'Just odd. Hard to explain.' Valerie grimaced. 'I thought at first he was a respectable tramp, you know. Someone down on his luck. I was about to go and find some money to give him and then turn him away when he stated his business.'

She looked darkly at Edmund, and his heart plummeted. All he could think of was a visit from the police. But surely a member of the CID would never look like a tramp, even a respectable one? Or would he? One never could tell with the police, masters of disguise! He became anxious again.

'Can't you say I'm not in?'

'I have a feeling he'll stay here until you are. I mean, he knows you live here.'

'How?'

'He asked for you by name.'

'Well, Valerie, go and ask him what he wants,' Edmund said, impatiently turning back to his work.

Valerie folded her arms and leaned against the door. 'I know what he wants, Ed.'

Fearful again, Edmund looked quickly round.

'What?'

'He's come about the girl Giles has gone to Australia with. He's her father. You better come and see him, Ed. I can't get rid of him. The poor man is obviously very upset.'

'But we don't know her.'

'I told him that, though I'm not sure he believes it.'

'Oh, well.' Impelled by a sense of relief, by acceptance of the inevitable, Edmund pushed back his chair and got to his feet. 'What's his name?'

'Mr Chase. Albert Chase. He was very polite. I think he's a bit frightened.'

'Good.' Edmund walked purposefully to the door. 'Then we'll soon get rid of him.'

When he got to the living room, Albert Chase was standing by the window looking into the garden, his back to the door. He turned as Edmund came into the room, and began nervously to twist his cap between his hands. Edmund could see why Valerie might have mistaken him for a gentleman of the road. As well as a tired, careworn expression on his not unhandsome face, his suit was maybe a size or two too large for him and looked as though it might have been bought from Montague Burton in the fifties and hardly worn since. The collar of his freshly-washed shirt stood out from his scrawny neck.

Edmund had decided that lashings of upper-class charm was what was required to deal with the working classes and advanced towards his clearly nervous and unwelcome guest, hand outstretched.

'How do you do, Mr Chase? I'm Edmund Harvey. Sorry to keep you waiting.'

Albert mumbled something inaudible and returned Edmund's clasp with a limp hand.

'Do sit down, Mr Chase.' Edmund pointed to a chair. 'Can I get you whisky?' he said, going to the drinks table.

'Or would you prefer coffee, or tea perhaps, Mr Chase?'

Valerie said from the background, remembering that tea was the favourite brew of people from up north.

Albert looked mulishly in front of him as though inclined neither to sit nor accept the offer of drinks. But he had come a long way and he was tired.

'A glass of whisky would be very nice thank you, Mr Harvey.' Albert looked behind him and sat down carefully.

'Are you staying long in town?' Edmund gave him his whisky, had one in his own hand and took a seat opposite him while Valerie also helped herself from the drinks table and sat on the sofa, between Albert and her husband.

'I'm going back tonight. There's a train from Euston at around midnight.'

'And how long have you been here?' Edmund raised his hand in the manner of one accustomed to asking questions.

'I arrived at three, sir.'

'Today, and you're going back *today*?'

'I came specifically to see you, Mr Harvey. I have never been to London before and I have no reason to stay here. It also took me some time to find you,' Albert dramatically clutched his chest, 'and I have a bad heart.'

'Oh, dear.' Valerie looked concerned. 'Of course we'll call you a taxi when you go.'

'The bus is quite alright for me thank you, Mrs Harvey. I don't like tube trains, they make me feel nervous, and I can't afford a taxi. I have been unemployed for a long time.'

Edmund wriggled uncomfortably and glanced at his wife.

'Would you like to come to the point, Mr Chase? We should hate you to miss your train as you have such a long way to go.'

Albert, sitting on the edge of his chair, one hand round his glass, the other on his knee, cleared his throat.

'It's about my daughter, Mr Harvey . . .'

'Mr Chase,' Edmund decided that domination must now replace charm and got to his feet, 'I'm afraid we do not know your daughter. Neither my wife nor I have ever met her. We didn't know she existed until we had a letter from Giles which he posted from the airport shortly before he left for Australia. Giles did everything with the greatest secrecy apparently because this girl, your daughter – Laura is her name? – was practically engaged to Nick Constantine who was Giles's best friend. Now why Giles should have behaved in this wholly reprehensible manner I have no idea. I deprecate it, and so does my wife. The Constantines are friends of ours and I understand Nick is extremely upset. But it takes two to make a decision, you know, and Laura must have agreed to go of her own free will. I understand she is twenty, so she is of age. There is absolutely nothing I can do about it except to say that I'm sorry.'

'You must have known about it, Mr Harvey,' Albert insisted. 'You must have helped him, your son, to make off with my daughter.'

'I certainly did not help him . . .' Edmund began, but Albert was not to be stopped.

'Where did he get the money for the tickets? My daughter hadn't a penny. I consider that your son stole my daughter and he should pay for it, or you should.'

'Are you asking me for *money*, Mr Chase?' Edmund thundered, the veins bulging in his neck.

'I mean "pay" in the sense of being responsible for. No, I am not asking for money. But I want my daughter restored to me. I have not been well – I had a heart attack as a matter of fact – and she was looking after me. My wife left me and Laura replaced her. I need her and I want her back. It's all I have now. We still have a bit of pride in the community in which we live and we were proud of Laura. She was the first person in our family to get a place at Oxford and thanks to this Nick Constantine she lost that. Did you know that, Mr Harvey?' Albert stuck a finger out at him.

'Yes, I did. I mean I knew absolutely nothing about Laura

until this happened. Naturally the Constantines, who are friends, were upset on their son's behalf . . .'

'You said you'd never heard her name and yet you are their friend?'

'Well,' Edmund coughed, 'not *all* that friendly. I mean we don't socialise, though we used to. Our sons were at school together.'

'Oh, then you do know this Nick?'

'Oh, yes, we do know him. He's a nice boy.'

'Despite taking advantage of my daughter?'

'Really, Mr Chase. These days . . .' Edmund threw out his arms in a theatrical gesture. 'You don't think in those terms any more: seduction, all that sort of thing you know. It's what young people do. Standards which mattered to you and me when we were young matter no more. I do think however that my son's behaviour is inexcusable and I am very upset on your behalf.'

'Upset on *my* behalf. What a laugh.' Albert gave a wry chuckle. 'Until a year ago my daughter was a good, studious girl, of whom we were very proud. Now she goes down to this fancy university and runs amok. She gets seduced by a man and fails her exams – a fact I only learned from the chemist she worked for shortly after she left. She left without a word to him or a word to me. She did tell her mother, but her mother had no desire to help or assist me. She was aided and abetted by her mother and her sister.'

'But she left of her own accord?'

'Obviously she left of her own accord. She wasn't kidnapped if that's what you mean. But what has happened to my daughter that she goes to the bad in just over a year? Can you tell me that? Is your son going to marry her?'

'I have no idea.' Edmund sank back into his chair again. 'Frankly, as he explained it to us in his letter, she is a travelling companion. She was upset at failing her exams. She apparently didn't want to stay at home. She felt she couldn't tell you she had failed her exams and had to leave Oxford. I'm sure she'll write to you and explain. But as for romance,' Edmund shook his head, 'I don't think there is one. Young people these days do go off you know. It doesn't mean they're in love.'

Edmund looked abruptly at his watch and got to his feet. 'I will write and tell him of your concern when I have an address to which to write. They've gone off into the blue. I'll say we had this most interesting chat and ask him to get Laura to write to you.'

'I want her to come home,' Albert said stubbornly, also rising to his feet, clutching his cloth cap close to his body as though it were a sporran. 'I want Laura to come back.' He advanced a step or two towards Edmund, who began to feel threatened and put up a hand.

'My dear man, there is absolutely nothing I can do to bring your daughter back if she doesn't wish to come back. I have no power at all. Look, as soon as I hear, as soon as I have an address I'll let you know and you can write.'

Suddenly Albert's right hand shot out and he seized a fistful of Edmund's clothing, the sweater he was wearing, part of his shirt. He tried to pull Edmund towards him but lacked the strength. He was not as fit as Edmund, and in the end it was Edmund who was doing the pulling while Albert, clinging on to his clothes as though he was taking part in a tug of war, resisted him all he could.

It was a farcical sight and Valerie, while registering horror, couldn't resist seeing the comical side to the whole affair and had to stifle a giggle.

'Stop, stop,' she cried, holding up a hand. 'This is too dreadful, too absurd,' and she caught at Albert's jacket and tried to pull him away. The harder she tugged, the harder Albert resisted, and the more he pulled at Edmund's pullover until his shirt burst out of his trousers. Albert fell backwards on top of Valerie who tumbled onto the sofa, Albert on top of her, finally letting go of Edmund's shirt.

Edmund was now able to gain control of the situation and, stuffing his shirt back into his trousers and pulling his sweater firmly over his hips, he bounded over to the sofa, dragged Albert away from his wife and pushed him towards the door.

'Get out of here,' he cried. 'Get out and don't *ever* let me see or hear from you again, do you understand? I don't want to *see* you or *hear* from you ever again, and if I do I shall call the police. I'm a lawyer you know, and I could charge you with assault, coming into my house and creating mayhem.'

Still with his hand firmly on Albert's shoulder he led him into the hall and opened the front door, practically throwing him down the steps. Then, without seeing what happened, he shut the door and turned round to see if Valerie was alright.

He found her sitting on the side of the sofa tugging her jersey back into shape, convulsed now in helpless giggles.

'Are you alright?' he asked, sitting down beside her and looking anxiously into her face. 'What's so funny?'

'My dear,' she gasped, pushing her hair back from her face with both hands, 'what a terrible experience. But I can't help seeing the funny side.'

'I don't think it was funny at all.' Edmund didn't try to conceal his irritation. 'It *was* a terrible experience. And it calls for another whisky,' and rising, he poured them two stiff measures and downed his in a gulp.

'I mean, what on earth . . . Is he alright, Ed?' Her hand still on her brow, Valerie looked anxiously at her husband.

'How do you mean, is *he* alright?'

'Well, he said he had a bad heart. I hope he hasn't collapsed in a heap outside our front door.'

With an exclamation Edmund got up, glass still in his hand, went back into the hall and opened the front door. The path to the gate was clear, but the gate swung open. He went along the path looking to right and left, did the same on the pavement, and then shutting the gate after him returned to the house.

'Not a sign of him.'

'Poor man,' she said, shaking her head.

'What on earth do you mean "poor man"?' Edmund poured himself another drink. 'The fellow invades our house and then launches an attack on me.'

'I feel just a bit sorry for him, coming after his daughter. It was rather pathetic. You can hardly call it an invasion. Besides, you're much bigger and stronger than he is, darling.'

'It still doesn't give him the right to assault me in my own house.'

'Oh, basically I agree. I do.' Valerie hauled herself out of the couch, and still stroking back her hair, looked out of the window. 'I still feel vaguely sorry for him, vaguely uncomfortable. Thinking of him finding his way back to the station, no money.' She hitched her trousers up and sighed deeply then, rather shakily, poured herself a fresh drink. 'Still, it's a bad situation and, frankly, I can't help blaming Giles.'

'If I could get my hands on him I'd murder him,' Edmund said, screwing up his fist and looking darkly into his glass.

Andreas Constantine stood in the lobby of the club in St James's and raised his eyes to the high ornate ceiling decorated with intricate plasterwork: quatrefoils, rectangles, lozenges, rosettes, fleurs-de-lis and various heraldic devices of the aristocratic family to whom, many years ago, this town house had belonged. From the ceiling his eyes travelled along the walls, lingering on the portraits of the august members of the family who for centuries had helped govern England. Also hanging were portraits of distinguished former members of the club who had served in many of the outposts of the British Empire, and had in some cases given their lives for it.

Andreas would have liked to belong to a club like this, but he didn't know how to go about it. Unlike Edmund Harvey, who, doubtless, was born to it. He had no connections with the world of gentlemen's clubs, nor did any member of his family. Most of his friends were like him: thrusting entrepreneurs of the second or third generation whose forebears had been born abroad.

Andreas reckoned he despised snobs, yet he was in his own way snobbish. He had sent his children to public school, not only to get a good education but to mingle with the sort of people whose fathers, by right, belonged to clubs like this.

And he had been successful. Nick had made a best friend of Giles Harvey, and Edmund Harvey was the reason why Andreas was here.

The invitation had come, via secretaries, a few days beforehand. Would Andreas dine with him at his club? No reason given. As Lydia had not been invited and, Andreas gathered, nor would Valerie, it must be something to do with men's affairs. Andreas suspected business, unless it was the matter between Giles and that girl, in which case he thought the women would have been invited too.

There were a few men in the lobby presumably, like Andreas, waiting to meet a club member. The members were quite obvious because of the way they sauntered past, perfectly at home in their patch. The guests, on the other hand, looked slightly nervous, more humble, more in awe at being in a famous club in the centre of clubland.

It was ridiculous to feel awed, but Andreas did. He shuffled his feet impatiently and looked at his watch. Harvey was already ten minutes late. Was he trying to tell Andreas something? Demonstrate his superiority? Lydia would have assumed that he was, and would have started to talk about insults and so on. 'Shall we leave?' and that kind of thing.

Andreas didn't quite feel as Lydia did about the Harveys, never had. But men tended not to, especially if they felt, as

Andreas did, that they had their place in the world, had it made in fact. He was an extremely wealthy man with a son at Oxford and a Rolls Royce parked round the corner.

But still there was something missing. He was not quite sure what it was, but he would like to belong to a club like this.

'Ah, there you are!' Both hands extended in greeting, Edmund entered the lobby with confidence, smiled at the porter, affably hailed one or two members he knew: a chap comfortable and at home in his own territory. Both hands clasped Andreas's, who felt rather confused by the warmth of the welcome and wondered what he had done to deserve it.

'I'm so glad you could make it,' Edmund said, leading his guest into the bar. 'Lydia well?'

'Very well, thank you.' Andreas looked keenly at Edmund. 'And Valerie?'

'Yes, very well, thanks. Now what will you have to drink?'

Drinks in hand they stood in the bar chatting, Edmund occasionally exchanging a word with other members, all of whom he introduced to his guest. They kept the conversation general: politics, the weather, the economic situation (grim but improving) and what a pity it was that the Harveys had been unable to join the Constantines on the yacht.

'Did you have a good time?'

'Yes, excellent. The Thompsons wished to be remembered to you.'

'Oh, they were there again?'

'Never miss. I hope you'll come next year?'

'Well . . .' Edmund looked meaningfully at Andreas and then gestured towards the door. 'Shall we dine?'

The dining room was large, elegant, with a view of a walled garden adjoining the backs of houses on the other side of the street. These had probably been turned into clubs, flats or offices at about the same time that the noble family had left the present building for, doubtless, a humbler dwelling. This would mean restricted space, fewer servants or none at all, and therefore easier and less costly to maintain. The new rich now were the Constantines of this world, not that even they could have afforded a place like this, or necessarily wanted one. Their wealth was probably comparable to that of the former inhabitants when they lived here, but these days money had different values and was spent on different things. It was a changed world from the last decade of the nineteenth century, a hundred years ago.

New money had now superseded the old.

'I've ordered us a very nice wine,' Edmund said, bending enthusiastically towards Andreas as the waiter seated them at the table and handed them each a menu. 'I think you'll approve. It's a Haut-Brion 1980, just ready for drinking, isn't it, Mathieu?' He turned to the wine waiter who was hovering respectfully by his elbow clutching a basket which contained a bottle, as though he had just discovered the Holy Grail. He placed it reverentially on the table and handed Edmund the cork. 'I think you will find it perfect, Mr Harvey. One of the finest first growths in our cellars and also,' he hung his head sadly, 'alas, one of the last. Would you like to taste it, Mr Harvey?'

'I can't resist it, Mathieu, but I think we're having a bottle of Montrachet to start?'

''85 Mr Harvey. I've had it on ice for an hour.'

'Just a drop of the claret then.' Edmund leaned forward with the eagerness of a greedy schoolboy and watched the wine waiter as he poured a little of the purple liquid into his glass. Edmund raised the glass towards the light, scrutinised it, held it away again, brought it to his nose and sniffed it, twirled it between his fingers, sniffed it again and, applying it to his lips, gulped down the drop in the glass.

'Wonderful stuff,' he said, looking enthusiastically at his guest. 'Would you like to try it, Andy?'

'I'm no connoisseur.' Andreas diffidently put forward his glass and, as the wine waiter poured an amount that hardly covered the bottom, lifted the glass without any of the elaborate ritual that Edmund had performed and swallowed the lot.

'Very nice,' he said, putting the glass down. 'Excellent.'

'Beats all that Australian muck,' Edmund said with a conspiratorial glance at the waiter. 'Now bring on the Montrachet, Mathieu, and let's try that.'

'Certainly, Mr Harvey.' The man withdrew as Edmund began enthusiastically to study the menu.

Andreas, recalling all the Chardonnay and Shiraz they had drunk on board the yacht in the summer, and served to the Harveys the summer before, wondered if Edmund's remark about Australian wine had been intended as a snub. But, looking at him covertly from behind his own menu, he decided it wasn't. There was no malice in the man, no deliberate intention to offend, or at least he didn't think so. Surely someone as well-bred as Edmund Harvey would have considered such a remark, if made intentionally, bad form?

He good-naturedly fell in with his suggestions for food to accompany the wine – a plate of smoked Scottish salmon followed by fillet of beef – and approved of the Montrachet when that was brought forward for tasting.

'How do you become a member of a place like this?' Andreas asked, looking round. 'Do you have to be proposed?'

The question seemed to surprise Edmund. 'Of course.' Then, 'Why, would you like to join?'

'Well . . .' Andreas self-consciously rearranged the army of knives and forks in front of him. 'Am I eligible?'

'Of course you're eligible. You can pay the membership fee, can't you?'

'I hope so. I suppose so. But everyone seems well . . . top drawer, you know what I mean.'

'My dear Andreas, there is no such thing as *class* these

days. Thank heavens for it too. Don't you agree?'

'Not really. There aren't many people here who would seem to me to have grandfathers who were Greek peasants.'

'But you don't *know*, do you, Andreas? You go by appearances. No, as long as you're proposed and seconded by members in good standing – and accepted by the committee, that goes without saying – and you can pay the entrance fee and the annual sub, you'd be welcome as a member. The next time I'm in I'll have a word with the club secretary.'

'That's very good of you.'

There was a pause while Edmund too started to rearrange his knives and forks. Obviously they were approaching the reason for the meeting.

'How's Nick?' he said looking up.

'Well . . .' Andreas studied the tablecloth, 'I think he's thrown himself into his work.'

'I can't say how sorry . . . it was *nothing* to do with us.'

'We realised that.'

'We didn't even know the girl. We never met her.'

'It's not your fault. Don't think that. Actually, we weren't really sorry, but it was hard on Nick.'

'Didn't like her then?' Edmund looked curious.

'Nothing to like or dislike. Not quite the sort of girl we hoped Nick would choose?'

'Working class?'

'I thought there was no such thing as class any more? You just said . . .'

'You know what I *mean*.' Edmund loftily wafted a hand in the air. 'You see, we had a very unpleasant encounter with the girl's father and we know what sort of man *he* was.'

'With Laura's father?' Andreas looked astonished. 'How did you come to meet him?'

'He came to see us. Just appeared on the doorstep. No "May I" or "By your leave". He said he wanted his daughter back and blamed us for what had happened to her. We were extremely civil to him and gave him a drink – Valerie was actually quite sorry for the man – but in the end he went for me and I had to throw him out.'

'Went . . . you mean he *attacked* you?'

'Pushed me, shoved me, that sort of thing. There was an unholy fracas.'

'Well, I'm terribly sorry . . .'

'My dear Andreas, I'm not telling you this because I in any way blame you. On the contrary. I blame my son and I intend to have it out with him when I see him again as I undoubtedly shall, as sooner or later he is going to run out of money. Giles behaved very badly, to us, to Nick who was his best friend, to the girl, though I suppose she is responsible for her own actions. Is Nick very cut up?'

'Nick doesn't say very much. He was very quiet during the vacation and he didn't tell us that she'd been sent down. Of course when they went away we were still on the yacht. We went to Greece and Turkey this year. He only found out when we got back. He took it very much with a stiff upper lip I must say. Then he went back to Oxford early. Frankly, Edmund, Lydia and I were quite relieved.'

'Is she pretty, is she . . .'

'She is not exactly pretty, but she is what I suppose you'd call striking. Her features are bold, very pronounced. She is very tall, but rather blunt and down to earth. No dress sense at all. Not a "womanly" woman, if you know what I mean. I think, yes, we were a little disappointed in her and are not sorry that she and Nick are no longer together. We certainly think Nick could do better.'

'Giles says they are just good friends, no intention of marrying.'

'Do you hear from him often?'

'No. And we don't write often either. All we want to know is whether or not he's alright and apparently he is. I only hope that when he comes back this friendship can revive.'

Edmund looked at Andreas who didn't reply. The excellent salmon, accompanied by the Montrachet, was finished, and a waiter removed the empty plates replacing them with warm ones on which was served succulent looking portions of best fillet of beef. The sacred Haut-Brion was reverentially poured by the wine waiter, was admired all over again, like a libation to the gods, and the waiters retired to let the two men proceed with their meal.

There were no more references to Nick, Giles and Laura and the conversation reverted to politics, the state of the nation and the global economic situation. Edmund was relieved to discover that he and Andreas were at least united on one thing: they were still Tories to the core.

After dinner they repaired to the lounge where, ensconced in deep armchairs, cigars in their hands and a fine old Cognac and coffee on the table in front of them Edmund, having tested the waters, got down to the real purpose of the meeting.

'Andreas, I'm wondering whether you would be interested in a little business proposition.'

'Oh?' Andreas felt immediately on the alert. 'Of what nature?'

'Well,' Edmund took a few deep puffs, swallowed some more Cognac and proceeded. 'I am, as you know, a solicitor specialising in corporate finance. I have a number of clients with large funds to invest and others in need of capital.'

'And which category do I come into?' Andreas, unaccustomed to a large amount of wine, was feeling slightly drunk.

'Of course I don't suppose you need money, but if you do . . .'

'No, just joking.' Andreas waved a hand dismissively.

'I try and marry the needs of one with the capacity of another. Of course there's some risk, there always is, but on the whole I think I can say I have a list of satisfied clients.'

Andreas, no slouch when it came to matters of business,

even if he had had too much to drink, looked sharply at his companion.

'Is all this perfectly legit?'

'My dear Andreas,' Edmund appeared deeply affronted by the question, 'do you think I could possibly discuss anything with you that wasn't? After all, we have known each other many years and our sons have been best friends. No, the fact is,' he studied the tip of his cigar, 'no, it is simply that I know you to be a man of means and . . . well . . . if you've funds at your disposal . . .'

'I'm *quite* interested,' Andreas said cautiously, 'but I'd be happier if you could give me examples of people, companies you've had dealings with, naming names of course.'

'Ah . . .' Edmund put his head on one side in imitation of a wise old bird. 'You wouldn't like *me* to give people details about *you*, would you?'

'Well, then, examples, but leave out the names . . .'

'Right.' Edmund took a deep breath and, for the next twenty minutes or so, took Andreas through a number of cases involving many companies and substantial sums of money. All the time Andreas watched Edmund carefully. He was an astute man of business and always believed he could tell when someone wasn't straight. He didn't particularly trust lawyers, but it was hard to credit that, in the circumstances, and considering all that was at stake, Harvey would set him up. As he listened, his eyes roved from time to time towards the members, some of them somnolent by now, in their deep comfortable armchairs: the backbone of the nation, pillars of the community. For generations, Harveys had been members of clubs like these, clubs that had their own codes of honour that few would dare offend.

Yes, it would be very nice, very satisfying if one day he, like them, could also consider himself well and truly to have arrived, no longer a third generation Greek immigrant, nouveau riche to boot, but a member of the Establishment, just like the Harveys.

At the end of the recital, which was impressive, he nodded and, after a brief pause, said: 'How much are we talking about?'

Edmund appeared to consider, looked at the ceiling, at the man beside him and, finally, lowering his voice: 'In the first instance? A million?'

Then, glancing at the tip of his cigar, he noted that by now it had gone quite cold.

CHAPTER 12

The garish lights from the amusement arcade opposite combined with the noise from the disco next door, to say nothing of the heat and Giles's restlessness in bed, contrived to give Laura another sleepless night. There had been too many of these since they arrived in Sydney, having abandoned their plans for further travel in Australia due to lack of money. The dingy hotel in the Kings Cross area of Sydney had been their home for almost a month, although it was the last place in the world you could call 'home'. Home it was not.

Laura abandoned her frantic attempts to sleep, banged the pillow into a ball and lay on her back staring at the kaleidoscopic effects of the strobe lights dancing upon the ceiling. She recalled with a pang then, as she so often did these days, lying awake in the morning at home listening to the distant thunder of traffic up the motorway. She also remembered, more vividly and with a terrible feeling of loss and yearning, lying in her bed at Oxford, sometimes with Nick by her side, sometimes not, aware of the peace surrounding her, the great and beautiful silence. Then the nostalgia overwhelmed her and she wept silently into her pillow, so as not to disturb Giles.

She wondered how anyone could sleep in this town where there was no demarcation between night and day. Only sometimes, when dawn appeared on the horizon and the rubbish carts started their early morning clear-up and began a different kind of noise, did there seem a lull and one's eyelids began to close, but not for long. She began work at eleven and had to be on her feet by ten.

It had all been very different when, six months before, they had landed in Sydney, stayed at the Park Hyatt, ate at the Rockpool, attended a concert in the spectacular Opera House on the Harbour and seen all the sights of Sydney and beyond: the Blue Mountains, Ku-ring-gai Chase National Park, Berrima in the Southern Highlands – an almost perfectly preserved Georgian settlement – and Lake Illawarra, south of Wollongong.

Sydney was an enchanting city, or so it seemed on that first visit, and its environs equally varied, beautiful and spectacular.

Still on a high and, more importantly, still in funds, they flew to Darwin in the Northern Territory, hired a car and drove along the Stuart Highway through hundreds of miles of arid scrub and huge termite mounds to Alice Springs and Ayers Rock, known nowadays as Uluru, on the way catching their first sight of kangaroos. It was still the dry season but after that the weather turned and so, in a way, did their fortunes.

Money didn't exactly run out but became scarcer, and they began backpacking in earnest, hitching lifts and staying in cheap lodgings. They went into Western Australia, the original first home of the Aborigines, touching the deserted and the beautiful Kimberley coastline with its scattered tropical islands and sandy beaches, crossing the Bungle Bungle Range of sandstone mountains in a jeep with some more affluent tourists they fell in with. Then, saying goodbye to their friends, hitching more lifts and travelling via the Canning Stock Route, skirting the Gibson Desert and the Great Victoria Nature Reserve, into South Australia, where Giles would have liked to make for the wine areas of the Coonawarra and the Barossa Valley in search of work. But Australia was a huge continent, its distances compared to England immeasurable, and what looked a short distance on the map was proving the opposite. They wanted to get to Sydney before the Australian winter came, and Laura in particular was tired of travelling and longing for home.

So instead of proceeding south towards Adelaide, they hugged the northern extremities of the State; on past Lake Eyre and the Simpson Desert, via the Oodnadatta and Birdsville Tracks, into Queensland where they made straight for Brisbane, the state capital, and stayed at the YHA hostel in the hope of finding work.

That was really when the fun stopped and life began in earnest. Giles did a variety of jobs, none of which paid well, and Laura found work where she could in bars and cafés. They made their way down the Gold Coast with a brief stop and more work at Surfers Paradise, a glitzy, tatty resort, until they reached Sydney just as summer was ending. But this time they stayed not at the Hyatt or the Regent but found a room in a backpacker's lodge in the Kings Cross area whose seedy atmosphere resembled its London name-sake, housing pimps, prostitutes, drug addicts, down-and-outs and the general flotsam and jetsam of social derelicts and misfits.

By this time Giles and Laura were totally out of funds. Giles, who once had a rather glamorised vision of working on a sheep farm or a vineyard, found himself cleaning cars at a taxi firm in nearby Darlinghurst while Laura got a job in a bar/restaurant on Bondi Beach. At least she was away from the clammy heat of the city and within sight of the ocean though Bondi, apart from its famous crescent-shaped sandy beach, had little of the glamour she had expected, being flanked by tacky bars and eating places and third-rate shops catering mainly for tourists.

Giles stirred but did not wake, he lay on his back with one hand flung sideways away from him. His mouth hung open and he had a few days' growth of beard. Laura looked at him with distaste and began to get gingerly out of bed so that she would not wake him.

They had become lovers by accident, and not because they had fallen in love or were ever likely to, at least not from Laura's side. She supposed that with Giles it was lust, the normal male desire to copulate with a woman he found sexually attractive. With her it was because she felt she owed him so much. Their relationship moved from a platonic to a physical level because during their travels they were forced to share a room. The step from sharing a bed to sex was almost inevitable.

They had never had a great rapport as lovers. Laura found Giles clumsy and inexpert, insensitive too after Nick. She thought that Giles might never have heard of the female orgasm because he was strangely indifferent to her feelings. Consequently, for her, it was mainly sex without pleasure and from that grew dislike.

This was a pity because, for a long time, they had a good relationship as companions and friends. They enjoyed travelling, and the sights and sounds of that glorious country to which, she felt, one day she would certainly return. The relationship also began to deteriorate because of over-familiarity, being together all the time, petty squabbles. Giles had never really known poverty. She remembered how he sometimes stayed at the Randolph when he came to Oxford. He basically didn't like travelling rough and staying in flea pits, and it made him disagreeable and morose.

Yes, one day she would like to return to Australia, but not with Giles. Maybe with Nick.

Laura knew it was futile to speculate about that. She had not written to him to explain her rather thoughtless and disgraceful conduct – she had not dared – and she had not heard from him; but she still loved him and the part of her that had broken away from him still cried out, in self-reproach, daily.

Laura threw on some clothes and then went down the corridor to wash and do her teeth in the grotty shower room that served the whole floor. Later she'd have a swim, which was the main way of keeping clean. She crept back to their room, and was about to slide her washing kit and towel through the door when Giles called out: 'Laura!'

'Yes?'

'What the devil are you up to?'

'Going to work, mate,' she said, preparing to close the door.

'What time is it, Laura?' Giles was shaking his head in an attempt to waken himself up.

'It's gone ten.'

'Christ, Laura, why didn't you wake me? I'll get the sack.'

'You didn't ask me to wake you,' she said sulkily, preparing to leave again.

'Don't be such a little shit, Laura. You want me to lose this job?'

Laura leaned against the wall and gazed at him. He'd been out drinking the night before, without her, and he looked a mess. She realised that she really despised Giles. Once she had admired him, looked up to him, found him dashing, unusual, different from Nick. There had been something rather wicked about Giles whereas there was nothing wicked at all about Nick. On the contrary: Nick was good, he was reliable, he was faithful, loving. Was it that she had in a very short time found Nick just a bit dull? Had he seemed dull, or was it really only his money that had come between them? Or was it that she still blamed Nick for being rusticated?

Giles appeared to have dozed off to sleep again and Laura quietly took up the canvas bag in which she kept her things, slid out of the room and flew down the corridor.

As soon as the door closed Giles was immediately wide awake. He jumped out of bed and rushed to the door flinging it open.

'Hi, Laura!' he called, but she'd gone. He was naked, so instead of running along the corridor, and the chance of bumping into someone, he went back into the room and arrived at the window just in time to see her crossing the street and head in the direction of the bus stop. A man on the pavement glanced behind him as she passed and, stopping, stood watching her. She was a tall, striking girl who moved easily and confidently, her bronze curly hair billowing out behind her. The bloke seemed in half a mind whether or not to follow her. Laura created that kind of reaction. Men were always looking at her. He supposed he should feel jealous but he didn't. Frankly if someone had taken her off his hands he wouldn't have minded at all; but until someone did he felt a responsibility for her.

Giles remained at the window until Laura was out of sight. Then he turned and went back to bed. He felt depressed and he felt hung over. He sat on the bed and looked round the dismal room, which had the bare essentials to conform to Government tourist standards. It was a very far cry from the Hyatt where they'd stayed when they'd first arrived. In fact, Giles had never stayed in a place like it until he'd come to Australia.

He lay down on the bed and closed his eyes. His head ached and his mouth was dry. He'd had much too much beer the night before, going from bar to bar with a few cronies from work, hoping that he might hear of better jobs, maybe something in the wineries in the Hunter Valley about a hundred miles from Sydney. All he heard about were other badly-paid jobs locally, and he got propositioned by a couple of gays.

His relationship with Laura had been disastrous. He had been so keen to go away with her, but he thought guilt about Nick prevented him loving her. All the time he was aware of Nick's hurt and how he would face him when he got home. He, Giles, had offended against the sacred trust that bound men of their sort together: the old school tie.

Or maybe the truth was that, although sexy, Laura wasn't his type. Truth to tell he thought he preferred those clean-cut, well-reared young women, like the sisters of his friends who, in their middle age, would eventually resemble his mother.

He had been clumsy with Laura. He knew very little about sex, and hadn't wanted her to know that she was his first woman. She wasn't very expert either, and neither of them knew anything more than the basics about contraception. He was left to fumble about with condoms which he found messy and vaguely disgusting.

Though at times exhilarating, the whole Australian experience had frightened him. He hated not having money, being down on his luck, being with a woman he was not in love with, with whom sex was difficult and unsatisfactory. He longed, now, to go home.

Depressed with his thoughts, Giles decided he would go back to sleep rather than go to work, and that when he woke he would spend the day on the Rocks, the rocky promontory opposite the Opera House where the original convict tents were pitched in 1788. There he and Laura had had some of their best days when they first arrived in Sydney, exploring the place and the old eighteenth-century buildings – the first fort, hospital, bakery – that still remained. There, full of energy, hope and enthusiasm, they had dreamed of the adventures that lay ahead of them. Today he would really make an effort to revive those dreams and in the evening he would take Laura out to dinner and try and devise some more positive plan for the future to make up to her for the pig he knew he'd been.

Laura sat on top of the double-decker bus taking her to Bondi Beach and her destination at Leo's Bar/Restaurant in the Bondi Pavilion. As she had no work permit, the job was poorly paid, but any money was better than none and they were skint. What had once seemed glamorous had become a tedious chore, and she longed to throw it all in and go home. Sometimes on impulse she had thought of telephoning Nick and asking for some money; but right now she couldn't bring herself to do it. To go begging to Nick would be a complete capitulation, and she still had too much pride to admit defeat.

The bus came in sight of the sea and she prepared to descend, jumping off at the stop and making her way swiftly through the crowds drifting down to the beach, to the bar. The Australians really did say 'g'day'. They said it all the time and after saying 'g'day' to her boss she got on with her work, which was to prepare the tables for lunch.

Leo had come as a baby to Australia with his parents. When he was a teenager they had decided to return to Italy. Leo had stayed behind and, in due course, opened the bar which bore his name. It was a clean, well-run establishment with a smarter clientele than some of the other places around. This was reflected in the prices he charged, which were designed to keep away the druggies and the dropouts who were common in the area. When trade was slack Laura sometimes chatted to Leo, who was about thirty-five, married with children, and who lived in the fashionable suburb of Kirribilli, north of the Harbour Bridge. She wondered today if she might take him to one side and explore the possibility of a loan. On the other hand, if she did, he might be eager to replace her once he knew that she wasn't going to stay. Then she'd be without a job altogether.

At about three o'clock Laura was sitting in the kitchen having a cool drink when Leo came to the door and beckoned to her. She finished her fruit squash, jumped up and followed him to his office next to the kitchen, where he invited her to sit down. She was immediately apprehensive and wondered if it was something about her lack of a work permit.

'Laura,' Leo said, taking his seat behind the desk, 'this is very difficult for me to say because I'm very pleased with your work. But I know that you're backpacking and, well, I have an Australian girl interested in this job and . . .'

'But, Leo, I want to stay on.' Laura, suddenly panic-stricken, leaned forward. 'I like it here. We have no intention of leaving yet.'

'Come off it, Laura,' Leo said in a tone that was not quite as friendly as the one she was used to. 'You know you're not going to stay, and with winter approaching, I'm having to reduce staff anyway.' He stood up. 'Sorry, Laura.'

'You don't mean goodbye *now*?' she said, aghast.

'Yes, why don't you take the rest of the day off?' He looked at the clock on the wall. 'I'll pay you off and you can go right now. Spend some time on the beach.'

'Leo, have I done anything wrong?' Laura felt close to tears.

'On the contrary, Laura. You've been first class, and I like you. But I'm always worried in case the authorities check up on me. I have a good place here and I want to stay on the right side of the law.' He handed her an envelope. 'I've put a few extra dollars in the packet, Laura, and I do wish you every luck. Come back and have a drink with us before you go.' He reached out to shake her hand, but she withheld hers.

'I think you've behaved very shabbily, Leo. I've given you all I've got, worked late whenever you wanted me to and now I'm dismissed without notice.'

Leo put his head on one side. 'That's the way of the world, Laura. If you come and work without a permit you're taking a risk, and your employer is taking a risk too. I wish you luck, Laura. Goodbye.' And he turned his back, signifying that the interview was at an end.

Laura picked up her bag and went into the kitchen to say goodbye to the rest of the staff. She had only been there a few weeks and she didn't know them very well, but there had been something about the place and she was sorry to leave. Now that the summer was ending she knew it would be very hard to find a job and a feeling of complete despair suddenly overwhelmed her.

She left the bar and walked towards the beach, not wanting to go back to the hotel. She sat there for a long time letting the sand run through her fingers, watching the bathers in the sea and the surfers riding the waves.

She'd brought her bathing costume and towel with her, thinking that after work she'd have a swim. Now she changed rapidly, and leaving her things in a neat bundle – she had carried no money with her except the bus fare and some loose coins – she coiled her hair above her head and walked towards the waves, flinging herself in, relishing the sensation of the cold clear water on her skin. She was a strong swimmer and she struck out away from the shore, the sound of the surf drowning the warning that was being shouted at her by one of the lifeguards who had started to run in her direction.

Laura felt liberated by the sea and headed firmly towards the horizon. Maybe it would be nice to go on swimming until she was too tired to go back, let herself float on a tide of oblivion? To fade away on a sea of forgetfulness. She swam and swam, riding with the waves and being tossed back by them. Suddenly a huge wave rose towards her, she braced herself to withstand it and, too late, saw the surfer coming over on the crest above her. She dived to avoid it but she didn't stand a chance. The last thing she heard before darkness claimed her was an awful drumming in her head, which felt as though it had split open.

By ten o'clock Giles decided to go to Leo's and find out what had happened to Laura. All his plans for a nice evening had evaporated and he felt intensely irritated and annoyed and, just slightly, worried. He felt that if she was working late, as she sometimes did, the least she could have done was telephone. On the other hand, she'd been annoyed with him in the morning; he'd been rude to her and this maybe was her way of paying him back.

When Giles got to the bar it was full of people, sitting outside as well as in. It was a balmy evening with a warm breeze and the gentle sound of the surf breaking on the shore. Giles stood around for some time looking for Laura but there was no sign of her. The barman polishing glasses behind the bar knew him and kept looking in his direction. Finally Giles went up to him and said: 'Is Laura around?'

The barman shook his head and then from around the corner of the bar Leo appeared. He seemed surprised to see Giles.

'Hi, Giles!' he said, looking slightly nervous.

'Hi!'

'Something wrong?' Leo spoke again.

'I'm looking for Laura.'

'Laura's not here.'

'She hasn't come home.'

Leo shrugged in an offhand way and was about to turn his back when Giles said: 'What time did she leave?'

'About three.'

'*Three*!' Giles gasped. 'Three o'clock this afternoon?'

'That's what I said.' Leo looked around and beckoned to Giles. 'Say, Giles, come into my office for a moment,' and Leo lifted the bar and pointed towards the door, standing to one side as Giles preceded him. Leo didn't ask him to come in but spoke standing up, just outside the door.

'Giles, I gave Laura notice to quit this afternoon. Nothing wrong with her, she's very good, but I need permanent staff. I know you're going back to England.'

'Well, not right away . . .'

'I know, but eventually. Also, I get nervous employing people without a permit.'

'Was Laura upset?'

Leo looked at the floor. 'Well, she wasn't exactly pleased. I gave her some extra cash and off she went.'

'You've no idea where she went?'

'Well, no. I guess she's at home by now and when you get back you'll find her there. No hard feelings, Giles? I mean Laura is a great girl . . .'

One of the waiters en route from the kitchen with a tray balanced on one hand stopped to get past and glanced at Giles.

'Did I hear someone say that Laura was not at home?'

'Yes. Were you on this afternoon?'

The waiter shook his head. 'But I did hear there was an accident on the beach. Maybe you should . . .'

Laura looked very peaceful, a little smile on her face as though in her dreams she had found some happiness. If he hadn't been told differently, Giles would have thought she was dead.

'Is she still unconscious?' he whispered to the young doctor standing next to him, who shook his head.

'She's sleeping, heavily sedated. She had a nasty bump.' He pointed to her skull which was swathed in bandages. 'She was very lucky not to have been killed or severely brain-damaged.'

'How did it happen?'

'There was some surfing championship and the area where she was swimming was out of bounds. She either failed to see or observe the warnings and the lifeguard was too late to save her. She was knocked unconscious by the surfboard, but luckily the guard who had seen her, and tried to warn her, pulled her from the water and resuscitated her. She is very lucky to be alive.'

'And she's OK?' Giles looked at him anxiously.

'As far as we can tell. We did a brain scan and there is no

apparent damage. We'll keep her in here for a few days just to be sure. She'll probably feel very woozy anyway with that wound.' The doctor paused and looked closely at Giles. 'I don't suppose it could have been deliberate?'

'Deliberate?' Giles didn't appear to understand.

'You know, tried to do herself in. It seemed such a very dangerous thing to do, unless she was desperate about something. If you think it might be so, I'll have the psychiatrist come along and have a chat with her.'

'Oh, no.' Giles shook his head vigorously. 'I don't think she'd try anything like that. She's not that sort.'

'Oh, good.' The young man seemed reassured. 'Just thought I'd check.' He shook his head. 'It really was a stupid thing to do.'

Giles sat by Laura's side throughout the night, and wondered. *Was* it possible that she had indeed intended to kill herself? Everyone knew the beaches were dangerous, and when there were surfing championships they kept well away. Laura knew that as well as anybody. Yet she'd just had the sack. She'd had a row with him. They'd both been low for ages. He began to feel terribly responsible for what had happened to her.

Once in the small hours she looked as though she was about to wake. Her eyelids flickered but didn't open. Regularly throughout the night the nurses monitored her blood pressure and temperature, and in the morning another doctor came to supervise a change of dressing and inspect her wound.

Giles nearly fainted himself when he saw the gash on her temple, and how her head had been shaved when they stitched the wound, which was about four inches long.

Laura opened her eyes when they were changing the dressing and for a long time she gazed at Giles. He looked at her sadly, wanting to reach out and hold her hand.

'Hi!' she said eventually.

'Hi!' He gave a sheepish grin. 'Glad you're alright.'

'God, my head.' Laura lifted a hand gingerly to feel the wound but the nurse gently stopped her. 'Does it hurt, dearie?' she enquired and, when Laura nodded, 'we'll give you something to make you go to sleep again.'

'How did it happen, Laura?' When the dressing was finished Giles bent forward so that only she could hear.

'I can't remember a thing . . .' Laura's limpid eyes suddenly filled with tears and she stretched out a hand towards him. 'Let's go home, Giles. *Please* let's go home.'

Back at the hotel Giles shaved, had a shower, changed his clothes and went out to a bar down the road where he had coffee and a sandwich. It was nearly noon but at home it would be two in the morning. The earliest he could ring would be five o'clock New South Wales time. Giles tried to compose himself but it was very difficult. He felt in a turmoil. It was going to be hard enough to admit defeat and failure, and that they'd had a bad time. But worst of all he felt that he hadn't taken sufficient care of Laura and that her accident was really his fault.

If it *was* an accident. He couldn't rule out the possibility that, as the hospital doctor had suggested, what Laura had done might have been deliberate. The sacking, on top of everything else that had gone wrong, might have been the last straw.

Giles finished his food, paid for it, and then set off in the direction of the hospital on Macquarie Street, but when he came to the Victorian sandstone building he walked past it and continued towards the harbour in the direction of the Rocks. Reaching Sydney Cove he found a bar and had a beer, sitting for a long time looking towards the Opera House and the bridge and watching the busy ferries as they plied industriously to and from the wharves.

He thought Sydney was a place he would like to return to. Maybe one could start a new life here, begin again. Or would it have too many unhappy memories of fear and failure?

Maybe one day, armed with a work permit, he would make it to the wineries of the Barossa or Hunter Valleys. As it struck five, Giles finished his beer and went to the telephone at the back of the bar. He had plenty of change and he put the coins in the telephone, dialled several numbers and listened to the telephone ringing thousands of miles away. He realised his heart was thumping and he prayed that his mother would answer rather than his father.

But then the ringing stopped and that familiar, well-modulated voice said: 'Hello?'

'Mum, is that you?'

'Giles, darling, where are you?' Valerie sounded pleased but, as always, controlled.

'I'm still in Sydney, Mum. Did you get my cards?'

'A letter *would* have been nice.' The voice now sounded rather reproachful. 'Giles, why . . .'

'Mum, I can't talk. I'm at a call box. Look, Mum, Laura's had a terrible accident. She's OK, but as soon as we can we'll be on our way home.'

PART IV

The Silver Spoon: Emma

CHAPTER 13

Giles stood for some time looking round the room trying to acclimatise himself to the gloom and the noise. He did not really know why he'd come; driven, he supposed, by boredom. He'd found his old membership card in a drawer in his bedroom and decided to use it to get in, though he hadn't visited the place for at least a couple of years.

He'd explained at the door that he'd been in Australia and they gave him an updated membership card on payment of the required fee. He thought the last time he'd been here had been with a group of friends during the Christmas break while he was still at university.

Having accustomed himself to his environment, Giles strolled across to the bar and ordered a beer. Then, glass in hand, he went over to a corner where he found himself a table and sat down, surveying the scene. Couples gyrated in time to the beat of the music, some dancing closely, some doing their own thing, touching occasionally, joining hands briefly from time to time. As well as mixed couples, men were dancing with men and women with women. Anything went. In some ways it reminded him of Australia, though really the scene could be universal.

Giles sat sipping his beer and gradually the figures on the floor became more discernible. He could pick out faces, although it was not always easy to distinguish men from women. He was quite enjoying the atmosphere, the fact that he could be here on his own and no one took any notice of him or bothered him. It might have been nicer to have brought a few mates or a girl, but it didn't matter. Giles finished his beer, rose to get another and, bumping into a couple who had come careering across the floor towards him, politely stood to one side and said: 'I'm sorry.' Though, in fact, it wasn't his fault. The couple seemed to have difficulty regaining their balance and Giles reached out to help pull the woman to her feet, realising they were both probably very drunk, or stoned, or both. He took hold of both the woman's hands and gently pulled her up, and as he did the strobe pinpointed them and he could see her face quite clearly, head back, eyes closed, mouth a little open.

'Emma!' he cried. But the woman didn't register and Giles, looking down, saw that her partner had passed out on the floor at his feet. It seemed to him that Emma was semi-conscious and he tried to sit her down in the chair he'd been occupying, but as soon as he did she slipped sideways.

As no one else was taking any notice of his predicament, and he supposed it was one that was not uncommon in a joint like this, he hauled Emma to her feet and, half lifting, half dragging her, got her to a side door on which were the bold letters EMERGENCY EXIT. He pushed the bar and almost collapsed outside, where he propped Emma against the wall while he recovered, breathing heavily. Now what to do? Maybe he should have left her where she was. There was surely some kind of provision for people who collapsed in a club where drink and drugs were freely available. Maybe he should take her back and leave her inside the door? But he knew he couldn't. If anything were to happen to Emma he would never be able to forgive himself.

Giles was now in a quandary. Having gone to a Soho club for a few beers and a bit of relaxation, he now found himself in an unexpected predicament, due purely to an act of kindness. He was saddled with the sister of his former best friend who was drunk and helpless in a dark narrow alley off

Gerrard Street. It was nearly midnight, it was January and bitterly cold and Giles did the only thing he could do. Leaving Emma, who had started to slide down the wall where she stood, he went out into Gerrard Street to look for a taxi. He soon found one and, giving the driver instructions and asking him to wait, he went back to get Emma, who seemed to be reviving, maybe due to the cold air, and actually walked the last few steps to the cab.

The driver looked dubiously at Giles and his charge.

'I hope she's not going to be sick in my cab, guv.'

'I hope so too,' Giles said grimly, and slipped the driver a ten-pound note through the window. 'There'll be another one when we get to Lamb's Conduit Street.'

The driver pocketed the note and, without a word, set his cab in a westerly direction.

Emma Constantine woke in a strange place in a strange bed. She guessed from the faint aura round the curtained window that it might be dawn, or maybe a bit later. She had no idea where she was or how she'd got here. She had no clothes on except for her pants; she hadn't worn a bra but she could see in the gloom that her clothes were draped neatly over a chair next to the bed. She reached out an arm, fumbled about a bit, found a light and put it on. It was rather a nice room, well and tastefully furnished, definitely masculine with ties round the mirror of the dressing table and a suit hanging on the outside of the wardrobe.

She felt, as usual, dreadful, with a raging thirst and a terrible head. She wondered where on earth Philip had got to and who this place belonged to.

She staggered out of bed, sat on the side for a moment to overcome a feeling of nausea, and then made for a door opposite, which was ajar. She groped for a switch, found one and, as she'd hoped, lit up the bathroom. She was immediately sick down the lavatory and remained on her knees for several minutes gazing into the bowl. Then she staggered to her feet, swayed, caught hold of the towel rail and, balancing herself carefully, got to the washbasin, sluiced her face in cold water and took a long long drink.

She grabbed a towel, wiped her face and, feeling marginally better, went back into the bedroom and climbed thankfully into bed, drawing the duvet right up to her chin. The door immediately in front of her opened slowly and a face peered round. She looked at it with curiosity, without fear but also without recognition. The door opened wider and a man dressed in a bathrobe came into the room carrying something and stood looking down at her.

Emma couldn't believe what or, rather, who, she saw and felt she should pinch herself to see if he was real.

'Giles?' she said tremulously, almost in a tone of enquiry.

'Giles it is,' he said smiling. 'Would you like a cup of tea?' And he held out his hand and placed a cup and saucer on the table by her bed.

'But how, where?' Emma looked round shaking her head. 'I have no idea how I got here.'

Giles sat on the side of her bed.

'I guess you remember the club?'

'Oh, I remember we were at the club. But where's Philip?'

'Well, I left the bloke you were with on the floor, I'm afraid. I could only cope with one.'

'Oh!' Emma looked crestfallen. 'It was that bad, eh?'

'It was bad. I had to bribe the taxi driver to bring you home.'

'And this is *home*? Gosh your mum and dad . . .' Emma looked at him aghast.

'This is *my* home, not theirs. I rented a flat near the law courts and the school where I'm studying law.'

'Ah!' she nodded. 'It's nice.'

'I like it.' Giles rose. 'Hang on and I'll fetch myself some tea.' He stopped and looked at her. 'If you don't mind?'

'Of course I don't mind. Golly, I just don't quite know where I'd be without you.'

Giles went over to the wardrobe and, taking a light dressing gown from it, tossed it to her. 'You might like this to keep you decent.'

'Thanks.' She grinned rather shamefacedly, and after he'd left the room shrugged it on. When he returned she had snuggled back against the pillows, teacup in hand. This time he didn't sit on the bed but in the chair, on the back of which were her clothes.

'I don't suppose you've got any Paracetamol?' she said.

'That bad, eh?' He got up.

'Terrible.'

Giles went into the bathroom and came back with a glass in which two tablets were fizzing.

'You'd make someone a lovely wife,' Emma said, taking the glass from him. 'Tea in bed, headache remedies . . .' She drank the liquid, put the glass by the bed and snuggled down again. 'What were *you* doing at Mephistos?'

'Well, I was there by myself, believe it or not. I'd had a hard day. I remembered I used to belong to it and renewed my membership. I'd just been there about half an hour and was about to get another beer when you came literally crashing back into my life.'

'Oh, gosh!' Emma put a hand to her mouth, half amused, half contrite.

'It was the most extraordinary coincidence.'

'I'll say.'

'Emma,' Giles wriggled in his seat, 'if I hadn't been there . . .'

'They've got a room where you can chill off. It's called "The Cooler". They'd have thrown us in there until one of us was fit to make the journey.'

From what she was saying, Giles gathered that this wasn't the first time Emma had found herself in such a situation.

He also thought that, in the circumstances, she didn't seem to mind very much. If this was regular behaviour he wondered what her parents thought about it.

He could see Emma was staring at him as if she could read his mind. 'You're wondering how often?'

'Kind of,' he nodded.

'Quite often. And now you're wondering what my parents say?'

Again Giles nodded.

'I think they're worried, but they put it down to youthful high spirits. Usually I go home anyway, or back to Phil's. Last night was an exception. We both went over the top. Phil had lost his job and most of his trouble was drink. He doesn't usually pass out.'

'Is Phil,' Giles paused, 'the boyfriend?'

Emma screwed up her nose. 'He's *a* friend. A good friend. He is a very good friend as a matter of fact.'

'Won't he be worried?'

'He may be. I'll phone him later. He was told to clear his desk and leave, just like that, so he won't be at work. Maybe we'll meet for lunch if I can get myself out of bed.' She groaned and lay back on the pillows again.

'And your mother?'

'I'll call her. I've got a very good friend, Sue, and I always say I'm with Sue.' She looked at him defensively. 'This doesn't happen *a lot*, Giles. It happens *sometimes*. I'm a big girl now. I'm twenty-one.'

'Emma, what do you do with yourself?' Giles asked, putting down his cup.

'How do you mean? *Do* with myself?'

'Do you work? Do you have a job?'

Emma shook her head. 'Uh, uh.'

'Don't you want a job, don't you want to do anything? Go to college maybe?'

'Giles, you know I'm not academic.' Emma began to look

restlessly about. 'And please don't give me the third degree. After all, from what I hear you haven't done so brilliantly yourself, messed up poor Nick's love life, to say nothing of what happened to Laura. She nearly died I understand.'

Giles rose and, going over to the dressing table, began to sort through one of the drawers. Finally he took out a pair of socks and what were obviously clean underpants.

'That's a part of my life over which I'd prefer to draw a veil,' he said. 'It's not something I'm proud of especially.'

'I should think it isn't. Well, then that's what I feel too. I am not particularly proud of this lifestyle either. But for the moment and until something better turns up it's how I live.'

'Sorry.' Giles turned to gaze down at her and thought how vulnerable she looked. Tired, drawn, older than her years. She stared back at him rather defensively as though daring him to say more. 'I did screw things up,' he said. 'And you're right. Laura nearly lost her life. But that was nothing to do with me. It was an accident that could have happened to anyone.'

'If it *was* an accident.' Emma looked at him oddly. 'Nick said . . .'

'Nick knew absolutely nothing about what happened. He has not talked to me about it because we haven't seen each other, and I don't think he's seen Laura either.'

'No, he hasn't.'

'So how does he know?'

'I guess he's hurt. He loved her very much.'

'I know.' Giles turned away. 'And now two friendships are smashed up. His and mine, his and Laura's, and throw in a third and you can say Laura and mine too. I did her no favours, and it's an episode of my life I very much regret. But now I'm trying to make up for it. I'm taking the law seriously. I'm working hard and maybe one day I can make things up with Laura and Nick too. My parents have been brilliant. After an initial rocket from my dad there were no more recriminations. They're paying for my course, they give me an allowance, and they didn't even mind when I left home.'

Emma, sitting up in bed, her arms round her knees, rested her chin against them.

'Parents are great,' she said. 'Mine are great too. Say, Giles, thanks for the rescue. Maybe we can see each other again?'

'I'll give you a call,' Giles said, looking at his watch. 'Meanwhile I have to run. My first class is at nine.' And he went into the bathroom, shutting the door behind him, while Emma lay back listening to the swishing sounds made by the shower.

After Giles had gone, Emma got unsteadily out of bed and, with a hand that was beginning to tremble, hurried over to her bag which she opened. She only hoped that Giles hadn't inspected the contents, but being a gentleman she didn't think he had. Snooping into people's bags wasn't the sort of thing that a gentleman would do.

She took from it a hypodermic syringe, a small silver teaspoon and a tiny packet of fine white powder, which she spread out on the table by the side of the bed. This she mixed on a teaspoon with a little water from a glass by her bed and carefully fed into the syringe. With the aid of a silk scarf that she'd worn the night before, she assembled a tourniquet round her arm and spent some time selecting a vein into which she then plunged the syringe, leaning forward tensely for a moment while she waited for the blessed feeling of relief and elation slowly to surge through her, and the trembling to cease. She packed away her kit and lay down on the bed letting her mind drift pleasantly towards oblivion, wondering what dear old Giles would say if he knew.

During that day and the ones that followed, Giles found himself preoccupied with thoughts of Emma. He knew he had always rather liked her, in a way fancied her. Maybe, because she was Nick's twin, there was something incestuous about his feelings for her. She and Nick hardly resembled each other, but there was something about them that indicated their closeness.

Of course, too, in a way Emma had always been a mate. He had known her since she was thirteen when he and Nick had established a rapport on their first day at school. There was a cosy, casual informality about his relationship with her, but that morning he had been particularly aware that they were alone together in a bedroom, and that when he had put her to bed the night before he had removed most of her clothes.

Was that the first time he had been conscious of an erotic sensation about Emma? He wasn't sure. He thought maybe not. During the holiday on the yacht, he had been very aware of her as a woman rather than a chum, had been interested when she sunbathed topless on the boat as it ploughed through the warm Mediterranean waters.

In a way she would have been a better companion for his Australian trip than Laura; but at that time it was Laura who obsessed him, not Emma. Now, Laura no longer interested him at all. And Emma was beginning to.

It was a chastened and much wiser Giles who had returned nine months before from Australia, as soon as Laura had recovered. They had parted immediately on their return despite the invitation to Laura by his mother, who met them at the airport, to spend a few days in London. Since then they had hardly communicated, though he rang her every now and then to see how she was. She reported no ill effects from the accident and that she was now back working in the chemist's shop, looking after her father and studying hard for her exams to return to Oxford.

It was as though Australia had never been, but it had. It was an experience Giles couldn't get out of his mind. There, for the first time, he had been at his worst and most vulnerable. There was a lot about Giles Harvey he had discovered he didn't like. Nick didn't like him either. There was no forgiveness there, no willingness to re-establish their old and long friendship, no invitation to the yacht the previous summer.

And now Emma and the Constantines had come back into his life again in the most unexpected of ways.

Giles waited a week or two before he telephoned Emma. He was rather nervous about ringing the house, but to his relief the phone was answered by Maria, the domestic who was still with the family, and Emma was in. They saw each other that night. They went to a film in Swiss Cottage and then to Lemonia, the fabulous Greek-Cypriot restaurant in Regent's Park Road. It had been a good evening and there were many others like it. They slipped into the easy-going camaraderie of their adolescence and enjoyed each other's company.

Then one night there was sex, back in Giles's flat. It was impetuous, passionate and very good. There was a harmony between their bodies he had never known with Laura. He couldn't believe it, nor could Emma. Neither could believe that at last they had found someone with whom they could be happy.

Yet there was something about Emma that worried Giles. She was so moody, at times distant, at times loving, at times she was offhand and rude. He didn't quite know what to make of her.

Another complication was that the affair was a secret both from Emma's parents and Giles's. Giles was still considered to have betrayed his best friend, to have behaved shamefully and, well, the Harveys would not have been delighted by the news either. This added spice to the relationship, a touch of the Romeo and Juliet scenario enacted in the unlikely setting of London of the nineteen-nineties.

One day, when the relationship was about four months'

old, Giles returned to the flat to pick up a file for one of his lectures that he had forgotten. As usual, he had left Emma in bed in the morning and they did not expect to meet again until that evening.

It was about eleven, and at first the silence was so profound that he thought Emma must have left. But when he pushed open the bedroom door he heard sounds from the bathroom, Emma singing, and he smiled to himself, relieved that all was well because the night before she had been in one of her moods, as though she had formed a barrier between them he had been unable to penetrate. At times like this he began to despair, and to wonder if they would ever be able to form the strong and enduring relationship that he was hoping for. Because, finally, he realised that he was in love. That Emma, mysterious Emma, was the one for him. Giles was about to go back into the living room to collect his file, and leave Emma to her ablutions, when a metallic gleam by the side of the bed caught his attention. It was a dark room and the bedside lamp was usually left on, and it was this light that illuminated an elongated object lying by its side.

Giles went over and, as he stooped to examine it, he was aware of a faint smell in the air; as he sat down heavily on the bed, he knew.

He thought perhaps he had always suspected, ever since they met, and that her preferring to make love in the dark was so that he would not see the tell-tale pinpricks on her arms. It also did much to explain her moods.

Giles sank his head in his hands just as Emma, wrapped in a towel, came out of the bathroom, her hair wet, still singing, and then stopped when she saw him. She put her hand to her mouth and gazed at him.

'Golly!' she said, and came and sat down beside him, putting an arm round his waist as if trying to comfort him. She leaned her head on his shoulder and for some time they sat like that in silence.

'Why did you come back?' she said at last. 'Did you guess?'

'I wanted a file for a lecture I have at twelve.'

'In that case you'd better go,' she said, glancing at the clock, 'or you'll be late.'

'I can't go now.'

'Didn't you guess? I was sure you knew and didn't say. I can give it up, you know, any time.'

'Then give it up.'

'I don't want to. I like the highs. I need them to stop me feeling so bloody miserable. That's why the sex is so good. That's why when I'm on a high everything is so good.'

'I thought you were only E-ing.' Occasionally they bought Ecstasy tablets at the club, or smoked a joint together. 'When did you start with heroin?'

'Well, Philip was into heroin, that's why he could never hold down a job. I just tried it for a lark. We smoked it to begin with, then we started to jag.' She looked at the syringe beside the bed. 'You get more of a high with the needle.'

Giles turned and seized her roughly by the arm. 'Then give it up for Christ's sake. Give it up *now*. Don't you realise, Emma, what it will do to you? Give it up and I'll help you. I love you. Oh, Emma, I love you so much, I need you so much, and the last thing in the world I want you to be is a junkie. Give it up for my sake, *please*.'

And he held her tightly in his arms and wept, because of all the pain of finding someone he realised he loved so much so deeply flawed.

Mary said: 'I thought you'd be so happy, Ed, that Adam passed the Common Entrance.'

'I am happy,' Edmund said woodenly.

'You don't sound happy.'

'Well, I am.'

'Trevor, the Head, said he's got a great future.'

'You call him Trevor now?'

Mary tried to hide the fact that she was blushing by taking a step back and walking behind him as they circled the pond in Regent's Park while Adam had a piano lesson in Camden Town. It was a chilly summer's day, below average temperature, with a steady drizzle, and they looked a miserable pair; a pair completely out of sorts and out of love with each other.

'Well, of course Trevor has been of enormous help to Adam. But for him he would never have passed Common Entrance and got into a good school. We owe Trevor a very great debt indeed.'

Edmund stopped and looked behind at her, waiting for her to catch up with him.

'Mary, about the school . . .'

'What about the school, Ed?' she said sharply, always on the defensive, alert for some underhand trick of Edmund's, something devious at the back of his crafty mind.

'Does it operate the Assisted Places scheme?'

'How do you mean does it operate the Assisted Places scheme?' She reddened again, but this time from anger rather than coyness. 'You're not suggesting that we should *demean* ourselves by applying for government help with all the disadvantages that would have for Adam?'

'I don't see why not. It's a perfectly respectable thing.'

'Is Paul on an Assisted Places scheme? Is Alice?'

'You know they're not.'

'Well, then.'

'Mary . . .' Edmund paused and breathed deeply several times. 'You know that, for my children, my income is assessed. For Adam, *your* income is assessed and I should have thought you were qualified to receive support which as far as I'm concerned,' he held up a hand as she tried to intervene. 'No, let me speak, let me finish what I have to say. Don't be so impetuous, Mary. As far as *I* am concerned, such help would be very welcome. I have the entire burden to bear of Adam's fees which I understand will amount to some nine thousand a year, and that's just for starters. In addition, I am supporting all my children, including Giles, and frankly the strain is wearing me down.' Edmund got out a handkerchief and mopped his brow. 'Sometimes I don't know how I can go on and that's a fact. The worry, the strain, is enormous. There is no shame in Assisted Places, no disgrace, none whatsoever.'

'I would feel ashamed,' Mary said, flopping suddenly on a dry patch of grass by the side of the lake. 'I would feel deeply humiliated. Just because poor Adam has not the advantages of your other children . . .'

'Mary,' Edmund flopped down beside her, 'how often have I heard this in the last few years? It's like a never-ending litany of whining and complaining. I have done all I can for Adam and for you. You know that. I think in the circumstances I have been a good father. I have done my best. But recently things have been very difficult financially and, frankly, you don't seem to care. You've become very hard, Mary, and since we're no longer lovers I feel I don't understand you.'

'Maybe you'd rather not see me again?' Mary said.

'I didn't say that. I want to see you and I want to see Adam, but I also want you to apply for the Assisted Places scheme because, if you don't, I don't think I can afford the fees for the school, the very expensive school you have chosen for Adam.'

Edmund was about to rise, but Mary made a grab for his coat and pulled him towards her. He felt so angry he almost struck out and hit her, but the curious gazes of the passers-by stopped him. They were almost eyeball to eyeball, Mary still clinging fiercely onto the lapels of his jacket.

'Listen, Ed,' she said in a tone of voice he had never heard before, 'you pay that money, and you be sure you pay it and on time. I have fooled around with you for too many years solely because of my son. The only good thing that came out of my relationship with you *has* been my son. I am not going to have him, already disadvantaged, going around a pauper, dependent on the state. I have often threatened to disclose Adam's existence to Valerie and, believe me, if I hear any more nonsense about Assisted Places, this time I bloody well shall!'

Edmund wondered just how much a man could take as he drove shakily home, leaving Mary to pick up Adam on her own. One part of him thought that maybe to unburden himself to Valerie would be the best thing. Tell her the truth, all of it. But the other part knew that he couldn't risk it. If he told Valerie that he had been deceiving her for so many years, that he had a son she knew nothing about and, not only that, but he was in deep financial trouble because he was also cheating on his clients and could possibly go to prison . . . Well, it was a bit much to suppose, certainly to hope that she would take it all on the chin. He knew he couldn't do it. The only chance he had now was to try and prolong the bluster. After all, it had gone on for a long time already, and there was always the possibility that one day everything he had gambled on would come good, that the tide would turn in his favour.

At last he was free of Mary. Their relationship had ended some time ago now. It had simply petered out. He nearly always saw her together with Adam. He was quite sure she was involved with someone else, maybe the Headmaster, and he didn't care. Sometimes he entertained a fantasy that one day he would simply pack up his gear and disappear and leave the rest of the world to get on with things without him.

Valerie wasn't at home when he got in. She was on one of her 'do good' missions among the hapless poor of East London, or some disadvantaged community or other north of the city, and had left him a cold meal in the fridge. Alice was with one of her friends, and Valerie said in her note that she would pick her up on the way home.

Edmund had a few whiskies, watched the news and then had his meal in the kitchen with half a bottle of wine.

Afterwards he climbed a little unsteadily to his study and, unlocking the drawer of his desk, got out the notebook in which he kept details of all his secret transactions. Finally he poured a fresh whisky from the bottle he kept in his study and put the telephone receiver to his ear, punched in a number and listened. He realised he was sweating heavily and the handset was sticky in the palm of his hand.

'Hello?' a voice said at the other end just as Edmund was about to put the phone down.'

'Andy?' Edmund boomed with false joviality. 'Is that you?'

'Yes.' The tone of voice was chilly. 'I was about to ring you, Edmund.'

'Oh, were you? Good. Well I have good news for you.'

'Oh!' The voice at the other end became more amiable. 'Were you? That's great.'

'I have found a seconder, at last, who is willing, despite the fact that he doesn't know you – he goes on my recommendation of course – and your adoption as a member will go up at the next selection meeting of the club.'

'It's taken a long time, Edmund.'

'It has and I'm sorry. But these things do.'

'But what I was going to telephone you about,' Andy's tone of voice was more assured, 'well, that little financial matter between us.'

'Yes?'

'How's it going?'

'It's going fine. Nothing to worry about . . .'

'I'm not exactly worried . . .'

'These things take time . . .'

'I know they do. But . . .'

'Another half a million would speed things up . . .'

'A *what*?'

'Half a million. My client is on the brink of great things. Look, maybe I can come round and show you the preliminary results?'

'That would be *very* good of you.' Andreas didn't attempt to hide his sarcasm. 'After all, I have expended a lot of money on vague promises. Some people might doubt my business acumen. I am regarded, I know, as a pretty tough customer to deal with, but you seem to have taken me for a patsy.'

'I say.' On the other end of the line, Edmund was visibly sweating. 'I do object to that.'

Andreas's tone grew more heated. 'I've trusted you because we have known each other a very long time. Our boys were at school together. Maybe I've let myself be taken in. A million quid is a lot of money, and now you're telling me you want more . . .'

'Look,' Edmund made a great effort to keep his tone soothing, moderate. 'This can easily be sorted out over lunch. At the club? I'll explain everything in detail then. Would Wednesday suit you. Say one o'clock?'

After agreeing, Andreas put down the phone and remained where he was for a few seconds, his head bent in thought. He had a profound feeling that his wish for social acceptance had overcome his sound business instincts. Yet, this was different from the usual cut and thrust of the marketplace he was used to. It was difficult to know just how to deal with a man, a respected solicitor of many years standing, who was about to propose you for a pukka London club. The last thing you wanted to do was insult him.

'Who was that, dear?' Lydia, passing in the hallway with a huge vase of freshly arranged flowers, paused and looked at her husband.

'Edmund.'

'Edmund Harvey?' She seemed surprised.

'Yes.'

'Haven't heard from them for ages, thank God. What on earth did he want?'

Lydia's love affair with the Harveys and her desire to emulate them and be approved of by them was long since over, and her tone was censorious.

'He wants money,' Andreas said with a sigh, following her into the drawing room.

'Money!' She swung round, nearly dropping the vase.

'It's a business matter. I should have told you about it but I didn't. It was after that trouble with Nick and I knew you'd be unhappy about it. Some time ago I let him have quite a considerable sum for investment. His projects sounded promising. I have yet to see a penny back and he wants more.'

'How much more, dear?' Lydia put down the vase and, sitting on the sofa, helped herself to a cigarette from an onyx box. Andreas leaned over and lit it for her with a matching lighter in the form of a dragon, the flame leaping from its mouth.

'Half a million. I let him have a million in the first place.'

'You must be joking!'

'I'm not. He took me to his club and set up the deal. It all seemed OK. I trusted him – after all, he *is* a Harvey – and I'm still not sure that it isn't all kosher. He wants to have lunch with me. I shan't give him a penny until I know more.'

Lydia leaned back in her chair and blew a long stream of smoke in the air.

'I never trusted that man, you know. I wouldn't have lent him a penny.'

'It wasn't a loan exactly. It was an investment.'

'Same thing. I wouldn't have invested in him either.'

'Why not?' Andreas looked at her uncomfortably.

'Well, look how Giles behaved, running off with that girl and then leaving her in the lurch, to say nothing about deceiving his best friend. Oh, I know they think they're better than the rest of us, and they certainly act like it, but, if you ask me, Andy, there are bad genes in that family.'

And through a cloud of tobacco smoke she gave her husband a knowing smile. 'You should have consulted *me*, dear, before you gave any money to Edmund Harvey.'

CHAPTER 14

As Laura came through the door Maggie looked up, a wide smile on her face.

'Greetings,' she said, rising to welcome her and, to Laura's embarrassment, kissed her on the cheek. 'And congratulations.' She pointed to a chair and Laura sat down, feeling almost overwhelmed by her tutor's reception.

Maggie had gone over to the kettle which she plugged in, and then fiddled around with mugs and coffee, chatting animatedly over her shoulder.

'You must have worked really hard. What sort of year did you have at home? How was Australia?'

Laura laughed.

'What will I answer first?'

'Whichever one you like.' Maggie brought the mugs over and set Laura's down in front of her. Then she squatted on a cushion on the floor and lit a cigarette. Laura thought it was very good to see Maggie, who hadn't changed a scrap in the past two years, and it was very good, very good indeed to be back in Oxford.

Laura had heard in July that she'd passed the exam and would be readmitted to the second year. It had enabled her to survive the summer, as working for the exam had helped her through the difficult time since her return from Australia. It had been hard to get away, to say goodbye to Mr Boothroyd, who had enjoyed having her work for him. It was harder still to say goodbye to her father who, she realised, was a sick man and who now only had his teenage son Gordon to look after him, and that wouldn't be for long as Gordon was ambitious and would follow his sister into higher education.

'Australia was a long time ago.' Laura tossed back her hair and paused to sip her coffee. 'It was an experience, but it wasn't a very happy time. Things with Giles didn't work out. We grated upon each other. We ran out of money and had to work. Giles wasn't used to roughing it. We had to do menial jobs as we hadn't a work permit. Giles didn't like the hardship.' Laura delicately fingered her brow, where Maggie could see a slight scar which disappeared into her hair. 'Then I had an accident swimming in the sea at Bondi, and we decided immediately to come home. In a way the accident was a blessing in disguise. Giles had some crazy idea I'd tried to kill myself, but I hadn't, although, to be honest, as I swam towards the horizon I remember thinking how nice it would be to get away from it all, a kind of natural reaction I guess to all that was going on.'

Maggie nodded sympathetically.

'And did you see Giles again?'

Laura shook her head. 'He telephoned a few times to keep in touch. I promised I'd pay him back the money for the fare, but when that will be I don't know. Not for a while.'

'And Nick?' Maggie lowered her eyes.

'I haven't seen Nick. I hear he got a very good degree?'

Maggie nodded. 'He also got his fellowship. But he's working on some project at the LSE. The future looks very bright for him.'

When she saw Laura's downcast expression she reached up and patted her on the knee. '*And* it's very bright for you. Your exam papers justified all the faith I had in you and, you know, I think your experiences these past two years have helped you to mature. They've broadened your mind.

You're not quite the girl you were when you left here. No experience you know, Laura, is ever wasted.'

No indeed. No experience was ever wasted but it was a pity, Laura thought, as she walked along the High swinging her bag, that one had to discover things the hard way, at so much personal cost. She felt wiser, more mature as Maggie had pointed out, but she felt older too, much much older than her fellow students in the second year, most of whom were nineteen whereas she had turned twenty-two in August. There seemed a big gap between nineteen and twenty-two.

Despite her joy at being back in Oxford, she also felt rootless, lost and a little depressed. Being there reminded her of Nick and the brief, beautiful doomed months of their love affair. It had undoubtedly been the best time of her life, but it also contained all the seeds of a Hardy novel; that such a love would inevitably founder because of the violent opposing forces of a savage and unrelenting destiny. Nick was rich, gifted, dedicated. She was poor, not nearly as gifted and lacking his dedication and self-control. And in the end it was she, the less gifted one, who had hurt him and, by betraying their love, destroyed any chance they might have had of being happy together.

Obsessed with these gloomy thoughts, Laura realised she had come to the café where she and Nick had first met, and she slowed down and found herself gazing through the great pane of plate glass at the table where he'd asked if he could join her, as if hoping, in some miraculous way, to see him there now. But another couple sat there, hands joined across the formica, gazing into each other's eyes.

What did the future hold for them? They suddenly looked up and saw her staring so intensely at them, and she gave them a little self-conscious wave and walked on back to college.

At the gate the porter stopped her.

'Oh, Miss Chase. I've let a gentleman into your room. He said you knew him very well. He didn't want to give me his name. He said it was a surprise.' The porter looked at her anxiously. 'I hope I did the right thing?'

'Yes, that's OK,' Laura said thoughtfully, wondering who of her past acquaintances would want to surprise her in this fashion. She supposed she could immediately eliminate Giles or Nick, the names that first sprang to mind.

'Shall I come with you, Miss Chase?'

'No, no, I'll be fine.' She smiled reassuringly at him and swiftly crossed the quad looking up at her window as she did, but seeing no one there. Maybe she *should* have asked the porter to chaperone her?

She smiled at the thought and sped up the stairs, standing outside her room for a moment listening. She turned the handle and pushed open the door, and for what seemed like a long time she stared at the still figure sitting in the chair by the window, head bent over a book. She realised that she had been hoping all the time it was him and her heart, literally, missed a beat.

Nick looked up at her and, for several seconds, they gazed at each other. It was such a long time since they had parted, but nothing had changed, physically at least. They looked the same; but did they still feel the same?

'Hi!' she said shyly, closing the door behind her and slowly entering into the room.

'Hi!' He stood up, also shy, and put down the book. Then, awkwardly, he approached her and kissed her on the cheek. For a moment they clung to each other and then they separated.

'I heard you were in Oxford?' Nick cleared his throat.

'I heard you got a very good degree,' she said. 'Congratulations.'

'Thanks.'

Awkward pause. Then: 'Would you like a coffee?'

'I thought we might have a bite to eat in the pub?' He looked at his watch. 'Nearly time for lunch.'

'That would be nice.'

The conversation was stilted, awkward. Of course that was natural, given what had happened and the time that had passed. They walked almost in silence to the pub. When they entered, Laura discovered it had the same air of nostalgia as the coffee bar. It even had the same barman, who recognised them, and they chatted to him as Nick ordered a beer for himself and a white wine for Laura, just as he used to, without consulting her, a fact she rather liked.

They even went over to the table they used to sit at in a corner and Nick raised his glass and turned to her. 'Cheers!'

'Cheers!' she said, raising hers.

'This is like old times.'

'It certainly is.'

'Why didn't you ever get in touch with me, Laura?' Nick said quietly after the barman had brought over their sandwiches. Laura looked at them, feeling around in her mind for the right reply.

'I guess I felt ashamed,' she said at last. 'I behaved terribly badly.' She raised her eyes and studied his face. 'After all we'd been to each other I didn't have to treat you like that.'

'It must have been partly my fault,' he said.

'How do you mean?' That searching look again.

'There was something I didn't understand. Something I didn't do right.'

'I was very hurt at fluffing my exams, hurt and humiliated. I think I blamed you which was stupid.'

'Blamed me?' Now Nick looked confused.

'You know, falling in love, all that crap. I thought you could take it in your stride and I couldn't. It mattered terribly to me letting my folks down.'

'I'm sorry.' His hand closed over hers, but she thought it felt like the clasp of a brother rather than a lover. There was no electricity there. She realised then that too much had happened for them to resume their relationship, as though time had not intervened.

'I know. I'm awfully confused, Nick,' Laura's eyes were swimming with tears, 'and I don't know why I did what I did.'

'You fancied Giles more.' His tone hardened and he removed his hand which had comforted her a little.

'No, I didn't fancy Giles; but he offered an escape.'

'I offered you a home with me in Oxford. We might have been married now, or on the verge. Something like that. Losing you was bad enough, but going off with Giles . . . I nearly had a breakdown. For weeks I simply couldn't concentrate on anything. I don't know what kept me going.'

She reached for his hand and ran her thumb up and down along the back.

'I lost a friend and a lover . . . Don't,' tears sprang to her eyes again, 'please don't reproach me. I simply can't bear it. I had a lousy two years. My mum left my dad. My dad, who we always thought was a hypochondriac, turned out to have real heart disease. He went off by himself, after I'd gone, to remonstrate with Giles's parents and they kicked him out of the house, and when he got home he collapsed again and this time the heart attack was worse than the one he'd had before.'

'Giles's parents kicked him out of the house?' Nick looked aghast.

'Pushed him into the street, but he was a silly old bugger to have gone. He'd never even been to London before. It was all too much for him, but he felt so angry. He was angry really at losing a nurse, not at my morals. As for Australia,' Laura paused and sniffed, 'that was a disaster. It was not "the experience of a lifetime" I can assure you.'

'But you and Giles were lovers?' The bitter tone had entered Nick's voice again.

Laura sighed. 'Well, we fucked, yes. I wouldn't call it love. It was nothing like what happened between you and me. Giles felt guilty too about you.'

'Oh, tough.'

'I know you're hurt, Nick. That it's difficult to understand. I can't understand it myself. Last year I paid for it dearly, working in the chemist's shop, looking after my dad. All I did was work, studying at night. It was the most dreary, awful year of my life and if there is ever retribution in this world, I paid it.'

Nick and Laura left the pub at about three and he took her back to college as far as the porter's lodge. The porter seeing him smiled, rather conspiratorially, and Nick winked as though they shared some secret.

Nick stood watching Laura cross the quad and then he turned and walked to where he'd left his car to drive back to London. The compulsion to see Laura had been overwhelming. He'd felt there was something he needed to settle before he could move on. And even now he was not sure that he'd settled it, that he'd got Laura out of his system.

And that was what he wanted to do. He didn't want to begin an affair with her again although he knew he still loved her. But it was the sort of irrational, obsessional love he despised. To love someone who had hurt you as badly as she had was absurd. Having done it once she would do it again. She had the power.

A woman like Laura was a very dangerous person to have under your skin.

When Nick realised he would be spending most of his time in London rather than Oxford he decided to move out of his parents' house and rented a flat in Covent Garden, a short walk from the LSE.

The LSE had grown from small beginnings at the end of the nineteenth century into a huge institution housed in a hybrid collection of buildings in the Aldwych, which formed what must have been one of the ugliest campus sites in the country. It was part of a dense jungle of buildings, somewhat randomly constructed, and a bridge ran over the narrow street which connected one part of the school with another. Round it was a warren of smaller houses and buildings, even a converted pub, that now contributed to the amorphous whole that was one of the greatest and most prestigious academic centres in the world.

Nick was very proud to have been given a research job in government at the LSE which enabled him to combine work with research for his doctorate. Eventually he hoped this would land him a lectureship at Oxford, LSE or some other comparable seat of learning.

Nick arrived home shortly after six, put his car in a mews garage which he rented at great expense, Covent Garden's parking restrictions being punitive. He occupied the second floor of an eighteenth century house that had been converted into flats, and although it could be noisy at times, due to the perpetual congestion in the streets around, he loved his flat and thought he was lucky to have acquired it in such a central and atmospheric location.

It was near the school and within walking distance of the West End. It was surrounded by nice pubs, some of the best restaurants in London and, of course, was a stone's throw from not one opera house but two, where he could indulge his favourite form of entertainment. Nick saw his parents at least once a week, sometimes twice. He usually dined with them on a Friday, though he didn't stick to the day because it was dangerous and also tedious to get into a routine.

Occasionally he had them to dinner or took them out and Emma was usually there too. She wanted her own flat and would quite like, he thought, to have moved in with him. But he thought Emma, with her love of a good time, involving late nights, would be too much of a liability when he wanted to apply himself to serious study. Nick rather liked his lifestyle and he felt that if only Laura hadn't deserted him he would have been the happiest man in the world; but now it was too late, far too late, to turn back the clock.

After his meeting with Laura, Nick flung himself into his work more than ever in an effort to forget her. Laura was no use to him; there was no point in being haunted by her, in craving her presence. He had a good life and career ahead of him and Laura would only mean trouble. Apart from that, he had seen nothing in her attitude to make him think she wanted to start up again.

He would never be able to trust her again.

One day, having sat in on a seminar on the European Union at the LSE, Nick was making his way from the new building to the old when, passing the porter's lodge, he noticed a tall familiar figure seemingly in consultation with one of the staff who, seeing Nick, suddenly hailed him.

'Mr Constantine! You've got a visitor. Someone asking for you.'

Giles turned in surprise and saw Nick just about to mount the steps to one of the lifts. Nick stopped and looked at him.

'Oh, hi!' he said, with little enthusiasm in his voice.

Nick saw the porter watching him with interest. To refuse Giles's outstretched hand would be churlish, so he took it and shook it.

'I was just passing,' Giles said, feeling awkward and thinking that, maybe, this chance encounter was not such a good idea. 'You know my law tutorial college is just round the corner in Lincoln's Inn Fields?'

'No, I didn't know.' Nick's tone was cool, indifferent.

'Well, it is. Look, Nick . . .' Giles's manner changed and he looked urgently at his former friend. 'I need to talk to you.'

'Well . . .' Nick looked as though he was going to refuse, but Giles caught hold of his arm. The porter turned and pretended to be busy with something else.

'It is something quite urgent, quite personal, and it concerns you.'

'Really?' Nick's expression was puzzled.

'Yes, really.'

'You'd better come to my room then.'

Nick rang for the lift and Giles stood beside him waiting for it.

'It's not exactly Oxford, is it?' he said, looking around.

'No. It's not. I think maybe it's what's meant by a blackboard jungle.' In fact, almost to prove the point, in the entrance hall were blackboards on which were scribbled in chalk a number of announcements and messages.

The lift came and they got in. A number of others piled in too. They got out at the third floor and Nick led Giles along the corridor, up a small flight of stairs, and opened the door of a room at the top. It was a room without charm or beauty, a functional room, very small and crammed with books, papers and on the desk, a computer. The narrow window looked onto the roof garden which, in summer, was one of the few places where the thousands of students and staff could get an unrestricted view of the sun. Now, on a cold November day with a keen wind blowing, it was deserted.

No, squashed in a corner of the Aldwych, opposite Bush House, the LSE was certainly not Oxford. That wonderful city with its quads filled with trees and flowers, its huge stretch of central meadowland and its ancient buildings hallowed by time.

'This is home, is it?' Hands in his pockets, Giles looked around, and Nick was reminded of that slight air of arrogance that his mother always hated and resented so much.

'It's not home,' Nick answered brusquely, 'it's merely where I work.'

'I hear you got a very good degree.'

'Thanks.'

'And a fellowship?'

'Can you come to the point, Giles?' Nick perched on the end of his desk and pointed to one of the two chairs in the room.

'I realise this is very difficult, for both of us.' Giles paused to clear his throat. 'And it's no use saying "I'm sorry".'

'Too late to say you're sorry.' Nick folded his arms and gazed out of the window. 'In fact, I can't think why you even considered coming to see me. What happened was a long time ago. It's over,' he turned and looked at Giles, 'but it is not forgotten, either for what you did to me or for what you did to Laura. Laura is deeply scarred by her experience, and I can't say that I'm unmoved either.'

'Laura was a free agent you know,' Giles said quietly. 'She wasn't kidnapped, or even coerced.'

'That's what you say. You paid her fare. It must have been tempting.'

'Laura insisted that the fare was a loan, and I agreed. If one day she can pay it back I'll accept it. There was more to it than that, Nick. I'll agree that the issue was complicated, and Laura is a complicated human being, maybe far more than you, or I, realise. Basically, she was upset by your wealth, or rather the fact that your dad was so wealthy: the yacht, the Rolls. She never felt happy about it or being your "concubine", as she called it, if she returned to Oxford to live with you.'

'My concubine!' Nick exploded angrily.

'Her very word. I swear I didn't make it up.' Giles gestured helplessly. 'But what is the point of raking over the past, Nick? It happened, and I'm very sorry. It didn't work out for Laura and me. It was not a happy time for either of us. If you like we were both punished. You and I had a great friendship which I thought would last all our lives and that has gone too. You are right to be angry and upset, but I have come to you not to rake over the past. I've come to tell you something else which I'm afraid is also going to upset you a great deal. However I feel I need your help.'

Nick looked puzzled and started to fiddle with some things on his desk.

'Go on,' he said at last.

'Nick, I have been seeing Emma for nearly a year.'

'*Emma*!' Nick bawled. 'My sister?'

Giles nodded. 'That may sound horrifying enough, which is the reason we kept it a secret.'

'But how . . .'

Giles raised a hand. 'I'll come to that in a minute. What I want to tell you, which is why I need help, is that Emma is a drug addict. She's addicted to heroin and I can't handle it alone any more.'

Nick buried his face in his hands and stood there for some time saying nothing. Then he slumped into the chair behind his desk and sat there staring at the blank computer screen.

'This needs a hell of a lot of explanation,' he said.

'I can't think how no one else in your family seems to have noticed. She leads a completely wild life and no one seems to try to rein her in – except me.'

'My parents are very worried about Emma,' Nick nodded slowly in agreement. 'But she is over twenty-one. If they ask her where she's been or what she's doing she flies off the handle. My mother finds she can't speak to her. I've tried . . . but heroin,' he put his hands over his face again. 'I can't believe it.'

'When I met her she already had the habit. It was just under a year ago. January this year in fact, and I didn't know for some time. She was very moody, either up or down, and this I realised, when I knew, was according to whether she'd had a fix or not. She had ample funds of course, well supplied by your father. She could get the finest heroin, only the best. When I first got to know about it she claimed she could give it up any time; but she can't. She's hooked and she's getting worse. She craves it more frequently in bigger quantities as her tolerance rises. Luckily, because she has money and is an intelligent woman, she knows the ropes. She would never, for instance, share a needle. She doesn't mix with the riffraff on the streets because she doesn't have to. But I have found it increasingly difficult to control her, and now I know she needs, and must have, professional help. If not, before she's thirty she'll be dead.'

Nick rose and, finger on his chin, went to stand at the window.

'What on earth can I do?'

'You'll have to speak to your father.' Giles's tone was firm. 'He'll have to cut off the money, cut off the supply and then, so as not to drive her underground, try and persuade her to have the best treatment. I will do all I can because I love her. I know this will not be good news to you or your family; but I think my love is strong enough to help and support her.'

'I don't suppose it will be good news to yours either.' Nick gave an ironic chuckle. 'Do they know?' He turned and looked at Giles, his expression somehow softened. He could feel that, imperceptibly, the tension between them was breaking down.

Giles shook his head.

'No, they don't know anything about me and Emma. I met her by accident at Mephistos, the nightclub. I was a bit lonely, at a loose end, and I went there alone one night for a few beers. I just bumped into Emma.' Giles thought he would leave out the rather sordid details of that occasion. 'We kind of hit it off.'

'You always liked each other.' Nick, to his surprise, felt himself warming once again to his old friend.

'Yes, we did. Well we started to meet and the friendship grew.'

'And you had no idea about the . . .' Nick could hardly bring himself to say the dreaded word.

'No. I mean we used to smoke hash and take Es at various clubs and parties – I mean everyone does, don't they? – but I didn't realise she was on a steady diet of heroin until I came back to my flat unexpectedly one day and found all the paraphernalia. Ever since then I've been trying to control it, but now,' Giles despairingly flung his arms in the air, 'I've had to confess to failure.'

'God knows what Dad will say.' Nick again slumped in his chair. 'He'll hit the roof. Yet in a way he has himself to blame. They've always spoiled Emma. She was born with a silver spoon in her mouth and has led a privileged lifestyle. She has a good brain but was never encouraged to work or to use it. It's their fault, as much as hers, that she turned to drugs. What else is there to do when you have everything? Dad, like Mum, had his ideas still anchored in the past. Women are not expected to work or have a career. Dad just wanted her to be decorative, happy, spend as much money as she liked on nice clothes, and marry well. They're worried that she hasn't already. Heavens, she's twenty-*two*.' Nick's expression mocked the amazement and concern of his parents. 'But then there was a man, Philip, she saw a lot of and they didn't like him either. No one is quite good enough for their princess.'

'I think Philip introduced her to H,' Giles said. 'I met him and I didn't care for him at all.'

'He was always losing his job. They were relieved when she seemed to have stopped seeing him.'

'Well, at least I'm not heavily into the drug scene, even if I am a Harvey.' Giles gave a rueful, self-deprecating smile. He went over to his old friend and put a hand on his shoulder. 'Perhaps this will help us to patch things up between ourselves, Nick? I'd like it more than anything, because maybe one day we'll be brothers-in-law.'

'You'd really do that?' Nick looked at him incredulously. 'You'd marry a junkie, with all the trouble and difficulty that entails?'

'I wouldn't marry a junkie, but I'll marry Emma when she's free from dope. If she'll have me.'

And at that moment Nick felt a resurgence of love for his old mate, companion in arms, friend of his youth.

Impulsively, he stood up and flung out his arms and embraced him.

CHAPTER 15

'You won't see a return on your investment overnight,' Edmund said with a trace of impatience in his voice. 'I think I've told you that before. Be reasonable, Andy.'

'I think I'm being very reasonable,' Andreas replied, gripping the receiver tightly in his hand. 'A million and a half is a lot of money.'

'I agree. It is a lot of money. But when this product comes on the market and you see your dividends, you will be thanking me for the rest of your life.'

'Well, let's hope so.' Andreas glanced round to be sure Lydia was not within earshot. 'Any news about the other matter?'

'What other matter?'

'The club.'

'Oh, the club. Yes, that's going through.'

'When?'

'Well, again, it's a matter of time.'

'But my name has gone forward?'

'Oh, definitely.'

'And I will be elected?'

'Don't see why not.'

'Well, I'll wait to hear about both matters.' Andreas felt a curious and untypical sense of defeat. It was not a sensation he was at all accustomed to. ''Bye, then,' he said, and replaced the receiver.

There was something about Edmund and his tactics that,

to an experienced man of business, smelt of rank dishonesty. Yet Andreas still couldn't bring himself to believe that someone of Harvey's background, with family traditions rooted deep in English soil, could deceive him. If he was engaged in some tricky transaction, Andreas was quite sure that Valerie knew nothing about it.

'Was that Emma?' Lydia asked, coming to the door of the dining room from where Andreas had been phoning.

'No.'

'I'm very worried about her.'

Andreas consulted his watch.

'It's only ten.'

'Last night she didn't come home at all.'

'You know she stays with Sue.' Andreas, still with a worried frown on his brow, followed his wife from the room.

'But *is* she with Sue?' Lydia turned anxiously towards him as they reached the drawing room.

'Why shouldn't she be? Look, darling, she's not a child.'

Andreas switched on the ten o'clock news. After watching it for a few moments he impatiently flicked off the remote control and, flopping into a chair, took up the *Evening Standard*.

'Andreas.' Looking tense, ill at ease, Lydia sat opposite him, perched on the edge of her chair. 'I do wish you'd take this seriously.'

'My dear, I am taking it seriously.' Andreas allowed the paper to fall to the floor. 'But Emma will soon be twenty-three.'

'She seems to have no permanent boyfriend, so where does she go? What does she do?'

'Do you want me to talk to her?'

Lydia clasped her hands together. 'Oh, Andy, I wish you would.'

'What shall I say?'

'Well, say we're a bit worried, concerned at the unusual

hours she keeps. She's also getting through a tremendous amount of money and I don't see it reflected in the clothes she buys.'

'She doesn't buy clothes?' Andreas looked surprised.

'Not with me any more.'

'Then what does she do with the money?'

'You'll have to ask her, Andy. You'll have to find out what's going on.'

They both listened at the sound of the front door closing.

'Oh, there she is,' Lydia said, relief in her voice.

'I shan't talk to her tonight,' Andreas murmured, rising to his feet. 'It's much too late.'

'Oh, no. Try to get her when she's fresh, not tired out. Take her to lunch or something. She'd like that. Lorenzo's, somewhere smart.'

'Hi, Mum. Hi, Dad!' Nick came into the room and both his parents stared at him in surprise.

'Where did you spring from?'

'Sorry, is it too late?'

'Is Emma with you?'

'No.'

Nick looked uncomfortable. He stooped to the floor for the paper his father had thrown down and stared at the front page for a few moments.

'Well, to what do we owe the pleasure, darling?' Lydia watched him a little anxiously. 'Is anything wrong?'

Nick put down the paper again and looked from one parent to the other.

'I don't really know where to start,' he said.

Andreas came downstairs into the living room, quietly closing the door behind him.

'Is she OK?' Nick asked.

'She's taken a sleeping tablet. She'll soon go off.' With an air of profound exhaustion Andreas sank into a chair opposite his son. 'I do wish you could have found another way to tell us all this.'

'I tried, Dad, but I could think of no other way. I thought I'd just tell you alone, but I knew Mum would have to know. I decided it was better to see you together.'

'It's had a terrible effect on your mother.' Andreas paused and looked at the floor. 'It's had a terrible effect on me.'

'And me,' Nick said. 'Don't forget, I heard it first.'

'And Giles Harvey of *all* people.' Andreas savagely banged his fist into the palm of his hand. 'I blame him for a lot of this.'

'I don't think you can blame him for any of it. He said that when he met up with her again she was already an addict.'

'And that was almost a year ago! Why couldn't he have told us then?'

'Well . . . he fell in love. He was in a quandary. Knowing how you felt about him, Emma didn't want you to know she was seeing him. He tried to get her off the habit himself. Frankly, I don't think his influence has been anything but good.'

'Rubbish!' Andreas snarled. 'He was probably after her money, just as his wretched father has been after mine.'

'I beg your pardon?' Nick looked up startled. 'I thought the Harveys were very well off, thank you.'

'Some time ago I let Edmund have some money towards a so-called investment. At the time it sounded promising, but I have yet to see a penny of my money back.'

'Well, I'm sure Edmund is a very straight guy. And Giles is very straight too.'

'You call him straight?' Andreas looked incredulously at his son. 'After what he did to you? He went off with your girl and you call that straight?'

'It's all over and forgotten now. I don't want to talk about it again.'

'Look how he treated her? Don't you think that might be relevant to how he might treat your sister? Has treated her, for all we know.'

'No, I don't and he is very supportive of her. He has tried desperately to get her off. He came to me as a last resort.'

'I don't believe a word of it. I don't like young Harvey and I don't like his father and, like your mother, who has shown much wisdom in all this, I bitterly regret that our paths ever crossed. To think of my daughter being involved with them is almost more than I can bear.'

'Dad,' Nick sat down next to his father and grabbed his hand urgently. 'You've got to think of Emma's welfare. We've got to see her together, and we've got to get her to agree to treatment.'

'However, I must insist,' Andreas said firmly, 'that she gives up seeing Harvey. It's got to be a clean break.'

'I don't think you can insist on that, Dad.'

'I can and I do. I will not tolerate Giles Harvey sniffing around my daughter.'

Andreas came out of the Greek Orthodox Church in Camden Town, went to his car which he had parked at a meter round the corner, and sat for a long time in the driver's seat staring in front of him. He felt like a man who had been crucified, and not even God could help him.

Andreas was not religious, didn't even go to church on holy days. But his children had been baptised into the Orthodox faith and he contributed to church charities and helped to support the priest.

The previous day, he and Nick had taken Emma to a clinic in rural Hampshire, to try and cure her of her addiction. It was costing him nearly two thousand pounds a week, but he didn't care about the money. He cared about his daughter who, the doctors had assured him, he would lose at an early age if she wasn't cured.

It had been a ghastly time with Emma. Once confronted, she had denied it and then she had tried to disappear, run away. Giles brought her back and was asked immediately to leave by Andreas, who still could not believe that she could have got into this condition without his help. Emma promptly had, or manufactured, a sort of fit and Giles was asked to come back.

Inevitably the Harvey family became aware of what was going on and they too tried to intervene, with all sorts of theories and good advice that Emma's increasingly tense and irritated parents could have done without.

They took Emma on a cruise in the yacht round the coast of North Africa, the only place to be sure of the sun, but they had to make an emergency run to Alexandria for her to see a doctor. Without her fix she was hallucinating and having fits. Finally she became frightened and consented to enter the clinic.

Giles assured her parents that, in the interests of her well-being and recovery, he would not see her unless they asked him to. By this time Emma hardly knew what was going on.

And now it was spring, but that didn't seem to help. Andreas had always felt a lift with the arrival of the season, the glimpse of leaves on the trees in the park, the blossom on the streets in the Wood. He was a naturally cheerful and buoyant man, his outlook on life one of optimism rather than pessimism. He could never in his life recall having felt so low; so low and depressed that he had driven to the Orthodox church to seek the help of one of the priests who listened to him most sympathetically and then invited him to come into the church with him and pray before the icon of the crucified Christ.

He had asked the Father what had he done to deserve this? He had always been a faithful husband and loving father. He had made money, but by honest means, never cheated; and had paid his taxes. God what a lot of those there were. He knew he liked nice things, expensive things like the boat and the Rolls, but was this wrong, was it a sin? He had not, he thought, been overly greedy, he gave generously to church funds and helped numerous other good causes. He had never stolen money or cheated people. He had never had a mistress.

He had, he thought, been vain in wanting so desperately to belong to a gentleman's club in St James's, a club that admitted people only from the very top drawer; but surely that was a weakness rather than a sin?

What, then, had he done to deserve that his beautiful, well-educated, well brought-up daughter, the light of his life, who should have everything to live for, should turn out to be a junkie. One so bad that the doctors gave her a limited lifespan of a few years maximum, unless she was cured?

The Father told him how difficult it was to explain or understand these things, said he would pray for him and his wife and their daughter and asked him to trust in God.

Father Spiros's final words had been ones of comfort and hope, but Andreas felt no hope, only a bleakness of spirit. And, as he started his car the tears that had lurked for so long began to roll slowly down his cheeks.

But, by the time he arrived at the West End offices of Frank Thompson, the tears had dried and, greeting Frank, it would have been hard to tell that here was a man who, half an hour earlier, had been in the grips of despair.

Frank greeted him warmly, and enquired after his family.

'Fine, fine,' Andreas replied.

'We're looking forward to our trip on the yacht this year.' Frank sat himself behind his enormous desk and, leaning towards Andreas, offered him a cigar. Andreas shook his head. 'It is on, isn't it?' Frank began the ritual of cigar lighting, removing the band, inspecting the tip, taking a cutter from a tray on the desk and puncturing the end. Then he looked at Andreas. 'Will the Harveys be there?'

Andreas appeared taken aback by the question: 'I don't expect so. Why do you ask?'

'Just wondered.' Frank began thoughtfully to examine the burning tip of his Havana. 'Now to business, Andy.' He reached over for a folder which he opened, and started going through the documents inside. 'We have a very large consignment of the finest pure virgin olive oil. It's not cheap, but all the best places will take it: Harrods, Fortnums. Guaranteed . . .'

'I just wondered why you asked about Harvey?' Andreas interrupted him.

'Well . . .' Frank, who was a bulky man, leaned forward and joined his hands on his desk. 'I have come across him again in a rather strange way.'

'Really?'

'Coincidence is a very funny thing.' Frank wriggled his bulk in his chair. 'Well, it's like this, Andy. I won't beat about the bush. I have been looking for money to expand. As you know, interest rates are competitive and the banks are tight. We're already over-geared. A friend of mine, Arnold Smart, who is in the fruit business, knew through a friend of a friend a lawyer able to lend money on favourable terms. I realised I knew him. We'd met on your yacht.'

'Edmund Harvey.' Andreas nodded.

'Oh, you know he does this sort of thing?'

'I certainly do.'

'Oh, that's a relief.' Frank sat back as if Andreas had taken a weight off his mind.

'Well, I don't know that it should be a relief. Harvey has taken a considerable amount of money off me and I have yet to see any return on investment.'

'Well, he is offering to advance me a million.'

'That's probably the money he took off me.'

'Thing is, I haven't had it and he wants twenty thousand pounds upfront.'

'For what?' Andreas looked amazed.

'Security.'

'And have you given it to him?'

'I was about to.'

'And in exchange for twenty thousand pounds he is going to let you have a million?'

'Approximately, at fifteen per cent over base.'

'Over what period of time?'

'Five years.'

'At fifteen per cent over base?'

Frank nodded. He suddenly looked a crumpled individual, rather than a giant of a man.

'And you haven't seen any of it yet?'

Frank shook his head.

'Why didn't you ask *me* for the money, Frank?' Andreas leaned forward and looked at him earnestly.

Thompson put his head on one side, studied his nails. 'You know how it is with friends. Doing business is one thing, but asking favours, borrowing money, is another. It may have made you doubt us financially and, commercially speaking, the business is extremely viable. We just have to pay more upfront for goods before receipt. You know how it is . . .'

He looked ruefully at Andreas, who slowly shook his head.

'It doesn't really work out, does it?' Andreas asked. 'The terms are ridiculous. In the meantime he's getting other loans while you and others repay theirs. It seems to me a highly risky, dubious enterprise. From what you tell me, I definitely think I'm going to have to make some enquiries into the business dealings of Mr Edmund Harvey.'

'Look, don't get me wrong.' Frank nervously held up his hands. 'I mean, I don't want to get the guy into trouble. He's a family friend of yours I know. The boys were at school together. I'm sure he's legit.' A look of disbelief spread over his homely features. 'He must be. He took me to lunch at his club. His grandfather was on the committee of the MCC.'

'Why do we trust these people?' Andreas said in a despairing voice. 'Is it because we think they're better than we are? It's nothing to do with brains or money, is it, Frank? It's to do with class. Something you can't buy, no matter how you try. Do you remember the way they behaved on the boat? Didn't bring the right clothes, tried to put us down at every turn, criticised the wine. Patronising. Acted as if they owned it. In a sense you'd think *we* were their guests. Lydia took to her bed because of the nervous strain of trying to entertain them. Now I've parted with a million and a half, and you have nearly parted with twenty thousand for nothing, just because he took us to dine at his club and his grandfather was on the committee of the MCC. Doubtless another grandfather was a High Court judge and an uncle or two an Admiral of the Fleet and a General in the British Army.'

Andreas, slightly frenzied by now, agitatedly stabbed the air with his finger. 'Do you know that his son lured my son's girlfriend to Australia, thus breaking up her relationship with Nick, and abandoned her after she nearly died in a swimming accident? Do you know that I have discovered that this very same son has been having an affair with *my* daughter and has introduced her to drugs? Emma is in a clinic at this moment in an effort to rehabilitate. That's the sort of people we're dealing with, Frank,' Andy continued, his voice finally breaking. 'If you ask *me*, they're the scum of the earth.'

When Andreas reached home later that same day, he ran his car into the garage beside the Rolls. He seldom used it for business in the city; it was too big, and too precious, to risk damaging in the narrow streets of London, the chances of a collision, or an act of vandalism were too great.

He got out of the Jag, locked it and then ran his hands lightly along the side of the Rolls. It was pale blue and it was very beautiful, over one hundred thousand pounds' worth of top-rate car. Not just a miracle of modern engineering and design, but a work of art. More importantly, it was a symbol of success.

And there was the yacht, *The Lydia*, at anchor in the port of Monaco, waiting the next trip. Its crew were fully paid throughout the year, ready to cast off at a moment's notice, on the whim of the boss: him, Andreas Michael Constantine.

He left the garage, closed it with a flip of the remote control, and stood for a few moments looking up at the house. His house, bought with his money. No mortgage, and now worth in today's inflated prices three and a half to four million. Inside it had several good paintings, many antiques, bought with taste and care by his wife, who kept a lovely home, a fitting place for a successful man. Not a greedy man, not an outrageous, bullying man, not a boastful, arrogant man, but a successful one. And what was wrong with success? Why, nothing, unless it meant that, perhaps, it had contributed to the loss of a daughter.

Andreas punched in the numbers at the door that gained him admission to his high-security home, vigilance that was important and necessary in these days when there were so many villains about. He had no doubt that Edmund Harvey and his ilk would have been outraged at the thought of breaking into someone's house and stealing their possessions, yet what they were doing was no less harmful, no less destructive.

There remained however a part of Andreas that found it difficult to believe that Edmund Harvey was a crooked lawyer, a con man who could end up behind bars, investing money he didn't have, offering to lend clients spurious loans. There were all sorts of things in business that were marginal. Maybe he should give Edmund the benefit of the doubt. Confront and warn him? Maybe that would be the decent, honourable thing to do.

Hadn't their sons gone to the same public school? Yet, when you thought about it, that being the case, didn't you deserve to be better treated by that self-same friend?

Inside, the house was quiet. Andreas guessed Lydia would be upstairs resting. She was still on tranquillisers and had been absolutely unable to face the journey to the clinic with Emma. It was almost five and, after depositing his briefcase in the hall, Andreas went into the kitchen, which was empty. This was the time of day that Maria and her husband usually had off. By six she would be back on duty again preparing the dinner. When Andreas used the Rolls, or had a particularly busy day with a round of engagements, Marco acted as chauffeur. Today had probably been spent doing jobs around the house or in the garden.

Andreas got a bottle of mineral water out of the fridge, poured some into a glass and drank it. Then with the glass still in his hand he went back to the drawing room and, after consulting the telephone directory, punched in a number.

'Good afternoon,' he said after asking for the club secretary, 'this is Andreas Constantine speaking.'

Polite pause.

'Does my name ring a bell?'

'I don't think so, Mr Constantine,' the plummy-toned voice replied. 'Are you a member of the club?'

'I was hoping to be elected,' Andreas replied. 'I understood my name had gone before the club committee. Some time ago, as a matter of fact.'

'Ah! In that case just let me look at my records. I'm afraid these things do take time.' The voice sounded regretful. 'May I ask the name of your proposer, Mr Constantine?'

'Mr Harvey. Edmund Harvey.'

'Edmund Harvey . . .' The voice went on repeating 'Harvey, Harvey' and then, finally, 'I'm afraid I have no record of a person with your name being proposed by Mr Harvey, Mr Constantine. I'm so sorry. I feel there must be some mistake.'

'But I think *you* must be mistaken,' Andreas insisted.

'Could you consult your records again, please?'

The plummy tone became less friendly.

'I have, sir, I assure you. Now that we are computerised, everything is here before me on the screen, and I'm afraid there is no one answering to the name of Constantine. My advice is that you should consult Mr Harvey again. Good day to you, sir.' The voice sounded very final.

Upstairs, when Andreas put his head round the door of their bedroom, he found Lydia still asleep. The curtains were drawn and it was so cool and peaceful that for a moment his terrible feeling of tension seemed to evaporate and he longed to throw himself by the side of his wife and go to sleep too. Instead, he sat by her side, still with the glass of water in his hand, and looked at her.

How she'd suffered. She didn't deserve it. She had been everything a man could ask for and more. Not only a good wife, but a good mother, too. A loyal companion and friend.

Yet in some way both of them had failed Emma. Had they been too indulgent? Demanding in one way, but not demanding enough in another? They had given her freedom, but should they really have been asking more questions?

In this day and age it was so hard to know the answer.

They had treated both their children the same, and yet no one could fault Nick, who had turned into a splendid specimen of humanity. A true Renaissance man: academically brilliant, cultured, good and kind.

Lydia's eyelids fluttered, and when she opened them and saw Andreas beside her, she reached out and took his hand.

'Is anything wrong, Andy?'

These days she was so nervous and anxious, fearful about everything, that it seemed that for her nothing could go right. Well at last something would go right.

'I've got Harvey,' he said, clutching her hand hard.

'You've got *what*, Andy?' Still frightened, she half-sat up in bed, running a hand nervously through her hair.

'Harvey's a crook. Edmund. Though the son's a crook too.'

She lay back on the bed, an expression of triumph on her pale, ill-looking face.

'I told you he was no good.'

'He's been defrauding people of thousands, perhaps millions. I've spent part of the day doing some checking and I am absolutely sure of my facts. Frank Thompson is one he nearly got, but I think I saved him. Alas, I also think I can kiss goodbye to my million and a half.' He squeezed her hand more tightly. 'My father and brothers won't be pleased.'

'Oh, Andy, it wasn't money from the business . . .'

'No, no. It was mine. But it was almost all the spare cash I'd got.'

'But *why* did you let him have it, Andy?'

'I guess I was stupid. Vain. I wanted to show off, impress him. I shall have to tell Father that I'll need a float for a while just to make it up. I'm afraid the yacht will have to go.'

'Well, I shan't miss *that,*' she said firmly.

'Maybe the Rolls.'

Silence. Like him, Lydia loved the beautiful car.

'Well, it may not be necessary. It's up to Father and the boys. They may let me keep it. They may want me to sell. Things are quite good business-wise, but they might want to teach me a lesson. I was taken in by Harvey. I let him blind me. I thought he was going to put me up for his club and even that was a lie. He made a fool of me. He had no intention of it. Nouveau riche, I guess. Not good enough. Now I'm going to shop him. I'm going to turn him in. Notify the police.'

Lydia put a hand to her mouth.

'Oh, *Andy,*' she said, 'do you think you should?'

'Yes,' Andreas said firmly, going over to the window and gazing out on to the tree-lined streets of St John's Wood.

Beautiful St John's Wood. The best part of London. *His* part of London. Turning to Lydia he nodded vigorously.

'Yes, I most certainly do. Edmund Harvey and his like have had this coming to them for a very long time.'

CHAPTER 16

Dr Pascoe had a youthful, unlined face, clear blue eyes and a sunny expression, which was remarkable, because his entire time was spent trying to solve the heart-rending problems of others. He looked not much older than Emma, but in fact he was nearly forty, had been married fifteen years and had three children.

It was not so much that David Pascoe was young, but that Emma had aged. She looked about thirty-five, and for a young woman of twenty-three who should have been on the brink of life, this was a terrible thing.

David, during the months he had been treating her, had become fond of Emma. He, too, thought it was a very terrible thing, even though for most of his medical career he had specialised in drugs and addiction. No matter how experienced you were, you never really became used to the effect drugs had on people. When they were young, beautiful, rich and had everything going for them, it was almost impossible to understand.

But perhaps that was the key to it. Emma *had* everything. She had only to ask, and her merest whim was satisfied by doting parents. It was not only the deprived and the disadvantaged who took to drugs; the clinics were unfortunately full of rich, beautiful and talented people, too.

Even though Emma looked much older than her years, she was still beautiful. Added to which, she had a nobility of expression and a serenity that was probably due to the suffering she had endured. For she had suffered, but she had overcome. She was cured of her heroin addiction, but remained on prescribed drugs and would be for some time.

But what to do with Emma now? She was ready to leave the clinic; but was it wise to allow her to go home, back to the environment that had been the cause of the whole thing in the first place? That was the question.

Emma and David sat in his pleasant office, facing each other. They were both smoking. Smoking tobacco was permitted. Though bad for you, it was better than smoking dope. It was the one concession the clinic made to those of its patients who were victims of addiction.

Emma had on jeans and a T-shirt. It was a long time since she had worn designer clothes. She didn't use make-up. She was the sort of girl who would have made a fabulous model. Now she was probably too old.

'What to do with you, Emma?' David murmured, tapping his pencil on the table. 'What to do?'

Emma had just been told she was free to leave, and she didn't seem too pleased. Here she felt safe, in an attractive environment, surrounded by helpful people, people who cared. It was not that her parents didn't care; but she knew that when she went home they would scarcely let her out of their sight. Her father could be bad-tempered and her mother was prone to hysterics.

But she knew she had to go because the expense of the clinic was causing difficulties. Six months in a place that cost two thousand pounds a week was a lot of money, even for her father. He had recently experienced some business reverses and had to get rid of the yacht and the Rolls. That much she knew, no more.

In the safe confines of the clinic, Emma had been protected from the harsh realities of life outside.

Emma watched David cogitating. She felt very peaceful. Away from the pressures of life, she had tried to come to terms with herself. The treatment in the clinic was a mixture of drug therapy, psychotherapy, healthy eating, exercise, and early nights. It had suited her. She didn't want to leave.

'What about this boyfriend of yours?' David asked, as he shifted through her notes. He looked up. 'Giles. Have you missed him?'

Emma wasn't quite sure whether she'd missed Giles or not. At the beginning she had been so ill that she didn't remember much about anyone; but now she thought about Giles quite a lot and where their relationship would be at when she got out. In a way it was a bit like getting out of prison after being deprived of sex and normal companionship for six months.

'Daddy made Giles promise not to contact me.'

'Ah, Daddy again!' David nodded and wrote something down on a notepad in front of him.

'Daddy's lovely,' Emma said defensively.

'I'm sure he is.'

'He just thinks Giles had something to do with my addiction. He hadn't, but Daddy has convinced himself of this, and nothing anyone can say or do will change his mind.'

'Why is this?' David looked interested.

'He doesn't like Giles's family. They're rather snobby, upper class. Toffee-nosed, you know the type. Giles and my brother Nick were at school together and the Harveys, Giles's family, always had a bad effect on my mother.'

'What kind of effect?'

'She kind of went to pieces. Freaked out.' Emma smiled at the recollection. 'Poor Mum. She was so anxious to please despite the fact that we'd pots more money than they had. They *were* kind of arrogant.'

'But Giles is not like that?'

'Not at all. Unfortunately he also went off with Nick's girlfriend, and although Daddy didn't like her either, he thought Giles didn't behave very well.' Emma grimaced and shook another cigarette from the pack. 'Well, frankly, he didn't, did he?'

'I don't know the circumstances.' David scribbled something more. 'I can't judge.'

'You're being very tactful, David.'

'Tact is my business,' David said with a smile.

'I shall miss you.' Emma looked at him rather wistfully.

'And I, believe it or not, shall miss you. But I'm always here, on the end of the telephone line.' David tapped the desk again with his pencil, still looking pensive.

'I would somehow rather you didn't go straight home when you left here, Emma. Is there a relation, a friend you can stay with?'

Emma looked doubtful. 'But what will Daddy say?'

'I'll speak to Daddy if you like. You have to stand on your own feet, and I feel that if you go home you'll be Daddy's little girl again, and Mummy's. You'll be smothered all over with parental love. Not good for you. You've got to be Emma: a person in her own right.'

'I can always stay with my brother.'

'Where does he live?'

'In London. He has a flat in Covent Garden. I don't think he'll mind for a time. As long as it's not too long.'

'I think Nick is a good idea.' David put down his pencil and stood up. 'Time to make some phone calls, Emma.'

They sat opposite each other, conscious of a feeling, now that they were alone, of strangeness, unease. It was the first time they'd seen each other since Emma entered the clinic. Giles had kept his word, anxious to do nothing that might impede Emma's recovery. He felt in a way that he'd been in rehabilitation too.

Giles had chosen the restaurant with care: Hampstead, classy, expensive. Afterwards, if all went well, they could go for a stroll on the Heath.

They each had a glass of wine while they studied the menu. Emma sipped hers nervously, as though it was a long time since she'd had a drink. She looked very pale and she was still underweight but, as he gazed at her furtively round the menu, almost drinking in her beauty, Giles knew he was as much in love with her as ever. More so, in fact.

Absence had driven the heart to desperation.

Much to his relief, Giles had picked her up at Nick's, with whom she was staying after being discharged from the clinic. He didn't think he could have faced Andreas and Lydia.

They hadn't spoken much in the car as they drove through Covent Garden, except for Giles to ask her approval of the restaurant.

When they stopped outside, he had reached out and tentatively taken her hand. Her responding squeeze was encouraging.

The waiter, pad in hand, approached, and they ordered. Emma said she wouldn't drink any more wine, so Giles only ordered half a bottle. The waiter whisked their menus away and again they were alone, staring at each other.

It was Emma who broke the silence.

'It seems like years,' she said, her features suddenly relaxing, breaking into a smile.

'A lifetime,' Giles replied.

Avoiding his eyes, she gazed at the tablecloth. 'I guess it's as well I'm staying at Nick's.'

'You mean to avoid me meeting your mum and dad?'

'It's an awful situation. I wasn't sure you'd want to see me.'

'Don't be silly.' His hand closed over hers. 'I've thought of nothing else. It wasn't your fault.'

She raised her eyes and stared into his. 'I want you to know neither Nick nor I approve of what Dad did. Going to the police. We think he should have discussed it with your father first. After all, they were old family friends. We think he had some sort of brainstorm, you know, a kind of mini-breakdown. He was full of so much anger that your father had deceived him, about the money, that stupid club.'

'And he always thought I was responsible for your addiction.' Giles looked rueful. 'I guess he boiled over.'

'That was rubbish, as I told him.' Emma frenziedly crumbled the bread roll on her plate. 'What . . . what's happening with your father now?'

'He's on bail, following the hearing at the magistrates' court. He is to be sent for trial, charged with conspiracy to defraud, false accounting. He will almost certainly go to prison.'

'It must be terrible for you.'

'It is terrible. It has thrown the family all over the place; but above all it means the end of Dad's career, his livelihood. He admits he was foolish, that he did wrong. He says, and I believe him, that he didn't mean to defraud, not at the beginning, anyway. He thought he could control it. He just found himself in a jam, lots of expense, things getting out of hand. Panic. We've never been really wealthy, though Mum has money of her own. She says she wishes like anything he'd told her, but he couldn't talk to Mum, couldn't talk to anyone. I feel so desperately sad that he felt he couldn't confide in the family, but we've all rallied round now. We're closer. Mum has been terrific even though she was as shocked as we were to learn that he had a mistress.'

'A mistress!' Emma gasped, putting down her glass.

'He'd had her for years, apparently. That was part of his financial problem. We knew her. She used to be his secretary. The worst part was learning they had a son, Adam. He's about twelve. Obviously we were upset, but somehow we also felt sorry for the woman, Mary, and the poor kid.'

'Have you met him?'

'Who? Adam. Not yet. It's a difficult sort of thing to arrange, and Mary is very uncooperative. I mean with Dad.'

'He's very lucky that you are all so understanding.'

'Well, we love him. He's a good father, a kind man. This is where it pays off, even if you find he has been dishonest and deceitful. We all have lots of happy childhood memories, and in a way we helped to get him into this mess. We've had a very expensive education. We were very selfish. I guess we thought money was like a bottomless well.'

'It makes me feel worse for what my father did.' Emma looked close to tears and Giles reached out and clasped her hand.

'It had *nothing* to do with you. Sooner or later Dad would have been found out. He was an idiot. He was the one who had the nervous breakdown. Must have. He lost millions of pounds. He could never have concealed it forever. Darling, Emma, it must not make any difference to us. We have our lives too. We've weathered this separation. We can weather anything.' He looked at her intensely. 'Do you feel as I do? Still?'

She nodded, eyes now blurred by tears. They were in a corner of the dimly-lit restaurant and Giles, rising, went round to her, bent and kissed her, indifferent to the surreptitious glances of their fellow diners.

'Darling,' Giles impulsively pulled his chair closer to her and took her hand. 'We shall have to go away.'

'Go away?'

'If we want to be together, we shall have to go away. Eventually, that is. I mean, I want to support Dad when he comes up for trial, but he's going to plead guilty to save embarrassing the family. Even so, I think he'll go away for quite a long time. After I'm certain that Mum and Paul and Alice are settled and OK, I want to start a new life, and if you and I are to be together, and want to avoid the press, we'll have to get away.'

'I think David would like that.'

'David?'

'My therapist at the clinic.'

'Oh, you think he'd like it.' Giles seemed amused. 'Good.'

'Daddy's girl. He helped me discover a lot about myself.' Suddenly she looked excited. 'But where shall we go?'

'How about Australia?'

'Australia?'

'It's a great place, a young place. It really is a new country, hot, alive.' He gazed thoughtfully at the wine in his glass. 'I'd like to go into the wine business. I know I've made a few false starts, but I'm pretty sure about this. There's so much opportunity with Australian wines.'

'I'd love to go to Australia.' All at once Emma looked better, happy, a changed person.

Giles realised at that moment that her whole wellbeing, as well as their future, depended on him. He might have failed his father, but he could help now to rebuild Emma's life. He felt a new, welcome but altogether strange feeling of responsibility and saw how, after a long period of darkness, could come the light.

Once again Nick found himself the bearer of bad tidings. He looked from one parent to the other, wishing these awful jobs didn't always fall on him.

Whichever way you looked at it, things were in a terrible mess. Not only had Edmund Harvey suffered, the Constantines had suffered too.

The trial at the Old Bailey had been reported in the papers, but it had not made national headlines. In view of the sum of money he'd lost and the people he'd involved, some of them well-known names, and many respectable companies, Edmund's case might have produced a bigger stir. The recession, however, had produced a number of crooked lawyers, and one who pleaded guilty had not as much interest for the media as a long, juicy, bitter fight with as much scandal as possible thrown in. The only real interest in Edmund was from the *Financial Times* and his local paper, both of which were read, unfortunately, by too many people who knew both families.

Oddly enough, there was a lot of sympathy for the Harveys, and it was the Constantines who seemed to have to bear the brunt of ostracism by local people and some who remembered them from the school. Moreover, Andreas's family had acted with incredulity. His father and brothers came down on him particularly hard for bad judgement; an abandonment of good business principles. The loss of money seemed second place.

They helped him out, of course, but the yacht had had to go; the Rolls, naturally, a particular wrench. At least they still had the house. Andy's family had wanted them to sacrifice that and move into something smaller to release capital, but so far so good. Andy had eaten humble pie, and they held on.

Visiting her parents since Emma had come out of the clinic had been a particular ordeal. Andreas, especially, resented the fact that she had moved in with Nick instead of returning to the nest. He felt that she would resume her old, bad habits away from the protective eyes of her parents. He didn't seem to realise that the combination of their adulation together with too much money had probably brought on and encouraged her addiction in the first place.

Daddy's little girl no longer.

Emma usually accompanied Nick to dinner, but tonight he came alone, mumbling some excuse. He felt unhappy and ill at ease, and knew that this transmitted itself to his parents. His mother was particularly jumpy, her wine disappearing very rapidly from her glass.

During the meal, Nick tried to keep the conversation more or less neutral. He told them about his course, enlivened with tales of mutual friends. But all the time the real reason for his visit weighed heavily upon him, like a lodestone, and frequently his words faltered.

After dinner they moved into the drawing room. Marco brought coffee and closed the door quietly behind him. Lydia helped herself to a brandy while Andreas, watching her anxiously, gnawed at a fingernail, noting the level in her glass, frowning at her as she sat down as though to say that one addict in the family was enough.

'Emma's where?' he asked at last.

His parents gazing at him expectantly, Nick cleared his throat.

'Look, I've got something to tell you. Well . . . Emma and Giles have been seeing each other. They want to go to Australia together.' He finished in a rush and waited for his mother to burst into tears and his father to start performing.

'Now I've heard everything,' Andreas said. 'But this I can't believe. Can you believe it, Lydia?' He stared at his wife who, as Nick had foreseen, was having trouble controlling her emotions. Lydia wordlessly shook her head.

'I'd instructed him not to see my daughter,' Andreas went on.

'That was while she was in the clinic, Dad.'

'I forbade him ever to see her.'

'Then I'm afraid you can't do that. You can't behave like a Victorian father. He obeyed your wishes while Emma was in the clinic because he loved her, and he desperately wanted her to get better. He didn't want you to blame him if she didn't.'

'And now, as soon as she gets out, round he trots . . .'

'That is not the case.'

'I don't know why you're so nice to Giles,' Andreas said peevishly, shaking his head. 'I can't fathom it out. It just doesn't seem natural to me. This is a man who pinches your girl, leaves her in the lurch and now runs off with your sister. Who knows that he won't do it again?'

'I know he won't do it again. He loves Emma, he's proved that. And if he does do it again, he will have me to reckon with.'

'You didn't reckon with him before.'

'Because I don't think he loved Laura, and she didn't love him. There were all sorts of complex reasons for what happened. It wasn't a straightforward situation. She had a hang-up about me having money; she was desperately insecure. Giles wanted a travelling companion and, finally, you keep on saying he left her in the lurch, but he did not. She wanted to come home and he brought her back. He kept in touch to see if she was OK. Alright, at the time I was confused, I was hurt, but now I think I understand. Besides, a lot of water has flown under the bridge and we are all older. Perhaps a little wiser.'

'You are too nice, Nick.' Lydia began with a wail, but Andreas, clearly still angry and unconvinced by Nick's defence of his friend, butted in.

'That clinic cost me an absolute fortune, coming on top of everything else. I had to sell the yacht.'

'And the Rolls.' Lydia's tone was aggrieved.

'Emma has a lot to answer for,' Andreas mumbled and, looking across at his wife, got up to help himself to a brandy, pointedly not inviting Nick to have one as if he too shared some of the blame.

'Dad, it wasn't just Emma's fault,' Nick crossed one leg over the other, and calmly regarded his father. 'It was also your fault for lending over a million quid to Edmund Harvey.'

As his wife and son turned their reproachful eyes on him, Andreas resumed his seat.

'I think it was the only bad business mistake I ever made in my life. I shan't make one like it again; but I am hurt, Nick, and I emphasise "hurt" rather than "annoyed" that Emma chooses to live with you rather than us, now that she's out of the clinic. Here she has her own room, her mother and father who love her very much, her freedom . . .'

'It wasn't really Emma's choice, Dad.'

'I know, and the psychiatrist spoke to me trying to explain the reasons. I'm not saying that I agree with all this mumbo jumbo these people talk. Basically, the medication cured Emma, I'm convinced of that. And I hope she doesn't remain under his influence now that she *is* cured.'

'Dad!' Nick looked angrily at his father. 'Emma can relapse any time. This is the trouble with addiction.'

'But if she stays on the medication?'

'Well, she doesn't want to stay on it forever. She wants to be permanently cured. She took the advice of Dr Pascoe and moved in with me. But that's not the issue, is it? We've moved on from there. It's what happens now, between her and Giles.'

'Australia . . .' Lydia murmured, raising her eyes to the ceiling and, finally, burst into tears. Her husband ignored her while Nick rose and, crossing the room, gazed helplessly down at her, simply not knowing what to do.

'You'd think that with all the harm Giles's family has done to mine . . .'

'And you have done to him, Dad. Don't forget that.' Nick turned savagely towards Andreas, beginning to feel that he was entitled to lose his temper too.

'What harm have *I* done to his family?'

'You reported him to the police.'

'Because he was a crook.'

'He'd hoped to get out of his difficulties. He had enormous financial problems he felt he couldn't tell anyone about. He did not intend to steal or dishonestly defraud anyone. OK, he knew what he was doing was risky, but he hoped and wanted to pay it all back.'

'Huh. That's what they all say. He must have known he could never pay it back. He owed millions.'

'He was in a jam. You could have gone to him, talked to him, warned him. You chose not to.'

'Because I knew he was dishonest.'

'Because,' Nick answered hotly, 'you didn't get into some stupid gentleman's club he'd put you up for.'

'He never put me up for it.'

'He did.'

'He did not.' The two men were now bawling across the room at each other, while Lydia, still ignored, quietly went on weeping.

'He put you up and you were blackballed. He didn't know how to tell you.'

'Blackballed?' Andreas gazed incredulously at Nick. 'Did you say blackballed?'

'They didn't want you. Sorry, Dad, you're not the right type. Surely you must have realised that these gentleman's clubs in St James's are full of assholes? Of course they wouldn't want you, a third generation immigrant from a Greek peasant family. They'd hardly want the Royal Family because they came from Hanover, and that was over two hundred years ago. There's nothing so rotten as the entrenched ruling classes in this country.'

Andreas leaned back in his chair, his mouth hanging open like a fish gasping for air.

'But I rang the secretary. He said he'd never heard of me.'

'Probably being tactful. They don't like to admit to that kind of thing. You were blackballed, Dad, and that's the truth.'

Whether it was the truth or not, Andreas was certain he would never know.

A month or so later, Giles and Emma flew to Sydney with Emma's parents' blessing, but without them to see her off. There was a loving farewell at the house, and they even shook Giles warmly by the hand. They were too afraid of meeting the Harveys, who also stayed away from the airport. They, too, were afraid of meeting the Constantines.

Nick alone, prey to many conflicting emotions, stood waving at the huge plane as it lifted into the air, en route for a new life for at least two of the people on board. As for him, he had his own life to get on with. Not quite the one he had perhaps at one time wished for, or expected, but a good life nevertheless.

And, in time, there would be other Lauras, other loves.

CHAPTER 17

Alice, Edmund's darling, was nearly sixteen. She was a tall, rangy, good-looking girl with long straight fair hair and a rather superior expression that she had inherited from her mother. It seemed to go with the breed. She was very casual and laid-back like most of her generation, but maybe she'd miss Whiteboys more than anybody, Valerie thought, watching her from her bedroom window as she took her horse Tuppence through his paces in the paddock.

But Alice was a sensible, self-contained young person who, in common with the rest of the family, could see nothing so dreadfully wrong in what poor Ed had done. It was an awful pity, and quite unfair, that he'd landed up in prison. They all went to see him as often as they could to cheer him up and bring him nice treats like cigars from Dunhills and chocolates from Bendicks in Wigmore Street.

Edmund had got seven years, but with remission for good behaviour he would be out after four.

The house, just outside the pretty village of Montacute, a few miles from Yeovil, belonged to Ed, so it had to go on the instructions of his trustees in bankruptcy. Fortunately the London house was Valerie's outright. The estate agents were due any moment to give a valuation before putting it on the market. It was ridiculous really, because what it would fetch in its dilapidated state would hardly pay legal fees and certainly not a penny would go to the people to whom he owed so much money.

Nothing to the wretched Andreas. Valerie, who was not a very vindictive woman, was glad of that. She *was* vindictive, though, in her feelings towards Andreas Constantine. It just showed how little breeding the man had, that instead of coming round to see Ed and discussing the problem like a gentleman, he'd gone to the police and poor Ed never stood a chance. After all, they were supposed to be *friends*. Their sons had gone to the same school. They'd socialised together and spent a holiday on that horribly vulgar yacht.

Valerie turned away from the window and pulled the duvet and sheets off the bed, dumping them violently on the floor as though it was the sort of thing she'd like to do to Andreas. Yes, *and* she'd stamp all over him, too.

The blasted Constantines seemed to have dogged their lives, Valerie thought, as she gathered up the bedclothes and threw them into the landing, where they joined another lot from the room next door. And now it looked as though one day they might be united by marriage, Giles being clearly in love with Emma and she with him.

Everything had to be reasonably tidy for the estate agents, not that she cared much because they wouldn't see any of the money. There was five bedrooms in the house and, frankly, she'd be quite glad to see the back of it. It was a lot of work when they were there, a constant worry when they were not, and they had thought for some time of putting it on the market. However, the children, who had happy childhood memories of it, resisted.

Valerie went back to the window and, waving her arms about to get her attention, called out to Alice indicating that she wanted her back in the house.

The summer holidays had just begun. Normally the whole family would have descended on the house and done the jolly, sporty, horsey things they invariably did when they spent time there. Alice was mad about horses. Paul and Giles not so much. To everyone's astonishment, after he left school

Paul had settled down and got a menial job in the futures department of a City merchant bank, starting in quite a humble capacity as a runner; but he had learned fast and was doing well. He was quick and agile and quite bright, and it seemed that soon he might start to deal and perhaps, eventually, he'd help to revive the family fortunes again.

Valerie went downstairs to make a cup of coffee, and then walked to the door to see if Alice had done as she'd asked. Yes, there was no sign of her in the paddock, and then she could see her making her way slowly round from the stables towards the house, her fair hair glistening in the sun.

The odd thing was that Giles, who had appeared so bright, so gifted, was the one who kept on changing his mind about his vocation. Paul, on the other hand, who had always been considered a bit dim and unreliable, now seemed so single-minded. Of course he had made a lot of valuable contacts at his expensive school (not public, but for the intellectually challenged sons of the wealthy and well connected) which had got him into the bank in the first place.

Maybe it was the example of his brother and father that had helped to give him a sense of direction. Giles had given up psychology, then law, and was now working at a winery near Adelaide in South Australia with the hope of making it a career.

Alice came into the kitchen and threw herself into a chair by the table, saying how tired she was and just how much she would love a cup of coffee.

'Coming up,' Valerie said and pushed a mug towards her. 'I could do with a bit of help in the house, darling.'

'Of course, Mum.' Alice glanced across at her mother as she seated herself opposite her. 'You look tired.'

'A bit tired,' Valerie acknowledged, pushing her hair back from her forehead. Alice thought her mother had been magnificent, stoical and stalwart, and had made the very best of a bad situation. But Alice knew that, beneath the sang-froid, the stiff upper lip, it had taken a lot out of her.

Apart from the trial itself, which wasn't quite as bad as they'd expected because Dad had pleaded guilty so it was short, the worst part in a way was discovering that Dad had a mistress and there was a half-brother, none of them had known anything about. Mum had been absolutely amazing about that.

'How are you *really* feeling, Mum?' Alice insisted. 'I think you bottle it all up.'

Valerie sat opposite her daughter, drew her mug of coffee towards her, suddenly, completely unexpectedly, feeling too overcome by emotion to trust herself to speak. Darling Alice. She was such a comfort, a caring, helpful companion despite her youth. A real little trouper. Yet Valerie had been brought up not to show feelings, except those of pleasure or satisfaction, never grief or, horror of horrors, despair. These virtues, if they could be called virtues, and in another era they had been, were inculcated in her from a young age, from the nursery and a series of strict, disciplined, nannies; through her girls' boarding school with its thick serge uniforms and grey felt hats, its motto of '*Labor omnia vincit* – work conquers all', and is certainly better than making an ass of yourself in public, it seemed to imply.

In its philosophy, its emphasis on hard work and games, it aped the better known public schools for boys. Emotions were to be firmly hidden, kept under control.

In many ways Valerie knew now, too late, that this had been responsible for the way she and Ed conducted their marriage. She was so awkward about sex that he had turned to someone else for pleasure. Yet when they were engaged she had found it all rather thrilling and exciting, perhaps because it was dangerous and, by implication, forbidden. After marriage and especially after children, all the pleasure went, and it became a duty.

Then there was their inability to talk, to confide in each

other, and Ed had kept all his terrible problems from her because he felt she would not understand, would disapprove.

At that moment another awful thing happened: tears began to roll down her cheeks and, as astonished as her mother, Alice urgently whispered: 'Mum?'

'Pretty terrible,' Valerie said at last, hastily producing a handkerchief and wiping her eyes. 'I feel pretty terrible really, darling.'

'Oh, *Mum,*' Alice swiftly rounded the table and flung both arms around her mother, pressing her cheek close to hers. This was a mother she didn't know, but nevertheless was glad to see. This was a mother with the raw, human emotions of everyone else, not someone whom nothing ever seemed to move very much. For instance, it was very seldom that they hugged, or touched as closely as they were now.

'Oh, Mum, have a good cry, let it all hang out.'

'You're such an angel.' Valerie put her arms more closely round her daughter's body and pressed it to hers. It was so warm, vibrant and alive; so comforting. 'I was always brought up, you know, darling, to hold things back, to be in control. It was considered a weakness to cry or show emotion. I felt when it all came out about Daddy . . . and Mary, and the boy, my whole world had collapsed. But all I knew how to do, had been taught to do, was to carry on as though nothing had happened. Then Giles going to Australia so soon after the trial . . .'

'Because he thought you were alright.' Alice brushed the hair back from her mother's damp forehead. 'You *told* him you were perfectly alright.'

'I know. I *was* alright. I am alright, but sometimes I think, darling, it doesn't do to be too strong, keep things back. People value your weaknesses. I'm glad I didn't send you to boarding school. You're a kind, sweet, understanding girl, older than your years. You're a great support to me and I'm sure you will never make the mistakes in your marriage I made in mine. Now then.'

Valerie made a visible effort to pull herself together, reverting to type. She released Alice, blew her nose several times and drew a crumpled letter from the pocket of her jeans. 'Enough of this nonsense. Look, I heard from Giles today. He wants to go into the wine business seriously.'

'That means he'll stay in Australia.'

'I suppose so.' Valerie pushed her untidy mop of hair away from her face again. 'Maybe it's just as well. Start a new life. I mean it's not the end of the world, though it does seem so far away.'

Alice reached for the letter and opened it. 'Does he say anything about Emma?'

'Emma *loves* it. She likes the wine business too, the people they're staying with, and she seems like a new person.'

Alice swiftly scanned the airmail letter and nodded, tossing it back to her mother. 'I always liked Emma.'

Valerie seemed to agree. 'Emma was the last person I thought would go off the rails.' She stuffed the letter back in her pocket. 'She seemed so sensible, not like her mother who was an hysteric. So detached.'

'Maybe that's why she went off the rails.' Alice assumed an expression of wisdom that made her look older than her years.

'You mean it was because of her parents?'

'Probably.'

Valerie sniffed. 'Emma and Nick were certainly *most* unfortunate in their parents. They simply had no breeding, no manners. I liked Nick too, frankly, but this whole ghastly business would never have happened if Andreas had had the decency to talk to Daddy.' She paused and sighed deeply. 'Or if he, Daddy, that is, had talked to *me*. I could have gone to Grandpa, who I'm sure would have helped, not only with money but with good advice. What Daddy did was stupid, not criminal. He never meant to steal, but to pay it all back. As if a person like him would *steal*! But I blame myself that he felt he couldn't talk to me. He must have suffered such agonies, poor lamb, deeply in debt, that accursed woman round his neck sponging off him.'

'Oh, Mum, you *are* a brick.' Impulsively Alice reached out and seized hold of her hand. 'I do so love you.'

'Don't be *silly*, darling,' Valerie said in a wobbly voice, taking a hankie from her pocket and blowing her nose really hard. 'We Harveys must stick together. Show a united front. Noblesse oblige, and all that, you know.'

Edmund leaned on his spade, got out a large handkerchief from his pocket and mopped his brow. Digging was hard work but it was very satisfying. Curious that, because he had never taken much interest in gardening before; woman's work he called it, and now he was in charge of the open prison's kitchen garden. Winter was coming on and he was preparing the ground for the planting of next year's crop of potatoes.

He was very into gardening catalogues, and the tomatoes he'd produced in the summer had been judged by his fellow inmates, some of whom had been there for years, as the very best.

In so far as he could say he was happy, Edmund *was* happy, perhaps really happy for the first time, or one of the few times, in his life.

There was this glorious freedom, a complete absence of responsibility. He had to make no decisions for himself or anyone else except what seed potatoes to plant, and what fertiliser to use. He was strongly in favour of organic gardening, so that was the difficult choice: how to produce spuds that were free from pests without the use of pesticides? Ah, that was the question. But there was no sweating and no sleepless nights about that, as had been the case in the bad old days. He slept like a baby, dreaming about seed potatoes and ripe plum tomatoes, organic fertilisers, mulch and manure.

Everything was ritualised from morning until he retired to bed at night to sleep the sleep of the just. No decisions. No worry. No fevered schemes for robbing Peter to pay Paul. No demanding mistress with ideas far above her station. No fear of discovery, because now all was out in the open. It was wonderful. He'd gained half a stone in weight.

Edmund tucked his handkerchief back in his pocket and bent his back over the spade thinking of the lucky break that had landed him here. At the time he hadn't called it luck. It had seemed like disaster, the end of the world.

But then the unexpected happened. He found he could talk to his wife, unburden himself, tell her about Mary, about Adam, about all the hideous deceit of the years gone by; the increasing demands, growing financial difficulties, the fall in property prices, the decline in the market. And while Val had been wonderful he'd had nothing but trouble from Mary who, of course in her awful lower-middle class way, was deeply ashamed of him. He was terribly fond of Adam, dear little boy, but there was now no question of him paying private school fees. So sucks to you, greedy Mary!

It was beginning to get dark and Edmund decided to finish his digging. A fellow inmate passed and he waved to him, had a word. It was really like being at school again, he thought, looking towards the large ivy-clad country house as, spade over his shoulder, he made his way through the fields and across smooth lawns, past well-filled herbaceous borders, round the back to the prisoners' entrance. Ah well, one couldn't have everything. The main entrance was reserved for people who were not detained at the pleasure of Her Majesty.

There was a stimulating atmosphere about the place with lots of good conversation. Doubtless, over the time he'd be here he'd make a number of valuable contacts for the future, though whether he'd be allowed to practise again was another matter. Doubtful. Perhaps he could act as a consultant? Consultancies were highly profitable. You didn't actually have to know much except your way about and, of course, the right people.

Edmund shook his head thoughtfully, went into the cloakroom and began removing his muddy boots, shaking out the soil and putting on clean socks. He would go upstairs and have a shower and then go to the common room for a jaw with fellow guests of the Queen.

If you looked carefully you found a lot of kindred spirits in an open prison. There were, inevitably, thick-necked brutes and hardened felons such as he'd encountered in Wormwood Scrubs. After all, in a democracy you had to give everyone an equal chance; you couldn't just have an open prison for gentlemen, nice as that would be. But it was quite easy to make one's way around the riffraff, because they enjoyed one another's company just as much as he did people of his own kind.

No, here, one also found lawyers, accountants – quite a lot of these – income tax inspectors, barristers, of course, plenty of ex-senior policemen, a few doctors, a surprising number of teachers, even a former High Court judge who had been at school with his uncle.

People of one's own kind. People like him.

In a way, when the time came, Edmund Harvey thought, he would be sorry to leave this sanctuary and return to the battles that, inevitably, he'd find in the real world.

There would be the struggle for existence, trying to make a living, patching up his marriage, dealing with Mary, facing old friends. Naturally he'd already resigned from the club. That club, the source of so much trouble.

Dear, oh dear, Edmund thought, shaking his head as he made his way along the corridor. Better not even to think about what lay ahead, but make the best of the present good times. And who'd have thought he, a man of the law, would ever say that about prison?

As for Laura Chase, she too was a survivor, discovering things about herself in the past few years every bit as profound as had someone she'd never known, never met, Edmund Harvey.

She'd read that he'd been sent to prison, but not about the involvement of Andreas Constantine, because the trial was a short affair, mostly ignored by the press.

She didn't write to Giles. 'Sorry your dad was sent to prison.' Somehow it sounded false. Also, she'd been quite glad. What she knew of Mr Harvey she hadn't liked. It seemed such a long time ago, and it was.

She had worked very hard at Oxford and gratified her tutor with a 2:1. But getting a job had been less easy. Even Oxbridge graduates were not wanted, and she'd had little alternative but to work at Mr Boothroyd's while endlessly applying for jobs.

Finally, persistence paid off. She was about to start as a trainee reporter on a local newspaper. She'd been one of three successful applicants out of over a thousand. The bottom rung of the ladder, but a ladder nevertheless.

It was very sad to say goodbye to Mr Boothroyd. He'd become like a second father, and the last day had been almost painful. He was a good and kind man, and in a way she loved him like she now loved her dad, although there was a distance between them and always would be. She would never, for instance, have dreamt of using his Christian name, Cecil, even in these days of easy familiarity.

There was something old worldly about Cecil Boothroyd, just as there was about his shop, and Laura, who in many ways was old worldly too, preferred it like that.

She took a long time getting her coat, her bag, the carrier

with the usual provisions for the evening meal. Early in the day she'd taken flowers to Mrs Boothroyd who was going into hospital in the near future for a hysterectomy and spent a great deal of time resting.

Laura never thought of Mrs Boothroyd as a second mother. In fact, she scarcely ever saw her and she sometimes wondered if she was not, in fact, jealous of Laura's relationship with her husband. It was absurd, of course, but there was always a funny air, a distance about Mrs Boothroyd that was hard to fathom. And as Laura handed her the flowers, had she perhaps discerned a gleam of pleasure, of relief in Mrs Boothroyd's eyes?

Finally it was time to go. Mr Boothroyd, in paying her her wages had added a generous sum of money, two hundred pounds, to help her, he told her, through the first few weeks until she drew her pay. She'd almost kissed him, but no, it would not do, even if there was no Mrs Boothroyd nursing her diseased womb upstairs. Besides, it would have embarrassed Mr Boothroyd who was not a demonstrative man.

Mr Boothroyd came to the door to see her off, held out his hand and shook hers.

'This isn't goodbye, Laura.'

'Of course not, Mr Boothroyd. Who knows, I might be back?'

Mr Boothroyd smiled and shook his head.

'No, young woman, I think you're on the up and up. But good luck.'

'Maybe I'll come and help out on my days off?'

'That would be great.'

Now that she was leaving, she didn't really want to go. The great, frantic, outside world of newspapers seemed a frightening place.

Laura had always liked writing. She had won an essay prize at school and her name was on a scroll in the school hall. 'The Deirdre Simpson Essay Prize' it was called, though everyone had long forgotten who Deirdre Simpson was. But writing an essay with loads of time in which to do it was very different from the succinct hack work required by a daily newspaper.

It was very cold, mid-winter. The wind blew in from the Pennines and people scurried, heads bent, along the street, as Laura, her head also down, hurried home.

Inside the house her father was waiting for her, looking expectantly towards the door, his face lighting up as she came in. Some days he never left his room, but others he came down and lit a fire and made tea for her. His isolation and dependence on his daughter had revealed a kindness neither he nor she knew he possessed.

Laura, who had once despised him, now loved her dad. They lived alone, her brothers having left home. They hardly saw Gary, or his wife and baby, who now lived in another town. Gordon hadn't made it to Academe, but had joined the regular army instead and was stationed somewhere abroad.

Occasionally Laura went to see her mother who still lived with her sister, a council flat having not yet materialised. They never visited her or her father, who thus far was entirely dependent on Laura.

Her father was excited about her job, which was starting the next day, but he was fearful too.

'I'm sure one of these days you'll leave me, love,' he said over tea, which they had sitting close to the fire. One of these days too, when Laura was a wealthy, successful journalist she told herself, she'd have central heating installed.

She smiled at her father and spread butter on her cake. Butter on a piece of fruitcake was a lovely indulgence.

'If I go, I'll take you with me, Dad.'

'Promise.'

'Promise.'

'Excited, Laura?'

She popped the piece of cake into her mouth.

'I'm excited,' she said, 'and a bit scared.'

She'd done a computer course, she'd done shorthand. She was well prepared. She didn't know why she was scared, but she was.

Little Laura going out into the big world. Well, not so little, she was speaking figuratively but, really, all she had behind her was her Oxford degree and her father, no rich powerful friends like Giles and Nick.

After tea, she washed up and they sat watching television. This was the ritual every night. She hardly ever went out and she had few friends. Her time was given to her father, and her dreams. She daydreamed a great deal.

But all this would change. Inevitably, it would change. She was ambitious and she would climb. She would go to London, maybe abroad; but not while her father was alive. The doctor had told her in confidence that he didn't think he'd last long. One more heart attack . . .

She kissed him fondly after taking his milk to him in bed, chatting for a while before saying good night.

Laura went to her room and, for a long time, remained standing by the window looking out on the sleeping city: ugly, ramshackle, a huge mixed conurbation yet exciting too – the place of her birth.

She knew for sure that however far she travelled from Salford, Manchester, she would always retain her regional accent, her forthright, uncompromising manner, and be at one with the people among whom she'd been born. She would always return home again, back to her roots.

But nothing ventured, nothing gained.

Then her thoughts went back, as they often did, to Nick and Giles. To her brief ecstatic love affair with one, her travels and not so ecstatic love affair with the other.

The trouble was that she had never really fitted in with either, with their manners, their outlook, their lifestyle or their folks.

Look at the way Edmund Harvey had treated her father; thrown him out into the street like a tramp. No respect, no dignity for the father of a girl they also doubtless thought of as a tramp. She'd only met Giles's mother at the airport on their return from Australia. She'd fallen over herself to be nice to Laura in a patronising kind of way. But how relieved she must have been when she knew the romance was over.

Despite what was said about modern times, democracy, equality, the rest, there was still class distinction about, and it mattered. You spoke differently, you behaved differently, you held your knife differently, your values and expectations were different. If you wanted to move up to the middle classes from the working class, you had to unlearn everything you already knew.

Some people said that you were born into a class, just as you inherited your genes. It was not something you could acquire.

But others said that you could change class if you were rich enough. Or maybe some people would say she had changed it by being educated, having an Oxford degree and aspiring to a profession like journalism.

Class mattered with the Constantines. They had looked down on her and she was aware of it. Never mind that the grandfather had been a Greek peasant; huge wealth had changed all that. The recollection of that overpowering visit to the house in St John's Wood still made her uncomfortable: the exquisite furnishings, the trappings of power, the high security with little screens and cameras all over the house showing you this section and that, the butler and maid, the Rolls in the garage. And the yacht . . . the yacht she had never seen and now never would.

Sometimes she thought she would write to Nick, tell him about her change of fortune. But then she knew she wouldn't. Nick and Giles were strangers to her now, alien. There were some barriers that could never be overcome.

Or was it, simply, that you moved on?

Laura knew then that, for the rest of her life, somewhere beneath the surface, no matter what happened to her, however much she changed or altered her views, she would be imprinted with the memory of that strange encounter in her youth with the children of the rich.

NICOLA THORNE

WORLDS APART

This book is for
my dear friend Jane Biran
who not only said it was high time
she had another of my novels
dedicated to her,
but suggested the theme.
So she deserves it.

But prisoners though we all were in a world apart, we were somehow conscious of the passage of winter into spring and spring into summer.

From *Memories* (Chapter Ten) by Frances Partridge

CONTENTS

PART 1

A Full and Useful Life

CHAPTER 1

Anna got tired of the joke: 'Mrs Livingstone, I presume?' She would react to it with the sort of polite, world-weary smile that she reserved for difficult clients, arrogant barristers, or patronising magistrates.

'Mrs Livingstone, I presume?' echoed down the years.

Anna reached across the desk, shook her client by the hand, and offered her a seat. Outside the window, the traffic at the busy road intersection rushed by, almost drowning her opening words.

The woman on the other side was pale-faced, thin, swamped by a heavy coat several sizes too big. Her spindly legs were encased in black leggings, and she wore a heavy pair of Doc Martens boots. Her spiky hair, sticking out like petrified electric shock waves, was a hectic shade of purple. She had rings on every finger and one through her nose. She was perhaps about thirty. Her name was Joyce Egan.

'I bet people say that to you all the time?' She smiled a cheeky, challenging kind of smile, as though pleased with her own cleverness.

'You could say that.' Anna glanced down at her notes. 'Now, what can I do for you?'

She joined her hands on the top of the desk and, for the umpteenth time that day, assumed the helpful air, the encouraging smile which she hoped would get her clients to like her, confide in her and, above all, trust her.

'It's like this,' Joyce began, crossing and uncrossing her legs.

Suddenly she seemed more vulnerable than self-confident.

Her story was about a landlord who had attempted to cut off the water and electricity, dumped rubbish on the stairs outside the back door, shoved excreta through the letterbox, anything to get her to leave. But, of course, she had nowhere to go. The kids were ill all the time, and her partner didn't have a job. He was on invalidity benefit, having served with the army in the Falklands. He was not, however, the father of Joyce's children.

But, still, there was the question of obvious harassment. Anna scribbled a note.

She had heard this tale so many times before it would be easy to be cynical about it. In a way people got themselves into their own messes and relied on others to get them out. But if you took that attitude you would condemn two thirds, if not more, of the human race.

There was still a lot Anna could do. The landlord was clearly acting illegally. He could be taken to court, but it would take time. The best thing was to refer her to the housing authority, the social services, and let the full panoply of bureaucratic welfare, now grinding rustily along on a treadmill, take control.

She explained to Joyce, whom she liked, her rights in a clear, firm voice, emphasising each point with a nod of her head. Joyce, who had at one time seemed on the point of tears, cheered visibly, reached over and shook Anna's hand warmly, stuffing into her vast pockets the sheaf of papers she'd given her.

Anna saw her to the door, looked out into the corridor which was empty. The front door was locked and the staff had gone home.

'Sorry to have kept you.' Joyce turned with a grateful smile as Anna followed her to let her into the street.

'No trouble at all,' Anna assured her. 'Let me know what happens.'

She drew back the bolt, unlocked the door and stood on the steps as Joyce blended into the flotsam and jetsam of mixed nationalities, people of all ages, shapes, colours and sizes, from all walks of life who swirled along the pavement round the corner from the tube station.

It was about seven o'clock on a summer evening and the heat rose from the stale city street, blending with the fumes of petrol and the noise of traffic.

Anna was very tired. She had come straight to the Law Centre from her office in Wigmore Street, pausing only to drink a plastic beaker of tea thrust into her hand by one of the volunteers who followed her to the empty office with a sheaf of files to brief her about the cases she was to see.

Twice a week, sometimes three if they were unusually busy, she helped out at the Law Centre set up by a bunch of lawyers, supporters of the Labour Party, who gave their services free. Usually they closed at about nine, but on this particular evening, due to staff shortages, they closed the door at seven. Anna had already telephoned her husband Peter to say she would be late, because she had at least another half-hour making notes on the files to be left ready for the staff when they arrived the following day.

Anna opened a window that gave on to a narrow, airless cobbled passage that bisected the warren of streets. Its size and location were redolent of its nineteenth century origins, maybe earlier. Halfway up the wall of the building opposite were a door and a derrick, indicating that it had once been a warehouse or a storage area for grain. Recently it had been turned into a trendy art gallery, part of the transformation of Camden Town into the radical chic of the late nineteen eighties. At weekends, people flocked to the street markets, the canalside cafés, fashionable bistros and Greek restaurants offering amazing value for money.

Anna returned to her desk and drew the top file towards her, brow puckered, as she momentarily attempted to recall the first of the many clients she had seen in her two hours at the centre. Approximately five an hour, possibly a little longer than the average patient was allowed in an NHS surgery.

The law was a kind of surgery too (in fact these sessions were called surgeries): a catharsis, a laying open of wounds, broken bodies and minds.

Forty minutes later she made her final note about Joyce, whom she'd rather taken to, put the files neatly together with a scribbled note on top for Mandy who ran the centre and, taking the jacket of her lightweight suit from the back of the chair slipped it on, grabbed her bag and briefcase, made her way to the outside door, locked it carefully behind her, and slipped the key back through the letterbox.

Then she wove her way cautiously through the stationary traffic of Camden High Street and strolled up Parkway towards the park where she'd left her car.

Inside the house all was quiet, except for the distant murmur of the television.

A quarter to nine. Anna felt guilty as she swiftly deposited her bag and briefcase in the hall, and stole towards the lounge, the door of which was ajar.

Peter, slumped in front of the TV, was fast asleep, long legs stretched before him, hands resting on his chest, head back, mouth slightly open.

Anna went over to the TV and was about to switch it off.

'Leave it, darling. It's nearly time for the news.'

Straightening up she smiled. 'I thought you were asleep.'

'I nodded off. Late again, Anna.'

'Sorry, darling.' She crouched at his feet. 'It was my night at the Law Centre.'

'Why don't you give it up?' His hand affectionately ruffled her hair.

'Are you crazy?'

'Yes,' deep sigh, 'I suppose I am.'

'And you're not eating enough.' He looked at her critically. 'I'm not the first person to notice you're too thin. Fiona said just the same thing yesterday when you dashed out before breakfast.'

'Well that's quite deliberate.' Anna placed her hands neatly on either side of her waist, breathed in deeply. 'I did actually feel I was putting on weight. All this sitting around.'

'Well, now it's the opposite. Haven't eaten tonight, I suppose?'

'I'll get a sandwich.' She looked at her watch. 'Are the children in?'

'Fiona's in her room. Guy had cricket practice.'

Once a week Guy went to the nets at Lords. This year Fiona had GCSEs.

The signal for the nine o'clock news came on, and Peter leaned forward.

'Turn it up, Anna.'

She waited to see the headlines and then, returning to the hall, took up her bag and jacket and went upstairs to her bedroom, passing Fiona's shut door on the way. She paused, momentarily seemed to steel herself, and then tapped firmly on the door.

No sound.

She braced her shoulders, tapped again, then almost simultaneously turned the door handle.

The room was empty, desperately untidy with clothes scattered on the floor, a pile of books flung on the unmade bed, and papers thrown on the desk, upon which was a light, still turned on as though she'd left in a hurry.

Well, nothing unusual about that.

Anna knew better than to try and tidy Fiona's room. She would be accused of interfering if she did, so she left it as she'd found it, closed the door firmly on the mess, and made her way up the short flight of stairs to the large back bedroom she shared with Peter, which overlooked the garden.

Here at least was peace and tranquillity. She even seemed to breathe more easily.

She switched on the small TV to get the rest of the news as she changed from her work clothes into a track suit and slippers.

As the weather forecast came on she went downstairs again and into the kitchen, which was also untidy with dishes on the draining board and, something that always irritated her, the door of the fridge left half-open.

She closed it with an exasperated sigh and, as she turned, she saw Peter lounging in the doorway, hands in his trouser pockets.

'I meant to clear up before you got home.' He sounded apologetic. 'I know how it irritates you.'

'Why should you? Let they or, I suppose to be truthful as well as accurate, I should say "she" who made the mess clear it up.'

'Fiona is busy working.' A defensive note came into his voice. 'She went straight up to her room.'

Anna got salami from the fridge and put two slices of bread into the toaster. 'Well, she isn't there now.'

'Fiona's not upstairs?'

'Nope.'

'She might have told me she was going out.'

Anna said nothing, plugged in the kettle to make a mug of instant coffee.

Watched by Peter, she put the salami between the slices of toast and placed mug and plate on a tray. 'Anything interesting on the news?'

Peter shrugged and followed her into the lounge, and as she munched and sipped her coffee he poured a whisky from a decanter on the table.

'I'm dreadfully worried about Fiona.' He sat opposite her, hands clutching his glass. 'Not only the lack of commitment to her work, but the company she keeps.'

Anna dreaded what was coming next. All her fault, as she had opposed sending the children to private schools and wanted them educated by the state in accordance with her socialist principles, even though they were not her children but Peter's by his first marriage.

'She could have met those sort of people anywhere. This is the Metropolis. A private education doesn't mean you only meet the right people. Not in London, not out of it either if we are to believe what we read in the papers and see on TV. Don't blame me.'

'I'm not blaming you, Anna, you know that. I'm just saying that if we knew then what we know now we might have acted differently.'

'I tell you I don't think it would have made any difference.'

'And Guy should be home from cricket practice.' Peter's tone was querulous as he looked at his watch. 'It's nearly ten. It finishes at eight, eight-thirty.'

Peter used to insist on picking Guy up, but now that he was nearly fifteen he resented being treated like a baby.

Guy and Fiona went to the large comprehensive school nearby, and although they had different sets of friends they led similar lifestyles, except that Guy had a deep love of all forms of sport, especially cricket, while Fiona's main object in life seemed to be to have a good time.

Another restless, maybe sleepless night, was in the offing. Anna yawned, suddenly aware that she was dead tired.

'You go to bed. I'll stay up,' Peter said.

'You've got to work too.'

'Yes, but they are my children . . .' He stopped, realising too late the gaffe.

Without a word Anna went into the kitchen, and with her usual speed and thoroughness put her dishes, along with those stacked on the draining board, into the dishwasher. It was such an easy thing to do as she kept on telling the children;

Peter was also an offender. It just took a few seconds, and look at the difference it made.

She wiped down the draining board, the kitchen table and work surfaces, set the dishwasher, put out the lights and went upstairs without looking into the lounge from whence came the sound of the ten o'clock news.

She passed Fiona's room, resisting for the umpteenth time the urge to go in and tidy it, past Guy's where the condition would be the same: unwashed socks and pants in a corner, dirty towels, sports gear all over the place.

She shut the door of her bedroom, opened the window and leaned on the sill, for a moment breathing in the warm, fragrant stillness of the garden.

The house in Belsize Park was a large, three-storeyed building that Peter and his first wife, Nancy, had bought when they married. It was a comfortable family house, with a sizeable garden, close to Haverstock Hill, Swiss Cottage and to all the amenities.

Anna had felt no aversion to living in a dead woman's house, because by the time she and Peter married all trace of Nancy had evaporated.

Actually she loved the house; its lived-in feel, its homeliness. When the children were small, bikes, balls, cricket bats and tennis racquets piled inside. The carpets were now rather shabby, and the whole place could do not only with redecoration, but with refurnishing as well.

The garden backed on to another garden, the huge trees now in leaf, and except for the sound of distant traffic, the red glow of the lights of London in the sky, one could almost have imagined oneself in the country. A gentle breeze fanned her face.

She closed the window, drew the curtains and began slowly to undress. Thoughtful. Somewhere out there were Guy and Fiona, and somewhere, perhaps, not very far away, staring through windows or prowling restlessly about were anxious parents like Peter and herself, wondering where their offspring were, what they were up to.

She was anxious about the children, but not as painfully anxious as Peter – maybe because the blood bond was lacking. Yet when they were small, she'd felt for them as though they were her own.

Eighteen months separated them: they were two and three when their mother died, four and five when she married Peter, knowing quite well what lay in store.

Anna had been twenty-three when she met Peter at the home of Claude Rigby, the then senior partner, who was giving a dinner party to celebrate the completion of her Articles, her emergence as a fully qualified solicitor. Peter, whose wife had just died, was a friend of the Rigby family.

She remembered how sorry she'd felt for him, how hard and successfully he had tried to conceal his grief. He was a tall, distinguished looking, attractive 'older' man, but she wouldn't have dreamt of taking it any further. She was studious, a little naive, still sexually immature and unsure of herself. Besides, in the circumstances, it had never crossed her mind.

Six months later they met again when Claude Rigby, who was something of a socialite, took a crowd of people to Henley for the Regatta, and again, Peter was among the guests. This time, there was no doubt that Peter and Anna were attracted to each other; there also was a meeting of minds. Gradually he introduced her into his life. She visited his home, met his children; they became lovers.

When she married him eighteen months later she knew exactly what she was doing. She loved Peter and she loved his children, even though children as such had never figured very high on her list of priorities. She was willing, temporarily, to abandon her career and devote herself to them; the archetypal female sacrificing her ambition for the sake of husband, home and children.

They were adorable children. It would have been hard not to like them; tiny looking, intensely vulnerable, badly in need of a mother's care.

Loving Peter as she did, she also loved his children, had no jealousy of the woman who had borne them, and had died prematurely and painfully of cancer of the spine.

Somehow you wanted to love the children all the more because of that. Give them everything; maybe too much. Maybe spoil them.

She had a bath, got into bed, and so had begun to read when she heard voices raised in the hall two floors below. The shrill whining voice of Fiona protesting innocence, the harsh angry tones of Peter. The voices rose to a crescendo and then there was the sound of hurried footsteps bounding up the stairs, a door banging. Probably tears on the other side.

Anna knew better than to go and try and comfort her step-daughter. Anyway, the door would be locked.

Silence again in the house. She became drowsy and was putting down her book when there was another commotion. Guy. Guy and Peter at it again, as they always were. But Guy could shout louder than Peter and his voice had almost broken. He was tall, well-built, mature for his age. If only he would stick to athletics and not worry his father so.

Everyone said they were normal children, that all teenagers were like that. It was not all that long ago that she'd been a teenager herself, but she was an only child with a single, working mother who had not had much time or patience for unruly offspring. Besides Anna seemed to have been born conscientious, ambitious and anxious to succeed. Clever at school, good at games, always occupied, with lots to do. Painfully aware that her gentle, self-effacing mother, lacking the educational opportunities Anna had had, had been abandoned by her husband and left to raise Anna on her own. They'd lived in a suburb of Leeds and there was no way you could compare it, even then, to life in the Metropolis, though in the years since she'd entered adulthood the suburb had developed adolescent problems and a drug culture of its own.

The voices downstairs sank to murmurs and then stopped, and Anna guessed they had gone into the kitchen. Unlike rows with Fiona, which ended in explosions and tears, with Guy they tended to simmer down. Guy, perpetually hungry, always went in search of food.

Anna left the light on on Peter's side of the bed, put out her own, and tried to compose herself for sleep. She was desperately tired, overtired, and she had to be at the magistrates' court in the morning to try and prevent a teenager from being sent to a youth detention centre. A teenager from a bad home with lots of problems. Never the chances that Guy and Fiona had.

The door opened and Peter crept in. Anna remained with her eyes closed not wanting to talk; tried to make her breathing regular, controlled. Finally she rolled on her back, head propped on the pillows, and gazed across at him, taking in his dejection, his utter weariness.

'I'm so sorry,' she said, stretching out a hand.

'And I'm sorry.' He went over to the bed, unbuttoning his shirt, and flopped by her side. 'I'm sorry about what I said . . .'

'It's true.' She shrugged. 'They are your children.'

'But I know you love them, care for them, worry about them as much as I do.'

Anna wasn't sure about that, but knew how hurt Peter would be if she said so. She knew she didn't have quite the agony, the almost visceral feelings of pain that he, and other parents had. Somehow although she cared, cared deeply and always had, she was detached. She knew that whatever happened to Fiona or Guy affected Peter in a much more profound way than her.

But she had to be the one to remain balanced, to keep sane. No use the pair of them going to pieces every time the children offended or did something they shouldn't, which was almost every day.

She knew that if she felt as Peter felt, her career would be adversely affected, her life.

Despite Anna's eloquent pleading, the magistrates, in their wisdom, decided to send her client to a youth detention centre for two years. They felt it was in his best interests. Anna knew that Mrs Bridges, the chairman of the magistrates, was a caring, compassionate woman, and she and her fellow magistrates would have taken time to consider the matter and reach a conclusion that they believed was just and fair.

But was it? Anna got together her papers and went into the lobby to confer with her client's probation officer, before going down to see the young man about to be taken into custody.

He was only sixteen, and none of his family had been present. He was a pale, pimply, unprepossessing yet infinitely pathetic youth, who clearly no one loved. The sort of person disadvantaged from the start, who had absolutely no chance in life, none at all; who flourished in the seed-bed of petty crime, and whose life henceforth could be predicted with utmost certainty. His time at the youth detention centre almost certainly would lead to more serious crime, and at some stage in his life incarceration, maybe for years, in prison.

The social worker grinned at her sympathetically. 'You did your best, Mrs Livingstone. Maybe if his parents had been here, or someone to give him a hand . . . I think Mrs Bridges thought so too.'

'Maybe.' Anna didn't like to give up on a client.

She felt depressed and anxious, not only on behalf of the young man. She'd had a bad night and was awake well before the alarm. As usual she had taken Peter a cup of tea in bed, called the children, and left the house probably before anyone was fully awake.

She went down to the cells for a final word with her client,

Joe. He looked more wan, more hopeless than he had in the dock, and she resisted the urge to put an arm round his shoulders and give him a comforting hug. How long ago was it, she wondered, since anyone had done that?

'Joe,' she said sitting opposite him, 'I'm very sorry you got done in. I know the magistrates thought it was in your best interest.'

'Sod the magistrate,' Joe mumbled, wiping his nose on the sleeve of his T-shirt.

'Well I suppose you think that. Now, Joe, I'd like to contact your mother and try and persuade her to come and visit you. Could you let me have her address?'

Joe remained sullen, silent, staring at the surface of the hard wooden table between them.

'Dunno,' he said.

'You don't know where she lives?'

'Somewhere in the norf'.'

'The north of England?' Anna shook her head helplessly. 'The north of England is a big place.'

'I don't want to see my ma.'

'Don't you really?' She looked searchingly into his eyes. They were shifty, evasive. 'I think everyone wants to see their mother,' she continued softly, 'truthfully.'

'You don't know my mother . . .'

'And father? Brothers or sisters, Joe?'

Apparently there was an elder sister whom he sometimes saw. Anna would get her secretary to try and find her, have another word with the probation officer. She looked at her watch and stood up.

'Joe . . . I am sorry.'

It seemed so inadequate to say 'take care' or 'good luck'. Hypocritical, too. Besides, there was this awful seemingly lack of interest in his fate on the part of Joe, as though he were swept along by a tide he had no means of controlling.

She went back to the lobby to seek out his probation officer but she had vanished. Too many clients on her mind to concentrate on Joe.

Joe, now swept up in the impersonal, majestic, inexorable processes of the law, was no longer the officer's problem.

Neither, strictly speaking, was he Anna's.

She had spent most of the morning in court waiting for the case to come up, and there was a heavy schedule of work back at the office. It was half past twelve, and she was reminded that she had had no breakfast. Nor had she had time for coffee. There was a pleasant snack bar up the road, and she would allow herself half an hour. If she hurried she would get a table before the place filled up.

Coffee and a toasted sandwich. She shook out the *Guardian*. Time to unwind. She became absorbed in the day's news.

'Mrs Livingstone, would you mind if I joined you?' She looked up to see Mrs Bridges, cup and plate balanced precariously in her hands, looking apologetically down at her. 'There doesn't seem to be any more room.'

'Of course.' Anna moved along the bench and put her newspaper aside.

'I expect I'm disturbing the only peaceful moment you're going to have all day?' Mrs Bridges' cultured tones sounded more apologetic than ever.

'That's perfectly alright.' Anna smiled.

'Actually I'm glad of a word with you,' Mrs Bridges put her cup and saucer and plate on the table, 'because I do know how you felt about that young man. But,' she sat down next to Anna and slipped her jacket round her shoulders, 'I really do think it was for the best you know. We were all in agreement.'

'I think it was a little severe for a first offence.'

'We had his best interests at heart. No parents. No support. Desperately sad, isn't it?'

Mrs Bridges – comfortable, well-off Mrs Bridges, whose husband was a distinguished ENT surgeon, doubtless with a lucrative private practice and whose children most likely went to private schools. They lived, probably, in a large house without mortgage, up the road in Hampstead. But who was Anna to judge? Comfortably off, a middle-class professional herself.

'Have you any children?' Mrs Bridges enquired, stirring brown sugar into her coffee.

'I've got two step-children, a boy and a girl.'

'Oh!' There was always the pause after she announced her relationship to the children. It was, she imagined, a bit like saying you were adopted and had never known your parents. Out of the ordinary. People didn't like to say 'why haven't you any of your own?' although, of course, they wanted to know. 'It's not quite the same then, is it?' Mrs Bridges stared at her brightly.

'What isn't the same?'

'Well I never know.' Mrs Bridges waved a hand in the air. 'I hope I'm not being tactless. I probably am.' She buried her face in her cup.

Anna said nothing, deciding to let her suffer.

'I've three children,' Mrs Bridges went on hurriedly. 'All flown the nest. One is a doctor like my husband, the girl is a nurse and my youngest son is still at university.'

'Mine are both still at school,' Anna said without volunteering where and, glancing at her watch, 'I really must fly. I have a conference at two.'

'Is it that late already?' Aghast, Mrs Bridges looked at her watch. 'And I said the court would resume . . .'

'No you've got plenty of time. I have to think of the traffic.'

'So nice to talk to you, Mrs Livingstone, and please don't think you failed that young man.' She sighed. 'Frankly I think he's a hopeless case.'

Anna sped down the hill fuming with indignation. It would be a very different kettle of fish if one of the Bridges' offspring had appeared in court. Not for the first time she thought about the injustice of middle class people sitting in judgment on those who, for lack of any precise or better description, would be considered their social and intellectual inferiors. Probably the same could be said about representing them too.

Yet somewhere in the middle, between the hapless Joe and the Bridges' children, were Fiona and Guy. Their mother had died; their professional father loved them, provided a good home for them and, eventually, a good surrogate mother.

And she had been a good mother. After she and Peter were married she gave up work for a time because his took him abroad a great deal. It was difficult getting to know someone else's children, growing to love them, wanting them to love you and trust you in return.

Halting outside the chemist at the bottom of the hill just before the magistrates' court, Anna, thinking of children, remembered something, ferreted frantically around in her bag, searched the side pockets, her wallet, and then heaved an exasperated sigh and muttered under her breath, 'damn!'

If only one didn't have to have prescriptions repeated for the oral contraceptive pill, life would be so much more simple. Then she hurried on towards her destination, through the doors of the courthouse.

Peter and Anna remained deeply physically in love, even after ten years and the trials, fairly recent, of the children growing towards adolescence. They had their rows, disagreements and moments of discord; but they shared a deep physical passion for each other that enabled them regularly to make the best of the brief time between going to bed and falling asleep. Somehow, no matter how tired, Anna was excited by Peter, his proximity, his touch. Willingly she made love, often she initiated it.

But tonight as Peter reached for her, she turned her face towards him and shook her head.

'Darling?' His brow puckered as he began tenderly to stroke her hair.

'I've forgotten my prescription for the Pill. I was due to start taking it again today.'

'Bugger the Pill,'Peter said, a hand continuing to stroke her hair, while the other began gently to fondle her breast.

Their lips met. His hand moved from her breast to her waist, further down. The desire for him was uncontrollable. Besides they were married, a couple together.

'It makes it more exciting like this,' he murmured, slipping into her with the easy familiarity of the practised lover. She folded her legs around his, locking him into her, linking her hands around his back, binding him indivisibly to her.

The excitement was intense, urgent. They thrashed about the bed like combatants, and afterwards they lay breathless, revelling in the kind of primitive joy that, although it was familiar, was also somehow new.

They joined sticky hands and looked at each other exultantly.

Maybe, their eyes seemed to say, unprotected sex occasionally was a good idea in a long, safe, happy marriage.

CHAPTER 2

The cottage in Dorset was part of Peter's past. It belonged to Peter, Fiona and Guy and their memories of Nancy, Peter's first wife, who had died at the age of thirty. She had lived in the house in London too, but somehow there wasn't the same association with Nancy that the cottage, where she died, possessed.

Although born in South Africa, she had no roots there and had lived in Dorset before her marriage to Peter. She had money of her own, and eventually bought the cottage in the Blackmore Vale where she used to take the children in the holidays and paint.

Nancy seemed to have been a beautiful, carefree woman, and although Anna was not considered conventionally beautiful, she had a natural élan and gaiety of spirit that made many people, who had known both women, say that in some ways, they resembled each other.

Like Nancy, Anna had ash blonde hair, blue eyes, well defined features, a hint of stubbornness about the chin. But here the resemblance ended. Nancy was considered elfin, petite whereas Anna was tall. Anna was athletic and liked to walk and swim, while Nancy had cosseted herself and had preferred to stay indoors, except when she painted her pretty rural scenes.

Because it was so far from London, the Dorset cottage was used mainly for holidays. It was really too far to travel just for weekends. This was just as well, because Anna was often busy, and the children, now that they were older, much preferred life in London to that in the country.

They had protested vigorously this time at being dragged away from their favourite haunts, if only for a relatively short time, but Peter put his foot down. He had taken a week off, so had Anna, just to be with them. Besides, they both wanted to encourage Fiona to get down to some serious studying as her exams were not far away.

Although a local woman came in regularly to air the cottage and make sure everything was functioning – no burst pipes in the winter – when the family arrived it always felt cold, deserted, almost neglected.

The garden was overgrown and untended, and Peter liked to don green wellies and do some serious digging. Then he and Anna toured the local garden centres and arrived home with a variety of plants and shrubs. By the time they left, the place was just about looking lived-in, and they were all sorry to depart until the next break, when they had to start all over again.

Fiona had arrived in a rebellious mood, but even she seemed to mellow under the influence of the peace, the calm, the beauty and, above all this year, the good weather. The village lay just under Bulbarrow, that great escarpment rising above the Blackmore Vale, giving spectacular, panoramic views for many miles around.

In many ways Little Halton was a picture postcard village, with a manor, a turreted church, two prosperous, well-stocked farms and a row of thatched cottages, of which theirs was one. It was at the end of the row, consequently it had a larger garden than the others, and also three bedrooms. Nancy had made a studio in the garden, and this was left as a sort of shrine to her. She had never enjoyed or really attempted any commercial success, regarding herself as an amateur painter. But her pretty, delicate canvases of flowers and rural scenes were still stacked against the wall, and the painting she was working on when she died was as she'd left it, on its easel.

The door of the studio was hardly ever unlocked or the room itself visited; but it remained as a memorial to Nancy who lay buried in the local churchyard under an elderberry tree.

The family left London on Friday at midday and were in Little Halton by five. They stopped for lunch at the service station on the M3, and again in Shaftesbury for petrol.

Mrs Hanson, the farmer's wife, who looked after the cottage, had left bread, potatoes and milk. The rest they'd bought. The fridge had been cleaned and switched on. The place was also clean and there was a large vase of flowers on the deal table in the kitchen, but still there was that slight air of must, of neglect, the feeling that windows should be flung wide and doors left open.

Peter immediately became transformed from a man of business and corporate affairs to a bluff, jolly countryman. Within minutes of arriving he was in his wellies and inspecting the garden, while Guy disappeared to look up his mate, Martin Hanson. Fiona and Anna were left with the woman's role of unpacking and preparing the evening meal, something which, surprisingly, Fiona seemed to like, though the atmosphere these days was always one of an armed truce.

Or perhaps it was only Anna who was aware of the tension in the cottage as if, instead of leaving their problems behind, they brought them with them. Maybe it was the close, enforced proximity that would last the week of the half term, and sometimes Anna felt that it was as though the shade of Nancy, though long dead, somehow remained to hover around them.

Or the simple explanation may have been that Anna, who worked so hard and for whom there were not enough hours in the day in which to accomplish everything, felt ill at ease with time on her hands.

By Sunday they had all settled in and established a routine.

The church bell rang in vain for them, because they never attended service. It was the kind of village where people kept to themselves. It was quite a distance from the nearest town, and houses had become so expensive that the local population had tended to move out. Therefore it was full of people like the Livingstones, who had second homes and went to the country to get away from busy lives. Thus they felt disinclined to socialise.

Some people – admirals, army officers and diplomats – had retired there, and they also kept themselves to themselves. No, it was not a friendly village, and the Livingstones rather liked it that way.

Fiona seemed to have decided that she was here to work, and she remained in her room attached to her Walkman, though Anna could never understand how the young continued to study while listening to their favourite pop music.

Guy, always a sociable boy, spent most of his time with his crony Martin, the farmer's son, who was keen on cricket, and they took over a field in which they endlessly bowled and batted to each other.

After they had settled in, Anna went up to thank Mrs Hanson at the farm and to buy some eggs. She was met in the strange reserved way the family seemed to have not only for her but for all newcomers. The Hansons were true Dorset people, and it was very easy to believe here that you came from a foreign land. Ted Hanson was a bluff, taciturn countryman, who actually seemed to harbour a feeling of resentment against all strangers, perhaps because he could see how they were encroaching on his land. Two of the Hansons' three daughters worked in Blandford Forum, seven miles away, and one was married and lived in Bournemouth.

Ted Hanson ran the farm virtually single-handed, which could explain much that he had to be angry about. He always seemed to Anna, who tried fruitlessly to communicate with him, an angry, overworked and resentful man.

'Mr Livingstone well?' Mrs Hanson enquired of Anna as she packed the eggs from her cool larder into cartons.

'He's fine. He's started on the garden.'

'And the children?' Mrs Hanson didn't look at Anna, but her tone of voice subtly changed.

'Oh, they're very well. Fiona has her GCSEs this summer, in a few weeks. She's working hard.' Anna tried to make her tone sound convincing.

'What does she want to do then?' Mrs Hanson finished packing the eggs and gave them to Anna who stacked them carefully in her basket.

'She's not sure. Is anyone these days?'

'Will she go back to school?'

'Oh, I suppose so.'

As they came out of the pantry and into the yard, they could see Guy and Martin practising their cricket in the far field.

'Sometimes I think Guy would like to be a farmer,' Anna said. 'He hasn't much inclination for intellectual work.'

'You don't have to be a fool to be a farmer,' Mrs Hanson said crisply, examining the notes in her hand with which Anna had paid for the eggs, and for her care of the cottage.

'Oh I don't mean *that* at all.' Anna was acutely embarrassed. 'Please don't think . . .'

Mrs Hanson gave her a frosty smile. 'Not that I don't think Ted hasn't made a lot of mistakes, and this so-called "agricultural policy" doesn't help us at all. In fact,' she paused as if considering whether or not she should continue, 'we'd like to get rid of the farm, I don't mind telling you, Mrs Livingstone. It's hard work. Our girls aren't interested, and our boy doesn't show much aptitude for it.'

Anna followed her gaze.

'What does Martin want to do?'

'I wish I knew. Always dissatisfied is Martin. Children can be a problem, can't they, Mrs Livingstone? But then,' she gave her a slightly patronising smile, 'as you never had any of your own . . .'

'Believe me, I know all about the problems of children,' Anna said firmly. 'I've looked after Fiona and Guy for ten years, watched them grow up.'

'Yes, but it's not as if they're your *own*, is it?'

'I feel they're my own.'

Irritated, Anna put her purse into the pocket of her jeans and picked up the basket. 'Thanks ever so much for these eggs and, by the way, thanks for all you do at the cottage. We do appreciate it.'

'It will be about ten years since Mrs Livingstone died,' Mrs Hanson seemed determined to pursue her point. 'The first Mrs Livingstone, I should say.'

'It's ten years since I married Peter,' Anna said politely. 'He was a widower for almost two years when I married him. So she must be dead twelve years.'

'Twelve.' Mrs Hanson sucked her lower lip. 'I wouldn't have thought it was as long as that. She was a lovely lady. Very clever. Always pleasant and smiling. Well thought of, but then in those days the village was more of a village, if you know what I mean.'

'More local people lived here?'

'Oh yes, and that cottage which she bought, so she could have some peace to paint, was the only one that belonged to a "foreigner", as we call them in Dorset. After that, house prices began to rise and the rot set in, though we all liked Nancy. Don't think we didn't.'

Nancy. So they did call her by her Christian name, a familiarity they never attempted with her, and yet she had been coming here year after year for ten years.

But she still felt a stranger.

'Bye for now, Mrs Hanson,' Anna raised her hand.

'How long will you be staying, Mrs Livingstone?'

'Just the week.'

'Sometimes Nancy stayed here all summer, with the children. But then of course you're so busy aren't you, being a professional woman?'

Anna smiled. 'I couldn't stay here all summer, even if I wanted to.'

'Don't suppose you could stand the quiet.'

'Don't suppose I could.'

Anna smiled again and turned, walking carefully along the muddy track that led from the farm to the road. Though the weather was good now, it had been very wet and the ground was still soft. She passed Guy and Martin in the field, but they were too busy to see her wave. Beneath her, the valley simmered in the sunshine, and fat lambs basked in the protective shadow cast by their mothers. It was calm, it was idyllic, it was peaceful, and yet inside, Anna did not feel at peace. She felt somehow that this was the calm before the storm; that eerie stillness that presages thunder.

There was also that nagging worry that had haunted her for two weeks: a most unusual occurrence as far as she was concerned. Meticulous in all things, it seemed that her mind governed her body, and she was also used to regular periods governed by the Pill, routine bleeding lasting a few days, usually beginning twenty-eight days to the dot at the end of her menstrual cycle. But, for the first time for many years, the expected hadn't happened, and then she had recalled those carefree nights, no not just one but several, when, having forgotten to renew her prescription for the Pill, she had missed it altogether.

The theory in her mind at the time was, she supposed, that it was so unlikely she would conceive after all these years anyway. Some doctors were of the opinion that a number of years on the Pill could make you sterile, at least temporarily, and she had been on it continuously for twelve years, and on and off before that as her sex life waxed and waned. She first had it prescribed as a first-year student. There was the fumbling and groping leading to uneasy sexual intercourse which made her visit the college doctor. There had been a period of abstinence, and then a more profound affair at twenty which broke off when the man in question, a graduate law student, returned to the States.

Yes, it was very silly. It was unlike her, too; careless. They made love so regularly that a few nights without wouldn't have been a great deprivation. And yet, it would. The more you had of a thing the more you wanted it, so that sex became like a drug, or alcohol, or food: one became addicted.

There had been that curiously uninhibited joy at making love without the Pill, illogical, but true. Peter had said it was like flirting with danger. Subconsciously, did he want her child? Subconsciously, too, did she?

When she got back to the cottage Peter was at work in the back garden, planting out some bedding plants they bought at a brief stop at a nursery on the way down.

He grinned at her, running his forearm across his forehead.

'Hard work, this gardening.'

'Better give it a break and have a beer.' Anna kicked off her wellies at the door before entering the kitchen. 'Eggs from Mrs Hanson. No pork.'

'Pity,' Peter grimaced. 'How are the Hansons?'

'As well as the Hansons ever are, I suppose.' Anna went into the cool larder and began unpacking the eggs from their cartons and placing them carefully in open trays. 'They don't give much away.'

'Country people are like that.'

'She did, however, seem fond of Nancy.'

'She mentioned Nancy?' Peter looked surprised, and getting a can of lager from the fridge, opened it and drank from it.

'She said Nancy was much loved in the village, and that I wouldn't really know about the problems of children as I hadn't any of my own.'

'You soon put her right on that!' Peter smiled, and raised the can again to his lips.

'I said I regarded Fiona and Guy as my own.'

'Quite right.' Peter put an arm round her waist and pressed her to him. 'You've been a marvellous mother to them. Better, I think, than Nancy would have been.'

'Really?' Now it was Anna's turn to express surprise.

'Oh, yes. I mean Nancy loved the kids but she didn't take her maternal duties very seriously. She came here for weeks on end to paint.'

'But the children came with her.'

'The Hansons' eldest daughter looked after them.'

'She didn't tell me that.'

'Darling, Nancy has been dead for twelve years. Why are we bringing this up?'

'That's what I keep asking myself.'

'There is nothing to be jealous about . . .'

'And I'm not, I promise.' Anna looked reassuringly at him, closing the door of the larder. 'It's just that, for some reason, the fact that the children are not biologically mine seems to have come up a lot recently.'

'Has it?'

'Well you mentioned it a few days ago. Before that no one seems to have given it a second thought.'

'And I apologised.'

'I know. Then the chairman of the magistrates, Mrs Bridges, mentioned it.'

'In what context?'

'Oh, I can't really remember.' Anna's hand brushed her brow. 'But I'd had rather a sad case at court of a young boy whose parents neglected him, put into custody for some petty theft. Mrs Bridges and I met by chance at lunch afterwards, and we talked about the case. She asked if I had any children and I said two step-children, and she trotted out with the business of it not being the same as having your own. I told her it was.'

Peter sat in the cane chair beside the kitchen table and stretched his legs. 'It is.'

'But *is* it? Is it, Peter? Am I as worried about them as you are, at a basic, visceral level?'

'Well, I think you are. You seem worried enough.'

'But you said . . .'

'I was a fool, and I apologised for it afterwards.'

'I know you did; but I *don't* think I worry quite as much as you do. I mean I can see in you a kind of exasperation which I don't feel. I love them, I'm anxious for them, I'm annoyed by them, made happy or sad by them, but not I think to the same extent as you.'

'That's because of the sort of person you are.' Peter put his lager on the table, got up and, walking over to her, stood behind her, placing his arms round her waist, hugging her tightly. 'You're a sensible, level-headed, unemotional woman. You wouldn't be able to do the kind of job you do if you weren't.'

'You really think I'd be like this if I were their biological mother?'

'I do.'

'You're saying I can't feel intensely?'

'No, I'm not.' He nuzzled her face with his mouth. 'I wish we were here alone, don't you?'

Oh yes she did. If they were here alone things would be very different.

Whenever they were away together, apart from the children, she didn't feel the same anxiety, the same feeling of tension, or the guilt.

That afternoon they went down to the coast, to the beach at Studland. Though it was still too cool for a bathe, some intrepid souls took to the sea, including Guy, who had brought Martin Hanson with him. The Livingstones had a hut on Studland beach which had been in the family since Nancy had first bought the cottage some sixteen or seventeen years before. They'd been down here at Easter but it had been too cold and wet to do much with the hut. This time, they spent the afternoon cleaning it out, and Peter did a bit of banging and resolved to come and start painting if he could accomplish all he had to do in the garden.

'I could do with two weeks here or even a month,' he added, and looked as though he would enjoy it.

'Maybe you're really a countryman at heart?' Anna was brewing tea on a butane gas stove. Fiona lay on her tummy on the beach, her Walkman clamped over her ears, letting the sand run through her fingers. Her feet rose up and down in time with the music.

'Do you know I believe I am. Let's retire.'

'Chance would be a fine thing. We couldn't afford it.'

'Besides, you wouldn't want to.' Fiona who, despite the drumming in her ears, missed nothing, rolled over on her back and, hands over her eyes, squinted at Anna. 'Would you?'

'I don't expect so. Besides,' she paused in the act of pouring tea into mugs, 'I would never have the time. By the way, I've been asked to stand for the Council.'

The lack of an immediate reaction from Peter and Fiona was highlighted by the sounds of people playing on the shore, calling to one another, by the breaking of the waves, and the cries of gulls.

'What Council?' Peter, standing on a ladder, paused in the act of battening down the roof, and asked abruptly.

'Our local Council.'

'You're joking!' Hammer in hand, Peter jumped down on to the sand.

'I'm not.' With a tense expression, Anna continued her pouring. Fiona's gaze never wavered.

'Who asked you?'

'Jimmy Wharton of the League of Labour Lawyers, among others. Several people have asked me.'

'You're sure to get on as a leftie,' Fiona said.

'I thought you were a leftie yourself?' Anna glanced at her sideways.

'I am. I didn't mean it nastily.'

'Well, the way you said it, it sounded nasty.'

'I didn't mean to. It's just that you misinterpret everything I say.'

'I try not to, really, Fiona.'

'You're too critical of Anna,' Peter said sharply. 'She feels it just as much, as if . . .' he paused and glanced at Anna, 'as if she were your own mother.'

'*If* she *were* my own mother I mightn't be so critical of her.'

'Fiona!'

'Well I mightn't, might I? Anyway,' she turned over again on her stomach and resumed pouring the sand through her fingers, 'we will never know as my own mother's dead.'

'But what makes you want to bring it up now?'

'Bring what up, Dad?'

'This.'

'I didn't bring it up.' She turned round and stared at him. 'You did.'

'Yes, you did, Peter.' Finishing pouring the tea and looking, but not feeling, very calm, Anna sat back on her haunches and began sipping the brew. 'I think it's come up more in the last few weeks than it has ever since I married you.'

'Has it?' Fiona looked interested.

'Yes it has, and I think for some reason you're suddenly feeling it too. It's because you resent the criticisms I have of you, thinking your own mother would behave differently.'

'Well she might.'

'And she might not.' Peter carefully put his hammer and nails inside the hut and joined them on the sand, taking the mug Anna held out to him.

'I think Anna has been more than a good mother to you;

she has been a wonderful mother. When I married her she gave up her career for a while to look after you . . .'

'Big deal,' Fiona muttered. For a moment, Peter, normally a controlled man, looked as though he would hit her. The mug shook in his hand.

'Best stop this conversation,' Anna said abruptly, jumping up. 'It's quite futile. I guess all parents and children have a time when their feelings for one another verge on hostility. All people I know seem to go through it. This really came on because I said I might be standing for the Council. Of course it won't be until next year so there's plenty of time to think about it, and if you all are dead against it, then I won't.'

'*I'm* not against it,' Fiona said robustly. 'I'm all for it.'

'Don't you think she has enough to do?' Peter took up his hammer again, and began slowly to mount the ladder to continue his repair of the roof. 'She has a busy practice; she does a lot of voluntary work. She goes to bed late and gets up early . . .'

'But she must *like* it, Dad, or she wouldn't do it.' Fiona looked gravely at her stepmother. 'You *do* like it, Anna, don't you?'

Anna collected the mugs and put them in a bowl. 'I don't know that "like" is exactly the right word. I mean a lot of it I do from a sense of duty. I feel there is a whole segment of our society that needs help, and if I can give it, I shall.'

'So you will seriously consider standing for the Council?' Peter looked down at her, hammer poised in his hand.

'Yes,' Anna swallowed, 'I shall.'

She took the bowl containing the mugs and went across the sand to the sea where she knelt and began rinsing them. Glancing behind her, she saw that Fiona was standing by the ladder in conversation with her father.

For the first time she felt a sense of exclusion, of apartness, of being a stranger from the family. Oddly enough, this was a new sensation. She had been so wanted by them, so needed, when she married Peter, that the alienation as she, and they, grew older, was insidious. Ten years was a long time, but it was not a lifetime, and Fiona had been conceived between Nancy and Peter, and carried in her womb. She gave birth to her, and for three very special, formative years lived with her.

When Anna married Peter the children seemed already to have taken to her and welcomed her into the family. And it was true that, out of love for him but also for them, she had abandoned her law practice and devoted herself to the two motherless children in her effort to bond with them. This step had, in fact, held back her career. It was the reason that, at the age of thirty-six she was, though a senior member of the firm, not yet a partner. She had given a lot for the children and she realised that a real mother might feel it was her duty, whereas a stepmother might feel she had no such obligation and expect, somehow, to be rewarded.

Anna hadn't even expected that.

She knew how Peter agonised over them since they'd been teenagers, and realised that she never experienced that special sort of agony felt by Peter. Worried, concerned, but not agonised. What was it that Anne Elliot's sister said to her in *Persuasion*? 'You, who have not a mother's feelings', when she asked her to look after her sick child. How perceptive of the author, the childless Jane!

When Anna got back to the hut, Peter was hammering away at the roof and Fiona had disappeared, maybe to get an ice cream at the kiosk, or to wander away into the dunes.

She looked up at Peter, but he avoided her eyes and, wondering what had passed between father and daughter, the feeling of isolation, or alienation on Anna's part, deepened.

All week, Fiona, who ostensibly had come to Dorset to study, scarcely touched her work. She seemed to prefer the company of Martin and Guy and a girl called Honey who lived in a cottage along the lane. Honey, hitherto an acquaintance, was rapidly becoming a bosom pal.

Peter worked hard in the garden, occasionally helped by Anna who had, however, brought a load of her own work, to try and catch up with a backlog.

'I wish Fiona were like you,' Peter said one day, looking into the bedroom where Anna had put a working table. 'I don't think she's done a stroke all week.'

Anna removed her spectacles and smiled at him.

'You've done all you can. She said so.'

'We've done all we can,' he corrected her gently.

Anna sat back in her chair and gazed out of the window at the gentle slopes of Bulbarrow. 'I feel at the moment I must take a back seat with Fiona, so as not to isolate her. She may yet need me.'

'How do you mean?'

'She's going through a difficult phase. It's obvious she feels very close to you and somehow resents me. She's prickly and brittle towards me.'

'I think you exaggerate.'

'No, it's true. I realise now that it has been getting like that for some time. We know she's not going to get good grades, don't we, Peter? She's going to have to resit and then there will be the question of what to do and where to go.'

'You think she'll have to leave the comp?'

'Yes, don't you? A crammer, I think, that is if she wants to go to university.'

'Which she says she doesn't.'

'I don't want her at the age of twenty-one wishing she'd got A levels. Some people do, you know. So when these results come out, that's when she'll need me, and you too.'

'What about the Council? That will take a lot of your time.' His tone was aggrieved and she knew that although he hadn't said as much he didn't, in fact, want her to stand.

'Well the Council's not until next year. *If* I do it. I have been asked before, you know, but I did consider the children. Now as they're older I'm getting older too.'

'We'll have you standing for Parliament next,' Peter slumped despondently on the bed. 'Don't you ever think of *me* as well?'

Ten o'clock and neither Fiona nor Guy were back. Peter was in his pyjamas, and feeling angry.

'I really think this is too bad. Heavens, we need our sleep for God's sake!'

Yet again Anna opened the front door and, going to the garden gate, looked up and down the deserted lane. It was no use worrying. At least the children were together.

She saw a light in Honey's house, the girl who Fiona played with, though 'play' was not exactly the right term at their age. Fiona usually picked up the girl, so Anna knew next to nothing about her. She slipped back into the cottage for a jumper, and as she shrugged it on said to Peter: 'I think I'll just pop along to that cottage down the road and see if they know where Fiona and Guy are. If they don't know, I'll try the farm.'

'But it's dark. I'd better come with you.'

'Don't be fussy, darling. It's perfectly safe.' Anna opened the drawer in the sideboard and rooted inside. 'I'll take a torch.' She turned and looked at Peter, who seemed tired and unhappy.

'Peter, do go to bed. Don't worry.'

'They are extremely trying.'

'Well, they're on holiday.'

'Fiona was specifically told she must work. We've hardly seen Guy at all.'

Anna went over to him and gently tried to erase the creases in his brow with her thumb. Then she stood on tiptoe and kissed him. Anna was considered tall for a woman, but Peter was six foot three. 'Go to bed, darling. *Don't* worry.'

'I love you,' Peter said reaching for her hand and taking it to his lips.

Clutching the torch Anna walked swiftly down the garden path, through the gate and along the road towards the only house in the village with a light on. People tended to go to bed early in rural Dorset.

When she got there she sensed her instincts were right, and immediately felt relief surging through her. The curtains were drawn, but the sound of youthful voices came from within.

She stood outside the door for a moment feeling apprehensive. She could just imagine what sort of reception she'd get from Fiona; the accusation that she was being spied on. For a moment she thought of turning round and persuading Peter that, after all, it *was* his job. But on reflection she decided it was hers too; until recently she would never have thought otherwise. Firmly she tapped on the door and the voices suddenly fell silent. There was no reply but she could hear furious whispers break out at the other side.

She knocked again, more firmly, and after a few moments a light went on round the side of the house and a female voice called out: 'Who's there?'

Anna hurried in the direction of the voice. In the light over the back door she saw a rather pleasant looking, youngish woman, dressed like her in jeans and a T-shirt. The woman had a cigarette in her hand and flicked the ash on to the garden path.

'Can I help you?' she enquired.

'It's just that . . . I'm afraid we haven't met, but I think my daughter Fiona knows . . . is it *your* daughter? Honey?'

'Oh, you're Fiona's mother,' the woman said pleasantly enough, but without inviting her in. 'How do you do? I'm Sal.'

'I'm Anna.'

'Yes, Honey is my daughter.'

'Are they there?' Anna, feeling rather chilly, looked towards the house.

'Yes. They're watching telly. They'll be home in a minute.'

'Is Guy there too?'

'Yes, and the boy from the farm. Martin, is it? They're alright, Anna. No need to worry.'

Sal turned towards the door, as if that was the end of the matter, but for Anna it was not.

'I'm sorry, Sal,' she called as pleasantly as she could, 'but I want to take the children home. Their father's worried about them.'

'There's no need to worry. They're *perfectly* alright. Watching a video. As soon as it's finished I'll send them home.'

'They have to come now, I'm afraid.' Anna's voice tightened. 'With me. Right away. Now.'

'My goodness!' Sal said mockingly, tossing back her hair. 'We *are* a disciplinarian, aren't we?'

Anna didn't like the woman's tone, or, now, her manner.

'Sal, it's well after ten. Fiona is supposed to be working for her GCSEs. Her father is very tired and so, in fact, am I. It's late and we want them both home.'

'What is it, Mum?' a younger voice called from inside.

'It's Fiona and Guy's mum. They have to come home. Get them would you, pet?'

'But Mum . . .'

'I said get them.' The friendly tone now became a sharp command, and Sal stood looking at the door. Anna began to shiver. From inside the house she could hear raised voices and then shrieks of laughter. Honey's voice, this time fainter, sounded from inside.

'They say ten minutes, until the end of the video . . .'

'Now,' Anna said in a commanding voice and walked firmly towards the door. 'I'm sorry, Sal, but I don't like this at all.'

'They're not watching dirty videos, if that's what you think.' Sal's tone was now contemptuous. 'I wouldn't allow it.'

'But I think you allow them to smoke pot,' Anna said quietly. The sweet, sickly smell that wafted towards the door was unmistakable.

'And you don't, I suppose?'

'I certainly do not.'

'Well they *all* do, you know. You might not know it or like it, but they *do*.'

'*If* they do, they do it without the knowledge of me or their father.'

'More fool you.'

'You realise that it's illegal?' Anna knew she was sounding like a schoolmistress and thoroughly alienating Honey's mother.

'What? Going to report us to the cops, are you?'

'Of course not, but it *is* against the law.' Anna pushed past Sal and into the kitchen, which was untidy, the sink and draining board stacked with dishes. The smell now from the living room was overpowering, and she guessed that Sal was smoking too. She went to the door and peered in. Through a thick haze she could see several people, including her stepson and stepdaughter, lounging about, propped up on cushions on the floor or lying on the sofa, draped in the large comfortable chairs. The television in one corner of the living room was on, but no one appeared to be taking much notice of it, if any at all.

When they saw her, however, the atmosphere changed completely as lethargy turned to panic. Guy rolled off the sofa on to the floor, face downwards as if to disguise himself, and Fiona turned her back to the door.

'Fiona, Guy,' Anna called. 'Time to go home.'

No one moved. Martin rose rather sheepishly to his feet, but Honey and a girl Anna didn't recognise and another youth remained where they were, gazing at her with expressions of derision on their faces.

'We'll come in a minute, Anna,' Fiona mumbled at last.

'*Now*, Fiona. Please.'

'Fiona's not a child,' Honey said aggressively.

'As a matter of fact, she is.' Anna crossed the room, stirred Guy's body with her foot, and took Fiona by the arm and tried to jerk her up.

'*Please*, don't make an exhibition . . .'

'You already have,' Fiona said petulantly, trying to release her arm. She aimed a vicious kick at Anna's shins, but missed.

'I'll go and wait outside the back door, and I expect you to join me in five minutes. OK? Five minutes. No more.' Neither of them looked at her. 'If not, I shall go and get your father. You give me no other choice.'

She went back into the kitchen where Sal, lounging against the draining board, a fresh cigarette in her hand, had now been joined by Honey, who was whispering feverishly into her ear. It was not hard to guess what.

'I don't think smoking pot is any worse than whisky,' Sal said in a tone of defiance to Anna. 'In fact it's probably better for you.'

'I don't think any of them are particularly good for teenagers. Guy is only fourteen.'

'They grow up very fast these days.'

Anna sized up Honey, who could have been eighteen but was, she knew, nearer Fiona's age. She was a tall, slim, attractive girl with crinkly brown hair, a smiling unmade-up face. With the right expression she would probably be pretty, but now her face was disfigured by an ugly scowl.

'I just want Fiona and Guy *home*,' Anna said in the same quiet, patient voice. 'Their father's worried. So am I.' She looked at her watch. 'It's after ten, and we didn't know where they were.'

'I feel sorry for you,' Sal said nonchalantly. 'Seems you have a lot to learn about kids nowadays.'

Anna opened the back door and breathed in deeply, feeling like a diver coming up for air.

Shortly after she was joined by a subdued Guy and Fiona, who followed several paces behind her, dragging their feet all the way up the lane and back to the house.

CHAPTER 3

Anna's doctor was a personal friend, a woman a little older than her, whom she'd known since their university days when they'd lived in the same hall of residence. Anna, who was hardly ever ill, took her few complaints to Katie Ward, who practised as a gynaecologist, was married to a GP and had two children.

The two women were of similar temperament; brisk, practical, outward looking, with well-developed social consciences. Katie did a lot of lowly or unpaid voluntary work in mother and baby welfare clinics in the disadvantaged areas of London, far from the fashionable ambience of Harley Street and its environs.

Katie gave Anna a yearly check-up, smear test, breast examination, heart, lungs and, after pronouncing her fit, as she usually did, they would go off to have lunch. Katie's consulting rooms were in Wimpole Street, a short distance from Anna's law office in Wigmore Street.

Apart from that, they socialised occasionally, attended the same dinner parties, had one another to dinner. Katie's husband, Donald, was younger than Peter, but the two men got on well. The Ward children were considerably younger than Guy and Fiona, so the socialising was confined to adults.

If Anna made an appointment to see Katie apart from the annual check-up it was never for something trivial so, as Anna loosened her coat and sat down, Katie took a seat opposite her preparing to listen attentively after they had exchanged the usual preliminaries: how were husbands, children, etc?

Katie opened Anna's file and flipped through the few papers it contained. 'I last saw you six months ago for the usual. Everything was fine.' She gave a brief professional smile, joined her hands together and looked across at her friend. 'What's the problem?'

'Well,' Anna, betraying her nerves, fidgeted with her rings, 'I think I might be pregnant.'

'Oh?' Katie's expression registered mild surprise. She was a small, neat woman with short dark hair, warm brown eyes, rather delicately featured, fine bone structure, and always discreetly but expensively dressed. Every inch the professional. 'Is that good news or bad?' She stared at her notes again. 'I see that I'm still prescribing the Pill for you. Did you stop taking it?'

'Briefly.'

'Oh!' Katie leaned back and nodded.

'I'd run out but I realised I'd left my prescription at home. Well, that night . . . you know how it is.' Anna fidgeted nervously again, and Katie nodded understandingly. Oh, yes, how well she knew.

'I thought that after taking it for so long there'd be no problem.' Anna's hands fluttered towards the desk in front of her as if seeking reassurance. 'I've said nothing to Peter.'

'Let's see,' Katie said jumping up. 'Put you out of your misery.'

'You can tell? *Now?*' Anna looked amazed.

'Not absolutely. But pretty sure, ninety-nine per cent.' Katie went over to a cupboard and began searching through the contents. 'No need to inject it into frogs and wait for ages.'

'*It?*' Anna looked puzzled and Katie turned towards her and smiled.

'Pop into the bathroom and give me a sample, there's a dear. You know the routine.'

* * *

Moments after the sample was delivered, Katie emerged from the examination room next to her consulting room smiling as she wiped her hands on a towel.

'False alarm.'

Anna felt she could have wept with relief.

'You're *sure*?'

'Pretty sure. Ninety-nine per cent.' Katie tossed the towel to one side and, resuming her seat at her desk, drew Anna's file towards her and scribbled a note. 'There is absolutely no trace of the dip stick changing colour, and if you missed two periods,' she looked up with a thoughtful expression and began to count on her fingers.

'Yes, two.' Anna found herself choking back the tears. 'Gosh, I was so worried.'

'Were you?' Katie sat back and regarded her friend solemnly. 'As much as that? Why?'

'Well . . .'

Katie was surprised by the attitude of the normally articulate Anna. It was so unlike her, losing her cool like this. 'Did you never *seriously* consider having a family, Anna?'

'Yes, we considered it. Naturally. But that was years ago before I resumed work.'

'And not since?'

'No. Guy and Fiona seemed to need all the parenting I could give.'

'And you didn't tell Peter you thought you were pregnant?'

Anna shook her head like a guilty schoolgirl.

'You thought he might be pleased?'

This time Anna nodded, then said: 'But I don't think in his heart of hearts he wants a baby. He's not quite sure about how *I* feel.'

Katie nodded understandingly again.

'Nevertheless, it is a very natural instinct to want your own children, the blood tie as it were.' She paused. 'But not you?'

Anna shook her head again, this time emphatically.

'Not me.'

'I see.' Katie got up and wandered to the window of her consulting room where she stood looking at the busy street below. 'Then why don't you opt for sterilisation?'

Returning to her desk, on which lay a sphygmomanometer which she opened, she took up her stethoscope and, asking Anna to bare her arm, bound the rubber cuff around it.

She looked thoughtfully at the instrument as the mercury rose and then fell and, removing the stethoscope from her ears, placed it on the table. 'Blood pressure OK. But last time it *was* a tiny bit up.'

'Oh?' Anna immediately looked anxious.

'Not enough for me to comment on. I know you lead a pretty stressful life and put it down to that. However, this missing two periods for no reason might indicate it's time you came off the Pill. Let me see, you'll soon be thirty-six,' she paused as she counted on her fingers again, 'what, sixteen, eighteen years?'

Anna nodded.

'Even with the low oestrogen dosage I give you I think it's long enough. I had my tubes tied two years ago.'

'*Did* you?' Anna looked impressed.

'There's nothing to it. A couple of days in bed, a tiny bit of discomfort. I can even do you as an outpatient and have you home the same day. However, I dare say, like me, you'd value a couple of days in the comfort of a nice private hospital room. How about the Princess Grace?'

'You're really serious about this, Katie?'

'Perfectly serious.' Katie sat down again and drummed her fingers on her desk. 'That is if *you* are.'

'But I'm not ill or anything?'

'I can assure you that you're not ill. I'll take another smear, just to reassure you before you go; but this is not uncommon with busy women who are not yet menopausal but are past the halfway mark of their reproductive lives. Sometimes the cycle starts to misbehave, or miss out altogether. I just thought it was silly to continue dosing myself with, what is, after all, a powerful drug – the long-term effects of which we frankly don't know. They're making new discoveries all the time. It *is* rather worrying. And if you are serious about not having children I would suggest you think about it.' She glanced at the clock on the wall. 'Do we have time for the ritual lunch?'

'Just a bite. I'm due at the magistrates' court at two.'

'And I'm due at the hospital at the same time.' Katie capped her pen and got up. Then she studied her friend who remained seated.

'Anything else worrying you, Anna? You look terribly anxious today. I thought you'd be relieved knowing the test was negative.' She leaned towards her and studied her closely. 'What else ails you?'

'Well,' Anna fidgeted with her rings yet again. 'I couldn't face a baby while Guy and Fiona present us with such problems.'

'Ah!' Katie sat down again. 'As you hadn't mentioned it, I hoped things had improved since I saw you last.'

'They haven't improved at all. They've got steadily worse. Fiona just took her GCSE exams and has probably flunked the lot. Guy does them next year with not much hope of success there either. Peter is really at his wits' end.'

'And you?'

'Obviously I'm very worried too; but you know although I love them and regard them as my own, I . . .'

'*Do* you?'

Anna seemed surprised at the sharpness of Katie's tone.

'Do I what?'

'*Really* regard them as your own?'

Anna examined her hands.

'Frankly, since you ask . . . not really.' Her face, when she looked up, was strained. 'I did when they were small and lovable, but now they seem to have grown away from me. I would only confess this to someone like you. Sometimes I feel I dare not even admit it to myself.'

'It's not a sin,' Katie protested. 'Biologically they are not your own children, and there's nothing quite like the blood tie.'

'But when they were young . . .'

'They were beautiful, vulnerable. They needed you. Teenagers are very different. Sometimes it's only the fact that I'm their mother that makes me tolerate my own children. Even though they're so much younger they're very demanding. I resent them.'

'Really?' Despite herself, Anna looked surprised.

'They irritate you, they annoy you. But some of my patients and friends with teenage kids are nearly demented. They seem to go out of their way to be as much trouble as possible. They don't know what to do with them.'

'Oh, I'm so *glad.*' A look of immense relief flooded Anna's face. She put her hand to her mouth. 'I mean. Oh I *don't* mean . . .'

'You mean you're glad that their biological parents feel as you do. My dear, most of the parents in this country would say the same if they were honest.'

'Yes.' Anna looked at her solemnly. 'Sometimes I confess I hate them. They are so uncaring, so thoughtless. They cause so much grief to Peter, and they make me feel guilty. Peter wanted them to go to private school, but I was a keen supporter of State education.'

'It *is* a mess, isn't it?' Katie looked sympathetic. 'But, believe me, others pay a fortune in fees for them and their problems are exactly the same.'

'Drugs?' Anna whispered.

'If you mean pot, yes, I suppose so. Frankly, I'm not really against pot; but I don't think encouraging drugs or any other form of narcotic at their age is a good thing. I'd say the same about drink and cigarettes, but after the age of eighteen . . . well, people will do it anyway.'

'We found Guy and Fiona smoking pot in Dorset in the half term holiday. The tiny little hamlet where we have our cottage is just about the very last place you'd think of. There was a group of them including the mother of the girl Fiona was friendly with.'

'Doesn't surprise me.' Katie glanced at her watch again. 'I wonder it surprises you, with all your experience.'

Anna rose, shook herself. 'Perhaps because it touches me, impinges on my private life.'

'If we're going to have that sandwich we'd better hurry.' Katie opened the communicating door between her and her secretary, had a word with her and then, gathering up her bag and briefcase, joined Anna by the door. 'Anna, I'd think very seriously, if I were you, about being sterilised. I mean at the moment you seem to me to be a bit unsure of your role as a mother. Maybe in your heart of hearts you actually do want a child of your own?'

'That's ridiculous.' Anna's reply was immediate as Katie closed the door and they waited for the lift.

'Anyway, it can't be done this summer,' Katie said. 'I'm going to America for a conference. Donald is joining us, and bringing the children for an extended holiday. We'll be away about a month. If you still feel the same, come and see me in the autumn.'

It was Peter who opened the buff envelope as Anna stood by with a sinking heart. He took the enclosure to the window, studied it for a few moments and then wordlessly passed it to Anna.

It was as they feared. Fiona had got hopelessly bad grades in all of her subjects except English and History, which could possibly be interpreted as a scrape pass.

She placed the letter down on the table and, going over to

Peter, put her hand on his arm, pressed her head against his back.

'It's no surprise, is it? Maybe it will jolt her.'

'Jolt her into what?'

'Trying harder.'

'But she doesn't want to try. She will use this as a reason to leave school.'

As Fiona was already sixteen there was no reason why, if she wanted to, she shouldn't.

'What do you believe she will think she is qualified to do at the age of sixteen?'

'She won't think about it. She's opted out. She's trying to tell us that as clearly as anything.'

'Maybe that will bring her to her senses. She will realise you can't get anywhere without qualifications and then . . .'

'Oh, Anna, don't deceive yourself. You know Fiona as well as I do. She's telling us by her attitude that she hates our middle-class lifestyle and all it stands for. We've failed her.'

'She's failed *you*.'

'Why me especially?' He looked up at her.

'Because you care so much.'

'But you care too.' He appeared anxious to convince himself.

'Of course I do, but you, as her biological father, care more.'

'I often wondered,' Peter paused and studied the floor, 'if you really did care.'

'I *do* care.' Anna sat opposite him clasping her hands between her knees. It was a Thursday morning and, knowing the results were due and Peter would probably need her, she had arranged to be late at the office. 'But I'm not quite as torn apart as you are . . . Darling, it's better that way. Same as I can sleep at night when they aren't in, and you can't.'

'You should have a child of your own, Anna,' Peter said with uncharacteristic sharpness, 'and then you'd know.'

Anna rose and, without replying, went over to the door.

'I'm sorry,' Peter called out, but by that time the door had shut behind her and he didn't know whether she had heard him or not.

Peter felt like crushing the paper containing the exam results into a ball and hurling it out of the window, or tearing it into tiny fragments and stuffing it into the wastepaper basket.

But no. Fiona was on a school trip to France – how convenient to arrange it when the exam results were due – and he had to keep it for her. He wondered if he should go after Anna, but at that moment he heard the front door shut and seconds later her car started up.

She had stayed home specially to be with him and he had behaved like a pig. It was at times like this that, subconsciously, he thought about Nancy and his guilt became acute, because Nancy would have been far less use, help, or support to him than Anna was.

Nancy had never taken herself or her responsibilities seriously. She was not an especially good or doting mother to the children. She was a spoilt, beautiful woman who only really cared for herself.

Yet he had adored her and had never loved Anna in quite the obsessional way that he had loved Nancy.

Nancy was the sort of woman who besotted men. Despite her many failings, her selfishness and idleness, they fell recklessly and helplessly, illogically in love with her. She was fascinating, a charmer. She had only been thirty when she died and he had never forgotten her.

Of course he loved Anna, but in a different way. He loved her, but had never been 'in love'. She was the sort of sensible, practical woman even at the age of twenty-five – five years younger than Nancy – who he had known would be a support to a man, someone he could lean on; a conscientious hard-working stepmother to the children.

She had been clever and ambitious in a way Nancy never was; smart, well groomed, whereas Nancy never felt it necessary to adorn her beauty, could hardly have been less interested in clothes and slopped around all day in jeans and loose sweaters. People said that Anna and Nancy were alike but they weren't. It was true they resembled each other slightly, physically and in colouring, so that people said he had fallen in love with similar types of women as men often do, but that was all.

It may have been that the children would have turned out better with Nancy as a mother just because she would have been less caring. Left to their own devices, they might have tried harder. Whereas with Peter and Anna, concerned parents who read all the books and knew all the rules about development and awareness and so on, they seemed to leave everything to them as though asking themselves what was the point of making an effort when their parents were so hardworking, successful and, inevitably, wealthy?

Peter had also trained as a lawyer, but after being called to the Bar he joined a huge oil concern and had been with them ever since. Now he was head of the legal department, a member of the board and a man with a six figure salary, one who could easily have afforded the priciest public schools in the country for his children's education.

Nancy, ill-educated herself, would have left it to him to decide. But Anna had very firm ideas about equality of opportunity, fair shares for all, and there was never any question but that the children went to the local comprehensive and mucked in like everyone else.

It was easy to relate the kind of effect this had had on the children to the kind of person that Anna had become. She had firm ideas about everything. She seldom wavered or changed her mind. She was so busy that she believed in planning well ahead, thinking that if she didn't, inevitably everything would fall apart.

She was well organised, meticulous to a fault. Yet no one could call her uncaring or accuse her of lacking compassion and, in effect, he had.

Peter sank into a chair and put his head in his hands. He felt his life and his children's were a mess. But without Anna he could hardly begin to know how to handle it.

The firm of Robertson, Askew & Cole was nearly a hundred years old. It had been founded at the end of the nineteenth century by Andrew Robertson in the very premises it still occupied. Only then it had been in one room and now it occupied not only the whole house but the one next door. Cecil Askew had joined it in the thirties bringing his own clients and considerable expertise of litigation, and after the Second World War it merged with the respectable City firm of Cardew Cole.

It was extremely prestigious and well regarded, yet it still maintained an air redolent of an earlier age: leisured, civilised, unhurried and compassionate. Despite its upmarket West End address, it accepted Legal Aid and a number of its lawyers were, like Anna, engaged in voluntary work.

Anna, a clever student with a first-class law degree, had been accepted by Robertson, Askew & Cole as an articled clerk. Although full of bright promise, after completing her Articles and on her marriage she resigned to look after Peter's young children, returning to work at the age of thirty. Her old firm were glad to have her back; she was well thought of by her colleagues and highly regarded by her clients.

She was considered typical of that breed of women who successfully combined running a home, a family and a career. Little was known about her private life, and it never intruded on her work.

But did it? Anna gazed out of the window above Wigmore Street from which she could just see the trees in Cavendish Square and propped her chin on her clasped hands.

Even if she conceived now she would be well into her thirty-sixth year when her baby was born.

With a jolt she looked at the calendar and realised that Katie

Ward would soon be back from her extended trip to the US and expecting a call from her.

Somehow she knew it was crunch time. A time for decisions.

If they had a baby, perhaps it would take their minds off the problems posed by Fiona and Guy. On the other hand, was it fair, either to the new child or its elder half-brother and sister? Did not Guy and Fiona need *more* help now in their difficult adolescence rather than less, and what would be the effect on them of a young sibling in the home? Also, how would it affect her own career? Would she abandon it, or simply take maternity leave?

The intercom buzzed, rudely disturbing her reverie, and she pressed the button.

'Anna, I wonder if you could come into my office? Could you spare a few moments?'

'Of course. Is there anything I should bring with me?'

'Just yourself, Anna.'

David Dugdale Cole, the grandson of Cardew Cole, senior partner and the only descendant of any of the original families still to be with the group, sounded quite jovial. Maybe he'd got back from a good lunch, though she knew him to be abstemious in all things, and he ate and drank sparingly.

Although possessed of considerable charm and impeccable good manners, David was rather dry and remote. He didn't socialise with the staff, although there was an annual Christmas party, usually at Brown's Hotel, to which he brought his attractive upper-class wife, June. He had two children whom Anna had never seen, didn't even know how old they were. It suited her that the relationships among the staff were business-like. Few of them knew much about one another's lives out of the office; she didn't have one person she confided in, but as they were mainly men that was perhaps understandable.

She put her head into her secretary's office to tell her where she was going, and then descended the two floors to David's spacious office on the first floor. She tapped on the door and he called out inviting her to enter.

Before she could turn the handle the door was flung open by Henry Atherton, also one of the partners, and standing next to David's desk with a smile on his face was Michael Norden, yet another.

'Come in, come in, Anna.' Henry genially reached for her hand and then, standing back for her to enter, closed the door after her.

'Welcome, Anna.' David got up from his desk to greet her, and Michael nodded. It struck Anna that the welcome was unusual. Something, decidedly, was up.

She felt a flicker of alarm but said nothing and, returning their smiles, took the chair indicated by David just to one side of his desk. Henry sat in the other and Michael, his hands clasped, perched on the side of David's imposing desk which, legend had it, had once belonged to the founder, Andrew Robertson.

'Well, Anna.' Resuming his seat, David, too, joined his hands together on the desk, and gave her a smile, the kind that must have reassured many an anxious client, or nervous junior barrister. 'I imagine you're wondering what this reception committee is in aid of?'

'I did wonder.' Anna tossed back her head and stared him straight in the eyes.

'Well, Anna,' David looking earnest, leaned forward, 'the object of this meeting is two-fold. As you know, we have been in these premises for nearly a hundred years. Although we have expanded and our space has increased – we now have two houses whereas in the days of the founder he had one room – we still haven't enough space for all the work we have to do and the staff we need to take on. We therefore propose to move.'

'Oh!' Anna's heart sank. If they were relocating out of

London, and firms bent on enlargement usually did these days, there would be no question of her moving with them.

That might provide the solution to several troubling domestic questions. More time to give the difficult adolescents and perhaps, at last, to have that baby whose possible existence always seemed to lurk at the back of her mind, however much she denied it.

She began to feel more relaxed and crossed her legs, her expression attentive.

'But,' Michael, head of human resources, leaned across the desk, 'there is another reason for our decision to move. We're increasing our corporate business. It has quadrupled since we've been in the EC, and we therefore propose to move to the City, which will give us more space and, at the same time, put us nearer some of our major clients.'

Mystification set in. Was she to get the sack? Made redundant? Well that would still give her the opportunities that had been at the back of her mind, but maybe with ignominy, which she didn't exactly relish. To get the push wasn't quite as heroic as giving up work voluntarily. But that's what it looked like. Her speciality was civil, family and divorce cases. She never touched corporation law.

Michael stopped talking, and she wondered if he was finding the next part of his task difficult.

'Seems like I'll be expendable,' she prompted him. 'Is that what I'm here for?'

The men looked at one another and simultaneously burst into gruff, clannish laughter. Michael rubbed his hands together as though in glee that his teasing approach had paid off.

'On the *contrary*, Anna,' David too gave a self-satisfied smile, 'we are hoping to keep these premises, for which we have the freehold, for our family and civil cases and we would like *you* to be the person in charge. We are thus offering you a partnership and making you a full member of the firm.'

'Wow!' Anna exclaimed, and they laughed again as if in self-congratulation. There really was something quite childlike about grown men.

'What about Arnold?' Anna asked before the laughter had subsided. Arnold Webster was the partner in charge of the civil and family division, her immediate boss.

'Arnold is nearly sixty and wants to retire. He will remain as a consultant to help you settle in. That is, if you agree.'

Anna remained silent for a moment and then said quietly: 'I don't think there's any doubt about that, except of course I'll want to consult Peter.'

They nodded in understanding, but David asked: 'Is there any reason why Peter should say "no"?'

'Oh, no. I don't think so.'

'He's not near retirement, is he? No plans to move?'

'Not at all; but we are a partnership. We do consult. He consulted with me before taking up his new position a few years ago, and I feel I should do the same.'

'Naturally.' The urbane David Cole stood up and held out his hand. 'The plans do not come into operation until the New Year so take what time you need. Please accept my congratulations, Anna. We shall hope your acceptance is a foregone conclusion, shan't we, gentlemen?' The others nodded and moved forward to press her hand. 'I think if you do accept, and naturally we hope you will, you'll be the youngest partner we have had for many years.'

'And the only woman,' Michael interposed.

'So far,' Anna said smiling.

'Yes, I do believe we must move with the times. Oh, and Anna,' David called out as she turned and walked to the door, 'my wife and I would be delighted if you and Peter would have dinner with us. Just a small party you know, to get to know one another better.'

Anna shut the door behind her, leaned on it for a second and then sped upstairs, two at a time.

A full partnership, a private dinner with the boss. Barriers falling down, horizons expanding, the future unlimited.

Anna left the office earlier than usual, scarcely able to contain her excitement. She realised as she never had before that she was truly ambitious, she wanted to get to the top, she valued the respect the partners held her in, the chances they offered her.

They had no garage, and she parked the car outside the house as usual, noticing Peter's on the other side of the road. He had got home even earlier than she had, and then she remembered, and a curious little chill clutched at her heart dispelling her euphoria.

Of course. Fiona was due home from the continent, and she in her excitement had forgotten all about it.

So much for being a good mother.

Tomorrow she would ring up Katie Ward's office and make an appointment to get her tubes tied. She couldn't be a partner *and* have a baby as well. No question now of that.

That decision, if Peter agreed – and of course he would – had been taken out of her hands.

She put the key in the lock, and the front door swung open. She paused for a moment and knew immediately, from the unnatural stillness in the house, that something had happened.

No sound of the TV, no voices. It was as though someone had died. In place of the chill, fear seemed to grip her heart, and her mouth felt dry.

She stood in the hall and called out in as natural a voice as she could muster: 'Hi! Anyone at home?'

There was no reply, and then she thought that perhaps she was silly and that the silence was because there *was* no one at home. She was in a hyper-sensitive mood. Peter must have taken a taxi to meet Fiona because of the difficulty of parking at Victoria.

But the door of the sitting room, usually open, was shut. She turned the handle, and as it swung away from her, she could see Peter sitting in the chair next to the TV, his face sullen and angry, his hands firmly grasping each arm as if to give him added gravitas or, maybe, simply more support.

The door was wide open now, and then Anna saw Fiona, her face white, her eyes red with weeping, sitting opposite Peter. Her body was squeezed up into the chair in embryonic fashion. Like her mother, she was petite, and the large armchair dwarfed her. Her hand was pressed into her mouth as though she were sucking her fingers like a baby.

Anna crossed the room in silence, put her briefcase and bag on the floor and flopped into a vacant chair.

'Hi!' she said looking across at Fiona. 'Welcome home.'

Fiona didn't reply.

'Hi, darling!' Anna turned to Peter who gave her a wintry smile. 'Did I interrupt something?'

'No, you didn't.' Fiona uncoiled herself from the chair looking as though with one bound she would spring out of it. Yet she hesitated as though uncertain now what to do.

'Have a good time?' Anna tried to keep the tone of her voice natural.

Fiona still didn't reply.

'Fiona, Anna asked you a question.' Peter looked sternly at his daughter.

'I'm not deaf,' Fiona said.

Anna rose and reached for her bag and briefcase. 'I think maybe I did interrupt something. Call me when the conference is over.'

'Anna, please stay.' Peter pointed to the seat. 'I think this is something you should be in on. Naturally it's about Fiona's results. Her future. As her mother . . .'

'She is *not* my mother,' Fiona said angrily. 'How many times do I have to say that?'

'As your stepmother then.' Anna was determined not to provoke Fiona. 'I am that, I think.'

'I wish you wouldn't take this attitude of rudeness and hostility towards Anna,' Peter said peevishly. 'She has always been a support and help to you. Yet now you seem to want to exclude her from the family counsels entirely.'

'Look, if I'm not wanted and can't help, honestly I don't mind.' Anna remained standing, uncertain whether to sit down again or go. Peter's eyes seemed to implore her to stay, but Fiona's remained implacably hostile.

'I *want* you to stay, Anna,' Peter insisted. 'Please sit down again.'

Anna sat, feeling foolish but also rather angry. Sod Fiona, on this day of days, *her* day. The day she was offered a partnership.

'You'd better give me a résumé about what's being said. And I'll see if I can help.'

'Well, you can't!' Fiona spat at her. Anna ignored her and looked at Peter.

'I gave Fiona her results. Naturally she's upset.'

'But hardly surprised, I'd have thought. She did absolutely no work and unless you're brilliant you can't expect to pass, so she didn't.'

'Not brilliant like *you*,' Fiona said. Anna ignored her. Useless to argue with someone in this mood, this frame of mind.

'Is that all this is about?'

'No.' Peter studied his fingers. 'I've told Fiona that you and I had discussed the matter and we thought she should go to a crammer for a year and retake.'

'Yes, we did think that, Fiona.' Anna, despite her feelings, managed a smile, trying to remember that, although this girl was not the daughter of her body, she did have a long and close relationship with her, claimed that she loved her. Could she *still* say she loved her? No, not at the moment. Did Peter? Probably, because his was a blood tie. If she and Peter had a baby that would be a blood tie too.

Then she remembered the partnership and she knew that the challenge of running her own division, the opportunity to succeed and maybe, above all, the chance to be away from this place all day was irresistible. Yes, maybe that was it. She couldn't bear the possibility, with all its concomitant irritations and responsibilities, of being at home all day long.

As no one answered, Anna looked over to Peter, and spoke as though her stepdaughter were not there.

'What did Fiona say, Peter?'

'Well, naturally she's confused.'

'I am *not* confused.' Fiona's tone was louder and more forceful than was necessary. 'I am quite clear about it. I am sixteen and I want to leave school.'

'And what do you want to do?' Anna tried to sound relaxed, friendly, cheerful, but it was very hard. She guessed the truth was that she sounded artificial and insincere.

'Dunno,' Fiona shrugged.

'You don't want to do anything?'

'What is there to do?'

'You think you're going to be kept by your father?'

'Why shouldn't he? He has plenty.'

'That's not the point, Fiona.'

'Lots of people do it. Before the War, girls never worked.'

Anna could hardly believe her ears.

'Did you say "before the War"?'

'Yes, I did.' Fiona's expression was defiant.

'But that was over fifty years ago.'

'Even I can't remember it.' Peter's laugh was relieved as though somehow the ice had been broken.

'It does seem a bit daft, Fiona, if you don't mind me saying so, to quote what happened many years before you were born.'

'Maybe it was a good age. All this emphasis on work. Why can't everyone relax and be themselves? What's wrong with me staying at home if Dad can keep me?'

'Because the idea of your selfishness appals me, that's what.' Peter's tone was brusque. 'Even in the thirties women wanted to work, unless they were married with children.'

'And that happens now,' Anna nodded. 'Many women with children have no choice but to stay at home. Most people want to work.'

'But why?'

It was a good point. One, actually, she'd never thought of.

'Because work is fulfilling,' she declared after a while. 'Also, these days, most people need the money.'

'But you and Dad have got plenty.'

'Yes, but we didn't say we wanted you to live on it.'

'But I do live on it while I'm at school, and if you send me to a crammer it will cost a bomb, and you will *also* have to keep me, whereas if I stayed at home and didn't go to the crammer it would save a bomb.'

There was logic in her argument.

'What a day.' Peter sat wearily on the edge of the bed, tugging at his shoelaces. He had taken off his tie but not changed when he came home.

'Exhausting!' Anna, looking by contrast fresh and pretty, emerged from the bathroom in her robe, rubbing moisturiser into her face.

The argument with Fiona had raged well into the evening, whereupon exhaustion, also repetition, set in, and they had all gone into the kitchen for something to eat. During the meal Fiona unexpectedly called a truce and told them quite animatedly about the holiday. She'd obviously had a good time which made her mood of hostility when she returned home all the stranger.

They sat round the supper table for some time and the discussion about her future began again, only with less heat. It was decided that they would talk about it at the weekend when they intended to have a few days together before term began.

Fiona had assumed anyway, and so had her parents, that she would be starting back at school in the normal way.

At the end of the evening, to their surprise and gratification, Fiona announced that she was going to bed. She came and kissed them both, and went upstairs to her room.

Anna had anticipated a drama about her going out to see her friends. So, for the time being, there was a temporary respite.

It could only be a respite, a truce.

The emotions of the evening had taken all the gloss off her news, and she was in half a mind as to whether to tell Peter about it or not. On the other hand, David would be sure to ask her the next day and she could hardly say it hadn't been mentioned.

'Darling,' she perched on the bed next to him, 'I have some rather momentous news.'

He turned to her immediately and his face had a curious expression on it – a kind of expectation that she had no difficulty interpreting.

'Not that!' she said, putting a hand on him. 'You thought I meant pregnant?'

He nodded.

'Of course I wouldn't have done anything like *that* without consulting you. No, Peter, I've been offered a partnership, a full member of the team with my own department. They're relocating to the City, but I'm to stay in Wigmore Street in charge of the Civil and Family Law side of the firm.'

'What's happened to Arnold?' Peter mumbled as if either unable to, or disinclined to assimilate the news.

'He's close to retirement. Staying on as consultant to see me in. Peter, I haven't accepted, but you'd want me to say "yes" wouldn't you? I mean,' her voice faltered, 'I mean I said

I'd discuss it with you, but I thought it would be a foregone conclusion.'

Peter sat staring in front of him, silent.

'Peter,' feeling suddenly anxious, 'aren't you *pleased*?'

'If it's what you want, yes.' Peter rose slowly from the bed. He got out of his City trousers, took off his shirt and went into the bathroom emerging almost immediately in his robe.

'Well, it's what I want, and I'd have thought it was what you wanted.'

'Why should I want it?' He scratched his head as if the whole thing perplexed him.

Anna felt astounded.

'Well, why *shouldn't* you want it? I mean I wanted your promotion. I was glad for you. Why shouldn't you want me to be a partner?'

Peter slumped down on the bed again and an arm encircled her waist.

'Because I think I wanted you to have a baby,' he said.

Anna looked at him incredulously.

'Peter, you *can't* want to begin this whole ghastly business again.'

'What ghastly business?' He sounded hurt. 'You loved the kids when they were little.'

'Yes but "little" grows up. I don't want this drama in another sixteen or so years with our son or daughter.'

'Times change.'

'Peter, you aren't serious are you? I mean the last time we talked about it we agreed . . .'

Peter lay full length on the bed, his head resting on his arms.

'I think that was *quite* a long time ago.' His eyes fastened on the ceiling.

'Soon I'll be thirty-six.'

'Yes, I know.'

'If I had a baby . . .'

'You'd still be thirty-six. It's not very old. Lots of women do it.'

Anna ran her hands through her hair.

'Peter, I feel horribly, terribly confused. I really don't know what to do.' She looked at him wildly. 'This is all so unexpected.'

'Can't you be a partner and have a baby?'

'Not really. I don't think it would be fair.'

'Why is it unfair?'

'Because I'll have to take time off.'

'We could have a nanny.'

'I'd have to take a lot of time off! Don't be absurd. Anyway, I think David and the partners would feel cheated, offering me a partnership and departmental headship and then finding that I'm pregnant. It's just not on, Peter. It's one thing or the other. And we must decide. Quite soon.'

Peter clasped his head suddenly with both hands as though he had a headache. Anna, overcome with love, pity, sympathy, and remorse, bent over him to kiss him. As she did, one hand flew away from his head and he grasped at the belt of her gown which fell open to display her nudity. Undoing the cord of his bath robe, he drew her to him kissing her there, just where she stood above him, arousing in her immediate feelings so intense, erotic and overwhelming that she straddled him quickly as, her hands straining against his chest, the moment of intense mutual pleasure overwhelmed them both.

She lay upon him, savouring him, listening to the steady pounding of his heart, licking, with swift darts of her tongue, the sweat that trickled down his neck.

After a while she rose, went into the bathroom, washed herself, slipped on a nightie and tiptoed back into the bedroom.

Peter still lay where he was, eyes closed, and as she approached the bed, he held out a hand for her.

'I want you to do what you want,' he said, drawing her on to the bed beside him.

'How do you mean?' She turned towards him, stroking his hair back from his damp forehead.

'You know what I mean.'

'About the baby or the job?'

'Both.' He opened his eyes and passed a hand over his brow again. 'If you're sure you don't want a baby then I'm content. Frankly, starting it all over again at my age would be traumatic. I hadn't thought it through.'

'Getting up at night . . .'

'The screams, the tantrums.'

'Babies are beautiful, but they're a tie. Besides, we love Fiona and Guy.' He turned sideways to look at her. 'Don't we? Despite everything?'

'We do. And they'd be terribly jealous of a baby. As they are now, it would cause all sorts of confusion and probably hostility. Frankly, I don't think I could cope.'

'I never thought of that.' He hesitated, looking at her. 'If you're *sure*.'

'I am.' She paused and ran a hand along his arm. 'It means having my tubes tied. Sterilisation. It's the sensible thing to do.'

'It seems very final.' His voice was flat, unemotional. Then, doubtfully, 'I *suppose* I could have a vasectomy.'

'You don't sound very happy about that.'

No reply.

'Besides,' Anna continued, knowing Peter had gone into his shell, 'I've discussed all this with Katie. She's had her tubes tied. Says there's nothing to it.'

'I feel it would . . . might, damage my masculinity. I mean one doesn't know. Vasectomy, I mean.'

'Whereas if I was sterilised, we could have an abandoned, carefree sex life.' She paused and smiled wickedly at him. 'Better than ever.'

'Better than ever.' He began to caress her. 'I don't believe you.' His voice sounded sleepy. 'If you don't mind, and you're sure . . . Besides, in a year or two we'd be able to go away for long, sexy holidays all by ourselves. Do it.'

And on those words he fell asleep.

How like a man. Changing their minds every two minutes, and yet they said women were the changeable ones.

Anna lay on her back, head propped in her hands. It was terribly final, but she knew it was what she wanted. How frightened she'd felt when she thought she might be pregnant. How trapped, unable to concentrate, terrified. It was so unlike her, even Katie had commented on it. *And* she had never told Peter. Even in marriage there was certain things one kept from one's spouse, and she thought that if she told him, Peter might be hurt she'd been so positive, so relieved, that his sperm and her egg hadn't fused to produce their child.

Anna drew the duvet carefully over them as Peter, fast asleep, turned on his side, his back to her; she pressed herself against him knowing that the ache, the longing she had for him would never pass.

CHAPTER 4

The comprehensive had been built in the sixties and, nearly thirty years later, it had already undergone extensive repairs. Even then it looked a jerry-built affair, a sort of concrete blackboard jungle, badly planned and of shoddy construction. It had two macadam playing grounds interspersed with patches of lawn, trees and an attempt at a garden which was invariably vandalised from the spring onwards. It was pathetic how regularly the attempts of the authorities to beautify this depressing place went unappreciated.

The school had about eleven hundred pupils, a tiny number of whom, due to a false Socialist Utopian idealism, went on to higher education.

Jessie Clark remembered very well the long and earnest talks she'd had with the Livingstones when first Fiona, and then Guy, came to the school. Anna had been a diligent member of the parent/teacher association and at first, as an eleven year old, Fiona had done well. She began to drop out when she was approaching thirteen, started bunking off and mixing with a crowd from one of the broken-down housing estates in Paddington, on the periphery of the school's catchment area.

No one's fault really, a case of mistaken, misdirected educational policies which were engendered by a Tory politician, Rab Butler, in the famous 1944 Education Act, with the best of motives: equality of education for all. But Fiona was one of the victims of this optimistic and impractical policy which didn't suit everyone. The bad, invariably, drives out the good. It had to be admitted that some pupils reacted best to discipline, an ordered society and a structured curriculum, even a uniform.

The comp had none of these things, and even its curriculum had been devised by its own staff to suit its own individualistic and, in the opinion of some, idiosyncratic, ends. It was unique; a few thought it was wonderful, but most thought it was dreadful and ill-equipped the children for a decent, even adequate, education. The gulf between private and State education was seen at its widest here.

Jessie felt a flutter of apprehension as the time for the interview with the Livingstones drew near. She looked out of the window at the traffic rushing up and down the busy arterial road out of London, at the stragglers in the playground, who should have been at their lessons, and wondered if she, a devoted educationalist and upholder of egalitarian principles, had contributed to that fundamental failure of the school to bring out the best, not only academically but socially, in those committed to her care?

Her secretary popped her head through the door.

'Mr and Mrs Livingstone are here.'

'Do show them in,' Jessie said with dogged cheerfulness and, hands in the pockets of her jersey suit, she went to the door to welcome them. Anna, who came in first, seemed her usual confident self, but Jessie thought Peter looked tired. She remembered, with a stab of guilt, how reluctant Peter had been to send his children to the school, but egged on by a determined Anna and given assurances by Jessie that a better, all rounded education could not be found elsewhere in the kingdom, he had agreed.

The three shook hands, and as the Livingstones sat down Jessie retired behind her desk, as if retreating behind a protective barrier.

Before her were Fiona's GCSE results which were, indeed,

awful. Outright failure in most subjects, a scrape through in English and History. But that was not the only thing. Beside it was a report from her form teacher, and those who dealt directly with her, which was every bit as damning as the examination results. Was it also a judgment on the school which had produced such an unsatisfactory pupil or, she studied them for a moment as they settled themselves into their chairs, the parents? Good, affluent, middle-class home it might be, but was it also a caring one? Above all, a perceptive one? Those with the most money were not necessarily the best parents. Had it in fact been the best environment for someone of Fiona's rebellious and unorthodox disposition? Did a stepmother *really* provide the love a vulnerable and sensitive child required? Was it actually possible? Especially with someone as hardworking and ambitious as Anna undoubtedly was.

'Well,' she braced herself as she began to speak, 'these results are very disappointing . . .'

'But not unexpected.' Peter, adopting an aggressive tone, shifted uncomfortably in his chair.

'No.' Jessie bowed her head in agreement. 'We *did* rather expect them. Nevertheless I'm still sorry they're *so* disappointing because Fiona did no work. Never once handed in written homework on time, if at all.'

'For years she didn't have any,' Peter interposed. 'I really blame the system, Mrs Clark.'

'Too late for that now.' Anna's quiet voice betrayed her unease. 'We didn't know at the time the children wouldn't have homework . . .'

'Well, they do in the fourth form . . .'

'But it was too *late*, Mrs Clark.' Peter struck the edge of the Head's desk with the palm of his hand. 'They should have been trained in the way of home study from the beginning and they were not. You don't just pick up these things. You have to learn them, be disciplined into them, get used to them. This sloppy attitude towards homework and the general uncompetitive nature of the school has worked to the detriment of Fiona and, if you ask me, most of the others like her. I take it the results as a whole weren't good?'

'Well, they *were* disappointing.' A flush stole up Jessie's cheeks.

'Then what are you going to do about it in future?' Peter's tone was growing more aggressive, and Anna slipped him an anxious sideways glance. 'Are you going to change anything, Mrs Clark? Are you going, for instance, *now* to introduce hard work and the competitive spirit? We have a son here too, you know. This year he begins to work for GCSE and the following year, if you ask me, we shall be sitting here having the very same discussion and hearing the same sorry tale about *him.*'

'I hope not.' Jessie knew she was projecting an air of defeat.

'You know it's very likely.' Peter leaned forward, aware of having gained the upper hand. 'Because Guy too has done *no* homework up to now, has had *no* annual exams as well, and he is to enter the fourth form with a lack of knowledge almost as complete – or should I say as incomplete – as Fiona's.'

Jessie by now was reduced to silence. Guy certainly was not a promising pupil. He seemed destined to follow the path set by his sister.

'There is absolutely *no* point,' Anna said, putting a restraining hand on Peter's arm, 'no point at all in getting overwrought about something that's in the past.'

'We're talking about the *future,*' Peter said.

'I know, I know,' Anna soothingly stroked his arm, 'and, yes, we should start thinking about the future and what to do about Guy. But for the moment we're here to discuss Fiona.'

'That is the question.' Jessie nodded thoughtfully, looking up. 'Fiona I understand doesn't want to stay on at school?'

Jessie and Anna had spoken on the telephone that morning to try and prepare the ground before the meeting.

Both parents nodded.

'We would like her to go to a crammer,' Anna swallowed, 'and retake her GCSEs.'

'And what does Fiona say to that?'

'She doesn't want to. Consequently, we would like her to stay on here and resit.'

Jessie neatly joined her hands in front of her, her expression grave. 'I really think, Anna, she would be wasting her time, and I think you and your husband agree in your heart of hearts, don't you?'

'But what are we to *do*?' Peter burst out as if prompted by some inner agony. 'She has no ambition, no motivation, nothing.'

'She expects us to keep her,' Anna went on in a level tone, trying hard to calm the proceedings. 'She knows we have the means. Peter and I have talked it over, and we really think, Jessie, that if she came back to the school that *would* be the best, if not the only thing to do.'

Slowly, regretfully, Jessie shook her head from side to side.

'I'm terribly sorry to say this, Anna,' she included Peter in her remarks with an inclination of her head, 'but I think it would be completely futile to send Fiona back here. In fact I would not *want* her.

'Furthermore, as she is already sixteen, I have no statutory duty to educate her.'

'What do you mean you have no statutory duty?' Peter spluttered, almost out of control.

'What I say. There is no obligation to educate anyone beyond the age of sixteen, especially if, as is clearly the case here, the person in question does not wish to be educated. Fiona obviously doesn't. I can't force her. What is more, with her attitude she is extremely disruptive and a bad influence in class. She unsettles people and makes them discontented, rebellious like herself.' Jessie reached out for a sheet of paper that lay beside the school report and exam results. 'I have here an account of Fiona's visit to France with the school. I'm afraid that her behaviour *there* was anything but satisfactory. She never came in at night when she was expected, and was considered a very bad influence on others who slavishly followed her. Moreover, I am sorry to report that there was a suspicion of drugs. Some substance, possibly Ecstasy I believe it is called, being ingested in the company of some others, including a crowd of local French boys and girls in the town where they were staying. They were all considerably the worse for wear and lacking coherence . . .'

'And *where* was the teacher in charge at this time?' Peter demanded, standing up and leaning threateningly over Jessie's desk. 'Tell me that!'

'Mr Livingstone,' Jessie leaned back in her chair folding her hands in her lap with an air of one whose patience is extremely tried, 'these were mostly boys and girls fifteen or sixteen years of age, some older. I am not saying that Fiona was a ringleader or even procured the drugs; but she did seem to play a very prominent part and her particular cronies were concerned to protect her, cover up for her. After this episode a member of staff did insist on accompanying the children everywhere, but of course it was extremely difficult. They enjoyed giving the poor harassed teachers the slip. The members of staff have returned completely exhausted, one close to a nervous breakdown, and a similar visit will not be repeated next year . . .'

'You mean *my* daughter has been taking a number of drugs?' Peter's voice could surely by now be heard on the other side of the door.

'It seems like it, Mr Livingstone.' Jessie's clasped hands pressed closer together. 'Believe me, I am very sorry to say it, but the staff are convinced she was no novice to the drug scene either, was, indeed, an instigator. Frankly I would not have Fiona back in the school even if requested to by the Education Authority. Were she here, I should probably expel her. I consider her a totally bad, pernicious influence and, sad though I am to say it, because I know you both to be devoted parents, I shall be very glad to be rid of her.

'As for Guy,' she reached wearily for another document and held it up, 'his report was terrible too. He did not do well in his end of term assessment, as you know. I believe him to be of a higher intellectual calibre than Fiona, and he has more discipline because of his devotion to sport, but if you would like to try and place Guy elsewhere, since you have the means and can afford it, I should strongly be inclined to do so.' She rose to her feet.

'I feel we at the school have failed you and I am humiliated; but I have nearly eleven hundred other children to think about and the more disruptive and unruly elements I can weed out the better.' She nervously straightened her skirt, and pulled her jacket closely around her hips. 'Believe me, I'm terribly sorry. But we at this school have done all we can. I consider myself to be an enlightened, caring educationalist. I have been in my profession for nearly thirty years and the principles we have in this school are ones I strongly believe in and adhere to. I think Anna does too. But they don't work with everyone, and they haven't worked either for Fiona or Guy. But then many parents consider themselves let down by the private sector too.' With evident pride she pointed to her desk. 'I have an application here from the parents of a boy at one of the very top public schools.'

'God help them,' Peter murmured as Jessie held out her hand, but he turned away. 'I shall be making a report to the Education Authority,' he said stiffly. '*And* about the destructive and malicious influence this school, and its barmy ideas, has had on my son and daughter.' He stood by the door, his hand on the handle, and looked back. 'Don't think for a moment you've heard the last of this matter, Mrs Clark.'

Sal, happening to be passing, saw a light on in the cottage owned by the Livingstones and hesitated by the garden gate.

Then, as if suddenly making up her mind, she opened it and walked up the path and knocked on the door.

As Anna answered, Sal noticed she was still in her dressing gown.

'Oh, I'm terribly sorry,' she said. 'I hope you're not ill?'

'No, not at all.'

'I'm Sal, you know, from down the road.'

'Yes, of course,' Anna said frostily. The memory of the last time she'd seen her was not easily forgotten. They hadn't met since, and she really didn't much want to ask her in. But Sal was not easily put off.

'Are the family with you?' she enquired chattily.

'No, I'm here by myself.'

'Everything alright?'

'Fine. I had a minor operation and just came for a few days' break before starting work.'

'Oh!' Sal nodded understandingly. 'Everything alright?' she asked again, clearly wishing that Anna would spill out the gory details.

'Fine. Look,' Anna found it very difficult to bear a grudge, to be rude. The woman was obviously trying to make up for that evening. 'Why don't you come in for a few moments? It's cold outside. You must think me terribly rude.'

'Oh, no,' Sal waved a hand in the air, 'I wouldn't dream of intruding. I just wanted to be sure that everything was alright. Not often you're down this time of the year.' She shivered. 'Do you have enough logs?'

'Plenty, thanks.' Anna flung the door wide open. 'Do *please* come in. I'm just about to have a coffee.'

'Oh, well, if you're sure.'

'I'm quite sure.'

Sal entered rubbing her hands, then held them out towards the fire.

'Oh, it's so lovely and *warm* in here.' She looked round. 'You've central heating too, I see.'

'Yes. My husband's first wife had it put in. She lived down here for quite a long time. Nancy. I don't know if you knew her.'

Sal shook her head. 'I've only been here a couple of years.'

'And your daughter,' Anna paused, recalling that night in the summer, 'Honey, is it?'

'Yes, Honey.' Sal nodded and moved nearer the fire as if mesmerised by the flames.

'How is she?'

'Oh, she's *fine*. Left school now. Works in a shop in Blandford, for how long I don't know. Fingers crossed.' Sal held up crossed fingers and smiled cheerfully.

'She must be the same age as Fiona.'

'Sixteen, going on seventeen. How are your children, Mrs Livingstone?'

'Do call me Anna. And please sit down.' Anna pointed to the chair next to the fire.

Sal settled into the chair and crossed one leg over the other. She wore leggings and a long warm cardigan that looked as though she might possibly have knitted it herself. She had on a rather cheap pair of boots, and it could have been quite a while since her hair had had the attention of a comb.

She was not an unattractive woman, nor quite as unprepossessing as Anna had thought her the night of the pot smoking episode. She had a fresh, open face, devoid of make-up. Yet her skin was incredibly good and she looked in her early thirties, though it was reasonable to expect she was older if she had a daughter of nearly seventeen.

Anna went into the kitchen to make the coffee, and emerged after a few moments with two cups on a tray and a plate of biscuits. Sal seemed hungry and Anna wondered if she had enough to eat. She suddenly became curious about this odd woman whom she had reluctantly allowed into her life.

'I was *ever* so sorry about that night.' Sal bit eagerly into her second biscuit before she had swallowed the first. 'I haven't had the chance to explain since. I know how upset you were; but you know you shouldn't be.'

'Oh?' Anna, her hands clasped around her coffee cup, eyed her companion. 'You approve of drugs? I gather you take them yourself?'

Sal bristled immediately. 'How do you "gather" that? Did Fiona say anything?'

'Fiona said nothing about that evening, but from what little I saw of you I felt you were smoking in the company of the young people.'

'And you think that's bad?'

'To be honest, I think I do.'

'Well, I don't agree with you, Mrs Livingstone. Pot isn't a *drug,* you know. It's a harmless substance, much better for you than alcohol or cigarettes.'

'Possibly.' Anna nodded. 'Expert opinions seem to differ.'

'Oh, you *do* think that then?' Sal looked interested.

'No, I do not think it necessarily; but I accept that there is an argument. The argument against is that marijuana and allied substances might lead to harder drugs, and in Fiona's case that seems to have happened.'

'Oh, dear.' Sal looked crestfallen.

'She certainly had taken Ecstasy and probably hard drugs on a trip abroad in the summer.'

'Oh, *dear.*' Sal reached for a fourth biscuit. 'She's not at school then now?'

'No.'

'Working is she?'

'No.'

'Oh!'

'She's at home, probably in bed, where she spends most of the day. Then she gets up, and after an elaborate, almost ritualistic washing and dressing ceremony, goes out at night.

We hardly ever see her. Even her father isn't as worried about her as he used to be.'

'And you don't worry?' Sal looked at her keenly. 'I thought you were ever so worried that night.'

'Yes, I do worry, but in a different kind of way. I don't know if you know this, but Guy and Fiona are my husband's children by his first wife.'

'Oh!' Sal looked thoughtful. 'No, I didn't know.'

'I wonder Fiona didn't mention it to Honey.'

'Well, she might have. But Hun would keep it to herself. They do, don't they, at that age? Very secretive.'

'Oh, yours is secretive too?'

'Very.'

'Is she living at home now?'

'Oh, yes. She has a friend who collects her every morning to take her to Blandford and brings her home again. Of course she's bored to death here. There are so few things for young people to do. She would like to get a room in Blandford and I have said that when she is seventeen she can.'

'Aren't you worried about what she'll get up to?'

'Look, Mrs Livingstone,' Sal reached in her pocket and drew out a packet of cigarettes and a lighter. After asking Anna if she minded and being told that she didn't, she lit a cigarette and blew a long stream of smoke towards the fire. 'Look, Mrs Livingstone, I mean, Anna, what I say is this: kids are not like they were in our day, are they? I mean I don't know how old you are, but I guess about my age. We were bad enough, but not as bad as they are today. Don't ask me the reason: affluence, too much welfare, a lapse of moral standards. Don't ask me because I don't know. I reckon young people have got to sort their lives out as we had to.'

'But the drugs scene *is* very worrying.'

'Oh, very worrying. And so is Aids, and of course the two are related if they inject. Dirty needles, I don't need to tell you. But what I say is that it is up to Honey to make what she can of her life. She didn't like school. She didn't pass *any* exams. A lot of them don't. Tough. Let them find out for themselves that it's a hard world. It's their responsibility.'

'Don't you think that at sixteen a young person still needs guidance?' Anna asked, thinking it rather ironical that she should be valuing the opinion of this odd young woman.

'No, I don't frankly.' Sal finished her cigarette and threw the stub in the fire. 'When Honey leaves home she can lead her life and I'll lead mine.'

'And what do you do?' Anna asked tentatively. 'Do you do anything?'

'No. Just please myself. I'm on benefit, single parent. I like to read and watch the soaps on TV. Frankly I don't really like it here, Mrs Livingstone – too quiet – but I didn't have much choice. It was either this or a council flat in Gillingham which frankly did not please me. You work, don't you?'

'I'm a solicitor.'

'Oh, I see.' Enlightenment appeared to dawn on Sal's face. '*That's* why you were so worried about the children smoking pot.'

'I'd worry anyway.'

'But why if they're not yours?'

Anna flushed.

'They *are* mine. I've had them since they were very small. I do worry about them.'

'But still it's not the same, is it?'

'Yes,' Anna stared at her boldly, 'it is.'

'Sorry.' Sal lowered her eyes. 'Didn't mean to offend.'

'I'm not offended, but it's an assumption people make and it's not true.'

Sal was anxious to change the subject. 'Ever think of having any of your own?'

'I did.' Anna paused. 'But I decided not to.'

'Very wise.' Sal got up and stretched her arms. 'Given my time again I would never have kids.'

'Oh, you've got more than one?'

'Yes. I've got a boy of nearly twenty.'

'And what's he doing?'

'He's at Bristol University learning to be a vet. Loves the country which is really how we came to be here. His father, my husband, was a farmer who got mangled in a tractor accident and was killed, silly bugger.' Sal's voice sounded gruff.

'Oh, I am sorry!' Anna put her hands to her face. 'How terrible.'

Sal looked solemn.

'It *was* terrible at the time; but it happened a long time ago. I've been a widow ten years, Anna. Ten very *lonely* years, really. I can't think I've made as much of a success of my life as I suppose you have of yours.'

Anna ran her hands through her hair. 'Not really.'

'Oh, I'm sure being a solicitor in London must be terribly important. Fiona did say you were clever. She spoke of you quite admiringly. I would never have thought she wasn't your real daughter.'

'Really?' Anna felt gratified, surprised.

'I think she's *really* fond of you.'

'You could have kidded me.'

'Seriously, I do. Why don't you ask her down? A spot of country air would do her good.'

'As a matter of fact, I think they're all coming down here for the weekend to take me back to London. Why don't you come over and have dinner with us on Saturday night? You and Honey.'

'That would be lovely.' Sal looked at the clock on the mantelpiece. She didn't wear a watch and gave the impression that time would not really be of much concern to her. She seemed such an urban creature that it was difficult to imagine her as a farmer's wife. 'I bet you want to get on with what it is you're doing, or maybe go back to bed.' She looked at her with concern. 'Feeling alright now are you?' Once again the hint that she'd like to know more.

'Oh, yes. It was just one of those things.'

Sal nodded understandingly as if to say: women's problems. Weren't they all the same?

Anna saw her to the door and stood on the threshold watching her as she walked back down the road to her cottage. Sal stopped at the gate of her own home and waved, and Anna waved back. Then she shut the door and went back to her chair by the fire, sat down feeling suddenly weary.

It was very funny how one had one's preconceptions shattered, one's prejudices excised. She knew that *she* had assumed that Sal was an unmarried mother with a difficult teenage daughter. That she would milk the system for all she was worth and get all the benefits to which she was entitled. She, Anna, would never have guessed that she was a widow whose husband had been a farmer and whose life had been blighted by tragedy. She would have assumed that Sal was comparatively uneducated, and perhaps she was, but not that she had a son clever enough to read veterinary science at a university.

In a way she herself was a woman of prejudices and presumptions, the traits she tended to condemn in other people.

Anna decided then that she rather liked Sal; that she was open, plain speaking and honest. She was pragmatic, a realist for whom life would hold few surprises. An engaging sort of woman.

In a way, Anna felt she had shown herself to be a middle-class moralist of the type she professed to despise; a champagne socialist who buried herself in her work because she could not really face up to the reality of an unsatisfactory home life, two appalling step-children and a husband whom she loved but who was becoming increasingly unreasonable and remote.

She climbed slowly upstairs to her room and lay on her unmade bed.

She had in fact felt dreadfully tired since the simple operation of sterilisation. She had spent two days in a private clinic. The operation was carried out by Katie and pronounced one hundred per cent satisfactory. She could now never have children. She could have sex without worry.

At first Anna felt elated, free from a great burden, a solution to a dilemma. She expected to feel totally free and happy, but to her surprise she didn't. She felt tired and rather depressed.

Katie said she thought this was a natural reaction, one many women had after a similar operation, or an abortion. Only there was no need for Anna to suffer from any kind of guilt. She had not killed anything. She was now free to enjoy her sex life unfettered by fear, either of ill-health, brought on by the Pill, or of an unwanted pregnancy.

But Anna felt neither of these things. She just wanted to be alone, and so she took a week off from work and had come down to the country in order to try and work things out.

But all she felt instead was muddled, depressed, angry. She didn't even look forward to the new job starting in January. The family were planning to spend Christmas and New Year skiing in Switzerland. Oh, and she was going to allow her name to go forward for election to the Council.

So why didn't she feel great? On top of the world?

She put her head on the pillow and wept.

CHAPTER 5

Peter thought Anna looked surprisingly well, a little pale but cheerful as she greeted them on the doorstep the following Friday.

Peter had taken the day off and they arrived in time for lunch, earlier than Anna had expected.

'I haven't got anything to eat,' she said, flinging her arms round his neck.

'Never mind, we brought plenty of stuff with us.' Peter encircled her waist with his free arm and kissed her, murmuring, 'How are you?'

'I'm fine,' she whispered back.

'Really?'

'Yuk.' Guy screwed up his face.

'What's the matter now, Guy?' Peter disentangled his arms from Anna's waist and turned to his son.

'All this lovey dovey. Yuk.'

'Sorry if it displeases you,' Peter said. 'I'm just glad to see Anna.'

'Oh don't let's *start* a row, for God's sake.' Anna bent swiftly to kiss Guy on the forehead, taking him by surprise, but she wouldn't have dared attempt any such gesture, not at the moment, with Fiona. Instead, noticing her usual sulky expression, she squeezed her arm.

'Hi! OK?'

Fiona grunted again and Anna's heart plummeted a little more. If only Peter had been able to come alone. The children had been told the reason for Anna's visit to hospital and why. They'd received the news without any comment, although their faces spoke volumes. Sex between old people was disgusting. The thought of babies . . . 'Yuk' as Guy would have said.

'Let's go to the pub for a sandwich,' Anna suggested, 'then you and I, Peter, can run into Blandford for some provisions for the weekend.'

'I tell you we've brought everything. Everything you can think of.'

'But we're having guests for dinner tomorrow.'

'Oh?' Peter looked surprised. 'Who?'

'Sal and her daughter Honey.' Anna glanced at Fiona. 'I thought you'd like that, Fiona.'

Fiona grunted and reached into the car, evidently searching for her Walkman.

'Is Honey home?' she asked, emerging from the car.

'I don't think so. She's working during the day. Martin will be home from school later,' she added, addressing Guy. 'You'll be able to walk up to the farm and wait for him after we've been to the pub.'

'There's really no need to go to the pub.' Peter began unpacking the stuff from the car. 'We've brought enough for an army.'

It was true, there was more than enough food for the weekend. Peter seemed relaxed, glad to be at the cottage, and Fiona appeared to have decided to make an effort to be civilised, going so far over lunch as to ask after Anna's health.

'Did it hurt?' she enquired.

'What, the op? I had an anaesthetic. It didn't hurt at all. It hurt a bit after, a vague pain.' She gently massaged her lower abdomen.

'What do they *do* exactly?'

'They tie the Fallopian tubes, so that the egg can't get to the womb to be fertilised.'

'What happens to the egg?' Guy wanted to know.

Anna looked at Peter, hunched her shoulders and burst out laughing.

'I don't know, what *does* happen to the egg?'

'Or all the eggs,' Fiona said loftily. 'There are millions of them.'

'They're so tiny.' Anna squinted up at a small aperture made by her two fingers. 'I guess they shrivel up and die. I'll have to ask Katie next time I see her.'

'And you don't have any regrets?' Fiona looked searchingly at her.

'Why should I? Why should I want children when I've got you?'

There was a rather embarrassed silence as if they didn't know whether she was being sarcastic or not. Finally Guy spoke: 'Why didn't you do it before? Weren't you sure that you didn't want a baby?'

'No, I was sure.' Anna put down her knife and fork, tucked her hands under her chin. 'It just seems rather a final step to take when you're in your thirties. But I do feel committed to you, to your father, my work and,' she took a deep breath, 'I *have* decided after all to stand for the Council.'

'My God, now you'll *never* be at home.' Peter stared at her in dismay. 'I'll see even less of you than I do now.'

'Why don't *you* do something, Dad?' Guy looked questioningly at his father.

'Like what? Don't you think I have enough to do?'

'You don't have any hobbies,' Fiona said slyly. 'You don't collect stamps or garden. You're not very keen on sport. You don't ever watch TV, except the news, you don't read except the papers. If you had an interest you wouldn't be so jealous of Anna.'

'I am *not* jealous of Anna.' Peter's expression was indignant.

'I never thought your father was jealous of me,' Anna concurred, trying to conceal the awful feeling she had that Fiona was up to something again. Always stirring things up, always making trouble, never a moment's peace. 'Your father is absorbed in his work. He brings a lot home. Always writing reports . . .'

'I garden when I'm here,' Peter protested. 'I like it very much. In London I don't have the time.'

'Yet you're always sitting around moaning about when will Anna be home. You ought to get yourself sorted out, Daddy,' and without asking permission Fiona jumped up and left the table.

''Scuse me,' Guy said and, wriggling off his seat, followed her. The door slammed behind them as they both went into the garden.

'Well I'll be . . . jiggered.' Peter, hardly concealing his irritation, also rose from the table and stood in front of the kitchen range. Peter was a tall well-built man, with a rather craggy, bluff featured sort of face and a receding hairline. He had a long nose and rather thick tufted eyebrows and looked as though he might have been a sailor rather than a lawyer. Anna gazed at him with love.

'I wish you could have come alone,' she said getting up and laying her head on his shoulder. 'I know I'm not supposed to say this, but I do. I can't help myself.'

'Why aren't you supposed to say it?' Peter said tenderly, beginning to stroke her hair.

'I'm always supposed to be so *nice* and *understanding* but I find it terribly difficult.'

'Darling,' he nuzzled her hair with his chin, 'they *are* very difficult children. I always try, you know, Anna, to concentrate on having a happy home. I *long* for it; but just recently it's been so difficult. And who is Fiona, I ask you, to talk about having nothing to do! She never gets up until three in the afternoon! What does *she* know about what I do with my life? Sometimes,' Peter tightly clenched his fist and punched the air, 'sometimes I feel like throwing her out. I really do.'

'You *don't.* You'd go mad if you didn't know where she was. I'm afraid, Peter, that for the next few years, or for as long as it takes, we'll have to accept Fiona as she is; helping her, tolerating her but, basically, putting up with her rudeness, her selfishness and her spite. It will take its toll but we'll win in the end. I'm sure we will, darling.'

'It makes *me* so hateful,' he said. 'The horrible things I've said to you.'

'I understand,' she murmured. 'I say horrible things back. Neither of us means them.'

'Does it hurt?' Peter tilted her chin to look at her.

'Does what hurt?'

'The tummy?'

'Why?' Her hand gingerly pressed the place where there was a little scar.

'I thought we might take a little nap.'

'With the children here running about?'

'They'll have gone off. They won't be back.'

'Oh!' Doubtfully Anna looked at the table. 'Shouldn't we do the dishes?'

'We can do them after,' Peter said and, with his hand tight round her waist, he pushed her gently towards the stairs that led to the bedroom.

It was late afternoon when Anna woke, and she lay for a moment trying to orientate herself. She had fallen into a very deep, relaxed sleep after the gentle caressing, the mutual stimulation, that hardly amounted to lovemaking but was pleasing in itself. Besides, it did hurt, and the last thing she wanted was to have to explain to Katie that the scar had burst open because she had behaved like an impetuous teenager.

Peter looked so peaceful asleep, the tired lines round his mouth and eyes had vanished, and for some time she lay contemplating him, the face that she loved, thinking what a perfect partnership they had, or would have, were it not for the children. How easily they forgave each other and overcame their misunderstandings.

Yet it was true that Peter had no hobbies, but neither had she. They were both workaholics and, apart from that, they enjoyed dinner parties with friends, occasional trips to the theatre or opera, and holidays abroad.

As for Anna, politics was work rather than a hobby because it involved ensuring, or trying to ensure, that people had a better life.

Peter didn't have her belief in or commitment to politics. He was an analyst rather than a believer. He voted Labour because she did, but she suspected that, at heart, he was probably an enlightened Tory. He believed in competition and the operation of a market economy.

Peter opened his eyes and stared straight into hers.

'Penny for them,' he said.

She reached out and touched him.

'Just thinking.'

Peter turned and looked at the clock by the bed. 'It's nearly four o'clock,' he exclaimed, sitting up. 'No sign of the kids?'

'No sight or sound. They'll be OK.'

'Remember last time you said that you found them smoking pot.'

Anna wriggled herself into a comfortable position, propped up against the pillows, her body touching his.

'Peter, we can't keep track of them all the time. You know that and I know it. Fiona, particularly, is independent, her own person.'

'She's still a child.'

'In your eyes, yes. In hers, no. I'm quite amazed, actually, that she came down with you.'

'She wants to look at her mother's things.'

'What things?' Anna turned to him sharply.

'Her paintings. She says that she wants to paint.'

Anna tried to conceal her astonishment.

'But she's never shown any interest before in painting or drawing, has she? Or any talent for them, as far as I know.'

'Well, I think drawing was her best subject.'

'No, that was English. If she had a "best" subject it was English. At least she passed in that. History too.'

'Well maybe it's been dormant. Maybe she has some of her mother's talent, who knows? Personally I'd be delighted if she got any inspiration from Nancy's work. If she wanted to train. It would be ideal, don't you think?'

'Ideal.' Anna snuggled down in the bed beside Peter. 'If we could get her focused on something it might be a whole new ball game.'

'If we could get Fiona interested in something and Guy concentrating on his work,' Peter slid an arm round her bare waist, 'it would be a whole new ball game for *us*.'

'How do you mean?' Anna felt a flicker of apprehension.

'We could have more time to ourselves.' He planted a kiss on the top of her head. 'We could really begin to enjoy life which, let's face it, we haven't for some time while concentrating on the kids. There'd be no need for you to stand for the Council.'

Anna didn't attempt to hide her concern.

'How do you mean, no need? I don't "need" to. I want to.'

'But, darling, *I* don't want you to.'

'You never said as much before.'

'But you must have realised it. Well I'm saying it now. I haven't been keen ever since you first brought it up.'

That was true. All the time she could detect a strong undercurrent of disapproval from Peter, a disapproval she hadn't wanted, perhaps because she lacked the courage, to challenge him on.

'We always agreed we wouldn't dictate to each other about our lives, Peter,' she said quietly.

'I never realised you'd grow so far away from me.'

'But I *haven't* grown away. Any division,' she paused to try and get her words just right, 'any split, if there has been a split, is because for some time you and Fiona, and others, keep on emphasising the fact I'm not her real mother. That is quite new, and frankly, I don't like it. It's hurtful.'

'I never . . .'

'You never *meant* to but you did,' Anna said firmly. 'Remember, I remarked on it? It made me feel that I was not part of the family. That somehow I was on my own.'

Peter shifted so that he lay on his back, hands on his stomach, and stared pointedly at the ceiling. 'I'm beginning to believe, Anna, that your work *has* superseded the family in your affections. It is of overriding importance to you, and standing for the Council is just part of it. Maybe that's really why you wanted to be sterilised.'

'That's ridiculous! And very unfair.'

'But,' he went on relentlessly, 'now that you can spend more time with me you want to spend less. I shouldn't think you'd ever have a night in if you're on the Council.'

'I think if *you* had any interests of your own you'd understand.' Anna thrust back the duvet and began to get out of bed. 'If the boot was on the other foot and you were the one thinking of standing for the Council, I'd be expected to support you.'

'No, you wouldn't.'

'Yes, I would. Look at all these MPs whose wives, though victims, are willing supporters of their husbands' ambitions. And usually men *are* more ambitious because they want power. I'm ambitious because I want to help people and now, as I have no children of my own and none are now possible, I feel free to do just that.' She got out of bed and put on her robe. '*And,* Peter Livingstone, I would be very glad if you would support me as you can be certain I should have supported you.'

And with that she went into the bathroom, seething with

a rage, a sense of indignation, a ferocity she hadn't experienced for years.

The next morning after breakfast, which to Anna's surprise she had eaten with them, though Guy remained in bed, Fiona said: 'Has anyone seen the key to Mum's studio?'

'It's behind the door I think.' Anna looked up from the washing up, Peter drying and carefully putting everything neatly away. On his best behaviour. He was taking a lot of trouble to be nice to Anna and she was taking care to reciprocate. The place was too small for tension, and it would never do to let the children sense this new feeling of unease between their parents. Peter didn't usually help in the house, regarding the garden, his province, as a more manly diversion. He found messing about in mud with thick wellies and producing a lot of sweat a gratifying occupation, especially if it was followed by a couple of pints in the pub.

'Not here,' Fiona said, after inspecting several keys on the back of the door.

'Maybe in the dresser.' Anna, with soapsuds up to her elbows, jerked her head in the direction of the large pine dresser that occupied a whole wall at the back of the kitchen.

Fiona went over to rummage in the drawer and, after letting out the plug and drying her hands, Anna joined her.

'We can't have lost it.'

'It's ages since anyone went in there,' Peter said. 'Maybe we have.'

'Is there anything in particular you want?' Anna kept her tone casual, offhand.

'I want to look at Mum's paintings. That's really why I came down here.'

'Fiona thinks she might like to paint.' Peter gave Anna a warning glance.

'What made you feel that?' Anna asked politely.

'Well, I was drawing something one day at a friend's and

he said he thought I had some talent.' Anna noticed the 'he'. Who Fiona's friends were or where they lived was a complete mystery.

'Did you ever feel that way before?'

'No.' Fiona was immediately on the defensive. 'But it's never too late, is it?'

'I think it's a splendid idea if you have talent and it's what you want to do. Maybe we could break open the lock, Peter?'

'Oh there's a key,' Peter said. 'I know,' and he disappeared into the larder and emerged with a handful of keys tied to various pieces of string. 'It's one of these. Let's go to the shed to see, Fiona.'

Fiona looked excited, happy, even relaxed, for a change. She wore her pretty fair hair plastered in fashionable spikes and the inevitable leggings and Doc Martens boots. At home she wore no make-up but when she went out she did herself up to the nines, purple lipstick, purple eye shadow and eyes deeply ringed with kohl. She'd had her ears pierced and talked about having a ring through her nose as well.

Anna was by now accustomed to the sight Fiona presented when she left the house to go wherever it was.

She saw it not as an expression of individuality, but as a uniform too often presented by those clients she saw either at the Law Centre or in Court.

The hair spikes had taken some getting used to because Fiona had soft, pretty hair with a deep wave. She must have gone to endless trouble to sleek her hair back with the thick gel and train it into sharp points like the caps of Swiss mountains.

Anna remained by the kitchen window looking out as Fiona crossed the garden with her father, who began to try the assorted keys he had in his hand, one after the other. They appeared to be almost on the verge of giving up when one Peter had inserted turned and, with a cry of exultation, Peter pushed the door open and entered.

Anna went over to the vegetable stand and began to do the

vegetables for dinner, plenty of potatoes to peel, cabbage to cut up. They were having beef that Peter had brought down, with smoked salmon to start, red and white wine. Anna filled the sink with fresh water and soaked the muddy potatoes in it, her eyes going from time to time to the shed at the other side of the garden. She could never recall Fiona ever expressing the slightest desire to visit it in all the years she had known her.

Fiona with a talent for art? Anna frowned in an effort at recollection as she began to peel the potatoes. If so, it was a light she'd kept hidden under a bushel, but if it was there by all means let her develop it.

After a while Peter came out, recrossed the garden and came back into the kitchen.

'I thought I'd leave her alone.'

'Good idea.' Anna nodded, but went on with her work.

'She seems happy.'

'I thought she looked happy when she came down to breakfast.'

'Shall I call Guy?'

'Let him sleep if he wants to. Doubtless when Martin appears he'll get up.'

She felt Peter's hand on her shoulder and involuntarily she stiffened. His lips brushed the nape of her neck.

'I do love you,' he said. 'Sorry about last night.'

Anna turned, potato and potato peeler still in her hands, and leaned against his chest.

'I won't stand for the Council if you don't want me to.'

He looked into her eyes, touched her nose gently with his finger.

'Let's wait and see, shall we?'

'Wait and see what?'

'What happens. You never know. Right now I'm going to go on with my digging and then a pint, or a couple of pints and a pub lunch.'

'Good idea.'

'I think I should be putting potatoes in for the spring.' Peter, a gardening amateur, looked unsure. 'Do we have a book?'

'Not here, but you can ask Fred at the pub at lunchtime if we see him.'

Fred was the local horticultural expert.

'Good idea.' Peter reached out and ruffled her hair. 'I love you.'

'And I love you too.'

Anna enjoyed the trivia of life in the cottage, so different from her usual daily routine. At home she had her daily, Paula, and was not much into cooking, but in the country she and Peter reversed their normal roles. He became transformed into a gardener and walker, a swiller of pints of Badger Beer, whereas in London he always drank wine, gin or whisky. Anna became the domestic animal she had never been, planning and cooking large meals in between washing up, making beds and keeping the cottage tidy.

It was a bit like Marie Antoinette and her court playing at being milkmaids in the opulent surroundings of Versailles because they had little else to do.

No, that was a bit far-fetched, Anna thought to herself with amusement as she straightened the duvet on her and Peter's bed, fluffed up the pillows and then turned her attention to tidying out one of the wardrobes, half of whose contents could go to Oxfam.

She wore a jersey and blue jeans, a smear of lipstick, no other make-up except foundation cream. For a moment she carefully studied her face in the wardrobe mirror and then, putting her fingers up to her eyes, smoothed out the creases underneath. She had good skin, she knew that, and a good figure. Her thick hair was in tip-top condition, well cut, and sprang back from her head, falling into a thick, neat bob half-way to her shoulders. Her clear blue eyes looked back at her appraisingly in a rather detached manner, as though she were measuring up a stranger, comparing herself to someone she didn't know.

Anna had always been at ease with herself. She supposed it would not be egotistical to say that she liked herself, and that this self-approval was not vanity or self-aggrandisement, but a genuine feeling of being at home in her body. Thus when people disliked her it worried her, and the gradual alienation of her two stepchildren had disturbed her profoundly and she sought for a cause, even though she knew that the experience of most people of the troublesome teenage years was similar to her own.

Her early years with the children had, she supposed, fulfilled her needs as a mother, stifled any natural biological urge she might have had to have children of her own. She used to do the school rounds, walks in the park, children's tea parties, outings to the zoo. They had been well behaved, good looking children, polite and well mannered, and in no time at all she came to see them, feel them as her own.

Peter was away a lot and she and the children were thrown together. She had to entertain them and care for them, supervise their activities and devise games for them, and when Peter came home it was like an endless celebration. There were special treats all round, holidays abroad or in the country. Very seldom, in those days, at the Dorset cottage because it still reminded him of the wife he had lost. It had been too sad a place to be too close to, the scene of Nancy's death.

When both the children went to junior school Anna resumed work part-time. An au pair was engaged to help in the house but Anna always made sure she was home on time to be with them while they had tea, bath them, put them to bed and read them a story.

Very slowly, only gradually, did it all change. Peter stopped travelling abroad so much, as he was given a senior position in the legal department at home, and Anna felt free to work longer hours and take on all the voluntary work she believed in.

She threw all the clothes on the bed and began briskly sorting through them. Jackets, old anoraks, jeans, tweed skirts which nowadays she never wore in the country – heaps of these.

She put the ones she knew they would never wear again into black plastic sacks. When it was all done she looked at her watch and was amazed to see that it was nearly twelve. She tied the tops of the bags, rearranged what was left in the wardrobe and shut the door. One day she would start on the spare room, but not now.

She looked in the mirror, ran a comb through her hair and glanced out of the window. The spade was stuck upright in the middle of the vegetable bed, but there was no sign of Peter. He'd already gone to the pub to slake his thirst or seek the advice of Fred, or maybe the two were not incompatible.

Anna smiled to herself. How Peter loved playing the role of the country gent, far from the tortuous and complex legal negotiations of his demanding job in the City.

Then her eyes travelled across to the shed and there was no sign of life there either. The door was shut. Probably Fiona had abandoned her examination of her mother's work and gone with her father. Well, in that case she'd join them.

Anna went down to the kitchen and into the pantry to check again that they had everything for the dinner with Sal and Honey that night. She slipped on her anorak, wound her scarf round her neck and put a woolly hat on her head. Gathering up her gloves she went to the front door and then stopped. Just as well to make sure that Fiona had gone, otherwise she would feel neglected and make a big deal out of that.

She unlatched the back door, walked quickly across the garden and turned the handle of the door to the studio, which yielded immediately.

Anna paused. The shed held a strange dread for her. She

had never been in it, never wanted to see the canvases that Nancy, her predecessor, had left behind. It was not that she tried to avoid mention of Nancy because she never had. In the early days she had encouraged the children to talk about their mother and her photographs were scattered round the house.

It was not that she felt jealous of Nancy or resented her, yet inevitably over the years her memory had receded.

Why now, then? Strange.

Finally she pushed open the door and found Fiona on her knees in a corner, crouched over one of her mother's paintings, whimpering softly like a kitten.

In a second Anna too was on her knees by Fiona's side, an arm round her shoulder.

'Pet,' she said using an endearment she hadn't used for years. 'Whatever is it?'

Fiona didn't reply but, her body shaken by sobs, she leaned against Anna who, gratified by this unaccustomed reaction, pulled the stricken girl close to her.

'Pet . . . Fiona. What has upset you so much?'

Fiona shook her head, buried her face in her hands.

'Mum–m–y's pictures,' she blubbered, 'they brought it all back.'

'Brought all *what* back?'

''Bout Mummy, 'bout missing her.' Fiona began to talk in a babyish voice.

'Oh, Fiona I'm so sorry.' Anna felt that unreasoning chill, rejection, like an abandoned child herself, pushed away to the corner, far from contact with the family.

'All Mummy's pictures *neglected,*' Fiona pointed towards them, 'lying here covered with dust as though we had forgotten all about her.'

'Well we haven't. We have her photos all over the house. You've talked about her quite a lot recently. Look,' Anna leaned forward and gently brushed the dust off one of the pictures, 'why don't we spend the afternoon dusting the pictures, going through them and then deciding which ones we'd like to frame? Would you like that?' She looked around. 'We could tidy the whole studio up and, look here, there is an easel, some unused canvases. Why don't you see if you really can follow in your mother's footsteps? Maybe you really do have a vocation to paint?'

If one had to be honest, the paintings done by Nancy so many years before really weren't up to much; blobs of paint on a canvas, a few wishy-washy country scenes, mostly in pastel colours. Swirls of mist merging with cloud, patches of sunlight streaming through branches. But then she had never pretended to be a professional artist, made no claims, and no one said she had.

But in Fiona's eyes they were perfection, and now the most attractive ones stood around the kitchen propped up against the dresser, the walls, the kitchen units, as the dinner party progressed.

Nancy was very much the main topic of conversation, and Anna bore it all with determined good humour, encouraging Fiona to talk about her mother and her feelings about her mother's art.

Sal and Honey had enthused over them too, Sal confessing that she didn't know much about art but she knew what she liked and she liked these very much, all of them, apparently.

Peter joined in the acclaim, saying the best ones would go to be framed and hung in the London house, and Sal wondered if a local art exhibition could be staged? Fiona assented to this with enthusiasm and said she would help Sal look into it. Anna was rather relieved to be able to say, truthfully, that she had absolutely no contacts in the art world and wouldn't know where or how to begin.

Sal and her daughter were an honest, engaging couple, and Anna felt her prejudices melting, until they dissolved altogether in a torrent of goodwill and bonhomie. The meal was plain but good, and so was the wine, of which a tolerable amount was drunk.

Fiona, all animation now that her tears were forgotten, said that she would spend all the next day doing out her mother's studio, tacking the canvases, and sweeping out the cobwebs so that she could start work on her own.

Peter, gratified at his daughter's show of interest in something positive at last, however, demurred.

'Darling, we're going back to London on Monday. Couldn't you wait until the next holiday?'

'Oh, Dad *do* I?' Fiona pleaded. 'Do I have to really?'

'But you can't stay down here, darling, on your own.' Peter looked at Anna for support. 'Can she, Anna?'

'Well,' Anna was again being cast in the role of villain, always having to sound negative, to dampen ideas, always the fly in the ointment. There was no earthly reason really why Fiona should be doing something, or at least attempting to do something, here as doing nothing in London. Yet Fiona was young and really too irresponsible to be left on her own. But how to put it without alienating her?

'Won't you be *lonely* on your own, Fiona?'

'Lonely is not the point,' Peter said heatedly. 'Heaven knows what Fiona will get up to . . .'

'You don't trust me,' Fiona burst out petulantly. 'You treat me as a baby . . .'

'Couldn't *we* help?' Sal said in a quiet, authoritative voice. 'After all, we're practically next door. Here to reassure you. To keep an eye on Fiona if that would help. We all *know* she's not a baby, wants to spread her wings. Perfectly natural. I'll certainly keep an eye on her if that will help. I mean, I know she can look after herself, but if she needs anything, you know what I mean? Then Honey will be here in the evenings and at weekends. Frankly, I'd like the company for Honey. She so misses people of her own age.

'Besides we can get to work on trying to arrange an exhibition for Fiona's mum.' She looked around expectantly, but there was only silence. Suspense seemed to hang in the air as Peter and Anna each searched silently within themselves for a reason to refuse, wishing that they'd been offered the question in advance, allowed time to think.

'Oh, Dad,' Fiona, face plaintive, infinitely appealing, leaned towards him and grasped his hand. 'Please, please say "yes".'

PART 2

Horizons New

CHAPTER 6

Anna stood looking at the gaunt warehouse building which had been part of the derelict site beside the railway bridge since the nineteenth century. It was in that run down part of north London which had escaped development for some reason or another: bureaucracy probably. Or maybe it was lack of interest on the part of developers looking for prime sites to which to attract the high flying yuppies of the eighties, who had begun to find parts of London north of Euston and King's Cross attractive.

Some of the windows of the building were without glass, like sightless eyes, and part of the top storey was missing. All around in the yard were pieces of broken machinery, upturned crates, empty boxes, rubber tyres and cases of empty bottles. A few dogs ran around relieving themselves when and where the fancy took them, a couple of wild-eyed cats threatened war from the vantage position of the high, broken fence.

In the background, the noise of a goods train trundling past made conversation temporarily impossible. When it had passed, the young man beside her, eyes gleaming with an enthusiasm she found, in her heart of hearts, hard to understand, waving his arms about with an air of ill-concealed excitement, continued: 'You see, Mrs Livingstone, this site has *endless* possibilities.'

'For what?' Anna looked searchingly at him.

'Why, for all kinds of things. The yard could be a play area for children; we could house workshops which would give employment to our members inside; some we could let. We could have sideshows, happenings, you name it.' As he stopped, his expectant gaze seemed to invite an enthusiastic response from her.

He was an engaging young man with his blond shoulder length hair, tuft of beard and moustache. His brilliant eyes were of an unusual turquoise colour, and in his long hessian robe and sandals he almost resembled the popular image of Jesus Christ: vibrant, alert, alive.

'How old were you when you left school, Damian?' she asked, abruptly changing the subject.

The man's smile vanished.

'Why do you ask that, Mrs Livingstone?'

'I just wondered. You're such an intelligent man . . .'

His expression turned swiftly from pleasure to derision.

'You've already made up your mind about us, haven't you, Mrs Livingstone? Like the others.'

'I don't know what you mean, Damian.' Anna perched on one of the upturned boxes and gazed earnestly at the man beside her.

'All you people, you "do-gooders", councillors and the like,' he went on, 'come here either to condemn or patronise us. You think we're all hippies, drug-addicts, layabouts . . .'

'No, Damian, I don't think that at all.' Anna stood up, and putting on her sunglasses again, surveyed the scene around her. 'You have asked for Council planning permission to develop the site and I am the Councillor on the Planning Committee. I'm here to help you. Believe me.'

He stared at her solemnly for a moment or two, and then lowered his eyes.

'I'd like to believe you, Mrs Livingstone. In fact I like *you*. I liked you when you first came. We all liked you and thought you were straight. Unpretentious and straight.'

'I'm flattered by your verdict, and I like you. I just wondered if you personally had any form of higher education. If, for instance, if need be you could teach. That was all I was getting at.'

'Oh!' He blinked. 'As a matter of fact I've a degree in Maths.'

Now it was Anna's turn to blink.

'Oxford,' he said. 'Magdalen.'

'Did you have difficulty getting a job?' Anna asked, wondering why and how this alert, obviously intelligent young man had ended up as the leader of a group of squatters who called themselves the Pilgrims.

The Pilgrims were a motley collection of people, of both sexes and all ages, who had somehow got together and formed themselves into a collective. For the last six months they had been illegally squatting in this disused warehouse, doing no harm to anyone, it was true; but maybe for this reason causing considerable irritation to their neighbours who lived either on the high-rise Council estates or in the neat rows of Georgian houses which had exchanged hands for large sums of money, due to the late eighties boom in the housing market.

It was also true that the Pilgrims did occasionally give loud and persistent voice to the sense of euphoria their freedom gave them. They chanted, banged drums, blew trumpets and bounded through the streets, flinging their arms in the air to the accompaniment of wild, enthusiastic shouts, hops, skips and jumps. There were several binges induced by drink, drugs, or a combination of the two, which also caused offence and, of course, no one doubted that a considerable amount of drug abuse went on which gave the Council its most powerful lever to try and evict them. That, and the fact that the Borough Surveyor had condemned the building as dangerous. The task of sorting out this knotty problem had, unfortunately but, perhaps, understandably, fallen to Anna, in view of her legal expertise and experience in these matters. It was one of the first jobs she'd been given since her election to the Council in May.

She had a great deal of sympathy with these people. She knew a lot about them, not as individuals but as a type of semi-vagrant, an offshoot of the gaps in the Welfare State, eroded increasingly now by various kinds of punitive local authority and Government action.

She would like them all to have had homes, families, jobs. Most of them had none of these things. Families who were either non-existent, who didn't want them or whom they didn't want; homes because they had not the wherewithal to buy, rent or otherwise pay for them, and as for jobs . . . well, one went with the other.

Some dropped out voluntarily, and she guessed that Damian was obviously one of those. Probably somewhere in London or the home counties there was a family rather like hers and Peter's, who bitterly regretted the waste, in their eyes, of a talent he undoubtedly had: the ability to be a useful, productive, wage-earning member of society. Criteria that in middle-class eyes were of such overwhelming importance.

Damian and Anna had continued their tour of the yard and they now went inside to a large, dark hall, welcomely cool after the heat outside. The atmosphere seemed, in many ways, like a very busy railway station, with people scurrying about on their various tasks, and every now and again an announcement being made on some kind of hailer. There were perhaps forty people in the hall, including several children, some toddlers and babes in arms. Their busy mothers were working in a space which had been set aside as a cooking area, obviously preparing the noonday meal. Others were working among the neatly laid out mattresses on the floor, making up the beds or sweeping the floor.

Several older men and women sat about on makeshift chairs or boxes, and one of indeterminate age and sex was sitting against the wall curled up, his or her face pressed against bent knees. Several animals were to be seen wandering around, or scavenging where the cooking was being done. Everyone looked reasonably happy and well fed. One or two came up to greet her, obviously sensing a meal ticket.

Yet withal it was very sad, certainly a condemnation of society. However at the same time it was somehow heart-warming, that this gathering of disparate people from all circumstances and walks of life should be brought together by common need.

The cooking was done on butane gas and paraffin stoves, none of which looked too safe. There was electric light, but no apparent heating and it must have been freezing in winter, a fact which made it pleasantly cool in summer. The upper floors of the warehouse were derelict, and a chink of light could be seen at the far end, approximately under the spot Anna had noticed from outside where the roof had given way.

'I think the Council want you out of here because the building is fundamentally unsafe,' Anna said, pointing to the chink of light. 'That is right under the broken roof. The water must come in in the winter. In fact, in the winter,' she put both hands round her shoulders involuntarily and shivered, 'it must be horrible. Frankly to rehouse you will be more costly than keeping you here; but it can't be done. The building is unsafe.'

Where to put them? That was the problem, particularly as, having formed a community, they now wished to stay together.

A few people had risen to greet them as they entered the warehouse, and they stood studying Anna as though she were a being from another planet. They registered various degrees of emotion: hope, anxiety, fear. One or two regarded her with loathing. Clearly, neatly dressed and well turned out, she was Authority, representing for them that section of society they had come to hate.

'You know Councillor Mrs Livingstone,' Damian gestured towards her, and one or two nodded.

'You see it's got such *potential.*' A young woman with scraped back hair and a ring through her nose came eagerly to the front of the group. 'You must see that, Councillor. We could make little cubicles and here,' she inscribed a wide circle with cupped hands, 'the communal area. Crèches,' she pointed to the far corner where the chink of light came through, 'for the children and,' another sweeping gesture with her arm, 'the kitchens over there.'

'Where are the toilets?' Anna asked.

'Well, at the moment . . . we have to use the public toilets up the road.'

'How *very* inconvenient.' The men and children, she suspected, probably used the yard. 'And washing?'

'There's a tap in the yard.'

'And you *all* use it?' Anna tried to conceal her amazement.

'We can go to the public baths.' The woman sounded defensive. 'They're not far away. Usually when we go to get our benefit.'

Once a week they would go to the local office of the Department of Social Security and collect the various benefits to which they were entitled: probably, in most cases, the maximum: family allowance, income support, the lot.

'What do *you* think, Mrs Livingstone?' The young woman joined her arms and stood beside Damian. Maybe she was his girlfriend.

'I think . . .' Anna hesitated, 'I would be deceiving you, I honestly would, if I said I thought you had any hope of convincing the Council to let you stay on here. The costs of repair would be enormous.'

'But the potential . . .' the young woman's face darkened.

Anna nodded vigorously.

'Oh, I agree. What's your name by the way?'

'Hope,' she said with a self-conscious giggle.

'I agree, Hope, that the potential *is* huge, but it would cost an awful lot of money and that,' she screwed up her face, 'we ain't got.'

'But we could raise it.'

'How?'

'All kinds of ways.'

'You could raise it, or attempt to, if you had all the facilities you want: the workshops, and so on. I have no doubt that between you all you have enormous talent: a great range of skills that in the end would bring in money. But, you see, first of all this . . .' she gestured around with a broad sweep of her hands, 'has to be changed. I should think the place would have to be *gutted* quite honestly, pulled down and a fresh start made. Then again in the eyes of the Council it has valuable potential for development into industrial premises, or houses that could bring in much needed income.'

'You mean if it's sold?'

'Yes.'

'To rich developers . . .'

'Well,' Anna hesitated, 'developers certainly, people who would want to build something on the land.'

'But *we* want to build something on it, Mrs Bloody Councillor Livingstone,' a woman hissed from the back, stabbing a finger at Anna. 'We the meek, the fucking poor, want to make something of it. But we ain't nothing.' And she spat on the floor.

'Please don't swear at Mrs Livingstone, Rosie,' Damian said in the sharp, authoritative tone of a leader. 'It's not helping our case.'

'Sorry,' Rosie mumbled. 'But you know what I mean, Mrs Livingstone. I get carried away.'

'I know, of course I know.' Anna smiled sympathetically. She wanted to put her arms round her and assure this woman of the streets, who looked only in her early or mid twenties, that she was her friend; that she believed in her cause, her freedom to please herself, and wanted to help her as well as everyone else.

But she couldn't. Why? Just because she was who she was: a member of the Council, a qualified solicitor and, she had to face it, a member of just those middle-class forces of society whom Hope, Rosie, Damian and their friends were retreating from and revolting against.

* * *

Anna got home very late that night. She'd gone from the squat to her office where the rest of the afternoon passed in legal business including a complicated matrimonial case where the parents were fighting to the death for custody of their so very vulnerable young children. That, too, was an agonising business, even though the parents lived, or had before the split, on The Bishop's Avenue, and had more money than Croesus.

She'd seen both parties separately – the father with his solicitor, as she was representing the mother; but she knew already, and so did the husband's solicitor, that neither parent was prepared to compromise.

Weary from this ordeal, she had thrown down a cup of instant coffee, made hurriedly in the office, and then gone to the Town Hall to report to the Chairman of the Housing Committee the result of her inspection of the warehouse squat at noon that day.

The Chairman was frankly unsympathetic towards squats. He thought that they did the image of the borough, and the Party, no good at all, and that they should be broken up and their members forced to find refuge elsewhere.

'But where?' she had urged.

The Chairman had shrugged his shoulders, said that was really up to the people concerned who milked the state enough as it was – well, didn't they?

Anyway, it would come up at the next meeting of the Council and no doubt an eviction order would be served.

As usual, Peter was in bed and, as usual, Anna crept into their bedroom, conscious of his bulky back turned to the door as if to emphasise his disapproval, his distance from her.

A solitary light burned on her side of the bed.

Whacked, Anna sank into the chair in front of the dressing table and gazed at herself in the mirror. Tired, very; lines . . . she peered more closely. Surely they had *increased*, especially the crows' feet by her eyes? She raised her fingers in a fruitless effort to try and smooth them out, perhaps even to erase them, but was left with the sinking feeling that no amount of anti-wrinkle cream would disperse the ravages of age.

She found herself wondering how old Damian Bradley, the Pilgrims' leader, was. Twenty-five, twenty-six? He didn't look any older. He could even be younger by a year or two. She was at least ten years older than he was. And if so, so what? And what precisely was she doing thinking in this absurd manner about a young, unemployed man who seemed to be going nowhere?

Yet he intrigued her. He had breeding, class. She hated the terms – of course, they were against her principles – yet they were here, nevertheless, at the back of her mind. He was extremely good looking, charismatic. He walked with a kind of languid elegance, and from his accent his family were certainly middle, possibly even upper, class.

Damn. There she went again. Labels, which, as an egalitarian, she abhorred. She tugged at her earrings feeling angry with herself – a successful, contented, happily married woman indulging in such fantasies.

Anna removed her rings, except her wedding ring, and undid the bow of her tie blouse. She took it off, rose and stepped out of her skirt and then went into the bathroom to complete undressing, did her teeth, cleansed and moisturised her face, brushed her springy hair.

Tired, exhausted, but at the same time mentally awake; the events of the day racing through her brain. She thought she'd go downstairs and watch some television to try and divert her mind from the myriad of things that seemed to possess it; but it was nearly midnight, and perhaps a book would do the trick instead. She crept into bed beside Peter and picked up a volume of political memoirs she seemed to have been reading for months. Just a few pages whenever she got the time.

She put on her reading glasses and turned to the bookmark. She knew Peter was awake, but his back remained turned to her and she felt too tired, too keyed-up, for a confrontation, the usual question and answer, reproach and defence.

Maybe they should have separate rooms? It didn't mean the end of the marriage, as some people thought or assumed, just practical good sense when one partner came in later and left earlier than the other. Usually it was the man, and the woman was meant to understand and be more accommodating. Besides, in those circumstances the woman wouldn't move out of bed; wouldn't dream of it. It was her place, and if the tired-out, overworked husband wanted sex to send him off to sleep it was her job to provide it.

Sex didn't send Anna to sleep. It was, anyway, the last thing she wanted at the moment.

Peter stirred.

'It's nearly a quarter to twelve,' he murmured peevishly.

'I know.'

'I suppose you don't really consider me.' Back still turned. Anna put down her book, the bookmark carefully in its place.

'Peter, would you like us to have separate rooms?'

Now he turned, his expression dumbstruck.

'Did you say separate *rooms*?'

'I didn't say separate *lives*. I simply thought it might be better, as I'm so busy at the moment.'

'At the *moment*. You're always busy, but since you've been on the Council. Well . . .' he puffed his pillows up behind him and lay back with an exaggerated sigh, 'I told you it would happen.'

'Peter, what if *you'd* gone on to the Council, or stood for Parliament?'

'I would never have dreamed of it. You know politics don't really interest me.'

'I'm speaking hypothetically. Supposing you were a political animal – as I confess I am – and you decided to combine civic duties with your work?'

'What are you getting at, Anna?'

'Whether I wanted to or not, I would have been expected to be your helpmeet, provide meals at any time, welcome you home at all hours; maybe sex last thing and then again first thing in the morning. Be a proper woman, in fact.'

'You are a proper woman.'

'You know what I mean. I'm acting out what has, for centuries despite women's lib and all, been considered the male role, and you are behaving like the wounded female is meant to behave: touchy, brittle, uncooperative, petulant, uncommunicative, and you've been like that for some time, Peter.'

'We used to go to the opera, the theatre . . .'

'It will all settle down. After all, I've only been a councillor for a few months.'

'And you threw yourself into it with almost indecent enthusiasm, *and* so soon after becoming a partner and taking charge of the Wigmore Street branch.' He looked across at her. 'Tell me, Anna, is there something missing from our life, honestly? Maybe you should have had a baby. Maybe all this . . .' he waved a hand in the air, 'desperate search for something to do, filling in every minute of your time, is a kind of substitution for the baby you should have had, the maternal role, now that Fiona has left home and Guy appears to have settled down a bit.'

Anna lay listening to him, conscious of a rising feeling of anger, wondering if, in fact, she should make the move to the bed in the spare room that very night.

Flounce out of bed, seize the pillows and march to the door? No, far too dramatic. Not her style. Throwing down a gauntlet instead of offering an olive branch?

'I think to throw this back at me about the baby is unworthy of you, Peter. It's cruel and unnecessary. It's not as if we didn't discuss it well and truly at the time.'

'It was obvious you didn't want one. You were determined to have the sterilisation.'

'I was not. All things considered, it seemed the best thing

to do, you *know* that. Then the opportunity of the partnership came up . . .'

'And that swayed you, didn't it?'

'No, it did not.' Her tone grew more heated. 'It brought it to a head. It was time to think about horizons new.'

'You'd been talking about the Council before that . . .'

'Fiona fluffing her exams and leaving school was a big worry . . .'

'You can't blame it on her.'

'I'm not blaming it on *anyone*, Peter, can't you see that? I'm just saying that, at the time and in the circumstances, I thought what I did was right. Anyway it's done and can't be undone.'

'You can't have them untied?'

'No, I can't,' emphatically, 'most certainly can't, and wouldn't want to if I could. And it's not just the practice and my Council work. The children are still unsettled. Guy is not preparing for his exam year with much enthusiasm and we really don't know what Fiona gets up to in Dorset, do we?'

'How do you mean?' Peter looked at her anxiously.

'As far as we *know* she's OK and she's painting, but what influence does Sal have on her? Honey? We don't really know. Perhaps we'd rather not because we haven't faced up to the dope business. In a way we've shut that aspect of our lives away, put it in a corner.'

'I thought of going down this weekend.' His expression became critical. 'You really haven't been much of a mother to those kids you know, Anna.'

'Peter,' she sat bolt upright and stared at him, 'how *can* you say such a thing?'

'It's true.'

'You said once upon a time that I was a wonderful mother. The best they could have had.'

'That was when they were young. As soon as they began growing up and you went back to work and they became more difficult, you kind of opted out.'

'I did *not*. I was very concerned and I said so.' Her tone grew more and more heated.

'But you only said recently that you didn't feel the way I did. You said it several times.'

Anna was silent, her sense of outrage quickening her heart rate until she thought it would burst. Finally she said: 'I was being honest. What I meant was that it was hard for me, for any non-biological step-parent, to feel the tug at the gut that a biological parent feels. I understand other step-parents feel it too. You know the thing about blood being thicker than water? Well that's how I interpret it. I worry about them, I love them and I agonise over them, but in not quite the *same* way as you . . . but to say I was an uncaring mother . . .' She felt unwelcome tears prick against her eyes and then Peter's hand stole comfortingly around her shoulders.

'Sorry.'

'You're always saying that, Peter.'

'I mean it. I shoot my mouth off. I thought this weekend we might both pop down to Dorset just to see how Fiona is getting on.'

'You mean *tomorrow*?'

'I know,' tone of resignation, 'you've a lot of things to do, a fête to open, a . . .'

'No,' firmly, 'I can come. I can put everything off. I will put everything off.' Features drawn, she glanced sideways at him. 'Despite everything you say, I want you to know how much you and the family really do matter to me. How they come before everything else.'

They reached the cottage at about eleven, having left after an early breakfast. First of all Guy said he didn't want to go and then he changed his mind. When they pulled up outside the cottage they sat for a moment looking at it as if each was wondering, a little guiltily, a little too late, whether they should have forewarned Fiona. It had seemed a good idea at the time to spring a nice surprise on her.

'She'll probably be at the back, painting.' Anna jerked her head in the direction of the silent house.

'She'll probably be asleep,' Guy said more prosaically.

Guy was right. The front door was locked and the shed round the back was deserted, though an easel was set up in a corner and a number of half-finished canvases lay around.

They went in by the back door and the kitchen was, as usual, in an appalling state: dishes stacked in the sink, on the draining board, the remnants of a half-eaten meal on the table.

Anna's heart sank. Well, it had been Peter's idea. If anyone was to blame, he was.

'This was rather a stupid idea after all,' she murmured, thankfully putting the two bags full of food she'd been carrying on the floor. 'We should have warned her. She's not going to change overnight you know.' Anna saw that Peter was making an effort to conceal his disappointment. He nodded; no words came.

They all looked at the staircase as if wondering who should be the first to go up.

'You put on the kettle, I'll go and see if she's awake.' Anna flashed Peter and Guy a cheery smile and gingerly mounted the stairs.

She stood outside Fiona's door for a moment, aware of that old familiar feeling of dread rearing its ugly head.

Fiona had been living on her own for over six months and, so far, things seemed to have gone well. Peter gave her a modest allowance. They came down occasionally to see her – they'd all, for instance, spent Easter together. She came up to London, not often but ostensibly to buy paint and materials, see friends. No one really knew how she was getting on as she was so secretive about her work but, to all appearances, she was well and happy, happier she said than she'd been for a long time.

Anna realised now that they *had* been fools not to forewarn Fiona they were going to visit her, and her courage nearly deserted her. Finally she braced herself and knocked firmly on the door.

'Fiona,' she called, 'it's us.'

Silence. It then occurred to her that Fiona might not be there. She was, after all, a young woman they didn't really know, and now, since she'd left home, how she got on or whom she met. Truth to tell, and if Anna had reason to feel guilty about anything it should have been this: they'd been so glad to get rid of her, to have that awful disturbing presence out of the house, that they didn't enquire too much. A terrible abnegation of the parental role but true nevertheless. They simply didn't really want to know.

She tapped again and, turning the handle gently, pushed open the door. She saw immediately that the curtains were drawn and in bed, fast asleep, was Fiona. Anna breathed a sigh of relief and was about to leave the room when Fiona's eyes flickered and opened. For a moment she stared incredulously at her stepmother and then reached up and rubbed her eyes.

'What . . .' She sat up in bed and gaped at Anna. 'Is something wrong?'

'No.' Anna gave a rather fake, pseudo laugh, and perched on the end of the bed. 'We simply decided we wanted to come and see you. The weather forecast was good.' She clicked her fingers in the air. 'Did it on the spur of the moment.'

Fiona looked at her suspiciously without smiling.

'Checking up on me, I suppose.'

'Oh, Fiona!' Anna got up and walked over to the window, drawing aside the curtains. 'Why *must* you always be so suspicious? I tell you it was an impromptu, friendly gesture. No ulterior motive at all.'

'The place is in a hell of a mess.'

Anna said nothing.

'I'd have tidied up if I'd known you were coming, I know you hate it. Hell,' she sat up in bed, tossed back the duvet angrily and sat with her feet on the floor. 'What a *hell* of a thing to do, arrive unannounced, just like that.'

'It really was well meant. Dad wanted to come and see you. Guy's here too.'

Fiona stared at her.

'*You* didn't want to come and see me, I suppose. You were dragged here?'

Anna decided to make a last effort and sat again on the bed next to the angry girl.

'Fiona. You are now seventeen and I've known you since you were four. For most of that time I've been married to your father. When I married him I took you as well as him, you and Guy, and I loved you and still do. Sometimes, I'll admit, it is hard. In recent years it hasn't always been easy; you haven't made it very easy for me . . .'

Fiona suddenly put her head in her hands.

'For Christ's sake I don't want a bloody lecture! I've only just woken up. Give me a chance to sluice some water on my face, clean my teeth and I'll be down.'

'Right.' Anna got up. Once again she felt rebuffed, but when had she really felt anything else when it came to trying to have a heart to heart with Fiona? Better really not to try at all.

When she came downstairs there was no sign of Guy. Peter still stood in the kitchen looking bewilderingly about him as if he didn't quite know what he should be doing. Well he could have done the dishes for a start, started to tidy up, Anna thought angrily, but decided to say nothing.

'Is she there?' He looked up as she came into the kitchen.

'Of course. Where did you think she would be?'

'Well,' Peter scratched his head, leaving a volume of words unsaid. 'Is she alright?'

'She was asleep. Didn't seem very pleased to see me. That's nothing new though.'

'I'm sorry we came. We should have rung.'

Anna moved over to the sink, biting back more words. She'd had three weekend engagements to put off, making what sounded like lame excuses to the disgruntled organisers on the other end of the phone first thing in the morning.

She'd put a lot of people out, upset a great many. For what? She tugged on the washing-up gloves with more strength than they required. For what? For this!

'Could you make the coffee, Peter?' over her shoulder as she began to tackle the mound of dirty dishes.

'I'd rather have a beer.'

'I dare say you would, but you did come down to see your daughter. I'd like a coffee, please.'

'Well, is she coming down or did she go back to sleep?'

'She said she'd have a wash and be down in a few minutes.'

'Does she seem alright?' She could feel Peter's breath on the back of her neck, his voice a mere whisper.

'Yes, she seems fine.' Not turning round. 'Only tired.'

'Tired at noon, for God's sake! We should have rung.'

Anna plunged her hands into the soapsuds. 'Peter, we should have planned this, say, for next weekend or the weekend after. That way I could have got out of my engagements and not offended so many people. As it is I had to lie. I know it sounded like a lie and I felt awful about it.'

'You didn't *have* to do it.'

Anna straightened her back and gazed out of the window. 'I think I did have to do it.'

'What do you mean?'

'I had, was forced to show you that I loved you and Fiona and Guy. That I was the wife and mother, part of the family. Somehow by your saying that I wasn't a very good mother, you made it essential for me to do this. Well I've done it and I've made the best of it, so let's get on with it. Let's try, really, once Fiona has come down, to make the best of it, and if we possibly can, have a really good time.'

CHAPTER 7

When Fiona came downstairs she was in a better mood than she had been half an hour before, not surprisingly perhaps, Anna acknowledged to herself as Fiona kissed her father and gave her a fleeting smile, a fluttery wave of the fingers, nothing too intimate. It had been rather stupid to descend on her unannounced. Few people, when it came to it, liked surprises, and Fiona was not one of them. They should at least have telephoned.

But then, when you came to think of it, it was Peter's fault. He had formulated his plans almost at midnight the night before. It was once again a case of men doing and women following. One had supposed that all that sort of thing was in the past.

Anna decided to let the children go off with their father to the pub for lunch while she made the excuse that she had a lot of odd jobs she wanted to do. Such as? Doing out the spare room which, she thought, could be made into a more comfortable studio for Fiona, a proposal that found favour with Fiona who contrived, from that moment on, to be more pleasant to her stepmother. Moreover, the spare room faced south and there was the possibility that they could put in a decent sized window to give it more light.

Anna assured them that she only wanted a snack anyway, and the three of them went off happily in one another's company. She stood at the window of the spare room watching them walk down the road, Fiona's arm linked through that of her father. A family togetherness. Did she fit in there? Had she ever? Would she ever?

She turned from the window with a heavy sigh and surveyed the rather unprepossessing sight: the spare room which had an unmade single bed in it but which was also a sort of glory room, a junk room.

It was really the fourth bedroom and would have made a nice guest room except that they had always made a point of never inviting guests to the cottage. It was a place where they went to get away from it all; where they wanted to be alone. There was enough entertaining and excitement and socialising, after all, in London. Here one wanted a rest.

Not that it was very easy for someone of Anna's temperament to rest. She scarcely knew the meaning of inactivity, of repose. She was either rushing from one appointment to another, attending meetings, committees or conferences and when she sat it was either to eat, to read legal documents, counsels' opinions, judgments and, of course, endless Council reports.

She was someone who, like Peter, could be said to have no hobbies. Maybe that's what had made her a bad stepmother. Had it also made her a bad wife?

She flopped on the side of the bed and gazed around her. This had been Nancy and Peter's room. Their bed had been sold and the decision was made to move to another room when she and Peter married. It wasn't so much that she would have minded using either Nancy's bed or Nancy's room, but Peter had. Now the room was very much as it had been when Nancy died. She, Anna, was sure that the children had completely forgotten it was their father and mother's bedroom, the room where she had died.

Anna tried to visualise Nancy as she must have been, the kind of person she was. How much of her was in the children? Certainly her looks were reflected in Fiona. But was her talent, or did she even have any? What of her temperament, her charm? The first certainly possessed by Fiona, and the second by Guy who could get away with a lot of things because he exuded it.

The striking of the church clock nearby jolted Anna from her reverie. It chimed for one o'clock, and Anna realised that it was a lovely day outside and once she had finished her self-appointed chore a number of pleasurable things could be done in the afternoon. Doubtless Peter would want to garden and she thought she might stroll down to see Sal, maybe invite her and Honey to supper. Or would they consider that always being asked at the last minute was patronising? Should she have telephoned first? But the whole visit had been arranged in such a hurry . . . Decisions, decisions. Always decisions.

Anna bounced off the bed and flung open the double doors of the wardrobe which was literally stuffed with clothes. They were mostly country clothes: jeans, shirts, anoraks, a couple of jackets that clearly belonged to Peter, but which she never remembered seeing him wearing, and several dresses which had belonged to Nancy. It was odd that no one had considered going through this cupboard for over a dozen years – maybe Peter did from time to time, but she suspected he didn't and that Fiona had no interest in it either.

Anna gathered most of the clothes into her arms and threw them on the bed, hangers and all. Then she began to sort through them. She'd make a pile of Nancy's things and then the family could decide what they wanted done with them. She would ask Peter if he wanted any of his things, and if he didn't, they could bundle them up and send them to Oxfam.

Nancy had been much smaller than Anna: petite, fine-boned, and beyond colouring and superficial facial characteristics there was no resemblance. Nancy, it was agreed, was lightweight, a scatterbrain. If Peter was to be believed, and there was no reason why he shouldn't be, she took very little interest in her children. Conversely, they adored her for it, venerated her memory more than ever now, since the passage of time seemed to have eclipsed the years.

Anna found the process of sorting through and folding the clothes oddly satisfying. There was something soothing, she decided, in the sameness of domestic routine.

She liked peeling potatoes, preparing the simple food they ate in the cottage, even washing up. In London it was all microwaves, precooked and frozen food usually made in advance by her excellent daily who doubled up as a housekeeper. But so many meals were eaten out, or not eaten at all.

She liked making beds, dusting, hoovering, tidying. She felt at one with the chores of the house while Peter preferred the manly role of digging and muck-spreading. Of course, it was all fantasy. She would hate it all the time. But, for a while, to play Marie Antoinette and the milkmaids was kind of fun.

At the bottom of the wardrobe was a selection of boots and shoes of various shapes and sizes, male, female and unisex. Nancy had small feet too, and her taste in shoes seemed unexceptional. Apart from casuals they were mostly sensible court shoes, such as one would wear with a good dress for a dinner party in the country.

There were few signs of the artist; nothing outlandish or bizarre, like her daughter wore now. Just unmistakably middle class, in good taste with, perhaps, a liking for bright colours: blue, turquoise, shocking pink and leaf green which would give her the sort of bright, bird-like effect Anna imagined Nancy had.

She left the footwear where it was and went down to the kitchen to get some black bin liners in which to put the clothes. To her surprise she found that Fiona had returned and was ferreting in a drawer as though she'd lost something.

'Oh!' Fiona looked up sharply when she saw her. 'I didn't realise you were still here.'

'I was tidying the spare room. Have you had lunch?'

'I had a sandwich. Daddy and Guy are still in the pub. Daddy loves jawing away to farmers as though he knows what he's talking about. He and Fred can keep each other bored for hours.'

Anna grinned. This confidential, friendly tone was like the Fiona of old. She wondered if she dared hope that a rapprochement was taking place?

'I'm sorry I was rude to you this morning,' Fiona said, as if she could read her mind.

'That's OK. You were half-awake. We should have rung. It was your father . . .'

'I know. He said over lunch that you had cancelled any number of engagements just to come and be with us.'

'It's the least I can do.' Anna, mollified, perched on the edge of the kitchen table. 'I realise I haven't been a very good mother of late. I have taken too much on and . . .' she paused, not quite knowing how to proceed.

'But why should *you* reproach yourself?' Fiona sat down in the chair facing her. 'You've had a rotten time with us. I know I've been hateful, and I so meant to be different this time, but I started out badly. I feel I've let you down and I let Dad down. We said horrible things to you about not being our real mother. After all this time it was a nasty, silly thing to do.'

Anna could hardly believe her ears. What had brought this on? Surely in such a short time it couldn't be due to anything Peter had said? As if answering her unspoken question Fiona rapidly went on. 'Sal thinks you've been a brick. She likes you.'

Ah, Sal, that was it.

'You mean you confided in Sal?'

'Sal's a mixture of youth and maturity,' Fiona said thoughtfully. 'She can be as young as us and as old as you. She can do the things we do and understands us. She and Honey are more like sisters than mother and daughter. In a way she's a teenager herself. She knows she can be irresponsible and lazy. She looks up to you and admires you enormously.'

'Really?' Anna felt gratified. Also surprised.

'You know I was beefing about you always being busy and not understanding, and she said that you also had the right to your own life. She said you had done a lot for us and obviously loved and believed in us even to the extent of foregoing having babies of your own. I never thought of it like that.'

'Look,' for a moment Anna felt almost overcome by emotion, 'I wasn't a martyr. Don't think that for a moment.'

'Oh, I don't. Neither does Sal. But you see there are things I never thought of. Then I know you persuaded Dad to let me stay down here, and it's been great. It really has.'

Anna thought it was not quite the best moment to ask this stepdaughter, who was acting as though she had undergone a Damascus-like conversion, to come and decide what to do with her mother's old clothes. It would break the bond, rather the fragile thread that drew them together. So she said: 'Why don't you show me what you've been doing? I'd love to see your paintings.'

'Oh, would you? Really?' Fiona's expression suddenly reflected the self-doubt and insecurity she'd often had as a little girl.

'Yes, I would. And then we can go up and have a look at the room. See what it would be like as a studio.'

'You're very good to me really, Anna.' Fiona reached out for her hand, pulling her off the table and towards the door like the excited, trusting little girl of old.

Anna followed Fiona across the garden, standing aside as she threw open the door, the expression on her mobile face suddenly registering not excitement but doubt.

'I don't *know* exactly if you'll like them.'

'I'm sure I shall.'

'They're not much good.'

'Well, let's see.' Anna smiled at the excited girl and pushed her inside.

Whatever their quality, there was no doubt that Fiona had not been idle in the months she'd had to herself in the cottage. Canvases were stacked around the wall in various stages of completion, and there was a half-finished painting on the easel by the window. The place was in Fiona's usual state of clutter, and it was obvious she didn't go in for cleaning paintbrushes which must have been rather expensive. Many of them lay congealed on the pallets as if Fiona had carelessly thrown them down, too impatient to clean them.

Casting an eye swiftly around the assorted canvases, Anna saw at once that Fiona's untutored talent was even less than her mother's. The pictures were of a uniform chocolate-boxey effect, simple subjects amateurishly executed, in wishy-washy colours. Yet there were dozens and dozens of them and it was obvious that Fiona painted feverishly, probably mostly all the time, dashing them all off with little consideration given to perspective or style.

It was very difficult for Anna to dissemble, even more so as she knew that Fiona almost breathlessly awaited her verdict.

'You *have* been busy.' She began thoughtfully to walk around, examining each one carefully. It was rather like looking at the work of a class of untrained young artists such as one would find in the average school. There was no real evidence of natural ability, of talent at all. But why, after all, should there be?

The whole enterprise had been one of Fiona's whims in order, Anna suspected, to stay down in the country. It was rather like people who wanted to write or act without any real vocation whatever.

Anna knew that Fiona was watching her, so she took as much time as she could on her tour of inspection while turning over in her mind what she could possibly say. Finally, standing in front of the unfinished canvas on the easel she said: 'Fiona, I like very much what I see, but,' she turned to study the anxious face, 'it seems to me you could do with some training. I mean you haven't had any, have you?'

'You mean to say I'm no good?' Fiona's features recomposed themselves into the familiar mulish stubbornness.

'No, I don't mean that at all; but most artists, even the best, have trained for many years. I think if you had a teacher you would learn more about form and colour . . . and perspective,' she finished knowing very well how lame and unconvincing she must sound.

'You just don't like them. Don't pretend.'

'I do, really. I like them. I'm simply saying that if you want to go on doing this, you can. No one's stopping you. Your father is prepared to support you, to help in any way. Having seen your work I feel personally that it would be better all round, and more productive from your point of view, if you studied with a teacher, and I'm sure someone can recommend one. Or you might try art school.'

'You're *saying* I'm no good,' Fiona insisted.

'Fiona, I am *not*. But you don't want me to lie to you.'

'Just when I was trying so hard to be *nice*.' Fiona petulantly stamped her foot. 'Just when I tried so hard for us to be friends you have to be horrible and negative about my paintings.'

'Fiona . . .' Anna's outstretched hand went instinctively towards her, but instead of taking it, Fiona slapped it away from her, her face contorted in that familiar frenzy of anger, loathing and, perhaps, fear. 'You know you don't like me, Anna. You don't like anything about me. So why do you *pretend*?'

She then turned her back and ran out of the door, across the garden, round the house and out of sight. Probably on her way to try and get comfort and reassurance from Sal, or her father, or both.

'You could have pretended you liked them,' Peter said later when, in the seclusion of their bedroom, they could discuss the events of the day; the exhausting events of the day: Fiona's renewed tantrums, her outburst against her stepmother, her threat to destroy all her canvases and make a bonfire of them in the garden. (It was so tempting to say 'let her'.)

Finally Fiona disappeared without saying where she was

going, but they were determined that her behaviour would not be allowed to spoil the day. After all, there was Guy, who appeared unusually subdued, to consider as well. They ate dinner virtually in silence, and at nine Sal rang to say Fiona had been with her and Honey, and was on her way home.

She had gone straight to her room where, eventually, Peter was allowed in. He now relayed the results of his talk to a more than usually exhausted Anna who would rather have had any number of events to open or committee meetings to attend than this.

'I didn't say I *disliked* them.' Anna, already undressed, lay on the bed longing for sleep. 'I suggested she might like to have proper training.'

'Well, she misunderstood.'

'She said I'd never really liked her,' Anna said bitterly. 'She uses every excuse she can to make the thing personal. Look,' Anna propped herself up on her arm on the bed, 'I don't honestly think the paintings *are* very good, but what do you expect? She has had no training, given no indication ever that she liked art and suddenly she decides she wants to be a painter and expects us to say she is a genius. It's not reasonable. It's not fair.'

'It's true though, you *are* rather critical of her. After all, the poor girl is trying to do something.'

Anna turned over, reached for the pillow and thumped it hard, wishing it was someone's head.

'Oh, Peter, you make me so angry. I am not *saying* that Fiona can't paint. I am just suggesting that, if it is what she wants to do, she might go to an art school, take lessons, learn more about the techniques and craft of being a painter. Oh, for God's sake . . .' she thumped the pillow again, and then kneading it into a ball climbed beneath the duvet and buried her head in it.

Peter remained for a long time by the window staring into the darkness before he joined her. He felt Anna's body stiff and unresponsive beside him, and knew that another idea he'd had was doomed to disappointment. A relaxing, rather sexy weekend in the country.

'What a day!' he murmured as he put out the light. He lay still for a while and, realising that Anna wasn't asleep, his libido still charged, his hand tentatively moved across the space between them and landed on her thigh. She didn't move.

'Anna?' he whispered. 'You awake?'

'You know I'm awake.'

'Let's try and relax.' He moved closer to her. 'It will do us both good.'

'For God's sake, Peter,' she turned over, 'you can't solve *everything* with sex you know.'

'It helps.'

'Well, it doesn't help me.'

'It used to.' The tone of Peter's voice changed, and he removed his hand. 'I thought that having your tubes tied was supposed to make our sex life better?'

'No, it wasn't. It was so that I could come off the Pill and possibly avoid an unnecessary and premature death.'

'Don't be so dramatic.'

'I'm not being dramatic, but that was the reason. Anyway,' she paused and he could feel her gazing at him through the gloom, 'you never complained about our sex life before.'

'I'm not complaining now.'

'You said "it was supposed to make it better".'

'Well it was a silly thing to say. I didn't think. I suppose I meant . . . more spontaneous.'

'Peter, our sex life was always spontaneous while I was on the Pill. It had nothing to do with spontaneity.' Pause again. 'What are you trying to say, Peter?'

'Nothing. Oh forget it.' He pulled the duvet over his shoulder, turned his back on his wife and closed his eyes.

'Peter, you can't just go to sleep and pretend this never happened.'

'I can try.'

'You make a pretty insulting remark and then . . .'

'It was *not* insulting, nor not meant to be.'

'You said you thought our sex life was supposed to be better. Better than what?'

'I got my words wrong.' Peter turned restlessly in the bed again, ran his hand over his face. 'Look, Anna, I'm tired. Forget it, for God's sake. Anyway look, it isn't very good now, is it? I mean at this moment. I feel like relaxing, making love to try and unwind. You don't.'

'Is that a sin? Or do you want me to pretend?'

'Look, Anna. Let's face it. Since you had your tubes tied, since you got promotion in your job and, especially, since you joined the Council, our sex life has been pretty non-existent. Pretty lousy.'

'If you mean it's not as frequent, I say that's just because we're getting older. You can't go on fucking like rabbits when you've been married twelve years. I think it's quality not quantity that counts.'

'I think having your tubes tied has taken the fun out of it.'

'Oh, don't be absurd. What fun?'

'The fun of making love, the danger . . .'

'You mean pregnancy? The danger of pregnancy?'

'Yes, I suppose I do. It's silly, but there it is.'

'But there was no danger of pregnancy with the Pill, you idiot. That is what it is all about. Women taking the Pill can't get pregnant.'

'They can if they forget.'

'Oh, I see. That's it.'

'Well, it makes sense, Anna, doesn't it? Something's changed. Something's happened.'

Anna was not going to be talked into doing something she didn't want by childish and largely unsubstantiated arguments and now she turned her back to Peter, but as he settled she was aware that something had happened between them. It was not only sex, not Fiona or Guy. It really was the state of their marriage. Peter was trying to tell her something. Many of their friends were getting divorced or contemplating it. She saw it every day, several times a day, in her office. Divorce was increasing, especially among their age group. People with a mountain of worries, busy lives and careers, difficult children.

It seemed to her that if a man's wife didn't support him he'd just get another wife. It seemed to be the nature of the beast.

With women it was different.

Sal popped her head round the door.

'So sorry we couldn't make it last night. I should have rung.'

'That's OK. We always leave things until the last minute.' Anna dried her hands on a towel and pointed to the chair. 'I was just going to make coffee.'

'What time are you off?'

'Well, now we're not going until tomorrow. Peter and I are so exhausted that we feel we need another day.' Anna shrugged. 'We shall both have to ring our offices, but there you are.'

'Busy lives, uh?' Sal lit a cigarette.

'Very busy.'

'Had a long talk with Fiona yesterday,' Sal said chattily, taking the cup of Instant Anna held out to her. 'She really is very sorry.'

'Sorry about what?' Anna faced her, sipping her coffee.

'Well, she's been trying so hard. She knows she flew off the handle. Didn't mean to.'

'She could have apologised.'

'She finds it very difficult. You must know that. Besides she feels you and she always get on the wrong side of each other. She really is very fond of you, you know.'

'Frankly, Sal,' Anna paused and swallowed a mouthful of coffee, 'I find that very hard to believe.'

'No, I think she is. She talks about you a lot when you're not here, I don't just mean now. Says you were very good to her as a child and she loved you like a mother.'

'I notice you use the past tense.'

'She thinks you don't have time for her, that you're so busy. I think she also envies you a bit your success.'

'Envies me?' Anna looked incredulous.

'Yes, jealous in a way. She feels an utter failure, and here you are: successful law practice, local councillor. She's sure you'll stand for Parliament.'

'Well, I won't.'

'No, but she's proud of you. She just feels so inadequate, and then when you attacked her paintings, my God,' Sal paused to light a fresh cigarette from the stub of the first, 'that girl has worked her little butt off painting away. She loves it . . .'

'I did *not* attack her paintings, Sal,' Anna said heatedly. 'I merely *suggested* that she might be better if she had proper training. I was trying to be constructive. Look, I don't give a damn if she goes on painting for the rest of her life, if that's what she wants to do. I was thinking of Fiona, of her own satisfaction, her success . . .'

Sal looked at her shrewdly, head on one side. 'You don't really think they're very good, do you?'

How to reply? Pondering the dilemma Anna gazed at the woman across the table. Then she did what she might have done in her law office, answered one question by another. It was a useful ploy.

'Do you?'

Sal smiled. 'Well we both know, don't we, to be honest? Not much. I mean there's nothing to them, and when you look at Nancy's they weren't up to much either.'

'The idea of the exhibition came to nothing?' Anna, too, put her head on one side.

Sal shrugged. 'It seemed to go off the boil. Fiona's not much of an organiser. Frankly,' she gave a fleeting, nervous smile, 'neither am I. It gave Fiona a reason at the time to stay on here. She never really referred to it again. Maybe she realised they weren't much good, but we all have to *pretend*, don't we?'

'Do we?' Mentally Anna pictured the scene between herself and Peter the night before.

'I think so.' Sal reached out to flick ash into a makeshift ashtray, as no one else in the house smoked. 'I think we have to compromise in life and, yes, that involves a lot of pretending, a good deal of the time anyway.'

'So in other words we should have said that we *liked* her pictures very much and left it at that?'

And I could have made love to Peter last night and pretended it was because I wanted to, Anna thought to herself, bitterly regretting now that she hadn't. When she'd woken in the morning Peter was already up and had gone for a walk.

'Maybe,' Sal shrugged and got up. 'Then let *her* bring up the fact that she'd like training. Now that you've put the idea into her head I think you'll find her willing if you suggest it again. If you could bring yourself to do so, that is.'

Anna leaned across the table and reached for Sal's hand. 'Thanks, Sal. I think you've been an excellent go-between and I'm grateful. You know I have a large office and I do legal aid work and run an advice bureau and I'm a councillor; but I still think I've a lot to learn.'

'I think that too.' Sal suddenly looked serious, vulnerable. 'About myself, I mean. I'm nearly forty. I've got two grown-up children, but sometimes I think when it comes to human relationships I don't know a thing.' She returned Anna's firm handclasp. 'It's always much easier to deal with other people than your own family. It's the blood tie . . . Oh . . .' her hand flew to her mouth, 'sorry, that was stupid.'

'Think nothing of it.' Anna also got up, but in that instant the feeling of hope and euphoria she'd had while Sal was speaking evaporated.

There it was again. The blood tie.

Anna saw Sal out and began the preparations for lunch, thinking about what Sal had said. Somehow, between now and tomorrow, she had to bring up, or get Fiona to bring up, the subject of training. Maybe Sal had been sent as a sort of emissary, and it would happen anyway.

They were going to have a late lunch; Sunday roast, Yorkshire pudding (from the freezer), the lot. She went to the larder and got out the beef, sirloin with the fillet which she and Peter had bought in Blandford the previous day, presumably while Fiona was pouring her heart out to Sal.

She shook her head as she carefully spread lard over the beef and peppered it before putting it in the oven. The blood tie. It would never go away, and Peter was trying to tell her that she had destroyed her chance of being linked to the family by blood by not having a baby. Her and Peter's child would have been linked to Fiona and Guy by blood, and thus they would all be related.

No chance of that now.

She looked up as the door opened and Guy sidled into the kitchen, a shifty, rather untypical expression on his face. Immediately she wondered what he wanted.

'Hi!' she called cheerily. 'Want a cup of coffee?'

'No, thanks.' Guy shook his head and sat opposite her, watching her carefully as she placed the partly boiled, floured potatoes round the joint in the baking tray.

'Why do you do that?' he asked.

'Do what?' She looked up at him.

'Put flour on them?'

'It makes them softer and crunchy.'

'Do you like cooking?' Guy put his face between his hands and stared at the tin. Anna thought he looked pale. In fact, he had been particularly subdued all tne time they'd been here.

'Sometimes.'

'But you don't have time at home, do you?'

'Guy, I do a fair amount of cooking and put it in the freezer. Just because we have a defrosted meal doesn't always mean I haven't cooked it.'

'I'm not criticising you, Anna,' he said carefully. 'I mean I think you're a very good cook.'

'Thank you, Guy.' She smiled, and taking the roasting tin carefully between her hands, popped it into the oven. Then she shut the door, adjusted the heat and, returning to the table, sat opposite him. 'That's that, then. Is Daddy in the garden?'

'I think he went to the pub.'

'You haven't seen much of Martin this weekend.'

Guy stuck a finger in his mouth and seemed to be struggling with some sort of inner battle or dilemma. Anna began to feel concerned.

'Anna,' he burst out removing the finger, 'supposing a friend of yours had done something awful, what would you do?'

Taken aback, Anna waited a second or two before replying.

'Something awful, like what?'

'Something that was really bad.'

'You mean, should *you* tell somebody?'

'Yes, or keep it to yourself. I mean if others got into trouble?'

'Oh, I see what you mean.' Anna's unease increased. 'You mean somebody, your friend, say, has done something wrong for which others might be punished?'

Guy nodded, and Anna noticed the high colour in his cheeks.

'And you feel your friend should tell the authorities?'

Guy nodded again and the blush deepened.

'What is it, Guy?' Anna leaned over towards him. 'What is

it your friend did . . . or was it you?' She rose swiftly from her chair, went across to him, putting a hand on his shoulder. 'And if it was, and you tell me what it was, I'll do my best to help . . .'

'No scolding . . .' Guy faltered, his body tense.

'Promise. No scolding.' Her grasp on his shoulder tightened as his head touched the table and he burst into tears.

'Oh, Guy!' Anna said, gently massaging his back, pressing his face close to hers and, finally, enveloping him in her arms.

Guy sat on the edge of his chair, hands clutching the sides, head bowed. Although he was tall, he seemed somehow to have diminished in size as he sat between Anna and Peter under the baleful gaze of the Head.

'I do very much appreciate your honesty, Guy, in owning up; but what you did was very terrible, very serious, and could have resulted in someone being killed.' The Head paused while the words sank in.

Anna closed her eyes involuntarily, visualising the scene, as she had several times since the extent of Guy's misdemeanour had become apparent. Together with two other boys he had thrown an old radiogram belonging to the school out of a fourth floor classroom window, regardless not only of the damage caused, the wilful destruction of property, but of who might have happened to be passing underneath on what was normally a busy walkway. Thankfully, no one had.

'I'm afraid I have got no option but to expel Guy from the school together with the two other boys he was involved with. Their parents have also been informed.'

The verdict was not unexpected. Nevertheless Anna felt a sharp sense of shock.

'But, Jessie, if Guy hadn't owned up . . .'

'Someone else would have been expelled instead of him. We had some idea who the culprits were, but we did not include Guy. Young people being what they are, loyal to the tribe, they would not have betrayed him. As it is, we can't keep Guy and let the others go. It wouldn't be fair.'

'But Guy wasn't in the same position as the other two,' Peter said. 'I understand they'd both just been released from young offenders' institutions.'

'One of them had,' Jessie corrected him. 'The other was on probation. And in any case Guy should have known better. Both came from underprivileged families.'

'And what kind of company was that for my son to keep?' Peter's voice rose.

'You may well ask Guy that question, Mr Livingstone.' Jessie Clark turned to Guy. 'What should attract you to people like that? Hey, Guy. Can you answer?'

Guy hunched his shoulders and said nothing.

'Guy?' His father looked at him, but Guy remained silent and, sensing he was close to tears, Anna shook her head at Peter and her hand groped for Guy's. To her surprise he gave it to her and let her hold it. She thought then of the number of pupils from the school who had appeared at the local magistrates' court and that if a fatality, or even injury, had resulted from the action of Guy and his friends, the committal proceedings would have been held in the same court. One of the things she had so often dreaded might, in fact, have come true. She could just see the smug expression on Mrs Bridges' face.

Peter broke the silence, the unnatural stillness, again.

'I might ask you, Mrs Clark, why disturbed youngsters like that are at a normal school at all. What were they doing here?'

'Mr Livingstone!' Jessie Clark's tone indicated that she was on the verge of losing her patience. 'This is a state school run for the benefit of all its citizens. Whatever you may or may not think of it, the boys concerned had paid their debt to society and were entitled to receive an education. I may doubt the wisdom of this, but I have to obey the rules set by the Department of Education. As it is, they have now been expelled from the school and so, I'm sorry to say, has Guy . . .'

'Couldn't Guy have *one* more chance?' Anna squeezed his hand very tightly in hers. 'After all, it is a first offence . . .'

'Mrs Livingstone . . . Anna,' Jessie Clark sighed deeply. 'It may be his first serious offence, but there are a number of minor ones I have had to take into consideration. I have been very patient with Guy, as I was with Fiona. But I am sorry to say that neither of them have responded to my kindness and tolerance. Guy has not been a satisfactory pupil. He has been lazy, workshy and has frequently been up for some sort of punishment in the time he has been in the school. We have found him a trial. Frankly, I shall be glad to see the back of him. And as this is nearly the end of the school year you will have plenty of time to try and find a new school for him.' She drew a line firmly under whatever it was she had written on the piece of paper in front of her.

'What about his sport?' Peter demanded. 'Captain of football, cricket.'

'If Guy could apply to his work and life in general the dedication he applies to football and cricket then I would have some hope for him. I would suggest that in looking for a school you find one which imposes very strict discipline, which places a great deal of emphasis on work . . . and,' she got up and joined her hands, 'which has none of the imperfections you have apparently found in us, if that is possible.'

She then looked pointedly towards the door, and as the Livingstones rose and filed slowly out there was no attempt to shake hands. Anna however remembered all the heart-to-hearts she and the Head had shared over the years and halted at the threshold looking back.

''Bye, Jessie,' she said.

Jessie smiled, winked and mouthed the words 'Good luck.'

CHAPTER 8

In a way, Anna's department almost ran itself. She had under her a team of good people, some of whom had been Articled to her as she mounted the firm's hierarchy. There were still, however, many things she had to do herself, and all the important decisions were made by her.

For anyone it was a full time job, but as the work of the Council encroached more on her time she sometimes had to leave essential work to others. She worked longer hours, left the office later and later to make up the time that she gave not only to Council and legal aid work but, increasingly, to the family.

Getting Guy into a school had not been easy, on two accounts. In the first place he had been expelled, so had a very black mark against him, and in the second his work was not up to the norm for a boy in the year before GCSEs. They had trundled him round all the London day schools because Guy deeply resented the idea of being a boarder. Valuable time was taken out, both by Anna and Peter, visiting these institutions, only to receive the discouraging news that nowhere was he wanted, not only because of his conduct but the low standard of his work. Even some expensive private schools, desperate for pupils, wouldn't take him.

Guy was a big problem, just now being tutored at home by a young man about to go up to university, to try and raise his overall standard of education before they tried again for the beginning of the autumn term.

A holiday was clearly indicated, but Anna considered it out of the question for her. Too many days off from the office, while she trailed round looking at schools for Guy, made her feel she was in danger of losing her position and authority at work unless she spent long hours making up for time lost.

There was a protracted row on the subject with Peter, but in the end he agreed to take Fiona and Guy to a hotel they'd stayed at before on the island of Rhodes, and on the whole it was a good holiday. Anna suspected not only that the children enjoyed the undivided attention of their father, but that they all got on better without her.

In the two weeks they were away she made up for a lot. Many cases were sorted out for the opening of the law term. Council work was largely in abeyance because councillors were on holiday, and Anna found that the problem needing her most urgent attention was the future of the self-styled Pilgrims: not only was their tenure of the warehouse almost at an end but, with the winter coming on, it would be impossible for them to live there. It was practically uninhabitable.

She found she had become very involved with the Pilgrims, and the outcome of their difficulties was important to her. As a lawyer she knew they had no chance, but as a councillor she hoped to be able to help bend the law. She felt it was terrible that so many lives were dependent on what was basically an unfair, uncaring and increasingly greedy society. Too many years of Conservative rule had provided a greater gap between the rich and the poor, the haves and have nots. She realised what little room there was for people who would not, or could not, conform, and she suspected that her experience with her two step-children gave her more insight into misfits than she had even a year before.

Peter, Fiona and Guy returned in the last week of August looking fit and rested, lots of tales to tell about the good time they'd had on Rhodes. Fiona produced some paintings she'd done, rather pretty, simple watercolours, and Anna felt that she'd made some progress, fancied she saw the shimmerings of talent.

Moreover, Fiona had decided that she would, after all, apply for art school, and Guy had agreed to the idea of being a boarder if a school could be found to take him. So progress had definitely been made.

Anna began to hope that the autumn would finally see a resolution, at least, to the problems of the family. There remained a tolerant yet disciplined school to find for Guy, and an art school for Fiona which would encourage her fledgling talent.

Anna was tired. Very. She had spent a long day in the magistrates' court and began to think she'd been short-sighted not to take a holiday. Maybe at Christmas a couple of weeks in the snow, or perhaps some sun in the West Indies? Anyway, it was something to look forward to.

It was nine o'clock. She'd phoned to say she wouldn't be in, but the answer-machine was on. Peter and Guy had been to see another school in the west country, one which specialised, discreetly, in adolescents with difficulties and charged accordingly, and Fiona had an interview with an art school in central London.

Anna expected no one to be in and was surprised to see a light in the living room. She called out, but there was no reply. Silence. She looked in, saw that it was empty and went into the kitchen to make herself a snack. She was starving. Her heart sank when she saw the usual messy pile up of supper dishes, the open fridge door. Fiona was back with a vengeance, and if she got her place at art school it would be as though she'd never left home. In her heart of hearts, Anna knew nothing would change.

She saw the back door was open as well, and went to close it. Something was stuck between the door and the outside path where the dustbins were kept, which meant it was unable to close. Anna put out a foot to remove the impediment and then stopped to look at it closer. She opened the door wider and gazed with some astonishment at a pile of junk that overflowed the dustbins and blocked the path.

Canvases, through which someone had put a fist or a boot or both. She had no need to examine them to know that they were the works of art produced by Fiona who, doubtless, lay now on her bed upstairs. The vandalised canvases seemed to tell the whole story.

Anna's hunger promptly evaporated and, with the greatest reluctance, she dragged herself back into the kitchen, across the hall and slowly upstairs to Fiona's room.

She didn't knock but gently turned the handle.

'Go away!' Fiona shouted, as Anna pushed open the door. Something was hurled at it, but Anna sidestepped the missile and stepped inside. Fiona lay on the bed. Around her were crumpled pieces of paper, probably the watercolours she'd brought back from Rhodes.

'Go away!' Fiona bellowed again, louder, and turned her face to the wall. Anna sat on the bed beside her, and put a hand on her shoulder.

Fiona tried to wriggle away but Anna wouldn't budge. 'I guess the interview didn't go well,' she said.

'I said go *away*,' Fiona shouted again. 'You are a pig and I hate you!'

Anna flinched but stayed where she was. Despite the fact that Fiona was now seventeen, Anna had to remember she was still a child.

'Tell me why I'm a pig,' she said after a moment, her hand on Fiona's shoulder firm, reassuring.

Suddenly Fiona, face streaked with tears, rose up on the bed. She'd made herself up heavily for the interview at the art school and the result now was terrible. She looked like a victim of war with black, red and purple blobs all over her face, her spiky hair, thick with gel, looking like a toppled blancmange. Anna felt infinite pity. Pity and love.

'Tell me why I'm a pig?' she asked again.

'Because,' Fiona pointed a trembling finger at her, 'because *you* should have told me the truth instead of pretending . . .'

'Pretending what?'

'That I was any good.'

'I thought you accused me of saying that you weren't any good, that was why you needed tuition?'

'No, no!' Fiona thumped her knee. '*You* said you thought I had potential . . .'

'Anyway what happened? They turned you down?'

'They said, the Head of the art school, said I had *no* talent at all and it would be a waste of time admitting me. He said . . . she said,' Fiona's lip trembled and she began to cry again, 'she said I was an *amateur* and no amount of tuition would do me any good. I had *no* sense of perspective, *no* idea of line or form, no talent at all. I was wasting my time, and hers.' Fiona flung herself face down on the bed again and her body heaved with heart-rending sobs.

Anna went on patting her back and then got up and wandered to the window, stepping carefully across the mangled balls of paper. It was almost dark outside and the lights of the houses all round were on, houses full of happy hopeful people. Or were they? Maybe everyone had problems like theirs. One always assumed one's own were the worst.

So she should have told Fiona the truth. But what did she really know about art? And was it fair to discourage someone when there was something they desperately wanted to do?

'There are other art schools,' she said without turning around. 'But I guess you destroyed your portfolio.'

'I'm hopeless, utterly *useless*. She said so. She was a hateful pig.'

'She certainly doesn't *sound* very nice.' Anna returned to the recumbent form. 'I am so very sorry, Fiona; but I'm sorry you destroyed your work.' As Fiona didn't seem to be rejecting her, she sat on the bed again. 'I think the trouble with you is that you give up too easily. I mean, who's to say this woman is right?'

'She is the Head of one of the top schools.'

'So, there are other schools.' Anna looked down at the floor. 'And now you've destroyed everything. I saw the mess outside the kitchen door. I wish to God I'd been here when you got back.' She bit her lip thinking of all the advice she'd given at the Law Centre to people who probably wouldn't take any notice of it anyway, whereas here was someone close to her whom she could actually have prevented from doing herself harm.

'I know this woman was right.' Fiona shook her head. 'I know I'm no good. I just liked to pretend . . .'

'But you do enjoy painting, don't you? I mean you did all that stuff in Rhodes? Frankly, Fiona, I liked it. I thought it was better than the watercolours I'd seen in the country and that you'd progressed.' Anna reached down to the floor and taking one of the pieces of paper began to smooth it out over her knee. It was a simple seascape with brightly coloured sails in a harbour setting. It had the air of an amateur Dufy, with stronger colours than before. As she studied it she was aware that Fiona's tears had ceased and she was looking over Anna's lap at the picture on her knee.

'Yes, I *do* like painting,' she said in a different, less whining tone. 'I love it. It helps me to lose myself.'

'What the Head of the art school meant was that you were not yet up to professional standard. There's no reason why, if you really have a strong urge to paint, you shouldn't have tuition of some kind, and then maybe try an art school later on if that's what you want to do. Or . . .' she looked at the girl now lying quietly beside her, finger stuck in her mouth like a baby, curled up, indeed, in rather a foetal-like position, 'maybe you'll just remain an amateur painter all your life like your mother; but it will be something that you enjoy doing, as she did, and which you'll gradually get better and better at. The main thing is that at last you've found something you really want to do. You hated school. You hated study, but you like to paint. I think you should stick at it and, please,' she smoothed the picture with her hands again, 'no more destructive urges like this. You want to start a portfolio otherwise no one will have any idea at all what you're like.'

She gazed down at Fiona who, in her foetal position sucking her thumb, reminded her more than ever of the fair-haired, little girl she first knew and came to love. The blue eyes gazed so trustingly up at her, and the expression was so innocent and adorable that she forgot the brittle confused unhappy young woman Fiona had become and remembered only the child she'd loved, loved like a mother. And still did. She stooped suddenly and, still afraid of a rebuff, planted a kiss on Fiona's cheek and, to her surprise and gratification, Fiona flung her arm round Anna's neck and hugged her close.

The school was an undenominational one whose principles were based on a spirit of Christian toleration and understanding. It had been founded by an enlightened educationalist in the thirties who realised that children's learning problems often stemmed from mysterious forces that were not necessarily to do with parents or their upbringing or environment, but probably went back to the womb.

The present Head, Dick Preston, was a man in the mould of the founder who had produced from the poor fodder that was sometimes sent to him, successful and happy citizens who not only prospered and did well, but went on to lead happy and fulfilled lives.

He wasn't sure about Guy Livingstone because, in so many ways, he did seem well adjusted. Yet the confidential report from his previous school told him differently. He was a youth whose looks and behaviour belied his age, and he felt that, perhaps, in the environment of an inner city comp with both a mother and father who were apparently workaholics, had high-powered jobs, he had matured too quickly. Some children, especially those living in cities, missed out on part of their childhood and grew up too fast.

The school offered a complete contrast to that of the city. It was set in fifty acres of green Wiltshire countryside, part of which was farmed and worked by some of the pupils, all of whom were encouraged to develop the skills they were good at or attracted to. This didn't mean that they were allowed to neglect academic work, but the principles of the school, although it was not Roman Catholic, were modelled on the ancient monastic foundation that divided the day into physical work, study and prayer. There was also ample time for recreation, which included plenty of sport.

The school itself had been the country house of a noble family which, like many of their kind, they had been forced to sell in order to meet debts or death duties. The house had been bought in the thirties by the school's founder with the help of backers who had faith in his educational methods and had turned the enterprise into an educational trust. It took both boys and girls and all of them had to board.

After the interview with the Head, Guy was set a number of tests which took up a couple of hours of his time, during which Peter wandered round the school and its grounds, which had made an immediately favourable impression on him. Term had not yet started, but there were a number of resident staff going about their various tasks, mostly domestic staff preparing for the new term or gardeners or farm workers who lived there all the time.

There was an atmosphere of peace and relaxation about the place, of order, routine and structured discipline. There was a chapel where prayers were said every morning and evening, and the pupils had small bedrooms instead of sleeping in large dormitories. The sixth formers had study-bedrooms to themselves in a specially built sixth form block behind the main house. Unlike some buildings in other schools they had seen which had grown up higgledy-piggledy in an assortment of styles, the new architecture here had been blended into a harmonious whole, with a neo-classical facade masking all the modern amenities of bathrooms, lavatories and central heating inside. Throughout, there were shiny parquet floors and a smell of fine old beeswax; well-polished furniture, maybe a few antiques among them, that had once belonged to the noble family. In the public rooms were comfortable chintz-covered sofas and chairs. The dining hall had long tables with benches, and various trophies of the school, and a war memorial for those who had fallen in the Second World War adorned the walls.

The outside of the house was covered with rust coloured vine, old rambling roses and ivy. While Guy did his tests, Peter stood for some time on the gravel in the drive looking up at the mullioned windows imbibing the sense of peace, and he wished Anna were there with him. He was sure she would approve. Now, more than ever, he wanted Guy to pass his tests because he knew the Head liked him and thought that Guy liked the Head, the staff he had met and the place – everything so unlike the inner city concrete jungle he was leaving.

Peter walked along the drive, past urns full of roses, petunia, lobelia and geranium now mostly past their best, and then he took the path across one of the lawns to a copse full of old yew trees, beech and oak, which framed the building.

Anna had nearly come, had wanted to come, but at the last minute, inevitably, something had turned up, a court case urgently needing her personal attention. He knew that Anna felt the opposing tug of two duties: one to family, one to her work. He knew that now in particular she would give preference in this war of opposing loyalties, to the family; but they had been to see many schools together. Then there was the problem of Fiona and trying to keep her on an even keel, her morale shattered by rejection of the art school, the cruel dismissive words of the Head, fatal to someone like Fiona, constantly in need of encouragement, who gave up all too easily. Anna had been trying to find another school or a tutor for Fiona, determined to build on that precious rapport they'd briefly shared and make it into a new and deeper understanding.

Peter was a worrier; he fretted, always imagining the worst. At these times he slept badly; he had an ulcer which modern medication now kept under control. He needed Anna's calm which he knew that he, and others, sometimes mistook for coldness, indifference, a kind of almost ruthless efficiency. This was what really had happened between her and the children recently and, to some extent, between her and himself.

He knew that in her heart she was a warm and caring person, but it was this iron will of hers, this control, that could mislead. She was a complex person who, in all the years he had known her, he felt he never completely understood. There was always that air of remoteness about her that could repel, but also intrigued.

He knew that in the year she'd been sterilised he'd felt a sense of ineffable loss that he and she had never had a child of their own, but it would be useless to try and make Anna realise it. This decision of hers, as well as many other things about Anna, he really failed to understand.

He was about to turn towards the school again when he heard a voice calling him and, in the distance, he saw Guy running towards him. He hailed him and quickened his step and when Guy caught up with him he was breathless.

'Hi, Dad!'

'Hi! How did you get on?'

'I think I was OK.' Guy stuck his hands in his pockets. 'Aptitude, intelligence tests really, a bit of maths.' He grimaced. 'I don't think that was so good.'

'Well, what do you think, son?' Peter put an arm paternally round his shoulders.

'I like it, Dad,' Guy nodded vigorously.

Peter's heart leapt. 'I like it too . . .'

'You don't think somehow,' Guy hesitated screwing up his face, 'it's too remote, too far from the real world?'

'Well,' Peter looked around him towards the beautiful old house in its lovely setting, the gracious lawns and colourful gardens, the well-stocked fish pond with an antique fountain in the middle. 'Well, it *has* got enormous charm. What's wrong with that? You've had quite enough of the real world, my son. At the most you'd only have three years here, one in the fifth, two in the sixth.'

'I'd have to work jolly hard. Mr Preston told me that.'

'I think you want to work jolly hard now, don't you, Guy?'

'I want to try and make up for the way I've messed things up. The misery I've caused you and Anna.'

Peter felt a strange emotion as though a great weight had been lifted from his heart.

It was nearly six o'clock and Anna shifted restlessly in her chair. But what her client was saying was important, important for her anyway to get the trauma of her impending divorce, her resentment against her husband who had gone off with his much younger secretary, and her anxiety about her children, all of whom were under fifteen, off her chest.

Sheila Jones was a smart, attractive woman, a buyer in a London store, a high flyer like Anna, and they seemed to understand each other well.

Anna had urged her to go for a clean break; not to be too vindictive, not to make the man suffer too much. After all he had gone, he wanted to marry the woman he was living with, they were expecting a child and she had absolutely no hope of saving the marriage. It had broken down irretrievably. He had offered a generous settlement and allowances, the family home, the children could continue their private education. What else did she want? Revenge. Mrs Jones wanted revenge.

This was where one could see the unattractive side of Mrs Jones, the reason, perhaps, why her husband had left her not only for a woman who was younger but who was also probably his intellectual and social inferior. She had obviously reached her position because she had just that extra degree of ruthlessness needed for a woman to succeed in a hard, competitive business.

Anna started, shocked more by her own thoughts than by what Mrs Jones was saying as she went on about getting her pound of flesh, squeezing until the pips squeaked, not letting him forget, making him pay, all that kind of thing.

What shocked Anna was the fact that she was thinking in terms of stereotypes, and her opinions about Mrs Jones could so easily apply to herself. Just that extra ruthlessness needed to succeed in a competitive world . . . like the law, a male profession if ever there was one, or the Council where he or she who shouted loudest was the one who got most attention and, inevitably, what they wanted. If she had to think in terms of men's and women's worlds, then she and Mrs Jones stood with a foot in each camp. If she called Mrs Jones hard then, perhaps, she was hard herself?

She had, after all, given up thought of having a child of her own not only because her step-children were so difficult, but because the idea of a small baby at her age was somehow frightening. What really was the truth about that decision, taken now a year ago? Whatever it was it had had unforeseen effects on her life, on Peter's life and that of the children.

'Mrs Jones, I really must go now,' she said looking at the clock. 'My husband has been away all day with our son looking at a new school and, well,' she smiled, 'it *is* rather important.'

'Oh, you've children of your own then?' Mrs Jones looked

interested. 'Somehow I didn't think you had. You gave that impression.'

'Two,' Anna said with a firm smile, 'a boy and a girl.'

'Well, you know what it's like then.' Mrs Jones's tone changed and Anna knew that she was about to become chatty, to confide as one mother to another.

'We could make an appointment for later on in the week.' Anna rapidly turned over the pages of her diary, her heart quailing as she saw how full it was, meetings all day, every day, going on into the evenings. A Council meeting on Thursday, a visit to one of the deprived area schools on Friday. 'I'm *afraid* it will have to be next week,' she said, flipping over the pages and seeing how full that week was too. She frowned. 'Look I'll get my secretary to call yours tomorrow and try and find a time.' She closed the book, her expression rueful. 'You know how it is.'

'Busy, busy,' Mrs Jones gave her a conspiratorial smile. 'I suppose *your* husband's jealous too?'

'I don't think he's jealous. Sometimes he gets a bit irritated.'

'You'd better hang on to him . . .' Mrs Jones was about to return to her favourite tack, but Anna steered her carefully, firmly to the door. Any minute now and she knew that Mrs Jones, a hurt and bitter woman, would start insinuating things about her own marriage, if she didn't take care.

Perhaps Mrs Jones would be right.

Peter looked up as Anna came in, arms flung out in apology.

'Sorry,' she said rushing over to kiss him, 'got held up by a client.'

'As usual.' Peter grimaced, returning her kiss.

'As usual.' She put bag and briefcase down and sat on the edge of the chair opposite him. 'How did it go?'

Peter leaned back in his chair, arms behind his head. 'It went well. It's a lovely place and the news is that they'll take Guy. Guy thinks he wants to go.'

'Thank *God* for that.' Anna also leaned back, sighing deeply. In the dreary rounds of the last few weeks she was so used to schools either which Guy didn't like or which didn't like him. Then she looked at Peter. 'What do you mean "thinks"?'

'He's thinking about it. He's gone out to consult with some of his friends. He feels it's too elitist.'

Anna groaned. 'In that case he'll come back . . .'

'No, I think he really liked it. He genuinely seems to have undergone a change of heart. He said he wanted to try and make up for the bloody awful mess, the misery he's made of our lives.'

'Guy said that?' Anna looked incredulous.

'He specifically mentioned you. "The misery I've caused you and Anna." His very words.'

'Well, I *am* impressed.' Anna got up. 'Did you eat?' She looked guiltily at her watch.

'I had a snack with Fiona.'

'Is she in?'

'No, she went out with her friends. I'm afraid she's getting more depressed again.' His voice became reproachful. 'She said you said you'd help her find another school or a tutor. Have you done anything?'

Anna rounded on him. 'For Christ's sake, Peter, you really should see my diary. I can't even fit in a woman I'm divorcing for at least another *ten* days.'

'But still you said you'd help her, Anna. It's important. Look,' Peter rose and went over to her, 'I know you're very busy and the kids take up a lot of time . . .'

'Peter, I've trudged all round the country looking for schools. I've taken days off I'm not entitled to, and now you both seem to have got on very well without me. Maybe you could do the same about art schools?'

'Anna, it was simply coincidental that we found a school when you weren't there. It could have happened at any other time.'

'No, I seriously think that you and the kids get on better when I'm not there. With each one of us individually it's alright. Fiona is fine with me. I mean when I see her, when we have a chance to talk.' Seeing the look of exasperation on Peter's face she sat down again. 'Peter, what is it you want me to do? Give up work?'

'Of course not!'

'The children are almost grown up.'

'I know, but they still need help.'

'Help I'm giving them, you're giving them. What else can we do?'

Peter rose and stood looking down at her.

'Look, Anna you've got to face it. Neither of these kids is much of a success. Both were expelled from school, well, virtually. Guy *was* expelled, and they wouldn't take Fiona back, which comes to the same thing. How do you think I feel as their father? I feel a failure, that's what. I'm trying desperately to overcome this feeling of failure. Anna, I need help too.'

Peter sank on to a chair and put his head in his hands. Watching him, Anna was aware of that feeling of anger and frustration she experienced so frequently with the children. She felt in a way that they were all children – Peter, Guy, Fiona, all needing her, all needing help.

She was not going to give Peter the sympathy he so obviously was agitating for, indulging in an orgy of self-pity really, so she picked up her bag and briefcase, dumped them in the hall at the foot of the stairs and went into the kitchen, which was in the usual chaotic state after Fiona, Guy, and even, Peter, had finished with it. There was no earthly excuse she thought angrily as she opened the dishwasher and started to stack, no excuse at all. When they'd finished their food they could put the dishes in the dishwasher instead of leaving them piled in the sink with remnants of food stuck to them. No one was actually asking them to wash anything.

Was it because they knew how angry it made her? Or was it simply because they didn't care? Or were they trying to tell her something?

She paused in the act of scraping the leftovers into the bin by the side of the sink and gazed out of the window into the dusk. Sometimes, really, she felt she'd like to leave home, strike out. Start all over again.

CHAPTER 9

'God save the world,' Arizona said. 'Joy to all.' She extended her arms over them as if in benediction as her rapt audience responded 'Joy to all,' and then, at the end of her homily, split up into small groups chattering animatedly.

Anna stood at the back of the room watching them wondering, as she always did, at the impact this small, fat, friendly woman seemed to have on the members of the Pilgrim community. For if Damian was the acknowledged leader, Arizona was the mother. Maybe because of her diminutive height, Arizona favoured flowing robes, large hats – with bells, tassels or feathers bobbing precariously about – long dangling earrings and pointed shoes with extremely high heels on which she managed, with difficulty, to teeter along. Above all, there was her long pretentious name which was almost certainly assumed: Arizona Washington.

No one knew her real name, or where she'd come from. She had been at the squat ever since it was formed. She had simply turned up one day with all her worldly goods in a bag slung over her shoulder, and a small, ugly, extremely pugnacious and snappy Jack Russell called Waffles at the end of a long piece of string. She was, and remained, devoted to the dog, giving him all her best scraps. Arizona had a vaguely transatlantic accent, was obviously well educated, had presence and charm and was a great asset to the community. In age she was between thirty and forty, it was impossible to be more accurate. She had an unlined, ageless face, an expression of calm that probably had more to do with drugs than religion.

'Hi!' Anna went over to Arizona as, her little homily finished, she lit a cigarette and perched on an upturned box. Waffles, snarling at Anna, jumped on to Arizona's knees and she kissed him fondly before setting him down again.

'Hi, Anna!' Arizona looked pleased to see her, and lifting her hand waved it about vaguely. 'Peace and joy.'

'Peace and joy,' Anna dutifully replied.

'Did you like my sermon?'

'Oh, it *was* a sermon?' Anna sat on the box next to Arizona and shook her head as she offered her a cigarette. 'I often wonder.'

'We always have a little gathering on a Sunday,' Arizona said piously. 'Of course I'm not religious, strictly speaking.'

'But you said "God save the world"?'

'I mean in the sense of the One, the Great Creator. The Other. There has to *be* a giver of life; but formal religion makes me puke.' Arizona made as if to spit on the floor. 'What did they ever do for the poor? What did *Jesus* do, for Christ's sake?' Anna felt inclined to agree, but she was not here to discuss polemics or matters theological. She was aware however that Arizona was gazing at her keenly. 'What brings you here on a Sunday, Anna?'

'It was the only time I could find,' Anna admitted. 'I'm already cast aside by my family.'

'In that case you must join us,' Arizona replied enthusiastically, her attention deflected by the approach of Damian who too raised his hand as he saw Anna.

'Love and peace.'

'Love and peace,' Anna replied. Whatever they thought of organised religion, the community was curiously ritualistic.

'Love and peace,' Arizona repeated, picking Waffles up and hugging him. 'Jump for joy.'

It really was amazing the way this bedraggled and disadvantaged group of people kept their spirits up, Anna thought, not for the first time. With few worldly goods, no place to live that gave them any security, comfort or stability, constantly harassed by the authorities, they maintained an outward show, at any rate, of joy, though what they really thought when lying on their makeshift beds in the cold and dark was anyone's guess.

'Do you know,' Anna hugged her knees, 'I just thought the other day I'd like to give *everything* up, run away . . .'

'Flee, flee, sister,' Arizona's head turned as though watching a bird in flight and then she looked anxiously at Anna, 'but don't forsake us, sister, for God's sake.'

'If Anna joined us she wouldn't forsake us.' Damian, perched next to Anna gazing at her with a similar expression to Arizona's, a semblance of serenity that in his case once again made her think of the Biblical representations of the Christ figure. 'We could certainly do with a lawyer in our midst,' he said invitingly.

'You have a lawyer in your midst,' she replied.

'But one to share our life.' And Damian leapt up and gave a little twirl, hands in the air, before settling down again. Surely there was a double entendre now in every word he uttered?

Anna experienced that slight frisson in Damian's presence that was a kind of attraction. Again she felt that sense of disquiet, of unease whenever her thoughts, however brief, lingered on him. She lowered her eyes to avoid his gaze, conscious of him, angry with herself for reacting like this.

'I've never actually seen *you* skip or jump, Anna,' Arizona said reproachfully. 'Do you really experience joy? You can't share our life unless you do.'

'I promise I'll give it my attention.' Anna suppressed a smile. 'But seriously, brother and sister, I am not here with good news.'

'We have to move?' Damian's expression showed resignation rather than surprise.

'You *do* have to move,' Anna looked around her, 'for health reasons as much as anything. It will soon be winter and this place will be damp, dark and rat infested. Now look, there are a couple of houses that I think the Council will grant you strictly on a temporary basis.'

'*Houses!*' Arizona looked aghast. 'How can we all fit into *houses*, sister? We are a community . . .'

'Yes, well . . . some of you will have to split.'

'The community cannot split.' Damian shook his head emphatically. 'We are indivisible.'

'But you keep on growing,' Anna wailed. 'I'm sure there are several people here today I haven't seen before.'

'So the Council absolutely refuses to let us do up these premises?'

'It is far too costly. They have to be demolished. Basically they are unsafe and, Arizona, as the mother, I think you should be concerned about the welfare of your children.'

'All my children.' Arizona looked at her gravely and lit a fresh cigarette. 'All are one.'

It was a terrible problem, but sitting there with the September sunshine outside, winter seemed very far away. There were at least forty, maybe more, people including three children who ought to be at school, five toddlers, two babes in arms and assorted animals – dogs, cats, a goat and three gerbils, one of whom was pregnant.

'I'll see if I can get another house.' Anna got to her feet. 'But it's *not* a long-term solution.' She gestured around her. 'Arizona, this is really no way to live.'

Arizona regarded her through heavily kohled, half-closed eyes, puffing away on her long expensive filter cigarette. 'Is that so? You just said yourself you longed to get away. Well we have. Don't you think we've got responsibilities we've left behind? People, problems? We've abandoned the lot. This life we live, though apparently uncomfortable as far as you are concerned, is freedom; we have put aside material things for the life of the spirit. We are pilgrims looking for the Promised Land, are we not, Damian?'

Damian seemed to agree, but his attention was caught by a tall, solemn looking young man dressed incongruously in a pale coloured double-breasted business suit with a black roll-top sweater, who was strolling casually over towards them. Anna's first impression was that he might be a Council official or a welfare worker, even though the designer stubble, long pony-tail and pearl earring dangling from his left ear might possibly, though not certainly, preclude such an occupation.

'Greetings, brother,' Damian hailed him, arm raised.

The young man too raised an arm, though he said nothing.

'Joy and peace,' Damian continued. 'Do you know Anna?'

The young man looked gravely towards Anna, and shook his head.

'This is Errol,' Damian said with an unmistakable note of pride in his voice. 'Our artist.'

'Artist?' Anna looked interested.

'He's very talented.'

So far, Anna realised, the young man had not uttered a word. It occurred to her to wonder if he was dumb, but just then he spoke in a very low, quiet voice with a pronounced northern accent.

'How do you do, Anna?' He reached out to shake her hand.

The members of the community gave many gestures of greeting including hailing, skipping, jumping, hugging and kissing, but shaking hands was seldom one of them. The hand-clasp was firm and cool, authoritative. Errol was decidedly different.

'How do you do, Errol?'

The introductions over, Arizona offered Errol a cigarette which he took, lit and sat opposite Anna on one of the upturned boxes. His scrutiny was rather unnerving.

'I know it's rude, but what sort of art?' she asked.

'I trained at the Slade,' Errol said, as if that explained everything.

'Really?'

'He has exhibited at some important London galleries, haven't you, Errol?' Arizona said proudly. '*And* he has drawn all of us for posterity.'

'I see. You keep a record of . . .' Anna looked around.

'When I feel like it.' Errol shrugged. His hand trembled slightly, he had a deep sadness in his eyes, and his shoulders drooped.

'Errol gets depressed,' Damian explained. 'That's why he joined us. No will to go on living.'

'I'm very sorry,' Anna said sincerely. 'Is it better here?'

Errol said nothing but went on smoking moodily, staring at the ground.

'I have a daughter who wants to paint,' Anna heard herself saying. 'She feels she hasn't any talent.'

'Perhaps she hasn't,' Errol said prosaically. 'Not everyone who wants to paint can.'

'Exactly.' Arizona addressed Waffles who wagged his tail in obvious ecstatic agreement.

'I wonder if you'd like to . . . I mean, well, it would be nice to have your opinion,' Anna heard herself saying.

'Oh, Errol will give you an opinion, won't you, Errol?' Arizona spoke encouragingly. 'Anna is *the* lawyer trying to help us to keep the warehouse.'

'Oh!' Errol momentarily brightened. 'What is it you want me to do exactly?'

'Fiona, my daughter, would really like some coaching . . . a bit of encouragement . . .' Anna tapered off. She wondered what had made her suggest this – Peter was sure to be furious. For once in her life she had acted with thoughtless spontaneity. Too late, now, to retract.

'I don't mind looking at her stuff,' Errol said offhandedly. Obviously he was not a man anxious to please. 'But don't expect me to say I like it if I don't, or to say she has talent if she hasn't.'

'She's got very little left to show,' Anna said, wishing now that she hadn't spoken. 'She destroyed most of what she'd done.'

'Oh! Why was that?'

'She also got depressed about her work. She hasn't had a very easy time.'

A glimmer of interest suddenly flickered in Errol's dull eyes. 'Now that I understand,' he said.

Errol looked round the large room and thought how nice it would be to live in a place like this. It had blue walls and a white ceiling with a plaster cornice. Town houses built early in the nineteenth century to house large families. Now they housed the small families of the rich.

The furniture was old but good; some was even shabby. There were books everywhere, from floor to ceiling, piled on small tables, on the floor. Books that were used, read, not just there to be seen. There was a fireplace, but he imagined no real fire was ever lit in this part of London where they had long gone out of fashion, and a tall window about thirteen feet high from floor almost to the ceiling looking out on a long, well-stocked garden. There was a decent carpet on the floor, again old, but of the quality which endured for years, and rugs on top of that. Perhaps a bit threadbare but good. The whole place was good, solid, monied.

In the corner was a large TV set with a video underneath, and a good supply of tapes, a stereo in the corner with speakers on either side of the room. Tapes here too, doubtless Bach, Mozart, Beethoven, perhaps Tippett and Benjamin Britten. The girl would have her own stereo upstairs and her own CDs, probably her own TV too. She would have been born here, or at least lived here for years, used to a room of her own, this kind of style, not realising how luxurious it would seem to someone who came from the backwoods and lived on the streets.

Errol turned from his inspection, his thoughts racing, as the door opened and Fiona came in, her mother behind her. Fiona no longer had spiky hair; it was short, fair and cut close to her head. She had on a dress to her knees over leggings, a flowered waistcoat unbuttoned. She wore pink eye shadow, mascara and a heavy blusher on her cheeks, her lips coloured magenta. He thought she was startling, but not unusual.

'This is Fiona,' Anna said. 'Fiona, Errol.'

'Hi!'

They shook hands. Errol realised his palm's were slightly sweaty because he was anxious. The cool sang-froid he had adopted at the squat was gone.

It was the weekend after Anna and Errol had met, and in the meantime Anna had managed to get a stay of execution about the eviction from the squat. Only it was near the end of September and the weather, benign at the moment, would soon be turning from autumn to winter.

Peter, having been briefed to stay away while the introductions were made, came in and met Errol. By that time, Errol and Fiona were chatting quite happily, both smoking, and Anna said she had to go to a very brief meeting in Hampstead but would soon be back. Would Errol like to stay on to supper later? Errol thought he might.

She said goodbye and surreptitiously jerked her head to Peter who, mystified, followed her into the hall.

'What the hell?' he said.

'Leave them alone, for God's sake. It's awkward enough. Why don't you run me up the hill and go for a walk while I have my meeting? That will give me an excuse to get away.'

'Why don't you give up the blasted meeting and come for a walk instead with me?'

'I'd love it, but you know I can't. They already delayed the meeting until three because of me.'

'But who the hell *is* he?' Peter slipped on his jacket and followed Anna to the car.

'He's an artist. I haven't seen his work but they say he's a good one. I thought he might help Fiona.' Ashamed of her impetuosity, she hadn't dared tell Peter the whole truth.

'Oh!' Peter seemed cheered by the news as he slid into the driving seat beside Anna and drove away, Anna glancing at the notes she'd produced from her bag. There was a campaign to section off part of the Heath, merely to build some very expensive houses and, of course, she was on the committee opposing such an act of vandalism. Once you began these things there was no knowing where they would stop.

Peter drove up Haverstock Hill and asked her where she wanted to be dropped off. 'But *why* on a Saturday afternoon?'

'There was no other time.' She leapt out, peeped through the window. 'I promise. Be back here in an hour, say, an hour and a half and we'll go for a cup of tea?'

She smiled brightly and walked quickly away.

'Big deal,' Peter said to himself and drove along the High Street, thinking that perhaps after all as the weather was nice he would take a walk on the Heath. Blow away some of the cobwebs.

Errol and Fiona sat looking at each other rather awkwardly as Peter and Anna left, Peter having popped his head round the door to say that he was going too.

'They seem rather nice, your mother and father.'

Fiona nodded.

'Get on, do you?'

Fiona nodded again, suddenly tongue-tied and wishing that Anna and Peter had stayed or, at least, one of them.

'Just you, is there?' Errol was making all the running which for him was unusual. Usually he waited for others to speak.

'I've got a brother. He's away at school.'

'Boarding school?'

She nodded.

'That fits.' Errol nodded too.

'What fits?' Fiona looked defensively at him.

'Well, all this, you know,' he looked round, 'the set-up. Rich people.'

'It's not like that at all.'

'Shall we look at your paintings then?'

Fiona coloured, the moment she'd been dreading.

'They're not very good.'

'Still, let's have a look. That's why I'm here.'

'And there aren't very many.'

'I know. Your mum said you tore them up.'

'Oh, she told you?'

'It's the only reason I agreed to come.' He looked at her. 'I fancied you were some rich, privileged kid, and then she said you had difficulties. Otherwise I wouldn't have bothered.'

'Where do you live then?'

Errol gave a half-smile, cupped the match in his hand, while he lit another cigarette.

'She didn't tell you?'

'All she told me was that you were an artist, not how or where she met you.'

'I live in a squat.'

Fiona's mouth fell open.

'Not *the* squat?'

'The one she's trying to save.'

'By the railway line?'

'That's it.' He looked sullenly across at her. 'Does it matter?'

'Of course it doesn't. I think it's very exciting and I hope you win.'

'I don't.'

Fiona expressed amazement.

'What, you don't *want* to win?'

'Have you ever seen the fucking place? The trains keep you awake all night. There's a hole in the roof, and it's going to leak in the winter. It's either perishing cold or too bloody hot.'

'Can't you sell your paintings?' Fiona's voice sank to an awestruck whisper.

'It's not that. It's other things. I don't want to talk about them really.' Errol got up and wandered across the room, turning sharply to stare at her. 'Well, am I to see those paintings or not?'

'You'll tell me *honestly* what you think?' Her expression was anxious, vulnerable, like a small child's.

'I'll tell you honestly what I think.'

Errol then suddenly smiled at her and Fiona thought that, although he was sexy, moody, had a lot of charm, he was full of hidden hurt like she was.

They were back by six. Anna's meeting had of course gone on longer than expected, and she had some shopping to do for an extra mouth at dinner. Peter thought they might all go out but Anna felt it was better the first time . . .

'First time what, for God's sake?'

'He may be able to help her. We'll see how they get on.'

'They're not getting *married*, Anna.'

Anna looked at him disparagingly.

'Of course they're not.'

'One thing leads to another.'

'Don't be silly. She's far too young.' All the same, she had felt it especially important to get home sooner rather than later. You couldn't chaperone young people these days, and they would do their own thing no matter what. But, still, maybe she had been idiotic to introduce Fiona to someone from the squat. A young man she knew nothing about; she didn't even know if he could draw, if he was an artist at all. God Almighty. In any case, how stupid to introduce one depressive to another.

She was appalled by her lack of judgment in her enthusiasm to get some sense of purpose into Fiona's life, and could hardly wait to get out of the car and rush up the path to the house, a heavy carrier bag in each hand. Peter watched her with some bewilderment, locked the car door and followed her.

The house was silent. No sound of voices. Anna stood in the hall and listened. Nothing. She glanced into the living room. It was empty. The kitchen looked as though no one had been there since she'd left. No empty teacups.

My God. She went into the hall and called: 'Anyone at home?'

No reply.

She climbed up the stairs two at a time and halted outside Fiona's room, took a deep breath and knocked.

'Come in,' Fiona called, and, before Anna even had time to turn the handle, the door opened in her face. Fiona all smiles. Errol, looking relaxed, was lying on her bed propped up on an elbow, his jacket off but otherwise fully clothed. In front of him were Fiona's still rather crumpled sketches which she'd tried to iron out and mount on thin board. Then a few of the canvases that had been thrown out had been salvaged and repaired with Sellotape. These stood on the floor, displayed in front of them. The stereo in the corner played quite softly for Fiona, and there was a very faint sweetish smell in the air.

'They're good,' Errol said bluntly, not bothering to get up as Anna walked slowly into the room. She would ignore the sweet smell because she knew quite well what it was. Pot. Her keen eyes took in every detail of the room and she was pretty sure they hadn't been to bed, or at least not in bed, and in a way she was more worried about that, though even in these enlightened times would people leap into bed *that* fast? That didn't mean they hadn't kissed or fondled, but somehow she didn't think they had. The atmosphere didn't exude sexual tension but relaxation, leisure, friendship, maybe – was it too much to hope for? – a mutual appreciation of art?

Fiona was looking pleased, her face flushed.

Anna perched on the bed beside Errol, and saw to her surprise that those doleful eyes actually seemed more alive.

'Do you *really* think they're good?' she asked.

'Oh, I do.' He held up one of the ironed-out paintings, one she'd done in Rhodes. 'I think she has a lot of talent. I'd like to help her.'

Now Anna knew she'd made a mistake, but it was too late to go back. 'You really could help her?' she faltered.

'Oh, sure. I think so.' Errol smiled conspiratorially up at the beaming Fiona looking admiringly down at him. 'I think I could help her, and that we'd get on.'

Fiona looked around her with awe. She had never seen anything like it in her life except on the TV or in the cinema. To one end of the large shed were rows of mattresses. Beside each one were a few possessions: bundles, boxes, clothes sometimes thrown on the bed, sometimes on the floor. There were one or two cots and, what struck her most, a total absence of privacy.

In the centre of the room was a long trestle table filled with bowls, plates, various cooking ingredients. Behind them were butane or paraffin stoves on which were a number of bubbling pots. A jolly hoard of women and one or two men were stirring the pots adding ingredients to them all the time, tasting, adding more seasoning. They all looked in high good humour.

In front of the trestle table were smaller tables with rickety chairs drawn up to them. The people sitting at the tables were mostly older, both men and women, some in groups, some solitary. Several small children ran about, watched over by the younger women, and there was an assortment of dogs, cats and small furry animals in cages at the far end.

Fiona felt that all that was needed was for someone to stride forward with a megaphone and cry 'action'.

From the grimy windows high up in the walls a little daylight struggled in, but although there was a curious atmosphere of cheerfulness mingled with resignation, when one paused to consider that here was a mass of breathing, living humanity who had nowhere to live, it was pretty awful.

Errol stood to one side of Fiona, closely watching her reaction. He hadn't wanted her to come, but she had insisted.

Finally she turned and looked at him.

'Which is yours?'

'Which what?'

'Where do you sleep?'

'Oh, come on,' he began to feel agitated.

'No, I want to see . . .'

They made their way through the people scattered about, some of whom greeted them, some ignored them. Errol's patch was a neat mattress on which was a pillow, a duvet and two boxes, a chest of drawers. Fiona stood looking about her. Not far above the place that apparently contained all Errol's worldly goods was the corner where the ceiling had started to fall away.

'You couldn't live *here* in the depths of winter,' she said aghast, pointing to the ceiling. 'And it's nearly winter now.'

'That's what your mother says.'

'But why can't it be repaired?'

Errol shrugged and began to roll a cigarette, using tobacco from a tin he kept in his pocket.

'I mean,' Fiona looked around, 'it *could* be a nice place with a bit of imagination.'

'But you see we don't own it. It belongs to the Council.'

'But Anna's on the Council.' Fiona looked indignant. 'She could *easily* . . .'

'No, she can't. She's tried.' Errol shook his head. 'She . . .'

'Joy to all. Greetings, brother.' He was interrupted by the arrival of Arizona who had been surreptitiously watching them ever since they had come into the building. She paused and stared with frank interest at Fiona. 'Who have we here? Another recruit for our community?' Arizona shook her head slowly from side to side. 'No. Somehow I don't think so.'

'Why don't you think so?' Fiona challenged her.

'I simply don't think so.'

'This is Anna's daughter, Fiona,' Errol said, and then to her, 'meet Arizona, she calls herself the mother of the community.'

'Don't scoff at me, Errol,' Arizona said reprovingly and then to Fiona: 'Anna's daughter?' Arizona examined her closely. 'I don't see the resemblance . . .'

'She's not my real mother. My mother died. Anna is my stepmother.'

'Ah!' Arizona nodded. 'I remember now. She asked Errol if he would look at your paintings.'

'Yes.' Fiona felt confused.

'Is she any good?' Arizona looked towards Errol.

'Very good,' Errol replied. 'She has talent.'

Fiona laughed in embarrassment.

'Oh, I don't think I really have. Errol's simply being very nice about me but . . .'

'So what happened?'

'He's tutoring me. Every day for the past week.'

'And now she wanted to see where you lived?'

'Exactly.'

'And what do you think of our little home?' Arizona got out a packet of cigarettes and lit one.

'I think it could be terrific. I can't understand why the Council won't do anything about restoring it.'

'The Council want to turn it into offices and homes for the rich,' Arizona said derisively. 'You know how it is near the canal? It could be just as swanky round here.'

'They want to take the area upmarket.' Errol's tone was equally sarcastic.

'But Anna doesn't believe that!' Fiona looked enraged.

'There's not a lot that Anna can do about it. She's tried. She has been very good. Some of those so-called "socialists" don't want to know, do nothing about it; but Anna has done all she can. The truth is we will have to leave in a few weeks and our community be split up. Just now we're trying to do all we can to keep it together, find a place big enough.'

'I think it's lovely,' Fiona said wistfully. 'I really do.'

'Join us, daughter.' Arizona piously raised a hand. 'See how the other half lives. Skip and jump for joy.'

'Don't talk nonsense, Arizona,' Errol said angrily. 'Fiona doesn't want to "play" at being poor, at having no home.'

'But think of the publicity for the cause. "The daughter of Mrs Councillor Livingstone . . ."'

'No, I wouldn't like that at all,' Fiona said quickly. 'And Anna would hate it. Besides, Errol's right. I have no real place in this community. I would be pretending, and people would despise me, but I assure you I will do all I can to help Anna to find you somewhere proper to live.'

'Very well. Then why not join us for lunch? Nothing wrong with that, is there?' Arizona extended a hand graciously as though she were showing Fiona to a table at the Café Royal. 'I think you will find that the fare we have to offer is excellent. Plain but wholesome.'

An orderly queue had formed at the trestle table and three women were doling out what looked like thick soup or stew into earthenware bowls. The children pushed eagerly up in front of their mothers, and another cheerful soul was handing out large chunks of bread.

'Don't you think I am taking food from people's mouths?' Fiona whispered anxiously.

'Oh, there is plenty for all,' Arizona said expansively.

The smell was good and the food did, indeed, look nutritious, chunks of meat and vegetables in a thick broth.

'Where does it all come from?'

'Local shops and markets.' Arizona and Errol took their places in the queue with Fiona. 'People are very good to us. They give us stuff that no one wants to buy. Oh, don't worry,' she laughed at the suddenly anxious expression on Fiona's face, 'there is nothing *wrong* with it. It would pass inspection, the vegetables are sometimes bruised but we make sure that the meat is always fresh. There are many good people locally who help to keep us fed and want nothing except a word of thanks in return. The baker will always give us bread left over from the day before, which means there is nothing wrong with it.' Arizona sniffed disapprovingly. 'Just that those with money like it fresh out of the oven. Spoilt brats.'

The woman who gave Fiona her bowl had a friendly smile for her.

'You new here, dearie?'

'This is Anna's daughter,' Arizona said with a proprietorial air, pushing her forward.

'Oh, Anna's *daughter*.' The word went round the group, heads nodding approvingly. Yet above the voices one suddenly rose stridently. It was the woman giving out the bread. She looked no more than about twenty-five, yet three small children, fingers in their mouths, hovered near her. 'Anna's *daughter*,' she said scathingly. 'What need has *she* of our food?'

Fiona flushed, and was about to return the bowl she'd been given, when Arizona snatched it from her and put it firmly back in her hand.

'Who do you think you are, mean minded slag?' she said, roughly addressing the speaker. 'Anna has been goodness itself to us. Can't we give something to her daughter in return?'

'You think you'll get preferential treatment, don't you, Arizona?' the bread woman replied, unabashed. 'By sucking up to her daughter . . .'

'If you don't take care I'll slap you across the gob,' Arizona threateningly raised her hand. At that moment, fraught with tension, Damian appeared and stood between Arizona and the bread woman, who happened to be Rosie.

'What's going on here?' he demanded. 'I can hear your shrieks at the back of the yard. Do you want a riot, the police called? What will happen to us then, do you suppose?'

Rosie's children by now had run up to her and were clinging to her long woollen skirt.

'I don't see why this rich bitch . . .' Rosie began and Damian thundered at her: 'Silence! Do you hear?' He then turned to Fiona with a smile of great charm. 'Did they say you were Anna's daughter? How do you do? I'm Damian.'

'Greetings.' Fiona, into the lingo by now, extended her hand.

'Fiona wanted to see where we lived,' Errol explained. 'Nothing wrong with that.'

'Nothing wrong at *all*,' Arizona chipped in, 'for all that *we* owe Anna.'

'I really am sick of the way you all kow-tow to Anna,' Rosie said in a tone of heavy sarcasm. 'Anna this, Anna that, Anna is so good and now we have *Anna's daughter*. What did Anna really do for us? Nothing. We have been under the death sentence for months, and we still are. The mighty Mrs Councillor Livingstone with a nice house in Hampstead . . .'

'Belsize Park,' Fiona said quickly.

'The same thing,' Rosie snarled. 'A nice *big* house, I hear, with a garden and two bathrooms, perhaps three. Everyone has their own bedroom. The children go to the best schools. I hear our champion councillor is a successful lawyer with a practice in the West End. She must make a mint of money. *And* her husband . . .'

'Oh, do shut up,' Damian commanded.

'Rosie *does* have a point,' a diminutive woman standing nearby piped up. 'We don't like being patronised by the children of the rich. We have our dignity. We have our pride. Does little miss here realise that? We'll have the TV cameras here next and an article in the *Big Issue*. We . . .'

Fiona put her bowl back on the table and looked at Errol.

'I really think she's right,' she said, and turned sharply on her heels towards the door. Arizona walked swiftly after her, teetering on her wobbly high heels.

Errol and Damian followed.

'Daughter . . . Fiona . . .' Arizona called after her, 'please don't go just like that.' Fiona paused and Arizona caught up with her.

'She is right,' Fiona said earnestly. 'I *do* see what she means. I mean we may have the best intentions, and we do. I know Anna does; but compared to what little people here have . . . just what do we know? We know nothing and I feel bitterly ashamed and she,' Fiona pointed in Rosie's direction, 'is absolutely right and I'm sorry.'

Fiona continued to walk quickly to the corner of the yard where she'd parked the car her father had given her for her seventeenth birthday just after she'd passed her test. She had been so proud of it, but now she saw it through eyes blurred by tears. She felt ashamed of it as a symbol of affluence, and herself. She would like to have gone right past the car and have pretended that she had nothing to do with it. It had been really crass to bring it here, a trendy Volkswagen Beetle, a real yuppy design car in hectic psychedelic colours. She was aware of footsteps next to her, Errol, the first to catch up with her.

'Take no notice . . .' he began.

'But I *do*, Errol.' She stopped and looked at him. 'I feel ashamed . . .'

'*She* should feel ashamed.' Angrily Errol looked behind him. 'She shoots off her big mouth and she knows *nothing*. Believe me, she knows *nothing*. She is a slag, she has a child by every man she meets and expects the State to look after her and them. She can't keep her legs together. She's a whore. Seriously, Fiona, she's a prostitute. We have to look after her kids at night while she skips off to King's Cross.'

'I still think she was right,' Fiona's eyes smouldered, 'and personally I'm sorry she has to do that.'

'Look,' Errol opened the car door for her and closed it after she had got in, 'don't waste your sympathy on these people.

You know . . .' he darted round to the passenger's side, opened the door and slid in, 'most of them are here because it is their *own* fault. It's *my* fault I'm here. We've given up. We're defeated by society. Others aren't. They go out and lick it. We've allowed it to conquer *us*. We all have something wrong with us, that's why we're here, Fiona. We're bums. Not worth wasting your tears over. Nothing to be ashamed about, honestly . . .'

Fiona was looking at him uncomprehendingly as she switched on the ignition and slowly let in the clutch before reversing the car out of the yard. Errol stopped speaking as she manoeuvred, anxious because she was such a new driver; but she had been well taught and passed her test on the first attempt. She came out of the yard and turned carefully into the main road, heading north towards home. She clutched the wheel firmly, her eyes on the road in front of her. She drove slowly, carefully, making the right steady gear changes because she knew that Errol was nervous. Then half way up Haverstock Hill she pulled into the kerb and stopped, switched off the engine and turned towards him.

'Why are you telling me all this, Errol?'

'Because I saw how upset you were. Honestly, no one there gives a shit. They are all on benefits, they scrounge off the State. They are jealous and envious. No one can help them because they're a load of bums, beyond help.'

'But *I* thought you identified with them?'

'Me identify with them?' Errol laughed loudly. 'I despise them. I'd give everything I could to get out of there. I'm ashamed of myself for living there, for taking someone like you there.'

'You didn't want to take me.'

'I didn't, and I was right. But I didn't dream that what happened would happen.'

'Then why are you there?'

'Because I gave up. Gave in. Look, I have a problem. I'm a

depressive. There are times when I can't cope and everything caves in. I couldn't sell my paintings. I got a bad review for a show. Someone said I couldn't paint, so I knew how you felt when you were told you couldn't. I'm not as successful as Anna thought I was.' He put a hand on her shoulder. 'I feel ashamed, Fiona, that I've involved you with this world, with me. Your mother will never forgive me for taking you there and she will be right. It's spoilt everything.'

'What has it spoilt?'

'Our relationship. It was coming on good.'

'Don't be silly,' impulsively she seized one of his hands. 'Of course it hasn't spoilt our relationship. It is good. Look I have an idea . . .' she put her other hand to her head and closed her eyes. 'I don't know how this sounds to you. It might sound mad, but you see I thought you *believed* in the squat. I thought it was a matter of principle and you identified with everyone there. Now I see that you don't, and that what Anna is trying to do is pretty futile. Maybe it is. I mean she has given much of her life to help the helpless, most of whom, according to you, don't need or deserve help . . .'

'Not everyone,' he said quickly.

'No, not everyone. I agree but,' she looked at him with her open, honest large blue eyes. 'If you really don't like it there you don't have to stay there. I've a cottage in Dorset. It belongs to me and my brother. I was working there for six months before I came back to London. London has made me depressed, made me destroy my work. Obviously you hate it too. What do you say, Errol, to life in the countryside?'

CHAPTER 10

'Young homeless people have no place in our increasingly materialistic and greedy society.' Anna paused and looked round at the faces of her fellow councillors listening attentively to her in the chamber at an emergency meeting of the Council. She was a good speaker – she had had a lot of practice – and she usually captured her audiences' attention and held it. Today was no exception, except for the handful of Tories who, acting as though they had heard it all before, and far too often, shuffled their papers, yawned, or simply stared at her with bored expressions, eyes sometimes half-closed, arms folded across their breasts.

'But it is not only the young who suffer. People of all ages are roaming the streets because they fall between the nets the increasingly hard-stretched Social Service Departments throw to them. They . . .'

She knew it was hopeless. Sympathetic though most of her audience was, the building occupied by the squatters was unsafe, the Council couldn't possibly vote enough funds to repair it. However she would go down fighting, which she did.

There were many who spoke in her support, people who genuinely wished to help the Pilgrim community but who would be accused of gross abuse of public funds if they did. The alternatives were in place: two derelict houses had been repaired for the most needy in the community, places in hotels or hostels for mothers with young children. Yet temporary accommodation was not a real answer to their needs. The problems of the homeless in inner London were insuperable.

The Council voted almost unanimously to close the squat, only Anna and a handful voting against as a protest rather than because they thought it would do any good.

Afterwards many of her fellow councillors came up to her and offered commiserations.

'First rate speech, Anna.' Jim Crowther was a supporter and a close colleague. He did a lot of work for the homeless and disadvantaged in all walks of life. He was also a journalist on a local newspaper and had written many articles in support of the Pilgrims. 'You should stand for Parliament where we can do something to change these disgusting laws which cap councils like ours trying to bring a little sanity to society.'

'I think my husband would really take off if I did.' Anna gathered her papers together and put a hand on Jim's arm. 'Thank you so much, Jim, for your support as always. To me now falls the ghastly duty of telling them they really have to get out. You wouldn't like to come with me, would you?'

'Of course I will. Gladly.'

'It will have to be first thing in the morning. I have a court case, but I think my deputy can hold the fort until the afternoon, or we could get an adjournment.'

'Would you like me to tell them for you?'

'Oh, no.' Anna looked gratefully at him. 'I must do it. After all, this time they'll think I've chickened out if I don't.'

'I think you'd better take the police with you, Anna.' Dorothy Singleton, the deputy-leader of the Council came up to her, 'They might turn nasty.'

'Oh, I wouldn't dream of having the police,' Anna said coldly. 'That really *would* be provocative.'

'Well,' Dorothy looked grim. 'Don't say I didn't warn you.'

Anna slept very badly that night and was up early to prepare herself for what would be a harrowing day. She crept out of bed, leaving Peter still asleep. It was so early that the central heating hadn't come on, and even the bath water was cold. Well it was nothing to what the people she had to talk to had to endure and, indeed, after the move most of them would be better off. The new premises had recently been put in good order, were newly decorated and passably furnished. There was electric light, running hot and cold water, gas fires and a proper kitchen. She herself had been several times to make sure the renovation was being carried out to acceptable standards.

However there were still those in the Pilgrim community who would say she had let them down, and others who would never fit in because they would never assimilate into any ordered existence, nor had they any desire to. Anna found it very hard to understand people like this, like Arizona and Damian, Rosie, Maeve, Hope, Biff Cassidy and others whom she knew would not want to live in an orderly society with decent accommodation and nearby schools and amenities, however much one tried. They were the vagabonds, the modern gypsies who also lacked the freedom of the road, being harassed by the authorities from pillar to post as their pathetic processions of unserviceable, unlicensed and uninsured vehicles made their way from county to county, only to be roughly moved on by unsympathetic councils and outraged local residents.

Anna quickly emerged from her tepid bath and dressed with care. By seven she was sitting at the kitchen table drinking black coffee and studying her brief for the law case that afternoon which concerned a woman trying to avoid being sent to prison for prostitution. She was an habitual offender, and the chances seemed slim as there were also several charges of breaking and entering for the purposes of theft to be considered. Yet another person whom Anna had spent many weeks desperately trying to help. But the woman needed the money. She had one child whom she adored and was bringing up alone. But it was not the answer, so one could only assume that, as she spurned other assistance, she rather enjoyed her job. She was also on drugs. In many ways prison might be the best place for her, but Anna didn't see it that way. She thought prison was to be avoided at all costs. The trouble was that there were not enough rehabilitation centres for people like her client, who would probably end up in some sort of squat until inevitably the drugs she pumped into her frail body killed her, and left the daughter she worked so hard to rear fend for herself.

Anna poured herself another cup of coffee and popped two slices of bread in the toaster. She wasn't hungry, but she didn't know when she'd next eat. The squat situation was bound to be an ordeal and then straight from there to court which would recommence at about two. Then when the court closed back to the office to see what additional work had accumulated during the day. In the meantime there would be a number of calls to make on her mobile, and she would want to keep in touch with what progress, if any, was being made on arrangements for the orderly dispersal of the Pilgrims. A court order would be obtained this very morning ordering their evacuation by Saturday. Many officials thought that the sooner they were out the better, before part of the building collapsed and there was an even greater scandal for which they would be sure to be blamed, Anna prominent among the accused.

It was rather eerie in the house in the quiet of the morning. Around her everything gleamed, and remained that way. Although it was curious to have no children in the house after all these years – the first and only time unless they had been on holiday – it was at the same time welcome and unwelcome. Above all she loved the order, the feeling that when she came home the place would look as it had when she went out, or even better as the cleaner would have been and would have met no opposition from Fiona or Guy about the state of their rooms or the kitchen or wherever else they chose to make their messes. This part was lovely, so was the absence of tension. But also Anna missed the presence of young people in a way she never thought she would, friends going in and out, and she knew Peter missed them too. Well, they might soon be back. There was no knowing how long Fiona would remain in Dorset, and Guy would be home first for half term and then holidays, of which private schools had a lot that seemed to go on for an awful long time.

It was getting light outside and Fiona finished her toast and marmalade, drained her coffee and then made a pot of tea for Peter which she put on a tray and took upstairs.

Peter was awake, lying in bed gazing at the ceiling.

'You're up early,' he said.

'I've got to go and tell the Pilgrims they have to leave,' she looked grim, '*and* I have to be in court this afternoon. I should be there this morning but Roger is holding the fort for me.'

'Another busy day, Anna.' There was a hint of sarcasm in his voice as he reached up and took the tea from her.

'I'm afraid so, dear.' She bent over and lightly kissed his brow. 'I'll try and make it back in time for dinner.' And before he could begin the customary whinge about how much she had to do, she fled downstairs and out of the house collecting her raincoat and briefcase on the way.

When she got to the warehouse Jim was already there. So too, to her irritation, was a policeman standing guard at the gate.

'We said "no police",' she hissed.

The policeman touched his helmet respectfully. 'I'm sorry, Councillor Livingstone, but we have instructions. It is just for your safety, ma'am. We will not enter the building unless it becomes necessary.'

'But it won't, and they are not being asked to leave today.'

'I know that, madam; but I have my instructions. I am here on duty by myself with orders to call my colleagues only if and when it should become necessary.'

'But . . .'

Jim Crowther put his hand on Anna's arm.

'You can't argue with him, Anna. It seems that the news may have got round.'

'But how?'

Jim shrugged.

'You know what the grapevine is like. Can't stop it, I'm afraid.'

By now the rain had started to fall steadily, so Anna returned to her car and drove it into a corner of the yard where Jim joined her after a further word with the constable on duty who had closed the gate after them.

'Let's hope this won't take long.' Jim put his umbrella over Anna's head as she emerged from the car. 'What a day.'

'A bloody awful day.' Anna gazed up to the skies. 'However it might make them realise that a move would be the best thing. The roof is sure to be leaking.'

And indeed it was. The first thing she saw as she and Jim quietly entered as inconspicuously as possible from the rear door was a collection of buckets, pots and pans under the portion of the ceiling where daylight usually came in.

Only today it was so dark that no light came, just a steady stream of rain not only from that corner but other parts of the ceiling too.

Some members of the community had not bothered to get up, but others were at the portable stoves making breakfast. The main lighting, which was not very good, was by paraffin lamps and candles, a hazard in itself. The Council had refused to pay for any more electricity and it had been disconnected two weeks earlier. Anna noticed several vacant spaces and guessed that some had already moved on. There was an air of palpable dejection and gloom in the building, and from the stares that greeted herself and Jim, she realised that everyone knew.

Having their meagre breakfast, heads close together in

earnest discussion so that they had not noticed their entrance, were Arizona and Damian. Anna and Jim walked across the room to them to be greeted in stony silence.

'I gather you heard.' Anna sat in one of the rickety chairs next to Arizona who was feeding Waffles on slices of buttered bread, thereby probably depriving herself.

'You might have told us,' she said reproachfully without looking up.

'The vote was only taken at nine o'clock last night. I didn't think you'd know. Besides I couldn't have come here at that time. The gate is always locked.'

Arizona and Damian exchanged glances, ignoring Anna and Jim.

'I came as soon as I could.' Anna glanced at her watch. 'It is only half past eight now, and Jim has come with me because he has all the details about the move.'

'We're not going to go, you know.' Arizona passed Waffles another choice slice of bread and butter, and licked her fingers.

Anna leaned forward.

'Arizona, you know you *have* to go. It is your duty to go and lead your children to a better style of accommodation. I have seen, you have seen, what we're offering. The Council has done its very best.'

'Anna made a marvellous speech.' Jim's voice was full of admiration. 'I was proud of her. Many councillors had tears in their eyes.'

'How very touching,' Arizona sniffed disdainfully. 'Wish I'd been there to hear it. The only tears I would have had in my eyes would have been for those with nowhere to live, not for those who live in posh houses and have the gift of the gab.'

'I do get so irritated when you speak like this,' Anna interrupted angrily. 'You *know* you can't continue to live here. It's falling to pieces around you. Look at the rain coming through the ceiling. Half the people here have got colds, and God knows what the effect on the children will be. They'll develop rickets.'

'You should have got somewhere for *all* of us.' Arizona gazed at her accusingly.

'Look, I'm going to talk to them now and explain. I can't guarantee you, no one can, *purpose*-built accommodation for a community that is largely composed of a group of itinerant people who have joined together to form themselves into a loose bond . . .'

'Loose!' Damian exploded. 'How do you think Christ's disciples came together?'

'I didn't think we were talking religion.' Anna looked surprised. 'You always told me you were an atheist, Damian, despite the fact that you call yourselves "The Pilgrims".'

'Pilgrims looking for a better land, as our forefathers did in the seventeenth century. Here we are talking of a so-called "Christian" society that treats people like outcasts.'

'But, Damian, as a qualified mathematician you know perfectly well that you could get a job, and probably a very good one. The fact that you don't happen to want to, that you prefer to live like this, is your decision entirely. As far as I know, you are neither an alcoholic, nor are you drug dependent. Your parents are ready and willing not only to help you financially but to give you a home. And this you have rejected to become leader of a band of people without direction in their lives, some through their own fault, others not. If you like this lifestyle, and I know you do, so be it, but please don't tell *me* about treating people like outcasts. *I* too could be an outcast if I wished, but I prefer instead to work from within society for the betterment of those outside it. I think you do it so that you can manipulate people, Damian. It satisfies some need for domination you can't find elsewhere . . .'

'Anna, please,' Jim interrupted, grasping her arm. 'Don't get yourself so worked up. It's not worth it.' He gestured towards the centre of the room, to where the rest of the community had gathered, slowly advancing towards them. 'Look: make it short and positive.'

'Right!' Anna stood up and faced the concourse of hostile faces gathering around her. Rosie was there, a contemptuous smile on her face, her children clustered, as usual, round her skirt. Merrylee, the mother of one of the babies, stood with the baby slung on her hip drinking contentedly from her exposed nipple. Biff Cassidy leaned nonchalantly against one of the tables and most of the others stood, squatted on the floor, or perched on the end of the table. Quite a few, mostly the older ones, remained in bed. It was bitterly cold and Anna felt she had never faced such a situation in such a depressing location in her life.

'Right,' she said again, 'I gather you all know why Jim and I are here.'

'*And* the policeman at the gate,' someone shouted.

'I specifically asked there should be no police,' Anna said. 'Jim will bear me out on this.' She glanced at Jim who nodded his head vigorously. 'But there is just one policeman at the gate, and although I asked him to go away he wouldn't.'

She paused and took a deep breath. Used as she was to making speeches, this was one of the most difficult.

'Last night the Council voted to seek an order to have the squat evicted. There is no appeal. The last day will be Saturday, that is in four days' time. In the opinion of the Council you have had plenty of notice and plenty of time to prepare. Other accommodation is available for you.'

'Not for us all,' someone shouted.

'For most of you.' Anna swallowed. 'Mothers with young children will be put in Bed and Breakfast accommodation, hostels or hotels until they can be rehoused. They will have priority. In the meantime . . .'

'Rich bitch,' someone yelled from the back.

Anna paused, her heart pounding.

'If you mean *me*, I am not rich and I am not a bitch. I have done all in my power to help you. I tried desperately, both as a lawyer and a borough councillor, to enable you to stay on here, to try and persuade the Council to agree to do the place up; but the estimates ran into millions, money which the Council felt could be better used elsewhere.'

'In the pockets of the fucking capitalists,' Biff Cassidy bawled in his rich Irish brogue. In his time he had worked as a builders' labourer, so he knew all about those who soaked the poor.

'This building will be demolished and the site redeveloped.' Anna felt her throat drying up. 'That I can do nothing about. We are not a rich council and we have an undue preponderance of people in need in the city as a whole. Others might object very much had we lavished millions into making what would in fact have been a sort of squatters' hotel. I spoke on your behalf to the very best of my ability; but the vote went against me by a large majority. I am,' as murmuring began around her she was forced to raise her voice even higher to make herself heard, 'I am very, very sorry. Many of you have become my friends. I have the welfare of you all very much to heart. The places we have got where most of you will be accommodated are of superior standard.'

'Good enough for *you*?' The woman's voice was shrilly accusatory.

'Only *temporary*,' cried someone else.

'They, too, are due ultimately to be demolished, but no time has been set.'

'What sort of way is *that* to live?'

'No way at all, I agree . . .'

'Not like the nice place you have got for your daughter and Errol.'

Anna stopped, momentarily winded. 'I had a lot of problems with my daughter . . .' she began.

'Yeah, and you'll have a whole heap more with Errol . . .'

screamed someone, and a general gust of ribald laughter swept the building.

'Please, friends . . .'

Anna suddenly felt a sharp sting on the side of her face and something smelly and horrible started to slide down her cheek. This was followed by another missile which hit her shoulder, another her hair. One hit Jim, another Arizona, for whom it certainly was not intended. Anna's eyes began to stream but she could still see that, from several parts of the hall, rotten eggs, fruit and vegetable were being hurled at them, obviously gathered early that morning or perhaps late the night before from the market.

Jim got one straight in the eyes, another landed squarely on her face. The smell was appalling. Suddenly Damian jumped up on the table and bellowed through cupped hand: 'Comrades, brothers and sisters, friends, I *beg* you do not . . .'

'Go and fuck yourself,' jeered a woman, and then, 'put it up your mother's . . .' Then Biff Cassidy ran forward like a rugger scrum half, and threw a violent punch in Jim's midriff, causing him to buckle.

'Judas!' Biff cried. 'Filthy, rotten, stinking swine in league with the capitalists . . .'

Some women began to scream in frenzy and the children, scattered to the far corner of the room, took up the refrain with gusto. The din was indescribable. The situation indeed looked menacing and Anna thought of the policeman at the gate and wished fervently that he were here. Suddenly a melee began in which Damian and Jim seemed to be the victims, and shaking from head to foot, trying her best to rub away the horrible egg and mess from her face with a handkerchief, she stumbled through the fracas towards the door and eventually found herself out in the yard where she raised her face for a moment to the life-giving rain.

At that moment the gates swung open and a number of

police cars sped into the yard disgorging their personnel who headed towards the door.

'Are you alright, Councillor?' She recognised the bobby who had stood at the gate, and looked at him with stricken eyes. 'I *knew* you'd have trouble, Mrs Livingstone.' He put an avuncular arm around her shoulder. 'You should have listened. You can't ever trust people content to live like animals. In time they come to resemble them, madam.'

And to her shame and horror Anna rested her head on the policeman's shoulder and wept.

Anna hardly ever rested, was never, or seldom, ill, and to find herself in the middle of the afternoon still in bed was an unusual, almost an extraordinary occurrence. One that hadn't happened since she'd had her sterilisation the year before. Then she'd had an excuse, but this time she felt she didn't, really, that she was merely indulging herself.

The house seemed incredibly silent, still, except for the distant sound of traffic racing up and down Haverstock Hill. It was odd, but it was not unpleasant to be in bed surrounded by the papers, the TV in front of her if she wanted to watch it, which she didn't. Daytime television seemed almost as sinful as staying in bed when there was nothing physically wrong with you.

The police had brought her home the day before and, despite her protestations, Peter had been summoned from work. The doctor too appeared and gave her a sedative. He said she should rest, take some days off yet not brood. Peter suggested that when she felt fit she should pay a visit to her mother in the north, a woman she loved deeply but felt she neglected.

Anna felt a bit of a fraud lying in bed, plucking at the bedcovers like some nineteenth-century damsel suffering from the vapours. Paula had been, cleaned, done some washing, brought her a light lunch and the latest editions of the newspapers and left.

The story had made national headlines: Tory supporters naturally cackling with glee.

Labour councillor pelted with rotten eggs

The members of the self-styled 'Pilgrim' squat in north London, whom Mrs Anna Livingstone had tried so hard to help, had a surprise for her when she went to see them yesterday: they pelted her with rotten eggs, cabbage and tomatoes.

Mrs Livingstone, thirty-seven, one of the most selfless, committed and respected Labour councillors, who devotes her spare time entirely to good causes, had tried to stop these people from being evicted from a condemned warehouse. This is the sort of reward she got. They have now been dispersed to alternative accommodation, at the taxpayers' expense, to other recently renovated quarters in the borough. Mrs Livingstone, who also has a successful private practice as a solicitor, was seen to be in tears as she left with a police escort. At her express request, no charges have been preferred, although two men and a woman who assaulted police officers were arrested.

Mrs Livingstone was unavailable for comment.

Mrs Livingstone was certainly unavailable for comment, but Mr Livingstone had appeared, reluctantly, at the garden gate to address reporters not only from the papers but from radio and television news. He'd made a short, dignified statement appealing for calm, denying that his wife would press charges ('Foolish', David Cole had remonstrated on the phone) and that was that.

Well, for the time being, though soon the story would be superseded by another disaster, a happening in another part of the city, and all attention would be focused on that.

It was after three, but Anna wasn't sleepy. She felt she

should get up, but she didn't know what to do. She'd telephone her mother, arrange to go north in a day or two, return the call Fiona had made while the daily was here and Anna was in the bath. Nice. Gratifying that Fiona was concerned.

The strident sound of the doorbell interrupted her reverie. She stiffened involuntarily, plucking again at the bedclothes, aware that the pace of her heart had quickened. Really, her nerves were shot to pieces. This was ridiculous. She lay where she was and listened. Maybe it was the press. The doorbell rang again and she got out of bed and, running lightly along the corridor, looked gingerly down towards the front door from the first floor window. She saw the brilliant, variegated tops of a large bouquet and, smiling to herself at her foolishness, returned to her bedroom, put on her gown and ran downstairs ridiculing her fears. Another bunch of flowers. The house was full of them already.

She opened the door, ready to take the present and then she stopped, the welcoming smile vanishing.

Damian was wearing jeans and a shirt, his hair tied at the back in a pony tail, his beard neatly combed. His expression was one of concern, contrite, difficult to fathom. He thrust the flowers towards her and she held out her arms to take them, not knowing what to say. For one who was so articulate she was momentarily lost for words.

'I just wanted to say . . .' he began as the flowers passed from his arms to hers.

'Come in,' she said tersely, stepping to one side and pointing the way indoors.

'Oh!' He scratched his head and looked uncertain as to what he should do.

'There's no one at home,' she added, wondering why she bothered to reassure him, and he nodded as if with relief and stepped inside looking round at the large airy hall towards the open door of the living room.

'Do go in,' she said, gesturing towards the room, 'and I'll pop these into the kitchen. It's very kind of you.'

'Anna,' Damian hesitated, stroking his beard. 'I just don't know what to say . . .'

'I'll make us some tea,' she said, propelling him gently towards the living-room door. 'Don't say anything.'

She went quickly into the kitchen, aware of the overpowering scent of the flowers. Beautiful roses, carnations. They must have cost a fortune. No question that these had fallen off the back of a lorry.

She realised she was trembling and her face was hot. She had been so totally unprepared to see him, here, in her home. She felt like a schoolgirl caught in some misdemeanour. She realised her hands were trembling as she filled the kettle, got out the cups and saucers, searched around for the teapot.

Why hadn't she told him to go away?

Biscuits. There were biscuits somewhere. In the tin. Where was the tin? Why, in the usual place, on the kitchen table.

The clock in the hall struck four. Supposing Peter came home early? What would he do if he saw Damian *here*? Silly. She wasn't doing anything wrong. But all the same she'd give him his tea and tell him to go.

Stupid to let him in. She should just have taken the flowers and . . .

'The flowers are really beautiful,' she said, kicking the living room door wider with her foot and bearing the tray towards a small occasional table as Damian jumped up to take it from her.

'Here, let me. You shouldn't.'

'They're just gorgeous. I love roses. Must have cost a bomb . . .' She halted. The implication was 'where did *you* get the money?' How tactless. What a stupid thing to say. She realised she was gabbling and that her gown had fallen open, a lock of hair hung across her brow.

She stooped, straightened up and looked at him.

'I must look a sight,' she said and she saw he was looking at her in that way, smiling.

'You look very nice,' he said. 'I've always thought you looked nice, from the moment you walked into the squat.'

She fastened her gown, tucked the lock back behind her ear and began to pour.

'Do sit down.' She jerked her head in the direction of Peter's chair, but Damian remained where he was, looking round.

'Nice place you've got here, Anna.'

'It was Peter's house before we married. Milk and sugar?' She looked up to see him still looking down at her with that curious, enigmatic smile. 'I mean, he lived here with his first wife.' She felt a bit calmer now, more in control, and passed him his cup. Of course she'd been taken unawares, she'd been silly, childish. Her hand no longer shook. She took up her own tea and sat down, indicating he should sit opposite her. But Damian remained where he was, cup and saucer in his hand, still gazing down at her.

'Anna, I can't tell you how awful I feel. I personally should have done something to stop what happened. I feel very responsible for it all. It was a terrible experience for you. I shall never forgive myself . . . Anna.'

She couldn't stop the tears. They just flowed spontaneously, burst out as from a great underground well. It was all the pent-up emotion, resentment, fear.

'I'm sorry,' she murmured, shaking her head. 'I'm in a stupid emotional state. I shall be perfectly alright.' She groped in the pocket of her gown for her handkerchief and blew her nose hard. 'I guess the doctor gave me some drug. And . . .'

'Anna, Anna, it's perfectly alright.' He was on his knees beside her, grasping her hand, stroking her brow, his touch so cool, tender. 'Relax, unwind, Anna.'

'Oh, *Damian*.' She put her head on his shoulder, as she had on that of the policeman, and once more gave herself up to unrestrained tears.

Damian's arms were around her, his lips, also cool, on her forehead. He slid one of his hands inside her gown and felt for her breast. She knew her nipple became instantly erect to his touch. She felt as though she had absolutely no willpower, that she was made of rubber. She raised her mouth and he kissed her. His lips were very firm and the feel of his beard and moustache was odd, prickly yet sexy. She had never kissed a man with so much facial hair.

She moved off the chair on to the floor. He took off his jeans and knelt beside her, raising her gown high over her hips and gazing at her, his hand very cool as it touched her flat stomach.

She knew that what was to happen was inevitable and she gave herself gladly to him.

Gladly and, at that moment, without guilt.

CHAPTER 11

The light filtered in through the tiny mullioned windows of Anna's mother's cottage on the outskirts of Leeds. Anna guessed it must be about eight, and she lay for some time gazing at the light, trying to guess the hour, too lazy to look at the clock. Then she made herself tea and got back into bed.

It was good to be out of London and away from the repercussions of the aftermath of the squat. But, more than that, she had had to put distance between herself and Damian as fast as she could, and to try and come to terms with what was a glorious adventure but, at the same time, an incredible folly.

It was glorious, reckless, total abandonment producing the deepest moment of orgasm she had had for years, perhaps ever. The others seemed like tiny tremors rippling on the surface. This time, the earth really had moved.

He had knelt over her when they had finished, staring into her eyes, and she had taken his face between her hands, kissed him and released him. She had told him matter-of-factly that he must go, her husband would soon be home. She had become the one in control of the situation, and it was he who was confused and trembling.

She'd felt utterly in command, asking him to take the tea-tray back into the kitchen while she straightened the room, opened the windows wide. The smell of sex seemed to her as pervasive as the chaos inside her own body. They'd stood briefly in the hall, arms linked, farewell kisses on the cheeks.

'I *must* see you again,' he said but she bundled him towards the door and shut it quickly after him, not even seeing him to the gate.

Then she'd gone slowly upstairs and had a long, long bath. She'd felt wonderful.

But the feeling didn't last. She felt less wonderful when Peter came home and a bit shabby. But her emotions varied. She kept on savouring the moment, that gigantic upheaval of the flesh, wondering if she could ever repeat it. But it was, after all, a sensation, and it passed. She'd known she had to get away, and the next day she pronounced herself fit and, despite Peter's misgivings, had driven north.

What to do about Damian on her return? Well, time, she guessed, would take care of that, but an affair was impossible. Besides, she wasn't sure she wanted one. She had too many messy marriages in her practice to contemplate one of her own.

She loved Peter. Just now there was a bad patch, but it would pass. What had happened between her and Damian was purely physical; in a way like dogs copulating in the street or the park only, she supposed, with more emotion, more cerebral pleasure, but just as quickly. She'd never had anything quite like it.

Anna took another sip of the hot tea, relishing the warmth from her electric blanket. It was a pretty room with white furniture and whitewashed walls, chintzy curtains. It was not a house associated with her childhood, for her mother had moved here a few years before in order to be nearer the countryside which she loved.

The house where Anna had grown up was semi-detached, also on the outskirts of Leeds. It was in a row of similar houses, all with a neat patch of garden in front, and a bigger one behind. It was not Council and it was not working class. In so far as people thought in stereotypes, and unfortunately they did, it was lower middle-class suburbia where bikes leaned against the railings, dogs ran about and children played in the streets.

Anna had not been born there either, although she had indeed been born in Leeds. Her father had left her mother when she was little, and the smaller house was part of the divorce settlement. Anna had never seen the house she had been born in, where she and her parents had lived before the split. Nor had she ever particularly wanted to. She was not a sentimental person which was, she supposed, the reason why she had chosen law as a profession. But she had heard it was a big house. Her father had been a successful businessman, like Peter, but he left her mother for another woman and subsequently showed very little interest in his daughter, even though he had no more children. Not long after his remarriage he died in a motor accident which left her mother financially rather badly off.

Anna and her mother had been close, but the relationship was a difficult one. They were very different kinds of people. Sylvia Wood was hurt by her husband's desertion and also diminished by it. She blamed herself, her lack of personality and attractiveness. It reinforced her low self-esteem, her basic lack of confidence.

For all that, she was an extremely good mother to Anna. She encouraged her and fostered her ambition, and Anna rewarded her by being a good and dutiful daughter, serious minded, devoted to her studies and, ultimately, successful.

Sylvia Wood had worked most of her life in the shoe section of a large department store in Leeds. She was one of those women who try hard to please, neatly dressed, self-effacing, efficient, rushing about with boxes of shoes, squatting on their knees to try them on the feet of sometimes capricious customers who spent more on footwear in one session than Mrs Wood could earn in a week.

Maybe it was her mother's unremitting air of sacrifice that

had made Anna determined to succeed where her mother hadn't.

Sylvia always said Anna was like her father. She had a hard edge.

Yet, needless to say, Sylvia was extremely proud of her successful daughter, her first-class law degree, her subsequent success, her election to the Council, her marriage to a man so like her father, in many ways. She had one sorrow, one rarely-voiced complaint: that she had no grandchildren and now she never would.

Anna turned restlessly in bed, gazed at the clock and was surprised to see that almost an hour had advanced since she woke. Her mother, who now worked part-time, didn't start work until the afternoon and she could hear sounds of stirring downstairs. She'd be laying the table in the little breakfast room, cutting bread, making tea, maybe watching the last few minutes of the breakfast programme on television.

Suddenly feeling guilty, Anna jumped out of bed, put on her gown, brushed her teeth and, taking the tray with the dirty teapot and cup, went downstairs to the kitchen where, as she thought, Sylvia, elbow on the table, was watching the nine o'clock news.

'Anything interesting? Morning, Mum.' Anna kissed her on the nape of the neck, and Sylvia turned, a smile of welcome on her face.

'Nothing much, dear.' She reached for the remote control to turn off the television. 'How did you sleep?'

'Fine.' Anna gently ruffled the top of her mother's hair and, going to the fridge, poured herself a glass of orange juice.

'Sure?' Sylvia looked at her anxiously.

'Sure. I didn't wake until nearly eight.'

'Oh, that's good.'

Sylvia always had this air of excessive concern for Anna, as though she were incapable of looking after herself, which her daughter found irritating. But she was so kind, so good-hearted, that she was careful not to show it.

Anna had driven up the day before, taking a few days off on David's advice to get over the publicity engendered by the squat, reporters at the door of her home, at the office. Peter had also taken time off and had gone down to Dorset to see Fiona, so the house was empty. Like many victims of the tabloid press before them, and doubtless many after, they hoped the fuss would die down. And it would. After all, no one had died.

'I thought I'd take you out to dinner, Mum. Anywhere nice you'd like to go?'

Sylvia thought, named a new restaurant not far away that she'd heard was good but, needless to say, had never tried. She only really ate out when her daughter and son-in-law came to see her. Ate out in style, that is. If she and a girl-friend went to see a film or a show, a preview of a London run in a Leeds theatre, they'd eat at a Burger King or a McDonald's, just have a snack.

Sylvia was very careful about money and always had been. She not only managed to live within her means, but also to save. It was a matter of pride, she felt, not to be a burden on her daughter and, hopefully, to leave her something when she died.

She made the toast, brewed the coffee, and mother and daughter sat facing each other across the breakfast table.

'I shan't be able to get away until six,' Sylvia said, continuing to look anxious. Being of a nervous disposition, she was always expecting something to go wrong, of giving offence or causing pain, ruffling feathers.

'That's OK.' Anna reached out an arm. 'Mum, do you still have to work at that place?'

'But what else could I do?'

'Do you have to work? You always told me you'd saved and saved, and you are nearly sixty.'

'I rather *like* work,' Sylvia said defensively. 'I can't think what I'd do with myself all day alone at home. In fact, I don't know what I'll do when I give it up, and there is talk of redundancies being made to make way for younger women.' Momentarily Sylvia looked indignant. 'They don't value the experience of older people who have been fitting shoes for thirty years; how important it is to the customer. I have some ladies who have been coming to me for years, and their daughters too. What will they do when I go?'

It did indeed seem sad, unfair that, in order to make way for young people who probably couldn't care less about a good fitting and wouldn't stay long anyway, the older, more reliable and loyal people had to go.

'I hope you're not brooding about the squat, Anna,' her mother said, anxious to change the subject. 'It wasn't your fault, you know, that those people behaved so badly.'

'No.' Anna sat back nodding her head. 'I'm not thinking about that, Mum. I'm thinking about you.'

'Me?' Sylvia proffered surprise.

'You've worked so hard all your life for, really, very little. *That* doesn't seem fair.'

'You can't compare my life with yours, you know, Anna. I never wanted very much. I was never ambitious, which was probably the trouble.'

'How do you mean the "trouble"?' Anna looked at her curiously.

'As far as your father was concerned.' Her mother lowered her voice, as though someone might be listening. 'You know. I think he thought I was rather dull. Pretty, but dull.'

'Mum, you *underestimate* yourself! You were *not* at all *dull*. You brought me up, gave me a good chance.'

'And you made the best of it, darling.' Her mother reached out to touch her hand. 'I'm so proud of you, Anna.' She removed her hand and gave a deep sigh. Immediately Anna knew what was coming, and braced herself. 'I only wish . . .' Sylvia began.

Anna interrupted her immediately. 'Well I didn't, Mum, and that's that.'

'But stepchildren are never like your own. I always wished that I'd spoken to you in the early years of your marriage, but somehow it didn't seem my place.'

'Spoken about what?'

'About having your own children; but at that time I didn't think you wouldn't. I mean, you were young. There was plenty of time. The years seemed to slip by. There still would have been time if you . . .'

Anna was beginning to regret the impulse that took her up the M1 to see her mother; partly guilt because she hadn't seen her for so long and partly because of a desire to get away. She in one direction, Peter in another, in order to throw what lingering press hounds there might have been off the scent. There would be a sad little homily now from her mother about no grandchildren, the loneliness of old age, etc., etc.

She got up from the table and went to stare out of the kitchen window.

'It's a bloody awful day. I think I'll go back to bed and read.'

'That's a good idea. I'll go shopping. You wouldn't like to come with me, dear?' She paused, looking a little wistful.

'I think not, Mum.' Anna nervously ran her hands through her hair. 'I'd just like to take it easy, mooch about.'

'Of course,' Sylvia said with forced cheerfulness. '*Must* you go back tomorrow?'

'Yes, I must. The heat will be off. These things are always a two-day wonder, and then something else of interest happens.'

After Sylvia had gone, Anna felt guilty that she hadn't gone with her. She'd set off with her shopping bag and a brave face. Stoical as usual. It would be nice to have a shopping companion but she wouldn't insist. Anna needed her rest.

Anna watched from the window of her bedroom as she got into her little car and drove away. It really wouldn't have been too much trouble to have a quick bath, throw on a sweater and jeans and go with her mother. It would have given her so much pleasure to be seen with the daughter of whom she was so proud.

Too late now. She'd make it up to her that evening. She also decided she would make an effort to see her mother more often, ask her to London, to Dorset. She'd never even seen the Dorset cottage. But then, at the moment, Anna wasn't terribly keen to visit it herself. She could imagine the state of the place with Fiona and Errol; but apparently they were getting on well, not only as far as the tuition was concerned, but personally.

It wasn't what either Peter or Anna would have wished, and Anna felt that had she not been so busy, so rushed, she would have stopped to think of the consequences of introducing Fiona to a personable needy young man. Fiona had acquired both a cause and a lover: a purpose in life.

Fiona had finally pronounced herself 'in love'.

Anna didn't go back to bed, but had a long leisurely bath and washed her hair which was the easy, thick, slightly wavy sort that set itself naturally. She was reading the *Guardian* when the phone rang and, cup of coffee in her hand, she answered it.

'Hello?'

'Hello, Anna?'

'Peter. Hello, darling. How are you?'

'I'm alright.' She thought his voice sounded strained and her brow puckered in concern.

'How are you, *really*?'

'Really, I'm fine. How's Mother?'

'She's fine. Peter . . .'

'Yes, Anna?'

'You don't sound quite yourself. Is everything alright? Those awful hounds of the press . . .'

'No, it's not them. Anna . . .'

Now she felt really anxious and put her coffee cup down on the table.

'What *is* it, Peter?'

'Fiona's pregnant.'

Silence.

'Anna, did you hear me?'

'Yes, I heard.' Anna bit her lip. 'Well, it's not the end of the world, darling.'

'But she wants to keep it. She wants to have a baby. She actually seems thrilled.'

'And Errol?'

'I think he's a bit bemused by the whole thing, as far as I can tell. He hardly says a word. I really don't *like* that fellow you know, Anna.'

Anna knew Peter didn't like him because he was the very opposite to the sort of man Peter would consider suitable for his daughter. He was a working-class northerner with a strong north-country accent. He had never worked and even his talent as an artist was suspect. He certainly painted, large abstracts whose worth it was impossible to evaluate. No one was even sure if he'd *been* at the Slade, if he'd ever really exhibited in London, or anywhere else. In short, he was possibly a con man who knew a good thing, a vulnerable girl with her own home, when he saw it.

Peter had wanted to have him investigated but Anna had stopped him saying what, after all, was the point? What was the point of investigating a past they both agreed, in hindsight, was probably made up anyway?

'If only you hadn't got involved with that squat, Anna, this would never have happened.'

'Well, I did and it has. We could never have known. She might have met someone else.'

'But not like *him.*'

His tone sounded outraged, accusatory.

'The point is, Peter, they're happy, or seem to be.' Even that was doubtful. Fiona was ecstatically happy, but Errol gave little away.

'And the place is the most awful tip.'

'I can imagine. Are you there now?'

'Oh, no!' Loud laugh. 'I'm at the pub, getting drunk.'

'That won't help matters much. How far gone is Fiona, Peter?'

'She says about three months.'

'It must have happened immediately.'

'I think he was her first man, Anna, you know. She knew absolutely nothing.'

'Probably.' Though with these worldly-wise young people of today, using make-up and smoking at thirteen, you never really knew.

'It's a hell of a mess, Anna.' He did sound rather drunk.

'I'm sorry, Peter, we'll discuss it next week.'

'Well, what are we to do?'

'We can't do anything. If Fiona really does want to have the baby and keep it, we must help her all we can.'

'Oh, hi!' Anna heard Peter say from the phone in his social voice, then to her, 'Anna, Fred has just come in and I'm going to buy him a drink. Will you be home tomorrow?'

'If I can. Yes.'

'Why? Is there anything wrong with your mother?'

'She just misses me, that's all. She makes me feel guilty.'

'But I miss you too. And I damn well wish you were here.'

'I'll see you tomorrow, darling. 'Bye.'

''Bye.' Kisses down the phone.

He did love her and he needed her.

Momentarily she felt quite dreadful about Damian, and sorry now it had ever happened. Really sorry. Anna sighed and brewed fresh coffee, looking anxiously at the clock. Just as well she hadn't gone with her mother. Just another problem, too, to solve.

She was not sure whether Sylvia would come home or go straight to work after shopping. Probably have a solitary cup of tea and sandwich in a snack bar. She could have taken her for lunch as well as dinner, helped her with the shopping. Guilt. Guilt all round. It was awful, in a way, to have so many people depending upon you, to be responsible for so many lives.

It was a small restaurant near Wetherby, and Sylvia was obviously enjoying herself, tucking in with gusto. She was very thin, even gaunt, a woman in whose life the pleasures of the table had never predominated. Really there had been very little pleasure in Sylvia's life, apart from the justified pride she felt in Anna's career. She'd chosen a pretty dress for the evening's outing, and a few pieces of costume jewellery to go with it. Anna wore the trouser suit she'd driven up in, but it was smart, a tailored black suit, the sort of thing that looked nice anywhere, and she'd chosen a red shirt to go with it. It became her tall, slim figure. But still she felt her mother was critical. She should have worn a dress.

However, Sylvia had the good sense to say nothing, and after they'd chosen and Anna ordered wine, Sylvia told her about the events of the day, nothing very exceptional apart from so and so she'd met in Marks & Spencer and they'd had a busy afternoon in the store. Suddenly she broke off the patter and looked at her daughter.

'I *wish* you didn't have to go back tomorrow, Anna.'

'I wish I didn't too, Mum.' True and also not true. Divided loyalties. Divided worlds.

'I so love having you here. I feel I don't see enough of you. You're all I've got.'

'I know, Mum.' Anna reached out and put her hand over her mother's. 'I've been thinking that I don't see enough of you too, and I promise I will come up more often, and you must come and see us. Really, Mum, I want you to start enjoying life more, and to consider giving up work. We can always help out financially, you know, if . . .'

'But, Anna, I really would *hate* giving up work. I'd miss having something to do. I have my friends there. The store is a kind of family. As it is, as I said, I might have to give it up anyway, and then I'd feel lost, I know I would.'

'But, Mum, you could travel. Go on a cruise. Maybe meet a man.' She smiled at her mischievously. 'Have you really never met anyone in all the time since my father left you?'

Sylvia shook her head and Anna was rather alarmed to see the suspicion of tears in her eyes. She always said 'my father', never 'Daddy' or 'Father'. She could never bring herself, never felt the need, to speak so intimately about a man she could scarcely remember. All Roger Wood was to her was a fuzzy face in a photograph.

They said a woman's relationship with her father affected her whole life; but she had never cared to delve too deeply into how it had affected hers.

'By the way,' she said quickly, in an attempt to forestall the tears, 'Peter rang this morning.'

'Oh, did he?' Sylvia liked Peter, good solid successful Peter. 'What did he have to say?'

'Fiona is pregnant.'

'Oh!' Sylvia put her knife and fork neatly side by side on her plate. 'I didn't know Fiona was married. Isn't she still at school?'

Fiona's dramas had always seemed too complicated to explain to her mother, who wouldn't understand anyway. She had always shown a kind of indifference to the welfare of her daughter's stepchildren who, she scarcely knew.

'Well, no, she's not at school. I think I told you she left in an attempt to become an artist.'

'Oh, yes, you did say something.' Sylvia picked up her knife and fork again, attacked her chicken suprême à l'estragon with vigour.

'Well she met, or rather I introduced her to a young man who we thought could tutor her. They went down to Dorset and . . .'

Sylvia put down her knife and fork again and her lips formed in a disapproving arc. 'I see. That was a bit risky, wasn't it? A big short-sighted? Of course, in my day and age such a thing would be unheard of.'

'Well today it's very common, Mum.'

In these days too there would be less of a chance of making the mistake of marrying a man like Roger Wood when you were also too young and ignorant about the facts of life. It was obvious that her mother and father had never been compatible, but that the then youthful apprentice engineer was at the time temporarily captivated by the good looks of Sylvia Marsden, who worked in the office, and in those days the thing to do was to marry and no nonsense.

Sylvia, who was thoughtfully chewing her food, paused and said, 'I still think it's wrong. Is she going to have the baby? These days they get rid of them, don't they?'

'Apparently she doesn't want to.'

'Something else for you to bear, Anna. Another responsibility, as if you haven't enough already.' Her mother went on chewing thoughtfully, swallowed, and took a sip of her wine. 'On the other hand she *is* Peter's child, not yours.'

'Mum, you know I never thought that way.' Feeling stung, Anna put down her knife and fork and leaned across the table.

'Anna, you can't tell me you've thought of those children as your own all these years? I know you tried, and when they were smaller it was easier. But since they've been teenagers it seems to me they've been nothing but trouble to you. And this doesn't surprise me in the least. Young girls given their head, no discipline. How different it would have been, Anna, if *you'd* had children of your own. You could really have cared for them then. And I,' Sylvia's voice became tremulous, and Anna braced herself for the inevitable, 'I would have had my very own grandchildren I could love and care for. I don't think you know, Anna, how much I wanted grandchildren, what joy they would have given me, a purpose in life. How I could have *loved* them and done things for them, and what pain it gave me when you had that senseless operation last year and finished for ever your chance of being a real mother.'

There, it was out, in a torrent of words towards the end. Sylvia put down her wine glass, and leaned across the table saying in a hiss that reverberated with spite, 'In many ways you think of no one but yourself, Anna. Sometimes, although you pretend to care for others, there's a very selfish streak in you. You're very like your father. He was a very selfish man.'

And for the first time Anna saw in her mother's eyes an expression of bitterness and rancour she had never seen before, and she felt shocked to her very core.

PART 3

The Blood Tie

CHAPTER 12

The corpse's sightless eyes seemed to stare reproachfully at Anna who gazed at the swollen, distorted face for a moment as though willing it back to life. Then, abruptly, she turned away feeling, somehow, that as she did the eyes followed her. But, of course, they didn't. The young woman had been dead for hours.

The governor put a comforting hand on her shoulder and propelled her towards the door which she opened and shut behind them.

'It's not our fault,' she said as she led Anna away from the infirmary block and along the corridor to her office.

Once inside the room, Anna sat down and gratefully took the cup of coffee offered by the governor's secretary. The governor sat opposite her, also with a cup in her hand.

'I thought I should call you, Mrs Livingstone, in case there was any more press comment. I know you've had a lot of it recently.'

'I don't see why there should be.' Anna looked curiously at her. 'If anything, I think it will focus on you.'

'It may come out that you failed to defend her because of the business with the illegal squat which, after all, wasn't so very far away or long ago.'

'That was extremely unfortunate, but my deputy was quite up to the job of defending Jansie.'

'Still, she felt you would have got her off. She brooded on it.'

Anna had brooded on it too ever since the telephone by the side of the bed had rung at seven that morning, and the governor had told her that Jansie Dicks, the prostitute she should have defended on the day of the riot at the squat, had been found hanged in her cell. The awful thing was that, with so much on her mind, Anna had hardly thought about the poor woman from that day to this. Events had seemed to follow one another in such rapid succession that the fate of a woman sent down not only for prostitution but other offences had entirely escaped her mind. Well, not entirely. From among the mass of papers waiting her perusal in the office each day she knew an appeal was being lodged which Jeremy had in hand. After all you couldn't, no one possibly could, keep all the problems of all your clients to the forefront of your mind.

'The point was,' the governor crossed her ankles, 'that you seemed to take such a personal interest in her. She totally relied on you.'

'I did. I did take an interest in her, and we are now very definitely considering an appeal.'

'If only she'd known . . . I mean, how much you'd cared.'

The governor was rubbing it in, Anna decided. Maybe trying to put the blame for the prison's lack of supervision on to the hard-pressed lawyer, probably with a possible enquiry in mind. Cheek.

'Really, Governor, I can't be *everywhere* at once,' Anna said with a touch of asperity. 'I can't see *all* my clients simultaneously, and thank heaven most of them do not think it necessary to take their lives if I don't. This is terribly unfortunate. But please don't put the blame on me.'

'Of course she was mentally rather unstable,' the governor conceded. 'I think however that she felt an attachment to you. But one does, Mrs Livingstone,' the governor smiled sweetly, 'you are so very persuasive, you *do* seem to care, I can quite understand your popularity and your success.'

'Well, I don't appear to have been very successful recently,'

Anna admitted ruefully. 'The squat was a miserable failure and everyone ended up hating me there. I was pelted with rotten eggs and vegetables. Red faces all round, especially mine.'

The governor uncrossed her ankles and rose to pour more coffee.

'No, thanks.' Anna put out a hand and rose from her seat. 'Well, there'll be an inquest and, of course, I'll give evidence. We were considering an appeal. We had not realised just how much her mental state had deteriorated.' Touch of criticism of the governor there.

'I don't think *any* of us had,' the governor said firmly, accompanying her to the door, 'otherwise we'd have put her in a secure wing. Such a *pity* about the little girl.'

The governor's words rang in Anna's ears as she drove from the prison to her office. 'Such a *pity* about the little girl.' Jansie had been a devoted mother. Anna had visited her in the high-rise where they lived in Highbury. The place was clean, the child well cared for. The only thing was that this was from where Jansie had plied her trade. How much had the poor child known about that?

And the fact that they were black and that their neighbours had informed the authorities, probably just because of that, didn't help at all.

Anna parked the car in the garage in the mews behind the offices reserved for senior staff and hurried round to Wigmore Street. The receptionists were busy at their computer screens in the hall, one or two clients sat waiting to keep their appointments. As Anna entered and proceeded to the reception desk to check her mail, a figure rose from a chair and called in an unnecessarily loud voice: 'Ah, *there* you are, Mrs Livingstone! I've *only* been here two hours.'

Anna turned, clapped a hand to her mouth.

'Oh, Mrs Jones, I'm so *terribly* sorry. An unexpected emergency . . . You could have seen my deputy. Didn't he . . .'

'I didn't *want* to see your deputy, Mrs Livingstone.' Mrs Jones's tone grew shriller by the second. 'I came here to see *you*. I do *not* expect to be kept waiting when I pay astronomical fees to have you, and you personally, to represent my interests. Now, see here, Mrs Livingstone,' she put a hand on her hip and stuck out a finger until it came within an inch of Anna's face. The gesture enraged Anna who felt as though a blood vessel was about to burst.

'And see *here*, Mrs Jones,' she retorted pointing her own finger at her obnoxious client before she could say another word, 'don't you suppose I have enough to think about without people like *you* making my life an added misery? Don't you think I have enough to do without rich, spoilt women thinking they have an exclusive right to my time when others are far more in need of it? I've just seen the body of a dead woman, Mrs Jones, a dead woman. I should have been in court to defend and wasn't because of people like *you*,' she concluded, stabbing her finger with each word again and again at the astonished woman.

Anna could hear the blood drumming in her ears. If she wasn't careful she'd give herself a stroke or a heart attack. Dead before forty. Why? What was the point? She was aware of Jeremy at her side saying quietly into her ear: 'Anna, maybe behind closed doors?'

'Do please come into my room, Mrs Jones.' Anna, visibly making an effort to control herself, lowered her voice and pointed the way upstairs.

'Thank *you*, Mrs Livingstone,' Mrs Jones drew herself up, 'but I shall be taking my business elsewhere. I wouldn't dream of remaining with this firm for another second. I shall also be making a complaint about your disgraceful conduct here today to your supervisors. Make no mistake about *that*!'

And Mrs Jones swept towards the door which a startled Jeremy rushed to open.

'Golly,' he said, following Anna as she climbed the stairs

two at a time to her room and shut the door behind them.

'That's blown it.' Anna tossed her briefcase on her desk. 'And she will. What with the squat, this and now Jansie Dicks has topped herself.' Jeremy screwed up his brow in an attempt at recollection. 'The black prostitute you defended on the day of the squat riot. The day I couldn't make it because I had to go home and get squashed tomato out of my clothes, to say nothing of trying to restore my emotional equilibrium.'

'You were treated abominably,' Jeremy said earnestly.

'Well that wasn't too much.' Anna reflectively fingered the side of her face. 'A few scratches really.' In fact she'd had to have an injection in case any of the putrid substances that had been thrown at her might have entered the bloodstream through the scratches caused by the egg shells exploding in her face. There was also the shock. It was easy to forget about that. She had indeed been very, very shocked, and there had been absolutely no possibility of her returning to court that day.

Jeremy sank into a chair, a hand to his face.

'I should have gone to see her.' Anna sat down in the chair behind her desk. 'I personally should have told her we were appealing, made an application for bail. I shouldn't have forgotten her. That's why I'm here. Everything recently has happened *so* quickly.'

'You can't take the blame,' Jeremy said loyally. 'I made a botch-up of the case.'

'Not your fault, you weren't properly briefed.' Jeremy, in fact, although talented, was a newly qualified solicitor, completely lacking in court experience. They should have asked for an adjournment. 'Sometimes I think this job is getting me down,' Anna said, staring at the wall. 'I've taken on too much.'

'Nonsense.' Jeremy rose and went over to her desk, picked up a bundle of legal documents bound with pink tape. 'About the squat incidentally, Damian Bradley is claiming police harassment. He has launched an official complaint.'

Anna sighed. The troubles with the squat were by no means over yet, even though, as she'd passed the site from the prison, she had noticed that where the warehouse had stood there was now a large piece of waste ground. The authorities had lost no time. What, she wondered, had happened to Damian?

For once, Anna spent the day at the office dealing with matters that were mainly routine but also important. The day that had started badly and had gone downhill thereafter, improved by degrees into one of normality and routine. She even had a sandwich lunch at her desk and found time to call Katie to fix a lunch appointment for the following week, and to say 'hello' to her mother before she left for home.

Anna had a handful of close women friends, some scattered around the country, others abroad. Most, like her, led busy lives and one tended to lose touch with them. With Katie, although there was a semi-professional relationship, she felt at ease, able to bare her heart and be sure of an experienced and sympathetic response.

Just now she felt problems, both personal and professional, were multiplying, partly to a lack of judgment and partly to bad luck. She hadn't realised how much her mother, although proud of her success, also perhaps resented it because Anna imitated her father rather than her. And so had come the dreadful – and Anna thought unfair – accusation that, beneath her apparent concern for others, she was basically a selfish person who had deprived her long-suffering and resentful mother of grandchildren.

Yes, Katie would be a good one to talk to. Anna looked at her watch. Nothing else dreadful had happened during the day; just routine conferences with her assistants, clients and, for once, she thought she'd leave early, surprise Peter by having a meal ready for him when he got home, usually about seven. It was a very long time since she'd done that. If she left now she could shop in the fancy delicatessens and smart butchers' shops on Marylebone High Street. Surprise Peter for once with a slap-up, gourmet meal.

Her telephone rang and she picked up the receiver, an eye on the clock on her wall.

'Anna, there's a call for you,' her secretary said in an unnecessarily furtive whisper. 'Damian Bradley.'

Anna felt her heart lurch, put a hand on her chest.

'I'll take it,' she said in a brisk, practical manner. 'Put him through,' and as she heard the phone click she said in a bright, artificial voice: 'Hi, Damian!'

'Hi, Anna.'

Pause.

'How are you?' they both said at once. Then laughed. Another awkward pause.

'Damian,' Anna realised that the nervousness she thought she had under control was showing, 'I hear you're taking action against the police.'

'The bastards.'

'Is it wise?'

'You mean it could involve you?' She was aware that his tone had hardened.

'I'm not thinking of me, actually; but yes, it would involve me. I'd be called. Is that why you rang?'

'I rang because I want to see you, Anna.' His voice softened. 'I haven't forgotten.'

The blush stole up Anna's neck, suffusing her cheeks. She visualised vividly how it had been that day: herself spread on the floor, Damian kneeling above her, bearing down on her like some Nordic god. She closed her eyes involuntarily seeing it now as from a distance, from a long long way. But almost sensing again that cataclysmic upheaval that had penetrated her belly, engulfing her entire body.

'Have you forgotten, Anna?'

'Of course I haven't. I think we'd better meet and have a talk, Damian.'

'But I want you . . .'

'Please,' nervously she glanced around as though someone was watching her. Her hands riffled swiftly through the pages of her diary. 'Look, can I give you a call? Where are you staying?'

'I'll have to call you. No fixed abode at the moment, as they say. My dad's not well and I may have to go home.'

'Well, give me a call next week.'

'You sound terribly impersonal. Please don't say you're going to end it, Anna?'

End what? It had hardly begun. 'Look, I'm in the office. Call me midweek,' she said. 'I must go now. 'Bye, Damian.'

She replaced the receiver without waiting for his reply, and sat for a long time with her chin in her hands staring at the phone. Supposing he said something? Tried blackmail? It would be his word against hers, but the effect on Peter would be shattering. She felt however that there was something good, almost noble about Damian; that he wouldn't stoop to such behaviour. She hoped she was right. Then she sighed and drew one of the many files awaiting her attention towards her.

Anna finished making the last notes on a file in preparation for tomorrow's load and packed her briefcase. She examined her face in the mirror of her compact and applied fresh lipstick a quick dab of face powder to take the shine off her nose, put on her jacket, when there was a tap on the door and before she could call out David Cole put his head round it.

Anna's heart sank. The vision of the gourmet meal and Peter's pleasure on seeing it somehow receded.

'Hi, Anna!' David sidled round the door while she tried to rearrange her expression into one of welcome.

'Hi, David!'

'You were just leaving, I see,' he said, closing the door behind him. 'Well, I shan't take too long.' But the way he eased himself into her most comfortable armchair seemed to indicate that he would in fact be staying for quite some time.

'Well, I did think that I would leave and maybe make Peter dinner for a change.' She glanced at her watch. 'Shop in Marylebone High Street on the way home.'

'Excellent idea.' David too consulted his watch. 'I shan't detain you. Peter and the family well?'

'Very well, thank you.' There was something unusually strained about David's manner and Anna felt a flutter of apprehension. The day had begun badly. Maybe it was going to end badly too.

David joined his hands together like a church steeple and stretched his long legs, encased in dark blue pinstripe, before him, looking at his most avuncular, almost judicial. He peered at her over the tops of his fingers.

'Things haven't been going too well for you lately, Anna, have they? I'm so sorry.'

Anna felt immediately on the defensive. She resumed her seat at her desk and rested her chin on her hands. 'In what sense, David?'

'Well, all these problems you've had to cope with.' David raised his hands above his head and cracked the joints of his fingers one by one. 'That dreadful business at the warehouse. The woman who just killed herself and now, today, I had a very irate call from Mrs Jones who accuses you of bullying and shouting at her in reception.'

'Oh, did she?' Anna, strengthened by a feeling of indignation, rested her hands on her desk and looked up at him defiantly.

'She was extremely upset,' David went on. 'We have been her solicitors for a number of years and,' he paused, looking at her levelly, 'apparently are not going to be any longer.'

'She is the *most* obnoxious woman,' Anna said heatedly.

'Nevertheless she's a very important client, and a very wealthy one. Her father deals with us too, and no doubt will follow her lead. He is Sir Harry Carter of the shipping line.' David paused ominously.

'David, am I supposed to be blackmailed by an angry and capricious client acting over my head? After all, I *am* in charge of this section and all complaints should come to me.'

David opened his hands in an eloquent expression of bewilderment.

'But if you, the head, have offended, to whom can one complain? Naturally she came to me who she has known for a very long time. Whether you like her or not, Anna, is beside the point. We're in this business to make money.'

'I realise that.' Momentarily Anna studied the shiny surface of her desk. 'But I am in it primarily to serve justice. However I *am* prepared to concede that I may have acted hastily. But as soon as I came into the building, Mrs Jones launched herself at me, shouting and bawling, poking me in the face with her gem-laden finger. Frankly, I almost lost control.'

'I realise that and, especially, why. I understand one of your clients had committed suicide and you had just come from viewing the body.'

'*That* has got to you very quickly. It only happened this morning.'

'These things do,' he replied urbanely, and Anna could somehow visualise the always polite but similarly urbane Jeremy getting quietly on the phone to his master. 'Anna's cracking up,' he might have whispered. Hence the visit.

'Naturally, Anna, when I heard about the scene I made a few enquiries and learned what had happened, and why you were in a state.'

'Did you by any chance learn why *she* was in a state?' Anna was aware that her voice was rising by decibels.

'My dear,' David languidly eased his lanky form out of the chair and, hands in the pockets of his trousers, strolled across to the window and gazed on to Wigmore Street, 'she is in a state because her marriage is breaking up. Her husband is trying to get as much of her money as he can . . .'

'I am aware of all this, David, and it is, or was, under control.'

David turned round and looked at her. 'She is also holding down a most important job, and if you feel your work is suffering, so does Sheila Jones.'

'I see.' Anna, hands in the pockets of her jacket, sat back. 'This is a reprimand then. Is it an official one?'

'My dear Anna,' David came over to her desk and leaned both hands on it, his face now very close to hers, 'it is *not* a reprimand. I am simply stating the facts, as I know them, to suggest that you may be overworked. You do look, if I may say so, desperately tired. Much much more tired than you have in all the years I've known you. What I am suggesting, Anna, is that the reason for this apparent exhaustion, unwise behaviour towards a client, is that you are taking on too much voluntary work in this firm's time.' The emphasis in his voice changed imperceptibly. 'The whole business about the squat, which got so much unwelcome publicity that you and your husband felt you should disappear for a few days . . .'

'I had leave due. Lots and lots of it. Besides, *you* suggested it.' She gazed at him accusingly.

'I am quite well aware of that, and I think you did the right, indeed the only, thing. But this firm was mentioned in the papers several times despite the fact that the incident had nothing to do with us at all. Nothing whatever, and now I am quite sure there is going to be an enquiry into this business of the death of the prostitute in custody . . . again work undertaken outside this office yet I believe Jeremy, your deputy, was asked to act for you in your absence. Again quite understandably; but . . .' David hunched his shoulders expressively and grimaced, 'hardly fair on *us*, is it?'

She had never, of course, thought anything of it. But she

should have. Formerly, she would have trusted Jeremy. Now she knew better.

'I considered it good experience for Jeremy,' she said, aware how lame she must sound. 'Legal aid would, naturally, have come to this firm for the time he appeared in court,' she went on, 'as it would if I'd represented Miss Dicks.'

'Legal aid,' David sniffed. 'Legal aid, you say, and then you saunter in this morning and lose us one, maybe two, of our most valuable clients. I'm sure having got divorced once, Sheila Jones will again. She's not the sort who will ever keep a man.'

Anna winced. David Cole was a closet chauvinist, and usually she would have remonstrated with him. They knew each other's political views and amicably disagreed about them. But at this moment she dare not. She felt her courage, her confidence, evaporating.

'Are you by any chance giving me notice, David? Asking me to leave?'

David looked horrorstruck.

'Oh my dear, Anna, by *no* means. Not at all. We value you highly. But I am going to ask you – and I have discussed this with the partners before I came – if you could give up some of your voluntary work or, at least, curtail it in the interests of the firm you work for and which pays you a very high salary. I'm also suggesting that we think of appointing a partner to *share* your duties with you and ease some of the burden you are under.'

'And who is this partner?' Anna felt a high colour rush to her cheeks.

'It's only an idea. Naturally someone you will like and approve of.'

'When you say "share" do you mean on an equal basis?'

'Well,' David studied the ceiling, 'it's all to be decided. Nothing's fixed.'

'If that were the case, it amounts to demotion. I will no longer be in charge.'

'That we shall have to think it out further, Anna. It is suggested we leave it until we see the response you make to my suggestions.'

'In other words it's a sort of blackmail?' she said bluntly.

David suppressed a shudder. 'That is a word I never thought I'd hear used against me, or any of my colleagues.'

'You're just saying "toe the line or else". That *is* blackmail.'

'We are *suggesting* that you are overworked, and I think you'll agree you are, and we're trying to help you in your own best interests. We value you, I assure you, Anna. You've a fine legal brain.' David resumed his seat and looked appealingly across at her. 'Anna, you're a young woman with a husband and family. You are not yet forty. Surely you don't want to burn yourself out yet. Do you?'

Anna put her key in the lock, dead tired, exhausted. She'd hardly been able to climb up the steps as a sudden overwhelming weariness had set in. As the key turned she pushed open the door.

The house seemed quieter than usual, empty, sepulchral. It was also cold as though the central heating had not yet come on. Seven-thirty. In the winter it usually came on about five. Perhaps something was wrong, and as it was a particularly cold evening they'd freeze.

Anyway, the meeting with David had dragged on and when she left it was far too late to shop in Marylebone High Street. Maybe they'd go out, except that now she wasn't hungry.

She knew Peter wasn't in. The house was too cold, too dark. Peter liked light and warmth. She went into the kitchen, switching on lights as she went. She checked the boiler and then she looked at the thermostat on the wall. It had been turned right down for some reason; probably by the daily by accident.

She flicked it to a higher number and she could hear the boiler spring to life. Relief.

She went back through the hall to the sitting room and glanced round. Peter definitely hadn't been back. The curtains weren't drawn and it was the first thing he always did on a winter's evening.

She thought maybe he'd come in and then gone out in a bad temper because she had promised to be home early and, once again, had broken her promise. But no, he hadn't come home. On the mat, just inside the door, was the local 'freebie' and some leaflets and he would have picked those up. He would never have left bits of paper lying around.

Anna switched on the answer-machine and played over the messages. Nothing important. Nothing from Peter. She sat down, head in her hands, feeling dejected, dispirited, close to tears if the truth be told.

Anna was not a woman who had ever been prone to tears. She was not emotional, and they had seldom been necessary. Her slight depressive outburst after the sterilisation, and weeping on the policeman's shoulder the day of the riot at the squat, had been two rare occasions in recent years. And yet here she was again, ready to blub. She felt so lonely, isolated. She craved Peter, needed Peter and he wasn't here. No, she was too resilient, too self-controlled to cry. She shook herself, got abruptly to her feet and drew the curtains firmly together.

Beware of pity, especially self-pity. She had had a lousy day and had been looking forward to telling Peter all about it – especially the conversation with David, and he wasn't here. No need to behave like a child on that account. But she did feel curiously empty, purposeless, rootless. She felt she had no props as other people had to get through the difficult spots in life. She didn't smoke, hardly drank, wine with a meal perhaps, but never spirits, and certainly never alone. That would somehow offend against the canons of the middle-class

Protestant ethic in which she had been raised: hard work, abstemious in all things.

Had her father drunk, she wondered? And she realised again, as she had ever since she returned to London from her visit to her mother, that she knew so little about him, what sort of man he was. She had always taken her mother's side, believed that her mother had been wronged and her father was to blame. Girls must stick together.

She didn't have a pet to stroke or fondle, an animal whose welcome, unquestioning love and obedience would be, if not as good as human contact, the next best thing.

It was absolutely useless getting maudlin. Peter was probably dining out, thinking maybe that, just for once, he would get his own back. It was, after all, a natural human desire to show his male assertiveness. Anna had never really thought of it that way.

She made a sandwich, watched the nine o'clock news and then read a brief for the next day. This time she was in court on behalf of one of the firm's clients; but it was a Crown Court case for which a barrister had been briefed, and she would be sitting on the sidelines, watching, helping. It could take several days.

At ten she put out the lights downstairs, except for the ones in the hall and the sitting room, and went upstairs, ran a bath and had a long soak.

She felt vaguely apprehensive, worried about Peter. She always left a message reporting on her whereabouts and so, usually, did he. Had he had an accident? Impossible. If he had there were any number of documents he carried about with him that would identify him. If he'd been taken ill, the same would apply.

Then where was he?

The idea slowly crossed her mind that he might be having an affair. Peter? Why not? She knew from her legal experience that it was just the people one least expected who had affairs;

seemingly faithful husbands' eyes suddenly began to rove in their late forties or fifties, just the age that Peter was now.

She and Peter had had a tough time recently. She knew he was worried to death about Fiona, and there was fresh anxiety about Guy who initially appeared to settle into and like his new school, but now wasn't so sure. Maybe Peter had gone out on a blind with some men friends and got drunk, but that seemed about as unlikely as him having an affair.

Anna knew she wouldn't sleep until he came in, so she settled down to read a book.

But by one o'clock Peter had still not returned and Anna began to become seriously anxious. She didn't think he would want to upset or frighten her and the conviction grew steadily that somehow he'd had an accident which had as yet been unreported.

What did one do? As a lawyer she should know. She put her book down and swung her legs over the bed. One rang hospitals, the police? But supposing, while she was ringing, Peter was trying to get hold of her? It was a dilemma. Supposing also he was in the arms of some woman while she was making a hysterical fool of herself?

She lay down on the bed again, took several long deep breaths to try and relax. Unlike her to panic. Very. She picked up the book, held it in her hands for some moments before she realised it was upside down. She righted it, put on her reading glasses and made a determined effort to concentrate. But it was useless.

She had an extremely busy schedule the next day, an appointment in court, a Council meeting in the evening and goodness knows how many other things to do. She'd planned on getting up at six, even earlier maybe, put a couple of hours in the office before rushing off to court. If Peter was doing what he was doing deliberately it was wicked and irresponsible of him.

By two o'clock she began to feel drowsy, the book slipped

in her hands. She reached for the light while she was still somnolent and let the book fall on the floor.

Suddenly the phone went. Her heart began to pound wildly in unison with the rings. She knew that her hand trembled as she picked up the receiver and said in a hoarse voice: 'Hello?'

'Anna?'

'Peter! Where in God's name are you? I've been worried sick . . .'

'I'm terribly sorry, Anna,' his voice sounded abnormally tense, strained, 'but I couldn't ring you before. I'll tell you why in a moment.'

'Are you alright, Peter?'

'I'm fine, really fine. Let me explain. I had a call from Fiona just as I was leaving the office. I knew we'd planned an evening in, but when I rang your office there was no one on the switchboard.'

Anna knew an involuntary plummeting of the heart. Fiona, of course, it had to be Fiona again.

'And believe it or not the phone at home was engaged. Your mobile wasn't working either.'

'I switched it off in the office. But please go on, Peter. Is Fiona alright? The baby . . .'

'Well she's in a fearful state. It's nothing to do with the baby, thank God; but Errol has left her. She came back from a day's outing with Sal and Honey and found he'd cleared out. Taken the TV, video, the hi-fi and all the money she had in the house. You know how careless she is. She had quite a lot lying around.'

Anna was aghast. 'Did he leave a note?'

'Nothing. But she knew he'd gone. He'd riffled through all the drawers, cupboards, for anything of value. The place was in a terrible mess,' he paused, 'I mean worse than usual.'

'Poor Fiona. I am sorry. But you could have rung when you got there . . .'

'Darling, I know I should have tried, made more effort, but

Sal rang me and made me seriously worried about Fiona. Said she was hysterical, she had to get the doctor. That wasn't easy because her phone was out of order,' he lowered his voice as if afraid of being overheard, 'as a matter of fact it's been disconnected. So when I got there . . .'

'OK, OK.' Anna ran her hands through her hair. 'I understand. Peter I'm so terribly sorry . . .'

'Anna, we need you here. We really do. Can you come down first thing in the morning?'

After all she had been through in the past few hours Anna felt a sudden surge of anger.

'Peter, please be reasonable! I have work to do. I can't just drop everything . . .'

The silence on the line was wary and palpable and then Peter's voice, sounding subdued.

'Anna, I thought this family meant a lot to you . . .'

'It does! Of course it does . . .'

'And that you felt as a real mother to Fiona and Guy . . .'

'Yes . . .' tremulously.

'Well then, I think a real mother would have wanted to be with her daughter, and a good wife with her husband at such a difficult time.'

'Peter, I know what has happened must have upset Fiona dreadfully, and I am truly very sorry, but it isn't as though anyone had died.'

'Someone might die. She might lose the baby.'

'Is it as bad as that?'

'It's a possibility, I suppose. She's still at Sal's. The doctor said she must be monitored for twenty-four hours. That's why we need you, Anna.'

'Peter, normally I'd be down at once, but this has come at a very unfortunate time. Please *try* and understand. David Cole told me today that he thought I was doing too much, and that he might appoint a joint head of the office.'

'Sounds like a jolly good idea.'

'Peter, how can you *say* that? It will mean loss of seniority.'

'Well, that's very important to you, isn't it, Anna? And you *are* doing too much as a matter of fact. The only thing that surprises me is that you don't have some kind of breakdown. It's dehumanising you, Anna, and as far as the family are concerned it's making you seem very selfish, thinking only of yourself.'

Selfish. There it was: that word again.

'I'll have a word with David first thing in the morning,' Anna said stiffly, 'and I will try and come down. Otherwise it will be the weekend. I'll let you know. Give Fiona my love . . .' But from the sound of the tone at the other end she already knew that Peter had rung off.

Fiona did indeed look very ill. By the time Anna got down early the following afternoon the doctor had visited her again and didn't want her to be moved from Sal's. Peter had paid Sal's outstanding telephone bill and the company had promised to reconnect the line as an emergency.

Anna went straight to Sal's where she was rather relieved to find her alone, with Fiona asleep upstairs. Peter had gone into Blandford to do some shopping.

'He'll be delighted to see you,' Sal said, leading Anna into her sitting room. 'Men don't know how to cope, do they?'

'Seems not.' Anna sank on to the sofa.

'You'll need a cup of tea I expect?'

'I do.'

After hardly any sleep the night before and an acrimonious conversation with David when she rang him at home that morning ('I can't understand *how* you can do this, Anna, when we only had the talk we had yesterday. It's not as though she's your own daughter'), she felt shattered.

While Sal busied herself getting the tea, Anna crept upstairs to look at Fiona. Even in sleep she was pale and exhausted, one hand clutching a handkerchief to her mouth like a baby would its comforter. Anna had stood for some time gazing down at her, but Fiona didn't move. Emotionally exhausted she was genuinely fast asleep, probably under the influence of a tranquilliser.

When Anna went downstairs there was a pot of tea, cups and a plate of biscuits on the table drawn up to the fire. It all looked cosy and inviting.

'You look as though you could do with a sleep yourself,' Sal said, passing Anna her cup as she sank back into the sofa.

'You can say that again. I was so worried . . .'

'Well, yes . . . it was too bad about the phone.'

'He could have gone to the cottage. So unlike Peter not to let me know. He's never wanted to carry a mobile. Thinks they're pretentious. I couldn't do without mine.' Anna thankfully sipped her tea.

'You've no idea how *worried* we were, Anna.' Sal's face creased with concern. 'Everything was chaotic. We thought she'd lose the baby.'

'Was she having contractions or anything? Pain?' Anna the lawyer wanted the rather woolly statement to be substantiated.

'Well, no; but she was that upset. The doctor had to give her a sedative.'

Anna sat staring at the fire, thoughtfully biting into the biscuit she'd taken.

'It's all my fault, really . . .'

'Oh, Anna, you can't blame yourself . . .' Sal looked shocked.

'Not this, but that they ever met at all. I introduced them. Peter never liked him from the start, but I thought that was just middle-class prejudice. Did you like him, Sal? I feel I hardly knew him. I just so hated the mess the place was in, that in the relatively brief time he was here I kept away.'

'Well with young people like that you feel you want to leave them to themselves, don't you?' Sal nodded understandingly. 'I *quite* liked him myself. I mean, deep down he was an ordinary kind of bloke. A bit sullen, not a great personality, not educated like you and Peter. But then Fiona's not educated, is she?'

'Well, not very.' Anna was aware of indignation rising again at the implied distinction, on the grounds of class, which she found offensive.

'I mean she didn't get GCSEs or anything, did she?' Sal, blissfully unaware of Anna's inner torment, pursued her point.

'Apart from scraping through English and History, she didn't.'

'Then perhaps they were quite suited? I mean everyone's the same these days, aren't they? No difference really. Did she ever meet his parents?'

'I don't think he had any.' Anna shook herself from the state of somnolence induced by the fire. 'I mean, I always assumed he had left home under some cloud, or perhaps he was an orphan. We knew very little about him.'

In that case how *ridiculous* to have introduced your step-daughter to a man you knew nothing about, a social reject who was part of a squat. Would she have done that if Fiona had been her natural daughter? Did it seem like carelessness, almost criminal in fact, to behave as she had?

If so, no wonder Peter was angry.

She ran her hands over her face. 'Did he give Fiona no inkling that he was going to do a bunk?'

'None at all. They seemed so happy. He even seemed pleased about the baby, that he was going to become a father, that he had a home and that this would give him the chance to settle down. I mean he had everything going for him, didn't he really? She kept him, yet he still got all his benefits. Not that I begrudge people their benefits because I get as many as I can myself. I mean I think we deserve them, don't you?' Sal's tone grew defensive. 'I mean that's what they're there for. For people to claim.'

Anna nodded.

Sal's eyes narrowed. 'Except that, for people like him who are being kept *and* leading the life of Riley, it doesn't seem fair, does it?'

'I suppose the social security system would have caught up with him sooner or later. In fact, it may be one way that we can find him again.'

'Would you want to find him?' Sal registered surprise.

'Of course.' Anna turned to her in astonishment. 'He's a thief. He has taken property that doesn't belong to him and, anyway, in a few months he will have a child he is one half responsible for. I'll certainly do everything I can to find him.'

'I don't think Fiona would like that,' Sal said quietly.

'How do you mean?'

'I think she still loves him. Silly I know. But I think she really does. Whatever he's done, if you ask me, she's crazy about him.'

CHAPTER 13

Mrs Hanson opened the door a crack and then, seeing who it was, flung it wide. Behind her lurked Martin, looking rather furtive as though he were anxious not to be seen. Maybe he was bunking off from school, or maybe it was the instinctive distrust of strangers that seemed to categorise the whole Hanson family, as though there were two distinct categories of people: locals and foreigners.

However today Mrs Hanson seemed initially friendly as Anna told her she had come to settle the bills run up by Errol and Fiona and collect more eggs.

The news seemed to please Mrs Hanson. Errol and Fiona had, indeed, run up rather a large bill: eggs, milk, bacon, pork, vegetables – anything, it seemed, they could get their hands on.

'I'm terribly sorry,' Anna said gaping at the amount as, after laboriously totting it up, Mrs Hanson presented her with a bill of over £100. 'I'd no idea they spent this much.'

'I dare say you hadn't.' Mrs Hanson looked sideways at her as Anna produced her cheque book.

'You don't mind a cheque, do you, Mrs Hanson?'

'Anything so long as it's legal,' Mrs Hanson replied. Then she turned abruptly to the boy behind her who had been surreptitiously watching the proceedings.

'Now don't stand there gawping, Martin. Get back to your work.' She shook her head wrathfully. 'I can't get him to do anything. Moons about all day.'

'Why isn't he at school?' Anna asked curiously.

'Woke up with a migraine, he *says*, but you've got to believe them, haven't you? Normally I would fetch him one and send him off to school, but today he really seemed quite poorly.'

Martin Hanson did indeed have the white, pasty face of a town boy rather than a country lad. Anna suspected that he spent quite an amount of his spare time in a smoke-filled room smoking pot, and that the rest was spent in front of the telly.

'How's your Guy doing?' Mrs Hanson inspected the cheque and popped it on the sideboard behind her.

'He's fine.' Truth to tell Anna still felt ashamed and embarrassed about the private school, a betrayal of her principles.

'Settled then, has he?'

'It seems so.'

'You're lucky you could afford to send Guy to private school. Something like that is just what Martin needs. A strict boarding school to discipline him.'

'I wouldn't say it was a "strict" school. In fact it's rather liberal. As a matter of fact it's something I feel rather ashamed about.'

Mrs Hanson looked puzzled. 'Ashamed?'

'I'm really dead against private education. It goes right against my idea of equality.'

Mrs Hanson's expression remained unchanged. She was not much over fifty but she had the careworn face of a woman overburdened with worries; of the family, the farm, the hard grind which was life.

'What's happening to Martin at *his* school goes against *my* idea of equality.' She paused sensing that the matter was a thorny one, as it emphasised the gap between the Livingstones, who could afford to send their children to private schools and didn't want to, and the Hansons who wanted to but couldn't afford it. 'How's Fiona?' she asked. 'I'm terribly sorry to hear what happened. You can't trust people, can you?'

She looked over her shoulder to be sure that Martin was out of earshot and then leaned conspiratorially towards Anna. 'I hear he ran off with everything?'

'TV, video, everything that he could put his hands on.' Anna gestured helplessly.

'He must have had an accomplice, someone to help him. Would you like a cup of tea, Mrs Livingstone?'

Anna felt honoured. She never remembered being invited to have a cup of tea by Mrs Hanson before. To have refused would have appeared rude.

'That's very nice of you,' she said.

'Come in and sit down.' Mrs Hanson led the way from the big hall to a sitting room that Anna had never seen. It was a lovely room, even a gracious one, overlooking a lawn that sloped down to the river upon which a family of ducks were now cavorting. It was a high-ceilinged room with an original plaster cornice, and had windows that ran from the ceiling almost to the floor. Anna had never been further than the hall, or the larder behind the big farmhouse kitchen at the back.

'What a lovely room,' Anna enthused as Mrs Hanson invited her to sit down.

'We like it.' Mrs Hanson sighed deeply. 'We shall miss it when we go.'

'Go?' Anna looked at her in concern. 'You're leaving?'

'Well we would *like* to leave. The farm isn't paying. We'd like to sell up. Ted's health is not good, bronchitis last winter turned to pneumonia and it took him weeks to recover. Martin is hopeless about the farm and the girls aren't interested. It's a big burden.'

'It must be. I didn't realise. I'm so sorry. Can't you get help?'

'No one wants to work on the land these days.' Mrs Hanson sighed wearily again and Anna felt she was glad to unburden herself to a virtual stranger, someone not local or a part of the family. 'I shan't be a moment,' she said pointing towards the door. 'I'll just get the tea, Mrs Livingstone.'

'I wish you'd call me Anna.' But Mrs Hanson had gone.

Anna stood by the window gazing at the river as it idled by. On the other side were water meadows, land which was subject to flood in winter and its lush greenery seemed to bear this out. It sloped gradually up to a coppice crowning the brow of the hill opposite, growing thicker towards the east and becoming sparser towards the west.

It was a scene of beauty, harmony and tranquillity, so different from the clutter they'd found in the cottage, the misery and chaos surrounding them there.

Anna knew she would always hate the cottage not only for its recent bad memories but for something that went much further back: because it had once belonged to Nancy and she had never truly felt happy or at home there.

She turned as Mrs Hanson laid the tray on a round mahogany table. All the furniture in the room was good, possibly antique, though the heavy red flocked walls would not have been to her taste. The carpet was well worn, but the great fireplace obviously saw service in winter; logs were piled up on one side and a brass coal scuttle stood on the other.

'When will you be leaving?' Anna asked as Mrs Hanson poured the tea, gave her her cup and proffered a plate of home-made cake.

'When we can sell. It's on the market, but so far no offers. Times are hard, aren't they, Mrs Livingstone?'

Anna knew she would never call her by her Christian name. There would always be that chasm sanctified by the formality of social address. She didn't even know Mrs Hanson's Christian name. It was the way they had of politely keeping strangers in their place.

'It will be dreadful without you. Whatever will we do for eggs and milk?'

Mrs Hanson gave a brittle laugh.

'Do the same as everyone else. Go to the supermarket. On the one hand we can't sell our produce because it's either too expensive or it falls foul of these daft European Community regulations. Our eggs for instance . . . well, you know, we're not supposed to sell those.'

Lovely big brown eggs fresh from the hen. It seemed ridiculous.

'Well, I hope you'll let me have a dozen today.'

'I will, Mrs Livingstone. When will you be going back to London?'

'I should go back very soon.' Anna looked uneasy. 'I have a job to hold down, you know. I'm taking unpaid leave at the moment. My husband has already gone back. We would like Fiona to return to London with us but she doesn't want to. Until that's solved I can't leave her.' Suddenly, acting on instinct, she said: 'Do you think I could see the rest of the house?'

'Are you interested perhaps in buying it, Mrs Livingstone?' Mrs Hanson perked up.

'Oh, no,' Anna said quickly, 'but I might know someone who is. It could, of course, be sold apart from the farm?'

'Oh, we'd sell all the animals. There would be nothing to stop it being turned into a private dwelling.'

The same heavy flock wallpaper lined the hall and stairways, the skirting boards and paintwork were stained or painted brown. The place looked as though it hadn't been decorated in the lifetime of the present incumbents, though it was by no means dirty or uncared for. On the contrary, everything was neat, tidy and clean. The beds in the bedrooms looked as though they had been freshly made, waiting for the next occupants. It was well-aired and welcoming. From every window there were extensive views, and the higher one climbed the better they got. There were two bathrooms with old-fashioned baths and basins, lavatories with solid wooden seats, old-fashioned cisterns and brass taps. It was all redolent of a past age, as though the Hanson family lived in a time warp.

'Won't you miss it dreadfully?' Anna asked looking from the window of what was obviously the master bedroom with a solid double bed, a pretty painted porcelain jug and basin on a stand in the corner and a huge double-fronted wardrobe, its highly polished surface gleaming in the afternoon sunlight.

Mrs Hanson, arms folded, stood beside her gazing out but not speaking. Finally, in a low voice she said: 'We've worked hard all our lives, Mrs Livingstone, with little to show for it. Our children are not keen, the first generation of Hansons not to want to farm. We did so hope that our married daughter's husband, or Martin, would show some interest but they don't. All they are attracted to these days are the bright lights of the city. When Ted was sixteen and school leaving age he knew almost as much about farming as his father. He'd worked on the farm ever since he could remember, getting up as a small boy to help with the milking, bringing the animals in from the fields when he got home after school of a winter's afternoon. It was a hard life, but it was satisfying. It was a different age.'

'It's a lovely house.' Anna sighed. 'I hope whoever buys it is as nice as you.' She felt impulsively that she wanted to kiss her cheek, but she didn't dare. The reserved, undemonstrative Mrs Hanson would think it extremely odd.

Once downstairs again, Anna put the eggs in her basket, was warmly thanked for paying the bill, and prepared to take her leave.

'I hope everything turns out well for you,' Mrs Hanson said. 'A young girl like that having a baby and no father.' She shook her head. 'It's a terrible thing. Not yet eighteen, is she?'

Anna shook her head. 'Well it *has* a father.' Instinctively she assumed the lawyer's sensible practical tone of voice. 'The trouble is, we don't know where he is.'

* * *

She took her time going down the hill towards the village and the cottage nestling in the centre; the place she so disliked. But her mind was on the farm, that house, the big, light airy rooms, the views which, as she entered the cottage, made it seem almost claustrophobic, its rooms so small and dark, and the sense of foreboding, the feeling of depression that now always seemed to go with it.

Fiona was a terrible problem, and Anna felt resentful that so much more pressure was being put on herself than anyone else. Peter had gone back to work. He said there were a number of knotty international problems that needed his personal attention. Anna was forced once more to get on the phone to David Cole, aware, more than ever, that her job, her career was in jeopardy. She was also missing meetings of the Council and the numerous committees she was on. The Law Centre had almost completely gone by the board. She hadn't been there for weeks.

There was the usual silence in the cottage as Fiona needed no excuse now to spend most of the time in bed. It was doubtless partly depression, partly her condition. She was pregnant, and she now had good reason to be depressed. Her partner had deserted her, and was she old enough, strong enough, to cope with motherhood?

Anna put the eggs in the larder and then climbed the stairs to Fiona's bedroom pausing with the customary feeling of tension before she knocked and went in.

Fiona was awake.

'Hi!' Anna said with forced jollity.

'Hi!' Fiona replied after a while.

'It's past noon,' Anna said, drawing the curtains and squinting at the wintry landscape. Since she'd left the farm the sun had gone in, which somehow seemed symbolic.

'I 'spect it is,' Fiona muttered, and Anna turned to see that she was curled up sucking her thumb, a child in a woman's body.

A child having a child. It seemed deeply, even morbidly, ironic.

With an assumed cheerfulness Anna went over to Fiona's bed and sat down on it.

'Fiona, do you feel up to talking?' She wanted to reach out and smooth her hair back from her sticky brow, but she didn't dare for fear of being repulsed. But in that crumpled figure before her she couldn't help seeing the Fiona she had known as a small girl: anxious, insecure, loving Anna to touch her, wanting her. Anna would reach out and smooth back her curls and then she would kiss her, hug her and perhaps sing to her until she fell asleep. They had once been very close, but it all seemed a long time ago now.

'Talking about what?' Fiona asked after she'd given it some thought.

'Things. The future.'

'If you mean am I going to have the baby adopted, no, I'm not.'

'No, I didn't mean that. I know you want it, and we want it.'

'Huh!' Fiona replied, eyeing Anna maliciously.

'We do really.' Anna's throat suddenly went dry and she coughed.

'How can you say that when only a year ago you got your tubes tied so that you could never have children?'

'It's different.' Anna coughed again, her throat feeling inexplicably tight and constricted. 'This is your baby. It exists. Mine didn't.'

'You can't have much of a maternal instinct to do a thing like that.' Anna realised that Fiona was sounding smug, implying in fact that she was one up on her stepmother.

'Fiona, please . . .' Anna struggled to find the right words. 'Just for once let's have a practical, sensible talk about the future. Let's forget about what happened in the past, or even a year ago, or why I did what I did which I thought at the time, and still do, was for the best. Look, I can't stay down here permanently with you. I have a job to do. Besides, you wouldn't want it, but your father and I would like it very much if you do come back to London. You'll be near the best hospitals, have the best care and treatment.'

Even as she spoke Fiona was shaking her head, eyes closed as if she didn't even want to listen.

'I don't *want* to come to London. You know I don't. I've said I don't, and I won't.'

'But, Fiona, isn't it more sensible? The weather . . . it's so remote out here.'

Fiona again stuck her finger in her mouth and went on shaking her head in that maddening way that made Anna feel she could cheerfully throttle her.

'You've got to think of the baby.'

'I am.'

'No, you're not, you're thinking about Errol.'

Pause. Then: 'What if I am? If he comes back he'll know where to find me.'

'If you're not here he'll know you're in London.'

Again the violent shaking of the head.

'He would never come and see me if you and Dad are there. You know that. He'd be afraid of what you'd say, or do. Being a lawyer, you might have him put in prison.'

'Which is something I'd dearly like to do,' Anna said savagely, and then, quickly, seeing Fiona's expression, 'only I shan't. But, darling,' instinctively she reached out and did what she'd wanted to do, stroked Fiona's brow and was pleased, and also surprised, to find that she didn't resist. 'Darling, Fiona, you must realise that it's unlikely Errol will come back.'

'Why?'

'Because he wouldn't have left as he did, especially,' curling her lip contemptuously, 'after pinching all the things he pinched.'

'They were no good to him. He'd want to sell them.'

'Obviously, but still it wasn't a very nice thing to do.'

'Nice,' Fiona burst out, 'that's all *you're* concerned about isn't it, Anna, with your horrible snobbish middle-class attitude? Nice, being nice. A nice person doesn't behave like that . . .'

'*Most* people don't . . .'

'Errol didn't want a baby. He didn't want the responsibility. He told me that. He said he was a free spirit, but he also said he loved me and I believe he does – *that's* why I think after it's born he'll come back. I'm staying here, Anna. You can do what you like. You can't force me to return, and I shan't.'

Anna stood looking around at the canvases stacked untidily in the shed. It was quite easy to see which were Errol's bright, vibrant colours as opposed to Fiona's, which were still rather wishy-washy, despite his tuition.

Yet how much tuition had there been? Anna didn't think he had any real talent. But then it was hard to judge something quite as abstract as the canvases before her. She might well feel the same about works of art, so-called, in some London galleries.

'Do you like his stuff?' she asked Sal who shook her head.

'Neither do I. He said he was at the Slade. I've no reason to think he lied. If he was, he must have had talent to have got in. They don't take anybody. Still, I should have checked up on him. I should have been more careful. I did so *much* that was wrong.'

'It wasn't your fault.' Sal touched her arm, running her finger up and down it, a sisterly gesture Anna appreciated.

'Everything *was* my fault. I acted out of a kind of desperation. I was so anxious that Fiona should be encouraged to get on with something she seemed so interested in.'

'It's still strange he took off though.' Sal continued to look puzzled.

'Why?' Anna bent down and began to flick through the canvases. 'I don't find that surprising.'

'He had a meal ticket, a home.'

Anna went on sorting through the canvases, putting them in three piles according to artist. It wasn't very difficult to distinguish Fiona's from Errol's (it showed how much he thought of them that he had left them behind) and the ones with any slight merit were Nancy's.

Nancy's house. She looked around. Not only the studio but the whole house belonged to Nancy. Still did. It was as though, even from the grave, she clung on to it and those inside it; made them her own, as she did with her children, or Peter. It was as though, after many years, she was reclaiming them. Anna felt alienated, somehow not belonging. Nancy's ghost resented her. Involuntarily Anna shivered and got up.

'Cold?' Sal asked sympathetically.

'Cold and a bit scared.' Anna glanced over her shoulder.

'Scared?' Sal looked puzzled.

'I always feel the presence of Nancy's ghost when I'm here.'

'It's because you've been looking at her pictures.'

Anna nodded and, crouching again, turned them all to the wall.

'There,' she said, 'that's better.' She dusted her hands and grinned across at Sal. 'You think I'm crazy, don't you?'

'No, but for someone so practical I'm surprised you're so sensitive. I mean ghosts don't exist. We all know that.'

'I think "presences", for want of a better word, do. I think something of Nancy lives on here and Fiona knows it and uses it against me. But to return to the subject of Errol. It's not so strange he took off. He didn't want a baby. That was too much. Fiona says that's the reason he left and I believe her. I can just see someone like Errol seeing it as the most enormous problem. The responsibility too much for him. Sal . . .' she turned to her and clasped her arm, 'do you think *you* could look after Fiona for us? She won't come to London, and I can't stay down here indefinitely.'

'Of *course* I will.' Sal's eyes earnestly sought Anna's, reassuring her.

'And as soon as anything happens, you'll let us know.'

'The very minute the pains start. You can rely on me.'

All the way back to London Anna thought about the farmhouse, about how beautiful the scenery around was on that winter's day, stark and severe in the December sunshine. How much more beautiful would it be in the spring, the leaves burgeoning on the skeletal trees, the birds busy nesting, the dawn chorus announcing the mating season. It was a time of year when everything in the country sprang to life.

It was true that in her part of London, near the Heath, the trees were full of blossom and the gardens of the well-heeled also seemed to spring to life. Driving through the park, though pleasurable, made you yearn for the country. Further towards the West End where her office was, you forgot about it altogether except for a glimpse of the tops of trees in Cavendish Square or the sight of a few bedraggled pigeons risking life and limb frenetically chasing one another around the streets.

There, the only indication of a change of season was the weather, or the fact that it got lighter or darker in the mornings or the evenings, or the streets were too hot, too cold or slippery with rain and ice.

But she also thought, couldn't help it, how much nicer it would be in the country, far away from Damian and the trouble he could cause.

It was with a feeling almost of discontent, of dissatisfaction, that Anna drew up outside the house and unpacked her bags. As she opened the gate she looked up and saw Peter standing by the window. She raised her hand and waved. He waved back before disappearing and reappearing at the door which he flung open running down the steps to welcome her.

'Darling,' he exclaimed crushing her to him, 'it's wonderful to have you back.' He released her and, taking her bags, preceded her up the steps.

Inside, the house was warm and welcoming. There was the smell of something delicious coming from the kitchen.

'Paula did a casserole.'

'How nice of her. It smells wonderful.' Anna put down her things and looked around. 'Yes, good to be home.'

'How's Fiona?' Peter asked stooping to kiss her again.

'Oh, she's fine. I'm still not happy leaving her but you can't force her, and Sal said she really would keep an eye on her, make sure she saw her every day.'

Peter put an arm round her and led her into the sitting room. The curtains had been drawn and he had evidently been reading the paper, a glass of whisky on a side table.

'Well here we are.' Anna sat down hands on her knees. She looked round, aware of a feeling of unease.

'Yes here we are.' Peter flopped into his chair and took up his glass. 'To you my love.'

She nodded. He was being especially loving and welcoming.

'Would you like a glass of wine?'

'No, thanks, I think I'll go up and unpack. I'm quite hungry actually.'

'It's ready any time you are, darling.'

In the hall Anna picked up her holdall, which wasn't very heavy, and went upstairs to her room, shutting the door behind her. She leaned against it and looked around. Her own room. Her own, familiar room. She'd lived here since her marriage. Nancy had lived here too, of course, and yet she didn't feel about this house the way she felt about the cottage.

She realised that the cottage *was* Nancy; it had her studio, her work, her canvases still stacked around, her pictures on the walls. Her daughter Fiona, and soon there would be her grandchild.

Anna thought of the farmhouse with its large airy rooms, painted white, restored to its eighteenth century origins, or maybe in Georgian colours: pastel blues, yellows, pinks and greens. She could see period chandeliers hanging from the ceilings instead of the very basic lighting fixtures there now. The beautiful original doors would be picked out in white with gleaming brass handles and fingerplates. It was difficult to know what was under the carpet. Was it parquet, boards or concrete? If concrete it would have to be recarpeted in a soft grey Axminster or Wilton. If parquet or boards they could be restored and waxed, covered with rugs. She could visualise the great range in the kitchen, still with the original coal fire, freshly blackened, with brass pots and pans hanging above it. In the garden, with its lovely views of river and coppice, would be a bird table for the robins, the woodpeckers, the chiff-chaffs and goldfinch . . .

She pulled herself up sharply as Peter's voice called out from below: 'Grub's up, Anna. Are you ready, darling?'

'Ready,' she called, and quickly fluffed out her hair, glanced at herself in the mirror, and without even applying fresh lipstick bounded down the stairs, two at a time.

They ate in the kitchen, serving the meal directly from the stove. Peter had put a candle in the centre of the table and she knew there was also a special bottle of wine. She toasted him and he smiled at her. 'I have missed you.'

'Me, too.'

'And thank you so much for doing what you did. I can't tell you how I appreciate it.'

'Doing what?' She looked surprised.

'Staying with Fiona.'

'It's my job. I wish I could have stayed longer. We can go down every weekend.'

'Can we?' He looked pleased, surprised. 'Oh good.'

'Peter,' Anna began, then paused not quite knowing how to say what she wanted to say. For once she was lost for words.

It was important to get it right, not to be misunderstood, to have him on her side.

'Yes, darling?' He looked up encouragingly.

'It's simply that the Hansons are selling the farm.' In the end the words all came out in a rush.

'Oh, dear, that is bad news.' Peter leaned back and broke into his bread roll. 'We shall miss them.'

'That's what I said. It's a lovely farmhouse. I . . .' She didn't want to get it wrong. 'Peter, I wonder if we should buy it.' There, it was out and even now she was surprised by her own words.

'Buy it!' he said in the crushing, almost derisory tone she'd dreaded. 'Buy the farm?'

'Yes. But not to farm it. You know what I mean.'

'I don't think I do. Don't you think we've enough on?' Peter got up to restock his plate with casserole and vegetables and looked across at her: 'Anna?'

'No, thanks.' She'd been terribly hungry, but now her appetite had gone.

'Yes, we have enough to do. It's just that I saw the house really for the first time the other day. Went all over it. I never realised it was so lovely. It's Georgian. I bet at one time it was the manor. It's got glorious ceilings. Mrs Hanson gave me tea when I went to pay the bill – enormous by the way – and get some eggs. It's such a beautiful house and the views . . .'

'Yes, those views are lovely.'

'It makes the cottage seem so claustrophobic.'

'You never liked it.'

'I think it's because of Nancy.'

Peter looked at her. *'Nancy?'*

'It was her place. Fiona is always more difficult when she's there. Somehow I think the presence, the memory rather, of her mother makes her irritated and dissatisfied with me.'

'Don't be ridiculous.'

'I'm serious. I always get depressed, frankly, when I go to

that cottage, and it's not just because of the time we've had there recently with the kids.'

'Then why not move away altogether if that's how you feel? Get somewhere else?'

'We couldn't sell that cottage, not at the moment, not with Fiona the way she is. Anyway, doesn't it belong to Fiona?'

'Yes.' Peter screwed up his nose. 'Nancy left it in trust for Guy and Fiona. I haven't thought about it, actually, because I've always regarded it as ours, you know, that is belonging to the family. To all of us.'

'So you can't sell it anyway unless they want to. Fiona might well make it her home. She seems to love it and we would want to be near Fiona and the baby.'

'I really believe you're serious,' Peter said wonderingly.

'I am. I mean I've thought a lot about it. Become obsessed by it, in a way, especially in the last few days. Mentally I've been refurbishing it.'

'Did you tell Fiona?'

'Oh, no. I told no one; but I think if we are interested, and I am, very, we must get a move on. It is on the market and we don't want the Hansons to sell it before we have the chance to inspect it properly, weigh the pros and cons and consider an offer. You see, darling,' she leaned earnestly across the table, 'I don't want to labour this point, but it will be hell on earth, once Fiona has had the baby, to keep on going there, expecting her to put us up.'

'You mean the place will be in a terrible mess.' Peter grinned and poured them each more wine.

'Well, that too. But it's her home. She can make it her home, and the farm is far enough away yet also near enough for us to keep an eye on her.'

'She'll move in,' he warned.

'If she did there'll be plenty of room. Six bedrooms.'

Peter whistled. 'It's a hell of an undertaking. It might mean changing your life.'

Anna smiled at him mysteriously and then abruptly left the table and went over to kiss him.

She felt like a little girl asking for a present, and offering something nice in exchange by way of a bribe.

Guy stood awkwardly, hands behind his back, as Peter and Anna shook hands with the Head.

'Oh, he's doing awfully well,' Dick Preston murmured, turning to Guy's form master who stood beside him. 'Isn't he, Tom?'

Tom Merton nodded.

'*And* he's a popular boy, too. The school seems to have brought out the best in him.'

Guy, in his neat blazer, striped tie, white shirt and grey trousers, well-polished black shoes, was hardly recognisable as the jean-clad boy from the comp who, only months before, had been expelled for hurling a radiogram out of a fourth floor window.

Involuntarily Anna's eyes closed at the memory. If he'd injured or killed somebody what a very different story it would have been. Incarceration, a life ruined, to say nothing of the person or people who had been maimed or killed.

Worlds apart. That's what came of having money. It enabled you to buy a new style of life, whether it was changing schools or swapping a cottage for a large country house.

It hadn't been easy, but it had been possible to transfer Guy to a fee-paying school where the classes were small and most, if not all, of the children came from well-off middle-class families like the Livingstones. Or from families who, if not well-off, had thought it best to scrimp and scrape, sell their homes, borrow from the bank, jeopardise their futures, to ensure that their child avoided the pitfalls offered in some parts of the country by state education.

Yet Anna still felt ashamed as she looked at the Bentleys and Jags in the drive, at the large hats worn by many of the mothers, the well-creased pin-striped suits of the fathers.

But then she and Peter were not so very different, though their car was a normal production model in the medium price range and she wore a woollen coat over a navy blue suit, while Peter wore tweeds. But it would be quite easy to tell that they were well-educated, affluent and that their son had his own room in a nice home and, possibly, a get-away place in the country.

Yes it would be quite possible to tell all of these things.

After chatting to the Headmaster and his form master, Guy took them through the school hall, along the highly polished corridors to his bedroom, which was small yet big enough for a bed, desk, chairs and a wardrobe, a basin by the window which looked out on to the fields at the rear of the school. There were posters of his favourite football team on the wall – Arsenal, of course – of the pop stars of the moment, of various sporting heroes.

The room was tidy but not suspiciously so. It still had the look of being Guy's room, and Anna guessed that if she opened the wardrobe or one of the drawers she would have found clothes tossed in any old how, crumpled shirts, creased underpants and socks with holes in them.

But she wouldn't.

'We're thinking of buying the farm in the village,' she said, unable to conceal her excitement, perching at the end of his bed.

'Which village?' Guy looked up.

'In our village, Little Halton.'

'Yippee!' Guy let out a whoop. For the first time since they'd arrived, he looked happy. 'Are you going to give up work and become farmers?'

'Not exactly,' Peter laughed. 'Anna's fallen in love with the house and the Hansons are selling up. Anna might work part-time, spend more of the week down there.'

'We want to be nearer Fiona after she has the baby. We feel she'll need help and support.'

Guy nodded, looked solemn, but also rather embarrassed. He couldn't see his sister, so near to him in age, in this unaccustomed role of future mother. Couldn't begin even to envisage it.

'Farming would be fun,' Guy said, and there was a sudden catch in his voice which made Anna look up.

'We're not going to farm, Guy. The Hansons are selling the animals and we'll buy the land to stop people building on it should the eventuality ever arise.'

'Oh!' Guy looked abashed.

There was something wrong with Guy. He was too quiet, too polite, unnaturally so. The atmosphere was awkward, strained.

'Is everything alright, Guy?' Anna asked looking at him intently.

'Of course.' Guy ran his finger along the side of his desk but avoided her eyes. 'Why shouldn't it be?'

'I don't know. It's just that you don't seem terribly at ease.'

'Oh, for God's sake, Anna,' Peter said irritably, 'don't encourage him, now that we've got him settled.'

'I hate this place,' Guy said suddenly. 'I loathe it.' His expression was bleak.

'Oh, *Guy*! . . .' Anna leaned forward and caught one of his hands. 'We thought you were happy, settled down. Your letters were fine. The Head said . . .'

'I don't like anything about it; the staff, the boys and girls are all snobs . . .'

'*All* of them?'

'Most of them. They look down on anyone who hasn't got money, and they know. They know whose parents have asked for help with fees, who are on assisted places schemes and they're horrible to them.'

'Then it's up to you to counteract that.'

'I do. I try, and they call me Trotsky, or Trot, you know the one who didn't fit in, who fell out with Stalin. The people here just cover all this up. The ones who are victimised put up with it for the sake of their parents, the sacrifices they made. They really are the nicest ones of all and my few friends are among them. But they want to get out, and so do I.'

Peter sat dejectedly on the bed next to Anna, his hands loosely joined in front of him.

'I knew it was too good to be true,' he said. 'I knew it was unbelievable.'

It had been hard to tell from Guy's letters home, and when they visited him he seemed well, happy in a controlled kind of way. But Anna realised now that it hadn't been at all like Guy. He'd been fooling them all along.

'Can you just bear it until you've done your exams?' she asked.

'Until the summer? Next summer?' He brightened at once, and the tears which had seemed to be lurking failed, after all, to flow. 'You mean I can *leave* in the summer?'

'We didn't say that,' Peter frowned at Anna. 'You might like it better by then.'

'Oh, I shan't.' Guy leaned against the wall, arms folded, and looked at them. 'I shall do as Fiona did and if you don't let me I shall still leave. I'd prefer to do it with your agreement. You know you can't make me stay here, but after all the trouble I've been I did want to try.' And then, suddenly, the tears came, first a trickle and then a flood cascading down his cheeks.

'Oh, *Guy*!' Anna leapt up and put her arms around him drawing him down on the bed. 'Really we didn't *know*. We wanted to do it for the best.'

'We wanted you to have a decent education, Guy,' Peter said tetchily, 'and you'd think that after what has happened to your sister that's what *you'd* want too.'

'I did. I do; but I just loathe it here.'

'But you loathed it at the comp.'

'I didn't loathe it.' Guy's tears dried up and his tone of voice became truculent. 'I just didn't like work. I had a lot of mates. Here I don't really mind the work but I don't like the people, and I don't like their parents,' he said viciously. 'A bunch of arty-farty snobs.'

'Well I don't know about "arty-farty" but I did think one or two of them didn't look too bad,' Anna demurred. 'However I know what you mean. It's not the real world.'

'Anna, why do you *say* these things?' Peter began to look really angry. 'Why are you encouraging him to behave like this?'

'What's the use of pretending, Peter?' Anna rose and went to the window. 'It's a lovely place, a beautiful setting, but it is an expensive minor public school. It's the sort of place I guess I knew Guy would be unhappy in.'

'Well *he* liked it. Christ, we went all over the bloody country.'

'I know, Dad, and I'm sorry. That's why I didn't say anything before. I know I've upset you and you've wasted a lot of time and money. I will stay here until the summer and I will do my best in the GCSEs. But after that I want to leave. I shall be sixteen and there will be no compulsive reason for me to stay on at school.'

'And do what?'

Guy shrugged.

'I quite like the idea of farming.' His face brightened, eyes looked hopeful. 'I mean if you bought the house and kept the land . . .'

Peter was silent for such a long time after they drove through the school gates that Anna wondered if he should be driving; he seemed to seethe with suppressed anger beside her and once or twice made a rash move.

'Shall I take over, dear?' she asked after a while.

'Why should you take over?' He looked at her savagely.

'I can see that you're upset.'

'Of course I'm bloody upset; and who was it that mentioned farming?'

'I saw absolutely nothing wrong in saying we were thinking of buying the farm. I didn't suggest he should farm there but, Peter, if we did and he wanted to, what's wrong with it?'

'Because I want him to do something with his life. I want him to get As and go to university.'

'Farming *is* doing something with his life. I mean, if you're so keen on an academic career for him and he is serious about it he could go to an agricultural college.'

'He's never said he was interested in farming before. If you ask me, the idea just occurred to him.' Now that they were actually discussing the subject that so irritated him, Peter's driving seemed to have improved and Anna felt easier.

'I seem to remember he did mention it once. Anyway, I didn't know I wanted to do law until I was in the sixth form. Even then I wasn't sure. Look, between now and the summer is quite a long time. He has agreed to stay on and that's the main thing. He might change his mind again.' She put out her hand and lightly touched his. 'One step at a time, darling. Don't make it too hard for yourself.'

The Hansons had been surprised but pleased by the Livingstones' interest in the farm. They would have preferred to sell it to working farmers, but in these days of recession the property market was sluggish and they had their eyes on a bungalow by the sea with half an acre of land, just enough for the amount of gardening they wanted to do. Time to put their feet up and retire, take things easy.

At Christmas all the family – Peter, Anna, Guy and Fiona – went round the house. Guy again affirmed his interest in farming and to emphasise this, helped Ted all over the Christmas holiday. On the whole, apart from the usual rows, misunderstandings and silences it was a happy time, a traditional Christmas with a tree, lights, turkey and a party for the neighbours including the Hansons, Sal and Honey, Fred and many more. All of them were delighted at the prospect of the Livingstones rather than strangers buying Hall Farm. Finally, Anna and Peter put in an offer only marginally below the asking price, and after further negotiation and deliberation the deal was settled.

A man called Michael Lawrence had been appointed to run the law practice in Wigmore Street jointly with Anna. They were equal partners and at first Anna liked Michael and got on with him. She swallowed her pride and found, besides, that having someone to share the workload gave her more time for her Council work and her voluntary sessions at the Law Centre. But she also felt increasingly that her many duties had become irksome. The purchase of Hall Farm and its future was much on her mind, and so was the question of Damian who had started to telephone her again.

Anna knew she couldn't go on stalling for ever.

Now was the time to do something about it.

McDonald's, off the busy Holloway Road, was hardly a romantic spot for a tryst. McDonald's at noon with people bustling in and out for an early lunch, a late breakfast, a snack.

Damian was already there when Anna arrived, having had difficulty finding somewhere to park her car. She stood for a moment in the doorway looking at him. It was not a large place, and had a back area, vaguely Art Deco, filled mainly with small tables and chairs. At one of the tables Damian sat staring moodily in front of him, hands clasped, fingers intertwined. He seemed bathed in a golden glow. His hair bleached by the artificial light, his beard full of red-bronze highlights, his earrings twinkling like tinsel. Anna remembered what kissing him had been like, and the supple firmness of his youthful body.

She swallowed and, as she did, he looked round, rose from his chair with the expression of an eager schoolboy and came towards her, one arm easily, briefly encircling her waist.

'Hi!' she said looking towards the counter. 'Sorry I'm late.'

'That's OK.' He removed his arm. 'Do you want something to eat?'

'Just a coffee. I'm between courts.' She moved towards the counter but he said: 'Hey, let me get it,' and pushed past her, hands in his pockets counting out the change. 'You get a place.'

In the fast food restaurant few of the tables were free, but she found one at the rear where she thought no one would notice them, busy metropolitans with no time on their hands. She had deliberately chosen McDonald's because it was an impersonal sort of place in a busy part of town where they were quite unlikely to see or be seen by anyone they knew.

Anna sat down, loosened her jacket, placed her bag and briefcase on the floor beside her, gave a deep sigh just as Damian joined her, setting her coffee in front of her, taking his place opposite.

'Thanks,' she said nervously, immediately putting her cup to her lips. She felt awkward, and wished she hadn't agreed to his request for a meeting.

She was aware that his eyes had never left her, and as she looked up he put a hand over hers. He'd gone to some trouble to groom himself for the occasion. He wore jeans, a clean shirt and a sweater, and the ribbon round his pony tail looked new.

'Anna,' he said, speaking hesitantly, 'I fancy you something rotten.'

'I like you too.' She lowered her eyes and clumsily tried to withdraw her hand.

'You know what I mean,' he urged. 'You're really sexy, Anna. You try to hide it . . .'

'I don't hide it,' she retorted angrily, looking up at him. 'But I really am in love with my husband, Peter. What happened was . . . well, a moment of aberration.'

He leaned forward as if he, too, were angry. 'You call that marvellous fuck a moment of aberration?' he hissed.

Momentarily she was speechless, and he grasped her hand again, his thumb and forefinger harshly rubbing against her rings.

'No,' she acknowledged, again avoiding his eyes. 'It *was* marvellous.' Then suddenly she looked straight at him, feeling liberated from her stupid middle-class inhibitions. 'Of course I enjoyed it.'

'Oh, *Anna*!' He squeezed her fingers so hard that the rings pressed into them and they hurt. 'Let's go on. I don't mind about Peter. Let's meet from time to time, do it again. I won't be around a great deal. My father is very ill. He's probably going to die. My mother says I've helped to bring on his illness, made his last years wretched, so I've promised to go home for a while. I've also,' he paused, 'called off the case of suing the police.'

'Oh, I'm so relieved.' She gave him a broad smile and returned the pressure of his hand. 'Not just for me. I think it's time for you to begin again, Damian. You haven't really got a squatter's mentality. You're a talented, educated man who could give a lot to society in other ways. Make a positive contribution. You could easily get a job.'

'You really *are* oriented to jobs, aren't you, Anna?' he said sarcastically. 'Success, money . . .'

'No, I'm *not*, but I think you're wasting your life.'

'Let's go on, Anna.' They had scarcely touched their coffee which was getting cold. Momentarily Anna thought that if anyone happened to be observing them they must have presented a strange picture: a woman in a black suit, white blouse with a briefcase and a man with a pony tail and three earrings through his ear, earnestly clutching her hand. 'Anna?' he said again.

'I was thinking we must look odd.' She smiled rather shyly. 'Look, we *can't* go on, Damian. Not only is it wrong, it's not sensible. Life is too complicated to do what you want to do. Let's just look at that day as something nice, memorable but unexpected that happened between us.' She touched his hand for a second, letting her fingers linger, and then her manner changed, becoming brisk and practical. 'Damian, do you know where Errol is? He left Fiona and we'd like to find him. She's having a baby.'

Damian whistled and shook his head.

'He just did a bunk,' Anna went on. 'I thought you might know. I always felt guilty, you see, that I never checked up on him properly: where he came from, anything about him. I mean he came from the north. Do you happen to know . . .'

Damian shook his head again and swallowed the rest of his cold coffee.

'You know that we never suss people up, Anna; but Errol was a genuine artist. He was properly trained. He suffered from depression. I guess he couldn't cope with the idea of a baby. It doesn't surprise me. But you'll never get any support out of him, Anna. He'd never . . .'

'It's not just *that.* I think she pines for him. She loves him. I'd like to think that if we find him we could reason with him, maybe offer him support.'

'Patronise him,' Damian said bitterly.

'No, not patronise. You're so damn defensive, Damian.'

'That's what it's all about, isn't it, Anna?' Damian suddenly slipped off his chair. 'The haves and the have nots. Patronise them, offer them charity, screw them . . .'

'Oh, Damian!' Anna shook her head and realised she felt wretched. One or two people had interrupted their meal to stare at them. Strangely she didn't care. 'That's *never* the way I thought about you.' Briefly, her fingers reached out and stroked his face. 'Just the time, the place, the moment, if you like; but a future for us? Never. Only heartache.'

She, too, rose from her chair, picked up her bag and briefcase and, followed by him, walked to the door.

Rather shyly, they stood facing each other on the pavement outside, as if neither knew what to say.

'Happy memories, Anna?' Damian stooped to kiss her cheek. Then he turned abruptly on his heels and walked quickly away, up the Seven Sisters Road, leaving a confused, unhappy woman not a little sorry about what she'd done, but, even more, for the unworthy thoughts that she'd harboured about him just because he was a squatter.

CHAPTER 14

Anna drove slowly along the lane that led from the farm to the village feeling, despite the normal worries and preoccupations that were so much a part of her life, very happy. It was late June and the hedgerows were lush with a profusion of wild flowers.

As if the beauties of nature weren't enough, she had another reason for her spirits to soar. She was a grandmother and how she loved it, surprising everybody, not least herself, by her reaction to Fiona's lovely baby, Harriet, who had been born a little premature, it seemed, but healthy at the hospital in Yeovil. Anna had been at Hall Farm at the time, the purchase having been completed two months earlier, and was there for the birth waiting, just as anxiously as any mother, for news of her daughter's safe delivery.

Fiona and Harriet had gone back to the cottage and Sal was persuaded to work full time as mother's help. She was needed. Everyone expected Fiona to be depressed, but curiously she wasn't. Instead she displayed a worrying apathy towards the child, a kind of indifference as though she could scarcely believe, indeed doubted, that she belonged to her. With time, hopefully, that would change. Fiona had all the help and support she could want, all the love except that of her baby's father: Errol.

Anna frowned as she approached the village. Momentarily her feeling of joy abated. Fiona remained a problem; probably she always would. The really amazing thing was how protective she herself felt towards the infant, maybe as a way of compensating. Anna simply doted on Harriet. The boot of the car at the moment full of useful gifts. Every day there was a visit, sometimes two, despite all the work there was to do in the house. And how she hated going back to London, longing to return to the country, her house and the baby again.

There was so much to see to at Hall Farm. So much to sort out. Workmen and decorators to be consulted, and somehow it seemed mostly to fall upon her. Not that Peter disagreed; he simply rubber stamped everything she suggested and came up with the money when it was time to pay.

But nevertheless there remained that tug between two worlds: the world of the city and the world beyond.

Anna had spent the morning with the interior decorator who had decided views of her own. She had come up from Bournemouth with swatches and samples of this and that, and the inevitable argument had followed. The decorator had rather grandiose ideas about the heavy use of silks and satins as hangings and coverings, and four-poster beds, while Peter and Anna wanted a simpler style, a place where their friends would feel at ease, not forced to dress up, the atmosphere as informal as possible. Sometimes Anna wished she had done the whole thing herself but there really wasn't time, and expense on this scale could not be repeated every few years. It had to be got right.

She'd travel down on Friday afternoon, sometimes with Peter and sometimes without, and back on Monday morning thus, in effect, taking a day off work, which continued as stressfully as usual and had to be sometimes crammed in. Peter told Anna that if she wasn't careful she'd have a nervous breakdown, to which she had replied that if she was that sort of person, she'd have had one a long time ago.

Peter had a conference in Scotland this weekend which Anna was rather pleased about. It gave her the chance to spend time alone in the new house and time with Fiona to help try and sort out what she was going to do with the next, say, eighteen years of her life while Harriet grew up. The time it would take Harriet to turn from the baby she now was, into a responsible woman like her mother.

Responsible? Well.

Anna, armed with various samples of material about which she thought it would be nice to consult Fiona and Sal, alighted from the car and went up the path, stopping for a moment outside the front door before entering.

It was such a lovely day, the countryside around so beautiful, the air so balmy, so different from London that it was odd still to feel this sense of foreboding that she had so many times experienced outside Fiona's bedroom door, a kind of mental taking stock, involuntarily bracing oneself for something unpleasant.

As she opened the door and entered, Sal looked up from the baby's cot, a smile of welcome, almost of relief, Anna thought momentarily, on her face.

'Hi!' Sal said.

'Hi! Everything OK?'

'Fine.' Sal looked tenderly at the baby sleeping in her carrycot. She was adorable, cuddly but not fat. She had wispy blonde hair, almost white, great blue eyes and dimpled cheeks. Thank heaven she seemed to have very little of the dark, brooding nature of Errol. It would be extremely difficult not to love her on sight, and Anna had fallen an immediate victim to her charms. She fussed anxiously over her, making sure that her bedding was right and her breathing regular. There was so much more these days in the way of infant welfare, yet there seemed to be a disproportionate increase in the amount of anxiety. Surely mothers hadn't worried so much in the past? Yet, years ago, mortality among children had been common. In a large family everyone expected one or two children to die. How agonising it must have been to watch a young life snuffed out and not being in a position to do anything about it. What anguish.

Anna made baby noises and then looked up at Sal.

'Isn't she *adorable*?'

'Adorable. She's a picture-book baby.'

Anna sighed and rose from the cot, looking in the direction of the stairs, her expression changing.

'Is Fiona still in bed?'

'Yes.'

'God knows how she could do without you.'

'I don't think we could leave her on her own with the baby.' Sal also rose and lowered her voice. Anna looked at her in alarm.

'You don't mean . . .'

'Oh, I don't think she'd *harm* her. Not for a moment. I just don't think she'd look after her properly, change her regularly, even feed her. That sort of thing. She'd forget.'

Mentally, Anna once more braced herself for that walk upstairs that sometimes seemed to resemble the march to the scaffold.

'Well, I'd better go and see how she is. Did she have breakfast?'

Sal shook her head. 'She didn't want anything.'

'I'll take her a cup of coffee.'

'I think she'd prefer tea.'

'Tea then. Look at these bits of material and tell me what you think.' Anna indicated a mass of stuff lying on the table. 'The decorator's got such fancy ideas. These came from Liberty's.'

Anna made the tea, put cups and teapot and milk on the tray and then, on impulse, toasted two slices of bread and added butter and honey as well. Honey was full of good things, vitamins, the nectar of the gods. Carefully she carried the tray upstairs and then outside Fiona's door she put it on the floor and tapped.

'Fiona?'

No reply, naturally.

Anna turned the handle, pushed open the door, picked up the tray, crept in. The curtains were still drawn and Fiona appeared asleep. Anna stood gazing down at her, her emotions the usual compound of irritation, anger and pity. She looked so vulnerable herself, scarcely out of childhood, someone who had never really grown up. Had she wanted a child because she herself was a child, wanted a companion to play with? Or had she thought, maybe subconsciously, that it would help her to hang on to Errol? That Errol would never leave her as long as she had his child?

'Fiona.' Gently Anna shook her and then realised from the rigidity of her body that she was awake. How long had she lain like that pretending to be asleep?

'Hi, you are awake!' Anna turned to the tray which she'd put on the chest at the foot of the bed. 'I brought you some tea.'

'I want my mummy,' Fiona said in a childish, little girl tone. She rolled her great eyes towards Anna. 'My real mummy, not you.'

Anna's heart froze. Even when you dread something, expect it, it's hard to be proved right.

She turned her back on Fiona and poured out two cups of tea, buttered the toast and spread honey on it.

She took one of the cups and the toast over to the bed and put it on the table near Fiona's elbow. Then she retrieved her own cup and sat in a chair facing it.

'We seem to have been here before, Fiona.'

Pause, then: 'What'd ja mean?'

'All this business about me not being your mother.'

'Well you aren't.' Fiona surreptitiously eyed the food placed beside her, then stretched out a hand and, taking the toast, began to eat it hungrily. This convinced Anna, as if she needed any convincing, that most of Fiona's attitude was an act rather than any form of depressive illness. In short she seemed prepared to do anything to get attention.

Anna finished her tea, put down her cup, joined her hands and contemplated Fiona. She had quite abandoned her spiky hairdo. It was pretty hair with a natural springy curl and it now tumbled about her face, half obscuring her features. She was an attractive girl, had the makings of beauty, had so much. Still only eighteen.

Anna felt a pricking on her temples, a tightening in her chest, all the symptoms of tension that seemed to go with Fiona. Soon it would develop into a headache and she'd want to creep away and lie down. This was something fairly new, an extension of her apprehension to her physical wellbeing.

'Fiona, what is it you want me to do?' she asked wearily.

No reply. Try again.

'I mean, do you want me to take Harriet to the house for the time being? I can easily do that and let you rest or, if you like, you can both come up to the house. It's a bit like camping but there is room.'

Fiona shook her head, gazing at Anna with those large, reproachful eyes, still saying nothing.

'You don't want to do any of those things?'

Fiona shook her head.

Anna began to feel exasperated and the pain across her forehead gradually grew worse as she knew it would. Fiona's eyes suddenly closed. One piece of toast had been eaten, the other not. The tea had been drunk.

'Fiona, I wish I could help you.' Anna sat on the bed beside her. 'I realise you're unhappy and it makes me feel helpless. I am also worried on Harriet's account. She must suffer.'

'She is not suffering.' Fiona's eyes flashed open. 'You know I love her. Sal loves her. She is very well looked after thank you, Anna!'

'I'm not talking about love. I simply feel the tension might somehow affect her.'

'What do you mean "tension"?'

'You staying in bed all day and not acting like a normal mother.'

'You're always so critical of me.' Fiona bounced around in the bed and buried her face in her pillow. 'I miss him so much.'

That was it. Errol.

'You haven't mentioned him for a long time,' Anna said gently. 'I'd hoped you might have forgotten him. Perhaps it will help to talk about him.'

'*How* can I possibly *forget* him?' Fiona, still with her face in the pillow, beat the bed on either side of her. 'He's Harriet's father. Don't you think . . .' she sat up, hugging her pillow as though it was her baby and looked pathetically at Anna, 'don't you think you could find him? You're so clever, Anna. You've got so much *influence* with all important people: the Council and so on. Couldn't you try?'

'My darling, what good would it do? Really, if we did find him? Would we be able to convince him to come here, to see you and Harriet? He would be afraid that the authorities would be after him to support the child, you know, the kind of thing you read about in the newspapers? Let's face it, basically, Errol has opted out of life with you. As long as he had it easy with you he was happy, but once you discovered you were pregnant then so many alarming speculations occurred to him.' Tenderly, gently Anna began to stroke her back. 'Dear, Fiona, and believe me, you are very dear to me, you must try and live for the present, for Harriet and yourself, and get Errol completely out of your mind.'

Anna looked round the house. What a wrench it was to leave it. Half-finished as it was, she knew that she loved it. It was her place. The walls of its high ceilinged rooms were now stripped and painted in soft pastel colours. Some of the doors, accretions of a later age, had been replaced by eighteenth century originals found in antique shops, sometimes dug up in junk yards, restored and rehung. The floorboards too had been stripped and waxed and a collection of beautiful rugs had been assembled, some newly purchased, some brought down from the London house.

Slowly everything was beginning to take shape. Some of the rooms had a modicum of furniture in them. In the master bedroom there was a double bed, and beds in two of the other rooms. The rest remained untouched. Some of the rooms were curtained, others not. In theory, therefore, it would have been possible for Fiona and Harriet to have moved in with Anna, but in many ways it was better they stayed where they were. When Anna had seen her that morning Fiona was up, dressed and playing quite happily with the baby in the sunlit garden. A different person altogether from the gloomy teenager of previous days, a creature of moods and impulse.

Anna had had another week's holiday, unpaid. She knew that she was beginning to stretch the amount of leave she could possibly take and even the status of part-time was being abused.

She went through the house checking that everything was in order; the last workers had left for the day and they would be there again at seven the next morning. The Livingstones had said they wanted the house to be ready by late summer. It was a tall order but with enough money you could get anything. Especially in times of recession people would work extra hard.

Anna went out into the sunlit yard and looked wistfully into the garden to where Peter, with the help of a part-time gardener, had already begun making inroads. The entire garden, which was a large one, was being redesigned. The Hansons had been practical people with a huge kitchen garden but with little time for herbaceous borders or ornamentation.

Looking around Anna realised that, for most of her life, she had in fact been starved of beauty, of the leisure time to enjoy the glories of nature. No time to stand and stare, to enjoy the hedgerows, fields full of corn and maize, the bright yellow of rapeseed in the spring. In London one knew sparrows, pigeons – plenty of those – and the odd blackbird, but little else. Here bluetits, robins, chaffinches and greenfinches were common and now and again one saw the green or great spotted woodpecker, a goldcrest or tree creeper, the swift flight of the tiny wren with its upturned tail, maybe a majestic heron rising from the river bank with a fish struggling in its mouth.

Once they were settled in they could have domestic pets, cats and dogs. She had always been an animal lover, but thought that to keep a pet in the London environment with its busy streets wasn't fair.

As Anna loaded the car for the drive back to London she thought that they would soon have to take the decision about what to do about the London house. They didn't really need a large house, especially if Fiona was going to stay in the country, and Guy wanted to farm. Perhaps a flat in the Barbican was the answer?

The idea of a flat wasn't very appealing, but the capital that would be released by the sale of the house would be a help now that Anna no longer worked full-time. However, she hardly felt part-time, what with all the toing and froing, and racing about she still had to do. She now gave Friday mornings to the Law Centre and drove down to Dorset in the afternoon. Coping with Fiona and the baby and the new house and its innumerable problems was hardly taking it easy.

She had an easy drive along the A303 and the M3, very little traffic about, and reached home at nine. The house was empty. Somehow she expected it would be and now, increasingly, Peter hardly ever left a note to say where he'd be. The thought uneasily crossed her mind again that he might be having an affair. After all, so many people did nowadays. If so, with whom? Would she mind? Well of course she'd mind terribly, but merely to speculate was a stupid waste of time, and she doubted that she would ever ask him outright.

She felt tired, a little headachy, and after playing the messages on the answer-machine and watching news headlines on the TV in the kitchen while she had a snack, she decided it was time for bed.

She rinsed the dishes under the tap, dried them and was in the act of putting them away when the phone rang. She quickly wiped her hands on the kitchen towel and, with a pleasant sense of anticipation, took the receiver off the wall phone.

'Hello?'

No answer.

She sensed there was someone on the line and she repeated herself.

'Hello? Peter, is that you?'

Still no response.

'Press the button' she said, beginning to feel irritated and remembering that these days people put the coins in the machine if they were calling from a call box. Or, perhaps they had a phone card?

It occurred to her that the caller was in fact calling from a private phone, and that he, or she, was there listening to her. It was an eerie, unpleasant sensation and she was about to replace the receiver when the line went dead. The person at the other end had done it first.

Thoughtfully Anna replaced her own receiver and slumped into a chair, leaning her elbows on the kitchen table.

This had happened before. Several times, now she came to think of it, but one often got wrong numbers, busy lines, and she hadn't given it another thought.

Supposing Peter did have a girlfriend? Some distraught woman who just wanted to hear the sound of his voice, know where he was or why he hadn't called? Or, perhaps, wanted to hear what his wife sounded like? A woman, maybe, she was crazily jealous of?

Anna rose abruptly, tucked the chair under the table, looked round to see everything was in place, though when Peter came in he would be sure to go into the kitchen. He always did. She put the light off and, leaving the one on in the hall, went upstairs, conscious of a dreadful feeling of depression, as though her body were weighted down with a huge stone.

Inside their bedroom she put on the lights at either side of the bed, went into the bathroom and turned on the bath taps, then back to the bedroom where she slowly began to undress. Well, supposing Peter *was* having an affair? Was she going to confront him or continue to torment herself with her suspicions? That green-eyed monster that denied peace of mind. How often had she counselled her clients to put it to one side and get on with their lives?

And what, if it came to that, of herself? Hadn't she had, well one could hardly dignify it with the name 'affair', but she had had sex here in this very house with a man she didn't love, hardly knew. She had been swept away in the crudest possible manner. It was quite outside any rational, sensible behaviour and, although it meant so little to her, knowledge of it would have devastated Peter, could possibly have ruined their marriage. But what about all these odd calls? If they *were* for Peter, from a woman, this was no casual fling. This was an affair and, yes, if so, it deeply worried her.

Anna returned to the bathroom determined to take the good advice she gave to others and put these, after all, very vague suspicions out of her mind. She would deliberately turn her thoughts to the country again, to the views from the house, the memory of changing seasons, the proliferation of colours, the sweet sound of birdsong and the peace and tranquillity it gave her.

She lay in the bath for a long time, ruminating. She felt the tug between the country and the town was unsettling her, almost, literally, pulling her apart. It was silly to lie there dreaming of lush green fields, of magpies on the lawn and squirrels chasing up the great oak trees in the fields when here she was in the heart of London with a very heavy schedule the following day.

After taking her bath and cleansing her face she got into bed wishing that, somehow, she didn't feel uneasy about Peter. Supposing he was having an affair and it was serious? Supposing he wanted to leave her, start a new life with someone else, a younger woman who would give him the baby he said she had denied him?

She had just picked up her book when she heard the key in the lock downstairs. She lay for some time listening to Peter moving around and then he came quietly upstairs and gently pushed the door open, looking at her.

'So you're awake? How long have you been in?'

'I got here at nine.' Anna put down her book. 'Where've you been?' She tried to keep criticism out of her voice. The last thing she wanted was to turn into the sort of nagging shrew, suspicious of her husband she met so often in her office.

'I had dinner in the club. Bumped into Matthew Thomson. I haven't seen him since university days.'

The name Matthew Thomson meant nothing to her.

'How nice,' she said.

'Anna?' In the act of taking off his shirt Peter paused and looked across at her.

'No, I mean, I just don't know the name.'

'It was the way you said it.'

'Sorry,' she smiled at at him, 'I feel tired.'

'I bet you do,' he paused, 'you're doing too much. More than ever now.'

'That's what I think. Sometimes,' she hesitated, wondering whether or not it was wise to go on. 'Sometimes I wonder if . . . it would be nice to live in the country all the time.' She finished in a rush. Peter, sitting on the bed to take off his shoes and socks, stopped abruptly and looked at her.

'Are you serious?'

'No. I just wonder. It was particularly beautiful when I left today. All serene and peaceful. The house is coming along well and, of course,' pause again, 'there is Fiona. She's a worry.'

Peter sighed.

'The other day she said she wanted her real mummy,' Anna went on. 'Then last night we had a perfectly civilised meal at the pub while Sal baby-sat and she was as nice as anything. Full of plans.'

'What sort of plans?'

'Oh, for painting, for Harriet's future. She's a female Jekyll and Hyde.'

'She's still very young. We mustn't forget that.' Peter got off the bed, removed the rest of his clothes and went into the bathroom.

She watched him as he walked across the room naked. Were there any telltale signs? Bruises? Marks on the neck? Bites on the body? Lipstick on the collar? She would never have thought of looking, but maybe now she should. If he was sleeping with someone else did they use contraception and, as it was natural to suppose they would, what kind? Peter would hate the condom. They had never used it and, Anna thought, if he *was* in fact sharing her with someone else should she worry too? Aids, Herpes, vaginal thrush, there were any number of things of which so far she had been free.

That was the worst of being a lawyer, of having an analytical mind. One could be objective about the most subjective, intimate things pertaining to oneself.

Peter came back, washed, teeth brushed, pyjamas on and climbed into bed beside her. He lay for a moment and then reached out gently, drew up her nightie, let his hand rest on her stomach and sighed.

'Nice,' he said closing his eyes.

Anna felt herself stiffen. Supposing, just supposing, in the past hour or two he had been having sex with someone else?

It didn't mean, did it, that he wouldn't necessarily want her now, that he'd had enough? In fact, the more you had the more you wanted. It became like a drug.

'Peter,' she asked, gently pushing his hand away, 'are you having an affair?'

She could sense his reaction before she turned and looked at him. You had to see people's eyes, their faces to know the truth.

'Why do you ask me, Anna?' He seemed more curious than angry.

'I just wondered.'

'But why *should* you wonder?'

'Because,' she paused, 'you are out an awful lot at night. I know you don't have any hobbies or belong to any committees, and maybe you don't think our own sex life is full enough. I just thought . . . I mean I don't think I'd blame you.'

'Really?' Now he sounded amused. 'You mean you wouldn't really care?'

'I would care, a great deal; but it's illogical, isn't it? I mean I see enough of it in my practice. The wife who doesn't know really what her husband does, or didn't until he asked for a divorce.'

'Do you think I'd have an affair with all that is going on in my life?'

'All what?'

'All this.' He spread out his hand. 'Moving to a new house, my teenage daughter with a baby, Guy about to do GCSEs and not knowing what to do with his life.'

'It might take your mind off it. You know, a fling, someone younger perhaps? *I* don't think you're the type, but one never knows. My work has taught me that the most ordinary people do the strangest things.'

'And I am an ordinary person?'

'Well you're not extraordinary. You're a nice, ordinary man. Yes.'

'Do you still love me, Anna?' He turned and looked at her with a sweet, sad expression.

'Yes, I do,' she paused, 'very much.'

'Because I, too, sometimes wonder.'

'You wonder about *me*?' She looked incredulous.

'Yes, I do.'

'You wonder if *I'm* having an affair? How preposterous.'

'No, I don't wonder, though of course one never knows. As you say you think you know someone and then find you don't. We're always being surprised by what other people do. You've always been a mystery to me.'

'How extraordinary.'

'You have. I always feel I never quite know you, understand you.'

She waited a long time before replying, because in a way she knew what he meant. Know thyself: she did, others didn't.

'I think we're *both* too analytical,' she said turning to him. 'I love you. I do. Take my word for it.'

'I love you.' He raised her nightie again and re-established his hand on her stomach. It would either travel upwards to her breasts, or down to her groin where, already, she began to feel a delicious anticipatory sensation.

She would try not to mention an affair again. But she would never really know the truth about Peter because, as they had now established, one never really knew the whole truth about another person, even if one was married to them.

There was always that inner, secret place that no one could reach.

And maybe there was also that other person, silent, listening at the end of the telephone line.

CHAPTER 15

The optician rose from his stool and switched on the lights, smiling at Anna as she blinked at the unaccustomed brightness.

'Everything seems absolutely fine,' he said. 'Your eyes are in very good shape, except for the slight problem you have seeing close up and this we deal with very effectively with your reading glasses.' He held them up. 'The prescription doesn't need changing at all.'

'Well, that's good.' Anna prepared to get up too, and looked around for her bag, but the optician indicated that she should stay where she was.

'How frequent are the headaches, Mrs Livingstone?'

'Well, fairly frequent.'

'Every day?'

'Oh, no.'

'Once a week, twice a week?'

Anna screwed up her nose in an effort to remember.

'They're intermittent. Every so often.'

'Do they relate to anything specific? Any time, not the time of the month for instance?'

'I wouldn't say so.' Then again, spontaneously, at the back of her mind the picture of Fiona formed. Fiona frowning, Fiona having a tantrum, Fiona turning her back to the wall as though in rejection.

'No!' She shook her head emphatically. 'They just come and go.'

The optician tapped his fingers on his bench, gazing at Anna's card and frowning.

'You do lead a very stressful life, I suppose, Mrs Livingstone, don't you? Family commitments, work, the Council . . .'

'I've cut down,' Anna said firmly, getting her bag and standing up. 'I only work part-time. Everything fits in very well.'

'Pressure *does* cause headaches.' The optician rose too. 'There's no sign of anything serious in the brain, as far as I can see, but it might be a good idea to get your doctor to check you over too.'

Brain? Anna eased her car into the traffic that moved at a snail's place along Wigmore Street. The lights by Cavendish Square seemed to be changing every two seconds, another rush of traffic would surge forward and she moved two more inches. She could feel the tension mounting in her breast, the fear that, once again, she would be late for a Council meeting, the gnawing anxiety that she was letting not only herself but the Party down by missing so many debates.

It was a Thursday, late-night opening in the West End and the traffic was appalling. After her optician's appointment she had stayed late at the office because there was so much more catching up to do now that she only worked a three-day week.

The traffic stopped again, someone had decided to sit on his or her horn. Probably a 'him' because men were inclined to show their impatience whereas women just suffered and simmered, as she was doing now. She gripped the wheel hard between her fingers and felt that familiar knot of tension and anxiety right in the middle of her solar plexus. It would be the usual excuse as she slipped into her seat under the baleful stare of the Council leader.

'Sorry, the traffic was bad,' she'd murmur.

Of course the traffic always was bad, every Londoner knew that. It wasn't an excuse either, so the thing was to leave in time to allow for the traffic. That was what she told people who were late for work, and what she knew others would like to tell her though, of course, because of the seniority of her position, they wouldn't dare.

The debate was drawing to an end as she slipped into the chamber, glancing at the leader, the word framed on her lips: 'Traffic.' He barely glanced at her before looking away again. But she was aware all round of stares, heads shaken, almost a palpable collective sigh of relief. She only realised how serious the situation was, or could have been, when the vote was carried in their favour by one. If she hadn't made it they would have lost. She screwed up her eyes and clenched her fist, rigid with embarrassment as the vote was announced.

It seemed to her as the chamber rose with much murmuring and shuffling of papers, people crossing the floor to confer with colleagues, that there was an attempt to isolate her; as though an invisible barrier formed around her as she sat alone to one side of the chamber, a gulf separating her from everyone else. No one came up to talk to her as they usually did.

Finally, as she was about to rise she saw Jack Fishwick, the leader, approach her, his progress towards her halted by individuals or groups who stopped to have a word with him, or tried to catch his attention.

'Glad you made it, Anna,' he said at last, his voice heavy with meaning as, hands in his pockets, he stood in front of her. 'It was a vital vote.'

'Sorry, Jack. You know,' her hand fluttered vaguely in the air, 'traffic. One *should* make allowances but one doesn't.'

He leaned towards her, lowering his voice.

'Do you think we could have a word in my office, Anna? It's more private there.'

'Of course.' She finished putting her papers in her briefcase and rose, looking at him eye to eye, not afraid. 'There's also something I want to ask you about.'

'Oh, good,' and together, chatting, to all extents and purposes amicably, they crossed the floor of the chamber into the corridor and walked down to the leader's room.

'I guess there's no point beating about the bush, Anna,' Jack said as he shut the door. 'You probably know what this is about.'

'My attendance record. Sorry. That's all I can say.'

'You nearly let us down tonight, Anna. When you first came on to the Council you were so diligent.'

'Things were rather different then, Jack; but I have tried to lessen my workload.'

'But you've taken on a house in the country, I hear.'

'Oh?' She looked up sharply, aware of a flush slowly creeping up her cheeks. 'Oh, you know about that?'

'Well I did hear about a large house . . .'

'How, may I ask?' She joined one hand across the other, irritated at being the subject of Party gossip.

'I guess these things get out.'

'I guess they do, though I'd like to know how.'

'Was it a secret then, Anna?'

'No, of course not.'

'Well, then, are you intending to live there permanently?'

'No, we're not.'

'Was it something to do with your daughter's baby?'

'In a way; but really, Jack, personal affairs and those of my family are nothing to do with my work on the Council.'

'I think they are, Anna.' Jack Fishwick sat down on the other side of the desk as though to emphasise his status as leader of the Council. 'There is also the question of a son at private school. That hasn't gone down at all well when the Party so rigorously opposes private education.'

Anna bit her lip. Obviously gossip had been rife.

'You know, I think, that Guy was expelled from the comprehensive. We had no alternative.'

'There are other state schools . . .'

'Jack, is this really the Council's business?'

'I'm afraid it is. It is not only the fact you've two homes, a house in the best part of London, and a son at private school, both of which ill become the image of a Labour Councillor; but you have either missed or been late for too many important debates recently. The Tories are saying "we can always rely on Anna Livingstone to send her apologies". In a Council where the balance is tight . . .'

'I think that's *very* unfair, Jack,' Anna paused thoughtfully for a moment while his message sank in, 'or should I say that I hadn't realised that I had so many enemies.'

'Not "enemies", Anna,' he said quickly.

'Well, people who obviously wish me harm.'

'No,' he shook his head emphatically, 'they don't wish you harm. They just want you to do what you were elected to do, and many of them do think you've got too much on, too many personal problems to cope with, and the idea of buying a large country house . . . when the country as a whole is in recession and people are being repossessed, didn't go down too well,' he murmured almost to himself.

'It is *not* a large country house in the sense that it is a status home or anything like that. It is a farm and my stepson Guy, who takes GCSEs this summer, may well think of farming.'

'Isn't he *lucky* to have someone to buy a farm for him?' Now Jack's tone was openly derisive.

'Jack, I don't think I have to make explanations to you . . .'

'And neither would I, Anna, were it not for your attendance record, your voting record, the fact that you resigned from the Housing Committee after the fiasco of the Pilgrim squat . . .'

'Oh, that's really what this is about, isn't it?' she asked. 'Come clean, Jack. It's about the Pilgrims and the way it ended, with me being escorted off by the police.'

'It didn't go down too well then.'

'Even though I did *everything* I could for those ungrateful people.'

'Well, we don't expect gratitude on the Council.' Jack stood up abruptly. 'I have several other people to see now, Anna, but I thought I should report back to my colleagues that I've had a word with you.'

'And what are you going to report back to them?' Anna again felt that icy finger on the back of her spine.

'Well, I shall say that we've spoken,' Jack began sorting through his papers, 'that you understand the situation and . . . well, Anna, quite frankly, if things don't improve, and improve dramatically, over the next few months or so I'm afraid that I shall have to suggest to you that you might resign and create a vacancy for someone else who will perform the job better than you appear to be doing at the moment.'

Jack crossed the room and, opening the door, held it for her. She hesitated for a moment and then she went through, stopping at the threshold to say in a low voice: 'I really am *very* sorry. I will try to improve and, incidentally, do you happen to know what has become of all the members of the squat? That's what I wanted to ask you.'

Jack looked surprised. 'Well, some of them were rehoused and others . . . just wandered away.' He looked at her quizzically. 'May I ask why?'

'Just wondered,' she said. 'Goodnight, Jack, and thank you for being so frank. I appreciate it.'

'I thought you would, Anna.' He gave her a polite rather than friendly smile and closed the door gently after them. 'It's our reputation I'm thinking about as well as that of our Party. But above all, Anna, the tide in the affairs of Labour is turning and we can't afford in a crucial marginal London Borough like this to let the Party down.'

It was wounding and it was humiliating to be accused not only of letting the Party down, but oneself too. There was the implication that she wasn't such a good socialist, in reality a champagne socialist – of whom the Labour Party had a fair number – with a son at private school and a 'large house in the country'. There was the implication that, somehow, if you were like this you didn't care as much for your fellow men and women as you might, couldn't strictly identify with them. She thought how much she'd agonised about the fate of the members of the squat – and what sort of reward she'd achieved as a result; of the countless hours she'd spent in the Law Centre and at court defending those who had the misfortune to come up against the law.

Was she somehow less humane and caring just because they could, in fact, afford to take Guy out of a school where he wasn't achieving, buy a larger house, alright partly for selfish ends too, so that Fiona would be able to bring up her daughter in some comfort in a house of her own?

Anna drove thoughtfully along, looking for a spot to park in Wimpole Street, and seeing a car emerge from a space nipped smartly into its place.

Katie was specially staying behind to see her and already she was late. Looking guiltily at her watch she nipped smartly out of the car, stuck some coins in the meter and ran up the steps to her consulting rooms.

Katie herself let her in with a rather strained smile.

'Sorry I'm late,' Anna said breathlessly. 'You know, the traffic.'

Katie smiled sympathetically.

'Unfortunately I have a meeting at the Royal Society of Medicine in an hour; but it won't take long, will it?'

She ushered Anna into her consulting room and closed the door.

'Just as long as it takes to check I haven't a brain tumour,' Anna said, sitting down and forcing a grin.

'A *what*?' Katie was looking through Anna's file in front of her on the desk.

'I'm joking, at least I hope I am. I've been having bad headaches and the optician said I should consult you.'

'Oh!' Katie, brow furrowed, went on leafing through the file. 'You didn't mention headaches before.'

'They're pretty recent, actually. They're so bad I have to lie down sometimes.'

'That's not good.' Katie got up and, going over to Anna, drew back her lower lids and looked at her eyes.

'Look up,' she said, and Anna obeyed. 'Look right, left . . . look down. The optician didn't find anything?'

'He said I only needed reading glasses.'

'Let's take your blood pressure.' Katie hesitated for a moment. 'Look, you might as well take off your suit, keep your bra and pants on and I'll give you a quick once over.'

Anna went behind the screen at the far end of the consulting room and began to undress.

The examination took about a quarter of an hour: heart, lungs, blood pressure. Katie took blood to run some tests, and asked for a urine sample. Then she told Anna to dress and went back to her desk.

'I know your smear is OK because you only had that done a few months ago.' She sat down and began to scribble some notes while Anna completed her dressing and sat down at her desk. Katie looked up with a reassuring smile.

'Like the optician, I'm glad to tell you I can find nothing wrong. Blood pressure fine, heart and lungs fine. I don't expect to find anything in the blood or urine samples. Tell me,' she leaned forward confidentially over her desk, 'you've been overdoing it, haven't you?'

'No more than usual,' Anna said defensively.

'But there's the baby now, and Fiona does need a lot of care because she's a baby herself?'

'Yes,' Anna nodded in agreement. 'I suppose that's half the trouble.'

'*And* there's a big new house.'

'Oh, I love it . . . I love *that*.'

Katie leaned back and looked at her. 'In that case why don't you spend more time there?'

'Well, I do spend more time there. I go down almost every

weekend now. I've gone on a three-day week at work and cut down on the Law Centre.'

'That's still quite a bit of toing and froing. And there remains the Council.' Katie tapped her pen on her desk.

'Good heavens, Katie,' Anna replied, 'look at all the work you do. You have a full-time medical practice. You're on the Council of this and the Council of that. You have a busy husband and two children.'

'Yes, but pressure takes us in different ways. So far, touch wood,' Katie tapped her desk, 'I don't have any symptoms of stress. The children are older and can look after themselves. Douglas has always been self-sufficient. I manage to juggle what I do reasonably well.'

'Well, so do I.'

'Yes, but you have these blinding headaches which have the effect of making you lie down. I think it is a form of migraine and that in your case, since you haven't had them before, it is a form of stress. Your body is telling you something and that seems to be saying "ease up". Do what you want for a change instead of what others want. You seem to love this house, and I suspect it's for you. It's your bolt hole, your security.'

'I still get headaches there.'

'Yes, but that's because Fiona is only a mile or two away. Couldn't you have moved, say, even further away?'

'I fell in love with the house and, yes, we did want to be near Fiona and the baby. The baby is quite adorable.' Anna's features softened for a moment. 'The baby I never had,' she concluded almost in a whisper.

'Are you sorry now?' Katie also lowered her voice.

'Yes, I think I am sorry now, just a little.'

'But you also know there is nothing you can do about it.' Katie got up and put Anna's file back in the filing cabinet. 'I mean, it is irreversible and frankly in the circumstances and at the time I think you did the right thing.'

'You really do?' Anna looked gratefully at her.

'Yes. It's all very well to moon over someone else's baby, but I think at the time you really didn't want one of your own. I also think there were contra indications to the Pill and these headaches may be a symptom. We *may* have avoided a thrombosis. Maybe you did come off just in time.'

'Oh, my goodness.' Anna clasped her hands to her face. 'You really think so?'

'So let *that* reassure you and cheer you up.' Katie glanced at her watch again and, patting Anna on the shoulder, handed her a prescription.

'I'm going to give you some medicine that you should take for a while to see if it eases the headaches. When you have a headache double the dose but they shouldn't be as bad.'

'Is it a tranquilliser?' Anna looked dubiously at the piece of paper.

'No, it's a new drug we prescribe to relieve migraine. I think you might find it helpful, and when that house is ready I'd love to see it.'

'You and Douglas must come down.' Anna got up and shrugged on her jacket. 'And thanks. I'm so sorry I kept you.'

'What are friends for?' Katie murmured as she saw her to the door. 'Oh, and of course there will be a bill.'

They both laughed, embraced on the steps and then Anna went to her car while Katie, with a wave of her hand disappeared round the corner into New Cavendish Street.

Anna sat on the lawn with baby Harriet on the rug beside her. Chubby and strong, she was growing into an even more beautiful baby and Anna drooled over her. Anna and Harriet were alone. Peter was up in London, Guy on holiday abroad and Fiona and Sal had gone into Bournemouth on a shopping expedition.

Anna sat back on her hands, face raised to the sun. Little Harriet, strapped in her baby rocker, chubby fists beating the air, gurgled with laughter, bubbles running down her chin. Anna turned and looked at her and was suddenly aware of such a profound maternal urge, a totally unexpected flow of feeling that was so intense that she knew she envied Fiona her baby and wished that she had one too; that Harriet was indeed hers.

She leaned over to Harriet and gave her a finger. Harriet grasped it in her podgy little fist and tried to stuff it in her mouth. Anna rolled over on her tummy and, undoing the strap that fastened the baby in, lifted her out so that she lay beside her, Anna's arm protectively round Harriet.

In a way Harriet was hers, or almost. Fiona seemed to have grown more and more distant from her baby, less interested in her, and had also taken to going up again to London while Sal was left in charge, or Anna or Peter came hurrying down to take over.

It was so awful that Fiona who'd wanted the baby had turned into such an indifferent mother, and Anna and Peter felt strongly the need to compensate. It was no chore. It was a pleasure but, still, it was a pity. There was no substitute for a natural mother as Fiona had so often pointed out to Anna. What an irony there was there!

Weatherwise it had so far been a glorious summer, at least in the West Country. But it had also been an anxious one, mainly because of the growing distance between Fiona and Harriet, the worry of what would happen if Fiona continued to be as bored with the country as she obviously was now and wanted to take her up to London. What rights would Anna and Peter have then if she did? Supposing they disappeared into a squat and Harriet ended up traipsing after her mother, if she adopted a hippy lifestyle?

It didn't bear thinking about.

One of the workmen called from the house and Anna looked up. It was almost finished and in record time. The rooms had been decorated, all the improvements made and the carpets laid. A lot of furniture had been brought down from the London house, which was now on the market, while Anna and Peter searched for a pied à terre. They enjoyed in their spare time making forays to auction rooms up and down the county and emerging with some piece of furniture which they bore triumphantly back to Hall Farm like a trophy.

Anna stood up, and taking Harriet in her arms walked across the lawn to the workman who, a pencil behind his ear and a plank under his arm, asked her which way she wanted the door to open, inwards or outwards.

'What do you think?' she asked shading her eyes from the sun.

'I'd say outwards,' the workman replied. 'That way you have more room indoors.'

'Of course.' Anna agreed and accompanied him round the house to look at the half-completed conservatory.

'It has to be big enough to hold a vine,' she said, looking at it doubtfully.

'Oh it will, Mrs Livingstone,' he replied genially. 'You could grow a palm tree in here.'

'Doubt if we'd want that.' Anna shifted Harriet, who had reached out to try and grab the workman's hair, from one arm to another.

'She's a lovely little thing,' the workman, whose name was Jerry, chucked her under the chin, 'your granddaughter, madam?'

'Yes,' Anna nodded.

'She's like you.'

'Thank you.'

'Not that you look old enough to be a grandmother,' he said, regarding her thoughtfully.

'I'm a step-grandma,' she said. 'My husband was married twice.'

'Ah, I see.'

Jerry returned to his task and Anna, still hugging Harriet,

who felt so natural, so at home in her arms, wandered through the garden inspecting the improvements that had been made, all the plants they had planted, the enlargement and development of several herbaceous borders, the beginnings of an arboretum, a fishpond being constructed in the middle of the patio that had been laid at one side and which caught the sun all day long. There would be a fountain in the middle which at night would be lit by spotlights at the side of the house. It was partly surrounded by a high wall which one day would be covered by honeysuckle, clematis and climbing roses already planted underneath.

In five years' time, Peter said, the place would be transformed. Anna hoped it would be very much sooner. She gazed for a while at the river and then, sensing that Harriet was sleepy, went indoors and took her upstairs for her afternoon nap.

Next to her and Peter's bedroom was a nursery where Harriet slept when Fiona was away. There was a room for Sal on the other side and then Guy's room beyond that. Guest bedrooms were on the top floor.

The whole house was light and airy. Sunlight flooded in from every aspect, and even on dull days its mellow, pastel-coloured walls and white paintwork dispelled the gloom. Anna had taken a month off work, though she had a computer, a fax, two telephone lines, and was able to keep in touch with the office, which anyway was slacker during the summer than at other periods.

Anna put Harriet in her cot and for a while remained with her, watching her eyes grow heavy, allowing her finger to be clutched in the little hand as a kind of comforter until Harriet fell asleep and the clasp slackened.

Anna loved her so much that she felt she was hers, a strange and dangerous feeling given the uncertainty, the precariousness of the situation. What would she do if Fiona took her away? Would they attempt to have Harriet made a ward of court? Better not to think, not to envisage such an awful situation which, anyway, might never happen.

Anna drew her finger away and, standing up, rearranged the bedclothes over the beloved baby's shoulder, not too tight and not too loose. To add to the anxieties of parents there was all this worry now about sudden infant death syndrome, something that had never been heard of twenty years before, though it must have been around for ever.

She tiptoed out of the nursery, switching on the baby alarm as she went which would take the sound of Harriet's cries, her lightest movement, to every part of the house. She went downstairs to her study where the fax and computer were installed. There were a couple of messages for her on the fax which she read and, discarding one, dealt with the other, faxing her London secretary back with the answer to the enquiry. She had chosen the room because of the view it had of the garden sloping down to the river, the fields with their grazing cattle rising on the other side. Even watching a cow chewing its cud could induce a soporific effect, and near her on her desk were powerful binoculars and a book to enable her to identify the many different birds alighting on the lawn.

In the background, but not obtrusive, was the sound of workmen banging, and outside the caw-caw of the crows and jackdaws, the cooing of the collared doves.

Anna closed her eyes and gently inhaled, as though she were breathing in the atmosphere of the countryside – no wonder it had inspired so many poets and writers, no wonder it had filled them with a sense of peace.

But how long would this peace last and what would happen if the restless Fiona took her baby to London, as she had every right to do, and one day disappeared? She could forbid them to see her daughter; she could in fact do anything she liked. The only hope was a judge, if it came to that, might be sympathetic. But what if, like Errol, she couldn't be *found*?

Anna cupped her head between her hands and stared out of the window. And what of her, Anna's complex emotions; the bond she had with Harriet? Was that natural, when she was not even related to the child by ties of blood?

She decided to abandon her profitless and futile line of thought and spent the afternoon in her office, resisting the strong temptation to return to the garden until she had finished her work. She was so used to keeping her emotions under control that she could achieve things that other people regarded as impossible: staying indoors on a hot day, refusing to be tempted out until the tasks she had set herself were done. Some people said she was inhuman, but she knew that for her a frame within which to work was essential.

At four she went to make a cup of tea for herself and the workmen, taking pleasure in the now completed and well-equipped kitchen with its huge stove, polished working surfaces, deep fridge-freezer, dishwasher and all the appurtenances of modern domestic aids that the Hansons would never have dreamt of. She took a tray to the men in the conservatory and then went into the garden, sipping her tea under Harriet's window so that she would hear if she cried out. The baby was sleeping for a long time today, the heat must have made her tired. Then, suddenly, a feeling of apprehension overwhelmed her and, leaving her cup, she dashed into the house and upstairs, threw open the door . . . Harriet, fully awake, kicked her legs in the air and, giving a deep-throated chuckle, seemed to hold out her arms to welcome Anna.

'Oh, my *precious*,' Anna cried, dashing over to the cot and taking the baby in her arms. 'Oh, Harriet, I do so *love* you.' She smothered her face with kisses only looking up when she realised that she and Harriet were no longer alone in the room.

Sal stood in the doorway, mouth agape.

'Did something happen? Is she alright?'

'Yes, she's fine.' Anna looked at her foolishly. 'I was just sitting in the garden enjoying it all so much. I'd put Harriet down about two and I suddenly realised she'd been asleep for a *long* time, you know usually it's an hour and I thought . . .'

'Cot death . . .' Sal murmured.

'I dashed upstairs and oh . . . there she was,' Anna pressed her cheek to the baby's head again. 'Oh, Sal, wasn't I *silly*?'

'Very silly,' Sal said prosaically, taking Harriet from her and lying her on the table where her nappies and creams and powders were kept. She put on a clean nappy and handed her back to Anna who cradled her gently in her arms.

'You're so *sensible*, Sal.'

'So are you.' Sal busily put the tops on the cream, the lids on the jars. 'Or you were.'

'When it comes to Harriet . . .'

Sal looked as though she was unsure whether or not to say what was on her mind and then decided she would.

'Anna, take care. You're *not* her mother.'

'I *know* that, Sal,' Anna said in a subdued voice, 'and I would never want to be or pretend to be. Fiona's her mother and we all do what we can to help Fiona . . .'

'Well, Fiona has gone off to London,' Sal said abruptly. 'Asked me to tell you. Said she'd be in touch . . .'

'London?' Anna looked aghast. '*Again?* Where, when?'

'She went to Bournemouth to buy a new suitcase and some clothes. She seemed very excited, somehow not quite all there. Like she was on a high. Then we drove home and she dropped me off at the gate. She said she was going to the cottage to pick up some things and she'd give us a call.'

'Did she say for how long?' Anna asked.

'No. But I don't think it was spur of the moment. There was something odd about her today, couldn't quite put my finger on it, you know. But she took me quite unawares when she put me off at the gate. I mean what could I do?'

'I'm going to ring the cottage,' Anna said. 'She can't just take off like that,' and, hurrying to the telephone, she dialled the number, stood there tapping her feet impatiently while it rang. Finally she put the phone down.

'Not there,' she said.

'Oh, she'll have gone by now. My feeling is that she was in a hurry, as if she was going to meet someone. She was all excited. Oh, and she had her hair and nails done in Bournemouth. Looked really nice in her new clothes, really pretty. I suppose I should have asked, but I didn't. I couldn't stop her, could I?' Sal suddenly looked worried, as though stricken with a sense of guilt. 'I mean I hadn't the right, had I? There was nothing I could do.'

As Sal stared at Anna and Anna stared back it was as though something had fallen from a great height and dropped to the ground without making any disturbance, any sound.

Anna paused outside the house and looked up at the lighted windows. The facade had been freshly painted, the brickwork repointed. It could have been a yuppy-type house on the fringes of Camden Town and Islington, not far from the Holloway Road. The neat black iron railing with its forbidding spikes had been freshly varnished. She rang the bell for a long time before she realised it might not be working so, as there was a large brass knocker on the door, she gave it a good hard bang.

Someone upstairs threw open a window and looked down.

'Yes?'

'Is er . . . May I come in?'

'Who are you?'

'Anna Livingstone . . .'

'Oh, Anna Livingstone,' a voice said, and she could hear someone inside bounding down the stairs. Then the door was thrown open and a large, big-breasted woman she recognised as Maeve stood on the doorstep. Fortunately, she had a smile on her face. Anna hadn't known what the existing members of the squat felt about her now after the eviction.

'Anna, what are you doing here?' Maeve asked, her smile friendly enough, but she didn't ask her in.

'I just wanted a bit of help.' Anna tried to look past the vast circumference of Maeve, but it was difficult. 'I wondered if I might come in?' She looked over her shoulder. 'It's pelting with rain.'

'Come in, come in, Anna,' Maeve said briskly and drew her into the hall shutting the door behind her. 'We have to be careful who we let in. So many people just try and barge in. Squatters you know,' she sniffed derisively and led Anna up the flight of stairs to the first floor landing where she recognised another amiable face leaning over the banister.

'Hi, Anna!' the man said, and held out his hand.

Biff Cassidy had always been a charmer, an easy talker despite a string of convictions for theft, pimping and drug pushing. He was about thirty-five with long flaxen hair and a ring through his nose. He was clean-shaven and wore jeans, a T-shirt and sandals. It was Biff who had attacked Jim, butted him with his head, but his manner was amiable enough now.

Biff led the way into a large front room which was well-decorated and quite tastefully if sparsely furnished. It had a full set of curtains held back by a tie.

Some of the furniture looked quite good, and in the corner was a large double divan with an attractive oriental throw-over and scatter cushions. There was a gas fire in the hearth and something cooking on a small Belling stove in the corner.

'Nice,' Anna said approvingly, looking round.

'Better than the warehouse, eh, Anna?'

'I think so.'

Biff pointed to a cane chair and Anna sat down on it.

'How many people have you got here?'

'About eight couples, four singles and some kids. Some are from the original squat and some are new; but we vet those we allow in very carefully. They have to be voted in and behave themselves, otherwise they get thrown out; we work very closely with the social services. They have to keep their rooms clean *and* help with the common parts. We take a great pride in the place and hope that once we can get jobs and pay rent the Council will let us keep it. We don't want people to think we're a bunch of hoodlums, because we're not.

'Though it's due for demolition,' Biff went on. 'The whole area is to be developed. A drink, Anna?'

'I'd like coffee or tea if you've got it.'

Maeve went over to the sink and filling the kettle with water plugged it in and switched it on. Then she got out three mugs from a rack over the sink and plopped a teabag in each. The room vaguely smelt of incense, or maybe it was hash. Old habits died hard, if they died at all, but there was a joss stick burning away in the corner.

'What help is it you want, Anna?' Biff lay on the divan, his eyes bright with interest.

'I want to try and find Errol. You remember him?'

'Errol?' Maeve turned from the stove, an expression of surprise on her face. 'I thought he went off with your girl?'

'He did. But he left her.'

'Oh, dear, that would be Errol.' Maeve chuckled, pouring water on the teabags and, after stirring and adding milk, brought Anna's over to her. 'Not what you'd call reliable.'

'An eye on the main chance.' Biff lit a cigarette and stuck it between his lips. 'Thought he liked the cushy life, so I wonder he left her. No, we've not seen him.'

'Would you know anyone who had?' Feeling dejected at the news, Anna looked at the people she had befriended and failed, but who obviously bore her no grudge.

'Why is it so important to find Errol?' Maeve joined Biff on the divan. 'Did he nick something?'

'Yes, he did when he left her. He took everything he could lay his hands on – TV, video, hi-fi. I suppose he wanted to sell them. But I'm not here about that. Fiona has now disappeared and we think she may be with him.'

Biff let out a whistle.

'Why would she want to do that?'

'She loved him I guess.' Anna found herself trying to avoid their scrutiny. 'Fiona had a child. Errol is the father.'

Biff whistled again.

'A dear little girl,' there was a catch in Anna's voice, 'called Harriet. Errol left Fiona before Harriet was born. She seemed OK at first and then she started to pine for him. She became moody and neglected the baby. First of all when he left she never mentioned Errol, but much later when she did we realised how much she'd missed him. I don't think she really wanted a baby, but it happened and she thought, wrongly, as it turned out, that it would tie Errol to her. It did just the opposite.'

'Poor kid.' Maeve, Anna remembered, had three children who didn't seem to be about.

'Where are your kids, Maeve?' she asked.

'Oh, they'll be with friends somewhere.' Maeve jerked her head towards the window. 'They're getting older now you know, Anna. The youngest is twelve, the eldest fifteen.'

'And doing very well at school,' Biff said proudly though Anna knew that Biff was a good bit younger than Maeve and the children weren't his.

'I'm very glad that things turned out all right.' Anna sipped her scalding tea and then carefully put the mug on the floor. 'It was an extremely painful business for me.'

'For us all in retrospect,' Biff said. 'We all behaved rather badly, especially towards you. It was a tough time. No hard feelings, Anna?'

'None at all.' She raised her head and smiled. 'What happened, by the way, to Damian and Arizona?'

Maeve snorted. 'They got married!'

'*Married?*' The statement amazed Anna.

'They went all respectable. Damian's father died and left

him some property so he and Arizona moved into the family mansion and kicked out his mother.'

'Well, I don't know.'

'Stranger things happen at sea.'

Anna rose. 'No idea at all then where I could find Errol?'

'Do you really want to find him?' Biff leaned over to the table next to the divan and stubbed out his cigarette.

'Of course I do. Why shouldn't I?'

'What makes you think the girl is with him?'

'Because of the way she left. She had her hair done and bought a complete set of new clothes. She also had her own car. The friend she was with on the day she disappeared said she was excited, as if she was going to meet someone, and she never had another boyfriend except Errol. We think he'd got in touch with her, or she somehow found out where he was and went to meet him.'

Biff slowly shook his head and Anna, feeling suddenly apprehensive, looked at him.

'What's the matter, Biff?'

'Errol was very heavily into the drug scene you know, Anna. There's no doubt that he couldn't do without the stuff. He would have nicked your daughter's property to sell to buy heroin or speed. I'm afraid that if your daughter has ended up with him she may be in trouble. Deep trouble.'

'Heroin?' Anna whispered.

Biff nodded. 'And he knew where to get the pure stuff. It's lethal.'

Anna put her head in her hands, her thoughts racing.

'Could you *please* help me find him?' she asked, raising her head. 'It seems absolutely essential that we do.'

'We'll do all we can. Leave us your telephone number. But we have lost touch. Mind you, one or two people may know. We'll ask around.' Maeve put a hand on Anna's arm and squeezed it. 'We owe you one, Anna. You did a lot for us and we were an ungrateful bunch of swine.'

CHAPTER 16

Anna looked up from her desk at the knock on the door.

'Come in,' she called, and then rapidly went on with writing her report ready to give to her secretary before she left. 'Shan't be a minute,' she said without raising her head. 'I've just got about five lines left to do.'

There was a distinctly masculine cough and she looked up sharply.

'Oh, David, I'm so sorry. I thought it was Joyce.'

'Carry on,' David said affably with a wave of his hand. 'We don't want to keep Joyce waiting.'

Anna glanced at her watch.

'As a matter of fact she's probably gone. I'll leave it in her "In" tray.'

It was Thursday and Anna's last working day of the week. So much had to be done.

'Do you mind if I just ring home?' Anna picked up the phone, smiling apologetically at David. 'It won't take a minute.'

'Go ahead, but I shan't keep you.'

'Sal,' Anna spoke to the person at the end of the line, 'everything alright? Good. Good.' Looking at her watch again. 'I should think about eight or nine,' she glanced across at David. 'The boss has just come in so . . .'

'It won't take a minute,' he hissed.

'Says he won't keep me long, but I know him. Good.' Anna listened to some more words from Sal at the other end. 'Give her a kiss from me. A big hug. Right. I'll see you.' She replaced the receiver and joined her hands, composed, smiling across the desk at David, inviting him to sit down.

'I'm all yours.'

'Everything well at home?'

'Everything is fine.' Anna sighed. 'As far as it can be. We keep the . . . tragedy of Fiona's disappearance as far to the back of our minds as we can, but of course it isn't easy. It's always there, like a wound.'

'Naturally,' David nodded sympathetically. 'How old is Harriet now, Anna?'

'She's just a year old,' Anna said with a sigh. 'We're having a party for her at the weekend. It seems incredible doesn't it?'

'How the time flies. Who would have thought, this time last year . . . Do you think Fiona will ever come back?'

'I don't know what we think, quite honestly. Of course we hope she will. We've done everything we can to find her. My old friends in the squatters' community are helping. It's possible she and Errol went abroad. Thailand, somewhere where drugs are easy to find.'

'Terrible for you and Peter.' David cracked his knuckles, raising both arms over his head as if in an effort to relax. 'All of which doesn't make this any easier to say, Anna.'

'Oh?' Immediately that little ball of lead lodged beside her heart, so familiar by now it was almost like a friend.

'Anna, you do *know* how much we appreciate all you have done while you've been with us and . . .'

'This sounds like the "goodbye", David.'

'No, Anna it is not "goodbye", emphatically not. At least we hope not.' He paused and looked at her. 'But the fact is, Anna, and it is *quite* understandable, that however hard you've tried, and I know you have, you have not been pulling your weight and Michael Lawrence has had a lot of the extra burden to carry.'

'I think that's unfair, David. I know I work part-time but I take work home. I am here sometimes at seven in the morning and don't leave until eight or nine at night. The fax and phone are going all the time I'm at home.'

'I'm sure of that, Anna; but it is the daily grind and it doesn't seem fair on Michael to have to take on much of your work as well as his . . .'

'That's quite untrue,' Anna interrupted heatedly.

'On the contrary, Anna,' David spoke quietly as was his custom when telling people unpleasant news, 'he had to appear at the Crown Court at the last minute last week because the little girl was ill.'

'That's true,' Anna bit her lip. They thought that she'd swallowed something that was making her choke and had to rush her to the Royal Free. 'I couldn't possibly have left Harriet . . .'

'Of *course* you couldn't, Anna.' His voice was very gentle now, 'that's my point. You're a woman standing in place of the baby's mother. I know how you feel about her, how much she means to you. We all are deeply sensitive of the trials you and Peter have been through in the last few years and think you have coped marvellously.'

'Come to the point, David.' Anna began to feel vaguely nauseous.

'I want to make Michael Lawrence head of the section and ask you to be a consultant, Anna. I know you wouldn't like to go into second place and this does seem the best way out.'

'Consultant?' Anna looked incredulous. 'I'm being kicked upstairs, is that it?'

'No, not at all, a consultancy is a most important position . . .'

'All the consultants in my experience have been people either well past their sell-by date, or who have committed some serious misdemeanour that nearly had them struck off the roll. Neither of which applies to me. I am not yet forty and remain in control of all my faculties.'

'Anna, *no one* is disputing that and, believe me, if the volume of work was not such and, above all, if Michael felt more amenable this wouldn't arise. But he doesn't. He's going to leave if he doesn't get overall control and I'm sure he means it.'

'I'm sure he does,' Anna said grimly and leaned her chin on her cupped hands staring in front of her.

The truth was really, in a nutshell, she and Michael Lawrence were incompatible. They respected each other but personally they didn't get on. Their relationship was polite but formal. She supposed it had been inevitable that Michael would use his position, his comparative youth, somehow to get her out of the way.

'Let me think about it,' she said at last standing up, getting her things together.

'It's no reflection on you personally, Anna.'

'Oh, but it is,' she said, her eyes flashing. 'I'm sure a lot of women would be able to keep down running a home, a busy law practice, a job as a councillor and so on.'

'But not many, Anna. Not without more support than you've got. Peter has his own busy job, and you have two rather difficult kids.'

Anna suddenly slumped back into her chair, feeling stupidly weak and vulnerable.

'I feel I've been a failure in my career, David, to be given the boot before I'm forty.'

David's expression was agonised, and she thought he was about to reach for her hand, then thought better of it. Instead he leaned forward, gazing at her earnestly. 'Oh, but you have not, Anna. You've been incredibly successful. You've made more money as an individual than anyone else in this practice.'

'Money isn't everything,' she said bitterly.

'Well, it helps. You have also combined with this a lot of voluntary work that only does you credit. Now you have the heartache of wondering what has happened to Fiona, the worry and responsibility of taking care of Harriet. As a family man, I know the toll all this has taken of you, and I think you coped brilliantly.

'But Michael Lawrence is young. He resents hanging about, referring decisions he is quite capable of taking himself, day to day routine matters, to you. You must appreciate his position and, believe me, as a consultant you will be very valuable to us indeed. Besides,' he looked at her slyly, 'apart from releasing you from the day to day trivia there is the money side. The fees consultancies bring can be quite substantial, and with your added responsibilities – a baby, a large home in the country, I'm sure that you'd want to feel the financial side as well taken care of. And it will be. Man cannot live on bread alone, Anna.'

Indeed man could not, nor woman. Anna turned off the A303 towards Shaftesbury and now she always felt she really was home, only a few miles and she would be there. Sal would have a meal ready and maybe Harriet would still be awake to greet her. The following day there was the birthday party with local babies. Peter was coming down in the morning and Guy driving over from the agricultural college where he was taking a course in farming after getting passable GCSE results the previous summer.

If only Fiona could be there. But there had been no trace of her. In the months since her disappearance, they had done everything possible, besides Anna's visit to the squatters. The police had been alerted, the Salvation Army and various missing persons bureaux had been informed. There had even been an appeal on a missing persons' programme on TV.

No one thought that Fiona was dead, but that she was alive somewhere and living with Errol. What they didn't know, couldn't know, was whether or not they would ever see her again or she would remain on the missing persons' list for ever.

When she arrived at the house Guy was already there, and Harriet had stayed up though it was past her bedtime.

As Anna came into the living room she stood at the threshold for a few moments, watching her playing on the floor with Guy who, despite his youth, was a devoted uncle. He had found it as difficult as anyone else to come to terms with Fiona's disappearance, and Anna knew that when he was in London he frequented old haunts they'd visited together to try and find news of her.

Harriet's demeanour changed when she saw Anna, and she tottered across the floor towards her outstretched arms.

'My precious one,' Anna said clutching her. 'How are you, darling?'

Harriet said, 'Mum, Mum,' and stuck her sticky fingers into Anna's face, eyes lit up with pleasure.

'Hi, Anna!' Guy held up a hand. 'Good journey down?'

'Very good. Any news from Dad?'

'He'll make it for the party. He's in Leicester.'

'Leicester? What's he doing there?' Really, they had so much to do now they scarcely saw each other.

'Some conference,' Guy shrugged his shoulders.

Sal came in, greeted Anna, said food was on the table and she and Guy should begin while she put Harriet to bed. This was a chore Anna enjoyed doing herself, but tonight she felt dead tired so she nodded and accepted Guy's offer of a drink while Sal took Harriet off to bed.

'Let's wait for Sal,' Anna said sitting next to Guy.

'Good idea. I'm not hungry anyway. How're things, Anna?'

'Well,' Anna gave a hopeless gesture. 'I don't suppose things will ever be the same until we find Fiona. If only people who do this sort of thing realised the suffering they cause.'

'They do. She must know, not only to Dad and me but you too. I don't mean,' he blushed, 'that you should care less. Oh, you know what I mean.'

The blood tie.

Anna nodded. No need to be reminded about the blood tie.

'Dad's terrifically cut up about it. He seems to be working flat out.'

'Yes, doesn't he?'

Always away. It never used to be like this. Maybe he'd taken comfort with a woman who could give him just that extra special bit of attention that Anna, with all she had to do, denied him.

'Oh, I've got a bit of news,' she said suddenly, and then seeing the expression on Guy's face said apologetically, 'no, I'm sorry, it's not about Fiona. That I would have told you immediately. David Cole wants me to give up being the joint head of the Wigmore Street practice. They've offered me a consultancy.'

'Oh!' Guy looked perplexed. 'Is that good or bad news?'

'Well, at first I thought it was bad. It's a kind way of giving me the sack. I've never got on especially well with Michael Lawrence. But he is a very capable lawyer and he's rather sick of having to consult on things with me. He's told them he'll leave if he can't take over complete responsibility.'

'And how do you feel about it?' Guy got up to refill her glass.

'At first I felt rather sick. But on the way down here – it only happened today – I thought maybe a consultancy is not such a bad deal. We're changing our lives, anyway, by selling the London house. When you've finished your course we'll start buying animals and restocking the farm. I *like* country life you know, Guy. Sometimes I feel I've had it up to here,' she drew an imaginary line across her forehead, 'with the city, office problems, the traffic, the noise, the rush. Maybe Fiona would not have gone off if I'd given her more time.'

'You can never know that. No one can.'

'I introduced her to Errol. I feel responsible for that.'

'Anna, it might have happened anyway. You can't go back

and say what might have been. You, above all people, should know that.'

Guy was right. He'd grown up so much suddenly, as if the absence of his sister made him more mature. Maybe, severally, they all felt responsible for Fiona, and if they never saw her again they would each spend the rest of their lives blaming not her but themselves, wondering where and how they'd gone so badly wrong.

Anna was up early the following morning anxious to make the best of her time in the garden before the final preparations began for the party.

Anna had found herself surprisingly adept at dealing with babies, not only Harriet. Sal, of course, was marvellous but when Anna had to cope by herself, cope she did. She knew it was this one-to-one relationship, especially at an early age, that made the bond between parent or, in her case, carer and child, so vital.

Maybe if she had been able to establish it with Fiona and Guy when they were babies the outcome might have been different. There would not have been the vague memory of Mother, producing a residue of bitterness and suppressed hostility which flared up during their adolescence.

What would Nancy have made of Fiona, had she lived, Anna wondered as she studied her plan for the border running south along the side of the lawn towards the river which allowed for a colourful display of lupins, delphiniums, pink and scarlet peonies, marguerites, dahlias, a splash that would be visible from the house and road alongside the river alike.

Trowel in hand, trays of bedding plants by her side, packet of blood and bone fertiliser at the ready, Anna sat back on her haunches. She wished she could have an instant garden full of these tall, brilliant flowers like those people who exhibited at the Chelsea Flower Show managed to produce. Instant gardening; but really to do that sort of thing one needed a full time gardener, and with all the expense of the house, Harriet, Guy's education and now her lack of a full-time job, they were going to have to rein in a bit and watch the money. The bright rays of the sun shining above the tall trees at the far side of the house began to burn her back, even at this early hour. It was going to be a hot day. Better to get everything in before the sun rose too high. Although most of the preparation for the party was done there was still the setting out to do, balloons to festoon round the house and hang at the gate.

Happiness. Anna felt herself slowly being infused by a sense of pure joy, and she closed her eyes momentarily to savour it. A slight breeze blew in from the river and the landscape seemed enveloped by an ethereal haze that made the moment a unique, almost mystical experience.

A life of solitude in the country would not mean abandoning London altogether. A consultancy would bring in some money and she could continue to give a few days a month at the Law Centre. But she decided she would resign from the Council. They wanted her to anyway – better to resign than be pushed – and all the other voluntary bodies to which she gave so much time.

She was already part weaned from the city, used to the slower pace of life in the country, the time taken in, say, the butcher's shop while one waited for ages while Mrs so and so explained what cut she liked and how she liked it and how much it should weigh and what it should look like. Then the butcher would disappear, the sound of chopping would be heard from his board around the corner out of sight and he would reappear with the joint that might, or just possibly might not, be what Mrs so and so wanted. If it was, there followed a discussion about how it should be cooked and some mention would be made, in passing, about the state of their various families, usually numerous and including children and grandchildren if they had any. If Mrs so and so did not like the joint the butcher would go back to his chopping block and try again.

It all took so much time that was both incredible and annoying to the person brought up in the city and used to the frantic pace of supermarkets, convenience shopping, traffic jams and city life.

Anna looked at her watch and jumped up. Harriet would be stirring if she wasn't already. She rushed indoors, washed her hands and then, two at a time, up to Harriet's room. But the infant, perhaps because of her relatively late night, was still asleep, although showing signs of stirring. Anna sat quietly by her side gazing at her, and then she knew how grateful she was to Fiona and Errol for giving her Harriet, a child of her own bound to her if not by blood then by a more invisible but precious commodity: love, pure and unadulterated.

Peter arrived just before lunch, his car boot packed with parcels and presents which included a large bunch of flowers for Anna.

A guilt offering? Could he have a mistress tucked away in Leicester, London, wherever? She'd looked into his eyes but saw only tenderness and love.

'How was Leicester?' she asked in the bedroom as they changed for the party.

'Very boring. We had a conference of all our overseas legal executives.'

'A likely tale,' she said doing up the buttons of her pretty cotton dress, and looking at herself in the mirror.

'But true.'

'I often do wonder if you're having an affair,' she heard herself saying, although she knew she hadn't meant to.

'Say again.' She saw him behind her looking at her in the mirror.

'You heard.'

'Don't start that again, Anna.' Peter put a hand on her

shoulder. 'You know it's like in a film or novel. It's not true.'

'You wouldn't say if it was.'

'I'm not,' his nails dug into her shoulder, 'and if you like I could ask you the same question.'

'Me?' She turned around, speechless. 'When have *I* the time for an affair?'

'I could say the same about myself.'

'Or the inclination?'

'Exactly!' He took her by both shoulders, spun her round and kissed her hard on the mouth.

Some people said that if you didn't desire your spouse you thought no one else would either. So maybe a little mutual suspicion was a good thing?

They finally came apart and, hand in hand, ran downstairs together to the lawn where already the party guests were foregathering.

Everyone knew that children's parties were exhausting. They'd hired an entertainer, but there was still a lot to do. There were the other parents to entertain as well with alcoholic refreshment after five when no one seemed to want to leave. One of the children was sick and had to be taken home, another had what was either an asthmatic attack or a spasm brought on by over-excitement and had to lie down. There was an anxious consultation about whether or not the doctor should be called but the child, one of the eldest who had had a previous attack, recovered and later rejoined the party.

By seven everyone had gone, and leaving the kitchen in a state of considerable disarray Anna, Peter, Guy and Sal collapsed on the terrace drinking white wine, while Honey went round the garden picking up the leftover bits. After a moment she was joined by Sal and Guy, leaving Anna and Peter alone on the terrace.

The swifts rose higher in the cerulean blue sky or dived low towards the trees, uttering their shrill reedy cries, while from the woods came the coos of pigeons or collared doves. Later a nightingale would start its song and later still the owls would begin their night-long dialogue as they hunted their prey.

Anna leaned back in her chair, briefly closing her eyes as Peter's hand stole into hers.

'Happy?'

'Very,' she gave him a warm, reassuring smile.

'You were wonderful.'

'So were you. So was Sal.'

'I could lead this kind of life always,' Anna murmured.

'Could you really?' Peter's clasp tightened.

'Yup.'

'Or do you just say it and you'd miss the city?'

'No.'

'Well . . .' Peter paused, 'why don't you do it?'

'Are you serious?'

'Yes, perfectly.'

'All the time? But what about money?'

'We'd manage.'

'I was going to tell you later but I'll tell you now,' Anna said. 'They want me out of the office.'

'Who wants you out?' Peter looked indignant.

'David wants me to be a consultant so that Michael Lawrence can run the place.'

There was silence for a moment.

'Sounds great,' Peter said eventually.

'You really think so?'

'Ideal.' As she turned her head their eyes met. 'Don't you think?'

'I'm gradually getting used to the idea.' Anna stretched out her legs and slipped off her sandals, rubbing her feet together, realising how tired she was. 'Trying not to feel kicked out, insulted, you know.'

From the house came the shrill sound of the telephone.

'Damn!' Anna said, opening her eyes.

'I'll get it.' Peter began to rise.

'No, I'll get it,' Anna pushed him back, 'it's bound to be some mother whose child has left a vital article of clothing.'

She almost danced to the phone. Happiness. Yes, it was within her grasp. She realised she was humming a tune sung by the kids that afternoon as they danced round in a circle.

The farmer's in his den, the farmer's in his den
Hey ho daddy oh the farmer's in his den . . .
The farmer picks a wife
The farmer picks a wife
Hey ho daddy oh the farmer picks a wife . . .

'Hello?' She lifted the receiver to her ear. For a long moment there was silence, and her heart suddenly skipped. Could it be . . .

'Anna, is that you?' a man's voice, kind of familiar, said.

'Yes. Can you speak up, you're rather faint.'

'Anna, it's me, Damian.' Anna then realised that the voice was not so much faint as cautious, as if he didn't want to be overheard.

'Damian!' Anna gave a false, rather embarrassed laugh. 'After all this time! Where are you? I hear you're married.'

He interrupted her quite brusquely. 'Anna, I can't speak for long but I've got something rather important to say and I want you to promise me that you won't get us into trouble.'

'What sort of trouble?' From joy to fear, that sudden transit that, after all, was so familiar to her.

'Anna, I know where Fiona is . . .'

'Oh my God, *Damian* . . . ' She clutched her chest.

'You've got to give me your word first. Anna . . .'

'Tell me quickly where she is.'

'You must give me your word you won't shop us to the fuzz.'

'But, Damian . . .'

'You must protect us. We've done nothing wrong, but something serious has happened and I'm running out of coins. I'm calling from a call box and if you don't give me your word I'll have to go.'

'Reverse charges!' Anna cried, but afraid he might not ring back said quickly: 'I give you my word. Where is she?'

'Your oath you won't let us get into trouble . . .'

'Look, my oath . . .'

'I *have* to go, Anna. But Fiona is sick, very sick. Now listen and I'll tell you where she is and you'd better get here soonest.'

CHAPTER 17

Peter and Anna drove at speed through the night, crossing Dorset and Wiltshire into the Gloucestershire countryside, pausing every now and then for Anna to consult a map. They spoke very little, preferring to listen to music on the car stereo, Mozart and some Vivaldi, to try and calm their agitation.

There was really nothing to talk about until they knew what had happened, Damian having rung off as soon as he had given them directions. In many ways, Anna felt this journey must be both the worst and longest of her life, though it took under three hours before they arrived at the open gates of the large house standing well back from the road.

It was a place of some size and the imposing front door had opened even before they stopped the car and Damian, followed slowly by Arizona, came over to greet them.

Peter wore a polo top sweater, jacket and flannels, Anna a baggy sweater and Marks & Spencer jogging pants. They had only stopped to pick up some money and pack an overnight bag.

'You got here very quickly,' Damian said awkwardly.

'Where is she?' Peter demanded looking at him.

'This is my husband, Peter.' Anna tried to temper Peter's annoyance, the result of his anxiety. 'Damian, Arizona,' she indicated them briefly.

Everyone nodded. It seemed no time for social niceties. Also, to Anna, it seemed light years had elapsed since her brief fling with Damian.

'Hi, Arizona!' she acknowledged her.

'Hi, Anna!' Arizona's voice sounded lifeless, frightened; all the former confidence and heartiness was completely lacking. She wore a caftan festooned with beads, but was very far from her old self.

Anna was looking impatiently towards the house.

'She's not here.' Damian's voice was strained. 'There's a cottage in the grounds. When my grandfather owned the place it was quite something and the gamekeeper lived there. They . . .'

'How did she come to be here?' Peter's tone was still threatening and Anna remembered how frightened Damian had been and nudged him, saying to Damian: 'You'd better lead the way.'

'I'll wait in the house.' Arizona turned towards the door. 'I'll have something ready for you when you come back.' She held out a hand to Damian as though giving him strength. Anna's feeling of apprehension mounted to panic. Damian turned and led the way around the house, across the lawn towards the outbuildings and a cottage that stood some distance away, a mere shadow in the dark. It was nearly midnight and the welcome, familiar hoot of an owl came from somewhere way back in the woods. How Anna wished they were home and not here; that Damian's nocturnal call had never happened. There was a light on in the cottage but the door was locked, and as they stood in front of it rigid with tension Damian produced a key, looked at them and gave a deep sigh.

'I'm terribly sorry,' he said.

Peter pushed past him, closely followed by Anna. They went immediately into the room where the light came from. A very low light was on by the side of a divan in which, huddled amid bedclothes pulled right up to her chin, lay Fiona, the tip of her head just visible. There was a noxious smell in the room which Anna couldn't place: not drugs, not urine nor faeces.

Maybe a mixture of all three, plus decay, damp. She shivered with horror at the notion that Fiona should end up in a place like this.

Damian lurked in the doorway while Peter hurried over to his daughter's bed. Then he stopped and looked over at Anna.

'You do it,' he said.

'Do what?' She went up to the bed.

'Touch her . . . see if she's . . .'

Suddenly the truth struck Anna; the stillness of the figure on the bed, the stench which she now realised was vomit.

Remembering that the female of the species was stronger than the male, two members of which species now seemed heavily dependent on her, she went over to the bed and slowly drew back the covers, stared at the ashen face, eyes closed as if in a deep sleep. But there was no sign of breathing; instead from her half-open mouth a sickly dribble seemed to have congealed, perhaps for days. Anna touched Fiona's jugular, put another hand against her cheek. It was as cold as marble.

'I think she's dead.' She turned to Peter. 'Oh, my darling, I am so so sorry.' She flung her arms round him as he raised his head and gave a cry like an animal caught in a trap. Anna cradled him for a moment feeling the tears on his face. 'I think she just fell asleep . . . I'm sure she felt no pain. She seems so peaceful.'

And indeed Fiona did look peaceful, curled up in her familiar foetal position, her finger resting against her chest looking as though it had slipped from her mouth. For some reason Anna thought of the tale told in the Bible of the daughter of Jairus: 'she is not dead but sleepeth'. Would that same miracle could bring Fiona back to life.

Peter still seemed incapable of movement so Anna turned to Damian and said quietly: 'We simply must call the police.'

'Anna, you *promised,*' Damian looked pathetically over to her.

'I didn't know she was dead,' Anna said in as gentle, as reasonable a tone as she could. 'The police must know,

Damian. If you had nothing to do with this you have nothing to fear.'

'Of course I had nothing to do with it.' Damian kneaded his hands. 'But I wanted to tell you first, to explain . . . We knew nothing. We found her like this. Called you at once.'

'You didn't know she was *here*?' Peter said looking incredulous.

'Oh, yes, of course we knew, but . . .' Damian hung his head as if lost for words.

'Why don't we go over to the house?' Anna said in a practical tone of voice, 'and you can tell us what happened. The police will be able to find out when Fiona died, and the longer you leave it the worse it will be.'

'But it was *nothing* to do with us.'

'Still, not reporting a death is an offence, I'm afraid. Let's get it over with. As you say you know nothing; and I believe you. All that will be required is a statement.' She looked around: 'I suppose Errol has done another bunk?'

Damian nodded. 'I think Fiona's been like this a day or two.'

Anna went back to the divan and drew the duvet up to cover Fiona's head. She let her hand rest there for a moment, wishing with all her heart that she could bring the dead girl back to life like the daughter of Jairus. Then she put her arm through Peter's and drew him towards the door.

Damian, having already preceded them, waited for them outside.

'Leave the light on,' Peter said suddenly turning to Anna as her hand reached for the switch. 'I don't want her . . .' and then he began to weep softly again. 'I don't want her to be alone in the dark.'

Anna left the light on and shut the door without looking at the bed again.

As they followed Damian back across the yard she thought it was like a mournful procession of hurt, bereaved, frightened people. When they got near the house the front door again swung open as if Arizona had been watching their progress through the grounds.

Inside it was cold. It also smelt of damp and neglect, as sinister as the doomladen cottage.

'I've made tea and sandwiches,' Arizona said as they trooped into the hall.

'Thanks.'

'I don't suppose you had time to eat,' Arizona went on.

'No, we didn't.'

'Maybe you'd like a whisky?' Damian led them into a room full of bulky, old-fashioned furniture.

'Whisky would be nice,' Anna said, rubbing her hands, and while Damian went out and Peter slumped into one of the chairs she looked around.

It was a large depressing room, almost a time warp of a past age. Obviously in its heyday the house had been one of the great places of Gloucestershire. The Bradleys were unknown to Anna but, doubtless, they had been a name in the county. The double entrance doors through which they'd entered gave way to a large baronial hall which, like the room they were now in, appeared to have seen better times.

The wooden floors were covered by rugs of undoubted antiquity, and probably value, but most of them were threadbare and beyond repair. The furniture was heavy, some of it good; but it must have been years since it had seen any polish. The sofas and armchairs were covered in a variety of materials: brocade, leather, even chintz, but they were all frayed and looked as though they were home to numerous small, unwelcome creatures. Heavy chandeliers hung from the smoke-darkened ceiling, their crystal lozenges yellowed by time, and on the floor and the rickety occasional tables were lamps, some with their shades askew, some with large burn marks; others lacked shades altogether and the naked bulbs winked unflinchingly in the gloom.

With an unsteady hand Arizona poured the tea into mugs which Damian passed round. His hands too were unsteady. Both had clearly had a profound shock.

Damian offered sandwiches which Peter declined. Anna took one out of politeness.

'Errol came to us about a year ago,' Damian said, sitting opposite Peter. 'He was looking for work and had heard through the grapevine that we lived here. Errol was in a bad way, depressed and heavily into drugs. He told us about Fiona and the baby which he guessed must have been born by then. He felt he couldn't cope with the baby, but I think he did love Fiona.'

'Love her!' Peter exploded. 'The way he treated her. You call *that* love? Leaving her in the lurch when she was pregnant and stealing everything he could lay his hands on.'

'He had a very bad habit.' Damian sat uneasily on the edge of his chair. 'He kept on trying to give it up, but he couldn't.'

'I wish you'd told me,' Anna said bitterly.

Damian gave an expressive shrug. 'How could I know what would happen? I didn't know he'd go off with Fiona. By then, it was too late anyway. The thing with Errol was that he couldn't take responsibility. When he came to us we were sorry for him and let him stay in the cottage. He said he wanted to kick the habit and go back to Fiona. You might have heard I inherited this place when my father died. I would like to restore it to what it was, but it's a terribly expensive business. The little money my father left went to my mother who wouldn't let me have a penny because she disapproved of my lifestyle. My grandfather had entailed the house for me. My mother and I never got on. When I turned up to claim my inheritance with Arizona she tried to prevent me coming into the house.'

'Called the *fuzz*.' Momentarily Arizona came to life, showing something of the old sparkle. 'His *own* mother.'

'Mother had no legal right,' Damian said, 'and it was soon

sorted out. She left and not long after that Errol turned up.'

'How did he know where you were?'

'He always kept in touch with some of the brethren who knew where we were.'

'What a pity,' Anna murmured.

'It was not a good day when Errol found us, but we didn't know that. There was something very likeable about Errol and I was happy when he went off with Fiona. I thought it would change him permanently. In many ways I do think he did want to settle down and come off drugs. But it's so hard once you've got a habit. He said he wanted to try, and would do up the cottage and give us a hand with the house.' Damian glanced towards the ceiling. 'It has almost as many leaks as the warehouse.

'For a while we all worked well. Errol seemed a lot better and to have ideas about making a nest for him, Fiona and the baby. He got in touch with her. Then she arrived one day in her car, some luggage, not much, but no baby.

'They seemed very happy together, but we never spoke to Fiona alone. We understood, however, that when the place was in order they would collect the baby, maybe get married.

'However this didn't last long. Errol was back on his habit and we think he got Fiona on to it. We saw less and less of them and there was obviously no work going on either at the cottage or here. They wanted to be left alone. We respected that. We had our own problems; what to do about the house, harassment by the social services who said we shouldn't be claiming benefits . . . you know, the usual sort of thing. Then Errol started to stay away and leave Fiona alone. I guess he was stealing to finance his habit. By then Fiona had probably started on it too . . .'

'If only you could have let me *know* . . . ' Anna tried hard to stem her rising anger.

'Look, we aren't into the business of grassing on other people, Anna. You know that. We let everyone lead their own lives, as we like to lead ours. Don't we?' He looked over at Arizona who nodded her confirmation. It was bitterly cold in the house and Anna felt as though her body was petrifying. 'Well this time he stayed away, and the car was there and there was no sign of Fiona. Arizona went over this afternoon . . .'

Arizona suddenly put her hands over her face, bent so low that she nearly touched her knees, rocked from side to side. 'It was so terrible,' she murmured, 'something I'll never forget.'

'She was dead?' Anna whispered, and Arizona nodded.

'I simply didn't know what to do. I knew it was too late to call a doctor and we should tell the police, but we have had *so* much trouble with the authorities. You know what bastards they are. And you are so kind, Anna . . .' as if pleading with her Arizona held out her hand, 'we hoped you'd understand that we did our best.'

Ex-Labour Councillor's daughter in drug tragedy

An inquest was held on Fiona Livingstone, stepdaughter of Mrs Anna Livingstone, once a prominent Labour Councillor tipped at one time as a future Member of Parliament. Mrs Livingstone and her husband Peter testified as to their daughter's mental state at an inquest held in Gloucester on Friday. Nineteen year old Fiona Livingstone was found dead in a cottage on an estate in a remote part of Gloucestershire where she had been living with a man who has since disappeared.

A pathologist testified to the cause of death as being due to an overdose of an unusually pure form of heroin compounded with a large quantity of alcohol. The Coroner heard evidence from Mr Damian Bradley, on whose estate the cottage is situated, that Miss Livingstone had missed her parents and her baby whom she had left in their care.

Police said that all attempts to trace Mr Errol

Murphy, who lived with Miss Livingstone, had failed.

Superintendent Francis Morris said that there were a number of deaths from overdoses relating to pure heroin in the area and attempts were being made to find the dealer with a view to charging him with manslaughter.

The Coroner expressed his condolences to Mr and Mrs Livingstone, who he said were in no way to blame for the tragedy. Mr Damian Bradley was also completely exonerated from blame.

Anna sat on an upturned packing case, the pages spread out on her knees. At times the report had been blurred by tears, and when she finished she gave her nose a good blow.

It was three months since Fiona had been found dead, the inquest having twice been adjourned while the police tried to find Errol, who they believed was the main supplier of drugs in the area. It was thought now that he had escaped abroad.

The Coroner had released Fiona's body for burial in Dorset in a grave next to her mother, and almost at the same time a purchaser had been found for the London house. Completion was due tomorrow.

One more trip from the removal lorry and the house would be empty, ready for its new owners. Anna put the paper on one side and got up, pacing restlessly to the window, looking out, and back to the paper again. All the papers had carried reports, one even giving a brief history of her career: prominent Labour Councillor, well known solicitor, regular do-gooder, the implication being 'look where it got you?' The business of the squat was revived and raked over again, and a link with it, Fiona and Errol established.

It had been a dreadful time; so much going on and so much speculation, which was unjust, which had caused the Coroner to emphasise that she and Peter were in no way to blame for what had happened.

But the papers didn't let it go at that. Why should a nineteen year old girl run away and leave her baby, if she was properly treated at home? If people understood her? Perhaps there was an element of disapproval on the part of her establishment-minded parents? Did she get all the help and understanding she had a right to especially from someone who spent hours, perhaps too many, doing voluntary work? To compound it all Anna was a *stepmother*: and the stereotype of the dreaded stepmother who made no effort to understand her step-children was reviewed, with many case histories presented from fact as well as fiction.

Anna saw the removal van draw up outside the front door so went down to greet the men.

'Just one load,' she called, 'and that's it.'

'All to the Barbican, Mrs Livingstone?'

'All to the Barbican. The stuff for the country all went down yesterday.'

She stood watching them while they put the boxes containing books and various ornaments, a couple of chairs and a small chest from the hall, into the van.

'That all, madam?'

'That's all.' She stood on the steps watching them as they shut the back of the van, locked it and, with a wave, jumped into the cab.

She followed the progress of the van as it went slowly downhill and disappeared round the corner, out of sight. In the front garden the SOLD notice creaked eerily in the wind.

She walked back into the house, and went slowly through the rooms, checking that they were all empty, nothing was missed. First, hers and Peter's. How many times had they made love in the double bed which had now gone to the Barbican? How many rows, reconciliations, talks behind the closed door? Too many to remember.

She closed the door and then walked along the corridor to Fiona's. Once again she stood outside, aware of that bunched-up feeling, the knot in the pit of the stomach, as she gently turned the handle and stole inside. Nothing remained of Fiona except a few marks on the wall where her pictures and posters had been. There had stood her bed, there she'd curled up, finger invariably in her mouth, eyes staring balefully, reproachfully, at Anna.

Anna's eyes suddenly filled with tears and going over to the window she leaned heavily against the sill. No, memories of Fiona, especially in later years, were not good. There had been good times in the early days, but later as a teenager . . . she shivered recalling the unkind press reports. The inveterate do-gooder who could not manage her own stepdaughter.

True or false? Anna wiped the tears from her eyes, but still the garden was seen through a blur.

She knew that, although she had meant well, trying to change the lives of others by good works had brought about disaster. If she had not been involved in the squat the meeting between Errol and Fiona would never have taken place and that, surely, was the biggest mistake she had made in her life. She had not checked up on Errol; his background, his ability as an artist. Would she regard *that* as criminal if she read about it in the papers? How could a woman introduce her daughter to a thief, a drug addict, some even suggested a murderer?

But she had, and she would never forget it. Good intentions gone sour.

Guy's room had fewer bad memories, mainly because the change in Guy had blotted out the bad ones. He was an industrious student at an agricultural college who had done well in his first year exams. He'd worked all summer at the house and with a neighbouring farmer looking after stock, cutting hay, learning some of the mysteries of farming.

She left Guy's room, checked on the two guest rooms, the bathrooms, and then ran downstairs and did the same with the kitchen, breakfast room, dining room, study, living room. She went over to the French windows that led on to the balcony and, opening them, stepped outside for a moment gazing into the garden which had the neglected rather bedraggled look of late summer, especially when those who had once tended it so lovingly had neglected it. She looked for the blackbird she had fed every day with scraps from the breakfast table. Sometimes he would be sitting on the railing waiting for her when she got home at night.

But today he was not there.

There will be other blackbirds she thought as, sadly, she closed the window, bolted it and, gathering up a few things in the hall, left the house by the main door.

She ran down the steps and put everything in the boot of the car. That, and the back seat, already bulged with the bric-a-brac of moving house.

She went back to close the garden gate and then stood for a moment gazing up at the house. How sad and empty it looked with the curtains all gone, either to the Barbican or the jumble. The new owners, who she had never met, wanted to do the place over, so even carpets had gone. She didn't blame them. It was how she had felt about Hall Farm.

Anna turned abruptly, got into her car and drove to the end of the road, eyes straight in front of her looking to the future, leaving the past behind.

It had been a heavy day and now, with a pile of files high in front of her, she sat scribbling in the last of them. Opposite her her client sat on the edge of the chair, eyes anxiously on Anna's face.

She was a young mother whose partner had left without giving an address and the authorities were after him and her because they felt she knew where he was. She didn't. Anna was sure of that. She was honest, caring and frightened. She lived in one room with her baby and was entirely dependent on welfare. Now the CSA were threatening to take her to court because they thought she was shielding her partner.

Anna finished making her notes, closed her file and leaned towards her client. Summoning up yet another smile for the umpteenth time that evening she said as gently as she could: 'Valerie, I'm leaving the Centre tonight. This is the last time we'll meet.'

'Oh, Mrs *Livingstone*,' the woman's concern was palpable, 'you said you'd come to Court with me.'

'I was hoping to see you through; but I have so many problems of my own at the moment that I'm giving up all voluntary work.'

The young woman continued to look dejected.

'There's a very *nice* person taking over from me. A caring person. She will know all the details of your case and,' she indicated the stack of files beside her, 'others. Believe me, she won't leave a stone unturned to get you justice.'

It was nearly eight. Peter would be waiting in their new flat in the Barbican. Tonight would be their first night there, but also the last for some time. The following day Anna was off to Dorset and there was a lot to do. She opened the door and ushered her client out. The last time she would do what had become a familiar task for several years now. The corridor was deserted and all the helpers had gone home. She had already said goodbye to them and promised to drop in to see them from time to time. The usual thing. One very seldom did. She was pretty sure she would never see her neighbours again, or her fellow councillors, though for the time being she would keep in touch with the law firm if only by fax, telephone and letter because of her consultancy work.

She saw Valerie to the door and stood for a moment while they exchanged mutual good wishes. Then she watched her disappear in the mass of people thronging the pavement on that warm September evening.

She was deserting them: the people of the streets, of the squats, of single bedsitters; the loners, the rootless ones, dwellers in a great city.

A breeze suddenly blew in from the street ruffling her hair. It was a warm dusty breeze with a whiff of curry from the take-away round the corner, but as she raised her head and sniffed it she imagined that it smelt of newly mown grass, green banks full of wild thyme, white cow parsley and yellow, lemony tansy.

Anna shut the door, locked it firmly, chucked the key back through the letterbox, walked along the street, turned the corner, not looking back.

AFTERWORD

The car slowly edged forward, the lights kept on changing from red to yellow, then green, but before she could make any headway they changed back again to red. She was terribly late and burst out in a sweat; her hands gripping the wheel of the car were damp. Suddenly there was an enormous crash from the rear and her car was propelled with lightning speed through the traffic, which seemed to part for her almost miraculously, allowing her, like the fast forward process on a video, speedy access along Wigmore Street up Portland Place all the way to the Council Hall.

She left the car in front of the steps and dashed out of it, despite the phalanx of traffic wardens advancing towards her, wagging their fingers. 'I'm late, I'm late,' she cried like the White Rabbit, and dashed up the steps to the Council chamber hotly pursued by the traffic wardens. As she entered, the debate taking place suddenly stopped, all sound ceased and those present turned accusingly towards her.

'I'm so sorry I'm late,' she began but David Cole rose from the leader's bench and began berating her.

'You're *always* late, Anna. How do you suppose you can do your job properly? You're letting everyone down. Letting the Party down . . .'

'Letting the *Party* down!' the members chorused in unison and, rising in a body, advanced towards her at the same time as the doors burst open and the army of vengeful traffic wardens surged in waving their parking tickets which they began to shower on her.

Anna woke with a start; sat upright in bed, heart pounding, nightie drenched, her face also covered with sweat, a choking sensation in her throat. There was an aura of light around the drawn curtains. Dawn.

The dream had been such a jumble of events from the past, not the first time she'd had it in the years that had passed since she'd settled in Dorset, abandoned the life in the town to become a country dweller.

Her hand sidled across the bed for the warm, comforting, reassuring presence of Peter. Empty. Peter was in town, she remembered. It was midweek and he came down at weekends, sometimes for longer in the summer.

Anna got up, spent a penny, drank a glass of water and returned to bed. She lay there for a long time, quite still, until gradually sleep reclaimed her again.

The next time she woke someone was snuggling into bed beside her, a little warm body next to hers.

'Good morning, Mummy.' Loving, warm lips against her cheek.

'Good morning, darling.'

That precious time of day she and Harriet had exclusively for each other, though at the weekends it was shared with Peter. She, unquestioningly, was 'Mummy' and always had been, Harriet too young when Fiona died to remember her. Peter, however, was 'Grandpa'. The division seemed strange but logical; no one queried it.

Harriet was now four, bright, intelligent, beautiful. She attended nursery school part-time to which Anna took her every morning and picked her up again at lunch time. Or, sometimes, if Anna had something to do, Sal picked her up, or Guy might go over and get her, or she'd spend the afternoon with one or other of her friends.

Anna sometimes wondered how they would deal with the problem of explaining to Harriet her origins, how they would be able to judge when was the best time and how they would be able to tell.

Harriet was a reflective child, not a prattler, and she and Anna lay companionably together, not speaking, Anna almost beginning to doze off again because of her disturbed night. She felt a finger on her cheek and opened her eyes to see Harriet staring earnestly at her.

'Are you alright, Mummy?'

'Just tired, darling.' Anna turned to look at the clock. 'Goodness, look at the time! We'll be late!' and with a squeal Harriet tumbled out of bed, and Anna followed her as far as the door and watched her scamper along the corridor to her room where she was quite capable of brushing her teeth, splashing some water on her face and dressing herself.

Anna went to her bathroom, ran a bath and jumped into it, lying there for a moment, eyes closed, as the horrors of the nightmare returned and then slowly receded again.

On the way downstairs she called into Harriet's room and found her dressed in her jeans and T-shirt, struggling with the laces of her little trainers. Swiftly Anna knelt and tied them for her, bows were still rather a problem.

'Done your hair?' she asked, gazing into the eager, upturned little face.

Harriet shook her head. She was still babyish enough to want Anna to do things for her, and Anna liked doing them. Grabbing a hairbrush, she began to brush the fair curls back from Harriet's head, making a semblance of a parting. Then there was the little ribbon to tie on for a top-knot.

Harriet sat on the bed watching her, and impulsively Anna leaned forward and kissed her.

'I do love you,' she said.

'I love you, Mummy.'

Anna held out her hand and together they went downstairs

for the quick breakfast that preceded the trip to school.

It was possible to love somebody as though they were your own, providing you began early enough, Anna thought as she walked the two golden labradors, Dover and George, along the path by the river. She had no misgivings at all about abandoning work and London life entirely to care for Harriet. She occasionally 'consulted', but cases were few and far between. Financially they made do, thanks to Peter's job and the growing success of the farm.

It was not the life she ever expected to have to choose, but now she was glad that, although to some extent it had been forced on her, she had wanted it, had prepared for it. She owed it not only to Harriet and Peter, but Fiona. Now she was making up to Fiona for her unwitting neglect of her in the past or, at least, she was trying to.

It was a beautiful June day and, in the distance Guy was inside the cab of the combine harvester harvesting the first of the grass crop that would be used to feed the cattle in the winter. They came to the spot where the dogs liked to take their dip in the river, and where Anna threw sticks for them as they splashed in and out retrieving them and laying them at her feet so that the whole absurd but pleasurable process could be gone through again. When it was all over, Dover and George shook themselves vigorously and she darted away just in time to save herself from a soaking.

They'd got George and Dover as puppies, part of a thoroughbred litter, and the names were on the pedigree George St George and Dover St George. They were that beautiful honey-gold, with soft almond coloured eyes and sleek heads, and as they sped ahead of her Anna saw that the combine harvester was coming towards them and the dogs ran eagerly towards it though taking care not to get too near.

Guy stopped the machine and climbed from the cab.

'Hi!' he called.

'Hi!' Anna called back, walking towards him. 'Lovely day.'

'Lovely.' Guy looked up at the blue sky, the tiny wisps of clouds scudding towards the distant hills.

'Will you have this field done today?'

'I expect so.' Guy addressed himself to the dogs who made a fuss of him.

Guy lived in the cottage. He was now twenty, had passed all his exams and ran the farm with the aid of two experienced hands. Anna did a lot of the bookwork, the tiresome details required by the Common Economic Policy which had finished the Hansons. She, however, liked this aspect, and with her neat and tidy mind was good at it. They were dairy farmers, with fields full of wheat, maize and rape whose golden glow had just faded. It was difficult to imagine in the strapping young man she saw before her now that sullen, difficult teenager. She thought that not only was Guy content with his work but Fiona's death had a lot to do with his transformation.

'Why don't you come for dinner tonight?' Anna asked.

'Anyone else coming?'

'No, just us.'

'I'll bring Honey,' Guy said.

'Do.' The dogs were now far ahead along the bank and Anna whistled at them. 'About seven?' she said.

'After milking.'

'See you.' Anna stood back as Guy climbed into his cabin, started the noisy engine again and, with a wave, drove on.

Anna hurried along the track after the dogs, her senses sharpened by the beauty of the scenery round her. The variegated greens of the trees overhead and the cut grass under her feet, the fading cow parsley mingling with the bright yellow buttercups by the side of the bank. The swift-flowing river as it cascaded over the waterfall by the bridge.

Honey and Guy, naturally it seemed, had, despite a slight age difference, teamed up and lived at the cottage together. Honey went on with her job and drove every day into Blandford, but at night and weekends she helped at the farm. It was a situation that seemed to suit everyone. Guy had a mate, Honey had a purpose and Sal nursed her hopes for the future.

Anna reached the gate by the bridge where the dogs obediently waited for her. She slipped on their leads and they trotted by her side as she walked along the main street of the village, up towards the farm. Her walk by the river brought her full circle. It was about three miles and she did it every day – winter, summer, rain, sun. She found in the country that one lived continuously in comfortable clothes and wellies. She thought you could hardly have walked up Regent Street in wellies, but in Blandford or Sturminster Newton they were *de rigueur*. No one cared. No one looked.

She passed Guy's cottage, a place she hardly ever visited, even though Nancy's studio was now a garden shed and all vestiges of her and her daughter's lives as painters had gone. She knew inside the cottage it would be clean and tidy, beds made, floors shining. Guy, now that he was a farmer, was meticulous, and Honey seemed to be a willing home-maker.

Anna walked past Sal's cottage but knew she'd gone to see a friend in Bristol. She passed the pub and waved to a couple of people who were about to go in, declining the offer of a lunchtime drink.

As she was about to turn up the hill she stopped by the churchyard. It was almost the anniversary of Fiona's death. They would go there on the day with flowers but, on impulse today, she went through the gate, tied the dogs' leads to the post and walked slowly up the path, past the church, towards the graves that, surrounded by simple twin headstones, lay by the wall shaded by an elderberry tree, just bursting forth.

It was difficult to assuage guilt and find peace. It took a long time.

But at last the Livingstone family had found it. And in

burying Fiona, Anna thought, they had finally buried Nancy too. Mother and daughter secure in each other's company.

Anna stole away from the graves, unhooked the dogs from the gate and began to climb the hill towards home. She realised that gradually she had been liberated from guilt and grief, free to enjoy her life with Peter and with Harriet, Fiona's child who, in some way, had become theirs, tied to them by blood.